# LAST OF THE DRAGORN

## THE ECHOES SAGA: BOOK EIGHT

PHILIP C. QUAINTRELL

Copyright © 2020 by Philip C. Quaintrell
First edition published 2020.
Second edition published 2023.



*Cover Illustration by Chris McGrath*
*Book design by BodiDog Design*
*Edited by David Bradley*

ISBN: 978-1-916610-07-1 (paperback)
ASIN: B08JDTR15R (ebook)

Published by Quaintrell Publishings

*This is for my Ma. Where would any son be without their mother?*

# ALSO BY PHILIP C. QUAINTRELL

### *THE ECHOES SAGA: (9 Book Series)*

1. Rise of the Ranger

2. Empire of Dirt

3. Relic of the Gods

4. The Fall of Neverdark

5. Kingdom of Bones

6. Age of the King

7. The Knights of Erador

8. Last of the Dragorn

9. A Clash of Fates

### *THE RANGER ARCHIVES: (3 Book Series)*

1. Court of Assassins

2. Blood and Coin

3. A Dance of Fang and Claw

### *THE TERRAN CYCLE: (4 Book Series)*

1. Intrinsic

2. Tempest

3. Heretic

4. Legacy

THE NIGHT SEA
THE DREAD WOOD
SILVYR HALL
STORM'S REACH
HYNDAERN
NIMDUHN
THE BROKEN MOUNTAINS
SNOWF
THE RUINS OF TOR VALAR
THE WATCHTOWER OF ARGUNSULIN
WHITE TOWER
DRAKANAN
THE DRAGON PATH
THE RAKAN RIVER
THE FOREST OF RUUN
DRAYSHON
DEMETRIUM MINES
THE BLOODED ROAD
THE RED FIELDS OF DUNMAR
LAKE SUNDRUM
SUNHOLD
FREYGARD
CARSTANE
THE TERRS OF NAGREL
THE DEEP
THE RUINS OF GELADOR
CASTLE HOLD
SILVYR VALES OF AKMAR
MOUNT KALIBAN
ERADOR
RIVERWATCH
THE EAST BANK ROAD
GRAVEN WOOD
VANGALA
THE BROKEN ROAD
THE TOWER OF JAIN
THE RED HOLD
ELDERHALL
THE RUINS
HEMON
THE HOX
FARNFOSS
THEDARIA
WARTH
THE MORN WOOD
LAKE TALON
THE CROOKED ROAD
TORINN
THE DAWNING PEAKS
CARTHAM
HARAN'S TOWN
ALLISANDER
THE GELDON FOREST
THE LONG ROAD
BROADCASTLE
QALANQATH
OLD DRIFT

VERDA
THE LONELY WASTES
HAL
N DORAL
THE IRON VALLEY
NAMDHOR
LONGDALE
HOMSTEAD
THE WHITE VALE
ILLIAN
THE BLACK WOOD
THE OLD WELL
DUNWICH
THE FROST MOUNTAINS
WOOD VALE
KELP TOWN
THE KING'S INN
ISIRITH
TONE
DARKWELL
THE EVERMOORE
THE UNMAR
THE NORD
LIRIAN
AL TARIEL
SHALARIA
VANGARTH
PALIOS
ELETHIAH
STOWHOLD
THE CRYSTAL SEA
THE SILVERLAND
KORKANATH
WHISTLE TOWN
VELIA
THE AMARA
WEST FELLION
THE ALBERIN LAKE
DRAGORN
THE MOORES
THE MOONLIT PLAINS
BAROSSH
ELANDRIL
THE NARROWS
GALOSHA
TOWER OF DRAGON
THE LIFELESS ISLES
THE ELMEER FOREST
MOUNT GARGANAPAN
ILYTHYRA
THE WILLOWS
LAKE NUBIA
THE ELMANT LAKE
TREGARAN
THE ADEAN
AMEERASKA
THE ARID LANDS
CALMARDRA
LAKE KAHEARE
AYDA
NIGHTFALL
THE Q'OL
THE OLD GARDEN
KARATH
THE RED MOUNTAINS
SYLA'S GATE
DROWNERS' RUN
ATILAN'S LANDING
THE FLAT WASTES
ITHILIA
THE MOUTH OF THE WORLD
DRAGONS' REACH
MALAYSAI
DAVOSAI
THE GREAT MAW
UNDYING MOUNTAINS
LAKE OBTHAN
GRAVOSAI
THE LIVING SEA

# DRAMATIS PERSONAE

**Adan'Karth (Adan)**
A Drake

**Adilandra Sevari**
The elven queen of Elandril and mother of Reyna Galfrey

**Alijah Galfrey**
Half-elf and self-proclaimed king of Verda

**Asher**
Human ranger

**Athis**
Red dragon, bonded with Inara

**Doran Heavybelly**
A Dwarven Ranger/Prince and War Mason of clan Heavybelly

**Ellöria Sevari**
The late Lady of Ilythyra

**Faylen Haldör**
An elf and High Guardian of Elandril

**Galanör Reveeri**
An elven ranger

**Gideon Thorn**
Master Dragorn

**Gondrith**
Reaver - bonded with the dragon *Yillir.*

**Ilargo**
Green dragon, bonded with Gideon

**Inara Galfrey**
Half-elf Dragorn/Guardian of the Realm

**Lord Kraiden**
Reaver - bonded with the dragon *Morgorth.*

**Kassian Kantaris**
A previous Keeper of Valatos

**Nathaniel Galfrey**
An ambassador and previous knight of the Graycoats

**Reyna Galfrey**
Elven princess of Elandril and Illian ambassador

**Rengyr**

Reaver - bonded with the dragon *Karsak.*

**Sir Ruban Dardaris**

Captain of the King's Guard

**Veda Malmagol**

The Father of Nightfall

**Vighon Draqaro**

The usurped king of Illian

**Vilyra**

Reaver - bonded with the dragon *Godrad.*

# PROLOGUE

The last days of summer were gone, taking with them the refuge of their warmth and hope. Gone were the good days. Autumn had been a brief gloom, passing entirely unnoticed by Illian's inhabitants. And now, as winter forced itself upon the land, there was no ignoring the lashing rain and skies of thunder that accompanied it.

Death itself was riding this storm...

The heavens hurled lightning across the freezing plains of The Ice Vales. With every blinding flash, ancient beasts, dragged from their eternal slumber, could be glimpsed in the sky. Their bat-like wings beat without need of rest, bringing their wretched riders ever closer.

Vighon Draqaro, the rightful king of Illian, yanked his sword from a Reaver's head and looked on in dread. *Three* dragons. How could they stand against such might? The northman narrowed his eyes, searching through the rain for those terrible features that would spell their doom. There was no mistaking the dragon that led the trio.

Malliath the voiceless.

And, of course, wherever he went, he carried the self-proclaimed king of Verda. Had the world ever known anyone so dangerous as Alijah Galfrey?

From this distance, it was impossible to discern which two of the four Dragon Riders accompanied him. It didn't really matter. Be it Lord Kraiden or any of the others, they would unleash an inferno upon the land and smother his men with flames.

For nearly ten months, Vighon had fought the good fight, leading The Rebellion into one skirmish after another. In all those battles, he had yet to witness anything worse than the all-consuming agony of dragon fire.

The sound of thundering hooves brought the northman back to the battlefield. His sword came up just in time to parry the swinging blade of a Reaver. Astride its horse, the knight from Erador continued on only to be brought down by the spear of a distant Namdhorian.

Foot soldiers quickly followed the charging rider, leaving Vighon no choice but to meet them with fury. How he longed for his flaming sword of silvyr in the fight. Still, he wielded northern steel - it did the job. One fiend after another fell to Vighon's skill with a blade, their heads parted from their undead bodies.

But more were coming...

From within the high walls of Grey Stone, every Reaver under Alijah's command was flooding the icy plains to meet the three thousand that had rallied to the true king of Illian. There was a chance, however slim, that they would defeat the Reavers and reclaim the city, but not before Malliath and the Dragon Riders arrived.

With only seconds to spare before clashing swords again, Vighon turned his sights to the east. He couldn't see them, but he knew The Carpel Slopes were out there. The scattered ruins that sprawled across the base of those slopes were, perhaps, their only hope of surviving to fight another day.

"Mount up!" he bellowed. "Make for The Carpel Slopes! Make for the ruins!"

His momentary reprieve was over when a Reaver came at him, its sword pointed at his chest. Sir Ruban Dardaris collided with the creature, shield first, before driving his blade through its rotten skull.

"We are abandoning Grey Stone?" the captain questioned, capturing the reins of a nearby horse, bereft of its rider.

Vighon looked up at the sheer cliff face of the ancient city. Light poured out of the central cut in the stone, illuminating hundreds of Reavers marching out to meet them. The northman had hoped to rally his men left there, months earlier, and take the city itself in the process, but they had greatly underestimated the enemy's numbers.

"We have the men," Vighon lamented. "That will have to be victory enough." He stole a glance at the approaching dragons, reminding himself that true victory was far from certain. "Mount up!" he reiterated.

The chaos outside Grey Stone's main entrance slowly began to dissipate as the Namdhorian force made for the east. The reinforcement of Reavers, however, simply marched over the dead in their pursuit.

Athis the ironheart made them suffer for it.

The red dragon swooped low and exhaled a torrent of flames that gave the Namdhorians a real chance at escape. On the ground, Inara Galfrey swept her Vi'tari blade in rolling arcs, dispatching any Reaver lucky enough to have evaded the inferno.

"Inara!" Vighon yelled her name as he galloped past. The Dragorn sheathed her scimitar and snatched his waiting hand. Her envious strength and agility saw the half-elf easily ascend onto the back of the northman's saddle.

"Come on!" Ruban shouted, ushering his king away from the relentless Reavers.

Vighon spurred his horse, taking them away from Grey Stone with all haste. The wind whipped through their hair and the rain stung as it lashed against their faces, but still they rode, and rode hard. Death was coming for them...

Inara leaned forward. "I can't hold all three of them off!"

Vighon dared to look. Malliath and the Reaver dragons were now banking east, coming up behind them. Inara was right - she couldn't hold them off. With that realisation, the last thread of hope he had been clinging to unravelled, setting him adrift into the darkness.

"Every campaign!" Vighon fumed. "If he knows I'm there, he rains all hell down on us!"

"Of course he does!" Inara replied. "There's no greater threat to him than your claim to the throne!"

"I've lost more men than I can count!"

Vighon could only claim one victory since The Rebellion first stood up to Alijah's reign. Since then, the new king had targeted the northman specifically, rallying his Dragon Riders and thousands of Reavers to his position every time. To ride with Vighon Draqaro was to ride into fire and hell. Yet he never failed to be surrounded by willing soldiers who bragged of the honour in fighting beside him. But how many more could he lead into such an *honourable* death?

"We should split up!" Inara suggested. "I will lead a contingent to the south and take them over The Unmar - save as many as we can!"

Vighon didn't like the idea of separating from her, and not just because she was the fabled Guardian of the Realm. They had grown closer over the last ten months - the only good thing to have come out of such dark times. Inara was also the reason he had survived Alijah's brutal retaliations that saw too many others perish.

"Go!" he growled over his shoulder. "Be safe!" he added.

Inara's arms squeezed a little tighter around his waist. "Be safe," she echoed quietly in his ear.

Vighon didn't even feel the Dragorn depart from his horse and, looking back, he couldn't see her on the ground. Instead he looked up to see Athis gliding overhead, his wings momentarily sheltering the northman from the rain. Inara was scaling the dragon's side, reminding Vighon that she was far from human.

Half of the force peeled off, following Athis to the south in an arcing wave of thundering hooves. Behind them, one of the dragons broke away from the trio and stalked the southern contingent. That still left Malliath and one Reaver dragon on Vighon's tail - his and that of a thousand others. Beyond the pursuing dragons, the Reavers that had been stationed at Grey Stone were riding their undead mounts, now surplus to requirement.

Malliath swept low overhead as they reached the ruins of The Carpel Slopes. His devastating tail carved up the ground, dividing the last of the Namdhorians to arrive. Vighon was practically dragged from his horse by Sir Ruban and shoved under a broken arch and into the old ruins. He looked back to see at least three hundred men cut off from the shelter, their horses rearing in fear. The Reaver dragon came in behind Malliath and let loose a jet of fire, boxing the riders in.

It was happening just like last time. They were all going to die and there was nothing Vighon could do about it.

Ruban clapped one soldier on the back after another, urging them to spread out amongst the ruins. Some were commanded to take up defensive positions while others were ordered to find escape routes and potential hiding places.

Inevitably, the Reavers arrived to assist Alijah in herding the captured riders. Their horses were discarded and the men themselves were disarmed and rounded up into rows. None dared to fight back while Rengyr and his dragon mount, Karsak, were circling them on the ground. Unseen inside his armour, carrying his battle-axe, Rengyr could have passed as human, but Karsak was unmistakably dead, his scales and rotten flesh hanging in strips from his ravaged body - a victim of a war so old it was consigned to the most ancient of history books.

Then there was Malliath, a dragon whose life exemplified the very meaning of ancient. His black scales were slick in the rain as he stood beside Alijah, who had ascended a cluster of boulders to the side of the prisoners. His black and red cloak was sodden, but the wind still picked up the heavy material, casting it about behind him. The green Vi'tari blade remained sheathed on his hip, though it wasn't known for staying there.

Vighon peered out through a jagged hole in the weathered stone. What a fool he had been. He should have waited for Doran and his Heavybelly warriors...

"I did this," he muttered, catching Sir Ruban's attention. "I actually thought we could take the city *and* liberate the men. It turns out we could do neither..."

"We couldn't have known Alijah himself would come," Sir Ruban replied. "Nor could we have known he would bring not one but two of his Riders."

"But *I* should have known!" Vighon hissed, watching the Reavers spread out. "My very presence jeopardises every campaign. How many times has The Rebellion lost because Alijah redirected his forces to my position?" The northman paused and gestured to a group of Namdhorians to move further down the ruins and ready their bows. "It would actually be a viable tactic," he continued, "if it didn't cost us so many lives."

Ruban adjusted the armoured collar around his neck. "The Rebellion can't afford to use you as bait, your Grace. You're too important."

Vighon looked out on the men who had believed he was worth their fealty. "The Rebellion might not be able to afford to use me as bait, but they also can't afford for me to lead either. I've doomed us all..."

"VIGHON DRAQARO!" Alijah's voice boomed across the gap, enhanced by magic. "HAS IT DAWNED ON YOU YET? WHEREVER YOU GO, I WILL BE THERE TO CRUSH YOU! I WILL BLEED YOUR LITTLE REBELLION TO ITS LAST DROP! ANYONE WHO SIDES WITH YOU WILL BURN! AND, VIGHON, YOU WILL BEAR WITNESS TO IT ALL! YOU WILL WATCH THEM ALL DIE CLINGING TO YOUR BANNER!"

Alijah half turned to regard the captured prisoners, shuffling nervously on their feet. "I KNOW IN THE PAST, THIS WOULD HAVE BEEN THE MOMENT I SPOKE OF MERCY! I WOULD LEVERAGE THE LIVES OF THESE MEN AND SEE YOU ALL IN CHAINS RATHER THAN

GRAVES! BUT YOUR RESISTANCE HAS PUSHED ME AGAIN AND AGAIN! NOW, IF ALL OF YOU STANDING BESIDE VIGHON DRAQARO COME FORWARD AND BEND THE KNEE, I CAN ONLY GRANT YOU A SWIFT AND PAINLESS DEATH, DELIVERED BY STEEL!"

Vighon pressed himself against the stone. "No..." He shuddered, fearing the worst.

Alijah faced the ruins once more. "STAND YOUR GROUND, HOWEVER, AND YOUR LOYALTY TO THE HOUSE OF DRAQARO WILL SEE YOU SUFFER THE SAME FATE AS THESE MEN..."

Malliath and Karsak turned on the prisoners and reminded them all why dragons were at the top of the food chain. From nothing there came fire, and it spread throughout the ranks of the captured Namdhorians, torching them alive. Their screams pushed through the rain to be carried on the wind, where they haunted the surviving rebels.

Vighon called out in protest and slammed the wall with his fist. The flames that burned their brothers-in-arms were reflected in every Namdhorian's eyes, the northman's included. Able to bear no more, Vighon turned around and rested his back against the wall. Looking at the men around him, he could see the fear that gripped their hearts, just as it did his own. He did not fear his own death, though, but rather theirs.

"You can keep your mercy, usurper!" one Namdhorian yelled from the ruins. The sentiment was echoed up and down The Carpel Slopes, swelling Vighon's chest with pride.

Sir Ruban placed a hand on the northman's shoulder. "We're not just Namdhorians. We're men of Illian and you are our king. We will fight with you. And we will die with you. That is our honour."

Vighon gripped the side of his friend's face, locking their eyes. "The honour has been mine."

"WHAT IS IT TO BE?" Alijah called, standing before a field of burning corpses.

The true king of Illian climbed up a broken wall to offer Alijah and his wicked lot an image of defiance. "If you want us, *necromancer*, come and get us!"

Alijah didn't move, but his forces did. The Reavers charged, directed by the half-elf's mental commands. Vighon jumped down and issued orders to prepare for battle. The ruins gave some advantage, forcing the Reavers' greater numbers to squeeze between the broken passages and fight inside the remains of ancient chambers.

Over the sound of charging armour and heavy rain, Vighon heard the unmistakable sound of wings. Karsak and Malliath had already taken off and were angling on the rebels' various positions. There was no hiding from them.

Malliath was the first to fly by, raining down fiery death along the northern edge of the ruins. His tail curled and smashed through a handful of walls, knocking Vighon and Ruban to the ground. Karsak took a higher vantage and attacked those in the hills, setting The Carpel Slopes alight.

Vighon staggered to his feet only seconds before the Reavers stormed the ruins. He timed his two-handed swing perfectly and decapitated the first Reaver to pass under the arch. An armoured shoulder-barge pushed him aside, however, and he was quickly separated from Sir Ruban. He backed up into another chamber devoid of a roof and engaged the undead fiends that followed him in.

The hammering rain had turned the mud beneath their feet into sludge, but it only worked in Vighon's favour. The Reavers, encumbered in heavy armour, struggled to maintain their balance and continued to slip and slide around the room. The northman, never one to wear full plate, dashed between their clumsy attempts and parted them from their heads one at a time.

Malliath flew overhead again. There was more fire and more screaming from further down the ruins. It enraged Vighon, driving him from the chamber and into the fray that had taken over the nearest passage. Sir Ruban, a diligent student of the sword, was displaying a few of the reasons that had contributed to his rank. The knight was as fearless as the Reavers themselves. Vighon fought his way to the captain, cutting down Reavers with as much savagery as he could muster.

"We need to get to higher ground!" Ruban yelled over the melee. "Our only hope is to find refuge inside the hills!"

As he often did, the captain of the king's guard forced Vighon in the direction he deemed safest. More Namdhorians rallied on them, fighting to be beside their king. Moving up the winding slopes, however, was dangerous, exposing them to Malliath's wrath. The black dragon, it seemed, was too distracted with those who had taken up positions inside one of the most intact buildings. He clawed at the stone and swung his tail through one of the walls until he could thrust his horned head inside. The flames he expelled filled the entire building and exploded from every crack and window. No one could have survived...

Entering the ruins set higher into the slopes, Vighon was able to see what remained of his men. Some had already vanished into the hills, chased by Karsak. Others cowered in dark corners, succumbing to their fears. The Reavers had found a way through every crack in the lower ruins. The Namdhorians still down there were quickly falling to their steel. There had to be a few hundred left, if that, and they were by Vighon's side now - a fact that would seal their fate.

"VIGHON DRAQARO!" Alijah was striding through the lower ruins, his green scimitar slicing through one Namdhorian after another. "ARE YOU WATCHING?"

The northman couldn't help but watch. The horror of it all was paralysing. So many had died and so many more were going to die. Because of him.

"Get away from me..." he whispered, backing away from his men. "Get away from me!" he yelled. "Run! You should all be running!"

"We stand with you!" Ruban argued.

"To what end?" Vighon countered. "You heard him? I walk hand in hand with death. Wherever I go, he will be there. Too many have died..."

"They're coming up the slopes!" a soldier warned, pointing to the advancing Reavers.

Vighon pointed his sword to the eastern valley, a narrow path that cut through the hills. "Run, you fools! I will ward them off!"

Without waiting, the northman made for the next slope, taking him higher into the hills. He shouted down at the Reavers again and again before Sir Ruban bundled into him, taking them both into the rocks.

"What are you doing?" he barked. "We need you! The Rebellion *needs* you!"

"Let go of me!" Vighon pushed the captain away and returned to the edge of the slope. "Over here!" he shouted. "I'm over..." His words died away, failing to find life in the shadow of his fears.

The Reavers ignored the path that led to the northman. They, instead, continued their hunt of the Namdhorian survivors with bloody swords in hand.

"No!" Vighon cursed and made to intercept them - but he was going nowhere.

The hill itself shuddered under the weight of Malliath the voiceless. So close was he that Vighon could smell his rank breath and feel the heat on his face. Purple reptilian eyes focused on him behind rows of bared fangs.

"I told you, old friend..." Alijah looked down on him from astride his dragon saddle. "You will bear witness to it all. In the end, The Rebellion won't know who is more to blame for their defeat: me... or *you*."

Sir Ruban brandished his sword. "Come down and fight us like a man!"

Alijah narrowed his eyes on the knight. "But I am not a man." Malliath inhaled a breath, preparing to reduce the captain to ash.

Vighon stepped in front of his friend, putting Alijah's threat to the test. Malliath closed his jaws, though his mighty head turned back to the west. Following his gaze, Vighon discovered a powerful light in the dark, at least a mile away.

Inara...

It was likely the crystal, fixed into the base of her pommel, that shone into the stormy night, daring to draw the enemy to her. The resurrected dragon who had broken away was still in pursuit and closing in on Inara and Athis.

The Reavers further down the hill stopped in the mouth of the narrow valley, listening to the will of their master. As one, they reversed their advance and began to descend The Carpel Slopes. Vighon struggled with the distance, but did his best to see through the rain. Inara and Athis had held back, parting from the soldiers who continued to flee south, towards The Unmar.

Vighon shook his head in despair. "Don't..." he whispered into the cold.

Malliath turned his whole body on the hillside, angling himself towards the light. His thick legs crouched, ready to spring off The Carpel Slopes.

"You can't!" Vighon snapped. "She is your *sister*!"

Alijah turned his head to look down on the northman. "She is my *enemy*. And like you, Inara is a symbol to others who would rebel. *Unlike* you, however, she would serve me better if she were dead. There can only be one true dragon in the skies..."

With that, Malliath launched himself from the slopes and flew west. Vighon could do nothing, a mortal bound to the earth. Seconds later, Karsak and Rengyr took to the sky and followed Malliath after their new prey.

The northman dropped to his knees, his sword pointed into the ground. Ruban was saying something behind him but there was nothing in Vighon's ears but the repeating sound of his men dying over and over across half a dozen battlefields. Soon, he feared, Inara would be added to them. And how many more would there be after her?

Vighon could see only one path that would give The Rebellion even a hope of beating Alijah. He rose from the wet mud and sheathed his blade, his eyes fixed on the west - Inara was taking them on a chase, saving as many lives as she could.

"Your Grace?"

"Fetch the men," he commanded without looking. "We need to reach The Black Wood." Sir Ruban hurried back down the slope. "And search for any survivors!" Vighon called after him.

When the captain of the king's guard returned, he would find no sign of Vighon Draqaro, nor would there be any man who went by that name again. The house of the flaming sword was lost to the summer, to those good days.

Now the dragon reigned...

# PART ONE

# CHAPTER 1

# KILLING THE PAST

*ne Year Later...*

It was a quiet night on The Shining Coast. Stars dominated the sky in their mysterious yet beautiful way; even the clouds dared not venture out for the crime of concealing their majesty. Beneath it all, The Adean lapped against the eastern shore, determined, through the eons, to wear down Illian's jagged edge.

Stepping onto the sand, Alijah Galfrey was momentarily taken back to his youth. How many times had he come down from the cliffs with Inara and Vighon? Their adventures, limited only by their imaginations, would stretch from dawn till dusk.

Those had been the easiest of days...

Now, he found himself on that same beach with the weight of the world on his shoulders. The ornate golden circlet, that ringed his dark hair, was a symbol of that weight, that responsibility. Such was the fate of the man who would be king of all the world.

There were none who could face the decisions left to him in these dark days. The half-elf told himself that a time would come when peace reigned from east to west, encompassing everything from Ayda to Erador and all of Illian in between. Until such a time, he would have to endure the hardships of his young kingdom.

Looking out over the black waves, he saw that The Adean had brought the next test of his rule. More ships than he could count were slipping out of the darkness, their elven sails illuminated by lanterns and moonlight. His grandmother, Queen Adilandra, had spent many months amassing her army to challenge him. With their might added to The Rebellion, the realm would be kept in a state of war for years to come.

Alijah sighed. How many elves would he have to kill this night to avoid that future? How many before they saw sense and turned back? The Adean would be red with blood come the dawn, an outcome the king found most undesirable. Elves were not only his kin; they were a race that had walked the face of Verda for thousands of years. It should not be forgotten, even in war, that elves are an ancient and immortal race whose experiences and wisdom surpassed all others. They had seen and heard so much of history that to kill them felt akin to erasing history itself.

As always, Alijah had his lessons to fall back on. The Crow's teachings were etched into his very soul, reminding him of his duty. Right now, he had three little words whispering into his mind, keeping him to the path laid out for him long before he was born.

*Sacrifice without hesitation.*

Soon, his grandmother would lead the charge against him and they would meet with one inevitable conclusion: either she would kill him, or he would kill her. If Adilandra of the royal house Sevari had to die for the sake of everlasting peace, then die she would.

Alijah watched the approaching ships from a small rise, behind his knights of Erador whose numbers were in the thousands this night. They lined the beach from north to south with more still atop the cliffs behind them, armed with bows. It had been Gondrith and his dragon, Yillir, who had first sighted the elves, their patrol taking them over The Adean for just such a thing. After hearing of their imminent arrival, the king had spent days - often without sleep - rallying his soldiers from Illian's eastern region and even a few thousand from the north.

The elves were not to be underestimated...

"Your Grace..."

Often surrounded by Reavers, Alijah had become unaccustomed to the sound of any voice that wasn't Malliath's. He knew this particular voice, however. He didn't need to look to see Veda Malmagol, the current Father of the Arakesh. To the king, Lady Gracen's successor was simply a passing figure, his death as inevitable as the tide. But, like the late Lady of Lirian, the Father had his uses, making him naught but a tool.

Veda made his way up the rise and bowed his bald head, his dark skin catching the moonlight. Like his predecessor, the Father wore a red blindfold, rejecting Nightfall's ancient tradition that demanded the ruler have their eyes removed. That wasn't the only thing he had in common with the deceased Mother. Like her, Veda had ambitions for his order; ambitions that would see them rise to something other than the cause of the fearful whispers of Illian's people.

Alijah looked over his shoulder, noting the dozens of Arakesh that accompanied the Father. "Veda, I didn't realise there were so many of you left." His remark was barbed, betraying his true feelings, but the assassin was too ambitious to hear the truth in the king's words. "I see he got close this time..." he added, glancing at the fresh scar that connected Veda's eye to his jaw line.

Veda tilted his head to hide the wound. "The ranger has proven himself nothing if not tenacious, I will admit."

"The ranger?" Alijah repeated. "Do you dare not say his name anymore?"

The Father puffed out his chest. "Asher will meet his end soon enough - he cannot hope to hunt us all." Veda steered the conversation. "The Arakesh would be in a better position if we were allowed to operate outside of the shadows, your Grace."

"I thought you did your best work in the shadows," Alijah replied, his attention out to sea.

Veda bowed his head again. "We have spoken before, as you did with Gracen, about our role ascending to that of the king's guard. Our order could be your greatest weapon in the war for peace."

"The king's guard is a sacred duty," Alijah stated, "an oath that binds one to service until death. *You* yearn for *real* power."

"Who doesn't, your Grace?" the Father posed, lowering Alijah's opinion of him even further. "With your banner and our unique skills, there would be no force in all of Verda that could challenge us."

Alijah imagined it - the realm's deadliest killers wandering the country with his banner on their chests and blindfolds over their eyes. They would be ruthless and prone to violence: neither of which was useful when creating a peace-keeping force.

"That time is coming, Veda," Alijah lied. "For now, I need the Arakesh to continue my work from the shadows. And do kill Asher; he's making your entire order appear weak."

Veda bowed deeply this time, no doubt hiding his reaction to the scorn he felt at Alijah's barbed words. "It will be done, your Grace..." The Father trailed off as his senses detected the Reavers digging hundreds of holes deep into the beach. "What are those?" he asked absently.

"Graves," Alijah replied without hesitation.

"You are anticipating quite the battle, your Grace."

Alijah almost laughed to himself. "Only a fool would position themselves into open battle with the elves. For all my numbers, their magic would prove superior."

Veda's cocked eyebrow was hard to see under his blindfold. "Your Grace? There is to be no battle?" The assassin turned his head as his senses took in the thousands of Reavers.

"Oh…" Alijah said casually. "They're just here to give our enemy pause."

"Pause for what, your Grace?"

The king was done speaking to the Father. Leaving him on the rise, Alijah descended to the soft sand where twenty rows of armoured Reavers moved aside and granted their master a clear path to the sea. With a hand resting on the hilt of his Vi'tari scimitar, the half-elf strode to victory.

Alijah entered the sea until the water was up to his knees, his cloak fanned out on the surface behind him. He waited, an age-old requirement when dealing with the legendary Mer-folk. They were, perhaps, just as loathsome as the assassins at his back but, like them, they served a purpose. They were creatures of ill-intent where surface dwellers were concerned and he would use them as such.

At last, there was movement beneath the surface of The Adean. The human eye would have missed it in the gloom, but Alijah missed little. The Mer-man slid from the water, breaking the surface without a sound as if some unseen force was pushing it up from the depths. A powerful tail coiled in and out of the water behind it, breaking the surface twenty-feet out to sea and shining brilliant silver in the moonlight. The dark scales of its lower half changed at the navel, blending into something more familiar to human eyes. The skin itself was a beautiful mixture of green and gold.

Long pointed fingers glided at its sides with translucent webbing between every digit. The Mer-man's chest was as chiselled as any statue, every muscle evolved to enhance their speed and agility in the water. Small spikes protruded from the skin in a perfect row, straight down the middle of the creature's body, beginning at the chin.

There were three gills on each side of the neck, all of which closed off completely as the Mer-man inhaled a deep breath through a nose devoid of cartilage. Everything above its neck was the stuff of nightmares, even for the king. Its wide-set jaw of razor-sharp teeth rose up to a pair of large eyes as bottomless as the ocean itself. From atop its head sprouted long tendrils, similar to seaweed though most certainly something else altogether.

"This is not the war you promised us, Surface-King." Its hideous voice came out in a wet rasp, as if several membranes were opening and closing rapidly inside its throat. "You said they would be distracted."

This wasn't the first time Alijah had conversed with one of the water-born and so he took its appearance in his stride. "They will be," he reassured. "Did you do as I asked?"

The Mer-man bared his fangs. "The elven queen possesses your *ball*."

The word primitive came to mind, but Alijah knew enough of The Adean's underwater inhabitants to understand that this particular Mer-man was only one of several species, some of which were potentially more advanced than any civilisation on the surface.

"Just be ready," he instructed. "You will know when it is time."

"Why are they not distracted now?" the Mer-man demanded. "We cannot stand their kind on the water!"

Alijah steadied his gaze, calling on that predator-like quality that Malliath lent him. "You will know when it is time," he echoed.

The Mer-man hissed before diving back into the sea, leaving the king to walk back onto the beach. He faced the elven ships as he removed the diviner from his belt. The black orb fitted neatly in the palm of his hand, just as its twin was now in the palm of Queen Adilandra. Alijah closed his eyes and poured his consciousness into the diviner, allowing it to connect him across the waves.

In a realm between the fabric of the world, where shadows and smoke were all that existed, Alijah's mind was projected into the form of an ethereal body. There before him was a vision of light and smoke that did its best to display Adilandra's exquisite beauty.

"In league with the Mer-folk now, I see." The queen wasted no time bartering with the pleasantries.

Alijah smiled and made no comment on her remark. "Greetings,

Grandmother," he began. "I was beginning to wonder if you were coming at all."

"Grandmother..." Adilandra drew the word out. "The name is hollow in your mouth - that much I can hear. Has your heart lost all its love?"

Alijah knew he would be lying if he didn't admit that his grandmother's voice was a relief to an older part of himself. "On the contrary," he replied. "I act only out of love. As the queen of a nation, I thought you of all people would understand my motivations."

Adilandra's image remained still while Alijah glided around her. "You would have me believe your actions are in *service* of the people," she challenged, "but you usurped their king, disbanded their army, and brought ruin upon Dhenaheim. I see hunger for power, not love for the people."

Alijah had expected her lack of vision, but he was still disappointed to hear it. "All that wisdom," he lamented, "wasted with such a narrow view."

"My view is clear," Adilandra said coolly. "My army will roll over your fiends and liberate Illian from your dark magic."

The king scrutinised his grandmother's words. "I have wondered if you have what it takes to kill me, your own blood."

"You stopped being my grandson the moment you murdered my sister and locked my daughter up."

"My mother is a guest in my house," Alijah corrected. "And... Ellöria didn't need to die, just like all of you. She chose her fate when she resisted my reign. It's *because* of what happened in Ilythyra that I'm talking to you right now. I give you this one—"

"Chance to bow the knee?" Adilandra finished, cutting him off. "I see your every move before you take it, child. And you can keep your mercy - I have heard of its *extent*..."

Alijah twisted his mouth. "Communicating with The Rebellion is treasonous and punishable by death."

"I do not recognise your authority, Alijah, neither in Illian nor

Ayda." The queen's ethereal head whipped around to face him. "You should have stayed in Erador."

Alijah was growing weary of the exchange. "And *you* should have stayed in Elandril," he replied threateningly. "If you had let me finish my work we could have avoided what is to follow this conversation."

"Use that bond of yours," Adilandra urged. "Look into the past. My kind stand undefeated in war."

Alijah nodded as if he was in agreement. "The dwarves said the same thing…"

The elven queen took her first ethereal step, bringing her closer to the king. "You have allowed your fate to be twisted. If it must be brought to an end by the steel of my sword then so be it."

"There she is," Alijah purred. "The warrior-queen… I never could match up the stories of you with the grandmother who held me close as a child. I will be interested to see you in action."

"Then come and get me," the queen provoked.

Alijah smiled. "We both know you have a shield around your entire fleet. It's the only reason you've sailed so close and the only reason I haven't wasted the arrows on you. Though, such a shield must be draining to say the least. I suppose that's why you haven't just opened a few portals…"

It was clear to see that Alijah's knowledge disturbed the elven queen. "You know nothing of the magic we wield."

"Oh, I know of the magic you boast, Grandmother. That aside, if you make it to shore, I will look for you. It is my *love* that will grant you a swift death."

Adilandra frowned, misting her expression for a moment. "Alijah, what have you done?"

The king retreated from the diviner and opened his eyes to the real. He reached out and found his eternal companion.

**Burn them,** he said into his mind. **Burn them all.**

For a few more seconds, the waters were calm. Then, in the middle of the fleet, an ancient wrath was unleashed upon the immortals. Malliath the voiceless exploded from the depths of The

Adean and plunged onto the nearest ship, his claws shredding it to pieces. His bulk alone was devastating, but his fiery breath ensured complete and utter destruction from within the elven shield.

The dragon quickly moved on, beating his wings to give him flight while staying low enough to remain inside the shield. A jet of fire tore through the next ship, sending elves into the water to escape the pain of his fire.

Then came the Mer-folk.

The water-born creatures launched themselves from the water and onto the elven decks. With tremendous speed and unbridled strength, the Mer-folk slammed into the immortal warriors before dragging them overboard, where they would succumb to the pressures of the deep. This was happening fleet-wide, across the expanse before Alijah. He heard the elves scream and the water splash, all between Malliath's rain of fire.

It was beautiful and terrifying all at once. He didn't want to watch but he couldn't look away. Then came the bodies, as per his instructions. The Mer-men splashed onto the beach one after the other with their victims in taloned hands. They slithered beyond the surf and left the elves in the sand before wriggling back into the ocean in search of more.

It wasn't long before a barricade of corpses lined the edge of the beach. The sand soaked up what it could of the blood, but the waves were soon awash with it.

"Your Grace?" It was Veda Malmagol again. This time, the Father had removed his blindfold to actually look upon the mounting bodies - a ghastly sight.

Without answering the Father's unasked question, Alijah mentally commanded several hundred Reavers to break away from their ranks and begin moving the bodies into the individual graves. His enemy or not, he refused to have his kin find their eternal rest in a watery grave - they deserved more than that.

Out to sea, the elves were retaliating. Arrows, spears, and magic were hurled at Malliath. There may have come a point when the enemy succeeded in overwhelming the dragon, but Malliath was burning more than one ship every minute. Eventually, and inevitably, he destroyed enough of them that the elves could no longer maintain the shield's integrity.

Like those of his mother's kin, Alijah was also connected to the magical realm, aware of its overlapping presence and the way it touched all things, especially those that existed as conduits between the two realms. It was this connection that lifted the small hairs on the back of his neck. He could feel the air crackle and the pressure change around him, just a fraction of a second before it happened.

The shield dissipated to nothingness.

Mer-folk be damned, Alijah commanded his forces to loose every arrow they had. The sound was soft yet thunderous as they were launched high into the air. Malliath, free of the invisible dome, took to the sky and evaded the incoming missiles.

The king raised both of his hands and called on the magic dwelling in his bones. From the centre and spreading out to the wings, every arrowhead was set alight with flames. Like a tsunami, the tidal wave of arrows swept over the fleet. This was shortly followed by another wave and another after that.

*This Rebellion is beginning to look like war,* the dragon observed, his deadly breath still laying waste to the elven warships lucky enough to have avoided the arrows.

The king had spent fifteen years planning his invasion of Illian, from taking control of Erador's throne to resurrecting an entire army of fallen knights. He had been meticulous in his strategy for the singular cause of avoiding war and minimising the death toll. It seemed he was failing, despite being the ruler of Illian now.

***Just burn it all,*** he fumed, walking away from the surf.

Fire was coming from the heavens in a scorching rage. Like dominoes, one ship after another perished within the engulfing flames. Elves young and ancient had nowhere to flee, with a hunter in the sky and more hunters in the water. It was chaos, and that was *before* the arrows came down.

Adilandra raised her closed fist and constructed a shield only seconds before the first wave of flaming arrows hammered the deck of her ship. Every arrowhead sparked against her magic and bounced away, but her elevated gaze shifted her attention from the creatures of the deep.

The elven queen twisted the scimitar in her hand, half aware that she wasn't going to get it up in time to defend herself. The High Guardian of Elandril, leader of Adilandra's army, skidded low across the deck, cutting a line between the queen and the Mer-man. Faylen's steel flashed, catching the firelight from the embedded arrows.

Adilandra looked down at the twitching tail end of the Mer-man's body, separated from its torso. There was no time to thank her old friend before more of The Adean's inhabitants clawed over the railing and threw themselves at the queen. With powerful strides, she dashed left then right, whipping the exquisite scimitar out with every lunge. By the time she reached the edge of the deck - two dead Mer-men at her feet - there was a call from the bow.

"Incoming!"

The queen raised her hand again and protected herself from the next wave of arrows. Conserving her magic, Faylen had crouched low and taken cover under an elven shield of glass. Two of the arrows impaled an advancing Mer-man, alerting Adilandra to the imminent threat. After the last missile had struck her shield, she turned to her foe and removed one of its clawed hands with a clean swipe. Her second swipe cut the top of its head off.

"We need to leave!" Faylen warned.

Looking to the rear of the fleet, it was clear to see that several captains had come to the same conclusion and were steering their ships back to the east. At least some would survive...

The queen moved to the bow and searched through the smoke

and chaos to find the beach. Auburn hair spilled out of her golden helm and her green eyes found him through the narrow gap that sloped down her cheeks. There was an element of fury in those eyes.

The royal guard crowded the deck behind her, their spears thrusting and jabbing at the relentless Mer-folk. Over their heads, Adilandra saw Malliath coming, his wings gliding across the field of stars.

"My Lady!" Faylen's voice directed the queen to the High Guardian's hand. The crystal had been kept on Faylen's belt for years, always in reserve for Adilandra's safety.

"Get us to Illian soil!" the queen commanded.

Faylen looked to question the order, but time was against them. Instead, she threw the crystal across the deck where it exploded into a reality-shattering portal. Sparks and lightning erupted from its edges, igniting parts of the ship's wooden structure. Adilandra had no idea where the portal would lead - Faylen had seen every corner of Illian. Her only limitation was the distance...

The royal guard rushed Adilandra towards the portal as Malliath swooped low, his jaws wide. Faylen's hand was on the queen's back as they leaped through the veil with as many warriors as possible. The last of the guard to emerge on the other side did so amidst a cloud of flames before they dropped to the ground, dead.

Adilandra picked herself up, immediately drawn to the south, where she could still see what was left of her fleet. A quick examination of their surroundings showed them to be standing on the wooden deck of Velia's harbour. Merchant ships and fishing boats littered the port while the city itself, beyond the harbour, was a quiet sentinel on the landscape, watching the elves burn.

The queen buried her scimitar in the decking and dropped to her knees in despair. She had underestimated her quarry, her blood...

"My Lady?" One of the guard approached. "Are you injured?"

Adilandra shrugged off the hands. If the queen was indeed wounded she didn't know and she didn't care.

"What now, my queen?" Faylen's voice was a balm, focusing Adilandra.

"Now?" The queen rose from the decking and retrieved her weapon, her eyes tracking Malliath in the distance. "Now we join The Rebellion, and we kill that dragon…"

Restless in the absence of real battle, Alijah had ascended the cliffs until he reached the green plains of Alborn. They were a familiar sight, one he had grown up with. He looked back to the east, over the edge. There, he saw an ocean of flaming ships and a bloody beach littered with immortals. It was a stark difference to the quiet and pristine land on top of the cliff.

The contrast wasn't lost on Alijah. He knew he would have to do terrible things if he was to create the peaceful and beautiful world he had always envisioned. He felt Malliath bolster that thought, strengthening him. Generations from now, there would be nothing but green pastures and endless peace. That would be worth the blood.

*Alijah…* Malliath's voice pulled him from his deep thoughts. *What are you doing?* the dragon asked.

The king blinked hard and came to his senses. Quite shockingly, there was nothing before him but the sheer drop of the cliff. His toes were hanging over the precipice as if he had been moments away from taking the last step of his life. Alijah shook his head and moved back.

Since bonding with a dragon as old as Malliath, Alijah's mind had become something of a well that knew no end. He could spend days reliving Malliath's life and only scratch the surface, but he could also enter new realms of his own thoughts that took him away from reality, blinding him to his environment.

Why he had walked towards the edge was beyond him. To think, his dream of a new world could have all come to a sudden end with a single step. He needed to be careful delving into his thoughts and those of Malliath for fear of leaving the world behind, never to return.

Heading away from the cliff edge, he caught sight of a dark silhouette. It could have been anything but Alijah knew immediately what it was - a house. In fact, it was the only house for miles around. To the king, however, it was more than the simple sum of its parts. To him, it was *home...*

So wrapped up in his thoughts of killing his grandmother, Alijah hadn't even considered the location from down on the beach. He walked further inland, around the fence, so that he could see the path that led to the front door. His parents' house. He had been born in there, only minutes before Inara. Without thinking, one hand moved to open the front gate.

*Alijah.* Malliath's tone was commanding, freezing him in place. *That is not your home. The boy who grew up in that dwelling was weak, undeserving of greatness, and wholly corruptible.*

The half-elf took in the house and the surrounding outbuildings. He wanted to go inside, to see his old room. To his right was the oak tree where his mother had taught him to hone his archery skills. To his left were the stables - he remembered Vighon climbing onto the roof and falling off, a broken wrist for his efforts. Everywhere he looked he recalled memories of playing with Inara.

From behind Alijah, Malliath's bat-like wings brought him over the cliff edge where he hovered above the Galfreys' homestead. Beyond the dragon lay a faint glow from burning warships.

*The past must die, so that the future may live...* There was no time to consider Malliath's statement before he opened his jaws of razored fangs and transformed the past into fire and flame. The Galfreys' home was blown to splinters in a cleansing blaze. The fire spread across the ground in one engulfing wave and ensnared the stables and outbuildings.

It was all reflected in Alijah's eyes. Malliath was right, as ever. His past would tie him down, restrict him in his efforts to right the world. He was above such trappings now, free of the bonds that had chained every king and queen before him.

The heat washed over him. It was all that remained of what he once was. Now and for evermore, he would simply be King Alijah, the last son of house Galfrey. That was all the world needed...

# CHAPTER 2
# APEX PREDATORS

At this the ironheart descended beneath the cloud bank, his red wings expanded to capture the currents. He glided over The Hox, hugging Illian's western coastline. Under a waning autumn sun, the land and sea came together in a beautiful vista of crashing waves and sandy cliffs.

Such beauty was lost on Inara Galfrey. There had been a time when the Dragorn had dreamed of adventuring across The Hox and exploring the foreign lands beyond. Now there was only The Rebellion - a life of constant violence.

Ignoring the natural splendour of Illian's coast, the Guardian of the Realm narrowed her eyes at the dark objects easily seen against The Hox's rich blue. Massive ships, sailing with the banner of the dragon - Alijah's sigil - were making their way south.

Inara had been watching them for days, making note of where they came from, where they stopped, and where they were going. Like all the others she had witnessed making this journey, they were heading for the island of Qamnaran - Illian's largest deposit of Demetrium, an ore that had assisted humans in the art of magic for millennia.

The ships had all come from Erador, sailing north along the coast until they found harbour by a small stretch of land between The Whispering Mountains and Vengora. There, the ships were stocked with hundreds of crates, all filled with silvyr taken from the abandoned kingdoms of Dhenaheim, and from where, Inara and Athis had stalked them south-east.

This was nothing new to the Dragorn, nor to her companion. The Rebellion had known of Alijah's activities on Qamnaran for some time and had surreptitiously tracked multiple vessels docking there over the last year. This was just the first time Inara and Athis had had the opportunity to actually investigate the suspicious movement of silvyr.

For nearly two years, both rider and dragon had been pulled in every direction, fighting on every front. Their presence was often the only reason Alijah's Dragon Riders hadn't decimated The Rebellion's numbers, though it didn't always mean victory...

Inara looked down at her hands, marred with scars. How many times had they chosen survival instead of victory? She possessed more scars, beneath her leathers, that all told the story of a failing resistance. Athis too wore the scars of battle. His scales were raked, his wings scored, and many of his horns and spikes had been chipped or worn down.

Of course, one no longer mirrored the other. Since entering the hidden cave, within their private sanctuary, Inara had taken a path known only to the Dragon Riders of an ancient time. Now, her mind and body were once again her own. They were both still coming to terms with their new existence, but it did offer a few advantages when it came to battle.

Inara clung on to that fact with everything she had...

**Let's disrupt their supply,** she said, eager to free her blade.

Athis's caution was felt across their bond. *We are expected to attend the next meeting, wingless one. If we do not make for The Black Wood now, we risk missing it. Besides, the sailors on those ships will likely be no wiser than we are to Alijah's schemes.*

Inara shook her head. *We haven't been watching them for days just to report what we've seen. Qamnaran has already received too much silvyr - we need to put a dent in the supply.*

The dragon could sense Inara's determination and knew there would be no arguing with her. *I can see people on the decks,* he reported. *The majority are guarded by Reavers, but there are definitely living humans steering the ships.*

*Good. If they're alive, they can answer questions. Drop me on one and destroy the rest.*

*The dwarves will not thank us for that,* Athis pointed out. *There would be advantages to regaining so much silvyr.*

*I agree, but since neither of us knows how to sail a ship and the dwarves are occupied inland, those ships only offer Alijah the advantage.*

Athis maintained his high altitude. *We are still none the wiser as to why he needs so much silvyr.*

*Exactly,* Inara replied, irritated that they weren't dropping into an attack approach. *I'll question the humans on board and see what I can learn.*

*This has been given to Galanör,* Athis reminded her, finally coming to his point. *The investigation of Qamnaran is his.*

*And how far has he got with it?* Inara retorted, growing impatient. *Or any of the elves under his command? I'm tired of being called to every battle just to avoid the loss of life. We need some victories. We need answers. We need...*

Inara held back, something she could never have done before entering the cave inside their sanctuary. It didn't matter - Athis knew what she was going to say.

*Vighon,* the dragon finished. *We need Vighon.*

Inara closed her eyes. It had been a long year since the northman had disappeared. Everything had become worse after that.

The Dragorn pushed it from her mind. In truth, The Rebellion needed a lot of things, chiefly answers as to what Alijah had been planning since conquering Dhenaheim and Illian. That started with questions, which had been hard to ask given that the majority of his forces were mindless Reavers.

Now they had a chance. ***Take me down. The meeting can wait...***

*They are armed with ballistas,* Athis warned.

He didn't need to say anything else; Inara knew of the dragon's strategy when dealing with ballistas. She held on tight and employed a touch of magic to keep her braced against Athis's scales - he was about to redefine the sailors' views on speed.

She felt his wings tuck in as if they were her own. Then, the world pulled them down into its embrace like a spear hurled by a god. The air raced through her red cloak and dark hair, dragging them out behind her. This was the easy part. From experience, Inara knew she would need to brace every muscle, ready for Athis's sudden change in direction.

The Hox rushed towards them, consuming their view. One by one, the ships disappeared until only one remained in their sights. Strengthening their bond, rider and dragon came together with a singular purpose.

As expected, Athis spread his wings before the sea pulverised them on impact. Inara had braced with magic and muscle, taking some of the strain off her spine. With tremendous speed, the dragon soared over The Hox, quickly catching up with the nearest ship.

*Be safe,* Athis offered.

Inara smiled. ***Be furious.***

Before embracing her human side, changing the nature of their bond, Inara would have hesitated to part with Athis in battle, their bodies having been so entwined, but now one could take all manner of punishment while the other continued the fight in earnest. This had allowed Athis to save her more than once when facing one of the undead Dragon Riders.

Inara tucked her legs up, finding her balance between the spikes, and sprang up, rolling her body backwards. Athis shot ahead, revealing the lone ship at the back of the convoy below. Twisting her body in the air, Inara angled herself to come down on the bow of the ship, feet first.

It was a considerable drop.

Mid-fall, she called upon the realm of magic to cocoon her, strengthening her feet, legs, and joints. The magic built upon itself as she fell, refracting the light around her in a myriad of colours. Those below had no idea what was about to happen.

Landing on the bow proved to be a devastating blow not only to the men and Reavers on board but also to the ship itself. The wooden deck shattered and splintered under the impact and was made all the worse when Inara released the magic surrounding her. The force of it rippled through the ship, cracking the mast and launching Reavers into the water.

Before the deck could give way beneath her feet, Inara leaped away and dropped into a roll. With elven agility, she launched out of her roll and removed her Vi'tari blade. She also removed the head of a Reaver in one smooth motion before her feet even touched down again.

Standing in the fifth, and most aggressive, form of the ancient Mag'dereth fighting style, Inara brandished her enchanted scimitar for all to see. There were none present who knew the weapon by its name, given by the Namdhorian soldiers she had saved in The Ice Vales, one year past.

There were so few to call allies that every man and his sword had counted - The Rebellion *needed* them. Ensuring their escape, beneath thundering clouds and lashing rain, Inara had raised her Vi'tari blade and poured her magic into the crystal.

What ensued was a fight for her life, saved only by Athis and his incredible speed. In the days following, word had spread throughout the Namdhorian soldiers and even through the ranks of The Rebellion. From that day forward, Inara Galfrey wielded *Firefly*!

The Guardian of the Realm had grown to love the name almost as much as she loved wielding the blade itself. And now, after days of sitting idly on her hip, Firefly was unleashed in her hands. Be it in seconds or minutes, the Reavers were all going to taste its steel.

The ship creaked and wood could be heard splintering throughout its framework, concealing the sound of Inara's movements. The Guardian darted to the port side, her scimitar slashing left and right, flashing in the sun.

The Reavers advanced, unafraid. Their lack of fear proved to be both their strength and weakness. A smart warrior would have assessed Inara and reacted accordingly, altering their strategy to one of running away. Instead, the undead fiends came at her with abandon. The Dragorn made short work of them. Some went over the side of the ship while others lost their heads. One was sent sprawling across the deck, smothered in flames.

The human sailors, natives of Erador, instinctively scattered with many considering The Hox's cold embrace over facing Inara's blade. One brave, yet foolish, man got in her way with a hatchet raised over his head. Firefly moved through his midriff with ease, dropping him to his knees.

The last Reaver to challenge Inara received a blast of magic to the face, the force of which blew its face into the back of its head. That only left one human sailor who appeared too petrified to do anything but freeze in a puddle of his own making.

Inara strode towards him as the mast snapped behind her and plummeted down over the deck and into the sea. The whole ship shuddered under their feet but she maintained enough balance to stay upright. The sailor, on the other hand, had fallen over and was now slowly crawling away on his back.

*The ship is sinking,* Athis told her, his fiery breath obliterating the last of the convoy.

Inara crouched down and adjusted her grip on Firefly to rest the edge of the blade under the sailor's jaw. With her free hand, she retrieved the spinning top from her belt and twisted it on the deck beside the man's head. "You are from Erador?" she asked, her words translated.

The sailor searched deep to find his courage. "Yes..." he stuttered.

"If you want to see home, you will speak only the truth. Lie and I will know." Inara could sense Athis's disapproving look from the distance. "Why is Alijah moving silvyr from Dhenaheim to Qamnaran? Why is he building that tower?" she demanded.

The sailor managed to look more concerned than before. "King Alijah's word is law," he blurted. "We are to serve without question - for the good of the realm!" Right now, the man looked to be regretting his vocation.

Inara pressed Firefly into his neck, threatening to spill his blood. "You must know something! Your journey has been months in the making. You must have heard something, seen something!"

*Inara,* Athis insisted. *He doesn't know anything.*

The Guardian dropped to one knee and adjusted the angle of her blade across his throat. "Speak!"

"This is the last shipment!" the sailor exclaimed, his eyes shifting between Inara and Firefly.

"The last?"

"This is all the silvyr the king requested," he elaborated.

Inara retrieved the spinning top and stood up, freeing the sailor of Firefly's edge. ***If this was to be the last of it, his schemes on Qamnaran must be nearly finished.***

*Troubling,* Athis agreed.

Inara made her way to starboard, so lost in thought that she barely registered the sailor as he leaped into The Hox. She had no idea what her brother was doing on that island and, all the while, she couldn't help but believe that Gideon Thorn would know. She knew of none wiser than the Master Dragorn and The Rebellion needed more than one dragon fighting for its cause.

Gideon's absence had become just as notable as Vighon's, though none had seen the Master Dragorn, or any of their order, in nearly seventeen years. Inara had lost count of the number of times she had attempted to make contact with her old master. Her attempts had lessened of late, consumed by The Rebellion's constant need of her.

*The ship is still sinking, wingless one.*

The Guardian pushed it all away - something she was becoming accustomed to - and climbed onto the half of the broken mast that still lay atop the deck. A run and jump had her and Athis brought back together and a flap of his wings took them both back into the sky.

Before they had even reached the clouds, Inara could sense that Athis was withholding something. Had he wished, the dragon could have concealed any emotion or thought entirely. This told the half-elf that he wanted her to ask about it.

Inara, however, already knew what her companion was thinking. **You believe I'm too aggressive...**

Athis turned his head to briefly lay a single blue orb on her. *You are Dragorn,* he stated. *Half of your nature is that of a dragon. Aggression is to be expected.*

Inara refrained from rolling her eyes. **That is not what you were thinking and you know it.**

Athis pretended to focus on his ascent, taking them over the cliffs and back into Illian's domain.

**You think my human side is to be blamed,** Inara concluded.

*No,* Athis replied calmly. *It is not the embrace of your human nature so much as it is the detachment from mine. There was a time when I was able to temper your aggression, an aggression formed by your bond to me in the first place. Now, it seems, it is up to you to control the dragon that lies within...*

Inara kept her response to herself. The entire subject was nothing if not sensitive.

*I can help you with this,* Athis continued, *if you would let me. Our bond has changed, but I can still guide you with words if not emotions.*

Inara rubbed his scales wondering, as she had done many times, whether entering that cave had been the right thing to do. In many ways, she missed their old bond, regardless of the invisible constraints that had put upon her.

**I would like that...**

# CHAPTER 3

# THE LIGHT IN THE DARK

Standing on Qamnaran's northern tip, where dark cliffs fell away into The Hox, Galanör Reveeri looked out on the remnants of a burning convoy. Four Eradoran ships, stocked with silvyr and Reavers, were quickly disappearing beneath the wild waves that slammed into Illian's coast.

It was the first time any of the ships had been destroyed since the elves had arrived on Qamnaran. It seemed too little too late, but Galanör embraced the scene for what it was - a victory!

Skirmishes had become a way of life on the rainy island, but none had felt like a win to the elf. The silvyr was still tended to by the imprisoned dwarves and the inexplicable tower continued to grow in height, to whatever gain...

For almost a year now they had monitored Alijah's schemes but, in all that time, they had failed to free a single dwarf or glean an answer as to the tower's purpose. The king himself had visited Qamnaran twice to oversee particular areas of the interior's construction. With so few under the banner of The Rebellion, however, they hadn't dared challenge him.

And so, in view of the flaming ships, Galanör had a smile pushing at his angular cheeks. Athis had reduced them to kindling in minutes, a predator over all things. Watching them fly away, and disappear over Illian's rocky walls, the elf found himself missing the mainland. The countryside, where he had once roamed as a ranger, called to him.

Now, as it had many years ago, duty kept him rooted in purpose. Caught up in the heart of things, he had discovered that fate had bound him to a life of the sword, a life that served others. He was content with that, for now. In months of late, however, he had woken from dreams of another place and another life, where the only duty he knew was that of a husband and a father.

Thunder rumbled overhead as dark clouds began to move in from the west. More rain then. Letting his dreams go, Galanör turned from The Hox and mounted his pale horse. Qamnaran was the largest known island in Verda, offering the elf a variety of paths that would take him back to his kin. Naturally, the elves had taken refuge in a small forest on the eastern side of the island, where they could make use of the cliffs and caves at its back.

These longer rides were the closest thing Galanör had to leisure time. He enjoyed what he could of the journey before the constant drizzle turned, inevitably, into a downpour. The ranger chose a path with a high ridge line, granting him a view of Qamnaran's western coast.

There it was, glistening in the last rays of light that punctured the clouds. Alijah's tower of silvyr was unlike anything Galanör had ever seen. Constructed over one of the Demetrium mines, it reminded the ranger of an elegant vase, with a wide curving base that ran up into a slender spout. From top to bottom, it appeared as one complete piece of silvyr, a feat only achievable in the experienced hands of the dwarves.

Today, like others in recent times, Galanör noticed that more of the surrounding scaffolding was gone. They were getting closer to finishing it. Much to the elf's chagrin, *it* was the most descriptive word for the tower. There were no apparent windows, doors, turrets, or anything that resembled a fortress.

Spread out around its base, dwarves could be seen - no bigger than ants from his vantage - working their makeshift forges. Numerous supply lines ran from the forges to the tower itself, where teams of dwarven engineers and labourers put the silvyr to use. Watching them, the Reavers patrolled endlessly. Even the camps, where the dwarves could find rest, were crawling with the knights of Erador.

Before he lost the light, Galanör guided his horse down the ridge and galloped back to the elven base. As always, he took a circuitous route in a bid to lose any potential tails - the Reavers knew they weren't alone on the island.

Approaching the tree line, his sharp eyes scanned the forest for any sign of those who guarded it. He was pleased to see nothing but foliage. Riding through, he eventually laid eyes on the archers nestled high in the trees, between thick branches. They offered him a simple nod of greeting and Galanör returned it, thankful for their dutiful watch.

His journey continued for some time before he finally came across the elves of Ilythyra. They were a resilient group and, in Galanör's opinion, capable of enduring far more than the soldiers he had trained with during his time in Elandril's army. They reminded him of their ancestral kin, from a time before their cities and expansion, when they were the simple, yet hardy, woodland folk of the world.

Dismounting, the ranger handed his reins over with a thanks and made his way towards the sound of rushing water. There wasn't an elf who passed him without a bow slung over their back or a scimitar on their hip. Though they had all come to Illian in the name of peace, the elves of Ilythyra knew how to defend themselves as well as hunt, whatever their prey...

As the cluster of trees thinned out, the waterfall cascading over the cliff dominated the clearing. From its base rushed a winding river that cut through the forest and out across Qamnaran's rough terrain. Looking up, Galanör could see more elves, on either side of the waterfall, moving along the narrow paths.

The ranger stepped into the clearing, surprised to see a shining moon instead of dark clouds and rain. Before he could take a second step, however, an arrow whistled down from above and embedded the ground between his feet.

"Come no closer, stranger!" came a call from the cliff face.

Galanör couldn't help but smile as he cocked an eyebrow. "I surrender," he replied, playing along.

From beside the waterfall, Aenwyn leaped from the edge with one of the hanging ropes between her hands. With quiet grace, she descended the cliff in seconds and navigated the pool's edge to meet Galanör. The ranger leaned forward but Aenwyn wasn't there to embrace. Fooling him, she had bent down at his feet to retrieve her arrow.

"I deserve that," he admitted.

"So long has it been I have forgotten your face," she told him with the hint of a smile.

Galanör broadened his own in a bid to reveal hers. "It's been a few days—"

"It's been *five*," Aenwyn specified. "That's three more than you were supposed to be gone."

"The perimeter needs scouting," he said confidently, even if he was getting further away from that smile he loved so much. "Alijah could send reinforcements any day. He would only have to send an extra battalion and our time on this island would come to an end."

"We already have scouts for that," Aenwyn stated. "You just enjoy riding up and down Qamnaran."

Galanör gestured at the cliff. "I can't expect any of them to do something that I wouldn't."

Aenwyn slowly shook her head. "They don't just follow you, Galanör, because you know the land or the enemy better. They respect you, just as they respect The Rebellion's leadership."

Galanör wasn't so convinced. "They respect me because Queen Adilandra commanded them to. I'm sure they would rather follow you."

"Well *I* follow you," Aenwyn declared boldly. "And not because the queen ordered me to. Your heart is in the right place, and that keeps *you* in the right place. You're always where you need to be, where you're *needed* to be."

Galanör took her in his arms and held her close. "With you is where I need to be." The two enjoyed a tender kiss that had been long missed by both.

Aenwyn stepped back first, her hands resting on his chest. "And did your scouting prove worth its time away from me?"

"I came across quite the spectacle in the north," he began, flashing his teeth. "A convoy of Eradoran ships sent to the bottom of The Hox..."

Aenwyn couldn't conceal her curiosity. "The Leviathan?" she asked incredulously.

"Now that would have been a sight," Galanör conceded, having never so much as glimpsed the legendary beast of The Hox. "They were set upon by Inara and Athis."

"I thought they were to attend the meeting tomorrow?"

Galanör shrugged. "I would rather they keep hounding the enemy than take time to converse with *us*."

"Their wisdom is amongst our greatest weapons against Alijah," Aenwyn pointed out.

"I agree. Though, I rank wisdom just under Athis himself, who can spit fire, has armoured scales, claws bigger than my arm, and a Dragorn on his back..." Galanör's smile was dripping with sarcasm.

"I see your time with the humans has done nothing for your wit," Aenwyn retorted.

The ranger considered her point. "But it has done wonders for my *charm*."

Aenwyn narrowed her eyes. "Thinking such does not make it so."

Galanör leaned down and kissed her again. "Then I am lucky that you think so."

Aenwyn gave him a playful scowl. "I wish I could have seen them sink. Perhaps I will join you next time."

"Just the two of us taking in the sights on a Reaver-infested island," Galanör mused. "Romance has never known such dizzying heights."

Aenwyn tried to contain her laugh before turning serious once more. "The loss of silvyr will have an impact on the tower. We should be ready to take any opportunity that might present itself."

Galanör was unsure. "I still want to see inside. Alijah has overseen the interior himself - it must be important."

Aenwyn displayed the same concern when he had last raised the issue. "Sneaking inside the tower is beyond dangerous, Galanör. There's only one way in and one way out and its guarded by more Reavers than we have elves."

"I will raise it with the leadership tomorrow," he assured. "Perhaps they can spare..." The ranger didn't even finish his sentence; it was ridiculous to think that The Rebellion would have any to spare.

Aenwyn cupped his cheek. "Do not lose heart, my love. The queen will arrive any day now, bringing with her an army. The tide is turning."

Galanör didn't believe that, but he gave Aenwyn a warm smile and held her close again. For all the darkness that had spread across the realm, he had found the only light still bright enough to shine through it all.

# CHAPTER 4
# THE REBELLION

After topping the cliffs and The Wild Moores that lined the western coast, Inara and Athis made their way across Illian on a north-easterly heading. Day passed into night before once again returning with a glorious sunrise. For dragon and rider, however, the journey was long and the sun continued to arch over their flight.

Beneath them, they followed a branch of The Unmar that snaked through the land until it brought them to the green pines of The Evermoore. They spent hours in the sky before leaving the great wood behind. From there they flew clear over The Vrost Mountains, a curving range of snow-capped tips.

Past the mountains, there was but one town to be seen, positioned on the edge of a glistening lake and cut down the middle by The Selk Road. Dunwich held nothing of interest to Inara, nor Athis, but the forest that lay just beyond it was of great importance.

The Black Wood, a relatively small and unassuming forest, was the home of The Rebellion. It was the last place anyone would look for a dwarf and, indeed, it was still an unusual sight to see their kind roaming between the trees. The elves, however, flowed through the wood as if they themselves were a part of the environment.

Mixed in between the two races were an array of humans from various backgrounds, all loyal to the flaming sword. Never, throughout all time, had anyone witnessed the three dominant surface races interact as they did now. There was friction, of course, but all had been brought together, unified by one enemy.

Athis landed in his usual spot, where Inara parted ways with him. The dragon usually stayed a while, however, to soak up the praise and affection given to him by the elves.

***Don't forget to hunt,*** Inara reminded him, laughing to herself.

Moving through the enormous camp of Heavybellys, there were clear areas where the elves had settled. The flowers were vibrant and the grass lush between the trees. The very air seemed sweeter around Inara's kin. The same could not be said of the dwarves, who stomped around the wood, their campsite dotted with fires and vats of stews and skewered meats. Their raucousness set an entirely different atmosphere, along with their unavoidable smell.

She did enjoy their laughter though. The children of the mountain were a hearty people who consistently chose to enjoy whatever they could of life, regardless of how terrible it might be.

Wherever Inara passed, she received respectful bows of the head from all races. The dwarves revered her power and battle prowess, which was quickly becoming legendary among The Rebellion. The elves had a very different angle on their respect for her. To them, she was a Dragorn - a title deserving of all honour. She was also a princess of Elandril by heritage, though Inara had often wondered if that was even considered in light of her title as a Dragorn.

The humans' love for her was better described as adoration and borderline worship. She was their saviour - at least that's what Inara had been told by Sir Ruban Dardaris a couple of times. There were always new faces when passing through the human areas, but most thanked her again and again for saving them from the Reavers.

As always, her journey was slowed somewhat. Many wished to

reach out and simply touch her arms or feel the fabric of her cloak. More than one even tried to give the Dragorn their baby in the desperate hope that she would pass on some of her abilities to their child.

After giving them all as much time as she could, Inara finally broke through and found the Heavybellys' royal tent. It was the man standing outside the tent, waiting for her, that brought a real smile to her face. The Dragorn collided with her father in a crushing embrace.

Inara found much-needed rest in his arms. The comfort she derived from such interactions was new to the Dragorn and likely a result of her new bond with Athis she had decided. Never before had she felt a sense of love or companionship from a simple embrace. Now, she almost craved them...

"Let me get a look at you," Nathaniel said, stepping back from his daughter with her arms in his hands.

Inara quietly laughed to herself. "Must you always?"

Nathaniel's eyes roamed over her face and leathers, lingering here and there over new scars. "You've been gone too long," he commented.

Inara's gaze dropped to her boots. "Yet it never seems long enough to have made a difference..."

The old Graycoat looked to reply but his mouth failed to form the right shape. It was his expression that told Inara something was wrong.

"What is it?" she asked. "What's happened?"

"The reason I came out to greet you..." He paused or, perhaps, hesitated - Inara couldn't be sure. "I wanted to tell you before you hear about it in there."

The Dragorn could feel her heart beginning to hammer in her chest. "What's happened?"

"The queen, your *grandmother*... The elven fleet never made it to shore. Our scouts report that some of their ships have washed up on the beach, but they're still on fire. And there are hundreds of unmarked graves at the foot of the cliffs."

Inara took the crushing blow in one deep breath so that she might ask her burning question. "What of my grandmother?"

"We've tried using the diviner we have, but so far there's been no response. We have to assume..."

Inara almost walked away, not wanting to hear it. "I can't believe he would..." The despair filling her heart was quickly being drowned out by anger. "How could he kill so many? He's half elf!'

Nathaniel said nothing, his expression blank. This wasn't the first time Alijah had come up and the old Graycoat had taken his mind elsewhere, to escape it all.

When he finally returned to the conversation, his tone was matter-of-fact. "We keep pushing back," he reminded her.

Inara was shaking her head. "That doesn't seem like enough anymore," she complained. "We still don't know what Alijah is planning. No one has reported seeing mother for three months now. We're scattered across the realm, fighting on more fronts than we can afford, and now our greatest allies have been decimated—"

Nathaniel cut her off as he offered a friendly nod to another human walking by. "You have told me more times than I can count," he said quietly, "and though I didn't use to listen, it is now the first and last thing I say to myself every day."

Inara knew what he was going to say and beat him to it. "Keep the hope alive."

He gave her a genuine smile. "A rebellion can thrive off nothing else."

"A few victories wouldn't hurt," she remarked.

"We should go inside," Nathaniel insisted, squeezing her hand.

Inara was reluctant to follow him. The meetings were always important for coordinating strategy, but it felt too much like standing still while Alijah and his Reavers gained more ground. Added to that, it seemed they had nothing to discuss except the latest loss of life.

As always, half of the interior was crowded with elves, dwarves, and humans. The other half was reserved for Dakmund, king of the Heavybellys. Since arriving in Illian nearly two years ago, the dwarven king had resided on that bed, clinging to life with the stubbornness his kin were famous for. The dwarves had insisted on the meetings taking place with the king present, awake or not, out of respect.

Lord Kraiden's poison had proven potent, beyond the magic of both human and elf. Together, they had found spells to keep him in this world but, ultimately, the elves - survivors of Ilythyra - had been forced to place the king in a restful sleep from which he could not wake. Dakmund was sustained only by magic now, while they waited to see if his body could overcome the nocuous wounds.

The dwarven morale had been crushed ever since, a burden on the shoulders of Doran, son of Dorain. Inara had no trouble finding the War Mason among his fellow warriors - he was the only one sporting an eye patch. His armour of black and gold revealed new battles since last they had met and, like Inara, he possessed new scars.

The son of Dorain spared the Dragorn a look and a nod of the head. This was not the right setting for any kind of reunion, though she could tell he was glad to see her. On the other side of the large table, two figures stood out more than any other, due to the fact that they weren't physically in the tent.

Sir Ruban Dardaris, captain of the king's guard, stood tall in his polished plate of armour, though its sheen was impossible to see. Like Galanör beside him, he was a projection, cast from the diviner in the middle of the table. Both figures were naught but ethereal ghosts given enough life to see and speak.

A little shorter, Galanör stood with his arms wrapped tightly across his chest, his expression pensive as he analysed the map on the table. He was likely the only one among them who didn't boast of new scars since it was damn near impossible to touch him with a blade. The Rebellion was made all the more terrifying with his scimitars on their side. At his back stood a handful of elves who were actually in the tent, one of whom was powering the diviner.

"Forgive my late intrusion," Inara said. "Please continue."

All eyes returned to Galanör. "You need no forgiveness, Inara," the elven ranger stated. "I witnessed your blow to Qamnaran's supply chain. I've never seen ships sink so fast."

Inara bowed her head to him in thanks. "According to one of the sailors, it was to be the last supply of silvyr."

Galanör was nodding along. "The tower appears to be in its last stages of construction. We were just discussing our options…"

"'ave ye been told, lass?" Doran asked without warrant.

Inara took a breath. "About the elven fleet on our shores? Yes, I've just heard." She looked back to Galanör. "We should continue to try and reach out. There have to have been survivors."

The ranger, clearly grieved, bowed his head. "The news has damaged the morale here. I'm trying to shift the focus back to the tower - I believe an opportunity is coming."

"Agreed," Doran announced. "If that thing is nearly finished there's a good chance Alijah 'imself will show up soon. Not to mention all the dwarves captive on that wretched island - they need freein'."

"I too am concerned for morale here," Ruban added. "The unrest stirring in the south is mounting and more than two sides are emerging. There are those trying to bring back slavery - highborns mostly - and they face a growing opposition. But there is also upset surrounding the fealty demanded by Alijah - they are the ones we are fostering. The men I have, however, are counting on elven reinforcements."

Galanör half turned to regard his ethereal comrade. "The Arid Lands are a source of reinforcements that you must continue to foster, Sir Ruban. We need the numbers."

"Do what you can, Sir Ruban," Inara encouraged. "Alijah's grip is weakest in the south, a fact we should continue to exploit. I will assist where I can."

Doran huffed. "Yer assistance isn' cuttin' it - no offence. Ye're doin' everythin' ye can, lass, an' this rebellion would already be dead if weren' for the blood ye've given. But we need *numbers*. We're losin' fighters faster than we can rally 'em."

"He's right," Galanör concurred. "The odds continue to stack against us. Nathaniel, how goes your work in the midlands?"

Inara's father didn't answer - he didn't even look up. As with most of these meetings, Nathaniel stood by the side table, poring over the reports from across the country, losing himself in the details.

"Nathaniel?" Galanör called again, this time catching his attention.

"Apologies," he replied, gripping one of the reports.

"Have you had any luck since last we spoke?" Galanör asked.

"I'm afraid not," Nathaniel reported. "I've reached out to several factions, ex-soldiers all, but ever since Alijah publicly executed Lord Carrington and replaced him with Lord Gydon, the people of Alborn are fearful of reprisals. There are those, just as there are in Lirian and Grey Stone, who would pledge themselves to The Rebellion, but we lack the one thing they all need to rally behind."

There wasn't a person inside the tent who wasn't thinking of Vighon Draqaro in that moment. The realm needed a king, they needed *their* king...

"This is madness," Galanör announced. "There were no more than a few hundred men who died in Alijah's invasion. Stripped of rank and armour, there is still an entire army of soldiers out there, most of whom fought for the flaming sword. This rebellion will die if we fail to amass a force capable of actually challenging him. Every day we are spread a little thinner and all the while he grows ever closer to his goal."

"Which is what?" Sir Ruban voiced the question they had all shared since Alijah had the dwarves split between Qamnaran and The Moonlit Plains.

Doran pressed his finger into the map, directing everyone to The

Moonlit Plains. "If I could get someone into that pit I might be able to tell ye."

"They're still digging?" Inara enquired.

"Straight down," Doran replied. "They 'ave me kin workin' day an' night. We've seen 'em takin' iron down there too, so we reckon they're buildin' somethin'."

Galanör cupped his jaw. "It makes no sense. On Qamnaran he's building up, and in The Moonlit Plains he's digging down…"

"Given our numbers," Nathaniel said, "we can only afford to focus on one site."

It all gave Inara a horrible feeling in her gut. "For the time being, we should concentrate on the tower. If an opportunity is coming to strike at Alijah directly, we need to take it."

"Finally!" came a call from the tent's entrance. "We can actually agree on something for a change."

All eyes turned to see Kassian Kantaris and two of his mages, as they filled the entrance. The Keeper was comparable to a vagrant by his appearance. His long coat had lost its grandeur, now stained with all manner of unpleasant things. His sandy hair was a mess and overgrown, matching his grubby beard. Only the sword on his hip and the wand holstered on his thigh looked to have been taken care of.

"Welcome, Kassian," Nathaniel greeted with some exasperation. "I thought you weren't attending these meetings anymore."

"You mean you *hoped*," Kassian replied. "Now did I hear right? You're actually considering a way to kill the king? I thought this committee was about the various ways we can watch dwarves dig holes and construct towers of silvyr."

"Reserve yer wit for those who would hear it," Doran admonished.

Kassian grinned, always eager to parry words. "Testy as usual I see, War Mason."

Nathaniel took up the fight. "Are we to take it that you consider yourself a part of The Rebellion today?"

The Keeper eyed the old Graycoat. "Rebellion..." he mocked. "You make it sound so small. This is a *war*. And my Keepers can achieve more for this war in a single day than any of you can in a month."

Inara took a step forward, her anger threatening to take control. She had gained too many scars and seen too many good warriors fall to hear such foolish words.

*There is power in words, wingless one - yours more than most. Stay your sword and use them...*

The Dragorn took a breath. "It seemed every other day we were hearing of your attempts on Alijah's life. Have you finally seen the folly in throwing lives at him?"

Kassian whipped his head around to face Inara. "At least we actually tried to end this war. While you watched Alijah flood the realm with undead fiends, we were attacking *him*."

"Then why have you stopped?" Nathaniel questioned.

Kassian chewed over his response. "Unfortunately it isn't because I wish for your son to live." He paused, as if something had caught in his throat. "In the chaos of this war, I have found a cause worthy of a Keeper, worthy even of my... of Clara's death."

Indeed, looking at the Keeper now, Inara could see that the man's sharp edge had been chiselled away. He was undoubtedly ruled by his grief and tormented by his wife's death, but it seemed he was finally beginning to find a glimmer of hope.

Inara caught his eye. "What cause could steer your path from such hatred?"

"My hatred is still very much alive," Kassian assured. "I've just found a way to *hurt* Alijah before he meets his end."

Doran threw up his hands. "Spit it out, lad; we've all got somewhere to be."

Kassian shot the dwarf a look before moving closer to the map. "There isn't one place, from Syla's Pass to The Iron Valley, that Alijah hasn't decorated with the dead. You must have seen them, nailed to posts outside every town and city."

"It's hard *not* to see them," Sir Ruban replied.

The Keeper nodded solemnly. "Do you know who they are? These seemingly ordinary people marked for death."

"It has something to do with those unnatural beasts - the Seekers," Nathaniel answered. "The Reavers keep them on leashes, like dogs."

"If only they *were* dogs," Kassian lamented. "Every month, Alijah imports more from Erador. They have a singular purpose - to sniff out any being touched by magic. There are hundreds, perhaps thousands, of people out there who don't even know they're conduits for the magical realm. They don't even know why they're being hunted down and dragged from their homes in front of their families."

Inara frowned, incapable of crying over her brother's monstrous decisions anymore. "He's killing anyone connected to magic?"

Kassian gestured to the mages behind him. "Not while we have anything to say about it."

Inara wished to pull on the thread a little further. "Why would Alijah be killing people who don't even know they're connected to magic?"

"He sees them as a threat perhaps?" Kassian suggested. "That is why he burnt Valatos to the ground and Ilythyra with it, after all."

"It's extreme if that's true," Ruban commented.

"Your cause is an honourable one," Galanör approved.

Kassian inhaled a deep breath and narrowed his eyes. "I would hold the honour in reserve. My group and I have taken a variety of avenues that have kept us from these meetings of late..."

Galanör rested his hands on his hips. "Would one of these avenues be the reason you have finally attended this gathering?"

Kassian revealed a mischievous grin. He held out his hand and one of his mages passed him a small cloth sack. The Keeper untied the binding and emptied the contents onto the map. Both Ruban and Galanör peered down, unable to make out the details through the diviner. Inara, unfortunately, could see them for what there were though - ragged patches of human skin. They had been dried out, but the tattoo of a wolf with a rose in its mouth was still clear to see.

*There* was that hatred he spoke of...

Kassian gestured to them. "For those of you not familiar with the Fenrig crime syndicate, *that* is their sigil. Everyone in their employ bears that mark upon their person."

"Not anymore," Doran quipped.

"Alijah has allied himself with them—"

"We already know this," Galanör cut in. "They are present at both the dig site and Qamnaran."

Kassian nodded in agreement. "That's because Alijah's using them to voice his commands to the dwarves. In our travels, we came across more than a few who were... *willing* to part with information."

"And what did they tell you?" Nathaniel pressed, without asking for the gruesome details.

Kassian tossed the sack cloth onto the patches of skin. "There's more going on in The Moonlit Plains than just a few dwarves with spades." Ignoring Doran's growl, the Keeper continued, "It's what Alijah's putting *inside* the hole that's interesting."

"What are ye talkin' abou'?" the War Mason grumbled.

"I understand why you're confused, Master Dwarf," Kassian replied. "I imagine it's hard to see *anything* from the ruins of West Fellion." Before Doran could curse the man, the Keeper continued. "I have knowledge from the very lips of a Fenrig who has been inside that hole and *it-is-deep*. Apparently, they're almost finished digging. Like the dwarves taken to Qamnaran, they've been instructed to start some kind of construction, only they aren't building *up*..."

Inara moved closer to the map. "What are they doing down there?" she asked, wondering if she really wanted to know.

"It's a prison," Kassian began. "Or at least that's what the Fenrig swore to. The dwarves have been ordered to build large cells around the surrounding wall, into the earth itself."

"Prisons are meant to keep people in," Galanör observed. "Who or what does Alijah mean to imprison?"

"And in The Moonlit Plains," Nathaniel added, confused with the rest of them.

"I don't have all the answers," Kassian confessed, "but at least I know where to look."

"Then perhaps we should be working *together*," Nathaniel suggested. "I told you once that you wouldn't get far without swords at your back. You've got what? Twenty mages? It isn't going to be enough to topple a kingdom. We need *numbers*, Kassian."

"You possess great passion," Inara added. "The Rebellion needs every ounce of it."

The Keeper shook his head. "Have you all forgotten your own history? How many of you did it take to bring Valanis down? How many fought the king of orcs on The White Vale and took his head? Or The Crow? Did you have an army at your back when you faced him? There are people in this very tent who are living proof that the few can topple the mighty..."

"Then let us hope that history intends to repeat itself," Galanör commented.

Doran threw up his arms. "Aye, well until then we need to build our forces. If we divert everyone to Qamnaran now, the rest o' the realm will be left to the damned Reavers."

The discussion continued in this desperate vein, but their words were lost beyond that of Athis's. *Inara,* he said, drawing her attention away.

***What is it?*** she asked, sensing elation in the dragon.

*Hope,* he replied.

Inara turned to the cut of sunlight that shone through the tent's flaps. The leadership stopped conversing at the sight of her sudden departure. More than one called after the Dragorn but she was already outside before any one voice stood out to her.

The camp was silent, filled with gawking on-lookers. Every elf had dropped to one knee and bowed their head in reverence. Striding up the central path, between the tents, a parade of armoured elves, cloaked in purple and gold, approached Inara. Leading them was her grandmother, Queen Adilandra.

The Dragorn couldn't help herself. For however long it had been, she had missed her grandmother, who looked so much like her mother. Inara made to bow her head, and even bend the knee, but Adilandra caught her arm.

"You will never bow to me," the queen stated softly.

Inara smiled with glassy eyes. "I have missed you—"

Adilandra pulled the Dragorn in and held her close. Even the queen's hugs were like those of Inara's mother's - strong and brimming with unconditional love. It felt comforting.

"We thought you were gone," the Guardian managed, pulling away from her grandmother.

"We very nearly were," Faylen answered, removing her encompassing hood.

Inara beamed at the elf who had always felt like an aunt. "Faylen!" They crashed together in a brief, yet tight embrace.

"It fills my heart to see you," Faylen confessed.

Her eyes shifted beyond Inara, turning the Dragorn to the royal tent. There, the leadership had come out to see what all the commotion was. Faylen was looking at Nathaniel.

"You're a sight for sore eyes," the old Graycoat proclaimed.

Their own embrace was inevitable, given their extensive history. It was good to see another genuine smile on her father's face... Of course, he bowed his head to Queen Adilandra, his mother in-law, before she blessed him with a kiss on each cheek.

"You are most welcome," he said to her.

"My Lady." Galanör's ethereal form, brought out by one of the elves carrying the diviner, genuflected before Adilandra. "We feared the worst."

Inara took a moment to look over the procession of elves who accompanied her grandmother. It wasn't an army. There were maybe three hundred of her kin, all of whom appeared haggard in some regard - an odd sight. Still, every one of them was a boon to The Rebellion.

"It is an honour an' a relief to 'ave ye among us, me Lady." Doran attempted to bow as much as his armour and girth would allow.

Adilandra bowed her head. "The relief is ours, War Mason. And it is an honour to meet you in person."

With Faylen alone, Queen Adilandra entered the tent beside the leadership. They were informed of the current situation and led to the conclusion that The Rebellion was facing its worst time.

"I will join you shortly, Galanör," the queen said, agreeing with the need to focus on the tower. "Our numbers will still not compare to that of the Reavers, but it may give us the chance we need. I will also use the diviner you have to contact what remains of my fleet. They should have already started their long journey, sailing south to The Shifting Cliffs. From there, they can travel on foot through Syla's Pass and into The Arid Lands."

Doran raised a hand to dismiss the dwarves whispering in his ears. "We will be grateful for the reinforcements, me Lady, but we don' 'ave the time to wait. If all o' the reports are accurate, this tower is only days away from bein' finished. We need to act now."

Adilandra looked across the table at Doran. "Can we count on your kin in this fight, War Mason?"

The queen's question set the dwarves off again, each offering their opinions and advice into Doran's ears. The son of Dorain scowled and waved them away like irritating bees. Before an answer could reach his lips, he studied the maps, his thoughts clearly in turmoil.

"I've got the bulk o' me warriors held up in the ruins o' West Fellion, jus' north o' this hole they're diggin' in The Plains. Movin' such a force in the open would be a mistake an', from what we can tell, the majority o' the prisoners are workin' on this hole rather than the tower. If we were to make a move an' give ourselves away, it should be to free the majority, not those on Qamnaran.

"Havin' said that," he continued, running a hand down his beard, "it would be easier to free the dwarves on that damned island, an' with them fightin' by our side we would stand a better chance o' freein' those in The Plains." The War Mason turned his eye on Kassian. "*Then* we'd have ourselves a real war..."

Nathaniel smirked. "Is that a long-winded way of saying you'll re-direct your forces to Qamnaran?"

Doran frowned. "It means I will accompany ye, me Lady. I'll bring with me as many from this camp as can fight an' hopefully those from West Fellion too."

Inara glanced at Andaljor, Doran's fabled weapon that boasted an axe head at one end and a hammer at the other. With the weapon of his ancestors in his hands, there were few among clan Heavybelly who would ignore his call to arms. She knew, however, that Doran hated such a fact...

"Take the path through The Narrows," Galanör suggested. "Follow it to the western shore - we will have boats waiting for you there."

Sir Ruban's ethereal image shifted. "I can divert my men north and meet you in The Narrows."

Nathaniel held up a hand. "I think it would be better if you and your men stayed in The Arid Lands for now, Sir Ruban. You're doing essential work - every soldier you recruit gives us a better chance of winning this."

"I agree," Faylen added. "We should not assume we will find victory on Qamnaran. Moving all of our forces to one battle right now could spell the end of The Rebellion."

"I don't want to be a survivor," the captain protested. "My knights are among the best in the realm - we want to *fight*."

More than one set of eyes fell on Inara, as they sometimes did in these situations. The wisdom of her order was often considered the deciding vote when the leadership failed to agree.

"What say you, Inara?" her grandmother asked.

The Dragorn didn't say anything as she allowed Athis's thoughts and feelings to flow through her. There were a multitude of options, each as dire as the next.

*Trust your instincts,* Athis advised.

Inara had hesitated to do such a thing since altering their bond, but what she finally said, however, felt right. "We need Vighon," she stated simply. "We need the true king of Illian."

There was no immediate response from the leadership, though their gaze remained fixed on the Dragorn.

"That is easier said than done," Nathaniel eventually replied.

"Yet it must be done," Inara insisted.

Doran sighed. "Not this again..."

"We spent months searching for him," Ruban added. "We've been through all of this before, Guardian. He doesn't *want* to be found."

Inara shook her head. "He believes he is doing the right thing for us all but he must be made to see sense." She paused, staring at the map. "Illian needs to resist Alijah's reign. We aren't going to convince an entire country without their king leading the charge."

"We've agreed on this before," Doran groaned. "But it still doesn' solve the issue o' actually findin' 'im."

Athis, whose mind worked far faster than any person, and on a multitude of levels they couldn't begin to fathom, gave Inara the answer to this conundrum.

Inara internally chastised herself for not thinking of the solution herself. "That's why we need Illian's greatest hunter."

The tent went quiet and more than one look was passed between the occupants. "*He*'s even harder to find than Vighon," Doran replied gruffly.

A subtle hint of revelation crossed Adilandra's angular face. "You are talking about the ranger," she surmised.

"He disappeared before Vighon did," Galanör pointed out.

"An' ye can bet he's droppin' bodies from north to south," Doran contributed. "We should leave 'im to it. He fought with us for what? Four months? He had too many demons on his shoulder - the old man needed to deal with them."

Demons was an apt description given that those who haunted Asher were none other than the assassins of Nightfall. The Arakesh hadn't been a priority to The Rebellion; a cause of friction between the ranger and the leadership.

"Well now it's time to bring him back into the fold," Inara concluded. "We're running out of time. The Qamnaran tower is almost complete. We have no idea what's being done on The Moonlit Plains. More Seekers are terrorising the people every day and the Reavers hold the country in an iron fist." She paused, allowing it all to sink in. There hadn't even been a mention of the four Dragon Riders patrolling the skies...

"It's time we were more than just a thorn in our enemy's side," she continued. "Whatever his reasons, Vighon *must* be brought back."

"A'right, a'right," Doran began. "Let's say we do find Asher an' let's say he does find Vighon. Who among us could convince the king to return? That northman's as stubborn as a dwarf!"

Athis poured all of his confidence and belief into Inara and she accepted it willingly. "I could," she stated. "I let him go last time..." The Dragorn refrained from voicing her full range of emotions where Vighon was concerned. "I won't let him go again," she promised.

Doran huffed, not entirely convinced. "But ye've got to find Asher first. We've left coded messages for 'im in every town an' city but he never responds. How in all the hells are *ye* goin' to find 'im?"

"I'm not," Inara answered, surprising the War Mason.

A host of quizzical expressions followed the Guardian's gaze to her father, the only person who didn't appear curious as to Inara's meaning.

"What are ye abou'?" Doran demanded irritably.

"I can find Asher," Nathaniel said, his eyes lingering on his daughter.

"How's that then?" the son of Dorain pressed.

The old Graycoat raised his hand, displaying his wedding ring. "It's bound to Reyna's," he explained, his tone relaying a sense of depression, "but, since I know where to find my wife, it seemed more prudent to keep track of Asher, given his quarry."

Doran beamed. "Very sly, lad - I like it!"

Kassian folded his arms. "So, we have to hunt down Asher and convince him to hunt down Vighon, who we then have to convince to stand with The Rebellion again... It sounds like a wild goose chase."

Inara stood her ground. "We've fought the good fight long enough without Vighon. He's tried to do the right thing and we've tried to limp on without him, something we might not have achieved had he remained. That time has come to an end."

"That's quite the declaration," Kassian replied with a bemused smile. "Aren't we supposed to have a unanimous agreement?"

Inara took in the leadership. "Do any disagree?" There came no protests, but neither were there any eager agreements.

"Inara is right," Adilandra announced. "Illian itself must stand up to Alijah. They need to see their king."

"True enough," Doran added earnestly, "but we can' spare the men, not with everythin' on Qamnaran."

"You can spare me," Nathaniel told them. "I can find Asher on my own."

"The price on yer head, lad, is so large ye've got more than jus' Reavers to worry abou' out there. All manner o' criminal an' bounty hunter will be lookin' to claim ye."

"He won't be alone," Kassian said boldly, much to the leadership's surprise. "*If* - and it's a *big* if - Asher can actually track Vighon down, the Keepers will ensure the king lives long enough to make a difference."

Inara cocked an eyebrow. "I thought it was a wild goose chase?"

Kassian gave a roguish shrug. "Who doesn't love a wild goose chase? Besides, I've tried enough times to know that, whatever happens on Qamnaran, you're not going to beat Alijah - you're just not." This caused more than a few sour expressions among the tent's occupants. "That isn't to say he can't be killed, because one day I *will* kill him, but, in the meantime, I'm going to make him *hurt*. Vighon turning the country against him is a good start..."

"I'm sure I'll appreciate the company," Nathaniel replied with an edge of sarcasm.

"I wish ye the best o' luck, fellas. If ye do find Asher, give him a smack round the head from me won' ye!"

Galanör unfolded his arms, drawing everyone's eyes to him. "We should discuss strategy regarding Qamnaran. Inara, I think you're best approaching from the west and attacking from the sea. They'll be distracted by our advances from the east and—"

Queen Adilandra briefly raised her finger. "I do not believe the Guardian of the Realm will be joining us..." Such a statement was cause for alarm.

Doran threw his arms up. "*Now* what are ye talkin' abou'?"

Adilandra moved around the table to face her granddaughter directly. "Never has a sovereign, elf or otherwise, possessed the authority to command a Dragorn. But I would urge you to take a different path in this battle."

Inara tilted her head, listening to her intuition. "You're not talking about Qamnaran, are you?"

Adilandra's eyes were piercing. "Just as it is time to bring Vighon home, so too is it time to bring the Dragorn home. It is troubling that Gideon Thorn cannot be reached. We must discover the truth of this. The Dragorn *must* come to our aid... or there may be none *to* aid."

Nathaniel stepped forward. "You're suggesting Inara goes to Dragons' Reach, in Ayda?"

Adilandra didn't take her eyes off her granddaughter. "There is no other way."

*The queen is right,* Athis said into her mind. *It is time...*

Judging by his face, Doran disagreed. "Without ye an' Athis in the sky, we will all fall prey to Lord Kraiden an' his Dragon Riders. We need ye!"

"Queen Adilandra is right," Galanör inserted. "Gideon took the Dragorn away to train for this exact scenario - we need them to turn the tide." Doran didn't argue with the elf but he didn't look much happier.

Nathaniel turned to each of the leadership. "It doesn't matter what any of us think or what we want. If this is to be Inara's path then she should choose it, and we should respect it."

Inara couldn't take her eyes off Adilandra. Her grandmother had once put all of her faith into the dragons, believing with all her being that they alone held the power to change the realm. She had been right. During The War for the Realm, she had arrived on dragon back with Galanör and a congregation of dragons, changing the outcome of the battle of Velia.

*There is more to this rebellion than just us, wingless one. They must stand on their own until we return.*

**With all the firepower of the Dragorn behind us!** Inara added enthusiastically.

"We will go to Dragons' Reach," she declared.

A little while later, as the setting sun was piercing the trees, Inara caught up with Nathaniel among the tents. The Dragorn had no doubt that she would spend most of the evening with her grandmother and wanted some time alone with her father first.

Approaching him from behind, she noticed the corner of a parchment protruding from his jacket pocket. "Something caught your eye?" she said, stepping in beside him.

Her father licked his lips, something he had always done to buy time while he considered his response. "It's one of the reports..." He retrieved it from his pocket and handed it to Inara.

The script was in elven, written by one of their spies in Namdhor. The report was short and to the point: it stated the date on which Reyna Galfrey had been spotted on the ramparts of The Dragon Keep. It also stated that, as every time before, the princess was accompanied by two Arakesh and a small group of Reavers. That was it.

Inara gave it back to her father. "I have them all," he told her. "The reports of her sightings. I keep them all..."

Inara wrapped her arms around his neck and held him close, hoping he could feel her love through such a tight embrace. "What do you think she's doing?"

Nathaniel rubbed his head, taking a moment to shut his eyes in a bid to keep them dry. "If I know your mother, she's trying to save him."

For just a second, Inara wondered if he was about to say her brother's name. Since the invasion, nearly two years ago, he had refrained from saying Alijah's name or even referencing him as his son.

"I fear he is beyond saving," Nathaniel continued, his eyes averted in shame.

Inara wished to agree, but she didn't have it in her to say it out loud. "Keep the hope alive," she managed with a faltering smile.

His dour expression broke just enough to allow the hint of a smile to shine through. "It's quite the journey to Dragons' Reach," he said, changing the subject. "Make sure you take plenty of supplies."

"Always the father," Inara replied, planting a kiss on his cheek. "When you find Vighon - and you will - bring him back here, gagged and bound if necessary. I will talk to him."

A shadow of doubt crossed Nathaniel's face and he lowered his voice. "I agree that bringing Vighon back is what The Rebellion needs, what the *country* needs. But Kassian wasn't wrong; this could be a wild goose chase. And, there's always the possibility that, whatever you say, Vighon will still choose exile."

Inara nodded her agreement. "I have to try. I can't see us winning any other way."

Nathaniel pulled her in for another embrace. "Will you stay with us tonight?"

Inara reached out to Athis and sensed the joy he was experiencing due to the elves' adoration - they had even cleaned his scales and claws. "I don't think we'll be leaving until first light..."

# CHAPTER 5
# BROAD SHOULDERS

All his long life, Doran Heavybelly had boasted of the ability to sleep anywhere, any time. He could also sleep most of the day away if he was so inclined, though a decent helping of mead aided him in this.

Now, like every day since his appointment as War Mason, the son of Dorain was awake before dawn. He could count the hours of sleep on one hand, but he never had time to dwell on such trivial matters - he had a rebellion to plan.

Camped next to the royal tent, there was no chance of him disturbing the quiet camp on his way to view the maps and reports. As always, he entered and bowed to his sleeping brother. He paused upon sighting his mother, Drelda, sitting beside Dakmund, asleep in her chair.

Doran sighed, his heart gripped with despair to see his family in such ruin. He walked over to his mother and adjusted the blanket on her legs to cover her shoulders as well.

Looking down at Dakmund, his brother was enveloped in faint wisps of golden dust, which clumped together and glided over his body. It had been too long since Doran had seen the king's eyes or heard his voice. Scrutinising the wounds on his shoulder and thigh, the War Mason had to wonder how long he would be kept in this elven sleep. Those wounds looked no better than they did over a year ago.

Doran shut his only eye, holding back the grief. He shouldn't mourn, he told himself. Dakmund was still alive which meant there was still a chance they would find a cure to Lord Kraiden's poison. And, like Doran, Dakmund was a descendent of Thorgen Heavybelly - there was no hardier stock than their bloodline.

The son of Dorain turned away, sure that if he were to dwell on the matter any longer he would see through the lies he told himself. Instead, he crossed the interior and pored over the maps. They revealed nothing he didn't already know. The territories carved out by The Rebellion continued to shrink, their numbers decreased across the entire realm, and the number of dwarven casualties - reported from both The Moonlit Plains and Qamnaran - continued to increase.

The Rebellion simply wasn't sustainable. Doran huffed and placed Andaljor on top of the maps. A cursory inspection of the axe and hammer informed him that the weapon hadn't seen nearly enough action...

He looked down at Qamnaran, still visible inside the curve of the axe blade. Perhaps there he would find a reason to swing the mighty Andaljor. Unlike many of his kin, who were openly opposed to his plan, Doran was looking forward to fighting alongside the elves, especially Queen Adilandra, a legendary fighter by all accounts. The War Mason had gone into battle beside elves before and knew it was better to have them as an ally than an opponent.

His finger tapped the table as he considered Inara's plan to find Vighon Draqaro. Doran agreed whole-heartedly with bringing the northman back into The Rebellion; he was the king after all! No one could rally the people like Vighon, regardless of whether he wielded the sword of the north or not. He was also a damned good fighter.

Then there was Nathaniel... The War Mason would rather have

the old knight by his side on Qamnaran, but they could move against the Reavers without him. Kassian and his Keepers were just unpredictable, something Doran had been loath to introduce to his forces for their own safety. So losing them and Nathaniel was acceptable if they could find a way to bring both Asher and Vighon back into the fight.

Losing Inara and Athis was something else altogether...

Without them in the sky, it felt to Doran as if they were already heading into defeat. There were plenty of Reavers on Qamnaran to provide a brutal battle, but if Alijah really did show up... *Defeat*. The War Mason's concerns began to spiral and he considered the possibility of running into one of the undead Dragon Riders on their journey to the island.

His head dropped onto his chest and he released a deep sigh into his bushy blond beard. How he missed the old days - roaming the land with axe and sword, a few coins in his pocket, and a monster to hunt. The thought of it was almost enough to bring a smile to his face.

"*Don't listen to them,*" came his mother's startling voice.

"Ma?" Doran turned to greet the queen-mother, a shadow of her former self.

"*The voices,*" she continued, coming up beside him. "*The ones that tell you to give up, that there's no hope.*"

Doran gave his mother a curious eye, sure that she had been reading his mind. "*Am I that easy to read?*" he asked.

"*I was married to your father for centuries,*" Drelda informed. "*And before that, I grew up around the royal family. I know of the burdens that haunt kings and queens. The doubts that eat away at us...*"

"*If only it were just the doubts that chip away,*" Doran replied. "*There's more than a few under my command who believe I'm not fit to be War Mason. Every decision I make is contested, my every step is judged.*"

"*Continue to prove yourself and their respect will return,*" Drelda reassured. "*You know, as well as I, that dwarves are slow to change their minds.*"

Doran looked over his shoulder to see Dakmund. "*The humans aren't the only ones who need their king.*"

The queen-mother kept her eyes on Doran as her hand rested on his pauldron. "*Your shoulders have taken on more weight than any crown of Grimwhal. You lead the Heavybellys, but every surviving dwarf of Dhenaheim is depending on you now. I see you preparing yourself for defeat,*" she added. "*But are you prepared for victory?*"

The son of Dorain raised an eyebrow. "*Prepared for victory?*" he echoed.

Drelda's eyes narrowed, yet softened. "*In defeat you would find death, and in death there is rest. But victory, your victory, will bring with it a new world, one you have tried so very hard to escape.*"

Doran pulled his head back, taking in all of his mother's words. It took a moment, but he found the meaning hidden within her words. It scared him. He shook his head, struggling to find the right response.

A noise outside the tent caught his attention, stealing any reply he might have conjured. Looking to the entrance, he could see that the sun had risen, its earliest rays cutting through the narrow gap in the flaps. Lost to his thoughts, the son of Dorain had missed the camp coming to life, though now it seemed there was something in particular happening outside.

Happy to leave the discussion with his mother, Doran retrieved Andaljor and made his way outside. There was no missing the hulking red dragon. Athis was surrounded by elves and gawking humans, his wings tucked neatly into his scaled body.

Inara was close by, talking intently with her grandmother, the elven queen. Doran slung Andaljor over his back and walked through the camp, nodding to Kassian Kantaris on his way. The roguish Keeper was content to stay among his dishevelled group and refrain from any farewells.

More than a few dwarves tried to stop Doran on his short journey, but he waved their issues away, promising to give them his undivided attention soon enough. Bar one, the Galfreys were counted among his closest friends and he'd be damned if he didn't say something before Inara left for Ayda's southern lands.

The War Mason frowned upon hearing the elvish that passed between Adilandra and Inara. They were holding hands and very close. Doran was sure he heard Reyna's name mentioned more than once...

He couldn't help but glance at Nathaniel, just off to the side. For most, The Rebellion was black and white but, for the old Graycoat, it was a shaded and complicated affair. Unlike everyone else, he was opposing his only son while his wife was a prisoner and his daughter was The Rebellion's sword *and* shield. Doran's respect for the man had grown over the last two years - something he didn't think possible given the high esteem with which he regarded Nathaniel already.

Finally, Adilandra gave Inara's hands one last squeeze and moved away. Doran returned the bow of the head she offered his way. As always, it was hard to tear his eye away from the elven queen. Her beauty surpassed all else in Doran's eye, a fact that he had decided to keep to himself - it was a very unnatural attraction and he knew it.

Inara took a step and looked down at him. "Care to join me?" she asked playfully.

Doran's good eye shifted to Athis and back. "Oh no, lass! Once is more than enough for this dwarf, I can tell ye!" Just thinking about their flight over The Vengoran Mountains made his stomach churn.

"That's a shame," Inara replied. "I would have enjoyed the company."

Doran considered the dwarves at his back. "An' I would 'ave enjoyed the break..." he cracked, drawing a smile from the Dragorn.

Inara bent down and planted a kiss on his cheek. "Be safe, Doran, son of Dorain. Remember: there is no rebellion if there is no one to fight it."

The War Mason scowled in confusion. "What are ye abou'?"

Inara expressed some awkwardness before lowering her voice. "I know you, Doran. I know that, should the opportunity arise, you would challenge Alijah or…" Her eyes flittered to the royal tent and back. "…Lord Kraiden."

Indeed, Doran had envisioned himself personally chopping off Lord Kraiden's head for what he had done to Dakmund. He had also thought about killing Alijah for all that he had done to the realm but, out of respect for Nathaniel, he had kept that fantasy to himself.

"Do ye doubt the swing o' me axe?" he argued.

"I would never be so foolish," Inara was quick to say. "It's just… This rebellion *needs* you. Your kin *need* you. We cannot afford to lose you. Alijah and Lord Kraiden, they're both…"

"Better fighters," Doran finished. "I might only 'ave the one eye, but I'm not blind. I know they're deadly, lass. But it wouldn' be the first time I've brought down a superior foe, let me tell ye!" His attempt at levity failed and he let his grin fade away.

"Promise me you won't challenge them directly."

Doran took a deep breath, touched by Inara's concern. "Ye know I can' do that. I'm the War Mason o' clan Heavybelly - I lead from the front, not the back."

Inara briefly closed her eyes before wrapping her arms around him. "I will return," she told him with an edge to her voice. "Make sure you're still in the fight when I do."

Rather than lie, Doran said, "Ye jus' make sure ye brin' the cavalry."

Inara nodded and smiled before turning to her father. "The same goes for you," she told him. "Don't get dragged in to Asher's crusade. Get him to find Vighon and then bring him back here. No fighting required."

"Shouldn't it be the father telling his daughter as much?"

"I've got *him*." Inara thumbed over her shoulder and Athis let out a sharp exhale through his nostrils.

"I used to say the same thing about your mother," Nathaniel quipped.

Inara gave a quiet laugh and embraced him. They were a family of heroes - Doran would fight any who contested that. They didn't deserve what was happening to them...

It wasn't long after their embrace that every neck was craned to watch Athis and Inara take to the sky. The dragon's wings buffeted the camp and surrounding trees. Then they were gone. What freedom they had, Doran mused.

"When are you leaving for Qamnaran?" Nathaniel asked, always quick to busy himself.

"Soon," Doran assured. "Our party isn' exactly small." He gestured to the elves and the wagons they were tending to. "We're splittin' into caravans an' staggerin' our departures. Their armour is as much o' a giveaway as their ears, so everythin' has to be carted. It'll slow us down for sure, but at least we'll 'ave the numbers on the other end."

"Your route?" the old knight enquired.

"South from 'ere, until we reach the road for Whistle Town. From there, we can cut across The Moonlit Plains an' join me kin in West Fellion."

Nathaniel's eyes glazed over. "It's been a long time since I've seen those ruins. Is Russell still there?"

"Aye," Doran answered. "He's the best scout we've got down there."

"Do they know about his... *affliction*?"

"He wouldn' be alive if they did. He keeps to 'imself mostly. Last time I was there, he told me he was usin' the old cells, beneath the keep, to... Well, ye know."

Nathaniel nodded his understanding but they discussed it no further. They were both aware that Russell's curse was getting worse.

"I wish you good fortune on your journey," the old Graycoat said instead. "If there is a victory to be claimed on Qamnaran, I hope it is you who takes the glory."

Doran replied with a sympathetic smile - it couldn't be easy to wish for such a thing when the likely conclusion was the death of his son. "We'll do what we can, lad. The priority is freein' the dwarves. After that, we'll try an' undo whatever this tower o' silvyr is meant for."

Nathaniel gave him a hard look. "Do whatever you must to end this."

The son of Dorain struggled to meet his friend's eyes. "Aye," he mumbled. "I could say somethin' similar to yerself. Asher can be stubborn, the northman too. Don' take no for an answer. Drag 'em both 'ere if ye have to. We need 'em..."

Nathaniel examined the wedding ring on his finger and watched his hand drift towards the west. "When Asher left, he was more assassin than ranger."

Doran chewed over that. "Well, if anyone can turn that old fool around, it's yerself."

Nathaniel tried to smile. "I'm almost afraid of what I might find."

"Bodies, lad. Ye'll find lots o' bodies..."

# CHAPTER 6

# ON THE HUNT

oney. That had been their mistake. The transaction of coin left a trail wherever it crossed hands, be it in the boast on a man's lips or in the ink on a piece of parchment. Trails were a foolish thing to leave when a predator was on the hunt...

Crouched low and perched on the lip of a three-storey building, Asher had caught the scent of his prey - the Arakesh. He had been trained to track down all manner of things, but never had it been easier than when dealing with the rich; a foolish breed.

Lady Gracen, before her death, had used the coin of her adoptive family to assist her brothers and sisters of Nightfall. They had infiltrated every tier of Illian's elite and there found more coin to help them create a new Nightfall. Now, they had lairs from north to south where they could recruit and train in secret, protected by the advantages of wealth.

It was elegant, if flawed. Indeed, it was now a lot harder to destroy their order but, with a trail of coins behind them, there was nowhere to hide.

Four days ago, Asher had entered Skystead, a sprawling city that curved around the southern edge of The King's Lake. It was home to thousands - nearly as many as Namdhor, further up the lake - the wealthiest of which were families and businesses invested in fishing. With that knowledge, the ranger had already whittled his list of potential suspects down to a handful. With no more than three conversations in local taverns, he had discovered the top two fishing businesses in the city.

He ruled out the wealthier of the two - an obvious choice the Arakesh would avoid. The second was a company owned by the Danebridge family. Entering their place of business was child's play to the ranger, as was leaving without a trace. Their files revealed a new partner, a rich merchant taken on five years previously, who heralded from Galosha. Since then, they had invested a lot of coin into the fishing lodge on the shore of the lake.

There was nothing suspicious about this and, of course, he had no way of verifying the merchant's legitimacy from Skystead. But, after more than a year of hunting the assassins down, he had developed a hunch about their new operation.

Having followed his hunch, Asher had dug a little deeper into the Danebridges, specifically the lodge by the lake. It was the largest building the family owned and, besides their fleet of fishing boats, their most valuable asset. The construction company paid to make the refurbishments had been harder to find, having changed their name twice before being bought by a Galoshan business that specialised in silk. This might have been curious to some, but not to Asher. For him the dots were all coming together.

After another day and night of investigation, the ranger discovered the foreman at the time of the refurbishments had gone missing and that the new owners were, in fact, the Danebridges, though their name had been difficult to find.

And so, from his lofty vantage, Asher now looked down, across the street, at the lodge in question. It should not be counted as one of their most valuable assets. By appearance it was tired and old and, certainly, in need of more than a few refurbishments. Asher failed to see where the coin had gone.

So he waited...

The moon eventually rose high over Skystead, amidst an ocean of stars, and all grew quiet. There was no fishing to be done at night and the popular taverns were all located in the heart of the city. To Asher's ears, there was naught but the sound of his cloak in the breeze.

There had been a time, decades earlier, when he had relished moments like this - the quiet before the storm. The anticipation had fuelled him as a young assassin but, now, he felt as though he lived only for the storm itself. He needed to be in the fight, making a difference, not watching from afar.

The moon was reaching for its apex when the first seeds of doubt began to creep in. Asher wondered if he had wasted four days on a fruitless investigation. He went over the information he had gathered in Vangarth, including the testimony of an assassin under extreme duress. Everything had pointed the ranger to Skystead...

Then, from an alley beneath Asher's building, a lone figure crossed the street and made their way towards the fishing lodge. Unlike others he had seen after dark, this individual didn't walk with a lantern or torch. They simply entered the lodge and disappeared.

Asher's suspicions grew when another appeared from along the lakeside. They too entered alone without torchlight and disappeared. He only had to wait another hour to witness five more arrive and vanish within the darkened lodge. This was it. Another nest of vipers located.

Asher smiled in the dark.

He descended the building and crossed the street. To the right of the lodge, he could see the flickering lights of Namdhor in the north, no bigger than a finger nail. It was the last thing he saw before the red blindfold covered his eyes.

The Nightseye elixir came to life in his veins, exciting his senses. He could taste the fish in the air and smell the damp wood of the harbour. Rats scuttled through the galleys of the ships docked in the water. Combined with his sense of touch, he could *feel* the vessels as if his fingers were running over their every imperfection.

There was one noise that caught his attention. He tilted his head, focusing on the sound of the breeze blowing through the narrow gap in a window left ajar. It was located on the top floor of the fishing lodge. Asher's nose pinched and he inhaled the scents from inside. There was no one up there - at least no one with a heartbeat.

That was his way in.

He always preferred to work his way down when facing multiple opponents; it decreased the chances of being flanked or ambushed. He ascended the side of the lodge in seconds and opened the window to accommodate his size. It was musty, dark, and everything creaked. It hadn't seen a single coin of investment in at least a decade.

Crouching on one knee, he placed a hand to the floor - no vibrations. A curious thing since there were only two floors to the lodge and he had seen seven people enter the premises. He waited there for a moment, allowing his senses to build him a picture.

There was something solid beneath the ground floor, detectable by the increased speed of sound passing through it. Under that was dead space, a hollow... a chamber.

Of course. The coin hadn't gone into the fishing lodge - it had gone into the foundations. The Nightfall of Skystead was underground, much like the original lair of the assassins in The Arid Lands.

Asher moved down to the ground floor, careful to avoid the oldest floorboards. He had a better picture of the stone beneath his feet now. It was one massive slab of stone that almost matched the lodge's outer walls. Except for the north-west corner. There, the ranger sensed a gap in the stone.

Approaching the corner, he rubbed his finger and thumb together, feeling the grooves that scarred the floor in a sweeping curve. His tongue ran briefly over his lips and he tasted steel. It wasn't old like everything else in the lodge and it wasn't in the room. A hand to the nearest wall told him everything he needed to know.

The ranger immediately began searching for the mechanism that would open the secret door, secured by a single bolt of steel within the wall cavity. His nose found it first. The oil, secreted by the human fingers, led him to the mantel shelf not far from the location of the secret door. It was hidden from sight, beneath the shelf, and the lever was small, requiring naught but a finger to switch.

A series of cogs and mechanisms ran behind the wall and the steel bolt was pulled away from the lock. It wasn't particularly loud, but to an Arakesh it might as well have been a knock on their front door.

Wasting no time, Asher gripped the apparent bookshelf and pulled it open until it fitted neatly into the scar on the floor. Beyond was a narrow shaft fitted with stone steps that spiralled down. Now he could hear distinct voices, sense heartbeats, and smell sweat.

The ranger waited an extra moment to analyse that sweat. He had, long ago, come to know the scent of fear. It was a good indication that they knew who was coming for them. And now they were cornered, trapped beneath the lodge with only one way out - through him.

Leaning his head into the stairwell, his gruff voice rasped, "I'm coming for you..."

His promise was met by the drawing of steel below, as fourteen blades were dragged from their scabbards. They were holding their ground, believing that together they stood a better chance of defeating the man who had killed more Arakesh than any other in history.

Fools to the end then.

"You should have learned your lesson," Asher said, descending the staircase. "You all survived the Darklings' attack on Nightfall because there was more than one way out of that hell. That's the trap, I suppose. Wealth gives you a false sense of security. You should have used *fear* to attain your resources, not *coin*."

Asher's voice filled the space around him, building a sharper image of the environment. Surrounded by darkness, he removed his blindfold and tucked it into his belt. Taking his last step, the ranger knew he faced two Arakesh barring his way. Behind them, a set of double doors had been closed to conceal a large chamber occupied by five more of their order. Every one of them was armed with twin short-swords in the pitch black.

This was no place for creatures of the light...

Asher grinned, eager to begin. "Do yourselves a favour: don't be the last one standing."

His ominous threat increased every assassin's heartbeat and drew even more sweat from four of them. They were all in their late twenties if he had to guess. A pity...

The ranger strode towards the double doors as if the two Arakesh weren't in the way. He already knew how he was going to kill them. The assassin to his right was poised to attack first if his stance was anything to go by. He put too much pressure on one foot - a declaration of his intended action. The assassin to Asher's left was cautious, willing to let his brother make the first move so he could sweep in and strike while the ranger was distracted.

They were already dead, they just didn't know it at that particular moment.

Keeping his weapons in their scabbards, Asher collided with his enemy using hands alone. The Arakesh to his right moved exactly as predicted, shortly followed by his brother. The ranger intercepted the blade, intended to cut him from navel to chin, and redirected the point into the approaching fool on his left. Impaled by his comrade's short-sword, he was dead before he hit the cold floor.

A boot to the survivor's knee broke everything between his calf and his thigh, dropping him down to Asher's waist. A single arm, wrapped around the assassin's head, was all the ranger needed to finish the job.

The acute senses of every Arakesh heard his neck snap.

A solid push-kick forced the double doors open, giving the assassins unbridled access to their foe. Their every sense informed them of the one standing in the threshold, including the two-handed broadsword he was slowly drawing from his hip. If they were too immature to detect the spiked pommel, they would soon learn of it another way.

Asher half turned as if to look over his shoulder. "If you run, you die slow…"

Two of them hesitated, telling the ranger that they had planned on fleeing the first chance they got. Good. Their fear would show through in their fighting style - he would drop them quickly. Of the remaining three, only one maintained a steady heartbeat in his presence. He would be the so-called master of this coven and therefore the one carrying the knowledge of more lairs secreted away across the realm. He would do his best to leave him to last.

Without verbal commands, the five Arakesh came at Asher as one, bringing ten blades to bear. He had faced more.

To the inhabitants of Skystead, it remained a night like any other. For any stragglers by the lakeside, staggering home in the early morn - their night of raucous festivities at an end - they wouldn't have looked twice at the Danebridge fishing lodge. Little did they know that, beneath its ageing walls, bodies had been piling up.

Death had come to Skystead…

Asher groaned as he removed the dagger from his hip, its blade red with his blood. It clattered on the floor and he pushed himself up, taking his knee off the assassin's throat. He couldn't be sure what had ultimately killed the Arakesh. It could have been suffocation beneath his knee or the knife he had plunged repeatedly into his chest.

Behind him lay three other bodies and beyond them two more. The floor was littered with amputated fingers, arms, one foot, and a copious amount of blood. Besides the dagger to his hip, Asher had taken some punishment for his victories. His beard - left to nature for months now - was splattered with the blood from his split lip and the gash across his right eyebrow. His ribs felt bruised, though one might be broken. On his feet, he could feel his left knee struggling to take his weight.

Limping, he made his way to the female Arakesh lying dead in the middle of the chamber. His senses guided his hand to the hilt of the broadsword standing on end in her chest. The steel slid out of her body and the only surviving Arakesh spat blood on the far side of the room.

"Come on then, old man!" the assassin goaded.

Asher tilted his head and took the measure of the man. He had his own injuries to speak of, delivered by the ranger to keep him out of the fight but still alive.

"Swing your sword, Ranger!" the Arakesh growled. "I will tell you nothing!"

"That's what the last fool said," Asher replied, sheathing his sword. "But here you are, right where he told me you'd be."

"Then he was weak!" The assassin paused, allowing his senses to feed back what Asher was doing.

"Can you smell that? Taste it?" The ranger had pulled two knuckle-dusters out of a pouch and slid them over his fingers. "That's dwarven steel," he boasted. They were each branded with the Heavybelly sigil, a gift from Doran before Asher parted ways with The Rebellion.

The Arakesh gripped the only short-sword he had left. "I'm not afraid of you," he said determinedly.

Asher clenched both of his fists. "You should be..."

Gathering his courage, the assassin leapt at the ranger only to be greeted by one of the knuckle-dusters. It broke his nose and immediately reversed his momentum. The sound of his short-sword hitting the floor bounced off the stone walls and was almost painful in Asher's sensitive ears.

"Give me his location," he demanded, punctuated by a heavy

blow to the assassin's ribs. Something broke and a sharp yell escaped the man's lips as he fell to the floor.

"Go to hell," he replied through gritted teeth.

Asher dragged him up and pressed him against the wall. "Give me his location," he repeated.

"Go to—" Three successive blows hammered into the assassin's midriff, stealing his last word.

Asher stopped him from sliding down the wall and pinned him in place. "When we took our oaths, we made a pact with death. Our end is inevitable..." The ranger pushed his fist into the Arakesh's jaw, letting his skin feel the cold metal. "...But *how* we meet it can be up to us. Choose your fate."

The assassin was either the bravest of his wretched kind or the most foolish. Using what speed he had left, the Arakesh swiped at Asher with a small dagger taken off the ranger's belt. Asher jumped back and heard his leathers take the brunt of the attack, which was quickly followed by another lashing strike.

"I'll die before telling—"

Asher snatched his enemy's wrist from the air and threw all of his weight behind the knuckle-duster that snapped the assassin's elbow. His reactionary scream drowned out the sound of the dagger hitting the floor. A powerful kick to the gut launched the Arakesh back into the wall where he crumpled to his knees.

Asher came to stand over him. In the darkness, none of the assassins had had need of their blindfolds, and so the ranger could *feel* the fine red fabric, tucked into his belt, just as he could smell the blood that stained it. He reached down and removed it from his enemy's belt.

"I've bloodied more of these than I can count," he said, ignoring the increasing pain in his hip. "Every town and city I visit your numbers drop away. There can't be that many places left for him to hide. Tell me, and the pain will stop." The ranger crouched down in front of him. "Where is Veda Malmagol?"

The assassin's breath was rapid, increasing to match the shock and pain in his arm. "Kill the Father... and another will take his place. You cannot win..."

Asher exploded into action and gripped him by the heel, dragging him into the middle of the training chamber. The Arakesh grunted in more pain as the back of his head knocked against the floor and slid through the blood. Amidst the corpses of his brothers and sisters, the assassin was left on his back and at the ranger's mercy.

Asher dropped a knee onto his chest. "Where-is-Veda-Malmagol?" Every word was a growl and accentuated with a blow from the knuckle-dusters.

The Arakesh spat blood over himself. When he started laughing Asher wondered if he had hit him too hard in the head.

"All your struggle," the assassin sputtered. "All your strife... You can't run away... from what you are." His next laugh was combined with a hacking cough. "You are not the warrior... they think you are. You will die... as one of *us*..."

With his fist clenched high, ready to deliver the next hammering blow, Asher hesitated. The assassin's words had cut through him deeper than any of their blades and struck at the heart of his turmoil, a turmoil he had spent over a year trying to ignore.

What was he becoming? What had he *become*?

"Nightfall will live on," the broken Arakesh continued. "It will live on... in all of us. You cannot stop us. We will go on..."

And there was the other side of his turmoil. The Arakesh would continue to kill for money if not the realm's new king. Asher couldn't live with either one. He also couldn't bring himself to torture this man for answers that would likely take hours to obtain. And, judging by the dizziness beginning to take a hold of him, the ranger didn't have hours before he succumbed to his own injuries.

Without another word, Asher slipped the dagger from his boot and drove it into the Arakesh's throat, angled to sever his spine at the back of his neck. It was a quicker death than the killer deserved, but the ranger was in no mood to prolong it any further.

Returning to his full height was a pain-inducing experience that nearly saw him fall over again. The Nightseye elixir was fighting his blood loss to maintain a map of his surroundings. Asher replaced his gifted knuckle-dusters and made for the spiral staircase. It was certainly a slower journey than his one to the training chamber, and he left bloody handprints up the curving wall.

He moved from corner to corner inside the fishing lodge, leaning on anything that would support him. There was no way he would be leaving the same way he entered - it would have to be the double doors that led out onto the street.

As he reached them, the effects of the Nightseye elixir were making his nausea worse and so he welcomed the faint light of the world. The very first rays of the dawn were piercing the windows and cracks of the lodge. There was no time to consider the way he would look in the streets of Skystead - he just needed to reach his room above the... He could no longer recall the name of the tavern.

The doors refused to budge under his shoulder. He shoved again and again only to find himself on his knees. It was there, on the floor, that he saw the blood running from his hip. What a careless fool he had been...

Throwing oneself into battle was a young man's game and the last thing he should have done considering his opponents. His training had taught him the art of despatching one target at a time with speed and efficiency, yet he continually charged into one nest of assassins after another. He should have been dead at least three times over. The only reason he wasn't dead was also the reason why he kept giving in to the storm that urged him to fight.

He had a Drake.

The double doors were torn from their hinges, splintered into pieces, and pulled out into the street. Standing there in front of the lodge, on the quiet road, was Adan'Karth. A flapping brown cloak hid most of him and a voluminous hood, draped over his head, concealed his horns, both of which had been filed down to flat protruding discs on his forehead.

"Adan..." Asher reached out for him. "Where in all the hells... have you been?"

The Drake rushed to his side with a raised eyebrow. "You told me not to leave our room."

The ranger left his attempt at humour behind and allowed the Drake to help him up. "Just get us back there," he insisted.

Adan'Karth looked over Asher with grave concern. "I need to heal you... *again*."

"Not here," Asher replied, gripping the Drake's wrist. "It's not safe." He made a cursory inspection of the street and the buildings facing them. Somewhere out there, in the city, were patrols of Reavers with their Seekers.

"Quickly then," Adan'Karth agreed, supporting Asher under the arm and onto the street.

"Wait," the ranger urged, turning back to the fishing lodge. "Burn it."

The Drake's lightly scaled face frowned under the hood. "That would be a violent action, Asher. I have promised to help *you*, not your cause."

The ranger was growing impatient. "There's no one inside, not alive anyway. And it's isolated - the fire won't spread. But it needs to burn, Adan. Purging fires are natural, remember. Do it..."

Adan'Karth looked from the ranger to the lodge, his moral code in question *again*. Eventually, the Drake flicked his wrist and unleashed a spell of fire upon the lodge's interior. It spread quickly and relentlessly as if set ablaze by a dragon.

Asher could feel the heat on his face. "Good..." At that moment, he didn't care that he was out of leads - he just wanted to watch it burn before passing out.

# CHAPTER 7

# MAKING PLANS

Galanör's feet could barely be said to touch the ground as he raced across Qamnaran. He skipped over the rocks, often using his momentum to gain height over the steep walls of jagged stone. The island's winding spine of pointed cliffs was the largest natural obstacle that kept the elven camp separated from the tower of silvyr.

Ascending the cliffs sapped his energy but he relished it. The elf *needed* to run off some energy before he actively sought out Reavers to temper the fury building up inside of him. The more he thought about his kin, washing up on The Shining Coast, the harder he ran.

Sprinting along a narrow ledge, the ranger jumped high to reach a precarious handhold. Experienced fingers found every crevice and elven strength pulled him up to the next ledge. Scaling the stone was akin to climbing the trees of The Evermoore and he made it look effortless.

A short fissure, just wider than the width of his shoulders, cut through the cliffs and opened up to the western side of the island. From up there, Galanör could see The Hox from north to south and the contrasting green and grey of Qamnaran below. Almost in line with his position was the colossal tower. Regardless of its intended use - and it was more than likely another weapon in Alijah's arsenal - the tower was beautiful, especially at night, when it would shimmer like diamonds under the moonlight.

Using a familiar route, Galanör made his way down the western slopes, aiming for the tall pine that dominated a mossy plateau. There, he found the elven scouts who had taken the night watch for the last three days. His approach was silent but their lookout had spotted him before he even touched down on the plateau.

Tyren, the leader of their watch, greeted the ranger and made room for him on the lip of the outcropping. *"We've been expecting you,"* he said with a glance at the pine tree.

Galanör didn't need to follow his gaze to know that Aenwyn was up there. She had always preferred a lofty vantage if there was one to be claimed - the mindset of an archer. Looking up, he could just make her out between the branches. She had left even earlier than Galanör, beating the dawn. Like him, Aenwyn had been restless since the fleet's crushing defeat and had chosen action over sleep.

Galanör kept his attention on Tyren. *"Has Aenwyn informed you..."*

Tyren's demeanour told the ranger everything he needed to know. *"We have lost many brothers and sisters to this evil,"* the scout lamented.

Galanör nodded in agreement, desperate to think of anything besides the number of their dead. *"You should all return to camp - you deserve rest. I will wait with Aenwyn until the next shift arrives."*

Tyren looked briefly at his fellow scouts. *"We believe we have found him,"* he reported.

The elven ranger raised an immaculate eyebrow, his interest piqued. *"Where?"*

Aenwyn dropped out of the tree with hardly a sound, be it in her impact or effort. *"Show us,"* she urged.

Galanör caught her eyes before Tyren directed them to the smoky camp below. There was recklessness brewing behind those exquisite orbs. The ranger had often given in to rash decisions in the heat of the moment, giving him an insight to where such impulsiveness might surface. For all Aenwyn's discipline and model restraint, she was prone, like so many elves, to her heightened emotions.

Crouched on the edge of the plateau, Tyren pointed to the north of the dwarven camp. *"Three tents in from the farthest edge, four tents up. He matches the War Mason's description."*

Narrowing his exceptional sight on the camp, Galanör searched the area Tyren had described. Like so much of the camp, both on Qamnaran and in The Moonlit Plains, the dwarves were mostly that of the Brightbeard clan - an easy distinction thanks to their eccentrically styled beards and hair.

*"Every morning,"* Tyren pointed out, *"the area around that tent fills with dwarves. Some of them, I would say, act protectively towards him."*

Galanör watched intently, waiting. At last, a large dwarf emerged from the tent under the morning sun. In the light, the dwarf's sizeable red beard and extravagant mane of hair was easy to see. He patted some of his fellow dwarves on the back and offered them words well beyond the hearing of the elves.

*"King Gaerhard,"* Galanör muttered.

Besides Dakmund Heavybelly, Gaerhard, son of Hermon, was the only surviving king of Dhenaheim. Doran had brought him to the elves' attention during a number of their meetings, stating his importance to the dwarven cause.

*"Is he treated differently by the enemy?"* Aenwyn enquired.

Tyren shook his head. *"The dwarves are given their orders by the Fenrigs, whose commands are enforced by the Reavers. They either don't know he's the king of the Brightbeards, or they don't care. He's put to work just like the rest. Most days he works on the supply line of silvyr from the forges to the tower."*

Galanör watched the crowd around the king disperse. *"Doran has insisted many times that Gaerhard is to be rescued if at all possible."*

*"That's a lot of risk for very little reward,"* Aenwyn opined. *"We have got word to the dwarves before, but never have we been able to rescue any*

*of them. I see no sense in endangering elven lives to save a dwarven king - we need numbers, not a crown."*

Galanör saw the logic in her words and even agreed with them to an extent. Her tone, however, was far from encouraging at a time when every one of them needed fire putting in their veins.

*"The dwarven culture is not our own,"* he began diplomatically. *"They often require a... pillar of sorts. Someone they can rally around and be inspired by—"*

*"You mean they're sheep,"* Aenwyn interjected.

Galanör took a breath. *"King Gaerhard is the pillar down there. He has the authority to turn those prisoners into rebels. We could use that to our advantage when the queen arrives."*

*"If he has such power,"* Aenwyn continued in ire, *"then why hasn't he already used it and fought back?"*

Galanör didn't answer her. Instead, he turned to Tyren. *"You have manned this post long enough, brother. See yourselves returned to the camp and..."* The ranger considered his words. *"Bring them what hope you can: it is much in need right now."*

*"What of our discovery?"* Tyren asked.

Galanör considered his options. *"Doran and the queen will be on the move by now. Have word of King Gaerhard sent to the dwarven camp at West Fellion."*

Tyren bowed his head and directed the other scouts to begin their climb. Galanör waited until they were out of earshot before returning to his conversation with Aenwyn.

Switching to man's tongue, he said, "I know you're hurting, Aenwyn, but—"

"I want action," she stated bluntly. "I want... retaliation. I want—"

"Revenge," Galanör finished.

Aenwyn's features softened a touch. "Yes," she confessed.

It was the first time Galanör had seen this side of his companion. After dedicating her life to peace in Ilythyra, Aenwyn had put her violent training behind her and embraced the lifestyle of their ancestors. Now, the ranger could see that much effort was applied daily as she battled the warrior she had been bred to be in what was once King Elym's army. Seeing her falter in such a noble endeavour only endeared her to him all the more.

"You," he said, "would be the first person to tell me that revenge isn't the path of an elf."

Aenwyn sighed. "I need to do something, Galanör. Living a life in harmony with nature was easy during my time in Ilythyra. Lady Ellöria guided me like all the others, but we were living in a time of peace. Our assistance against the orcs was brief and seen as necessary, but this... The Rebellion requires us to fight again and again. I see it in the others too. The soldier in us all is returning to life, demanding we take action. And now... Now we have lost so many of our kin to Alijah and his wretched dragon." She clenched her fist in an effort to regain some emotional control.

"I understand," Galanör replied honestly. "You know well of the demons I fight."

Aenwyn finally met his eyes and reached out for his hand. "You have come a long way since you arrived in Ilythyra," she praised with half a smile. "I see your control every day. Perhaps it should be *you* helping *me*..."

Galanör squeezed her hand. "Why don't we help each other," he suggested tenderly.

"We will get through this, won't we?" Aenwyn asked. "I mean, without losing ourselves..."

"If we get lost," he replied, "then we get lost together." He squeezed her hand a little tighter. "And we will find ourselves together."

Aenwyn found the rest of her smile and leaned in to kiss him. These were the moments he had come to live for. Whenever she kissed him, Galanör glimpsed that life he had begun to dream of in his sleep. Even for an immortal, it seemed like a lifetime away...

"Tonight then," Aenwyn said, only seconds after pulling away.

Slightly dazed, Galanör frowned at his companion. "Tonight?"

Aenwyn nodded eagerly. "We will sneak into the camp tonight and speak with King Gaerhard."

Stunned, the ranger replied, "You make it sound simple."

Aenwyn shrugged. "The Reavers possess human sight, diminishing their ability to secure the camp at night."

Galanör knew there would be no arguing with her, yet he still said, "We should discuss this with the others first."

Without taking her eyes off the camp, she replied, "We will tell the scouts when they arrive. We go tonight."

It was dangerous - that much Galanör knew without a doubt. But he needed a little danger, not to mention some sense of victory. And he had long ago learned that fretting over Aenwyn was a foolish mistake - she had saved him more times than he had saved her...

"Tonight," he agreed.

# CHAPTER 8

# AS THE CROW FLIES

As autumn considered surrendering its claim on the realm, the snowy tundras of The White Vale were becoming inhospitable. Strong and icy winds dominated the open stretch of land, buffeting any who dared to cross it. There was no refuge out there. No towns or settlements to call upon. A few more weeks from now and winter would ensure that any fool stupid enough to cut through the flat land would never see the other side.

Kassian, seated atop his horse, took in the surroundings from the roadside. To the south, beyond sight, was the green of The Evermoore and, to the north, reaching for the clear blue sky, were The Vengoran Mountains. The Selk Road was the only path that offered a safe route around the edge of the vale, though it was treacherous in other ways...

"We shouldn't be here," Fin remarked from his own horse. "We're too exposed on the road."

Kassian glanced at the young mage. Fin had only been days away from earning his title as Keeper before Alijah and Malliath razed Valatos to the ground. Kassian had found the fiery young man in a gutter in Whistle Town and in need of purpose. He had since more than earned the title.

"Fin's right," Quaid agreed. "The north is no place to be exposed."

Kassian didn't need to look at the older Keeper to know he was frowning - he was always frowning. His scraggy grey hair fell to his shoulders and concealed the burns that ran up his neck and over his left ear or, at least, what was left of it. For all his pessimism, however, Quaid was a brutal fighter with both magic and staff - an attractive quality as far as Kassian was concerned.

The sound of hooves crushing snow drew Kassian to his right, where he discovered Aphira bringing her horse in line with his own. The hood of her Keeper's coat was draped low over her head, though it could do nothing to contain her wild black hair. Her olive skin told of an upbringing in The Arid Lands and her stony expression spoke of a hard life.

Valatos had saved her from a path similar to what Kassian's had been in the wake of The Ash War. The south had been ravaged by the orcs more than most, its inhabitants left with nothing to call their own. Aphira had found her place in the Keepers' order and taken to destructive magic with frightening ease. In truth, she was the only one among their band who had not lost a loved one to Malliath's fire. But, like them all, she had lost her place in the world.

"They're not wrong," she said in a hushed tone. "We're too close to the capital to be just sat on the roadside. If this Asher is in Namd-hor, perhaps we should consider returning to our own path. There are plenty of towns and cities in need of our help, Kassian."

"Give him a minute," the Keeper urged, his eyes fixed on Nathaniel Galfrey.

The old Graycoat had dismounted and was now standing in the snow, thirty feet away from the Keepers. His left arm was outstretched and his hand raised to the west. Soon, Kassian hoped, that ring of his would guide them away from the region.

"Do you trust him?" Aphira questioned with a whisper.

Kassian had been considering that question since they departed The Black Wood. Of all those who fought for The Rebellion, none was so complicated as Nathaniel, the father of their greatest enemy.

"He's a Galfrey; of course I don't trust him." Kassian had, as ever, given the only answer he could. Anything else would make him appear naive.

"Then why do we follow him?" Aphira continued, likely voicing the question they had all been asking each other.

"Because he's the only one who can find the ranger." He kept his reply simple and clipped.

"You imply a degree of trust there," Aphira observed.

"How long have we been doing this, Aphira?" Kassian asked, taking control of the conversation. "How long have we been journeying from place to place trying to make a difference; trying to put some kind of dent in Alijah's reign? We all agreed that we wanted nothing more than to make him hurt."

"We save lives everywhere we go," Aphira countered. "That *is* making a difference. And it must be hurting Alijah - he's targeting magic users for a reason."

"You're right," Kassian said. "We do save lives wherever we go. But we also lose lives wherever we go. Layah, Demry, Erik... Good mages all. It's time we did something that *really* hurts, that *really* makes a difference."

Aphira looked to be considering his words. "And you believe that this *ranger* can help us to do such a thing?"

"The ranger? Who knows? I find half of what I hear about him hard to believe. *But,*" Kassian emphasised, "if there's even a chance that he can find Vighon Draqaro, then we need to take it."

"Some of the others have less faith in the house of Draqaro," Aphira commented. "They do not believe the king holds much promise."

Kassian sighed, trying to soften his scowl. "Then why are they here?" he asked without looking back at any of them.

"Because they have faith in *you*," Aphira asserted.

That was the last thing Kassian had expected to hear and it silenced him. He knew that those around him always did as he commanded, but he had never considered himself their leader. They were all angry and in need of action to settle their rage, like him. All the Keeper had done was give them an outlet. Hadn't he? When had he become someone they had faith in?

Nathaniel finally returned and such questions faded from Kassian's mind. "Well?" The Keeper shrugged.

The old Graycoat glanced at his wedding ring. "He's west of here - I'd say almost directly."

Kassian looked out on The White Vale, despairing at the never-ending horizon to the west. "At least he's not in Namdhor," he muttered. "What's west of here?" he asked Quaid.

The older Keeper narrowed his eyes, pulling at the lines that surrounded them. "The King's Lake stretches south." He took a breath, seeing the map in his mind no doubt. "Directly west of here... There's a good chance you'd hit Skystead."

Nathaniel mounted his horse, throwing his long coat over the back of the saddle. "As the crow flies then." With that, he spurred his horse from the road and across the thick snow.

Kassian could feel the eyes of his Keepers on him, his word the only thing that would get them moving. "We have our heading," he announced. "Keep your heads on a swivel - I don't want wolves adding to our problems..."

All eighteen riders broke away from the road and trailed Nathaniel into The White Vale. Not even an hour into the tundras and the wind pummelled them with the power of a thousand needles. Kassian used his wand to envelope himself and his horse in warmth, a privilege Nathaniel had declined in favour of bearing the cold.

Fool...

The old Graycoat was an enigma, something the Keeper struggled to live with. Since taking to his crusade, life had been simple and Kassian liked it that way. Spurring his horse on, he trotted ahead to come alongside Nathaniel.

"Has he moved?" Kassian asked by way of starting a dialogue.

Nathaniel lifted his hand from the reins and examined his rigid fingers. "No," he answered. "Wherever he is, he hasn't moved."

The Keeper nodded in acknowledgement, unsure what to say next. "A stroke of luck you giving that ring to the ranger, eh."

Keeping his eyes on the horizon, Nathaniel replied. "I didn't give it to Asher - he would never allow himself to be tracked."

With some alarm, Kassian turned in his saddle. "Then who are we tracking?"

"Adan'Karth."

Kassian's eyes danced over the landscape as he recalled the owner of the said name. "The Drake?"

"He travels with Asher," Nathaniel explained. "If we can find Adan, we can find Asher."

The Keeper was shaking his head. "This is sounding less like a wild goose chase and more like a needle in a haystack…"

"They're together," Nathaniel stated confidently. "Adan feels… *indebted* to Asher."

"Why?"

The old Graycoat struggled to find an immediate response. "Because Asher is responsible for Adan's existence," he said simply, shrugging his shoulders.

Kassian couldn't arch his eyebrow any further. "Come again?"

Nathaniel shrugged. "It's a long story. We just need to find Adan."

The Keeper let his curiosity fall away, something he could never have done before Clara's death. These days, he preferred to tackle what he could see or, more specifically, what he could hit with his wand.

"So we find Asher, he leads us to Vighon… then what?"

Nathaniel took a breath, his gaze dropping for just a moment. "He rallies the realm against our enemy. Then we take Illian back."

"I got that far myself," Kassian retorted. "I was talking about you? We find Asher who tracks down Vighon and then... What's your part in all this? You have to know this war only ends one way."

The old Graycoat, poised to respond, finally looked at Kassian. But he said nothing and quickly returned to the horizon.

The Keeper persisted. "You must have—"

"I don't recall you being so talkative," Nathaniel cut in.

"I don't recall you being so clipped," Kassian responded. "You're the only reason I didn't march to Namdhor and get myself killed. You told me I needed swords at my back. Well, now I have something better." He grinned.

"I know how this ends," Nathaniel said quietly. "I've lived through enough wars and seen enough tyrants to know what's coming."

"Yet you still help The Rebellion," Kassian pointed out. "You could be living the high life in The Dragon Keep. Hells, you could probably have your own city! Why are you here? What are you fighting for?"

"Why do you need to know?" Nathaniel growled. "Why do you even care?"

"I need to know what your place is in all this because it's my people at your back. You're the only person in the whole rebellion who has so much to lose from winning."

"So it's a question of trust," Nathaniel concluded.

"Of course it is. You're riding beside someone who has sworn to kill your son..."

There it was. Kassian could see it flash across the old Graycoat's face. Nathaniel was already grieving his son, considering him lost.

"My task is simple," Nathaniel replied. "I'm going to do what I can to put Vighon back on the throne. And I'm going to rescue my wife in the process. If the Fates are kind, I'll still have a daughter when this is all over."

"You're going to rescue Reyna?" Kassian considered the reports he had read. "It's never been noted that the ambassador is in chains."

"You don't need chains when you're surrounded by Arakesh and Reavers."

"You think she can't break free of them?" Kassian asked with some surprise. "Everything I've heard and seen of your wife suggests she could turn The Dragon Keep inside out if she wanted to."

Nathaniel was quiet for more than an awkward moment after that. "I'm not going to rescue Reyna from those who guard her. I'm going to..." Again, his gaze fell onto the horse beneath him. "I'm going to free her from herself. From her responsibilities."

It took a few seconds for the gravity of the knight's task to sink in. Convincing any mother to give up on their son seemed like a fool's errand to Kassian, but most mothers didn't have a genocidal tyrant for a son...

For the first time, the Keeper felt sorry for Nathaniel. Clara had been killed before they could have children, but he could empathise to a degree. Even that flicker of understanding made him pity the old Graycoat.

"Has there been any attempt to save her?" Kassian asked. "Since our earliest attempts, I mean." The Keeper remembered well the terrible casualties they had suffered trying to get Reyna out of The Dragon Keep.

"No," Nathaniel said blankly, perhaps recalling the same nightmare.

Kassian wanted to offer some suggestions where that predicament was concerned, but to infiltrate the capital, let alone the keep, was folly. Instead, they continued to ride through the snows of The White Vale with some semblance of understanding forming between them.

There was still a way to go...

# CHAPTER 9

# ALL THAT REMAINS

Vighon saw it coming. It was impossible to miss, given that there was nothing else to see but the closed fist hurtling towards his face. He considered evading the blow - he even considered the counter attack that would immobilise his opponent for some hours.

*Damn it all*, he thought...

The knuckles slammed into his face which, in turn, slammed his head into the surrounding wall of the filthy arena. It hurt like hell. He didn't care. In fact, he embraced the pain.

The northman groaned as he staggered back to his feet, using the wall as an aid. There was a familiar taste in his mouth and he spat blood onto the dirty floor, there to be lost amongst the rest of the grime. He didn't see the next punch coming, his sight blocked by a mane of matted dark hair he hadn't bothered to cut in some time.

The fist caught his lip, splitting it and decorating the wall with more of his blood. Vighon didn't have time to think about how much that hurt - his head was being dragged up by his hair. A swift uppercut into his gut relieved him of the ale he had been downing since sunrise.

His opponent jumped back, disgusted by the filth covering his feet. "You mangy beast!" the fighter growled. "I will beat you like a beast!"

Vighon finally succeeded in standing upright again, just in time to receive a flurry of punches to the midriff and one last strike across the face, knocking him down to one knee.

"Come on!" the fighter yelled over the baying mob that watched from above. "I thought you Ironsworn were supposed to be tough! Ancient history I suppose!"

Vighon spared a glance for the tattoo that ran up the underside of his forearm. How many years had he been branded by that vile mark? He had barely heard the name Ironsworn since his coronation, but his time in the fighting pits had brought it all back, their sigil laid bare for all to see. There could only be a handful of the gang left, if that. The northman had often wondered if he was the last of them...

More ale, he decided. He could barely hold on to a thought when he was in the pit, yet here he was thinking about the past. More ale would help and it certainly needed replacing now that most of his previous drinks were on the floor.

A bare foot hammered the side of his head and dropped him onto his front - another problem with *thinking* while in the pit. There was, however, a glimmer of hope in his future. Through the raucous din that filled the haze, Vighon heard the barkeep's voice bellow over it all.

"Black Forest Brandy!"

"Finally," he rasped.

Vighon had been waiting for the fresh keg. Just the thought of its sweet flavour was making his mouth water, though that could have been the blood... he wasn't sure.

"Get up, Ironsworn!" The fighter yanked Vighon up by his hair. "You're not getting out of this hole with your eyes open!"

Thirsty and eager to return to a state of blissful oblivion, Vighon ended the fight. A palm to the throat rid him of the hand gripping his hair again. For the first time since the fight began, the northman actually looked upon his opponent. The intricate burn that adorned his chest revealed him to be a member of the Yarl crime syndicate. Their entire gang were survivors of Dragorn and counted among the lucky ones who had escaped the island before the Leviathan flattened it.

Vighon sighed - he was thinking again.

His fist closed together, the knuckles cracking. He visualised his one and only attack, confident from years of practice that it would drop his opponent and end the fight. His arm snapped up like a snake, his speed previously unseen during the fight. Indeed, the right hook was enough to rob the thug of his senses and take him from his feet.

The northman didn't bother to wait and see if the man got back up before he ascended the ladder built into the circular wall. Only when he reached the top did he realise the crowd had ceased their cheering. Instead, they were all staring at the Yarl sprawled across the arena floor.

Shoving his way through the surrounding crowd, Vighon didn't pause as he took the bag of coins he was owed on his way to the bar. The bookie was already turning to the mob, his hands raised as he assured them all there would be another fight and, with it, another chance to win back the money they had lost betting against Vighon.

His sack of coins touched the bar no longer than a second before Davan, the barkeep, swept it up and tucked it into his belt. He didn't even ask Vighon what he wanted, but rather placed a tankard of Black Forest Brandy into the northman's waiting hand. It was lukewarm and sweet as it disappeared down Vighon's throat. He didn't stop until he could see the bottom of the tankard and his scruffy overgrown beard was drenched.

"Must be a new crowd," Davan remarked, refilling the tankard. "Any who have enough coin to return tomorrow won't be so foolish as to bet against you."

Vighon looked up at the tall barkeep and froze. It had been Davan speaking, but it wasn't Davan's face looking back at him. The northman saw Orvan's face, contorted in horror, just as it had been before the Reavers killed him. He turned away from the barkeep as a couple of patrons walked by. Each possessed a familiar face and their names came to him with ease. Qillian and Valwyn, brothers who had died in agony thanks to Malliath's flames.

"Brandy," he demanded without looking back at Davan.

More faces and names came out of the crowd, haunting the northman. Fathers, brothers, husbands, and sons, all loyal to the flaming sword, to his banner. They had suffered Alijah's wrath again and again for fighting beside him. With every new battle his ranks would be filled with new warriors to replace the fallen and they too would become Alijah's sole target. It didn't matter what he did, Alijah responded to every one of Vighon's campaigns with the full force of his might, regardless of other battles he might lose elsewhere.

There were only so many men the northman could lead to their deaths...

"Brandy!" he roared.

"Your tankard's full, Voss," Davan replied, using Vighon's pseudonym.

The northman inhaled the Black Forest Brandy, hoping that quantities of alcohol would be his ally against such memories. It usually did the job, but it took time. He looked down at the palm of his hand and saw nothing but blood. A memory flashed in front of his eyes, showing him Ailio's last moments before succumbing to his wounds, like so many soldiers of The Rebellion before him.

He could hear Alijah screaming his name. *"VIGHON DRAQARO!"* his voice had boomed.

It echoed in the northman's mind, refusing to go away. His oldest friend and now greatest nemesis had yelled above the battle, promising death and worse to any and all who fought with the fallen king.

The brandy wasn't working.

He turned to the fighting pit for his salvation. The bookie was already taking new bets for a fresh pair of fighters preparing to descend into the arena. The Vighon of old would have assessed each of the opponents and decided whether it was even possible to beat them, but winning the fight wasn't always his aim.

Pushing away from his stool, the northman forced his way back to the bookie, his bare chest still glistening with sweat and blood from the last two fights.

He jostled the old bookie to steal his full attention. "The next fight is mine," he told him.

The bookie shook his head. "This isn't your fight, Voss, trust me. You've had your win. I've got other fighters who want a chance."

Vighon gripped him by the collar and gave the man a comprehensive sample of his brandy breath. "The next fight-is-*mine*."

The bookie lifted his chin and pursed his lips. "I've already got two fighters..." he said, nodding at the men behind Vighon.

The northman grunted and released the bookie. Apparently, it was a simple problem of numbers and Vighon had just the solution. He tapped the nearest fighter on the shoulder before introducing the man to his forehead. The force of the blow knocked him back until the back of his head collided with a post, dropping him to the floor.

The bookie rolled his eyes, helpless to stop Vighon from entering the arena. It wasn't long before the bets were being changed and the northman's chosen name was being tossed about the din.

"Voss fancies his chances again! I should remind you all he's only just left the pit - he's pretty tired by the look of him!"

Vighon couldn't make sense of the crowd's reaction, their yelling lost on him as they placed their bets. He didn't much care either; he just needed the violence to start before the guilt weighed him down.

Down in the pit, he moved through his stretches, waiting impatiently for his opponent; another Yarl judging by his mark. There was nothing remarkable about the man, though he did possess shockingly large hands for his frame. Good. Those fists would knock Vighon's memories into oblivion before he dispatched the thug.

"Fighters!" the bookie shouted. "Take your marrow!"

Vighon looked up at the bookie with a wicked scowl. "Marrow?"

With a coy smile and a shrug, the bookie replied, "I told you this wasn't your fight!"

By the time the northman returned his attention to the Yarl, the thug was downing a small vial of brown liquid. He knew what came next - he had seen the transformation before. At least back then Sir Ruban and his king's guard had fought beside him.

The Yarl cried out as the Leviathan's marrow, taken from its gigantic bones, infected his body. The whites of his eyes disappeared behind a web of red veins and his pupils expanded to remove any trace of colour. His voice dropped several octaves until he sounded like a feral beast. The marrow increased his breathing, setting his chest to a rapid heaving beat.

There was a lot more happening that couldn't be seen by the naked eye. The Yarl's mind was being ravaged by the foul elixir, reducing him to no more than a raging monster. There would be no hurting him now either, his ability to experience pain greatly diminished. Vighon's choices were limited. Choking the Yarl was an option - the drug-fuelled idiot still needed to draw breath like the rest of them. Besides that, with no blade, he could only hope to evade long enough to see the marrow fade, leaving the man a blubbering mess.

Then he saw the flames from not one but two dragons engulf what remained of his captured forces. Those in the middle lasted long enough to scream before death claimed them as its own.

Vighon took a breath. Then he did nothing at all. What followed should have been brief but terribly painful. A lifetime of fighting, however, granted the northman a threshold against such a battering, keeping him conscious longer than most. And so what actually followed wasn't brief at all, but it was certainly painful, and most welcomed...

Vighon came to under a barrage of icy water. It was shockingly cold and drew a gasp from the sleeping northman. Autumn's cool breeze didn't help thereafter.

He was on his front, covered in mud, and wholly sore from head to toe. He could just make out the hubbub of the townspeople beyond the alleyway, though it only added to his disorientation.

"You're lucky to be alive, Voss," came Davan's voice.

It took Vighon an extra second to realise that *he* was supposed to be Voss. Then it took an another second to realise that it was the barkeep standing over him, holding an empty bucket.

"Lucky isn't the word I'd use..." Vighon wiped his face and rubbed his eyes. "Did I win?" he asked hopelessly.

"You should consider it a win to be *alive*, Voss. That Yarl almost tore you in half."

The northman closed his eyes, sure that - while intoxicated - that had been his plan all along. "Then how is it I've lived long enough to see your sorry face again?"

"The pit ain't exactly legal," Davan replied, shrugging his broad shoulders. "Getting rid of bodies is hard work and Mr Tawny ain't one for hard work. He declared the Yarl's victory and had the boys haul you out of the pit before he finished you."

Vighon let the name Tawny roll around his mind for a moment until it came to him - the bookie. "Well thank the gods for laziness, eh." The northman turned for the street and began to stagger away.

"Voss?" Davan called after him. "Do yourself a favour: don't come back tonight."

Vighon hadn't even bothered to look back as he left the alley behind. Left and right, the people of Kelp Town were going about their business, collectively avoiding the reeking odour that clung to the northman.

Unfortunately, there was still just enough alcohol in his blood to prevent him from recalling the location of his lodgings. The inn definitely had something to do with wheat, but the whole name escaped him. He decided on a westerly heading and put one foot in front of the other, confident that he would find another source of ale before long...

Rounding a corner, the northman's daze was knocked out of him. He was hurling insults before his eyes had even settled on the one who had shoved past his shoulder. The Reaver, clad in dark armour, whipped its head around to peer out through the narrow slits in its helmet. It said nothing, its threatening demeanour more than enough for most.

Vighon reined in his torrent of abuses and lowered his gaze, allowing some of his wet hair to hide his face. He had no idea if they would recognise him or if they were even capable of such a thing - it was just a habit now to hide who he really was.

With his sight lowered, Vighon ended up looking a Seeker right in the eyes. On all fours, the beast came up to his waist in height and was easily as long as the northman was tall. Its leathery albino skin was decorated with fine translucent spines, all angled down the length of its body. Pale red eyes, set deep within a pointed head, met Vighon's and two patches of circular skin, either side of its head, began to vibrate.

It was seeking its next prey, some poor fool to endure the wrath of Alijah and his terrifying reign.

The northman had seen people try and run away at this point, but the Reavers always let the Seeker go and it inevitably caught them. So Vighon remained as still as the alcohol in his system would allow. The thin membrane that covered its apparent ears finally stopped vibrating and the Seeker turned away from him. The Reavers lost interest and continued their patrol, leaving Vighon to take a breath.

He rested his back against the wall as they disappeared around the next corner. There had been a time when he would have slain both Reavers with their own swords. And he certainly wouldn't have suffered the likes of their pale dog.

A monstrous shriek blared out from around the corner, quickly followed by a scream and shattering glass. Vighon already knew what was happening before he reached the edge of the building. There was a man shouting now, his tone aggressive if somewhat fearful.

With eyes on the street, the northman could see the two Reavers standing motionless outside the tanner's shop. The window was broken where the Seeker had obviously leapt into the shop. There came a brief commotion from inside before a man came bursting onto the street with the Seeker tangled in his arms.

The two went down hard, but the man continued to slam one fist after another into the creature. He was covered in bites for his resistance, his clothes tattered and bloodied. A red-headed woman came to the open door in distress, screaming at the Seeker to let him go. The Reavers reacted to her potential interference and pinned her to the adjacent wall, where she was forced to watch.

The northman's uneasy gaze shifted from the woman to the man wrestling with the Seeker. Vighon had no idea why this man had been targeted. He had always assumed the Seekers were employed as a fear tactic, to keep the populace in line.

Vighon's fist clenched without direct command and his teeth clamped together. This wasn't the first time he had witnessed the atrocities Alijah's Reavers had inflicted on the people. Like all those other times, the northman asked himself if this was the moment. Was this the end of his exile? Would he finally allow the warrior out, where it belonged?

The man cried out when the Seeker's fangs gripped his forearm in a vice of needles. From the back of his belt, he removed a dagger and promptly shoved it into the creature's side, eliciting a pained yelp from the beast. As its jaws grew slack, he hammered the tip down into its head and stood over it victorious.

Vighon narrowed his eyes. He recognised the dagger as the standard issue for all Namdhorian soldiers. Looking at the man with a scrutinising eye, he did, indeed, have the look of a soldier. Everything from his build to his cropped hair told of a man who had been trained to fight and live with a sword on his hip.

He was one of Vighon's, forced into retirement by the Reavers who now pinned his wife to a wall.

The fight faded from the northman's bones and his muscles relaxed as he slumped into the wall. He would only make the situation worse - he always did. The man called out his love for the woman and burst into a sprint, shortly followed by the Reavers. His wife fell into fits of tears before those around her offered comfort.

Vighon had nothing to offer. The best thing he could do was keep his true self locked away, deep down where he couldn't bring harm upon those around him. Fighting his instincts, he couldn't help but think of the one thing that felt missing from his grip - the flaming sword of the north, a symbol of who he was... who he *had* been.

That, like everything else, had been taken from him. It wasn't *his* Illian anymore. It all belonged to Alijah now.

# CHAPTER 10
# JUST A PEEK

Under the light of a startling moon, the tower of silvyr radiated with the brilliance of a million diamonds.

Galanör had seen the beauty of silvyr when touched by the moon before, but never had he imagined the magnificence of an entire structure made from the exquisite metal. Even now, after months of observing the tower in the moonlight, the ranger still looked on with rapture.

Movement focused him, reminding the elf that he had a job to do. In the manner of a stalking panther, he moved slowly over the branches and looked down on the prey that had entered his field of vision.

Reavers, two of them. The undead fiends were patrolling the outer edge of the tower's territory, walking in complete and eerie silence. Galanör had chosen this particular tree after hours of watching the pattern of their patrol. Every two hours, they passed directly beneath its canopy.

Now to deliver true death...

The ranger pulled Stormweaver from its scabbard with smooth ease, careful to reduce the noise it made. Timing was everything, for his strike had to be clean and precise. He counted their steps, just as he had done hours earlier.

The leaves rustled as he dropped down, but the Reavers remained unaware of the threat. Before his feet hit the ground, the elf backhanded his scimitar, throwing all of his strength behind the swing. He felt the resistance, what little there was, as the blade sliced through the Reavers' necks.

Only a second after he landed in a crouch did their heads tumble across the ground. Aenwyn emerged from the shadows with her bow raised to chest height. Upon sighting the decapitated Reavers, she lowered her weapon and moved quickly to help Galanör drag the bodies into the long grass.

With no lack of disgust on her face, she said, "I'm really not looking forward to this part..."

Galanör shook both of the helmets to rid them of the heads inside. "You were the one who wanted to go down there," he replied with a sheepish grin.

Aenwyn narrowed her eyes at him. "I didn't think you were going to suggest we do that wearing the armour of dead men."

The elven ranger began taking one of the Reaver's armour off. "Well one of us had to think about how we get *out* of there. Just try not to use your nose too much..."

The armour wasn't a perfect fit on either of them - and it stank of death. As disgusting as the process was, Galanör found it much harder to leave his twin scimitars behind, hidden with the bodies. The Reaver's blade was poorly weighted in the ranger's opinion, but he was confident it would remain in the scabbard on his hip.

Putting on the helmet was the worst part. The narrow slit was disorientating and made Galanör feel closed in, though his vision was hardly the problem. Whether he breathed using his nose or mouth alone he felt as if he was inhaling the dead man who had inhabited it.

"You can't take that," he remarked, noting Aenwyn slinging her bow over one shoulder.

"Some of the Reavers have bows," she reasoned with a shrug.

"Not these two," Galanör replied. "We have no idea how they communicate with each other. We can't risk it."

Aenwyn sighed in her helmet. "I'm starting to think there isn't going to be any action at all..."

The ranger watched her add the bow to his scimitars. "Let's just find King Gaerhard. The fighting can wait."

Together, they finished the patrol route expected of the Reavers they were impersonating, bringing them to the back of the dwarven prison camp. They should have continued north and circled around the western edge of the island but, instead, they used the chaos of the forges to slip into the camp.

"Stay by my side," Galanör urged as they passed between the dozens of makeshift forges.

The thick muscled arms of dwarves beat down on anvils, crafting specialist tools to shape the silvyr, while others worked on the unique metal itself. Their bearded faces glistened with sweat, knuckles crushed white under their iron grip, and their eyes were lost to the flames and the glow of the heated metal.

They were not as Galanör had seen them in Dhenaheim. There, the children of the mountain sang as they worked the forge and cheered with each strike of their hammer. Here, every dwarf appeared haunted, stripped of their pride and honour as they wasted precious silvyr on their enemy's schemes.

They were a fierce people in all that they did. This was breaking them...

Maintaining their pace so as not to draw attention to themselves, the elves weaved through the field of forges. The cacophony of it all only worked against Galanör's senses, however, adding to the encumbering helmet. Before reaching the camp, he came very close to accidentally walking into one of the Fenrig men barking orders at the dwarves.

A pained growl gave the ranger pause, drawing him to the south. He quickly found the source - a dwarf being whipped for working too slowly. Others of his kin stopped their hammering and looked to intervene, but a small group of Reavers diverted from their positions. The smiths averted their gaze and reluctantly continued with their jobs.

It took every bit of Galanör's self-discipline to refrain from drawing his sword. Though crude by comparison to his scimitars, he could still gut every Fenrig and dismember every Reaver surrounding the punished dwarf. The remaining thousand or so Reavers, however, would become something of a problem...

Gritting his teeth, the ranger kept to Aenwyn's side and passed into the tented area. It wasn't nearly as hot as by the forges, but it was almost as chaotic. From months of observation, they knew the dwarves were given a short rest period between shifts. In this time, they had to recover from their labour, sleep, and eat. It was gruelling.

Two rows over, one of the Fenrigs was beating a stick against a tent pole. "Get up you lazy dogs!" he bellowed, rousing the dwarves still sleeping inside. The thug didn't wait for them to get up before he ordered his men in to drag them out. "Quarter rations for this lot!"

Aenwyn tapped the back of Galanör's hand, focusing him. They had to keep to their stride, resisting the instinct to step aside and give the dwarves their space. Heading north, they made their way to the farthest edge of the camp, garnering more and more looks of disdain as they did.

There was no mistaking King Gaerhard, even amongst his clan of bright bearded dwarves. It seemed there was also no missing them. The closer they approached, the more dwarves appeared from their tents. Gaerhard puffed out his chest and spat a mouthful of gristle on the ground at their feet.

"What do ye two fiends want?" he demanded, doing his best to keep some air of authority about him. "I've only jus' finished," he pointed out.

A pair of Brightbeards came up on either side of the elves, their fists clenched into tight knots of fury. They were likely the king's personal guard or, at least, they had been before their capture. Gaerhard subtly raised his fingers, warning them to back off.

"Well?" he growled.

Galanör made a cursory glance over the tops of the surrounding tents. There were Reavers everywhere and Fenrigs between, but most were more focused on work being done to the tower than the camp. The ranger took his chance.

"King Gaerhard, son of Hermon..." Galanör crouched on one knee and removed his helmet to reveal a face of elven features and chestnut hair.

The dwarven king immediately frowned before some semblance of revelation crossed his lined face. "Get inside," he instructed after a second's pause. He gave his fellow Brightbeards a nod and they quickly fell into subtle, yet defensive, positions around his tent.

It was cramped inside but it appeared Gaerhard was the only dwarf not sharing a tent. It certainly smelled like there was more than one dwarf calling it home.

Aenwyn wasted no time removing her own helmet, preferring the odour of dwarf to the rot of dead flesh.

"So ye 'aven' abandoned us then?" the king began eagerly. "Never again shall I hear yer lot be slighted. Ye 'ave me word as king!" Gaerhard looked over them both. "Now why am I only seein' two o' ye? Where's yer army? Where are the Heavybellys?"

By the look on Aenwyn's face, she had struggled to keep up with the dwarf's command of man's tongue. Were their situation not so dire, Galanör would have spared an amused smile.

"Doran Heavybelly is coming with his clan and a contingent of elves to add to our own," he explained. "He has stressed the importance of your survival, however. That is why we're here."

"Very soon," Aenwyn continued, "this island is going to become a battleground. We're here to see you removed from it before that happens."

Gaerhard raised a scarlet eyebrow to complement his look of disbelief. "Ye've come to take me away?"

"To rescue you," Aenwyn corrected.

Galanör refrained from sighing - she was only trying to help. "Rescue is a strong word," he interjected before the king could act on the offence. "Doran seeks your help with strategy. There are none better than yourself who know the lay of the land."

"Ye must be jokin', elf. I've met Doran Heavybelly an' I knew his father before 'im. Theirs is not a clan that seeks aid in any regard, especially with battle strategy. I've heard plenty o' stories abou' Doran's days as War Mason. He jus' wants me alive to keep the clans 'ere under control, an' because he an' I 'ave an arrangement where Dhenaheim's future is concerned."

Aenwyn adjusted herself in the close quarters. "Our window is small, good king. We must go now."

"I'm not goin' anywhere," Gaerhard articulated. "The place o' any king is among his people. If they are to suffer, then so shall I. Ye go an' tell Doran to raise Andaljor on that rise," he said, gesturing to the back of the tent. "Tell 'im to make sure he's got all manner o' Grarfath's rage at his back. *Then*, the Brightbeards will stand up to these monsters an' bring what's left o' the Battleborns, Hammerkegs, an' Goldhorns up with 'em." The king chuckled to himself. "Then we'll 'ave that battleground ye speak o'."

"We have risked much to get this far," Galanör said. "We must get you out of here. This might be our only opportunity to do so without violence."

"It sounds like violence is comin' anyway," Gaerhard replied with a shrug of his massive shoulders. "I'll be here waitin' for it. Until then, I suggest ye sharpen those sorry excuses for swords o' yers. We'll be ready."

Galanör chastised himself for having neglected to consider this scenario. He looked at Aenwyn, both silently agreeing that they were running out of time. But there would be no moving a dwarf that didn't want to, and that counted for double when dealing with a dwarven king - a special breed of stubbornness.

"Grarfath has given you his courage," Galanör remarked by way of a compliment.

"The courage is Yamnomora's!" Gaerhard corrected. "For who else could be so brave as to stand beside a god so ill-tempered as Grarfath?"

The ranger didn't know what to say to that but, rather than dwell on his lack of knowledge where dwarven religion was concerned, he asked, "What will you do about weapons? We have none to give you."

The king waved the concern away. "I could use me boot as a weapon if I needed to, lad. Don' be worryin' abou' us - we can fight." Gaerhard moved closer to him. "Jus' make sure ye're *bringin'* the fight. For too long have we been in chains. We would rather meet our enemy in battle and die than labour for King Alijah for another day."

Galanör put a hand on the king's shoulder. "Fear not - the battle is coming."

There were no farewells to be had. The elves replaced their helmets and, upon hearing that the path was clear, they exited the tent and continued their charade of patrolling the camp.

"That didn't go according to plan," Aenwyn commented.

"You're suggesting we had a plan?" Galanör quipped.

"At least they can prepare now," she replied, seeing the silver lining. "When we're ready to attack, the Reavers will face two fronts instead of one."

Galanör could certainly see the benefit of that but, without any real weapons, the dwarves would likely suffer great casualties. Any further thought on the matter faded in the shadow of the tower. The ranger stopped by the western edge of the camp and craned his neck to see its top. None from The Rebellion had ever got this far before...

Up close, its sparkling surface was harder to make out through the many levels of scaffolding. The dwarves called out from all over, directing each other on the best way to manage the construction. Torches were fixed at intervals to the railings, the firelight adding to the silvyr's diamond effect.

"Galanör," Aenwyn hissed, urging him to stay by her side.

A daring and impulsive plan came to the ranger in that moment. "Follow my lead," he whispered.

Aenwyn didn't have a chance to question him before he stepped away from the camp and fell in line behind a dozen Reavers, marching north across the tower's entrance. The ranger received a look from his companion but her helmet left it to his imagination.

Galanör kept with the Reavers' pace while stealing glances at the tower's singular threshold. It wasn't particularly large - a dragon would struggle to fit inside. That fact only confused Galanör all the more since Alijah made sure everything accommodated Malliath.

Dwarves and Reavers crossed the archway but never moved inside. Perhaps they were finished with the interior... Galanör had to know. He lightly rapped his knuckles against Aenwyn's hand. Her attention gained, they moved as one and departed the group of Reavers with smooth efficiency. They crossed paths with a handful of Fenrigs and were given way by a pair of dwarves carting tools. None challenged them.

"If there ever was a plan," Aenwyn remarked quietly, "then you're far from it."

"You were the one who wanted to do something," he reminded her, watching the entrance grow in size.

"I don't think dying counts as *doing something...*"

Galanör smiled inside his helmet and continued his purposeful stride into the tower. The walls were dull without the light of the moon to bring out their beauty, leaving the way to be lit by torches alone.

Aenwyn inspected the blank walls. "I was expecting something... *grander.*"

Galanör had the same expectations, surprised to come across a sloping ramp that curved around the tower's wide base. Together, they followed the only available path up and round until it brought them to a chamber nearly as large and circular as the base itself.

Looking up, Galanör removed his helmet to take it all in. "Is that grand enough for you?"

Aenwyn happily took her own helmet off and followed the ranger's wide eyes to the soaring interior. The space mimicked its exterior shape exactly, proving the entire tower to be hollow. At its apex, the relatively narrow opening was exposed to the sky, revealing a small circle of stars above.

"What is this?" Galanör asked absently.

Aenwyn shook her head slowly, her eyes captured by the immensity of it all. "I have never seen anything like this before."

Bringing his vision back to the base, Galanör quickly discovered more designs that compounded the mystery. Carved into the silvyr walls, all the way around, were numerous glyphs of all shapes and sizes. They even ran over the floor in intercepting patterns, leading, seemingly, into the very centre, directly in line with the apex.

"These glyphs..." He crouched down and ran his fingers over the groves. "They are from the time of The First Kingdom."

Aenwyn walked over to the wall and scrutinised the carvings. "I can read some of them," she said. "Though, even translated side by side, they make no sense."

Galanör didn't like any of what he was seeing. "This is ancient magic," he intoned. "Maybe even the oldest magic. What could he possibly be doing that requires a tower of the strongest metal in all of Verda and magic older than civilisation?"

Aenwyn met his concern from across the chamber. "And what does it have to do with digging a hole in the middle of The Moonlit Plains?"

The elven ranger sighed. "There is nothing left to learn here. We should retrieve our things and return to the woods. I want us to be ready when the queen and Doran arrive." He picked up his helmet, ready to don his disguise one last time. "Whatever Alijah has planned here, we need to stop him..."

After one last look at the mysterious interior, the elves descended the winding ramp and made for the archway.

"Oi!" came the obnoxious call of a Fenrig given too much power.

"Don't stop," Aenwyn hissed, keeping to her stride.

"Oi!" he yelled again, approaching them from the north. "What in all the hells were you two doing in there? No one is supposed to go inside - king's orders!"

The elves found their path blocked by the fool stupid enough to put himself in their way. Galanör quickly sized the man up and decided, quite confidently, that he could dispatch him with his hands alone. It was the other Fenrigs and copious number of Reavers that would prove problematic.

"I don't know how you do things in Erador," the Fenrig continued, "but here we obey orders!"

Another Fenrig made himself known. "Royce..." he warned, his eyes shifting from his comrade to the apparent Reavers. "Leave 'em," he urged, as if he had a sense that the knights from Erador weren't entirely human.

Royce had no such sense. "No," he replied, waving his friend's concern away. "These mute buggers do nothing but obey, so why were they inside the tower?" The Fenrig tapped his knuckles against Galanör's helmet. "We're in charge here. That means we're in charge of you lot. No one is to go inside, you hear?"

Galanör and Aenwyn could do nothing but remain silent, imitating the undead creatures. Silent or not, they were at the heart of a scene that was attracting more unwanted attention. Through the slit in his helmet, the ranger could see real Reavers pausing on their patrols to observe the confrontation.

"Tell me you understand," Royce demanded, exercising the inch of power he had been gifted.

Galanör, however, had mentally departed the interaction, sure that the Reavers were learning the truth of things in their own supernatural way. Instead of giving the Fenrig any of his attention, the ranger was scanning the environment, searching for solutions that would see them survive.

He caught the eyes of more than a few dwarves, but he couldn't ask any of them to help. The neigh of a horse drew the elf to the south, where a pair of Fenrigs on horseback were slowly approaching.

"Cat got your tongue?" Royce sneered. "Why don't we take that helmet off..."

Galanör offered no resistance, but the moment his mouth was free of the lifting helmet, he whispered, "Run."

Upon sighting the angelic face of an elf, Royce's cocky expression turned to one of genuine surprise. It was the last thing he ever did. Galanör's hands snatched at the Fenrig's podgy face and twisted with more force than was perhaps needed, given his superior strength.

Before Royce's body hit the ground, Aenwyn was diving and rolling towards his comrade who had warned of halting them. Her momentum came to an end when she hit the thug's leg, which she snapped with a powerful blow from her elbow. Dragging him down, Aenwyn finished him off with a swift strike to his face.

"Run!" Galanör barked this time.

The ranger kept his movements fluid. In one motion, he crouched down, removed a pair of daggers from Royce's belt, rolled across the ground, and came up launching the blades at the approaching riders. Both thugs caught a dagger in the chest and fell from their mounts.

In his peripheral vision, Galanör could see Reavers coming from several directions. Those closest to him were unable to intercept them due to the dwarves, who all needed holding back by the point of a sword. The ranger mounted the nearest horse, now absent its dead rider, and turned it south.

Elevated, he caught a glimpse of Aenwyn, now having removed her helmet, dashing through the camp, towards the forges and the rising cliffs beyond. Both Fenrigs and Reavers were pursuing her...

Without delay, he spurred the horse, guiding it around the northern edge of the dwarven camp. He made as much noise as possible while also drawing the sword from his hip. The captured dwarves cheered as he galloped past but the ranger's focus was on Aenwyn and those behind her.

A swing of steel sliced through the head of one Reaver breaking away from the camp. Galanör readied himself for the next swing - a Fenrig. Blood was sent high into the air with the flick of the ranger's blade, halting the thug's pursuit of Aenwyn.

Ensuring that he acquired the attention of them all, Galanör brought his mount to a rearing stop, bartered blows with a Reaver, and kicked a Fenrig in the face. On the other side of him, Aenwyn was putting her natural agility to good use and ascending the rise with great speed.

"Come on!" Galanör roared, provoking the enemy into following him.

His steed exploded with energy and sped away into the night, heading south. On foot, his foes were helpless to prevent his escape, but he was quickly set upon by riders, both human and undead.

The cheers of the dwarves soon faded, replaced by the beating hooves of his horse and the waves slamming into the shore on his right. The cliff had a significant drop into The Hox below and the path ahead was illuminated by the glow of the moon alone.

It wasn't long before arrows began whistling past his ears. The ranger dared to steal a glance over his shoulder, taking his eyes off the path. The Reavers, a far deadlier enemy than the untrained Fenrigs, had taken the lead and were nocking arrow after arrow from atop their horses.

Galanör ducked repeatedly and directed his mount to weave where he could. Here and there the arrows bounced off the path and skidded away while others found their end in passing trees. One careered off the black pauldron protecting the elf's shoulder and cut his cheek.

It wasn't long before a particularly fast horse brought one of the Reavers alongside the ranger, blocking his view of The Hox. Their swords clashed one way then another, each searching in vain for the opportune strike.

The path was treacherous, however, and Galanör knew he didn't have time to parry steel. Freeing his right foot of the stirrup, the ranger lifted his leg and shoved a boot into the side of the Reaver. The fiend's sudden and violent shift in weight took the horse with it, over the edge of the cliff to where neither would be seen again.

Galanör's attention was brought back to his route when his horse leapt over a rock. He kept his head low and continued to spur the horse on as more arrows hurtled through the night. The path zig-zagged left and right before coming back to a route alongside the lip of the cliff.

The ranger's stomach sank...

Up ahead, his elven eyes found the end of the cliff. The only way to navigate it would be to slow down and direct the horse to the left, where the edge of the island cut back to the east. From there, he could ride hard until the horse finally gave out, but it wouldn't solve the issue of his pursuers or the fact that they could track him back to his kin.

He couldn't let that happen.

His hands tightened around the reins. This was the only way. Galanör kept the horse on its shadowy track and prepared himself for the pain. A cautious voice passed briefly through his thoughts, reminding the elf that death was more than a possibility.

Unaware of its future and inevitable doom, the horse galloped as fast as it could until it ran out of ground. Before them both, far below, were the dark and uninviting waves of The Hox...

# CHAPTER II

# CHILDREN OF FIRE AND FLAME

Despite the sublime and panoramic view that stretched around The Dragon Keep, Alijah Galfrey's attention was captured entirely by his mother. Atop the ramparts, her back to him, she stood as a sentinel of Namdhor with her green cloak billowing wildly in the high wind.

Just looking at Reyna's whipping blonde hair threatened to bring back all the memories of his youth. Malliath, ever present, was there to remind him of the rejection he had suffered under his parents. They had always favoured Inara for her numerous accomplishments.

He had been the disappointment...

For years Alijah had held fast to the belief that there would be no climbing out from under his parents' shadow, or even that of his twin sister. They had all resigned him to the life of a rogue, direction-less and doomed to fail in all his endeavours.

They had underestimated him. They had underestimated the fate for which he was destined. Now, he stood atop The Dragon Keep, the king of Erador, Illian, and Ayda. Now he was strong.

The wind ran through his mother's hair and caught in his nose, filling his sense with her natural perfume, a familiar scent. He remembered her kissing him on the head, no older than ten years, and telling him that she loved him.

Alijah exhaled and clenched his fist, welcoming Malliath's steadfast presence. The dragon, his eternal companion, was all he needed. Yet here he was, approaching his mother on the rampart...

"Your Grace," came a gruff and unwanted voice.

Alijah refrained from gritting his teeth but he refused to turn and greet the Fenrig criminal. Instead, he held his hand out for the reports he had requested. The man stepped closer and placed the parchment in the king's hand and stepped back again, staying out of his eye line.

The half-elf tore his eyes from his mother and looked down at the numbers on the scroll, each one pertaining to the Drakes captured across the realm.

"More," he said.

The Fenrig hesitated. "*More*, your Grace?"

"I need more Drakes," he specified, holding the parchment out.

The criminal took the offered scroll. "I will have the rewards doubled."

"Good," Alijah acknowledged, returning his attention to Reyna. "Send word to every region," he added. "Begin transporting the Drakes at once."

"Your Grace." The Fenrig bowed to Alijah's back, delaying his departure from the rampart.

The king continued his approach until he was by his mother's side. "Do you grieve?" he asked.

"For your grandmother?" Reyna specified. "No. She is queen of the elves. If anyone's survival was ensured it was hers. I'm afraid you haven't seen the last of Queen Adilandra. Though... I do grieve." She turned to look upon her son's face. "I grieve for what you could have been. For what you were supposed to be."

Alijah briefly closed his eyes - he had heard this speech before. "You still haven't given up on me then. You still think this is about something as arbitrary as good and evil, the light and the dark. I won't pretend to know what forces govern our fate, but they are more powerful than either of us. Our place in all this is set and has been for eternity."

"I know you want to believe that," Reyna replied, her emerald eyes boring into him. "But I also know you are smarter than that. Life is about *choice*. Every branch in our path can lead to a new and different future if we but take it. There is no fate. Knowing your future allows you to rewrite it before it happens - that is all. In all my time, I've found nothing but false gods and tyrants who would declare themselves as gods."

Alijah heard it all and gave her the respect of letting her finish. "Choice is an illusion," he countered. "When I lived that life, one of a roguish young fool, I thought I was forging my own path every day. Yet every decision I made led me to this very moment; standing beside you in the capital of Illian with a crown on my head. Our fates are sealed before we are born..."

Finally, Reyna looked away. "And all those who have died for you to be king - was it their fate to simply perish before their time? How many more have the Fates put on this earth so that they might die as proof of your might? How much more blood must there be on my hands?"

Alijah glanced down at his mother and saw a tear running down her cheek. He was on the verge of feeling something, anything, when Malliath's exasperation bled across their bond.

"What are you talking about?" Alijah asked, intoning his companion's feelings.

Reyna took a steadying breath before looking down at her hands. "I can see it. Blood." She met his eyes and Alijah resisted the urge to look away. "I brought you into this world. That makes me responsible for every life you take. Your father too."

Alijah held up his hand. "Do not speak of him," he commanded. "Nathaniel Galfrey fights for The Rebellion. That makes him my enemy, not my father."

"Should I not receive such scorn?" Reyna questioned. "You know well that I do not condone your actions or even your right to rule."

"Be careful, Mother," he warned. "I am still your king."

Reyna lifted her chin in defiance. "Illian's king - *my* king - is Vighon Draqaro. You called him brother once."

"And you called him *son*," Alijah snapped, instantly regretting the envy that came out in his tone. "There was always someone else, wasn't there? There was always someone for you to love more than me. It never mattered what I did. You always had Inara and Vighon. It must have made you so proud the day he rose to king, the boy you took in and raised as your own."

Without giving her a chance to respond, the half-elf stormed away, heading for the large courtyard beyond the entrance of the keep. He could hear her feet close behind, following him. Alijah didn't look back but, rather, sent a mental command to the Reavers inside the keep.

"You cannot run away from me, Alijah. I will always be here. I will always remind you of who you were, who you could—" Reyna failed to make another sound under the shadow of Malliath.

The black dragon came from the sky and landed in the courtyard, his purple eyes trained on her. She stopped on the rampart, met by her escort of assassins.

"You can't outrun who you truly are!" Reyna called down. "And that is my *son*!"

Alijah stepped down onto the courtyard as a Reaver exited the main keep with a large black book in its hands and a slender box on top of that. Without words, he had the Reaver place them both on the table by the wall.

***Are you ready?*** he asked Malliath. He could sense the dragon's apprehension.

*I have been branded before*, Malliath replied flatly. *This is the only way.*

Alijah placed a soothing hand on his scales, a privilege reserved for him alone. ***None but us can bear this burden.***

Malliath curled his neck to lay his startling eyes on the half-elf. *We are the strong,* he declared. *Now do it.*

Alijah walked away from the dragon to peruse the black book on the table. He had read it from cover to cover more than once, but he still examined the pages relating to the correct symbols he needed - he had to get this right.

"What book is that?" Reyna asked from above.

Ignoring her, Alijah opened the book to the page that had been marked with a fine ribbon. The parchment therein was ancient. It had survived the eons thanks only to the Jainus and their protective spells, placed over it thousands of years ago.

*You know the glyphs from memory,* Malliath insisted. *I wish to get this over with.*

**That is the very reason I study them now,** Alijah replied, doing his best to calm the dragon. **I don't want to get it wrong and be forced to start again.**

With a simple spell, Alijah levitated the book and had it follow him back to Malliath's side, where he could refer to it at his leisure.

*You will have to remove the necessary scales,* Malliath cautioned. *You possess no magic capable of burning them.*

Wearing an armoured suit of Malliath's smallest scales, Alijah was very thankful for that fact. **Each glyph should be no larger than one of these scales,** he reassured, brushing his hand over the dragon's midriff. **I will need to remove thirty-three in total.**

Malliath growled deep in his throat and his claws dug into the ground. *As you say...*

A strong telekinetic tug pulled the first scale from Malliath's side, eliciting the slightest of twitches from the irritated hide beneath. Regardless of his magical skill, using his fingers to employ a fire spell would be too messy and likely cause his companion more pain. Instead, he raised his left hand and accepted the contents of the slender box, brought to his waiting grip by a Reaver.

His fingers coiled around the dark wand, a foreign tool to the king. Bonded to Malliath, he had no need of the thing, but it would allow him a degree of precision with the glyphs, much in the way he had once witnessed The Crow branding the bones of the dead Leviathan.

A brief examination showed there to be some blood splattered up the length of the wand. The blood had once belonged to Eatred Mannus, Vighon's court mage. Alijah couldn't even recall the man's death - perhaps he hadn't been present for it...

Pondering aside, the half-elf pointed the wand at Malliath's exposed hide. It was going to hurt and it was definitely going to bring up some of Malliath's worst memories. Just thinking about it brought images to the surface, taken from the dragon. Alijah saw his companion chained down and bombarded with spells to keep him as docile as possible. The human mages of Korkanath had branded him fiercely, taking a sick delight in his torment.

It ignited fire in the king's veins and refuelled his passion for completing their task. They would bear the pain. Then they would share it with their enemies...

The dawn brought with it a new day over The Adean and a new sense of hope in Inara Galfrey. For the first time since Alijah had taken the throne, the Dragorn felt as if she was finally doing the right thing. For all the risk that accompanied The Rebellion's new plan, they were each set to a task that could actually make a difference.

Inara had faith in her father to find Asher and there was none better in all the realm to track Vighon down than the legendary ranger. And, of course, bringing Vighon back was The Rebellion's best chance at rallying the people.

There was a sense of excitement in her gut. The thought of seeing the northman again had pressed on her mind since the day he had disappeared.

*Your emotions are torn over him,* Athis observed from within her mind. *You don't often let me in when you're thinking of him...*

Inara considered both of his comments. *I enjoy having some part of myself just for me,* she explained, *as well as the knowledge that they are my thoughts alone. But I am always more at peace when our minds are one. You understand me better than any and all.*

*And the king?* her companion probed.

Now there was a storm of emotions, many of which Inara wasn't even sure what to do with. It was only when thinking about Vighon that she truly felt the absence of Athis's influence. Without his support and guidance, even on a subconscious level, her emotions floundered, unsure of what to do with no consideration but her own.

Inara both enjoyed and hated how out of control that made her feel.

*That's complicated...*

Inara could feel Athis's temptation to tease more from her, but the dragon let it go. His respect for her human side only increased the Dragorn's love for him and she poured that feeling into their bond. It always made her feel whole when he embraced her feelings and reciprocated them.

And so they continued their journey south, over The Adean. Before midday, they were flying over the ruins of Korkanath. There was just enough of the school left to recognise it as once being man made. What did remain was charred black from dragon fire. Inara hadn't seen Malliath set the island ablaze but Gideon had described it as hell on water.

That memory set off a chain of memories. Alijah had been with Gideon then, astride Ilargo as they flew to Velia. From there, her brother had gone to The Bastion and his fate was sealed. What followed was a series of events set in motion by a necromancer of the highest order: The Crow.

Just ahead of them, Inara laid eyes on The Crow's resting place. The island of Dragorn was a graveyard for tens of thousands who had called it their home, but it was also the graveyard of a Leviathan.

The three-headed Cerbadon lay sprawled across what had once been the largest city in all of Verda.

A sense of pride rose up in Athis. Not only did it please him to recall their victory over the ginormous beast, but it also pleased him on a primal level. His oldest ancestors had fought the Leviathans for dominance over Verda. In the wake of the Leviathans' defeat, mankind was able to rise and enjoy the fruits yielded from working the land.

Soaring over the dead city, Inara adjusted her position to get a better look. After nearly seventeen years of decay, there was nothing left of the Cerbadon but a rotting skeleton. Its bones were thicker than any fortifying walls ever built by man, elf, or dwarf. All three of its skulls lay with mouths ajar, surrounded by debris.

*Come,* Athis bade. *Let us enjoy what time we have away from the misery of war. When was the last time we took to the sky for the sake of flying alone?*

Inara couldn't recall but she could certainly grin at the idea. **Let's fly!**

Athis brought in his wings and dived towards The Adean at such speed Inara's cloak threatened to disappear. When his wings unfurled at last, they shot over the waves and weaved left and right. It was invigorating, adding to the sense of hope rising in the Dragorn.

They were going to Dragons' Reach. There they would see Gideon again and reunite with the order she had missed so much. Together, they would fly back and reclaim Illian and even free Erador of Alijah's iron grip.

Everything felt right...

Athis shared in her joy and beat his wings, taking them back into the sky. Inara knew well that the dragon had missed the companionship of his kin. It would be a glorious reunion for them all!

They soon passed over The Lifeless Isles, south of Dragorn. It had been too long since either of them had returned to their old home. Gideon had charged them with protecting the library, hidden within the cliffs of the archipelago. Perhaps, she hoped, after the order returned to challenge Alijah, they would once again live together on the islands.

After leaving the familiar cliffs behind, rider and dragon continued on a south-easterly heading. They flew for many miles before sighting the white sails of elven ships.

*Down there!* Athis declared with glee.

Now they were soaring only metres above The Adean's surface and hurtling towards the back of the small fleet. They were all that remained of Adilandra's army, forced south in the hope of entering Illian's less guarded Arid Lands.

**Let them hear you,** Inara said with anticipation.

Athis cast his shadow over the ships and roared with all his might. The elves took to their decks with cheers on their lips, gathering wherever they could to glimpse the red dragon. Athis circled the ships three times, roaring as he did, before correcting their course to continue south-east.

Inara tried not to think about how few had survived Malliath's brutal surprise attack.

*However few their number,* Athis said, *every elf will make a difference in this fight.*

Inara watched the fleet disappear behind them. **Let's just hope we're back before they're needed...**

# CHAPTER 12
# A DWARVEN PROMISE

Astride his loyal, if troublesome, Warhog, Doran Heavybelly looked out on a world of green grass and fields of golden wheat. Alborn, a prosperous region that knew reasonable climates, was resisting winter's call. Having skirted around the town of Darkwell, seeing such a sight was the only way of telling that their party had finally put the north behind them.

Just east of their position, The Unmar glistened under the sun as its waters rushed southward. A ranger of the wilds, Doran knew well that they had but to follow the river until it took them near to Whistle Town. From there, they could avoid the town by hugging the southern borders of The Evermoore and simply cross The Moonlit Plains to West Fellion.

It sounded so simple when he thought of it like that...

Riding their horses, just ahead of the dwarf, were the elves of Ayda. Queen Adilandra was accompanied by Doran's old friend, Faylen Haldör, and a dozen of their warriors, all draped in voluminous cloaks to conceal their true nature. Along with Doran's twenty Heavybellys, they were the vanguard of the staggered caravan, though the next group was half a day behind.

"*I can't stand it,*" Thraal grumbled beside Doran. "*The breeze carries their scent - it's too sweet for my liking!*"

"*And mine,*" Thaligg, Thraal's brother, added to the complaint. "*Do they bathe in sugar?*"

"*Dead or not,*" Thraal continued, "*surely a Reaver can smell their lot coming a mile off.*"

Faylen turned over her shoulder. "*Perhaps, Master Dwarves,*" she began in their native tongue, "*you should try breathing through your mouths. That is what we have been doing...*"

The High Guardian's command of their language flushed more than a few cheeks among the dwarves - many of whom had shared unkind words between them.

Doran's eye rolled dramatically up into his head. "Idiots," he remarked, spurring Pig to catch up with the elves. "Forgive 'em, me Lady," he said, struggling to see both Faylen and Adilandra. "Thraal an' Thaligg are among me best, an' loyal to boot, but they share a single mind between 'em an' it's had more than a few rocks give it a beatin' over the years..."

Adilandra replied from within her hood, "Our skin may look fair, War Mason, but, I assure you, it is thicker than the trees of The Amara."

Having never been to Ayda, the son of Dorain had to assume the trees of The Amara were very thick. "As ye say," he agreed. "Yer dwarven tongue is very good, Faylen—" Doran cut himself off, stumbling over his own speech. "I mean *High Guardian,*" he corrected by way of an apology.

The elf looked down on him and replied first with a warm smile. "You can always call me Faylen," she said.

The stout ranger couldn't hide his relief. "An' ye can always call me Doran," he told her. He looked to Adilandra but the queen offered no familiarity where their names were concerned.

The War Mason cleared his throat. "If I might be so bold, *Faylen.* Is yer husband among us? Ye'll 'ave to forgive me; I've forgotten his name..."

"Nemir," Faylen revealed. "He is not among us, nor any of the groups I'm afraid. I last saw his ship escaping Malliath's fires on The Shining Coast. I imagine he is somewhere far south of here by now."

"Well, it's good to hear that he survived that damned dragon."

"Yes, it pleased me too," she understated. "*We* certainly came close to perishing."

"'aven't we all," Doran mumbled. "There ain' one among The Rebellion that wouldn' mind earnin' the title o' dragon slayer these days."

"That is easier said than done," the queen spoke up. "Even with a weapon such as that one..." Adilandra's gaze fell upon the legendary Andaljor, strapped horizontally across the back of Pig's saddle.

The son of Dorain patted the flat of the steel hammer. "I've no doubt Andaljor could crush even the skull o' a dragon," he boasted.

"Given enough *strength*," the elven queen added.

Doran let out a little laugh. "Am I barterin' words with the queen o' Ayda?" He caught a glimpse of a smile on Adilandra's face.

"Elves do not *barter* words," she replied coolly.

Doran thought of Galanör and had to disagree, though he kept such a disagreement to himself - after all, elves don't barter words.

Faylen examined the weapon from her horse. "It does seem a little... unwieldy."

"Aye, an' it is!" Doran chuckled. "The hammer is *heavy*, far heavier than the axe at the other end. Ye 'ave to know exactly where to hold it, how to swing it, an' what each side has to offer in battle. If ye get into a fight with this beauty in yer hands an' ye're not worthy o' it, Andaljor will see to yer end in no time."

"It is the sigil of your clan," Faylen stated, curious.

"It's more than that," Doran began. "Andaljor is a symbol o' what we used to be, before The Great War even. It's from a time o' heroes. We could surely do with a few o' those right now."

Faylen tilted her head. "It is cumbersome, ugly even. But it is the weapon of a king. Memorable, deadly, worthy of legend."

Doran was overcome with a shadow of guilt. Faylen was right; Andaljor belonged in the hands of the king, his brother. Wounded or not, it was a symbol of their royal blood line, a reminder to all that Dakmund was the king of Grimwhal. Yet here it was, strapped to *his* Warhog.

"You carry it well," Faylen concluded, returning her attention to their route.

The son of Dorain reminded himself that he was only acting as War Mason for a time. His brother had commanded it - to refuse in front of the generals would have made Dakmund appear even weaker than he already was. Doran would help to get his kin free of Alijah's grip and, if he could, help his brother and King Gaerhard to unite the clans until a new hierarchy could be formed.

Then, on that glorious day, he would put Andaljor down, take Pig by the reins, and return to the ranger's life. Only the guilt hanging over him kept his smile at bay.

A male elf, riding on the fringe of their group, turned his horse towards the queen. To any, the sound of an elf speaking in their native language was akin to listening to a pleasant melody, but this particular warrior had an unmistakable sense of urgency in his musical tone. Doran had no clue as to what he was saying to Adilandra, but he had no trouble following his pointed arm to the black dot in the sky.

"*What's that then?*" Thraal asked from the rear.

"*What's what?*" Thaligg sheltered his eyes from the sun. "*I can't see anything.*"

Doran knew what that black dot was...

"Dragon!" Faylen exclaimed. That single word lit a fire under the dwarves and elves alike.

"Into the trees!" Adilandra urged, directing her white mount towards The Evermoore.

"Pound the dirt, Pig!" Doran tucked himself in and gripped the reins with white knuckles. The Warhog defied the weight of its girth and kept pace with the galloping horses.

The trees of The Evermoore grew taller upon their fast approach. Doran didn't even look back to see of any pursuit.

"Find cover!" Faylen shouted to all.

Following their lead, the son of Dorain trailed the queen up a small rise, where the ridge line could hide their number. With swords and axes drawn, the company of elves and dwarves waited with bated breath. For a while there was nothing but the sound of the leaves around them and the occasional dwarf making more noise than they should.

Then, the birds stopped their singing. The forest drew in on itself as if it knew something was coming. They heard the wings first, buffeting the air. A shadow passed along the tree line in the rising sun, moving from right to left. Despite their distance, the group felt the ground shake from what could only be a dragon touching down.

Then there was nothing...

Doran had already dismounted and retrieved Andaljor before joining Adilandra and Faylen by the lip of the rise. Looking down the line, the War Mason's kin were looking eager for a fight, their weapons in hand and a hungry expression on their faces. Doran gestured for them to remain calm - fighting a dragon, Reaver or not, was a difficult task.

Bobbing his head above the rise, the son of Dorain searched for any sign of their enemy. There was nothing but damned trees getting in his way. His mouth moved to whisper a question to the elves when a shocking roar tore through The Evermoore. Doran instinctively withdrew from the rise, along with most of his party. Every bird and foraging animal, previously hidden from sight, made a dash into the depths of the forest, away from the dragon.

Faylen was the first to set her eyes on the distance. She froze, her face ashen. Doran had seen that face on many a warrior...

"What do ye see?" he whispered.

Faylen swallowed first. "'Tis a Reaver to be sure," she answered, her eyes fixed over the ridge. "Though I have never seen one such as this."

Doran sighed quietly. "The Dragon Riders are a wicked sight." He considered the remaining four that still haunted the land, his thoughts always leading to one in particular. "Can ye still see 'em?" Faylen nodded silently. "Do they wear a crown o' spikes, tall ones?"

Faylen tilted her head, focusing her sharp eyes. "Yes," she replied.

The son of Dorain gripped Andaljor so tight his knuckles cracked. He clamped his jaw shut until his teeth protested in pain. Through the dense muscle of his chest, the dwarf could feel his heart beating like a war drum.

"Lord Kraiden," he uttered.

"Their leader," Faylen elaborated. "And his dragon?"

"Morgorth," Doran breathed with contempt.

Queen Adilandra adjusted her position on the other side of the High Guardian. "This is the one who poisoned King Dakmund?"

"Aye." Doran's hand came to rest on the edge of the rise, his knees tucked under him. "I need that monster's sword," he asserted. "The elves o' Ilythyra told me there was a chance for a cure if we could get our hands on the poison."

"True enough," Adilandra said, nodding agreeably. "But Lord Kraiden has a dragon at his back. A degree of planning will be necessary if we are to claim the sword."

"Oh, I've got a plan, me Lady." Doran hefted Andaljor and prepared to give the Heavybellys their orders.

Adilandra reached around Faylen and placed a hand on the haft of Andaljor. "That is not a plan, War Mason. Look at our surroundings. Morgorth has but to open his mouth and the forest will see us engulfed in flames."

Doran's eye twitched. "I *need* that sword," he reiterated.

"Is your need of it worth the lives of every dwarf and elf beside you?" the queen countered. "As with every move The Rebellion makes, we must calculate."

The son of Dorain was finding it hard to absorb the caution. He wanted to attack Kraiden from all sides and hack the fiend into as many pieces as possible.

Faylen's hand came to rest on his shoulder, tugging at his attention. "Not today," she said gently.

Doran's breathing had become heavy. He looked to his left, where his kin lay awaiting his command. There should have been at least one of them who looked disappointed that their War Mason was taking counsel from an elf but, it seemed, none of them were eager to charge over the rise and face either Rider or dragon.

But none of them had a brother to lose...

There were, however, brothers, sisters, mothers, and fathers who would all lose members of their family if he commanded them to attack. How many lives could be sacrificed to try and save Dakmund's life? Doran didn't have an answer for that, but he knew there were too many accompanying him.

Andaljor was lowered to the ground. "As ye say," he conceded. Doran turned his back into the rise and rested there, letting his anger and desperation fade as best he could.

There came another hideous roar from beyond the forest. Morgorth's wings beat the air, pushing on the trees, and the dragon departed with the wicked Rider.

"Not today," Doran murmured to himself. "But the day *is* comin', mark me words, when that Reaver's head is parted from its body. An' on that day, I will personally put a hook through its wretched head an' tie it to me Warhog, where it shall be dragged from north to south!"

His description painted quite the gruesome picture, appreciated by his grinning kin. The elves among them weren't so taken by the image conjured by the vengeful dwarf. Doran couldn't say he cared much either way.

He just needed to save Dak...

# PART TWO

# CHAPTER 13
# THERE'S ALWAYS ANOTHER BIG STICK

Asher's eyes finally opened, freeing him, for a time, from the only prison he could never escape. In his sleep, he was shackled to his nightmares; images and sounds that had been with him since his earliest days in Nightfall. Of course, for the last seventeen years, they had become even more lucid, fortified as they were by Malliath's memories.

Yet, every night, the ranger would willingly close his eyes and endure the pain of his murderous past. It was all part of his atonement. He embraced Malliath's memories, however, for an entirely different reason. The dragon's long life provided Asher with no end of blood and violence, but it also gave him an insight into the voiceless one himself.

*"Knowing your enemy is half the battle,"* Nasta Nal-Aket had always instructed him.

Before moving, he inhaled through his nose, taking in the smell of his environment. The ranger knew immediately that he was resting on the single bed in his room above The Dancing Fox.

He sat up, bracing himself for the expected pain from various parts of his body. He still wasn't used to waking with full health after taking such a beating. It reminded him of his days in possession of Paldora's Gem, when he could call upon the magic of the stone to heal him of every ailment. Now, instead of a magical relic, he had a Drake.

His weapons, propped up against the far wall, caught his eye. They were all clean again, the blood and gore dutifully removed by Adan'Karth. Except for his trousers, which Asher was wearing, his leathers and cloak were missing.

"Adan?" he croaked, testing his legs out. His back and neck cracked as he rose to his full stature. "Adan?"

The Drake emerged from an adjoining room with Asher's green cloak in his hands. The fabric was soaking wet though noticeably absent the dirt and blood that had previously stained it.

"You rise," the Drake stated, apparently pleased by the look of the ranger. "You were especially broken this time..."

Asher clenched his fist, experimenting with the strength he discovered there. "You did a good job patching me up... *again*." He took a breath, unaccustomed to his next words. "Thank you." The ranger gestured to his gear. "And..." He couldn't say it again. "You didn't need to do that," he said instead.

"It is dangerous for me to go out during the day," Adan'Karth explained. "There is only so much one can do in this room."

As always, Asher was impressed with the Drake's command of man's tongue. He had picked up not only the words themselves but also a variety of local colloquialisms from their journey. Adan's ability to learn almost anything in such little time often made Asher thankful that his kin abhorred violence - they would easily be the most dangerous beings in the realm.

The ranger caught a glimpse of himself in the small mirror on the wall. He wouldn't have bothered giving the reflection a second glance except for the lack of beard that greeted him there.

"You shaved me." His tone implied the Drake had gone a step too far, a ridiculous notion he knew.

Adan shrugged his nimble shoulders. "You needed it - you were long past looking scruffy."

Asher ran his hand over the smooth skin of his jaw. He couldn't argue with the improvement it had made to his appearance. It was only a shame he didn't care for his looks...

Below the mirror, his eyes were drawn to the red blindfold laid out on the dresser, as if the fabric had known he was thinking about the most dangerous beings in the world. Asher picked up the blindfold, clean like everything else, and sighed.

"I've run out of leads," he confessed. "I have no idea where to go from here."

"The Arakesh told you nothing?"

Asher thought back on the assassin's last words to him...

*"All your struggle. All your strife... You can't run away... from what you are. You are not the warrior... they think you are. You will die... as one of us..."*

The ranger tossed the blindfold back onto the dresser. "He didn't tell me anything I don't already know."

Adan subconsciously stroked the flat of one of his horns. "Then what are we to do next?"

"*We* won't be doing anything," Asher was quick to reply. "Our time together has come to an end, Adan."

The Drake straightened out the wet cloak in his hands. "You say that every time." He shook the cloak vigorously before holding it high, revealing a perfectly dry piece of material.

Asher, who had become accustomed to such displays of magic made no comment on the feat. "I mean it this time," he continued, taking the offered cloak.

"You said that last time as well. Would you be rid of me because you see no injuries in your immediate future?"

Asher turned on the Drake and stuck a finger in his face. "That isn't why I've *tolerated* your company. You have..." The ranger hadn't given the argument enough forethought.

"I have a debt," Adan concluded. "Like all my people; we are indebted to the one who made us."

Asher shook his head and walked away as much as the small room would allow. "I've told you - I never intended to make you. I thought I was killing orcs, nothing more."

"That doesn't negate the facts," Adan countered with his calm tone.

Frustration was beginning to cloud the ranger's mind. "The facts? If you stay with me, you will die: fact." He moved to the side table and picked up a piece of parchment. "Look at this," he commanded, putting it in Adan's face. The Drake looked upon the ranger's likeness, sketched on to the poster. "The reward for my head is *thirty-thousand*. The only one higher than that is Vighon's."

"You are skilled in evasion," Adan observed.

Asher threw his arms up. "Do I look like I'm evading? I *seek out* my enemy. As we speak, word will be reaching Alijah that I am here and Veda Malmagol will move on again." The ranger took a breath. "Whatever big stick Fate decides to hit me with next, my end is sealed, as it always has been. I am to die alone, be that by the edge of my enemy's steel or in the maw of some great beast. I do not wish for you to be dragged down with me, Adan. You must leave me now."

Adan'Karth appeared genuinely upset, as if he was hearing Asher for the first time. "But where will you go? Without further information you have no direction."

"Like I said; word of my work here will already have reached Alijah. He will expect me to have moved on for sure, but he will likely send a few Arakesh to make certain." Asher began to gather his belongings. "I think I will go downstairs for a drink..."

"You will simply wait for your enemy to find you?" Adan's incredulous tone spoke of his lack of faith.

"Arakesh are trained investigators. It will not take them long. At least I hope not," he added. "I would prefer to meet them sober."

"Even if you succeed in acquiring answers from them, you may suffer grievous wounds. Without me you will—"

"Survive," Asher interrupted. "As any man should. I have already abused our companionship. I have made you party to violence and death. I will take my guilt to my grave for that. I only hope that you find some peace with what we've done. Eternity should help with that..." The ranger went about readying himself while Adan'Karth remained rooted to the middle of the room, his expression absent any hint of emotion.

"I do not want you to die alone," the Drake finally said. "Nor die at all."

Asher lifted his broadsword a few inches from its scabbard and inspected the steel before sliding it back into place. "Even if I best my enemy, the magic in my bones won't last forever - you know this."

A pall of deep sadness overcame Adan. "You are a good man, Asher. I have seen this, for all your endeavours to prove otherwise. A good man shouldn't die alone in the dark."

The ranger strapped his quiver and folded bow over his back, tucking them against his silvyr short-sword. "It wouldn't be the first time," he quipped, making for the door.

Adan's pointed ears twitched and his reptilian eyes shifted towards the window that looked over the street.

"What is it?" Asher asked, pausing by the door.

"Your name," the Drake answered. "It is being bandied around the street."

Asher raised an eyebrow. "Even for the Arakesh that is a fast response. They must have already been in the city..."

Moving to the window, the ranger kept to the frame as he peered out. Indeed there were men, Fenrigs by the look of them, moving from person to person with wanted posters in their hands. They accosted anyone moving through the street and hounded those who tried to take a different route. Standing silently in three neat rows were a dozen Reavers in their black armour and ragged cloaks.

Then he saw them. Two assassins of Nightfall, attired in their dark leathers, stalked the edges of the street. They were the ones in charge down there, despite their aloofness.

"Why do they not wear their blindfolds?" Adan'Karth asked from the other side of the window.

"That would identify them as Arakesh to the people. I don't think our *good king* wishes his subjects to learn that he is in league with them." Asher groaned. "I should have waited longer last night."

"Their numbers have varied in every place," Adan reassured. "You couldn't have known there were two more."

Asher stepped well back from the window. "They have Seekers." The ranger grabbed Adan's brown cloak and threw it at him. "You will take the tavern's back door, *now*. I paid the owner twice the worth of this room to be able to do such a thing."

"I will not leave you, Asher."

The ranger didn't have time to argue with him anymore. "Fine, but you must leave this place. I can't fight them and protect you at the same time. The alley I showed you, by the eastern gates, wait for me there. If I'm not with you by midday leave Skystead and search for your people."

Adan'Karth hesitated before nodding in agreement. "I will see you again."

Asher watched the Drake leave their room before strapping the last of his small knives and daggers to his person. Adan'Karth had cleaned them all - no easy task for one who loathed violence and bloodshed.

Quite calmly, the ranger made his way downstairs and entered the quiet tavern area. He took a stool by the bar and ordered a tankard of ale - he didn't care which brand. The barman placed the tankard in front of Asher, his expression contorted into confusion.

"Your *friend* just left," he commented.

"So he did," Asher replied ominously. He casually glanced over his shoulder, making a quick note of the patrons. Bar one man - a hunter by the look of him - it was the expected crowd.

The barman's fingers tapped incessantly against the surface, turning the ranger back to him. "Your business in Skystead is finished?" he asked in a harmless tone.

Asher heard the tavern door open behind him. "Not quite," he answered.

The Fenrig's boisterous entrance gave his identity away long before he started asking the scared patrons if they had seen anyone matching the poster's likeness. Asher slowly lifted his eyes to see the barman slinking away towards the other end of the tavern.

One by one, the thug interrogated every patron, working his way towards the ranger. His barking questions came to an abrupt end. Asher assumed he had finally laid eyes on him or, more specifically, the weapons on his back. At that moment, the thug should have alerted the Arakesh outside, but he was of an arrogant breed, typical of those who bore the Fenrig brand.

"You!" he snapped, marching towards Asher. "Let me see your face!"

The ranger fingered a fifty-piece coin from his belt and flicked it down the bar. The barman watched the coin come to a spinning stop and looked at Asher questioningly.

"For the window," he explained, grinning.

The Fenrig clapped a hand on Asher's shoulder. "I said—"

The ranger whipped his head around and spat a mouthful of ale into the fool's ugly face. As expected, the man closed his eyes, cried out, and stepped back in shock. Asher grabbed him roughly by the shirt and drove his head down on to the bar top.

Gripping the Fenrig by the throat, he then dragged the man through the tavern, towards the window. "Let's go for a walk…"

# CHAPTER 14

# NOTHING IS EVER SIMPLE

Though not unique in its appearance, as Namdhor was, Skystead was certainly the most beautiful city in the north to the eyes of Kassian Kantaris. The way it curved around the shore of The King's Lake, offering a magnificent view of the towers and ancient cathedrals, was a sight to behold. He only wished Clara could be beside him to share it...

Kassian closed his eyes. He had to take control of the anger that desired to be unleashed. They had a job to do in Skystead - a relatively simple one. If he could get in and out of the city without any of his Keepers suffering injury or worse, then he would.

His fingers hovered around the wand holstered on his thigh.

"You're not breathing," Aphira noted.

Kassian opened his eyes and exhaled. "Control lies at the heart of a Keeper's existence," he said, quoting the Keepers' Manual.

"True," Aphira agreed, her breath visible on the cold air. "But like all of us here, Kassian, your heart has been pierced. When you found me, you told me that letting go of our control would be among our greatest weapons against Alijah. Why do you seek such discipline now?"

*Because that's what Clara would want of me. And that's all I have left of her...* Kassian kept that particular thought to himself.

Instead, he said, "We're about to enter one of the largest cities in all of Illian. A measure of control might be the only thing that sees us ever leave again." With that in mind, Kassian turned on his horse to address the group. "We're only here to find one man - a simple job. But you can bet the Demetrium in your wands there's going to be a lot of Seekers in there. They'll sniff our numbers out in no time. Fin, Quaid - you're coming with me and Aphira. As for the rest of you: if we're not back by nightfall, move on and give 'em hell."

Following Nathaniel's lead, the four Keepers trailed behind on horseback until they reached a block of stables by the entrance. The old Graycoat suggested leaving the horses there so as to avoid notice in the streets. Kassian would have preferred to keep speed on their side but Nathaniel had experience when it came to moving undetected.

"You're sure he's here?" Kassian checked. "The Drake?"

Nathaniel was slowly eating his way through an apple, a ploy to hide the fact that he was following the directions of his ring finger. "They're here," he replied confidently.

Kassian moved through the streets, taking in the sights and sounds of everyday life. To his eyes it was missing something, as if the soul of the city had been dampened. There were few children playing in the streets and boards on windows. The market was quiet and those who were present rarely looked up from their feet.

"They live in fear," Quaid remarked.

"Of course they do," Fin said. "Any one of them could be a conduit for magic and have no idea. One day you're out selling your wares or buying food for your family. Then you're gone. There's no outrunning a Seeker..."

"This way," Nathaniel instructed, taking them east.

Fin, always the talker, continued, "Hester reckons the Seekers are from the shadow realm - beasts pulled from the dark ether."

Quaid tutted and shook his head. "Hester thinks everything comes from the shadow realm."

"They could be," Fin opined. "No one has ever seen anything like them before."

Aphira came up beside the young mage. "That's because they're imported from Erador - you know this. Now keep that tongue in your head and your eyes on the streets."

Nathaniel stopped with the apple in his mouth, his ring finger drawn to an alley on their right. "Down there," he said.

Kassian checked the streets before leading them into the alley. He trusted Nathaniel enough to know they weren't being deceived, but it was the perfect ambush spot. With the exception of a beggar, who was drowning in a ragged brown cloak, the alley was clear. Kassian would have been happy to continue past the crouching beggar and check the adjacent street, but Nathaniel came to a stop in front of the man.

A small nod alerted the three Keepers and they each rested a hand on either their wand or their sword. Kassian opted for his sword since it would be quieter if things got out of hand.

Nathaniel crouched down to the beggar's level and dipped his head in an effort to peak under his hood. "Adan'Karth, is that you in there?"

The Drake lifted his head and set a pair of reptilian eyes on the old Graycoat. "Nathaniel?"

The knight raised his left hand to show his wedding ring. "Glad to see you still carry it."

Adan'Karth stood up and removed the ring from a pouch on his belt. "I would have kept such a token safe with my life."

Nathaniel took the ring back with some concern. "No token is worth your life, Adan."

The Drake shifted his shoulders to look upon the Keepers. "You are here to save Asher!" he declared.

Nathaniel frowned. "Save him?"

"What's happened?" Kassian demanded, an uneasy feeling creeping into his resolve.

"The enemy has found him, not far from here. He is trapped inside The Dancing Fox!" Adan'Karth made for the end of the alley. "Come! I will show you the way!"

Aphira caught up with Kassian as they made for the next street. "Should we send for the others?"

Kassian shook his head. "Not yet. Let's see what the Drake means by enemy. If there's a handful of Reavers we can deal with them."

Rushing now, the group followed Adan'Karth through the twists and turns of Skystead, garnering the attention of every person they passed. Kassian could feel their plan unravelling and a simple job descending into chaos. There was a part of him that still craved that, a part of him that hoped today would be the day he fell in battle.

He had found again and again, however, that his skill with a wand prevented such a thing...

After journeying deeper into the city than any of them would have preferred, the Drake finally brought them to the corner that revealed The Dancing Fox. Kassian tilted his head to assess the street. His eyes only required a second to understand Adan'Karth's description of *trapped*.

Turning to his companions he relayed, "Reavers, Fenrigs, and a couple of Seekers."

"How many?" Quaid asked.

"More than us," Kassian answered.

Nathaniel moved to fit in beside Kassian, replacing him at the end of the corner. He peered out for a couple of seconds before returning his back to the wall.

"I count twelve Reavers, four Fenrigs, and two Seekers." Curiously, the old Graycoat had an amused smile on his face.

"Did I miss the joke?" Kassian asked quietly.

Nathaniel gave the Keeper a mere glance. "Asher isn't trapped."

Kassian scowled at the ridiculousness of that statement. "You're going to have to explain that."

"I don't need to explain it," Nathaniel replied. "We just need to wait. He'll be out in a minute."

Kassian looked back at his fellow Keepers and was met with a collective shrug. Adan'Karth gave nothing away, standing behind them all like an expressionless statue.

"We can't just wait," Kassian insisted. "He faces nearly *twenty* opponents."

Nathaniel shrugged with his head. "They could do with a few more..."

Kassian looked at the old Graycoat like he was mad. "You can't be serious. You believe the stories told of the ranger? I thought you were a man of reason."

"Believe the stories?" Nathaniel echoed. "I witnessed most of them, *boy*. Who do you think told the stories?"

The Keeper was shaking his head. "You've lost your damned mind. I came here for the ranger and I'm leaving with the ranger." Kassian made for the street.

"Kassian!" Nathaniel hissed, failing to keep him concealed.

The Keeper strode boldly out into the street and positioned himself in the centre of the crossroads. Within seconds the two Seekers were turning towards him, sensing the magic in his bones. Their attention caught that of the Reavers, who turned to see Kassian pull his long coat back, revealing his wand.

Before his fingers could grasp the handle, a shocking explosion erupted from inside The Dancing Fox and took out the front window.

Quite surprisingly, in that shower of splinters and glass, it was a Fenrig that hit the street in a crumpled heap...

Then there was chaos.

The Reavers and Fenrigs drew their swords. The Seekers, released by their masters, made a sprinting dash for Kassian. Asher leapt through the broken window and met them all with his broadsword.

Kassian took his wand in hand and threw his arm up, unleashing a staccato of lightning up the street and into the cluster of Reavers. It caught one of the approaching Seekers and tore the beast in half before going on to launch three of the Reavers into the surrounding buildings.

Aphira jumped out of the alley and cast a destruction spell into the ribs of the remaining Seeker, killing it before it could sink its teeth into Kassian.

Outside The Dancing Fox, Asher moved like a wraith between his foes. Kassian readied another spell but his intended targets were dead by the time he had aimed his wand. The ranger might as well have been Death itself, sent by the gods to collect souls. In the Reavers' case, he was simply sending them back to whatever hell they had been spawned from.

Quaid succeeded in bringing one of the Fenrigs down in the distance, his spell turning a deadly proportion of the thug's body to solid ice. The remaining three were cut down by Asher's blade, which never stopped moving. Even the Reavers, with their superior numbers, failed to surround him.

Nathaniel ran past Kassian with his own sword in hand, only the knight wasn't running towards the Reavers. One of the fiends, however, noticed the old Graycoat and swung for his head, an attack easily avoided by skidding along the ground. When Nathaniel jumped back up he was clashing swords with neither Reaver nor Fenrig.

"Who is that?" Fin asked, struggling to find an enemy to aim at without risking an ally.

Kassian knew who it was, having run into a few of them in the early days of The Rebellion. "Arakesh," he growled, drawing his sword.

Nathaniel had placed himself between the ranger and the assassin and employed every skill he possessed to keep the killer at bay. That was when a second emerged from the other side of the street. Kassian changed his direction and ran for the second assassin, directing his Keepers to help Nathaniel.

Before meeting the Arakesh in battle, Kassian ran the length of his blade over his left vambrace, activating the spell that bound both together. The result was blinding and fiercely powerful as the sword glowed a hot white from guard to tip.

Even without his blindfold on, the assassin knew the Keeper was coming for him. Using one of the last remaining Reavers as a jumping board, the Arakesh launched himself at Kassian with both short-swords held high over his head. That glowing white blade came up and blocked both swords from cutting its owner down, but there was no protection from the boot that caught the Keeper in the chest.

Kassian's back greeted the ground with some protest, but there was no time to give in to the pain - Arakesh gave no quarter. The Keeper rolled to the side, narrowly evading both points of the killer's blades. When he rose to his feet once more, the assassin was on him with fury. Kassian held his own, though every parry saw him take a step back, manipulated by his opponent.

Sparks showered the street with every clash of their swords, but every other swing of the assassin's blades cut somewhere new on Kassian's body. All it took, however, was one kick to the back of his knee and the Keeper was dropped to waist height, at the Arakesh's mercy. A short-sword batted his glowing blade away while the other came up, ready to plunge down into Kassian's chest.

But the sword was only one of the Keeper's weapons...

While down on one knee, he retrieved his wand from its holster and aimed it squarely at the assassin's chest. A flash of purple light erupted between the fighters and the Arakesh was sent flying back, his dark leathers smoking.

With a host of fresh cuts and new aches, Kassian stood up with a groan. The Arakesh squirmed on his back amidst a street littered with dead Fenrigs and dismembered Reavers. For good measure, Aphira put her wand to the man's temple and fired a spell that burnt a neat hole through to the other side of his head. Off to the side, Nathaniel was drawing his sword from the gut of his own assassin.

"No..." Asher muttered, looking over the dead assassins. "They're dead," he growled.

Somewhat surprised by the ranger's dismay, Kassian said, "Given your... *display*, I would have thought death the intended outcome."

"I needed one of them alive," the ranger grumbled.

Nathaniel sheathed. "Asher..."

The ranger's blue eyes settled on the knight for a moment, his expression that of stone. Then his shoulders sagged and he smiled at his old friend.

"I see you haven't forgotten how to kill an Arakesh," he commented, gesturing to the dead assassin behind the knight.

"I learned from the best," Nathaniel replied jovially.

The entire exchange was bizarre to Kassian. It was clear that these men had seen more than most if they could talk so off-handedly over the dead at their feet. Indeed, beyond Asher was a scene of butchery the likes of which Kassian had never witnessed. Yet Asher had done it all with finesse and a flowing style that spoke of deadly precision.

Perhaps the stories were true after all. Or, at least *some* of them. Kassian refused to believe that the man before him had brought down a mountain giant with his sword alone.

Then again...

The Keeper tore his eyes from the mass of bodies. "We should get out of here, *now*."

Adan'Karth, now standing among them, turned his head up at an angle. "More are coming," he warned.

Asher guided his sword into the sheath on his hip and gave the Drake a pointed look. "I take it you are responsible for this reunion."

The Drake gave an innocent shrug. "As I said; I do not want you to die alone." Asher narrowed his eyes disapprovingly at Adan'Karth.

Kassian had no idea what they were talking about. "Why are we still here?" he asked impatiently. "Every one of us is Seeker bait."

"Agreed," Asher said. "You have horses?"

"Waiting for us by the eastern gate," Aphira answered.

"As do we," the ranger replied, clapping Nathaniel on the arm.

"First we escape. *Then* we can talk of Vighon..." He moved past them all and made for the nearest alley.

Kassian turned a quizzical look on the old Graycoat. "How does he know—"

Nathaniel raised a hand and shook his head. "You'll get used to him."

Kassian doubted that.

Their route had been winding and overly complicated in the Keeper's opinion, but the ranger had successfully directed them to the stables free of conflict. From there, they fled unchallenged and raced away from the city.

Over the rise, to the south, they met up with the rest of the band and journeyed further still, wary of any patrols likely to be in the area after their public fight.

A little higher up, nestled within the woods that lined the southern curve of The Vengoran Mountains, they were still offered a view of Skystead and The King's Lake. Kassian surveyed it all, through the gap in the trees, before turning back to the group. At its heart, Nathaniel, Asher, and Adan'Karth resided on fallen logs and packs from their horses.

"We weren't followed," Kassian announced. "Hester, Garren: take up a patrol of the area anyway. We caused quite the stir back there - they'll be looking for us." He watched the Keepers leave before taking his own position beside the Drake.

Nathaniel tossed a waterskin at the Keeper. "For the pain."

Kassian followed the knight's gaze to the largest of his cuts, across his right thigh. "Thank you," he replied, swigging the cider. "You can handle yourself, Ranger, I'll give you that."

"I could say the same of you," Asher said. "It isn't easy to defeat an Arakesh, even without their blindfold."

Adan'Karth's expression soured within his hood. "Is it customary to compliment one's ability to take life?"

Asher eyed the Drake while taking a long breath. "So you want to find Vighon," he stated, ignoring Adan as he slowly shifted his gaze to Nathaniel.

"We do," the old Graycoat confirmed.

Kassian raised a hand to stop any further conversation. "How do you know that?"

"Why else would you seek me out?" Asher responded. "The Rebellion wouldn't spare all of you, especially Nathaniel, just to bring me back into the fight. I'm good, but one fighter isn't going to be enough to make a difference. A *king*, however... I heard he was gone. Which means you've sought me out because you think I can track him down."

Kassian swallowed, absorbing the ranger's impeccable intuition. "And can you? Track the king down?"

Asher looked him in the eyes. "No. I'm a ranger not a bloodhound. He's one man who doesn't want to be found in a realm that spans more than a thousand miles from north to south. He's likely travelling alone, moving often, and using a different name."

Kassian hadn't realised until that very moment what hope he carried. It faded quickly.

"Very good," the Keeper said, his tone dripping with sarcasm. "Well, it was a pleasure to see you cut down so many Reavers. If you will excuse us..." Kassian stood up and gestured for his band to prepare to leave.

Nathaniel waved his silent commands away and turned to the ranger. "You say you cannot track him but I can see it on your face, Asher. You know *how* to find him."

Kassian scrutinised the ranger and failed to see anything about the man or his demeanour that told of such knowledge. Again, the Keeper was forced down a path that required trust of Nathaniel. And so, he paused by the gathering and waited impatiently for an answer from Asher.

"To date," Asher asked, "has there been any report of Alijah being coronated as king?"

Kassian looked to be considering the answer but Nathaniel quickly replied, "No. I don't think he believes a coronation to be necessary."

Kassian shrugged in a questioning way. "What does that have to do with finding Vighon?"

"There's always been a way to find Vighon," Asher began, leaving his elbows on his knees. "But it's not without considerable risk."

With an air of confidence and a hint of urgency, Kassian declared, "We are not averse to risk, Ranger. Every day my Keepers fight for those who can't against an enemy that outnumbers them. We *need* the king to rally those who *can* fight. Nothing will hurt Alijah more. So tell us of this way and we will see it done."

Asher looked up at the Keeper with a faint smile. "We're going to need chains. Big ones."

Nathaniel raised an eyebrow. "And where are we going?"

Asher lost his smile. "Namdhor…"

# CHAPTER 15

# IGNORANCE IS BLISS

There was only one way in or out of Kelp Town - a broad path that led to The Selk Road. Arching over the entrance was a wooden sign, proudly informing travellers that they had, indeed, found themselves at Kelp Town, the last refuge before the unforgiving north. The two beams, either side of the road, were thick and the large plaque was of sturdy build, designed to weather the blasting winds that came off The Vengoran Mountains.

It had no trouble supporting the body that now hung from it.

Vighon stood in the biting cold a while longer, haunted by the dead eyes of a familiar face. It was the same man who had been attacked in the tanner's shop. He had slain the Seeker but been pursued by the relentless Reavers. Few escaped them.

The northman was plagued by one question, a question that rooted him to the spot on Kelp Town's eastern edge. Could he have saved him?

It seemed arrogant to believe that he could have done anything, but he had faced greater odds than two Reavers before and emerged the victor. He could have done something, *anything*. What did it matter if the Reavers had killed him in the process; at least the man would have lived and he would have died doing something good.

Seeing the man, a Namdhorian soldier, hanging there like a piece of meat infuriated Vighon. How many battles had he fought for the realm? For his king? Even if he had never found cause to raise his sword, the man deserved respect enough for a proper burial. Instead, he was being used as a tool by Alijah.

Vighon started to look around for something to cut the rope. He would get the soldier down and give him the funeral he should have been given in the first place. He didn't care who watched him do it. There was a part of him that hoped the Reavers would witness his crime and confront him. He would return them to death and hang *their* corpses from the entrance.

The northman made it half way to the soldier when he noticed a woman sitting on a partially broken crate, by the wall of a potter's shop. Everything about her appeared broken. Her shoulders were sagged, her hair matted and long overdue some attention. Dirt clung to every item of clothing she was wearing, obscuring any colour her dress might have once possessed. In fact, the only colour to be seen was the red around her eyes. Even now, she was sobbing, her raw eyes fixed on the hanging soldier.

His stride brought to a halt, Vighon paused in the road, his focus shifting between the dead soldier and the crying woman. Tilting his head to see her face from a better angle, he recognised her as the woman who had been pinned by the Reavers - the wife.

*Keep walking*, he told himself. *Forget all of this and walk away.*

Try as he might, there were still parts of him that he couldn't bury. Vighon approached the woman, his concern growing when he realised she wasn't wearing enough to protect against the weather. She had clearly seen him through her tears and chosen to ignore him.

"Hello," he said gruffly, his voice out of practice. "I'm so sorry," he continued in the absence of a reply. "He doesn't deserve—"

"I know your face," the woman croaked.

Vighon hesitated, not expecting to be recognised. "I was—"

"There," she finished, slowly rising to her feet. "You were there, in the street - I saw you."

The northman nodded. "I'm so sorry for—"

"For what?" she spat. "For standing there and doing nothing? You're just like the others," she accused. "It's easier to offer condolences than it is to actually do anything to help. Renan was a good man. He spent his life standing up for others." Fresh tears streaked down her face.

"I'm going to cut Renan down," Vighon told her.

"You won't touch him!" the woman shrieked. "You did nothing then and you can do nothing now! Just leave..."

The northman took a breath readying a new line of argument. "I just want to—"

"Leave! Now!"

Vighon offered one last apology and walked away with a heavy heart. How many women were out there like her, bereft of their husbands, brothers, and sons because of him? If he acted to help, they died. If he did nothing, they died. He was of no use to anyone - it was time to move on.

It was time to get a drink...

Rounding the corner, returning to Kelp Town's embrace, the northman located the nearest shop that would sell him the supplies needed to keep him alive between towns and cities. He did his best to keep one foot moving in front of the other and put Renan and his wife behind him.

Inside the shop, he began noting aloud everything he would need as well as a few replacements. He didn't have nearly as much coin as he should have, but ale and brandy weren't always cheap. Still, he had enough to buy what he needed and see him move on.

Approaching the store owner - or at least the young man behind the counter - Vighon reached for his coin purse when a particular item caught his eye. The northman made for the far wall and ran his hand down the length of a thick fur cloak. His own cloak, though tattered and dirty, was lined with fur and did an adequate job of keeping him warm and dry.

He thought of Renan's wife, sitting out there in the cold.

Vighon enquired about the price from across the shop and the young man informed him that it would be equal in price to all the items that he required. The northman squeezed the fur and sighed at his dilemma - where was that drink he needed? Perhaps he should have visited a tavern first.

The shop door opened and a freezing gust of wind whipped at Vighon's cloak. A glance and then a second look at the young man told the northman that something was wrong. He waited quietly by the far wall, unable to see past a stack of goods. There were multiple footsteps, heavy and confident by their stride. No armour to speak of, ruling out Reavers.

"Where's your old man, boy?" Everything from the man's tone to his choice of words told Vighon that a group of Yarls had just entered the shop.

The young man behind the counter stepped back with terror in his eyes. "He's not well," he stuttered, searching for his courage. "You're dealing with me now." There it was, far closer to the surface than it was in Vighon. Though his bold words could have done with an equally bold tone.

The Yarls finally came into view in front of the counter. The leader amongst them was a short balding man, whose hand rested permanently on the hilt of a long dagger. He was backed up by three others, each capable of killing the young man by themselves and with naught but their bare hands.

"Sick or not," the short Yarl continued, "he'd better have told you how this works. Otherwise," he said with a wicked grin, "we're going to have to instruct you as we once did him."

"You can't..." The young man licked his lips. "We can't afford to keep paying you. We don't even need protection!"

"Oh but you do," the Yarl replied menacingly. "This is the way it is, boy. Pay or bleed - the choice is yours."

From his angle, Vighon could see the young man slowly reaching for a small club behind the counter. "Just pay them," he announced from the corner, startling the short Yarl.

"Ah, a customer!" he declared happily. "And a smart one at that. You see," he said, gesturing to the northman, "you have coin coming in. We all pay for a service at the end of the day."

The young man's hand hovered over the unseen club. "Just pay them," Vighon repeated, his voice close to a growl. "Don't be a fool, lad," he added in a softer tone.

Reluctantly, the young man withdrew the required amount of coin and handed it over to the Yarls. The short one counted them out before a smile of satisfaction stretched his cheeks.

"Have it ready next time," he said threateningly. "Or the price of our *service* will go up..."

Vighon waited until they had all left the shop before approaching the counter with the fur cloak. "Do yourself a favour and get rid of that," he suggested, nodding at the concealed club. "Removes the temptation to use it."

"We can't all cower in the corner," the young man sniped before demanding the coin for the cloak.

"Any one of them could have broken your skull," Vighon pointed out, handing over the coin. "How will you provide for your family if you're nothing but a feast for the crows?" He took the fur cloak in hand. "Everything we do affects those around us. Be smart, not strong..."

Vighon left the shop and rounded the corner again, making for the town entrance. There was no ignoring Renan's body, hanging there for all to see. The northman walked over to the man's wife, still sitting on the damaged crate. Without a word, he placed the folded cloak down next to her. He didn't wait for a response nor did he look back to see if she wrapped the cloak around her shoulders.

Without enough coin to purchase the necessary supplies now, the northman returned to the heart of Kelp Town. He would be stuck here a while longer until he could acquire the coin needed to move on. Having already paid for his room for the week, he began the short journey to the tavern below.

Hoping to put the events of the day behind him and keep his true self buried deep, he decided to use what little coin he had left and buy a whole bottle of brandy.

He would let the Vighon of tomorrow figure out what to do next...

# CHAPTER 16

# THE SWORD OF NOTHING

Alijah looked out on the world, on a horizon that seemingly had no end. That was his future. Immortality. A single word that described a path with no end, much like the one Malliath had been on for so many eons.

Just thinking of his companion opened up his mind to endless memories. He saw all manner of terrain from places that had never even been seen by man nor elf.

It was all so fragile...

Alijah knew that if he reached out and touched any of them, the memories would shatter into a thousand pieces. It was all held together by wrath. None was so scarred as Malliath the voiceless and it broke Alijah's heart.

It was that boundless horizon, that infinite future, that would give him time to heal Malliath of his ancient wounds.

"Your Grace?"

Alijah's mind snapped back to his surroundings. He was standing on the dragon platform, outside the throne room. Before him was the southern horizon, over Namdhor and The White Vale. Below was a deadly drop into the keep's grounds, a fact he realised when he noted his foot was hovering over the edge, as it had on the Alborn cliffs.

The king brought his foot back and planted it firmly on the stone. He couldn't fathom why he had been in the process of stepping forward...

"Your Grace?" came the call again. Alijah turned to see one of the keep servants standing beneath the portcullis. "The court awaits you, your Grace."

Alijah dismissed the man with a flick of his wrist, his thoughts still swirling. **What's happening to me?** he asked Malliath, aware that the dragon was nearby.

*I have warned you before,* the dragon replied. *My life dwarfs your own - you must absorb it one memory at a time.*

Alijah understood, but he still didn't know why his subconscious would cause him to take a fatal step.

It was trivial, he decided. He was young by the standards of a Dragon Rider and there were none who had ever bonded to a dragon so old as Malliath. Putting it all aside, he turned to the throne room - he had a realm to run.

Seated on his tall black throne, Alijah called on every ounce of his self-discipline to remain still; composed as a king should be. He had held court many times before in the great halls of Erador, bringing justice to the people. He had always performed his duty to the best of his ability, confident that he was only ever improving in his endeavour to be the greatest ruler Verda had ever seen.

But he was on the edge of a new kind of victory, a victory that would secure his throne and ever-lasting peace all at once. He itched to be on the move, seeing his grand plans to their end. Malliath too felt the need for action, frustrated with the waiting.

They were so close...

The half-elf pressed his elbow into the edge of the armrest until the pain gave him focus. He took a breath and returned his attention to the small assembly before him. It was tedious, considering the work yet to be completed, but he was the king now. As such, there was king's work to be done.

"Our case is simple," insisted Hasta Hash-Aseem, lord of the southern lands, with no lack of aggression in his voice. "The Arid Lands no longer recognises slavery as law. No man, woman, or child is to be owned. To do so is punishable by death."

A few feet left of the lord was his opponent in the matter, Usani of house Relios. Alijah knew him to be the wealthiest highborn in Tregaran, making him influential and undoubtedly powerful. He was also a weasel of a man who had yet to experience a hard day in his life.

"Tradition, Lord Hasta. Tradition is the blood that courses through The Arid Lands. It is the one thing that ties every man, woman, and child together. For a thousand years we have practiced slavery - it is the way of things!"

Alijah shifted his position on the throne, drawing the attention of all, except for his mother, who stared blankly at the eastern wall. The king ignored his mother's distraction and addressed the men and their entourage.

"I am something of a student in history, Usani of house Relios. I am certain slavery was abolished before I was even born, by Tauren Salimson no less."

Usani bowed his bald head. "Indeed, you are correct, your Grace. However, that decree was forced upon The Arid Lands in the wake of The War for the Realm. It has been contested ever since and—"

"And now there is violence in the streets again," Alijah interjected. "Violence on *my* streets." His gaze turned to the lord of Tregaran. "Is it not your duty to prevent such bloodshed, Lord Hasta? Or do I have to come down there myself?"

Perfectly timed, Malliath descended from the heavens and landed on the platform extending from the throne room. His horned head snaked through the dragon door and rested in the air, his fangs slightly parted.

Through his bond to Malliath, Alijah could smell the fear permeating the air around the two men.

"No, your Grace," Lord Hasta reassured. "I have the matter in hand."

"Then why are you here?" Alijah countered. "I have three realms to unite, a task you cannot comprehend. Is it too much to ask that my lords ensure safety and prosperity in their provinces? Have I not given you the means to do so?" Alijah glanced at his mother, seated off to the side, and found himself increasingly aggravated by her distraction.

Lord Hasta raised both of his hands. "You have, your Grace. The Arid Lands uphold your word and appreciate your support in outlawing slavery. I have already taken strong measures to dissuade the highborns—"

"You executed the eldest son of house Orneese!" Usani snapped.

"He sold children!" Hasta bellowed.

"You will address me," Alijah commanded, drawing apologies from both men.

"They demand blood," Usani replied calmly, "but I have convinced them to settle for compensation."

"Is that why you are here, Usani?" Alijah questioned. "You speak for house Orneese?"

"I speak for every highborn in The Arid Lands, your Grace. They trust me to—"

"What?" Alijah cut in. "They trust you to bend my ear? Have you come all this way to convince me that slavery is the future of my realm? I hope not, Usani of house Relios."

A smile twitched across the highborn's face. "No, your Grace. But, perhaps, The Arid Lands could be allowed its most ancient of traditions. It worked for centuries and it would end many a conflict in the south."

"That's an absurd statement," Alijah replied. "The conflict will continue as long as there are those who oppose the tradition."

"Not if it was the king's law," Usani countered.

Alijah leaned forward. "Hear me well: it is not the king's law. Nor shall it ever be."

Lord Hasta had the beginnings of a broad grin on his wide face. "Praise for the wisdom of the king!"

"He executed Surka Orneese without a trial, your Grace! Is it not the king's law that regardless of stature, every man has the right to a trial? Surka was hung in the square with less respect than a common criminal. The highborns of The Arid Lands demand you take action, your Grace."

"I am to suffer demands now," Alijah mused. He raised a hand to stop Usani from saying another word. "Is this true, Lord Hasta? You executed one of my subjects without trial?"

Lord Hasta swallowed and glanced up at Malliath. "It is true, your Grace. Surka Orneese was arrested in the middle of a slave auction - an auction at which Usani of house Relios was present, I might add."

"Lies!" the highborn spat.

Alijah flexed his fingers to calm the highborn. "This matter would appear complicated, but my laws are simple. Slavery is unacceptable. Execution without a fair trial is also unacceptable."

*Let me eat them both.* Malliath's meaty tongue bathed his fangs in thick saliva.

"My predecessors would have bent many a law for the highborns of Illian, from Namdhor to old Karath. But those days are behind us all now. Let it be known that the King's Justice is swift and unwavering. I act only in service to the people, not just the rich," he added with a pointed look at Usani. "Lord Hasta..."

The large man stepped forward and bowed his head. "Your Grace."

"I have no doubt that Surka of house Orneese was guilty of his crimes. But you cannot dispense justice without a trial. The people must be a part of the process, so that justice might be experienced by all. You will pay Surka's weight in coin to the house of Orneese."

Lord Hasta looked to protest the judgment, but under the shadow of Malliath he held his tongue.

"Perhaps," Usani suggested slyly, "the lord should pay his own weight in coin..."

Malliath growled over them. "You will not speak while I am passing judgment," Alijah asserted. He composed himself on the throne and gave the highborn a long look.

Again, he spared a moment's glance at his mother. Reyna was staring absently at the eastern wall where Vighon's sword and shield had been mounted. Alijah's fists clenched together.

"I can see, Usani of house Relios, that you speak for a great many. Is that correct?"

The bald man bowed his head with an arrogant smile. "It is, your Grace."

"Can I trust you to inform every highborn in The Arid Lands that slavery is against the law?"

Usani hesitated. "If that is your will, your Grace, I will see it done."

Alijah tapped his fingers against his armrest. "I fear your words will not be mine, Usani. I am concerned that you will, in fact, return to the south and continue to sow seeds of unrest among my people. I think the highborns, such as yourself, require a powerful message. I'm sure, however, that your entourage is more than capable of spreading this message far and wide..."

Usani's confident expression had slowly slipped away until confusion ruled his face. By Alijah's last, ominous words, that confusion had transformed into fear. He opened his mouth to either question or protest the king's judgment, but none would ever know for sure.

There was no coming back from Malliath's maw.

Lord Hasta fell to the ground, shrieking with horror at the sight. The last thing anyone saw of Usani of house Relios was his bloody shaking legs before they disappeared down Malliath's throat.

Reyna didn't so much as flinch...

"See that recompense is made, Lord Hasta," Alijah told him, standing from his throne. "If this unrest continues in your province I will be forced to come down there myself and see to it personally. If that happens, be warned, you will not retain your title upon my departure."

Hasta scrambled to his feet and bowed so low the king could see the back of his neck. "It will be done, your Grace."

"Then be gone. All of you."

Alijah remained standing as he watched the chamber empty of all but himself and his mother.

*It would have been a powerful message to all the south had I eaten them both...*

The half-elf straightened his shoulders. ***We cannot solve every matter with your ravenous stomach. Remember the world we're working towards. In that world, words alone will prevail.***

*I forget nothing,* Malliath said. *Have you forgotten how we will forge this world? We do not have time to sit in court and bandy words with the foulness of highborns.*

Alijah looked at his mother. ***We will leave shortly,*** he promised the dragon.

Malliath grumbled in his throat. *You would waste more time with words. She may have brought you into this world, Alijah, but I gave you the strength to conquer it, to tame it. There is only us.*

The dragon retracted his head from the chamber and dropped away from the platform, his wings unfurled to glide over the city. Alijah was left with a stain of harsh memories concerning his parents, fuelling his underlying anger.

"How do you find my court, Mother?"

Reyna's eyes flitted to the dark puddle in front of the dragon gate. "Bloody," she said simply.

The muscles tensed in Alijah's face. "You have counselled kings and queens alike. Is that all you have to say? Since when has the King's Justice been absent blood. Do you have no advice concerning my approach to The Arid Lands?"

Reyna dragged her eyes from Vighon's sword. "Killing one high-born, even one such as Usani, will not bring peace to The Arid Lands. You will need to spend time down there, *personally*. Many meetings will be required and you will have to sit in on all of them as mediator. You will also have to divert more Reavers to each of the three cities in the south, so as to enforce your will."

"*Knights*, Mother, call them *knights*. And you're right, of course. Time will be needed in each of the cities - it will be a lengthy process. I take such harsh action now because I do not *have* that time."

"You refer to your work in The Moonlit Plains and on Qamnaran."

Alijah paused, his lips pursed. "I do."

Reyna once again let her gaze drift over the sword and shield. "What could you possibly be doing in either of those locations that is more important than governing the realm?"

"*Preserving* the realm," the king announced cheerily. "All will make sense in time. Until then, you will have to do the one thing you've always struggled to do."

Reyna took a breath. "And what would that be?"

"Have faith - in *me*, specifically..." Alijah's reply trailed off as his mother returned her attention to the sword of the north. "I left that up there out of respect for him; he was a good king, after all. But I see it serves as nothing but a distraction. Or worse," he added, "a *reminder*."

Alijah stormed across the chamber and ripped the sword from the wall. "Vighon isn't coming back, Mother. His reign ended. *I* am your son, not *him*! You should show your love for me!"

Reyna's expression cracked. "I do love you..."

"Liar! I can see your love for Vighon every time you look at his sword! Is this where your loyalties lie?" Alijah gripped the scabbard and the hilt and separated the two, revealing the silvyr length. He couldn't hide his surprise when the sword failed to set alight.

"It is the sword of the north," Reyna said gently. "The *king's* sword. It will not flame for you nor any other."

His mother's words, tone, and demeanour enraged Alijah just as much as the sword's insolence. "I AM KING!" he fumed. "This sword does not dictate who resides on that throne! The enchantment laid upon the blade was done by the elves for Vighon - it means nothing!"

"You care an awful lot for something that means nothing," his mother observed.

Alijah could feel the dragon in him fighting to be unleashed. His grip around the hilt was tight enough to break every bone in a man's hand.

"That rage you're feeling," Reyna said softly, taking a step closer, "belongs to Malliath. You must resist his influence—"

"Silence!" he barked. The king took a few more seconds to compose himself, running a hand through his long dark hair. "You know nothing of what you speak," he told her, walking out onto the exterior platform. "Malliath holds no sway over me; I saw to that years ago. I am of my own mind. And I am fated to rule from east to west with Malliath by my side. You must accept this."

The wind caught his hair and cloak, blowing both to the north. He looked out on Namdhor before examining the blade in his hand. It meant nothing. He could feel his mother's eyes on him and he met them boldly. Without blinking or straying from her gaze, he casually tossed the sword of the north over the side of the platform.

Reyna said nothing. She remained perfectly still as he passed her by and made for the doors of the throne room. Before he could pass over the threshold, her voice called out, giving him momentary pause.

"There is still good in you, Alijah. I know it."

"The fact that you believe there is anything *but* good in me speaks of your own failings as a mother..." With that, he slammed the doors shut behind him and rejoined Malliath in the courtyard.

His mother's sobs were the last thing he heard of her...

# CHAPTER 17

# WASHED UP

The sound of lapping waves finally broke through the deep slumber that had enthralled Galanör. His eyes blinked in quick succession, faltering under the oppressive light. Then cold water washed up around him and spilled across one half of his face. He could taste the salt...

The elven ranger slowly pulled himself up onto all fours and discovered he had been lying in the surf. One half of his face was coated in sand and he was dripping wet from head to toe.

His last memory came back to him and he recalled the shielding spell that had spared him most of the deadly impact. His swim to the beach had been arduous, requiring all of his discipline and training to get him through the icy water.

Finally, he realised, exhaustion must have got to him and he collapsed on what had been dry sand at the time.

Caught up with himself, he checked that both of his scimitars were still on his hip.

They weren't there!

Galanör pushed himself up onto just his knees and looked down in alarm, fearing that he had lost the blades. Seeing himself coated in the dark armour of a Reaver brought a flood of memories back to the elf. He looked over his shoulder and followed the cliff face to the very top. He remembered falling.

The ranger wiped his face and investigated the rest of the beach. There, further south of his position, was the horse he had been riding. The impact had killed the larger animal.

Staggering to his feet, Galanör thought only of Aenwyn. He hoped she had escaped and made it to safety. There was a fire igniting within him, driving him to learn of her fate as soon as possible.

The distinct sound of hooves ploughing through soft sand caught Galanör's pointed ears. They were moving fast and coming from the north, the direction of the tower. A jolt of pain ran down his neck as he turned his head to the left. He winced and gripped the muscles at the base of his neck while casting his vision up the beach.

Reavers were galloping towards him on horseback. Leading them was a Fenrig, pointing his sword at the elf and shouting something unintelligible. Galanör's hands drifted over his belt but failed to grip any sword - lost to The Hox. Judging by the sun above him, he had been lying on the beach for hours, giving his enemy plenty of time to find a way down to his position.

The ranger had no idea how he was going to survive the next few minutes. He counted four Reavers behind the Fenrig, all of whom would come for him until freed of their heads - a difficult feat with naught but bare hands.

He straightened his back and rotated his wrists to a series of audible cracks. Everything hurt. He decided to kill the Fenrig first. The thug was a human, after all, and would succumb to Galanör's superior strength and speed. Hopefully, he could then use the Fenrig's weapon against the undead Reavers.

If only he didn't feel like death himself...

The familiar sound of an arrow cutting through the air found Galanör's ears before his eyes caught sight of the missile flying from the tree line in the east. The arrow soared over the distance and demonstrated a degree of accuracy rarely seen in any but elves as it struck the Fenrig in the heart. The thug was jolted by the impact before his body slumped off the side of his mount.

Galanör searched the trees for any sign of his saviour. There was nothing to see but another arrow hurtling across the beach. It ended its magnificent flight in the head of a Reaver, dropping it to the beach. The next two arrows were fired in quick succession and angled slightly higher, so as to come down on the pair of Reavers from above.

The elven ranger only faced a single Reaver on horseback now. That was when Aenwyn stepped out from between the trees, her bow nocked. Her marksmanship never faltered, even to the last foe. The Reaver took the arrow in the head and flew back off its saddle.

Galanör took one sluggish step after another to greet Aenwyn. Her own steps were light and far swifter - she was crushing him within her embrace in seconds. It was good to hold her again, to inhale her natural perfume.

"I feared the worst," Aenwyn expressed, squeezing him all the tighter.

"Easy," he moaned, discovering new pains in his ribs.

Aenwyn stepped back from him and examined his body. "I can't decide if you were brave or foolish for making such a jump."

"Let's settle on brave," he uttered, looking back at the tree line. There, he saw half a dozen of his kin emerging with arrows nocked.

"Thank you," Aenwyn offered. "If you hadn't led them away I would never have escaped."

Galanör replied with a warm smile and a kiss on top of her head.

"We should leave this place," one of them suggested.

"Agreed," Galanör replied. He paused and gripped Aenwyn's arm. "My blades?"

Aenwyn almost rolled her eyes but, instead, settled on a brief sigh. "We have retrieved them. They await your return with open arms."

Despite her wit, Galanör managed a smile. "Then take me to them."

Half a mile beyond the trees, they mounted their waiting horses and made for the east. The ranger was thankful for the ride since his legs were still reeling from meeting The Hox at such speed and from such a shocking height. He held on to Aenwyn's waist and let his head rest on her shoulder while his mind ran through the events prior to his fall.

Inside the comfort and safety of their camp, Galanör was ordered to rest - he knew better than to argue with Aenwyn. To the sound of a rushing waterfall and his companion's gentle voice, the ranger eventually closed his eyes and slept well.

The elf was quite baffled when he awoke to a rising sun. He was also quite hungry. Thankfully, Aenwyn was there to help him with both. Greeting her love with a smile, she placed a plate of food next to his cot and a fresh cup of water.

"You slept through the day and night," she explained.

Galanör sat up and squeezed her wrist with one hand while shovelling food into his mouth with the other. He was more than pleased to see Guardian and Stormweaver standing upright against the end of his cot.

Aenwyn gave an amused laugh. "Sometimes you are more human than elf..."

The ranger swallowed his food and clenched his fist. "I feel much better," he observed.

"Helayna saw to some of your wounds while you slumbered," Aenwyn told him, speaking of the camp's greatest healer.

"I must thank her." Galanör stood up and took in the cave that surrounded them. Beyond its entrance was a wall of water, blurring the earliest rays of sunlight.

"She rests herself," Aenwyn replied. "Healing you took its toll on her…"

Galanör nodded his understanding, though his attention was gripped by the scrolls laid out on the wooden table, across the cave. He walked over with an apple in hand and scrutinised the sketches and glyphs scrawled over the parchment. He instantly recognised it as the tower's interior, expertly drawn by Aenwyn. One of the scrolls was simply line after line of glyphs.

"That was all I could recall in detail."

The ranger was impressed. "It's more than *I* remember." He fingered each scroll, examining them closely.

"I never imagined it to be hollow," Aenwyn commented. "Why would Alijah build something like this?"

"And out of silvyr no less," Galanör added.

"Inara and Athis might have destroyed the last shipment," Aenwyn continued, "but it doesn't seem to have affected construction."

"It was likely surplus," Galanör reasoned. "I want to check the boats today, by the eastern shore."

Aenwyn looked him up and down. "Are you rested enough for that?"

"I am rested enough to check over a few boats, yes. They need sending across to Illian's shore before our reinforcements arrive. Besides, there have never been any Reavers sighted that far from the tower."

"If there is to be a fight, Galanör, I would like for you to hold back - just this once. There is a real battle coming and we both know you will be on the front line."

The ranger wasn't sure he could keep to Aenwyn's wishes were they to be set upon by Reavers, but he agreed with her statement. "I will do my best. I just want to make certain the boats are ready for the queen and Doran. We will need to get them over here as quickly and quietly as possible."

"Do dwarves ever move quietly?" Aenwyn quipped.

Galanör laughed to himself. "Fair point." He took a large bite from his green apple. "Let us be going then."

Aenwyn reached out and held him back by the arm. "There will be time to check on the boats. I would keep you here with me a while longer…"

Galanör's beaming grin spread across his face. "Do you require help with meditation? You should know I've been taught by the best."

Aenwyn matched his smile. "Meditation can wait…"

## CHAPTER 18
# THE EYE OF GRARFATH

Under the cover of darkness, Doran Heavybelly led his companions, both elf and dwarf, across the northern stretch of The Moonlit Plains, to the ancient fort of West Fellion. Once home to the fearsome Graycoats, there wasn't much left of the structure to recognise it as a fort anymore. The circular outer walls stood tall for their part, but decades of neglect and the relentless force of nature had worn away at them.

With no torches or fires of any kind, West Fellion was steeped in shadow. Day or night, the fort would always appear a ruin, long forgotten and plundered to its last treasure.

Having approached from the north-east, they could see the broken archway strewn with heavy stone, barring the entrance where the gates had been. There were likely more than a few skeletons still buried beneath it all. The ditch surrounding the outer walls was filled with dirty water, though beneath the stars it was a moat of black that glistened in the moonlight. Dotted throughout, poking just above the surface, were sharpened logs that had been dug into the ground.

From their vantage, descending a small rise, it was clear to see from the outside that there was nothing taller than the surviving walls. The main tower, that had once looked out over the green plains, now littered the interior and had crushed more than one building upon finding its resting place.

"How do we get inside?" Faylen asked from atop her mount.

Doran looked up at the elf with an answer on his lips when he realised this wasn't the first time she had been to West Fellion. "Ye were 'ere, weren' ye?" he said, recalling the story from decades earlier. "Ye were with Asher an' the Galfreys when the Arakesh attacked."

"It seems like a lifetime ago," she whispered, her gaze drifting over the ramparts.

"It was," Doran remarked with a shrug, "for a *human*..."

"We should get out of the open," Queen Adilandra suggested, coming up beside Faylen. "We're too exposed on the plains."

Doran couldn't disagree with the queen's assessment. Much in the way that silvyr reacted under the stark light of the moon, so too did the green pastures of The Moonlit Plains. All around them, the fields glowed a beautiful shade of green that illuminated the land for miles around. So powerful was the glow that every dwarf and elf alike was cast in its eerie light. It also meant that their presence could be seen from afar...

"There's an entrance on the north side," Doran explained, pointing at the fort. "Though that might be too grand a word for it..."

With Thraal and Thaligg trailing him, the War Mason guided their party around to the north side of the curving wall. There they came across rickety boards that bridged the gap across the ditch. On the fort side was a pointed, jagged hole in the stone, leading to a dark interior.

"Where are your kin, War Mason?" Adilandra was looking over the fort from east to west.

"They don' man the ramparts or guard the exterior, me Lady. Like ye said: too exposed. West Fellion has been abandoned for decades; any sign o' life would give us away. But don' worry, ye'll get a warm dwarven welcome soon enough!"

One behind the other, they crossed the makeshift bridge and entered the ruins of West Fellion. One foot inside the keep and Doran was very quickly looking down the length of several spears.

"Easy boys!" he called. "The real warriors 'ave arrived!"

The Heavybellys greeted them eagerly, happy to see new faces and potentially receive orders more exciting than *sit on yer arse*. Doran climbed down from Pig and gripped the forearm of more than one dwarf, offering them praise for their duty. There were still those who visibly avoided him, however, and even scowled at his arrival. Doran let it go over his head - which wasn't hard.

The elves sent an audible ripple through the fort and tensions rose somewhat. They weren't enemies - Doran thanked Grarfath every day for that fact - but they weren't the best of allies either. Queen Adilandra handed her horse to another elf and surveyed their surroundings with a passive eye, her thoughts her own.

"Thraal!" Doran called. "Find Queen Adilandra somewhere suitable to sleep for the night." The loyal dwarf nodded his acknowledgment. "And Thraal! Suitable means *private*." The warrior paused before nodding his understanding. "Thaligg!" Doran called next. "Gather everyone in what's left o' the dinin' hall. I would 'ave words with 'em before the gossipin' starts."

Adilandra raised an immaculate eyebrow. "I wasn't aware dwarves were so susceptible to gossip, War Mason."

Doran replied with a mischievous tone. "Oh aye, me Lady. 'Tis our guilty pastime. That's why we try to busy ourselves with the likes o' swingin' our axes an' minin' the mountains."

An amused smile flashed across Adilandra's face, making Doran glad he hadn't blinked. She soon moved on to commune with her kin who, for the most part, were seeing to their supplies and tending to the armour they had stored on the carts.

Between the hub of activity, the son of Dorain caught sight of Faylen, standing by the entrance to the main courtyard, or what was left of it. Doran weaved between his clan, giving friendly nods where he could, and made his way to the elf's side. Her hand was resting on the stone, her gaze distant despite the lack of a view.

"Ye know, humans believe that our memories are kept in 'ere," he began, putting a stubby finger to his temple, "but we dwarves know better," he added with a coy smile. "The strongest memories are kept by the *stone*."

"I am inclined to believe it," Faylen said softly. "There, not ten feet away, is where we fought Adellum Bövö, one of Valanis's generals. Reyna delivered the final blow, killing him with his own bow."

Doran looked at the pile of rubble where Faylen had indicated. "Aye, I can believe it. I've seen that bow in action an' know well o' its power."

"We were all to die here," the High Guardian told him. "Adellum's death spelled the end of West Fellion and it should have taken us with it."

The War Mason frowned as he dredged up the story he had been told nearly fifty years ago. "It was Asher, no? He used that ol' gem thing - he had a ring, didn' he?"

Faylen contained her smile. "He possessed Paldora's Gem, or at least a fragment of it." She stifled a laugh. "The old fool had no idea how to wield it. But he still managed to save us all." Turning away from the courtyard, Faylen's eyes settled on the ruin of West Fellion's main entrance. "He certainly knew how to wield a sword though. I watched him hold back dozens of Arakesh in there, maybe even a hundred."

The son of Dorain craned his neck and cast a critical eye over her expression. "Ye could o' gone with Nathaniel an' Kassian, ye know. Ye'd 'ave seen him again..."

Faylen maintained her steady gaze. "Anything that might have existed between us... died with him in the pools of Naius. That isn't to say I do not hold a place for Asher in my heart. He is a good man, an *extraordinary* man. But, in truth, I do not believe he is for anyone - he belongs to the realm if not Fate itself."

Doran gave an agreeable shrug. "He does find 'imself bein' dragged into the worst o' things. But, me Lady, he is *only* human. The realm can' 'ave 'im for ever."

"Agreed," Faylen grieved. "But I'm afraid it is no longer within me to give him that peace he deserves. I fear he will only ever find meaning in his deeds alone."

Doran sighed and looked at his feet. "True enough..."

Faylen placed a gentle hand on the War Mason's pauldron and offered him a warm smile that promised him hope - such was the power and beauty of elves. "My place is by my queen's side."

Doran watched her walk away until a shadow moved in the dwarf's vicinity. He turned to find a pair of reflective eyes in the dark, where the moon failed to touch. He narrowed his vision and scrutinised the hulking form by the wall.

"Rus? Is that ye, lad?"

The shadow moved and the eyes with it. Stepping closer, towards the light cast by the moon, Russell Maybury's large frame took on new detail, bringing a genuine smile to Doran's bearded face. That smile quickly faded as he got a better look at his old friend, cloaked and hooded. His face was ashen, marred by dark rings under his yellow eyes. His usually cropped hair had grown into a knotted white mess and his jaw was rough with stubble.

Russell's head only poked out of the shadow for a moment before the old wolf quickly retreated again, his expression pained. Doran looked from his friend to the partial moon and back, putting a despairing picture together.

"What's the matter, Rus?" the dwarf questioned, sure that he already possessed the answer.

"I dare not step into the moon," Russell replied with a rasp. "Full or not, it gives the wolf strength..."

Doran closed his eye and briefly clamped his jaw shut. "I'm so sorry, Rus. I shouldn' o' left ye 'ere. I should o' been 'ere to help ye."

Russell managed something akin to a smile. "A War Mason's

place is not beside an ageing werewolf. You have responsibility now, Doran."

The son of Dorain stepped into the shadow of the ruins and embraced his friend. "Me place is beside those who need me - that includes yerself, ye damned fool."

Russell stepped back from their embrace, his grip still strong. "I hear your name a lot within these walls."

Doran refrained from wincing. "I can only imagine..."

Russell started walking, hugging the curve of the interior wall. "It's not all bad," he reassured. "Don't get me wrong; some of them really dislike you - especially one dwarf in particular."

The War Mason already knew that dwarf's name. "Ragnar," he muttered. "He's the son o' General Reggor, another *fan* o' mine," he added sarcastically.

Russell glanced down at Doran. "From what I can tell, he wishes himself to be War Mason, if not his father. But not everyone agrees with him." The old wolf continued in a hopeful tone, "Every time news arrives of your victories, the talk changes amongst your kin. Well, except for Ragnar..."

"Hmm. There are still those who reckon I haven' earned me title." Doran actually agreed with that particular opinion, but he didn't say anything to Russell. "Forget all that," he said, waving the subject away. "I'm more than aware o' the stir me brother's last command has had on the clan. I'm more concerned with *ye*."

Russell paused just before the edge of an entranceway. A Heavy-belly walked through, demonstrating the old wolf's senses were as sharp as ever. The dwarf, however, gave him a suspicious look before bowing his head to Doran and continuing on his way.

"I hear their whispers," Russell said. "They at least suspect that I am a werewolf, a *Lycan*. How could they not? When the wolf has its time, I lock myself away beneath the keep, but the stone cannot contain the howl of the beast."

Doran eyed those of his kin who were yet to enter the dining hall. "Have ye had any trouble?" he asked, promising himself that any dwarf to have even provoked Russell would get the blunt end of Andaljor.

"They avoid me mostly. I do not fear their judgment and I care little for their looks. I am more troubled by my own ability to be of service. I cannot give the wolf an inch. By night I am ruled by a cloudy sky for fear of the moon. Yet night is the only time we can venture out to spy on the dig site."

"Ah, Rus..." The son of Dorain hated seeing his friend so defeated. "Ye can still wield that pick-axe o' yers though, right?"

"I can. It seems that the closer the wolf gets to assuming full control, the stronger I get."

"Well that we can use," Doran assured. "Trust me, there's a fight comin'." The dwarf gestured to the gloomy doorway that led into the dining hall. "Come with me an' I'll tell ye all abou' it."

The War Mason led the way, his thoughts concerning Russell spiralling into a dark place. There was only one obvious outcome to his friend's curse though. Perhaps he was cursed all the more for being friends with a dwarf who killed such monsters.

Inside the dining hall, the dwarves were able to illuminate the interior with torches and candles without fear of giving their position away. Thanks to the light, the War Mason could see several hundred grubby faces looking back at him as he entered. The hall was packed from side to side and made all the worse by the added elves, who clustered together on one side around their queen.

Adilandra bowed her head to Doran, signalling his authority. He bowed in return and looked to his left only to discover that Russell was no longer with him and, in fact, had never even entered the hall. His keen ears would suffice, Doran assumed.

"What's goin' on?" one of the Heavybellys cried out, followed by similar questions.

Doran waved his hands down to calm the hall. "As ye can see, Ayda has come to The Rebellion's aid!"

"A few elves aren' aid!" came a barbed reply. Doran was sure it had come from Ragnar, who was seated amongst his loyal idiots.

"More are comin'!" Doran continued. "As are more o' our own! They will arrive shortly in small groups. The leadership has been in conference these past days. It seems that whatever our kin are bein' forced to build on Qamnaran is almost complete. We still don' know what the tower is for, but we know it ain' good."

"I could o' told ye that months ago!" Ragnar bellowed.

Doran gritted his teeth and ignored the young fool. "At first light, we're to march for The Narrows! From there, we will cross on boats to Qamnaran an' meet up with the elves o' Ilythyra! Together, we will attack the Reavers who shackle our brothers an' sisters!"

The responding cheer did not come from all parts of the hall. "What about' our brothers an' sisters here, in The Moonlit Plains?" demanded Ragnar. "They are closer! We could 'ave ourselves a battle tomorrow an' not 'ave to suffer so many elves!"

Doran's fist balled up until his knuckles cracked. "Our foe has proven 'imself meticulous in his plannin'. We 'ave to assume that the tower's early completion is deliberate!" The War Mason regretted giving his response immediately. He didn't need to justify his orders, simply enforce them.

Ragnar looked to protest further when all eyes turned to the door behind the son of Dorain. There, he found a dwarf and an elf stood side by side.

"War Mason," the dwarf addressed. "This elf claims to 'ave come from Qamnaran."

Indeed the elf looked haggard by comparison to those who had not long arrived, suggesting he had travelled fast with little rest. Upon noticing his queen, the elf bowed his head to his chest.

A little impatient, Doran said, "Ye've come a long way to bow ye head, lad."

The elf offered him a brief bow of apology. "I come with word from Galanör of house Reveeri." Doran took the small scroll no longer than his finger and unravelled it. He read the simple report to himself before relaying it to the hall.

"King Gaerhard of the Brightbeards has been sighted at the camp on Qamnaran!" That set a few tongues wagging amongst the Heavy-bellys. "This only confirms it - we are to liberate our kin on that wretched island!"

Again, not everyone cheered. "Why should we care about the king o' the Brightbeards?" Ragnar asked, continuing his verbal assault. "I say we attack the dig site!"

Doran sighed and found Ragnar in the crowd. "I gave King Gaerhard me word that clan Heavybelly would return to offer their steel!"

"Ye gave that word while an exile!" Ragnar pointed out. "Before ye brother saw fit to curse us all..." he mumbled a little too loudly.

"Ye'll call 'im *king*, boy," Doran replied with a threatening tone. "An me word is me bond, exile or not!"

Ragnar laughed to himself. "If that were true ye would never 'ave become an exile in the first place!"

"I don' care who ye daddy is, Ragnar; one more word out yer fat gob an' ye'll be so far behind our assault on Qamnaran that even the Mother an' Father won' see ye."

Ragnar squared his shoulders and sneered, his cheeks flushing red.

"Right," Doran continued. "First light - be ready!"

Ragnar stood up from his chair and pushed his friends aside. "I demand the eye of Grarfath!" he blurted. Again, the hall was filled with whispers.

Doran caught Faylen's questioning expression and shook his head in response. He took in the dwarves around him, assessing the environment to give him options. He could see, however, that something definitive was required to silence Ragnar and his loyalists.

"What say ye?" Ragnar called, aware that if Doran was to decline the eye he would be forfeiting his title and authority.

The son of Dorain reluctantly gave the slightest nod of his head and the hall erupted into chaos as the Heavybellys rushed to get outside.

Queen Adilandra came up on Doran's side. "If this is what I

suspect it is, we do not have time for it. Nor can we risk the loss of a strong arm."

"It's too late," Doran replied bitterly. "He's called for the eye o' Grarfath; I either meet his challenge or give 'im me title right now. Trust me, me Lady, ye don' want to be dealin' with that fool."

Adilandra looked down at him. "Can I trust you to bring a swift end to this matter? We must all rest before the journey."

Doran nodded as he made for the door. "Don' worry, me Lady. *Swift* will be the drop o' me hammer..."

Outside, a thick cloud bank had blown over, covering the dwarves of clan Heavybelly, who had organised themselves to create a circle in the open space. Judging by the eager faces in the crowd, many of them had clearly been terribly bored until now. Doran pushed his way through, closely followed by Russell who was carrying Andaljor.

"What about your oath?" The old wolf passed the legendary weapon to its owner. "You have sworn to never spill another drop of dwarven blood."

Doran hefted Andaljor, aware that such a weapon was designed to wash the ground with blood. "Don' worry, lad, I can beat this upstart bag o' spanners without spillin' his worthless blood."

Opposite him, inside the circle, Ragnar drew his sword from his belt with glee. "To the death, son of Dorain?"

The War Mason frowned at the barbaric suggestion. "It's the Fourth Age, ye dolt - such times are past! An' we can' be losin' dwarven lives on the eve o' a battle! First blood... or the first to *yield*!"

Ragnar laughed. "The son o' Reggor does not yield!"

"Oh, ye'll yield before the end, boy." Doran promised menacingly. He turned the latch in the middle of Andaljor's haft and separated the axe from the hammer. Since the axe was guaranteed to break his oath, he threw it into the ground beside his feet.

Ragnar gestured at the axe. "That was a mistake."

Now it was Doran's turn to laugh. "I've got a hundred years on ye, boy. An' I've fought in more battles than ye've had hot dinners at yer daddy's table."

That enraged the son of Reggor, but his urge to fight was forced to wait when Thaligg walked into the middle of the circle.

"The eye o' Grarfath has been invoked! Ye both know what this means! The Father is watching ye now. His eye will not close until his favour has been given. To that end, ye're stuck in here until blood is spilled or one o' ye yields!"

"Get out o' the eye, Thaligg!" Ragnar fumed. The moment the circle was clear, the son of Reggor roared from deep in his chest and ran at his opponent.

Doran didn't bother charging as Ragnar did - it was a waste of energy. Instead, he casually threw his hammer underarm, towards the ground. There, the heavy slab of steel collided with Ragnar's foot, halting his charge immediately. The young dwarf staggered forward and fell face first into the mud.

The War Mason pressed a boot into Ragnar's side as he tried to rise, pushing him over onto his back. Doran trod on his opponent's wrist, keeping his sword at bay, before dropping his knee onto the son of Reggor's neck.

Then he waited.

Ragnar spluttered and choked on his own spit, struggling to breathe a single gulp of air. His face quickly turned an unhealthy colour.

Doran bent down. "This'd be the part where ye yield, boy."

There was still some defiance in Ragnar's eyes as his free hand thumped again and again into Doran's hip. It might as well have been a tap on his shoulder for all the bother it caused the son of Dorain.

"Yield, boy!" Doran urged. "Or ye'll lose yer senses an' wake up in the moat!" Like every dwarf in West Fellion, the War Mason had relieved himself from the ramparts into that filthy moat.

Judging by the realisation that took a hold of Ragnar's eyes, the son of Reggor knew that to be a terrible fate, one which would taint his reputation far more than being bested by the War Mason.

His free hand ceased its continuous assault, though his lack of air could have been responsible for this. Doran maintained his pressure on the fool's throat and waited to see. A moment later, young Ragnar slapped the palm of his hand three times down on the ground.

The fight, if it could ever have been called that, was over.

Doran removed his knee from Ragnar's throat and the dwarf coughed and rasped as he inhaled as much air as possible. The crowd was silent, observing Doran as he rose the victor. Adilandra and her elves watched from the broken steps that failed to reach the northern rampart.

Without a word, the son of Dorain put Andaljor back together. He had given speeches before, both pre and post battle, and knew well to wait until he had everyone's attention.

"Ye all know who I am!" he began. "Some o' ye fought under me command in Dhenaheim, when me father, King Dorain, ruled over Grimwhal! Some o' ye fought by me side on The White Vale, against King Karakulak an' his orcs! Some o' ye," he spared a glance at Ragnar, "don' know me at all!

"I walked away from the duties o' War Mason once! I walked away from me duties as a son, a brother, an' a warrior o' Grimwhal! I had blood on me hands - a *lot* o' blood! I had been killin' Hammerkegs an' Stormshields all me life! Killin' dwarves was all I knew, whatever their clan! I knew then, jus' as I do now, that there has to be a better way! A way that doesn' 'ave to pit us against each other!

"The Heavybellys an' the Brightbeards 'ave the numbers - there's no arguin' that! We have to let go o' the old ways an' start thinkin' abou' survival, abou' allies! How many o' ye 'ave got little ones? Do ye want 'em to see a world where the children o' Grarfath can thrive?"

Doran took a moment for himself. He hadn't anticipated such a speech as this, but he knew it needed to be said; that much he could feel in his bones.

"Our king will have his day again!" he continued. "An' he will forge a future for us alongside the Brightbeards an' any o' the others! I can' claim to know how we're goin' to get there, but I know one thing: I will give me life for it! Some o' ye can' forgive me for walkin' away when I did! Fair enough. I don' need yer forgiveness! I just need ye to take orders an' join me on the battlefield!

"An' if, by some miracle o' Grarfath, I survive what is to come, then, an' only then, can ye raise ye grievances with me. But until that bloody day, ye had better pick up yer weapon when I tell ye to, an' swing it when I tell ye to!" Doran looked around, meeting as many eyes as he could. "ARE YE WITH ME?"

Thaligg and Thraal led the resounding cheer. Doran hadn't expected such a response, but it made the hairs on the back of his neck stand up. He refrained from smiling and maintained his serious demeanour, though such a thing was made all the harder when he saw Ragnar bowing his head in respect.

"Now get some rest ye lot!" he barked. "At dawn, the Heavybellys march for battle!" His last words were met by yet more cheers from his kin.

Russell clapped a hand on the War Mason's pauldron. "That was a damn good fight!" he praised, showing more life than Doran thought he had in him.

The son of Dorain waved the compliment away. "Ragnar's jus' a pup." Doran caught Queen Adilandra's eyes on him. She gave the dwarf an approving nod before moving away from the broken steps and disappearing into what was left of the main keep.

"Come on," he said to Russell. "Let's find drink an' talk like the old days. By the gods I miss huntin' monsters..."

# CHAPTER 19

# DREDGING UP THE PAST

Travelling along the shore of The King's Lake, the views were plentiful and serene. To the east, the land stretched on across The White Vale, but most were captivated by the snow-capped mountains of Vengora that reached around the western curve of the lake. To look back, to the south, the city of Skystead glistened, while ahead, to the north, the capital dominated the landscape.

Namdhor rose from the ground like a dark sentinel, placed on Verda by the gods to watch over the northern realm. For the second time in its lifespan, the city was the capital of Illian. It was a place of learning, where knowledge from centuries past was kept safe. It was a refuge for all who found themselves lost in the unforgiving cold. It was a place where a man could make anything of himself.

To Asher's eyes, it was a death trap.

Since claiming the capital, Alijah had flooded it with Reavers and employed as many criminal organisations as he could. To take the city was an uphill battle and The Rebellion certainly didn't have the numbers for such a campaign. The city itself was a maze of alleys, which was to say it possessed a maze of ambush spots.

The ranger couldn't help but wonder if he had made a mistake with his ambitious plan.

His green hood concealing his face, Asher turned to the water on his left. The magnificent view did nothing for him. He was thinking about the two mages Kassian had sent on ahead to purchase the required chains and rags from a merchant. They had entered the lion's den because Asher opened his mouth.

At least none of them had been interested in talking to him. It had been a while since he had journeyed amongst others - he had almost forgotten how to carry on a conversation.

There was at least one among them, besides Nathaniel Galfrey, who had no qualms about interacting with him. Coming up beside him on horseback, Adan'Karth cut off the ranger's view of the lake.

*"You seem ill at ease,"* he remarked in elvish, perhaps so the others wouldn't understand.

Asher met the Drake's eyes. *"You did hear my plan, yes?"*

Adan gave a half smile from within his hood. *"As unbelievable - and dangerous - as it is, we both know you have faced worse. Shall I tell you what I think is really bothering you?"*

The ranger sighed. *"You usually do."*

*"I can see it in you,"* Adan began. *"You believe you are dooming others to die. Though, it is more than that this time. You look behind you and everything that you were, everything that you were trained to be, tells you that travelling in company is simply wrong."*

*"Is that right?"*

The Drake didn't miss a beat. *"In your earlier years, the company of others compromised you if you weren't using them as cover. In later years, you have come to believe that those who surround you will die."*

Adan'Karth was very astute - an aspect of his nature - but Asher decided not to tell him as much. *"People die around me. Stick around any longer, Adan, and you'll learn that the hard way."*

*"Yet I hear so many tales of you saving people,"* the Drake countered.

Asher gave a short laugh. *"They often need saving because they're around me."*

Adan gently shook his head. *"You are restless. Because of this, you fail to see what is true, what is right in front of you."*

*"And what's that?"* Asher grumbled.

*"Your place in all this,"* the Drake replied simply. *"You wander the realm with nothing to show for your existence but blood and coin. I would say, for all your long and extraordinary life, you are yet to understand your purpose."*

Asher blinked slowly inside his hood before glancing over his shoulder to check on Nathaniel's position at the back of the group. *"My purpose,"* he pondered. *"My purpose is simple: I'm here to kill monsters, in all their forms..."*

The ranger halted his horse's progression and let Adan and the others continue ahead.

*"You can't walk away from your fate, Asher,"* the Drake called back.

*"No, but I can walk away from this conversation,"* Asher countered, waiting for Nathaniel to come alongside him. The old Graycoat rode along the shore with his gaze firmly fixed on Namdhor's dizzying heights, on The Dragon Keep itself.

"She's in there," Nathaniel announced without waiting for Asher to speak. "It is strange to be so close to her, yet so far away."

Asher could see the pain that tormented his oldest friend. "I tried to reach her once," the ranger confessed. "After I left The Rebellion," he elaborated for Nathaniel's quizzical expression. "Adan was healing me for days - I barely escaped with all my limbs."

"Thank you," Nathaniel uttered. "Thank you for *trying*."

"You don't need to thank me - it pains me that Reyna's trapped up there."

"Reyna *wants* to be there," the knight replied, confirming the ranger's private beliefs. "Even if I could walk in there, I don't think I could convince her to leave him."

"The fight isn't over yet," Asher reminded him. "We'll get another chance. She just needs time."

Nathaniel turned to the ranger. "There are those in The Rebellion who believe you are out of the *fight*, as you put it."

Asher offered an amused smile. "Well it's a good thing *you* never doubted me, old friend."

Against the odds, Nathaniel mirrored the ranger's smile. "I tried on several occasions to point out your angle on the fight, that killing Arakesh only served the cause. *But,*" he emphasised, "I have to admit, there were times when I wondered whether your crusade served only yourself."

The ranger didn't answer right away. "I have spent most of my life tied to the Arakesh in one form or another. I have run from them for too long. I decided to make a stand. I went to Vighon but his concerns lay elsewhere. So I took it into my own hands."

"Don't you always," Nathaniel quipped.

"I've never considered myself apart from The Rebellion," Asher continued. "I just had a different path to the same end."

"I'm afraid neither of us has found that end yet," the knight replied. "Beside us or not," he continued, "we knew you were doing good. The order of Nightfall has stained the realm for too many centuries. And there is none better suited to bringing them down than yourself." Nathaniel glanced at the group ahead of them before returning to the ranger. "I never doubted you, Asher. But I must admit, I was surprised you agreed to join us. I had prepared all manner of speeches to sway you."

Asher shrugged. "I ran out of leads."

Nathaniel turned a questioning expression on his friend. "The Arakesh in Skystead didn't tell you what you wanted to know? I thought you *always* got your answers."

The ranger released a breath, easily seen on the cold air. "They told me something. It just wasn't what I wanted to hear..." Asher turned to see Nathaniel staring at him expectantly, drawing more from him with just a look - it was a gift unique to the Galfreys apparently.

Asher groaned in his gruff voice. "You're not going to leave this be, are you?"

Nathaniel shrugged. "I've got time."

The truth of that statement made Asher silently laugh to himself. "Fine," he relented. "I came so willingly because..." The ranger narrowed his eyes - he hated words. "I'm not foolish enough to believe I can outrun death forever - I'm a *ranger*; it comes with the job. But if I stayed on that path there was only one end for me. I don't want to die an assassin..."

Nathaniel looked him in the eyes as a warm smile pushed at his cheeks. "Then welcome back. Now you get to die a rebel," he jested, sharing a laugh with the ranger.

"The Rebellion's cause has always been a worthy one," Asher stated, choosing not to dwell on the Arakesh's spiteful words. "And it needs Vighon," he added. "I was surprised when I heard he had left. The Fenrigs tried to spin it that he was dead, killed on The Carpel Slopes."

"You were there in the beginning," Nathaniel said, his gaze distant as if he could actually see the past. "You remember what it was like. Everywhere Vighon went, Alijah and Malliath would be there, the Dragon Riders would be there, Reavers from all over would be rallied right on top of him. It was always a slaughter."

"Why didn't Vighon just stay in The Black Wood and coordinate from there?" Asher asked.

"We considered that," Nathaniel replied. "But we needed the numbers. There were - still are - soldiers scattered across the land bereft of their sword and shield, but still warriors, warriors of the *king*. They needed to see Vighon stand up for them before they stood up for him. Alijah knew this of course. That's why he decided to personally challenge Vighon wherever he went."

Asher nodded with understanding. "He thought he was doing The Rebellion a favour by leaving."

"For a while there, I'd say it actually helped. We had our first streak of victories after Grey Stone. But we quickly noticed that we weren't replenishing the ranks like before. From that point on, it was just a matter of time before The Rebellion died."

For a moment, Asher said nothing, battling the creeping guilt that had begun to weigh on him from the moment Nathaniel started talking. How many more victories might they have claimed had he stayed with them and left his hunt of the Arakesh? How many people would still be alive that were now in the ground?

Perhaps, like Vighon, he had made a mistake in leaving...

A little further ahead, one of Kassian's mages turned his head to the sky and swore. It wasn't hard to find the source of the man's concern. Against the white of the clouded sky, a dark figure flew across the heavens, heading south. Asher looked upon Malliath and Alijah, the two beings who had haunted his dreams for over a decade.

Nathaniel looked up at his son and watched them disappear to the south. "They haven't seen us," he reassured. "Even to dragon eyes, we're just ants from this distance."

Asher wasn't so convinced of the latter, but he could see that it settled some nerves amongst the mages and Malliath had, indeed, paid them no attention. The ranger caught sight of Kassian, a little further out from the group. The mage had brought his horse to a halt to observe Alijah and Malliath. There was a man of conviction, Asher thought. Kassian was of the firm belief that Alijah was his enemy and that he would make that enemy suffer - it was all over his face.

Most would tell the Keeper that revenge serves no good and will offer no comfort, but Asher had acted with vengeance before and knew it to be quite cathartic, if bloody. Unfortunately for Kassian Kantaris, there was something of a line when it came to facing Alijah Galfrey and, in Asher's opinion, he wasn't at the front.

Together, they finished the rest of the journey along the shore, bringing them under The King's Hollow, a looming pillar of stone that supported Namdhor's rise. In relative silence, they made the skeleton of a camp - Asher had informed them that they likely wouldn't be there for very long.

"You're sure about this?" Nathaniel asked, looking out on the lake.

"He had better be," Kassian called, making his way over to them.

"This is the worst place for anyone to be if they've got magic in their bones."

Asher removed his weapons and cloak, the first of many things he intended to take off. "I know monsters," he stated confidently, meeting Adan'Karth's eyes briefly. "This is the only way."

By the time Asher was stripped down to his waist and his boots were removed, the two Keepers Kassian had sent to the markets returned on horseback. They were, apparently, the only two among his band who didn't possess magic, but had, in fact, lost loved ones to the Seekers.

"Did you get everything I asked for?" Asher called at their approach.

"We got what we could," one of them replied, gesturing to the chains on the back of her horse. "These are the longest ones we could find."

"And the hooks?" the ranger enquired.

The other keeper held up a pair of iron hooks usually reserved for hanging large meats. "We got this too," he said, holding up a very large hooded poncho, made from a dark leather that had seen better days.

"Good." Asher pointed at the lake. "Lay the chains out to the shore and attach the hooks to both."

Kassian was shaking his head. "This is madness," he opined. "I can't believe I agreed to this."

"Well you did," Asher pointed out. "So bring your magic, Keeper - we're going to need it."

Nathaniel came up on the ranger's side. "It's going to be like ice under there. Can you make that kind of swim?"

Asher flexed his arms. "It's been a while, but I see no other way. This is how we find Vighon."

Walking towards the shore, Asher inspected the chains and the hooks for himself, hoping they would be strong enough. Kassian organised his mages, some of whom were to use their wands to pull the chain while others were to simply stand at the ready with destructive spells.

"That won't be necessary," the ranger told him, gesturing to those pointing their wands and staffs at the water.

Kassian didn't look convinced. "If this doesn't go the way you want it to, Ranger, my Keepers are the only thing that's going to keep you alive."

Asher walked up to his waist into the freezing water with the chains wrapped over one shoulder and under the other. "If this goes wrong, Kassian Kantaris," he called back, "this is the last time you will ever see me..." The ranger was impressed with the control he had maintained over his voice before taking three deep breaths and diving beneath the surface.

The cold water was biting, attacking his every muscle in a bid to slow him down and welcome him to its murky depths. An oppressive force pushed against his head, numbing the skin. There was nothing left now but to fall back on his training. They were the worst of memories, but they had kept him alive through all manner of hell.

In his late teens, he had been taken in the night, with a handful of others in training, to a boat on The Shining Coast. There, one of the masters of Nightfall had taken them out into the shockingly cold embrace of The Adean's dark waves. Paired up, one of them was to be bound in chains and thrown overboard. It was the other's job to dive in after them and bring them back to the boat. Asher had endured both sides of that challenge and lived to recall it. Not all of them had...

With the weight of the chains, and no lack of determination, he put the land behind him and followed the declining ground to the lake's lowest depths. Thankfully, the clouds abated, allowing rays of startling sunlight to pierce the surface and touch the bottom.

His vision was blurred by the water and his head was really starting to hurt, but there was no mistaking the ominous figure standing motionless before him. It was like looking at some guardian to the gates of hell.

Sir Borin the Dread.

Feeling the burn in his lungs now, Asher went to work. Balancing speed with caution, he approached the Golem and took the chains in hand. Sir Borin had no reaction to the proximity nor the prodding finger that the ranger put firmly into his chest.

With his own time running out, Asher began to wrap the chains around the Golem, fastening them all together with the hooks. Wrapping one of the chains over Sir Borin's shoulder, the ranger came face to face with an opening pair of eyes. He waited for any kind of reaction, typically violent given the nature of Golems. Nothing. Sir Borin remained as motionless as before, his legs buried in dirt and rocks up to his knees.

Asher caught sight of an enormous claymore on the ground, beside the hulking Golem. It was rusted and useless now.

The ranger returned his attention to the chains. Satisfied that he had secured them all, he pulled himself along and finally pushed up, kicking his legs to reach the surface. Most would gasp for air, but such a noisy breach would have had him punished during his training. He filled his lungs with one measured breath and waved at the Keepers to begin dragging Sir Borin from his watery prison.

"Keep going!" he yelled as he swam for shore.

The chains were pulled taut in the air between the mages. Kassian was slowly pulling his wand arm back, directing the chain away from the lake. Asher eventually found the ground beneath his feet and staggered onto dry land, freezing from head to toe. Adan'Karth was there to meet him with a blanket and a warm dose of magic. His body steamed under the Drake's spell and he welcomed the waves of heat.

Moments later, Sir Borin was striding out of The King's Lake, matching the speed of the drawing chains. Every Keeper braced themselves as they looked upon a giant from their worst nightmares.

Asher walked towards the Golem, inspecting what was left of him. What flesh remained was white as chalk and riddled with old scars and nibbles where the lake's inhabitants had sampled the putrid meat. The hauberk on top of the faded black gambeson was rusted orange and there was nothing left of The Ironsworn sigil.

The ancient runes that had decorated his bald head were the only runes to have survived the watery grave. Asher was the only one brave enough to step right in front of the Golem, where he met the pale grey eyes of a dead man looking out on the world with passive interest.

"Asher…" Nathaniel called his name with a cautionary tone.

"Golems only defend themselves if attacked. Or," Asher added, "if their master is attacked."

"You're willing to bet your life on that?" Kassian checked.

The ranger answered the Keeper by throwing off his blanket and removing the chains and hooks, freeing Sir Borin. Without pause, the Golem turned right and began walking south, back along the trail they had taken to reach The King's Hollow.

"What now?" Kassian asked.

"We follow him," Asher said. He took his time replacing all of his clothes and weapons - Sir Borin wasn't going to be hard to follow. "Wherever Vighon is," he elaborated, "the magic that binds the Golem to the crown will ensure that he finds him."

The Keeper cast a questioning expression over that logic. "But Alijah is king," he pointed out. "Won't the Golem just lead us to him? He's even heading in the same direction we saw Malliath fly."

Asher shook his head. "Alijah was never coronated as the king of Namdhor nor Illian. Vighon was. Sir Borin the Dread is about to become a shadow the king can't get rid of…"

# CHAPTER 20

# GUARDIANS

The southern lands of Ayda were hot, much like The Arid Lands of Illian, though the landscape was vastly different to the eye. Unlike its larger sibling, Ayda's southern hemisphere possessed a dusky red desert, dotted with lush oases. The Trident, a single river of blue, cut through the land and divided into three snaking heads.

It was this river that Athis had followed having caught sight of the mouth in Atilan's Landing, a curve of land that reached back on itself in an attempt to touch Ayda's Opal Coast. The Trident soon brought dragon and rider to The Great Maw, a thick jungle that housed the ruins of an ancient and savage civilisation.

The Darkakin...

Inara raised herself up to see the approaching city of Malaysai. Growing up, the Dragorn had heard the tale of Gideon's adventures in these lands. Having heard more of the story than most, however, Inara knew the adventure to be something of a nightmare not only for her old master, but also for Galanör and, especially, her grandmother, Adilandra, who had been a prisoner in this very city.

Of the three, her grandmother was the only one reluctant to

speak of their time in this part of the world, though Gideon had revealed elements of her captivity that made Inara's skin crawl.

Athis glided over the remains of Malaysai, a desolate and empty ruin of burnt out buildings, fallen towers, and a charred pyramid at its heart. To the west was a large circular structure, held up by three columns of red rock. Inara knew it to be the arena in which her grandmother had been forced to kill in order to survive.

*You were here,* she said across their bond.

*I was,* Athis replied, his memories casting back to his younger days. *Rainael the emerald star led our assault.*

*Ilargo's mother,* Inara noted with a sense of joy. *I've always wanted to meet her.*

*Soon you will, wingless one.*

Inara took in the far-reaching destruction of Malaysai. *It's strange to think of you doing anything without me, but laying waste to an entire city...*

*We were many,* Athis told her. *Though most of what you see was Malliath's doing. He was unleashed upon the Darkakin. With the younger ones, I was kept away from him, but we could all sense his feelings. He enjoyed it.*

Inara turned her gaze to the southern horizon. *Galanör accompanied you to the other cities,* she recalled, having heard snippets of his time among the dragons.

*He did,* Athis confirmed. *First, we razed Malaysai to the ground.* The dragon's statement was evident by the total devastation that now surrounded them. *From here, we flew further south and torched Davosai, then Gravosai, the third and final refuge of their barbaric kind.*

Seeing the speed and ferocity with which dragons could wipe out masses of life, Inara couldn't imagine them losing the war to Alijah. For all his Reavers, Dragon Riders, and even Malliath, they would be no match for a congregation of dragons led by Rainael herself.

*Is that what I think it is?* Flying directly over the heart of the city, Inara could now see a great mound of colourful flowers, from which a number of roots had grown and wrapped around the nearby ruins. From these, tall trees had sprung to life, visible through the jagged holes in the buildings.

*The resting place of Angala the wise,* Athis began. *She was slain by the Darkakin, brought down with Crissalith.*

Inara knew of the green crystals Athis spoke of, an anti-magic that severed one's link to the magical realm. To a dragon, being separated from magic was a death sentence.

*One day,* Athis continued, *the magic expelled from Angala's death will see what's left of this city covered with new life. It will be unrecognisable. And it will be beautiful.*

It was bittersweet to see such a sight. No dragon should suffer an end or, in Inara's opinion, the realm should never have to suffer the loss of a dragon. But, at least, even in death, they continued to affect the land, sparking new life.

Athis turned his head to the east. *The Flat Wastes,* he announced, banking in that direction. *We must cross those lands if we are to find The Red Mountains.*

Just hearing of the mountains ignited a sense of excitement inside Inara. She had heard of The Red Mountains many times during her training in The Lifeless Isles, for there was one place, nestled within their embrace, that the Dragorn had wanted to see with her own eyes for as long as she could remember. It was an oasis in the harsh environment, created by the natural magic of dragons.

**Gideon always told me that if there was an afterlife, he imagined it to look like Dragons' Reach.**

A wave of warm joy emanated from Athis. *I would have to agree with him.*

The red dragon left Malaysai and The Great Maw behind as he flew over The Flat Wastes. There was nothing to see over the landscape but exactly that. With her mother's eyes, however, Inara looked upon The Red Mountains, the only thing between them and Dragons' Reach.

Athis called on his reserves and beat his wings with all determination. Just like his eternal companion, the dragon was eager to see the place he had often thought of as home. The wait to cross over the first peaks of the mountains felt like a lifetime, but the pair finally made it as the sun passed into the afternoon.

It wasn't a long journey from those first peaks to the first glimpse of a green oasis. Inara pushed herself up and Athis dipped his head to give her a better view. As the last mountain gave way, the majesty of Dragons' Reach was clear to see.

Though roughly circular in shape, the eastern wall of mountains protruded into the space and ended with a towering waterfall that filled a small lake in the heart of the Reach. Surrounding it were dozens of boulders and rocks, all varying in size from that of a horse to a small village. Of course, these landmarks were all the more spectacular due to their floating existence. Tethered by thick roots, they hovered above the dragons' home, creating the perfect perches and resting places.

Below, the forest stretched from north to south, an inviting wilderness that supported several ecosystems besides the dragons. It was truly a haven, a jewel set in the midst of a barren vista.

Not only had it been the home of the oldest dragons for a thousand years, but it was also where Gideon began his path to becoming a Dragorn, a destiny that would touch the lives of so many others, her own included. But, even more than all of that, Dragons' Reach was the birth place of Athis.

The dragon soared over the trees having found new life in his wings. Magic seemed to permeate the very air, an intoxicating aroma that filled both of them with energy. They weren't alone in the sky. Coming up on all sides, Inara spotted dragons of every colour, welcoming them with a wave of joyous emotion.

Inara breathed it in.

Without greeting a single person or even speaking to the dragons that now accompanied them, the half-elf felt content. It was like returning home after years of being away. Inara soon came to realise that a lot of her emotion did, in fact, originate from Athis. He was happy. It made the Dragorn smile and she gripped his spikes, aware that he was about to spiral in and out of his kin's flight path; a dance of sorts.

It was glorious. All thought of The Rebellion and Illian's troubles were melting away the deeper they flew into Dragons' Reach. There was a harmony here, among the dragons both ancient and new-born.

Amidst the growing congregation, familiar dragons began to appear. Coming down from high on her right, the distinctive scales of Valkor - a shade of oak - could be seen. So fast was his flight that Inara but glimpsed the blond rider on his back, though she knew it could only be Alastir Knox, a member of the Dragorn council like herself.

Flying up and over them was a dragon equal in size to Athis, though her scales were a burnt orange. Inara tracked the dragon's flight, looking for Rolan Baird astride Alensia's back.

Before any details could be gleaned, a third dragon cut through the sky and matched Athis's speed. Inara beamed as she looked upon the elven face of Ayana Glanduil, seated between Deartanyon's spinal horns. Ayana mirrored her smile, welcoming the half-elf, before angling down towards the waterfall.

Inara would have followed her path, but a shadow overcame Athis, turning the Dragorn to where the sun should have been. In its place was the largest dragon she had ever seen, perhaps even larger than Malliath.

*It is Vorgraf the mountain child,* Athis told her with a sense of awe about him.

Inara shared that same feeling as she watched Vorgraf beat his majestic wings and ascend into the clouds. ***He is the offspring of Garganafan!*** she exclaimed, referring to the late, if most notable, king of the dragons.

The half-elf could hear multiple voices now, distant, but each distinct, in her mind as Athis communed with them all. It had been years since Inara had been around so many of her own kind - the voices were jarring. Once upon a time she would have had to endure them, but not anymore. With thought alone the Dragorn was able to dampen her bond with Athis, quieting the voices.

*Inara...* Athis drew her attention back to what was in front of them.

As well as the dozens of dragons that spiralled and darted through the air, there was one dragon gliding off to the side, just in front of them. This dragon was longer than Athis but, perhaps, not as hulking in size. The scales were the green of a lush forest that sparkled with golden flecks in the sunlight.

For a moment, Inara swelled with anticipation, truly believing that she looked upon the beauty of Ilargo, but there were just enough differences to tell her otherwise.

**Athis, is that...**

The red dragon looked on with veneration. *Rainael the emerald star, the queen of my kin.*

By the way Rainael glided in front of Athis, the queen wished for them to follow her. Athis happily obliged and trailed the gold-speckled dragon down and round several of the floating boulders. Inara searched the ground and caught glimpses of Valkor, Alensia, and Deartanyon between the boulders, all drinking water from the lake.

Following Rainael, they too found themselves touching down by the shore of the lake. It all felt surreal to Inara, who had heard stories of Dragons' Reach as if it were some fairy tale. Yet here she was, jumping down onto a very real ground, under the shadow of very real floating boulders. It was on these boulders that Inara discovered several members of her order watching their arrival. She wanted to greet them all!

Athis dipped his head, bowing to Rainael, and Inara mimicked him, paying her respect to one of the oldest dragons. Valkor, Alensia, and Deartanyon came over and greeted Athis with affection, touching their heads together, one after the other.

More effort was required to keep their many voices out of her mind. Inara touched her temple subconsciously, feeling the edges of a headache taking hold. The Guardian briefly closed her eyes and applied more focus. The voices soon disappeared down a long tunnel until they vanished altogether, including Athis's...

The red dragon spared her a knowing look but made no attempt to re-establish their connection, instead, allowing her some time to greet the other *wingless* ones.

Ayana's arms were open wide long before the two met in a tight embrace. To the half-elf, Ayana had the aroma of honey and lavender - it had been long missed.

"My heart swells to see you," the elf proclaimed, flashing her perfect teeth.

"As does mine," Inara replied, squeezing her hands.

Alastir came up on Ayana's left. "I have wondered often when we would be graced by your presence here." His handsome face was made all the sweeter by his charming smile. Inara hesitated before hugging him, realising, for the first time, that she had never found Alastir attractive in all the years she had flown by his side.

Inara cast a guilty look at Athis but the dragon was blissfully unaware of her very human thoughts.

The Dragorn pulled away from Alastir, her smile fading. "I only wish I came to you with..." Her blue eyes naturally fell on Rolan Baird, who had, it seemed, held back from greeting her.

"Forgive my reticence," Rolan said apologetically. "Seeing you, Inara... It reminds me of my shame..."

"Those times are behind us," Alastir reminded him, motioning for the man to join them.

Inara hadn't forgotten the trouble Rolan had caused Gideon during the orc invasion. For a time there, she had harboured her own anger towards the man for disobeying their master and leading her fellow Dragorn into certain death. She had forgiven him and his brash ways at a time when he hadn't been quite so restrained, as he now appeared.

"I have found redemption in this place," Rolan told her, his face daring to attempt a smile.

"That is good, Master Rolan," Inara replied genuinely.

All three of them shared a questionable glance. "It's just Rolan now," he continued. "The same can be said for us all."

Inara frowned, searching their faces for an answer that wasn't coming. "I... I haven't come with good news - I wouldn't lightly leave my post. Where is Gideon?" she finally asked, her concern for his absence growing by the second.

Again, the three shared a look that Inara struggled to understand. It was Ayana who stepped forward and guided Inara away from the lake, under the watching eyes of Rainael.

"Why don't we go for a walk?" the elf suggested.

A sinking feeling was beginning to overwhelm Inara. "Has something happened? Where is he?"

Ayana led her through the trees and Alastir and Rolan walked casually behind them. Inara had had enough. She stopped between the trees and swept her red cloak behind her.

"I have travelled far and risked much to be here. I must speak with Gideon and I must speak with him *now*. Where is he, Ayana?"

The elf continued a few steps before coming to a halt. Appearing at home in the forest, she maintained her gaze with Inara this time. "Gideon isn't here," Ayana announced calmly.

Inara's expression dropped. "Where is he then? Hunting with Ilargo?" she asked hopefully.

Ayana shook her head. "Gideon left Dragons' Reach eight years ago. He and Ilargo flew west and have never returned."

Inara broke her eye contact with Ayana and turned away as her mind fell into turmoil. "I... I don't understand." She couldn't find the words to express all of her questions and confusion at once.

Alastir strolled past on Inara's right. "Eight years ago, Gideon came to us with concerns he had been holding on to since we left Illian."

"They weighed on him," Rolan added.

"What concerns?" Inara questioned.

"Your brother," Ayana replied. "He had spoken to us all of his fears for Alijah and what he might become, but for nearly a decade he tried to focus on our training."

"So what happened eight years ago to make him leave? Where did he go?" Inara's impatience was reaching boiling point. Ayana glanced at Alastir, who glanced at Rolan. It infuriated the half-elf. "Stop doing that! Tell me what's... Tell me everything. *Please.*"

Ayana motioned for Inara to continue following her.

"I want answers," Inara demanded, rooted to the spot.

"And you will get them," Ayana said coolly. "This way..."

Along with Alastir and Rolan, the half-elf followed closely behind Ayana, taking a pleasant path through the woods. Thankfully, it wasn't long before they reached their destination, a place Inara recognised from her childhood stories. They had entered a clearing occupied by a single rock, illuminated by a ray of light piercing the canopy above.

Ayana gestured to the rock. "This is where Gideon claimed Mournblade for his own. This is where the old order - *Adriel's* Dragorn - came to rest, and where our order began anew."

It was exhilarating to be in this place, but Inara's excitement was tempered by the rock's appearance. Attempt as she might, the Guardian couldn't hope to count all of the Vi'tari blades protruding from the stone, their magnificent hilts pointing to the sky.

Scrutinising her three companions, Inara could see that none of them possessed their legendary scimitar, nor any weapon for that matter. A picture was beginning to form in her mind and she didn't like the image it was creating.

"Is this all part of the training?" Inara asked, fearful of the answer. "You have to earn your sword?"

Ayana stared at Inara for a moment. "You have always had a sharp mind. You know what this means..."

Inara frowned and swallowed. "It cannot be true. I *know* it cannot be true." She looked at each of them, searching desperately for the crack that would reveal all of this to be a tasteless joke.

Rolan walked around the sword-covered rock. "We have left the path of the Dragorn, Inara," he stated.

His words, though simple and easy to understand, left Inara feeling dazed.

"This was not an easy decision," Ayana explained. "We arrived at it after years of long discussions and many debates."

Inara was shocked, a fact that slowed her responses down. "And Gideon?" she managed.

"He opposed us," Rolan said, his blunt tone reminding Inara of the man he claimed to have left behind.

"He wished to continue the order," Alastir attempted. "He even spoke of us returning to the days of the Dragon Riders."

"They were warriors," Ayana observed, "not peacekeepers." The elf held out a small black orb that looked like marble - Gideon's diviner.

Not a word of it made any sense to Inara as she took the orb in hand. "So, instead, you forsake your duty? Why not challenge Gideon on the matter, especially if the entire order was in agreement with you?"

"With every day," Rolan said, "Gideon became more and more concerned with threats that don't even exist yet. He wanted us to be something we are not."

"When did you *stop* being warriors?" Inara snapped. "I have witnessed you all fight for the realm."

"Our time among the older dragons has been influential to be sure," Alastir began, "but also enlightening."

Ayana picked up his thread. "Their perspective is ancient, Inara. Rainael and the others have lived through most of recorded history."

"And *unrecorded* history," Rolan added.

"They have seen wars ravage the continents," Ayana continued. "Dragon Riders, Dragorn, human, elf, all have dragged their kind into battles that should not concern them. We are immortal. Have you truly grasped the meaning of that yet? My own kin have not. But those of us bonded to dragons; we stand apart from the races tied to the earth. We soar above them, our existence our own, as it always should have been.”

“Enough dragon blood has been spilt for the wars of man,” Alastir declared. “There is peace here, *eternal* peace. For all the good we could enforce upon Illian and even Erador, they will continue to make war - it is their way. It doesn’t have to be ours anymore.”

“It is not just our strength they need,” Inara argued, “but also our wisdom. We are to guide the realm, not abandon it.”

“You are young,” Rolan said patronisingly. “As is Athis. Spend some time here. Commune with the older dragons as we have and you will come to see the world from a—”

Inara pointed a finger at him. “One more word and I’ll give you a reason to take back your sword.” The clearing’s inhabitants were taken aback by her biting words and she came to regret them. “I’m sorry. I just... We have had very different lives since you left Illian.”

Ayana looked Inara up and down. “I would say yours has been hard.”

“And filled with violence,” Alastir remarked.

Inara almost laughed at the statements. She turned away from them and walked further into the clearing, her thoughts scrabbling for purchase on anything solid.

“If you spend some time with us here,” Ayana suggested, “you will come to understand our point of view.”

“I will *never* see your point of view. How could you do this?” Inara gestured to the Vi’tari blades. “How could you abandon the realm? The people?”

“We are our own people now,” Rolan stated. “We bow to no king, we claim no land but this and the sky above, and we do not challenge others for what we do not have. We are a... tribe, if you will. This is how we were always supposed to live. The Dragorn, even the Dragon Riders, were appendages of kingdoms and realms that had nothing in common with them.”

“You see yourselves as better,” Inara concluded.

“No,” Ayana was quick to respond. “We are different. Different enough to live separate lives from the kingdoms of man and elf. That is all."

Alastir put himself between Inara and the scimitars. "Time and time again, the Dragorn have suffered fighting wars that need not concern them. We decided as *one people* to change that, to determine our own fate. You can be a part of that, Inara, should you wish."

Ayana offered a warm smile. "You are most welcome here."

Inara felt the weight of despair dragging her spirit down. "What of Gideon? You said he left."

"Yes," Alastir divulged. "He never stopped thinking about Alijah. He voiced concerns that The Crow had poisoned his mind and that, even in Erador, he posed a serious threat."

"He left for Erador," Rolan told her. "Since you haven't seen him, I would assume he's still there."

"Perhaps he found Alijah," Ayana posed, "and is counselling him. He always wanted to help Malliath."

Inara's despair quickly fell away, pulled down into an abyss of fears and terror. "Alijah..." She didn't even know how to sum up the horrors her brother had unleashed upon the land. "Two years ago, Alijah invaded Dhenaheim and then Illian." Inara paused, letting her words sink in. "He did this with an army of Reavers, fallen knights from Erador's past. He also has Dragon Riders, resurrected from their graves, fighting for him.

"He usurped Vighon within weeks of his return to Illian. More recently, he torched the elven fleet and nearly killed my grandmother. If, as you say, Gideon went to Erador to find Alijah, I would say he's been dead for eight years, and our only hope with him."

Ayana took a breath before replying, her expression as unreadable as the others. "What you say is grave and troubling. But..."

"It is not *our* trouble," Rolan finished.

"How can you say that?" Inara spat, finding their lack of reaction to be insulting. "Alijah seeks to control all of Verda, Dragons' Reach included."

"Should he seek to change our way of life," Alastir replied, "we will defend ourselves. But this is just another war, as we said. The truly grave news is that it will not be the last."

"But we have seen our last war," Rolan said, his tone as blunt as ever.

The half-elf sighed with glassy eyes. "You were supposed to come back. I have fought and bled and lost so much for the realm, waiting for all of you to return. We were meant to be warriors..."

Ayana's sweet voice cut through the air. "You *are* a warrior, Inara. Unlike us, it is in your blood. You are always welcome among us, but I do not believe you have it in you to choose anything other than the *fight.*"

Inara retreated into her thoughts for a moment. The idea of Gideon and Ilargo being dead would torment her until she knew for certain. It also crushed her to entertain it.

"You are to be the last Dragorn," Rolan expressed, tearing through Inara's reverie. "I tell you this because the hatchlings born in Dragons' Reach are to be raised here. You cannot bring people to try and bond with them, as Gideon did."

Inara hadn't even considered that line of thought, but Rolan was right; these were the only dragons in the world and they wanted nothing to do with the realm's affairs. She was alone...

*You are not alone,* Athis reminded her, his voice finding a way back into his companion's mind as her wall came down. *You and I are of that world, not this one. Our place is between the light and the dark, as it always has been.*

Inara did her best to absorb the dragon's confidence and beliefs, something she wouldn't have had to work at prior to altering their bond. ***Perhaps it is time we return to that world.***

The Dragorn gripped her hilt, taking heart in the feel of Firefly within her grip. "You have my word I will not return." With that, Inara made to leave the clearing and return to Athis.

"He accepted our decision," Ayana called. "Before he chose to leave, Gideon accepted the way we wished to live."

Inara paused, considering the harsh response she wanted to give.

Instead, she let go of her frustration, dampened as it was by grief, and exhaled. Looking over her shoulder, she met Ayana's gaze, then that of Alastir and Rolan.

"Then live well," Inara finally replied, intoning as much sincerity as she could muster.

Without giving the dragons much of her attention, Inara returned to Athis and urged him to take them far away from the Reach. Athis shared her feelings, though it was clear that the dragon would have stayed a while longer to rest if not to enjoy the company of his kin. Inara felt guilty insisting that they leave immediately, but she knew she couldn't stay a minute longer.

Before they even reached the peaks of The Red Mountains, Athis's fatigue became apparent. **We will find somewhere to rest,** Inara reassured him.

Athis turned his horned head to the left, revealing one of his rich blue eyes. *We are not alone...*

Inara looked back over her shoulder to discover Rainael the emerald star close behind. The beat of her wings was slower than Athis, yet she closed the gap between them with ease.

*She wishes to speak with us,* Athis informed her. *Both of us.*

**Then I would hear her.**

Athis opened his mind to Rainael and acted as a bridge between the queen and Inara. For just a moment, the Dragorn was touching the periphery of Rainael's mind, a place where she could glimpse the most ancient of memories. Her mind was like a bottomless well, rich with experiences that surpassed the stories Inara had been told of the dragon.

Rainael's voice cut through it all, pushing Inara back into Athis's mind where she could hear only their voices. *Ilargo has not passed to the eternal shores,* she said with boldness and clarity. *If he had, I would know.*

The Galfrey in Inara made her sceptical of this, but Athis spoke before she could say as much. *If Ilargo still lives, then so too does Gideon.*

Rainael came up on their left. *The same cannot be said of you two.*

Without words, Inara questioned Athis but the dragon seemed to be working furiously to guard the contents of his mind.

*Yes,* Rainael continued, *I can sense the change in your bond. Your roots go deep together, but you are no longer the same tree. You know why this path is a dangerous one, Athis the ironheart. I do not condemn it, but I do not condone it. You say you will not come back, but I am telling you: you will never return to Dragons' Reach.*

**There is nothing wrong with our bond,** Inara defended, ignoring Athis's plea to soften her tone.

*Not now,* Rainael replied. *But the potential now lies within you, Inara Galfrey. So long as you harness the power of a dragon, your human nature, even your elven nature, poses a threat to the people of Verda. Without our influence, our guidance, you will—*

*Our minds remain our own,* Athis interjected, mirroring Inara's harsh tone. *Unlike those we have just left behind, we still have our duty to the realm, an oath not taken lightly. Regardless of our bond - and regardless of your judgement - we will fight for the people of Illian, Erador, and Ayda.*

Inara was grinning from ear to ear on the inside.

Rainael was silent as they passed over the mountains, her contemplation there to see. *What will you do now?* she finally asked.

Inara only required the briefest of moments with her eternal companion to know what they needed to do next. **We will go to Erador and see for ourselves what has become of Gideon and Ilargo.**

Again, the queen of dragons was contemplative. *Then I will help you,* she said. *Open your mind further, Athis, and I will give you my memories of Erador. You will know the land as you do that of Illian.*

Athis willingly accepted her memories, though they were very specific from what Inara could tell. There was nothing but detail of the land itself, mostly from the sky looking down. It was a skill to transfer something so specific and yet so incredibly vast without events bleeding through.

*Close your mind to it, Inara.*

The half-elf heeded her companion's warning and allowed Athis to absorb the information. His mind was capable of storing a seemingly infinite amount of memory without the required time to process it all. Inara, on the other hand, would need to absorb the memories over time so as not to overwhelm her mind.

*I have it,* Athis confirmed.

Rainael acknowledged with a feeling rather than words. She continued to fly beside them for a while longer, their bond still bridged, if more tenuous while she considered her private thoughts.

*I was there,* she began, *when Elandril and Nylla declared themselves Dragorn. I witnessed their order grow, just as I had once witnessed the humans of Erador form their bonds with my kin and declare themselves Riders. Since the latter ceased to exist millennia ago, and you know nothing of their teachings, you are not of the Dragon Riders. And since you no longer possess the bond that lies at the heart of what it is to be Dragorn, I, Rainael the emerald star, queen of the dragons, declare that the world has already seen the last of the Dragorn...*

Inara felt the blow as almost physical. She could feel Athis's heart racing as he too felt the stinging blow of such a bold declaration.

*Take heart,* Rainael reassured. *Like us, you now belong to neither. As such, you are now free to choose your fate and live whatever life you so desire. There is no better freedom.*

Again, Inara only required the briefest of moments within the comforting folds of her bond with Athis to know their course. ***Our freedom is tied to that of the people. We don't need to be Dragorn to fulfil our duty. We,*** she promised with all her being, ***are the Guardians of the Realm...***

# CHAPTER 21
# THE YARLS

"Vighon?" came a distant call. "Vighon?"

The northman tried to catch on to his name and follow the call to its elusive source.

"Voss?" it came again with an edge of clarity this time.

Then, without an inebriated mind to let go, an old memory pressed itself upon him, taking him by surprise.

"YOU WILL WATCH THEM ALL DIE!" Alijah's voice boomed in his mind.

Soaked in sweat, Vighon's head shot up from the bar. His hand snapped down to his hip, searching in vain for a sword that wasn't there. Instead of looking up at Alijah Galfrey, he set eyes on the forgettable face of Davan the barkeep.

"Voss," he said again, "I've been saying your name for an age."

Vighon muttered some form of apology and attempted to take in his surroundings. He was back in the fighting pit, locked away in the darkest places of Kelp Town. How had he got here? The last thing he recalled was ordering a drink in the tavern below his room. He had no memory of leaving that place or taking his seat on a stool at this bar.

Worst of all, he was practically sober...

"What are you doing back here, Voss?" Davan questioned, his eyes shifting left and right over Vighon's head. "I told you not to come back," he hissed.

"You said..." Vighon clicked his fingers as he tried to recall his exact words. "You said not to come back *tonight*. That was days ago... I think."

Davan was shaking his head. "Do you remember that Yarl, the one you replaced in the fight?"

Vighon squinted and took a deep breath. "No."

Davan rolled his eyes. "Well he remembers you. An easy thing I imagine since you broke his nose with your head. And he wasn't just some enforcer neither. He was *Uthrad*."

The northman maintained his expressionless gaze.

Davan sighed with exasperation. "Unlike a lot of the ugly beasts who bear their mark, Uthrad's family name is *Yarl*. He is the son of *Bairnan*, the head of the Yarls."

Vighon shrugged. "So he's a prince amongst murderers and thieves. I don't much care," he added, searching the shelves behind Davan for a new libation.

"What is *he* doing here?" came an irritating and familiar voice.

"Ah, Mr Tawny," Davan greeted gingerly. "I was just telling Voss here—"

"Shut it," the bookie snapped. "I make my money with fighting in the pits," he explained, poking a finger into Vighon's shoulder. "I don't make money with fights out of the pit. The latter is exactly what I'm going to get if you don't clear off *right now*."

His words and tone were enough to get under the northman's skin, but the finger jabbing into his shoulder was ultimately responsible for his brash response.

"Fine," he growled, standing up with enough force to launch his stool across the floor.

"What are you doing?" Mr Tawny demanded, seeing that the northman was heading towards the pit instead of the door.

"I'm making you coin," Vighon answered, pushing and shoving his way to the walled off pit.

By the edge, he surveyed those that were packed around the circular arena. Many were spectators, gambling men. Others appeared to be fighters by the look of them. The Yarls were easy to spot, clumped together with scowls for expressions. Vighon had hated their kind as king and he hated them still as a vagrant.

Looking down, the pit was yet to be occupied. Vighon changed that dramatically. He swung his legs over the wall and dropped down. Vighon ignored the onlookers and locked his eyes on the only Yarl with an obviously broken nose.

"Baby Yarl!" he provoked.

Uthrad looked down at him with visible hatred. It seemed the young man had endured more than just physical pain from the humiliation of Vighon's previous surprise attack.

"How is your nose?" Vighon continued with an amused grin. "Why don't you come down here and I'll even out your whole face. That way, no one will notice a thing." Vighon wasn't the only one laughing, but he was certainly the loudest.

Uthrad sneered and then winced in pain. He slammed his fist onto the wall and jumped down with a display of grace and strength Vighon had not.

"I'm going to kill you, fool," he promised.

Vighon nodded in mock agreement. "Make your bets fellas! I promise to use my winnings to buy a round for all!"

Mr Tawny's reluctance faded in the sight of coins being thrust before him.

Uthrad shrugged off his leathers and stripped down to his bare chest. "I'm going to enjoy this," he said over the din. "You have no idea what a mistake you've made you old sack of—"

"Save it, boy," Vighon cut in. "I've stood up to things that would eat you for breakfast." The northman licked his lips and considered. "I'm quite hungry, now I think about it..."

The Yarl boy dismissed his ramblings as that of a drunkard,

failing to note his current sobriety. "Any man here who doesn't put his coin on me is a fool!" he yelled, looking up at the spectators. "I'm going to break every—"

Vighon hammered his fist into Uthrad's exposed throat.

Within seconds, the son of Bairnan Yarl was curled up on the floor, clawing at his throat, and desperate for air. The crowd went instantly quiet as all eyes fell on the young man, wondering if these were to be his last moments. Indeed, Vighon himself was wondering if he had killed him...

At last, Uthrad inhaled enough air to keep his fight to survive going. His face wasn't a good colour and his chest was heaving as if he had already endured a lengthy fight in the pit, but at least he was alive. Vighon was happy to stand back and watch, satisfied that he had taught the dolt a few things about opening his mouth.

It wasn't long after his first breath that Uthrad began to pull himself up the wall and find his feet again. Bloodshot eyes, filled with humiliation, fell on Vighon with a promise of savage retribution. With a bruised throat and ego to match, the baby Yarl managed to stand up straight and even clench his fists. What he couldn't do, however, was speak. Pain crossed his face as he tried to hurl an insult at the northman and he swallowed it instead.

"Kill him, Uthrad!" This cheer was quickly followed by more, encouraging the young man to get his head back in the fight.

"I had to watch my words too once," Vighon told him as they began to circle round the pit. "My every word carried weight. When I spoke, consequences followed. When you wake up, do your best to remember this..."

Uthrad had heard enough. The Yarl leapt across the gap between them with an obvious right hook coming for Vighon's jaw. Had he had the time, the northman would have spared a laugh. In times past, he had sparred with Galanör, the greatest swordsman in the realm. Not to mention the orcs, Golems, Reavers, and dark mages.

Unfortunately, his moment of reminiscing made him slow. Uthrad's right hook landed quite firmly, causing Vighon to spit blood up the curving wall before slamming into it. The Yarl gave no pause and quickly brought a knee up into the northman's gut before yanking him upright and pinning him to the wall.

The pain was giving Vighon longer moments of clarity. He had such a moment as Uthrad's fist was launching towards his face. The northman tilted his head to the right and the Yarl punched the wall with enough force to break at least one of his knuckles.

He reeled back in pain and Vighon decided it was time to end the fight - he really was quite hungry. Uthrad, seeing the northman's approach, forgot his damaged hand and threw a punch with his other hand. Vighon locked it in a vice-like hold he had once seen Asher use. There wasn't much force required to snap the elbow, nor dislocate his knee with a swift kick.

Falling onto his severely damaged knee, Uthrad couldn't even manage a scream due to his bruised throat. Putting the thug out of his misery, Vighon brought his elbow down and into the side of his head, plunging him into blissful oblivion.

Once again, the cheering came to an abrupt ending.

Vighon rolled his neck and stretched his arms before climbing up the ladder dug into the arena's wall. Every spectator, including Mr Tawny, watched the northman as he picked up his purse of coins, downed a tankard of ale - taken right out of the hands of one of the gawkers - and made for the doors. He tossed one of his coins over the bar and into Davan's grateful hand.

Outside, Vighon was surprised to discover the night awaiting him. He had no recollection of being out at night, though he couldn't recall the last time he was out in the day either. His breath filled the air in front of his face and he wrapped his cloak a little tighter around his shoulders.

There was no fighting his hunger any longer. Using some of his winnings, he took himself off to a tavern he had come to like in the northern quarter. There he enjoyed a warm meal and another tankard of ale, lest he begin to recall his memories with perfect clarity.

Finally in search of his bed, Vighon paid his coin and left, returning to Kelp Town's icy night. He had just enough awareness about him to know that winter was quickly approaching. What he failed to be aware of, unfortunately, were the men who had fallen in behind him since leaving the tavern.

It wasn't the first time the northman had been attacked and dragged into an alley. The first punch had startled him, adding to the pain. What followed was a barrage from more fists and feet than he could count and he soon found himself face down, bleeding into the mud.

Rough hands grabbed him by the arms and lifted him up to his knees. Another hand grabbed him by the hair and yanked his head back. It took several seconds and a lot of blinking to focus his vision on the looming figure that had come to stand before him.

"This is the one?" the large man asked to a chorus of nods.

Vighon spat blood on the ground as the man crouched down and gave him a scrutinising once over. He reminded the northman of his father, Arlon, if a little wider in the shoulders and the face.

"You... You must be... Bairnan Yarl."

"That I am," he replied with the same air of arrogance Arlon had always carried. "And you; you're the nameless sack of wine that just crippled my son."

Vighon knew there was to be more pain, so why hold back? "You should have... kept him on a tighter leash."

A single look from Bairnan, as he stood up, had one of the Yarls bury their fist into Vighon's gut. He tried to double over and give in to the pain, but the hands around his arms increased their grip.

"It's a shame really," Bairnan went on. "Had you not hurt my boy I would have gladly paid for your services. You could have been one of us, a made man. Winter is coming you know and she's an unforgiving mistress. Not a good time to be a wanderer."

Vighon spat blood again, making sure to aim for Bairnan's boots. "I'm not concerned," he muttered. "As long as there's... Yarls to bleed in the pit... I will always have a roof over my head."

Another look from Bairnan and another solid fist to the gut silenced Vighon in all but groans.

"Knights!" one of the thugs hissed from the end of the alley.

Bairnan grimaced. "You know," he explained, "these black knights have made my line of work very hard of late. You can't just kill a man like you used to - their retribution is merciless." The Yarl grabbed Vighon by the jaw. "I'm awfully tempted to gut you right here, but there's nothing like a long walk to a man's death to put fear in his bones." His fingers squeezed. "And I want you to see your end coming."

"What do you want us to do, Boss?"

The big man resumed his full height and looked to his men. "We'll take him north like the others."

"You're coming too, Boss?"

A wicked grin spread across Bairnan's wide face. "For what he did to Uthrad, I want to put the noose around his neck myself. Maybe we'll have ourselves a little fun too - see how much damage he can really take."

"Trust me," Vighon uttered, "nothing can be worse... than your breath..."

Bairnan sneered. "You're going to hang... *eventually*."

Vighon was forced to look at the sole of Bairnan's boot as it was thrust into his face. He didn't see anything after that...

# CHAPTER 22

# LAND OF MEMORY

golden sun pushed up from the east, its first rays bathing the ruins of West Fellion in warm light. The stars, lingering in the farthest reaches of the west, began to retreat in the wake of the moon. The lush plains blew in the morning breeze, carrying nature's calming aroma.

Queen Adilandra inhaled the scent, allowing it to take her back to Ayda. Though the terrain of Illian and Ayda was largely similar, the latter wasn't nearly as scarred as the land she now occupied. Illian held so much memory, especially for the elven race. They had loved, fought, and lost so much on this soil.

Now, Adilandra feared they were to lose more before the end...

The queen of elves sat cross-legged on an elevated slab of West Fellion's rampart. She had intended to keep her eyes closed while falling deeply into the folds of her meditation, but the sunrise demanded her attention. The colours sparked hope and the sheer magnificence of the spectacle reminded her that anything was possible.

It was hard to hold on to those feelings when she considered the truth of her reality. So much of it was falling to pieces and she couldn't grasp them all for trying.

Adilandra looked down at the crystal resting in front of her crossed legs. It sparkled with life, having captured some of the magic she poured into it, but there was room for more. Her focus had been spoiled by dark thoughts.

Light footsteps turned her attention to the walkway. Faylen approached, every bit the warrior in her leathers, scimitar on her hip, and her elven cloak blowing out behind her in the wind. She was as fierce as she was beautiful; two praise-worthy attributes that Adilandra only considered after Faylen's intelligence and insight.

"I sense unrest in you," the queen remarked, turning her eyes back to the horizon.

"I was going to say the same," Faylen replied, absent the formality all others would show in the queen's presence, especially when addressing her.

Adilandra smiled to herself, welcoming the comfort of their friendship. "You have always known what was in my heart. How I lived for six hundred years without you I'll never know."

Faylen came to rest against the short outer wall of the rampart, her back to the east so she was facing Adilandra. "What troubles you so much that you cannot fill a single crystal? I once saw you fill a crystal twice that size with nothing but a sweat to show for it."

Adilandra recalled the crystal; a gift for her granddaughter that now served as the pommel of her Vi'tari blade, Firefly. "This conflict," she began, "is set to break my heart. It would be ignorant of me to say that no other will suffer as I do - war is a ravaging beast. But my family lies at the heart of it all."

The queen blinked her glassy eyes, sending a single tear down her cheek. She quickly wiped it away and scooped up the crystal, vowing to continue her meditation another time.

"Qamnaran is where we can do most good," Adilandra continued. "Of that I have no doubt. Even if we fail to end the war on that island, we will save as many dwarves as possible."

Faylen gave her a long, hard look. "But…"

Adilandra inhaled a slow and calming breath. "But this is not the path my heart wishes to take. I would storm The Dragon Keep and find my daughter. With Nathaniel, Inara and Athis, I would take them all back to Ayda and close off our borders. We would forget Illian and its never-ending troubles and live together in peace… forever."

Faylen crossed her arms. "You would have to drag each of them to The Opal Coast," she remarked.

"Very true."

"I too would rather be heading north," Faylen revealed. "I cannot boast of a mother's love for Reyna, but I love her with all that I have to give. I also know what Reyna would say were we to arrive at The Dragon Keep instead of helping on Qamnaran."

Adilandra had to agree. "Reyna has always known what was in her heart. I am thankful that it is pure and righteous. It makes her steadfast in her duty, a duty she has chosen. Reyna has always been the best of us."

"You will see her again," Faylen reassured. "We both will. By all reports, she is treated well in the keep. Apparently Alijah does have a line."

"Alijah perhaps, but Malliath the voiceless? There is no creature in all of Verda so broken as he. From the first time I saw Malliath, it was clear that he has always lived on the very edge of his sanity. His mind was shattered long before The Crow got to him."

Adilandra recalled not only the dragon's recent and brutal attack on her fleet, but also the devastation he made of the Darkakin. Standing beside Galanör, they had witnessed hundreds, even thousands, of Darkakin fall to his fiery breath, his whipping tail, ferocious claws, and hungry maw. He hadn't stopped with the destruction of their cities - it hadn't been enough for his rage. He had chased them across the desert and reduced them to black husks.

"Regardless of The Crow's machinations," Adilandra voiced, "I fear Alijah is lost to Malliath's madness now…"

"Is that all that troubles you?" Faylen enquired knowingly.

Adilandra looked at her oldest friend, considering the list of things that plagued her. The queen knew from experience that it was better to talk it through, especially with Faylen, or risk succumbing to the weight of it all in her own mind.

"I fear that I have undone all our hard work by leading our people back into war. For decades, both of us have worked tirelessly to eradicate that violent nature that lives in us all. Then, one conversation with my sister and I amass an army and build a fleet..."

Faylen adopted a comforting tone. "You did what any other would have done. You did the right thing. Our ancestors were peaceful yes, but they always rose to the darkness that challenged the realm. We do not wish for war any longer, but that does not mean we *will* not and *cannot* rise to it."

Adilandra smiled into the light. "You remind me of her."

"It is an honour to be compared, in any regard, to Lady Ellöria. I still grieve for the loss..."

Grief had become a close companion for the queen. "There were many times I wished Ellöria had been born first. Then she would have been married to Elym - I can't help but think she would have steered him away from war with Illian. I miss her greatly..."

"You have always been exactly where you were supposed to be," Faylen insisted. "Fate has aligned you for the good of the realm again and again."

Adilandra disagreed. "I took my eyes off the realm years ago. I made the mistake of looking inwards, at our people alone. Regardless of our origins, it has always been our place to safeguard the land and guide the humans. I turned us away from that and Illian fell to the orcs. Now my own blood stains the realm with dark magic."

Faylen stepped closer. "Elym unleashed a part of us that should never have seen the light of day. Without you, the elves of Ayda would be naught but war-mongers. We must tread a fine line now. War is just as unavoidable as our part in it all, but our people must know *why* we fight. Where once it was for pride and arrogance, now it is for the good of all. You must see that."

"I see my sister fading to the eternal shores. I see my daughter imprisoned by her own son in that dreadful keep. I see my grand-daughter walking hand in hand with death itself - she risks more than any of us every day. And I see her brother, my darling grandson who could charm a skittish deer into lapping water from his hand, as he tears us all apart. His reliance on dark magic corrupts him more every day, to say nothing of Malliath's influence."

"I have never wished for ill-treatment against a dragon," Faylen said, "but in days of late I have cursed the mages of Korkanath for not slaying Malliath when they had the chance."

Adilandra had shared similar thoughts. "We can do nothing to change what was, only what is."

Faylen came closer still. "Have you considered the end of this journey? Of what change may come from our time on Qamnaran?"

"I have always appreciated your mind, Faylen. I would have you speak it, *plainly*."

The High Guardian glanced away. "Alijah is our enemy. He murdered Lady Ellöria. He has caused countless deaths and suffering. And, as you said, he wields dark magic to an extent we have never seen before. Even Valanis refrained from necromancy. By all rights, we should kill him."

Adilandra maintained her form of perfect calm and control, despite the turbulent emotions swirling just beneath the surface. She marvelled at The Moonlit Plains a while longer, waiting for her courage and conviction to reach her tongue.

"I will kill him, should I have the opportunity to," she finally said. "Reyna could not live with herself if the burden fell to her, and Nathaniel would fall on his sword before he harmed his son. Inara carries enough without her brother's death to shoulder. I would do it for them as much as I would for the realm."

"And what of you?" Faylen asked. "Could you live with yourself?"

Adilandra considered Alijah's power and wondered if she would even survive such a fight, even if it still resulted in his death. "I know I cannot live with him as he is."

Faylen turned and greeted the sunrise for a brief moment. "What of redemption? Immortality gives one perspective does it not? Is there no chance we can save him from himself?"

"If I see even a glint of my grandson, I will try and save him," the queen declared confidently. "But I fear he is long lost to us all. There are others in this fight, lest we forget, who would see him dead regardless of redemption. The choice may be taken from us..."

Faylen turned back and offered a glimpse of a smile. "You are Queen Adilandra of house Sevari - no one takes anything from you."

Adilandra tried to mirror her friend's smile. "If only that were so." The queen rose from her perch and jumped down to the rampart. "Should we win this war, our work in Ayda will begin again. Every elf who fights on Illian soil will need to purge their need for action and blood."

"Then it is a good thing we have eternity on our side," Faylen replied positively.

Adilandra reached out and squeezed her friend's wrist, silently thanking her for always being there. "Come then," she bade. "I would rather take the lead than be down wind of our dwarven cousins."

"Quite," Faylen agreed. "And I always thought the humans had the worst smell..."

# CHAPTER 23
## OLD MAGIC

Standing on the muddy banks of Qamnaran's eastern shore, Galanör sheltered his eyes from the rising sun as he looked out on Illian's distant coast. It was far, but he could just make out the rocky peaks of The Narrows. Having heard from Faylen Haldör, the elven ranger knew that the queen's party had left West Fellion and were on their way to the land he could see before him.

Not one to stand and watch, Galanör trod through the mud until he rejoined his kin on firmer ground. There, they removed the foliage hiding over a dozen boats and began dragging them towards The Hox. The ranger commanded one elf to every three boats, instructing them to use their magic to direct all three to Illian while being seated in one.

"You are to wait for Queen Adilandra," he told them. "Ferry her party across and that of the dwarves. It may take more than one trip to transport them all."

Aenwyn loaded the last boat with quivers and blankets before saying her farewells to the departing elves. They were like family to her, that much Galanör could see. There was a growing part of him that longed for those roots and a place to firmly plant them. Aenwyn had found some semblance of family in Ilythyra, no easy thing considering her past in the army. If she could do it, he thought, then there was still hope for him.

If he lived long enough...

How many more times could he fight his way from Death's clutches if he kept putting himself in harm's way? He lived a life of the sword and had done for nearly five hundred years - a fact that saw him, time and time again, put himself in the middle of the fight. Yet, the more he looked at Aenwyn, the more he imagined another life, one filled with comfort and the sound of young laughter.

Having helped to push the last of the boats out onto the water, Aenwyn turned to see Galanör's wistful gaze. She smiled and approached with a questioning expression.

"What has captured you so?" she asked.

Galanör broke from his reverie. "I was just... thinking of the future."

Aenwyn cocked an eyebrow. "I thought you warrior-types kept your minds in the here and now."

The ranger offered an amused grin. "Here and now I see only you. I can't help but think of what might be. For the last five centuries I have lived from order to order, day to day, but now... Now I find hope in the future, in *our* future."

Aenwyn's smile faded. "I too have considered what may come to pass. But I cannot dwell on it. I fear the battles to come will take you from me. I would be left a shade..."

Galanör reached out and cupped her beautiful face. "I now have something more to fight for, a future I could never have dreamed of before you. Nothing will take you from me nor me from you. I promise."

Aenwyn gripped his hands and pulled them down, matching her demeanour. "You cannot make such a promise. Your heart swells for me, I know this. But it is the heart of a warrior, as is mine. We will give everything to win back the realm. Our future is not—"

Both elves turned to the sound of galloping hooves. Aenwyn

instinctively reached round for her bow while Galanör rested a hand on Stormweaver. There had been no Reavers seen here to date, but their recent breach of the tower had likely upset the routine.

From the tree line, the female elf, Kaila, came riding out on her horse. She searched the elves who had remained on Qamnaran's shore until her eyes settled on Galanör. Kaila spurred her horse to come alongside the pair.

"Malliath," she said gravely. "He has been seen approaching from the north."

Galanör turned to his left where the island faded far from sight into the distant north. "You are sure?" he checked, making for his tethered horse.

"A black dragon," Kaila clarified. "There is no mistaking his likeness."

Galanör turned back to Illian's western coastline, eager to see any sign of their reinforcements. "I would see this for myself," he replied.

With Aenwyn seated behind him in the saddle, the elven ranger took a southerly route that brought them round the spine of cliffs in the middle of the island. A light rainfall had started during their journey and was now a heavy downpour, obscuring some of their view.

"We should climb up that ridge line," Aenwyn suggested. "We will get a better view from there."

Agreeing, Galanör tethered their horse to a nearby tree and began the ascent. By the time they had reached the plateau, his chestnut hair was matted to his head and the rain made an irritating sound as it bounced off his armoured vambraces.

They could make out the dwarves, working their forges and moving about the scaffolding that wrapped around the tower. The Reavers were dark figures gliding between them all, their dead eyes always scanning for any signs of trouble.

Galanör noticed their patrolling pattern was different since their recent intrusion into the tower. He decided it would be impossible now to get any closer than this without alerting either the Reavers or the Fenrigs.

"I see no dragon," Aenwyn observed.

As if hearing Aenwyn's remark, Malliath let loose a ferocious roar upon the land. His hulking form flew over them, sheltering the elves from the rain for a moment. Malliath's wings were beating the air, however, carrying him away from their location and towards the tower. The black dragon circled the sentinel of imposing silvyr once before landing on a stretch of land between the tower's base and the edge of the western cliff.

Galanör looked about him. "He's been patrolling the island..."

Some of the dwarves stopped their work and stared at the beast who had killed their greatest warriors and kings. The Reavers and Fenrigs were quick to raise their whips and keep order through pain.

"Can you see Alijah?" Galanör asked.

Aenwyn mirrored his frown as she tried to pierce the cover of rain and distance between them. "No. He's not on Malliath's back but..."

Galanör sighed. "Damn this wretched island."

"Alijah must be with him," Aenwyn insisted. "They have never been seen to travel separately."

The ranger was growing more anxious by the second. "Is he here to oversee another aspect of its design? Or is he here to finally make use of whatever it is?"

"I can see your mind," Aenwyn told him. "Hear me Galanör Reveeri; we are not going anywhere near that tower until we have an army of elves and dwarves at our back."

The ranger pressed his fist into the grassy patch beneath him. "We might not have time for that."

Aenwyn gripped his shoulder. "We barely escaped last time. Could you do the same with a dragon on your tail?"

"If I could get close enough to kill Alijah there wouldn't be a dragon on my tail. Or Reavers for that matter - his will gives them life."

"You forget Inara's words too easily," Aenwyn chastised. "Like her, Alijah's bond with Malliath is different to that of the Dragorn. They do not share pain, nor are their lives tied as one anymore. If you kill Alijah, there will still be a dragon to slay." She hooked his jaw and turned the ranger's eyes to her own. "Have you ever slain a dragon before? Because I haven't. Good sense and everything I have ever been told of them suggests it is no simple task."

Galanör struggled to let it go, but there was no countering Aenwyn's argument. "Then let us return to camp," he said. "We will wait for reinforcements."

Together, they descended the rise and returned to their horse. Galanör looked over his shoulder, catching a glimpse of Malliath's tail lifting into the air.

"I could slay a dragon..." he muttered to himself.

Alijah swung his leg over Malliath's saddle and jumped down onto Qamnaran's hard ground. An honour guard of Reavers awaited him, creating a tunnel that led from his dragon's side to the tower. Unlike those around him, the king was dry in the pouring rain, sheltered beneath a very simple, if effective, shielding spell.

"Your Grace!" Pelter, the Fenrig put in charge of the dwarves' efforts, came running to his side.

Alijah could feel the ripple that ran through his Reavers as they considered blocking the man's path to their master. With a mental command, the king kept them where they were, allowing Pelter to approach.

"You honour us with your presence, your Grace!" he called before falling in beside Alijah.

"There is still considerable scaffolding around my tower, Mr Pelter. Why is that?"

The Fenrig swallowed. "There was some confusion after we lost the last shipment of silvyr, your Grace. We weren't sure if we could get the job finished as planned, but the dwarves found a way with what they had. It's all coming down now," he assured.

"Be sure that it does, and swiftly, Mr Pelter. I would see inside."

"Of course." Pelter gestured for Alijah to continue along the path he was already taking.

Walking around the base of the tower, Alijah could feel the large deposit of Demetrium beneath his feet. The mineral would work as the perfect conduit, ensuring his human half didn't let him down. He smiled to himself, proud of what he had achieved: a feat that others had tried and then died due to their failure. But he was destined to succeed where all others had fallen...

Alijah marvelled at the craftsmanship of the tower, a structure of pure silvyr that rose even higher than the Battleborns' Silvyr Hall in Dhenaheim. Such a thought led the king's eyes to those who had brought his dream to life. Sweaty and covered in filth, dwarves from every surviving clan were working together. Though a strong hand was needed now, Alijah was confident that the generations to come would call him king and thank him for uniting the clans.

Entering the tall archway, the king ascended the winding ramp that led up onto the only floor of the tower. He observed the hole at the top of the tower, where rain poured down and splashed on the silvyr floor. The hole was an essential aspect to the design, drawn by his predecessors. So too was their work evident in the surrounding wall.

Alijah walked along the curve, his hand brushing against the indentations of the runes. "Your report stated that elves had breached this chamber, Mr Pelter - is that correct?"

The Fenrig wiped the rain from his eyes. "Yes... Yes, your Grace. Two of them. Unfortunately, they both escaped our pursuit. Quick they were, and *strong*."

"In all your time on Qamnaran," Alijah began, "have you ever caught or killed a single one of the elves who hide here?"

Pelter hesitated. "No, your Grace."

Alijah continued his inspection of the runes. "Yet I gave you numerous Reavers and allowed you to bring many of your thugs for company."

Pelter would have had to have been deaf not to hear the king's intended insult, but he knew better than to react accordingly. "My men are ill-equipped to hunt elves. Something they have in common with your knights..." he added quietly.

Alijah, of course, had no trouble hearing him. "Do you like your men, Mr Pelter? Do you enjoy their company on this dreary island?"

"For the most part, your Grace. They're good boys - they do as they're told, always have."

Without missing a beat, Alijah said, "I'm going to kill one of them."

Pelter stuttered. "Your Grace?"

"My knights have no blood to speak of and dwarves make for terrible conduits where magic is concerned. I require the blood of a human, any human - the choice is yours. I will also require the dwarf responsible for these runes - Malankor, I believe his name was. Make sure he has a brush too."

The Fenrig remained rooted to the spot, a battle raging in his pathetic mind. "Is that really necessary, your Grace? If this is punishment for the elves then—"

"Blood is necessary," Alijah stated bluntly. "Old magic always requires it." The king ceased his inspection and looked back at the bewildered Fenrig. "Quickly now, Mr Pelter; there is still much work to be done."

The Fenrig hurried out of the chamber, leaving Alijah to pick out the specific glyphs he had been looking for. There were quite a lot of them that needed coating in blood, but he knew better than most how far a man's blood could go.

It wasn't too long before Pelter returned with a human and Malankor, the dwarf he had personally instructed to carve the ancient runes into the silvyr. The Fenrig looked confused rather than terrified, informing the king that he had no idea why Pelter had brought him inside the chamber.

"Malankor!" Alijah greeted as if they were old friends. "Your work is truly exceptional. I would have you apply your skills to The Dragon Keep in time."

Malankor fidgeted on the spot and rubbed his dirty hands together. So filthy was he that Alijah could no longer see the sigil of the Battleborns the dwarf had tattooed on his upper arm. His belt was laden with tools, though the king failed to spot the one he would need.

"You have a brush, Malankor?"

The Battleborn's eyes shifted to the Fenrigs and back. "I do... your Grace." He removed a brush from the back of his belt.

"Excellent." Alijah motioned for the new Fenrig to escort the dwarf to his side.

Pelter cast his eyes to the floor.

"You see this glyph?" the king asked Malankor, pointing to a rune shaped like a crescent moon with a line through the middle. "It is laced throughout the text all the way around the chamber. I need you to take that brush of yours and paint the interior of only this particular glyph. Do you understand?"

Malankor's bushy eyebrows knotted together. "Paint, your Grace? Paint them with what?"

Alijah nodded at the young Fenrig. "This man's blood."

The thug's confusion only lasted as long as it took Alijah to retrieve his Vi'tari blade and slash it across his throat - that is to say, not very long at all. Landing face first on the silvyr floor, his blood poured out of his neck and pooled around Malankor's feet.

"Make sure you don't miss a single glyph," Alijah added, moving into the centre of the chamber, where his shielding spell continued to keep him dry.

**This is it,** he said to Malliath. **This is where we shall ensure our reign for all time.**

*I do not like that there are elves on the island,* Malliath replied in his usual way.

**The Rebellion cannot stop us now,** Alijah reassured.

*I will have to fly very high for this to work,* Malliath reminded him. *I will not be able to protect you.*

**I do not require your protection. Besides my own skill, I will have Reavers and even Fenrigs down here. When the time comes, a few elves will not be able to penetrate our defences.**

Regardless of Alijah's response, Malliath reached out across their bond with the Reavers, and indeed the entire realm, as he searched for Lord Kraiden. The dragon commanded the Rider to join them on the island at once. The half-elf could sense the dragon's general misgivings and took comfort in his companion's need to keep him safe. They had, after all, promised to keep each other safe for all time.

And, after their accomplishments on Qamnaran, they would have *all* the time...

# CHAPTER 24

# A GOLEM WALKS INTO A BAR

Situated at the top of The Ice Vales, bordering the northern realm, Kelp Town was a stone's throw from Vighon's homeland. The Yarls only had to march him in that direction for a few minutes before they were greeted by the sign instructing them on the distance to Namdhor and Skystead.

It was, perhaps, the most melancholic thought Vighon had ever entertained, but he couldn't help taking some solace in knowing that he would die in the north, where he had always truly belonged. A shame, he believed, that it would be at the end of a rope and not on the battlefield, but how many now lived because he had walked away from *all* the battlefields?

He groaned, and not because his wrists were tied to the back of a horse that forced him to walk for hours. The alcohol, it seemed, had completely abandoned him and, despite his thumping head - thanks to Bairnan's boot - he could still recall the past with horrifying clarity.

It wouldn't be long before he started seeing his men die across numerous battles again, their names etched into his mind for all time.

"Pick up your feet," Bairnan growled, coming up on the north-man's side.

Vighon yelled out as the big man's boot yet again connected with his head and forced him down into the northern snow. The horse continued to drag him along, ignorant to his protests. Comfortable astride their mounts, the Yarls shared a hearty laugh at the north-man's expense.

It took some effort, but after a humiliating couple of minutes, he found the leverage he needed to pull himself back up and continue walking. After another hour, his feet were thumping much in the way his head was. They had marched him for hours into northern territory, hugging the tree line of one of the few forests that dotted The White Vale.

Just as his feet were complaining, so too were the Yarls around him. They aimed their complaints at each other, never Bairnan, but ensured they were loud enough to be heard. For the most part, the chief Yarl ignored their comments about being tired or in need of a warm ale. His interest, however, was piqued when one of them mentioned chicken pot pie. He claimed to know of an inn, not far away, that made the best in the north.

"Alright, you bag of bones!" Bairnan declared. "I've heard enough of your ranting! Old Bill, where is this place you speak of?"

The Yarl by the name of Old Bill turned back in his saddle before returning to the north with a pointed finger. "Just beyond them trees, Boss! Not far at all!"

"They got beds for the night?"

"They won't say no to us, Boss!"

Bairnan looked down at Vighon as he addressed his men. "I say we prolong the inevitable then, boys! We'll wake up to a trembling mess of a man I reckon!" They shared another laugh and continued in the direction Old Bill had suggested.

Vighon looked down at the cosy path they came across between the trees. He could see that it led back out to the west where it would likely meet The Selk Road. In all his years, he had never found such a path or even heard of a place inside this patch of woods.

Sure enough, just as Old Bill had said, the trees opened into a clearing and a black and white building sat comfortably in the space. Smoke rose from its chimney and a couple of horses neighed in the stables off to the side. It looked warm inside, a place where the northman could dry off.

"What did I tell you?" Old Bill grinned.

The surprisingly young Yarl jumped down from his horse and Vighon got his first look at the name above the door. Frozen as his face was, an amused smile couldn't be helped as it broke through his permanent scowl.

The King's Inn.

Untethered from the back of the horse, Vighon's wrists remained bound in rope as they entered the inn. The woman behind the bar gave every one of them a critical eye, quickly coming to the conclusion that trouble had just entered her home.

"Whatever this is," she said, waving her hand at Vighon, "I don't want it here."

Bairnan responded with the arrogant smile of a man who always got what he wanted. "We'll take your rooms for the night - all of them," he added loudly enough for anyone who had already purchased a bed for the night. "Keep the ales coming and chicken pot pies all round - except for him," he instructed, thumbing at Vighon over his shoulder. "He'll have whatever gruel you feed the dogs."

The woman looked to protest everything Bairnan had told her, but experienced eyes caught sight of every sword and dagger hanging from the Yarls' belts. She may have had the right to refuse them, but she didn't have the clout. Instead, they were given a couple of tables side by side while two customers on the other side of the inn were refunded for their rooms.

Then began the merriment that accompanied warm meals, full bellies, and an endless amount of drink. All the while, Vighon sat with his head down on his chest, arguing with himself as to whether he should even bother escaping. He had already discovered a path that he believed would see him free of his captors, a path that became easier with every fresh tankard of ale they each consumed.

The woman placed a bowl of gruel down in front of him and the northman silently nodded his thanks for adding some chunks of chicken into it. Eating with his wrists bound wasn't easy, but a growling stomach demanded he tried his best.

"Eat up, northman!" Bairnan cheered. "That slop is the last thing that'll ever pass your lips! At dawn, I'm going to find the ugliest tree and watch you swing from it!" The Yarl snorted with laughter.

Every word out of Bairnan's mouth made Vighon more inclined to escape, since such an action would likely end with the big man swallowing a length of steel. But the northman couldn't help but wonder what he was escaping for? What was there to live for? He could never go by his real name again, never put down roots, and never enjoy what was left of life.

Perhaps he should swing and join his men in whatever lay beyond this realm...

"What's that then?" one of the Yarls questioned in an obnoxiously loud voice.

All heads turned to one of the wooden pillars that supported the inn. Of all the trinkets hanging from nails, there was but a single item that caught Vighon's attention and held his gaze.

It was only the size of a man's hand, but there was no mistaking the small banner adorned with his sigil, the flaming sword. He hadn't seen it in a long while - he had missed it.

"That's illegal that is!" Old Bill chipped in.

Bairnan eyed the sigil with a greedy look. "It seems we're not paying after all, fellas!" The Yarl made certain the owner of the inn was watching him as he said it. "Or perhaps we should report you to the black knights..."

"Leave her alone," Vighon uttered, his threatening tone surprising even himself.

Bairnan swivelled back to the table and eyed the northman. "What did you say, deadman?"

Vighon took a breath and met the Yarl. "I said: leave-her-alone."

Bairnan licked his ale-soaked lips. "Got a soft spot for the old lady, have you? Or maybe you're a supporter of the flaming sword. Either one is going to see you receive a beating. Maybe her too..." The big man nodded at Old Bill, who promptly got up and made for the woman behind the bar.

A singular thought occurred to the northman in that moment: he had nothing to lose anymore. The Yarls were to be his end one way or another and he preferred to die with a sword in his hand defending someone.

Vighon snapped up from his chair and rolled over the table, spilling several tankards as he did.

Such a shocking move made the Yarls slow to react, including Old Bill, who turned just in time to see Vighon steal a dagger from his own belt.

Wrists bound, Vighon could do nothing but employ all his strength as he plunged the dagger into the man's head. As the Yarl fell back with steel jammed in his brain, Vighon gripped the sword on Old Bill's hip and slid it free of the scabbard. There was a moment of silence from the stunned patrons and the Yarls.

Vighon looked at the woman behind the bar, who swallowed hard and shifted her eyes to the rising Yarls, behind the northman. Their chairs scraped across the floor and their swords rang out as they were taken in hand.

"Now," Bairnan asserted, "you're going to die slowly."

Vighon stood with his feet apart and a hunched back, ready to swing at the first fool to challenge him. Hands tied or not, he was going to rid the world of seven more Yarls before death came for him.

Bairnan turned to the ugliest of the lot. "Kalag, break every bone in his body, but don't kill him."

The thug named Kalag stepped forward and, in a surprising move, replaced his sword in its scabbard. Vighon felt some of the fight leave him when Kalag removed a small vial of brown liquid from his belt. He swallowed the contents in one gulp and stripped off his jacket.

The Leviathan marrow immediately went to work, altering his body in gruesome ways. He cried out, pained by the transformation, until a low growl escaped his lips. What looked back at Vighon was less of a man and more of a beast.

Deciding he would take the first swing, the northman lunged forward and lashed out at the Yarl's neck, a natural attack after fighting Reavers for so long. Kalag arched his back, evading the tip of the sword by an inch - having moved too fast for Vighon to note.

Never one to back down, the northman brought his blade up again and came down on Kalag's head. The Yarl's deformed hand whipped through the air and gripped the middle of the sword. Without the marrow, such a defence would have cost him his hand and then his life. As it was, he halted the blade mid-strike and squeezed. Blood oozed down his hand, proving that he wasn't invincible, but he might as well have been.

Vighon tried to yank the sword back, but Kalag's grip was unyielding. Finally, the Yarl's free hand shot up and shoved the northman back, leaving the blade in his monstrous grip. With a snarl, Kalag discarded the weapon and approached Vighon with a murderous look about him...

Closing in on the north's southern border, Kassian watched the goliath that was Sir Borin the Dread veer off The Selk Road. Though Asher had managed to cover him in the hooded poncho, the Golem was still a terrible sight to behold.

"Where in all the hells is he going now?" the Keeper called, noting the approach of a merchant caravan up ahead.

Asher had no reply but to guide his horse off the road and follow the giant. Kassian groaned and trailed the ranger with Nathaniel beside him.

"We could be following this thing for days, weeks even," Kassian complained. "I agree that finding Vighon is the best thing but there are people out there who need our help. Every day we sit atop our horses, looking at the back of that creature's head, is another day the Seekers add to their kills."

"Just when I thought you were starting to see the bigger picture," Nathaniel replied with disappointment.

"I see the bigger picture," Kassian argued. "I wouldn't have agreed to this madness if I didn't believe it was the best chance of sticking it to your son." Nathaniel tried to hide the sting. "I'm just saying," he continued, "that maybe we shouldn't have wasted so much time on the ranger…"

"You're new to this life," Nathaniel said without an ounce of what could easily have been a patronising tone. "After a while, you develop a sort of instinct. Now, sometimes, if you listen to this instinct, it'll put you right in the *middle* of it. That's when you have to fight for your life as well as what you stand for. On the flip side, ignoring it can see you avoid the hard thing and live to see another day. But you might not be able to live with the cost."

Kassian laughed quietly to himself and shook his head. "You *hero-types*… You don't half talk a lot of nonsense."

Nathaniel smiled and glanced at the Keeper. "Let go of your vengeance, Kassian Kantaris, and one day soon you might find *yourself* heralded a hero. Then *you* can talk out of your arse."

The Keeper couldn't help but laugh, despite his strong feelings towards Nathaniel's family. For a moment, however, he did ponder on the vengeance that lived deep in his foundations. It was the only thing that kept his legs moving forward. How could he exist without Clara, without this burning vengeance to keep him going?

"What's that?" one of his Keepers asked, drawing him back to his surroundings.

The trees of the small wood opened up to what could only be a travellers' inn. There were several horses in the stable, though none of them bore Alijah's sigil. Still, Kassian kept one hand on his wand.

"Is he thirsty?" Fin asked humorously.

Indeed, Sir Borin the Dread continued his march towards The King's Inn. Asher brought his horse to a halt and raised a hand to stop all those behind him.

"I suggest we wait here," the ranger said in his gruff voice.

"We're just going to let that thing walk in there?" Kassian asked incredulously.

"Do you want to stop him?" Nathaniel replied.

The door of The King's Inn was pushed open by the Golem and he ducked his enormous frame to fit inside. The door closed behind him. Kassian looked around at his fellow Keepers, all of whom shared his scepticism. He narrowed his eyes trying to see through the windows but there wasn't one clean enough to offer a glimpse of the interior.

"Now what?" he asked impatiently.

The quiet was instantly shattered as the window beside the door exploded outwards. Amidst the debris was a man Kassian had never seen before or, at least, it was the top *half* a man he had never seen before. The torso hit the ground in a shower of glass and splintered wood and came to land next to Asher's horse.

What followed was hard to listen to, but impossible not to watch.

Inside, men could be heard both shouting and screaming depending on who was in Sir Borin's way. Further up the inn, another man was hurled through a window with enough force that he skidded across the ground and slammed into the side of the stables. Judging by the variety of angles his limbs displayed, he was already dead.

The wall between the windows shuddered and even cracked in places. More screams. The tip of a sword pierced the front door until half of its length was protruding, dripping with blood. Thunderous feet beat against the ground from right to left and all manner of things were shattered, broken, and torn. Sir Borin's obvious charge ended with a man being launched through the far wall, on the side of the inn.

"Help me!" came the cry of a man trying to escape via one of the broken windows. Most of his body was outside before a meaty hand and a relentless grip snatched the back of his neck and dragged him inside. His scream quickly became distorted until there was no sound at all.

Kassian looked at his companions again but this time with horror in his eyes. "What have we done?" he asked aloud, concerned that they had just unleashed a monster on the occupants.

Asher jumped down from his horse and used his boot to roll the torso over, splaying the arms. Crouching, he wiped some of the blood and dirt away from the upper arm, revealing a tattoo.

"They're Yarls," Asher reported, looking back at the inn. "I'd say we've found him..."

The door burst open and two men, merchants by the look of them, fell over themselves, slipping on the blood, as they tried to navigate the corpse pinned to the inside of the door. They yelped at the sight of so many on horseback but never stopped to ask questions or warn them of the unspeakable things they had just witnessed. With tears in their eyes and unintelligible mutterings, they dashed to the stables and fled on horseback, never once looking back.

Kassian's eyes went wide as he took in the breadth of Sir Borin's devastation. He had read about Golems during his time studying in Valatos, but no amount of ink on parchment could truly describe the awesome power they wielded.

"Do you think he's finished?" the Keeper asked.

Nathaniel jumped down from his horse. "Well no one's screaming," he quipped.

Asher looked to Adan'Karth, hidden beneath his hood. "You should wait out here."

The Drake nodded. "I quite agree."

Kassian climbed down from his mount and instructed the rest of his Keepers to fan out and scout the area while he accompanied Asher and Nathaniel inside.

He did so with his wand in hand...

Covered in blood that wasn't his own - it belonged to several people in fact - Vighon rested on the end of a bench with Old Bill's sword hanging by his side. He had picked it up in the chaos before coming to the realisation that he didn't need it. Still, seeing Sir Borin, a monster from his past, tearing through men like sacks of wine had kept his grip on the hilt like that of an iron vice.

The elderly woman behind the bar had fainted at the mere sight of him, a blessing she would come to be thankful for when she laid eyes on the ruin of her home.

Everywhere the northman looked, the most violent kind of death awaited him. He had to tilt his head to recognise the blood-splattered face of Bairnan Yarl. Sir Borin had punched through his chest and strangled the man behind him. The big man's face was contorted in an expression of dread, befitting of the giant that had killed him.

Next to Bairnan was simply a pair of legs. The rest of Kalag had been launched through the window shortly after Sir Borin had parted his top from his bottom. All the marrow in the world wouldn't have stopped the Golem...

Now, in the gloom, Sir Borin the Dread stood motionless, looming over Vighon. The Golem was eerily still where any other would have been heaving from the exertion of such a fight. But the dead had little need of air.

"You missed one," he told the towering beast with a shrug of his shoulders. "Surely you have dragged yourself from that watery grave to finish the job." Vighon let his head drop. "Just do it," he groaned, resigned to a fate he had outrun for too long.

"He can't hurt you," came a familiar voice. "He is bound to you."

Vighon turned to the light that poured in through the open door. They filled the bloody frame, blocking his view of the man Sir Borin had nailed to the door with his own sword. Then the northman groaned.

"What are you two doing here?"

Asher and Nathaniel entered the inn with a third man behind them. Surprising as it was to see them, Vighon was still taken aback by their appearance. Both men looked to have been chiselled from stone, never to age. He had memories of Nathaniel from his childhood and the old knight was exactly as he saw him now.

"Having trouble with the Yarls?" Nathaniel enquired, ignoring the question.

Vighon gestured lazily to the gore that decorated The King's Inn. "Not anymore." He noted the third man step further into the tavern, inspecting the extent of Sir Borin's work. "I know you," he said. "You're the..." He wagged his finger in the air trying to catch the name that eluded him.

"This is Kassian Kantaris," Nathaniel introduced.

Vighon clicked his fingers. "The Keeper. I remember you now. You fought with us in Velia, in the early days."

"I did," Kassian replied, his eyes shifting nervously to Sir Borin.

Vighon swept his hand across the room. "Well do the owner a favour, lad, and wave that wand of yours. This place could with a spruce and then some."

Kassian's expression dropped. "That's not really my area of expertise. And you can't tell me what to—"

"Why is *he* here?" Vighon interrupted, thumbing at the Golem. "And why is he just standing there? I've just watched him butcher seven men with his bare hands."

"He's here to protect you," Asher answered simply.

"Protect me?" Vighon spat. "The last time I saw this lump of dead meat he was trying to take my head."

Asher nodded at the Golem. "Queen Yelifer made him for one specific reason: protect the king or queen of Namdhor."

Vighon dropped his head again, wishing more than anything that he had a bottomless tankard of ale in his hand. "Well that's not me is it..."

"The magic that drives him would say otherwise," Nathaniel explained. "If... If *Alijah* were truly the king, Sir Borin would have searched him out and not you."

Vighon could hear the strain in Nathaniel's voice - it wasn't easy talking about the one who had betrayed them all. "You should have left him at the bottom of the lake."

"We needed to find you, Vighon." Nathaniel went on.

The northman blinked slowly and rose from the bench, tossing Old Bill's sword aside as he made for the bar. Sir Borin moved, giving him a clear path. On the other side of the bar, lying on her back, the old woman who had served him chicken gruel remained passed out, he *hoped.*

"Be sure to leave her some coin," the northman instructed. "She's going to need it." Taking the only tankard he could find without blood on it, he helped himself to a jug of what smelled like Strider Cider.

Kassian picked up a chair and waved his wand over the seat, removing the wet blood before taking to it. "This is not the king Inara promised us," he remarked.

Vighon's tankard rested at his lips, failing to meet his thirst. It had been a long time since he had heard another say her name. It was sweet in his ears and, for just a moment, he recalled her perfume. In reality, it was disheartening to realise that the scent of death remained firmly lodged in his nose. Looking over his shoulder, he had to wonder if it was, in fact, Sir Borin's singular odour.

"Is that why you're here?" Vighon asked, putting the tankard down. "Inara made some grand promise of a king who could turn the tide of The Rebellion?" He was fishing and he knew it.

"She said what we've all been thinking," Nathaniel began. "The

Rebellion cannot sustain its fight against Alijah. The realm needs you to stand with us. *You* are the heart of Illian, Vighon. The people need—"

"They don't need *me*," Vighon cut in. "I lost Illian in a day. I tried to take it back at the cost of more lives than I can count. I do nothing but attract dragon fire..."

Nathaniel stepped closer and Sir Borin mimicked him, giving the old Graycoat pause.

It irritated Vighon. "How do I get rid of this thing?"

"You can't," Asher told him. "He'll take simple commands, but he will always return to your side."

Vighon laughed. "You think the people will rally to me with this monster standing beside me?"

"People are dying." Nathaniel's tone was clipped, cutting Vighon's laugh short. "We could *all* be somewhere making a difference. But we're *here*, with *you*. It's time to stand up, Vighon."

"I did stand up," the northman argued. "I fought and I fought and I *fought*. As good men died at my feet I still swung my sword. And everywhere I went more good men joined our cause and I led them *all* to slaughter. For what? We gained *nothing*! They all died for *nothing*! There wasn't one battlefield where Malliath wasn't waiting for us."

Something quite visible snapped inside Nathaniel and he crossed the gap between them in a heartbeat. "Didn't you hear me, boy?" he growled, taking Vighon by the shirt. "People are *dying*." Sir Borin dropped a threateningly heavy hand onto the knight's shoulder, but Nathaniel didn't so much as flinch. "Fight with us, run from us, people are dying all the same. They only died for *nothing* if you don't stand up. Now I have fought too hard and lost too much to endure your self-pity. This realm, *my* realm, needs its *king*. *I* need my king.

"You are like a son to me - I know you are stronger than this. You're like the old man behind me," he said, flicking his head towards Asher. "You always get back up. Well now it's time to rise. Be the king we know you to be, the king you've *proven* yourself to be."

Asher turned to Kassian and motioned for the mage to follow him outside, leaving Nathaniel and Vighon to their conversation.

"We cannot linger here," Kassian was saying on his way out. "Those who fled will alert the watch in Kelp Town..." His words were lost when the door closed behind him.

"The Rebellion doesn't need you to save lives," Nathaniel continued. "You're not Illian's defender. No one man can protect everyone. You're Illian's *king*. You're needed to stand tall, to be the light that rallies all against the dark."

The tears welling in Vighon's eyes forced him to shut them as he waved Sir Borin away. His entire youth had been spent looking up to Nathaniel Galfrey, the heroic knight who had stood up to the darkness and drawn a line. He had wanted to be him just as much as he had wanted him to be his real father.

The northman gripped Nathaniel's collar and he chewed over his response. "What if I don't know how to be that king? What if I'm not as strong as you think I am?"

"Then you will die on the battlefield, fighting beside me and all those who believe in you and what you stand for. None of us chose this life because we want to live. We chose it because we're willing to die for it, for The Rebellion, for the crown... for *you*." Nathaniel gripped the side of Vighon's hair, tears in his own eyes. "You should have come to me. As long as there's magic in these old bones, I will champion you to my end."

Vighon looked around helplessly. "What would you have me do?"

"For now?" Nathaniel gripped his arms. "You need only return to The Black Wood with us. Whatever Alijah has been planning, it's nearly finished. We're no closer to understanding what he's been doing on Qamnaran or The Moonlit Plains, for that matter, but we're all agreed that his motivations come from a dark place."

Vighon recalled the reports of a tower and a pit, both created by the dwarves Alijah had enslaved. There had been a time when that had set his blood on fire, just like everything else Alijah did. Now, he couldn't find the *passion* to move himself, but he felt the call to duty instilled by Nathaniel's words - words he should have told himself long ago.

There was also another reason, equal in power to his duty, that might see him return to The Rebellion. "How is Inara?" he asked tentatively.

Nathaniel concealed his smile before it broke out across his entire face. "She misses you. She might *hurt* you," he added with a touch of humour, "but she has missed you every day. As we speak, she is in Dragons' Reach."

That surprised Vighon. "In Ayda?"

"Yes. She intends to return with Gideon and the Dragorn. With them leading from the sky and you leading from the ground, what could stand against us?"

Vighon took a breath and walked away from Nathaniel. "I *want* to go back," he confessed. "I have thought about it every day. I would have fought to my death to keep The Rebellion alive." He shook his head. "But I cannot go back," he declared. "I left them, *all* of them, to fight without me. I do not deserve to be welcomed back nor bowed to as their king."

"You left to save us," Nathaniel pointed out. "We know that. In the beginning, some even appreciated it. Alijah and Malliath stepped back and we gained victories. But this fight is coming to an end; we can all feel it. If we don't fight back with everything we've got the realm will fall into ruin."

Vighon turned away from the old knight and leaned against the bar. How could he face them all again? How could he lead more men to die and keep getting back up?

*They only died for nothing if you don't stand up...*

Nathaniel's words echoed throughout Vighon's mind, plaguing him with the need to act, even if that was to simply die on the battlefield.

"What say you?" Nathaniel demanded an answer and he deserved one too.

"No." It hurt to even say it and the northman knew it would hurt even more to live with it. "I'm sorry you came all this way, but I chose my path because it's the best way for me to help the cause. I will not go back with you..."

Nathaniel had the look of a man whose world had fallen out from under him. The disappointment was easy to see and would be all too easy to remember after he had gone.

Picking himself up, the old knight placed a hand on the northman's shoulder. "Whatever Fate has in store for you, Vighon Draqaro, know that I am proud of the man you have become. For your time, Illian had its greatest king. I will believe that for all my days."

Vighon quickly discovered something was lodged in his throat, preventing him from replying.

Nathaniel paused before leaving the inn. "I will convince the Keepers to clean some of this up before we leave.

"And leave coin," Vighon croaked.

"*And* leave coin..." Nathaniel bowed his head. "Your *Grace*..."

# PART THREE

CHAPTER 25

# REMEMBER ME

Having crossed The Unmar into the western lands of The Moonlit Plains, there was a notable difference to all that lay east of the river. There, green fields and dense forests stretched all the way to Velia, with all manner of creature calling the plains their home. But west of the river...

Doran Heavybelly brought his Warhog to a halt at the top of a small rise, giving him the best vantage of the landscape. It was a swamp. A cursed place. Even under the touch of the moon, the grass that protruded from the boggy water failed to illuminate as the rest of the plains did.

Lying at the heart of the swamp was a ruin equal in size to Velia or possibly even the sprawling Tregaran. The dwarf had made an effort in the past to avoid the area - easily done since civilisation had long avoided Elethiah, the ancient elven city.

Returning his attention to the large caravan of dwarves and elves, Doran noted that a few of his kin had stepped out of the southern procession to gawk at the ruins. The children of the mountain loved a good ruin! There was potential plunder, treasures long forgotten, and secrets left for the taking.

"Thraal!" the War Mason called to his side - where naturally, his brother Thaligg accompanied him. "Get those dolts back in line an' keep 'em movin'." His eye turned to the pale sky, searching for their deadliest foe. "We're goin' to be exposed now until we reach The Narrows an' there's no missin' us, I can tell ye that!"

Indeed, having left West Fellion with the fort's entire complement of Heavybellys, and the remaining caravans that had staggered their departure from The Black Wood, there was now a line two thousand strong marching south on the open plains.

Thraal pointed his stubby finger further down the line. "The elves 'ave stopped to take a look."

Doran tilted his head to see from Thraal's angle. There, beyond the fools of his own kind, were Adilandra and Faylen. Astride their horses, they both appeared to be sat in silence as they gazed at the ruins of Elethiah.

"I don' command elves," he replied. "I command dwarves, like yerselves. Now get 'em back in line an' get 'em movin'."

The brothers spurred their Warhogs up the line and began barking orders on his behalf. Not much further up, he spotted the hulking back of Russell Maybury. He had opted to walk with those who didn't have mounts, stating his preference for exercise.

"A'right, Pig, pick up yer hooves…"

The son of Dorain didn't want to dwell on his friend's condition any more than he wanted to dwell on his brother's condition. Instead, he maintained his elevated position and rode along the narrow rise, above his kin further down the slope. Eventually, he came up alongside Faylen and the queen, both of whom appeared exquisite in the glow of the setting sun.

"This journey holds a lot o' memories for ye, lass," he observed. "How many buildin's 'ave ye had come down on ye head exactly?"

"Too many," Faylen replied. "That's why I appreciate the outdoors so much," she added with amusement.

Doran laughed, appreciating the humour on a long trip. "I must 'ave met ye not long after this," he said, emerging from his laugh.

"Yes," Faylen agreed. "Two weeks later if I recall, in The Pick-Axe."

"That were it!" Doran cheered, stealing a glance at Russell further along their caravan. "I tell ye, I've heard a lot o' tales in me time - had me own part in some - but I still remember the princess tellin' us yer story. I can still see everyone's faces when ye took off yer hoods!"

Despite the harsh memories brought on by Elethiah, Faylen managed a smile. "I believe we found it quite difficult convincing you we *were* elves."

The dwarf shrugged. "No one had seen an elf since me own daddy was jus' a boy." He looked under her horse's neck to see Adilandra on the other side. "Does Elethiah hold memories for yerself, me Lady?"

Adilandra's sight looked to pierce time itself. "It was once my home, for a time. I was only a child then."

Doran's only visible eyebrow reached for his hairline. "Ye were among those who sailed for Ayda, me Lady?"

"I was."

Faylen glanced down at Doran before turning to her queen. "Were you here during the last battle, your Grace?"

"No," Adilandra answered. "I have heard the rumours though. There are those who believe I saw Garganafan before his end and that I witnessed Valanis being trapped in the Amber Spell. Excitable hearsay I'm afraid. Had I seen either of those things I too would have been a victim of the spell, like the *ranger...*"

That was a part of Asher's history that Doran didn't give much thought - mostly because of how unbelievable it was. "Asher was trapped in there for... what? A thousand years?"

"He stood still while the world moved around him," Faylen elaborated. "It doesn't sound so bad..."

Queen Adilandra turned her horse away from the ancient rubble. "Elethiah had its time. I am more concerned with the eastern plains."

Doran guided Pig around, careful not to interfere with Faylen's similar adjustment. "What abou' it?" the dwarf asked, assuming she was speaking of the enormous hole being dug out there.

"From West Fellion to here, I did not see a single Centaur. Not even a scout among the trees. My daughter made allies of them, yet they do not approach, not even to greet elves."

The son of Dorain cast his eye out across The Moonlit Plains, a horizon of lush flat land. "Alijah's wicked grip has taken these lands," he reasoned. "I've spent some time among the Centaurs; they're a smart people. They're likely hidin' from anythin' on two legs... or anythin' with wings," he added, looking at the sky.

"They are fierce warriors too," Faylen imparted. "They would prove hard to bring down from a Reaver's point of view."

Adilandra kept her startling eyes on the plains a while longer, her thoughts her own. "Come," she finally said. "Such open ground is no place to camp. We must push on through the night if needed."

"I agree," Doran affirmed. "I'm more aware than ever that we 'ave no dragon o' our own to call upon."

"Soon," Faylen said, turning south, "we will have *dozens* of dragons to call upon. I feel a swift victory is coming..."

There was something about the elves that instilled a sense of hope in the War Mason. He found himself trekking along with them, accompanied by thoughts of a life and world after this conflict. His brother would recover, the clans would naturally fall into a new hierarchy, and he would return to enjoying a vocation in slaying monsters.

That future was coming, he believed that.

Until then, he led his people south, across the edge of The Moonlit Plains. They journeyed for two more days and nights before the dusky rock of The Narrows came into view. Seeing those cliffs told any traveller that they were entering the deserts of The Arid Lands.

Though such a sight was not required to alert the dwarves of Grimwhal that they had entered a desert. Up and down their caravan, Doran's kin were complaining about the dry heat. Many, including the son of Dorain, had stripped down to their waist, revealing an exotic collection of tattoos.

"Please don' tell me Qamnaran is like this!" Thraal groaned.

Doran laughed to himself. "Oh aye, it's a barren desert without so much as a tree to take shelter. The earth itself is a cracked web of hard ground that'll cover ye in sand."

"Truth?" Thraal enquired with a hint of apprehension.

"No, ye fool!" Doran barked with an amused grin. "We 'ave to take the southern pass to get into The Narrows. Once we're inside the valley, we 'ave to go back on ourselves, to the north. There's a break in the cliffs that'll lead us to the western shore."

"By all accounts," Thaligg chipped in, "the island is rarely dry."

"Praise Grarfath!" Thraal yelled.

Doran smiled to himself before he spotted Russell walking in the shadow of the cliff. The old wolf was still wearing all of his clothes, including his cloak and hood, which concealed his head. He had kept very much to himself on their journey thus far - no one could find him at night while they camped. The War Mason had wondered, more than once, if bringing the old wolf was such a good idea.

Breaking away from the line, Doran guided his Warhog to come alongside his old friend. "How are ye doin', lad?"

Russell turned his head to properly see Doran from within his hood. "I'm fine," he answered plainly.

Doran looked him up and down. "It's hot as hell 'ere an' ye're still wearin' yer leathers, cloak, an' hood. How can ye be fine?"

"The heat doesn't bother me," he replied.

"An' I've not seen ye without that pick-axe in hand," Doran added with concern. "Yer arm must've detached by now!"

Russell hefted the pick-axe and rolled his shoulder. "It's nothing," he remarked.

Doran let the subsequent silence fill the gap between them for a little while. "Are ye sure ye want to be doin' this, lad?" he asked quietly.

"I would rather meet my end on the battlefield than give in to the wolf."

"I respect that," Doran replied. "But—"

"You're worried I will turn into the wolf and become a hindrance," Russell finished.

Doran puffed out his cheeks. "Calling the wolf a hindrance ain't doin' it justice, lad. If the wolf gets out there's goin' to be bloodshed for those around ye."

"Not with you beside me," Russell uttered, turning Doran's head.

"What are ye abou'?" the dwarf demanded.

Russell continued towards The Narrows, keeping in step with Pig. "It has gone unsaid, but we both know what must be done. I would not live out my final days or even years in the shadow of the wolf. I can think of no one better to end my—"

"Don' say it!" Doran snapped. "I was jus' startin' to get a good feelin' abou' all this - a feelin' *long* missed I can tell ye."

"You can't bury your head in the sand, Doran. We've both known for a while how this has to end. You're a ranger. I'm a monster."

"Bah! If that were truly the case, Asher would 'ave lopped off yer mangy head decades ago! We're goin' to find a way, ye mark me words, Rus. We'll find a cure!" he declared. "Or at least somethin' to keep the wolf part quiet."

Russell cast an incredulous expression on the son of Dorain. "You and I both know there isn't a cure for this."

"That's because no one's ever bothered before!" Doran countered. "Ye *see* a werewolf, ye *kill* a werewolf. We jus' need to..." His arms went up left and right as he tried to pull on threads that simply didn't exist.

"We just need to accept the inevitable, Heavybelly. I for one am content. I've lived longer than most humans and I've done so with all my wits and strength. I've made friends, owned my own tavern, had the best of times. I've even managed to do my part for the realm here and there. A man can ask for no more..."

"Except ye bloody are askin' for more!" Doran pointed out. "Ye're askin' me to... to... How am I supposed to live with meself afterwards, eh?"

"You get to live knowing you ended my suffering, you stupid oaf of a dwarf."

Doran could hear the humour in his friend's voice, but he could also hear *and* see the suffering of which he spoke. Russell had been the epitome of strength and resilience for as long as he had known him - it was heartbreaking to see him this way.

"Ye said ye might 'ave years left in ye," the dwarf grumbled as the towering cliffs of The Narrows embraced them.

"Look at me, Doran. I think years was being optimistic. Don't focus on my death," he said, drawing a wince from the dwarf. "Instead, focus on my life. I have lived a better life than any with this curse. I don't wish to stain my memories with countless years of this torment. And I don't want you to remember me this way..."

Doran was shaking his head. "I'll remember ye," he grumbled, "as a stubborn git who charged too much for a Hobgobbers Ale."

Russell laughed deep in his gut, a sound the dwarf hadn't heard in too long. It brought a genuine smile to his face.

They continued into the canyon, enjoying the banter that had brought them together so many times over the years. For a while, it seemed Russell wasn't haunted by the wolf's bite. He pushed back his hood and exchanged jokes with Thraal and swapped recipes with Thaligg. Futile as it was, Doran couldn't help but *hope*, a very un-dwarven thing to do. To hope, however, was better than dwelling on the conclusion they were heading towards.

"Damned elves," he muttered to himself, blaming their disposition for his dream of a better outcome.

As they rounded the long bend in the canyon, Russell stopped walking and his head lifted to the sky. Doran was of a mind to halt the entire caravan given his friend's instincts, but stopping and starting that many marching feet and hooves wasn't easy.

Instead, he had Pig trot over to the old wolf. "What's ye nose tellin' ye, lad?"

"An old scent, one I haven't come across since my ranger days." Russell turned his head to the numerous rocky shelves above them. "Sandstalkers..."

Doran spat on the ground. "Foul creatures!" he cursed. "Keep yer head on a swivel, Rus. I'll alert the others."

"I thought you'd be itching for a fight," Russell remarked. "How long's it been since you swung your axe?"

Doran ignored the question. "There's more than enough fightin' to come, lad. I jus' want to get us to Qamnaran in one piece."

With his eye scanning the high cliffs, the son of Dorain returned to his kin and had the message dispersed down the line. He then, quite silently, prayed to Grarfath that they would make it to that miserable island with every soul that had left West Fellion.

He feared they were going to need every one of them...

CHAPTER 26

# A GAME OF RISK

Vighon groaned as he deposited the last of the Yarls round the back of The King's Inn. He had retrieved that final corpse, broken from head to toe, from beside the stables and dragged it by a pair of icy cold wrists. He stood, sweating in the freezing air, and stared at the gruesome sight before him.

Piled on top of each other, right where he had left them, were the rest of Bairnan Yarl's men and the big man himself. The sight of them was made all the worse by the fact that they weren't all in one piece.

Just beyond them, to the side, the cause of their dismemberment was busy digging the last grave. With a simple spade, Sir Borin had worked the ground and dug a grave for every man in a fraction of the time it would have taken the northman. The Golem simply didn't tire...

Vighon added the last body to the pile and wandered towards the back wall of the inn. He remained outside and perched on a bench, swigging water from a tankard. He could have commanded Sir Borin to amass the bodies *and* dig the graves, but keeping his hands and mind occupied had been essential, lest he chase after Nathaniel and the others.

Denying that side of him hadn't been easy for the last twelve months, but Nathaniel had directly challenged him to return. It was all Vighon wanted: to help. To help his friends, to help The Rebellion, to help his people.

*His* people...

The northman hadn't thought like that in some time. Yet only hours ago he had stood up to the Yarls in defence of Magatha, the owner of the inn. The weight of so much injustice, witnessed through his eyes, had broken the wall that kept his true self locked away.

It had felt good in that moment, like inhaling that first breath of air after being submerged for so long.

*They're better off without you,* he told himself, wiping his brow of sweat.

His lot was to wander the realm until he could wander no more. Of course, now he was lumped with Sir Borin. The Golem would prove to be something of a problem wherever he went. It wouldn't matter if he covered the beast's ghastly face, the sheer size of him would attract unwanted attention or simply see them turned away.

He wondered if it would be feasible to order the Golem to dig another hole - one far deeper than any grave - and jump in it. Something told him that would interfere with the magic that bound Sir Borin to him. It seemed that even beyond death, Yelifer Skalaf was still gifting him things, despite his hesitance to accept.

"When you're finished with that grave," he called, "bury the bodies in them. Oh, and try to put the right parts together..."

Sir Borin paused briefly in his work to nod his understanding. Vighon finished the last of his water and made for the back door of the inn. Thankfully, the Keepers had done as Nathaniel requested and cleared much of the debris up. There was nothing they could do, apparently, about the hole in the far wall. Vighon hoped the coin they had left would see to the refurbishments, including the shattered windows.

Looking around, he struggled to find much evidence of the dismemberment that had taken place. Some of the corners had traces of blood staining the wooden beams, while some of the tables and chairs were marred with cracks that hadn't been fused properly.

"That thing is to stay outside," Magatha warned him from behind the bar.

The owner of The King's Inn had required some care upon waking. She wasn't frail by any means, but just seeing Sir Borin walking around was enough to make even the bravest of warriors abandon their courage. A dark bruise discoloured her right cheek where she had hit the floor, though it had been the least of her worries given the Golem's proximity.

"Don't worry," Vighon assured, righting a chair under a table. "He won't come inside." An icy draft funnelled through the broken wall and the shattered windows. "The cold, however, will come in," the northman observed apologetically. "I'm afraid there's nothing I can do about that."

Magatha waved his comment away. "I'm not without my own skills - I can board it up until I can get some help from Kelp Town." She placed another tankard of water on the bar for him. "I would give you something stronger, but from the look of you I'd say you've had more than your fair share of a barrel or two."

Vighon couldn't argue with that and reached for the water instead. He noticed the slightest of tremors in his hand and felt a pang of shame. How many had died fighting for him? Their memory should never have been wiped away by every kind of ale, beer, brandy, and cider he could get his hands on.

"I would also offer you one of my rooms for the night," Magatha continued, "but I'm not sure I'd sleep with that thing even close to my home."

Vighon used the sleeve of his coat to wipe the excess water from his beard. "We'll both be long gone by the time you go to sleep. I promise."

With a look of guilt, Magatha busied herself behind the bar. She was a good woman - that much was obvious. Even if she had allowed him to stay the night, he would have refused - it wouldn't be long before someone came from Kelp Town having heard of Sir Borin's rampage from the two patrons who fled. Vighon decided that it would be better for Magatha if neither he nor Sir Borin were around when that happened.

"Where will you go next?" she asked. "I'm assuming you're in trouble with the Yarls."

"If only it were just the Yarls," Vighon quipped.

"I thought you had that look about you," Magatha commented.

"What's that?"

"You've the look of a man who attracts trouble," she clarified. "But then," she added with a thought, "the way you put yourself between me and those men... *You* don't attract *trouble, trouble* attracts *you*."

Vighon's smile suggested he agreed. "That would explain a lot about my life."

"Well, wherever you find yourself next, I hope you can help someone else like you did me today. Though maybe lose the giant - he's trouble you don't need."

"I'm inclined to agree with the latter," he replied tipping his tankard towards her.

Magatha cocked an eyebrow. "The way you speak and the way you look tell two very different stories."

"I had a good upbringing," he explained vaguely, not wishing to dwell on happier days on the Galfrey homestead.

"Highborn?" she enquired casually, as if it made no difference to her.

"Definitely not," he said with mirthless laugh. "My mother was the daughter of a fisherman and a servant for most of her life. My father... well he liked to *think* he was highborn. Only the worst of words could describe him."

"That doesn't sound like a good upbringing," Magatha opined.

"That's because I was mostly raised by others." Vighon thought then about telling her who he really was, just to hear himself declare that he was king. The feeling faded with the sound of hooves quickly approaching the inn.

Magatha scowled at the door, now absent the body that had been pinned to it. "This is turning into the busiest day of my life."

Vighon had an uneasy feeling. Leaving the owner to straighten out her clothes, he returned to the back door where, as he had expected, Sir Borin was trying to enter. The northman placed a firm hand against the Golem's chest, halting his lumbering stride in the threshold.

"Stay outside." His command was just as firm as his hand, but the giant didn't move. "If I need you, I will call for you. *Stay outside.*" With that, the Golem stepped back and returned to his duties regarding the numerous bodies.

Vighon made it half way back to the bar when he became aware of his hip, absent a sword. The Yarls' weapons had been collected in a pile out back, but it was too late to retrieve one before the door was barged open.

Three men entered The King's Inn - everything about them broadcast their vocation: bounty hunters. They were scarred from years of tracking down those who didn't wish to be caught and they each possessed enough weaponry to bring down any foe, human or beast. Their long coats were that of a thick hide, lined with dark fur.

"Forgive the state of things, gentlemen," Magatha pleaded. "The beer is good and I have warm beds available upstairs. You may use the stables as you—"

"We haven't tracked our quarry this far to rest, old woman," the lead hunter cut in, scanning the inn. "From Skystead to Namdhor and back down to this rat hole, our prey has remained ahead of us. We went to Kelp Town only to hear of a slaughter off the road." This time his eyes roamed from the shattered windows to the broken wall.

"There was a fight," Magatha told them. "Yarls I think. Not sure who the others were. As you can see, gentlemen, I came off worse." Vighon winced internally - she wasn't a great liar.

Judging by the lead hunter's intense gaze, he must have detected the same thing. Magatha, however, remained firm, turning the hunter to Vighon at the end of the bar. The northman gave them a nod, wondering how many more were outside. He had heard a lot more than the hooves of three horses and he had caught glimpses of men crossing the windows outside.

It was going to be another bloodbath.

"And who might you be?" the hunter on the right asked him.

"Name's Voss. Just passing through."

The hunters scrutinised him for a moment longer before determining that he wasn't anyone of interest. Vighon had discovered almost a year ago that those with swords cared very little for those without swords.

"We have not come looking for Yarls," the hunter continued. "The bounty we seek is more valuable than any Yarl." He marched forward and, from within his coat, produced a rolled piece of parchment which he separated into three sheets. "These men," he said, laying them on the bar. "Were any of them here?"

Vighon sidled up the length of the bar and viewed them with Magatha. They weren't the best drawings the northman had ever seen, but they each had enough of a resemblance to be Asher, Nathaniel, and Kassian. Asher's even had his black-fang tattoo under his left eye. The reward for each was substantial, though only Nathaniel's specified that the reward would be double if he could be captured alive.

"I've never seen these men in my life," Magatha declared.

Again, the hunter remained silent for a moment as he assessed her for any sign of a lie. "And you?" he questioned, looking at Vighon.

The northman pretended to take another look at the images. "I can't say I've come across any of them."

The hunter's eye twitched. He shifted his position. It was all subtle, but Vighon saw it all as threatening. These hunters had been on the road for some time chasing their bounty and were reaching the point of needing action.

"Do you know who we are?" The leader's voice was low and controlled; another precursor to violence in Vighon's assessment.

Maintaining his lowly demeanour, the northman ran a quick eye over the other two before finding a spot on his boots to look at. "Bounty hunters."

"We're the Bailey brothers," the hunter declared.

As it happened, Vighon had heard of these particular brothers. "I hear you're good hunters."

"The men out there are good hunters," he replied nodding his head at the door. "The three of us are the best hunters. We've never failed to catch our prey. Do you know why—"

"Alec!" came a call from outside.

The leader nodded at his brother who opened the door of the inn. "What is it?"

"Rake says he's found tracks - twenty plus!"

The brother holding the door open turned back to his brothers. "They were spotted in a group that size."

"They're skirting round the edge of the woods," the hunter outside continued, "heading east by the look of it!"

The leader offered Vighon and Magatha a predatory grin. "You have a good day." He led his brothers outside with a swift stride about them. "Let's go!" he cheered. "Cut through the trees! I don't want them to see us coming!"

Magatha waited until the sound of their hooves were distant before exhaling a long sigh of relief. "I thought for sure that was going to end in blood. Do you know those men?" she asked, gesturing to the parchments left on the bar.

Vighon barely heard her, his eyes fixed on the door through which the hunters had left. A cold pit was forming inside of him. There was a good chance that Asher and Nathaniel would survive an encounter with the Bailey brothers, but their chances diminished in light of a surprise attack.

"Voss?" Magatha's tone suggested she had said his name a few times.

Something awoke in Vighon. As the bounty hunters disappeared into the woods, he saw the Seeker attack Renan in the tanner's shops. He saw the man's wife held back and forced to watch, as she now watched her husband's body swing on the end of a rope. He saw the Yarls demanding coin from a young man who had displayed more courage than he had. Through it all he had done nothing but stand by and witness events unfold.

A flicker of his true self had allowed him to stand up for Magatha, though he knew in his heart he had been seeking a way to die in battle rather than hang from a rope. In refusing Nathaniel, he had attempted to extinguish that flickering flame before it turned into a blazing fire.

But now, under the weight of so much inaction, that part of him that he had allowed to fade away demanded his attention.

"Voss?" Magatha said again.

"My name is Vighon, of house Draqaro, first of his name, ruler of Namdhor and king of Illian." He turned to see a bewildered woman looking back at him. "I need a horse."

"Is that it then?" Kassian Kantaris called out.

Asher blinked long and hard but kept his sigh to himself.

"Is this what we returned to The Rebellion for?" the Keeper continued. "Our magic could be of better use *anywhere* else. And what do we have to show for our time on this wild chase? We dug up a fossil in Skystead and a fossil in The King's Lake and we don't even return with both..."

Asher looked to his right, where Nathaniel rode beside him. The knight didn't look to be listening, his attention adrift like the leaves on the wind.

"You're disappointed," the ranger commented, ignoring the Keeper as well.

"Aren't you?" Nathaniel replied. "Both of us have tipped battles towards victory and both of us have seen the beginning and ends of wars, yet neither of us has the power to pull the realm together like Vighon. We need him…"

"We haven't seen the last of the northman," Asher said casually, turning Nathaniel's head.

"Do you know something I don't?"

"It was in his eyes," the ranger explained. "I just needed to see it for myself."

Nathaniel continued to stare at Asher. "Are you going to make me ask?"

The ranger glanced at the knight with half a smile. "The warrior in him," he elaborated. "I see it in you, even in him," he added with a nod back at Kassian. "A year living in the gutters isn't enough to change who Vighon really is."

"He still said no, Asher. Even if he does return to us, if he doesn't do it *now*, it might be too late."

Asher took a breath - he always enjoyed the winter air and it was quickly approaching. "Have you ever played Galant?" he asked, surprising the old knight.

"It's a gambler's game, but yes. Why? Can you play? I never took you for one to play cards of any kind."

"To be a true Arakesh, you have to master the art of manipulation," he began, repeating the words of his old master. "You have to be able to manoeuvre your opponents to give you the best possible chance of eliminating your target. There are many ways Nightfall teaches this skill, but Nasta Nal-Aket always preferred Galant.

"It's a mistake to play the cards you are dealt," he continued, "but rather the players around you; people are far easier to read than the back of a card. Galant, however, is a game of risk. The cards are always moving and you have to persuade your opponents to pick up cards that will see them damage their hand. You have to create a narrative that will ensure the man opposite you takes the path you want them to—"

"Therein lies the risk," Nathaniel pointed out.

"Yes," Asher agreed. "If *they* out-manoeuvre *you*, your time in the game will quickly come to an end. All you can do is make calculated moves based on your knowledge of those around you. The more you do this, the better you get. As an assassin, you take these skills and apply them to the real world. You must always think ahead, predicting what others will do based on what *you* have done *first*."

Nathaniel was nodding along. "Why are you telling me this?"

"Back in Skystead, we caught the attention of the Bailey brothers - do you know them?"

The knight frowned. "The bounty hunters?"

Asher kept his sight on the horizon. "The same; though, from what I've heard, they're more of a *gang* these days. Whether they were tracking you, me, or the Keeper is unclear, but all three of us have *large* bounties on our heads. They followed us to Namdhor," he said, confounding the knight even more. "But they made the mistake of thinking we were in the city itself - that was *their* gamble. Mine was keeping quiet to see where things led—"

"See where things led?" Nathaniel interrupted in disbelief.

"There was nothing to gain by acknowledging them at that point," Asher replied with a shrug.

"Are you serious?" the knight asked incredulously.

"I have been chased by the world's greatest hunters. Sometimes, it's best to simply stay a step ahead than to challenge them. Trust me."

Nathaniel was shaking his head with a smile that told of both his curiosity and concern. "So where did things lead?"

"By the time the Bailey brothers realised we weren't in the city, we were already returning south with Sir Borin. But, they would have found our tracks again - a simple task given our number.

"Their next gamble was heading straight to Kelp Town."

"How do you know that?" Nathaniel enquired.

"Because we didn't face them at The King's Inn. That merchant caravan we passed on the road - they covered our tracks as we turned off. When they never appeared, I knew I had played my hand well and I was satisfied to leave it at that."

Nathaniel quickly shook his head in confusion. "What does this have to do with Vighon?"

Asher glanced at his friend with a hint of impatience. "Potentially nothing or, at least, I hadn't factored him into the game at that point. But Kelp Town is a small place. Those two men that fled? They more than likely rode to Kelp Town where news travels fast and the Bailey brothers would be all ears."

"This sounds like another gamble," Nathaniel opined.

"Almost my *last* gamble," he confessed. "And I would have acted on it and alerted you all to our pursuers had Vighon chosen to journey with us. But he didn't, and I saw an opportunity based on what I had seen in the northman.

"I'm betting the Bailey brothers have found themselves at The King's Inn by now," he added, looking over his shoulder at the western sun. "They'll be looking for us and there's only Vighon and the owner to question. My last hand is that look in his eyes. He'll either challenge them there and then or he'll come to our aid." He looked at Nathaniel with a coy grin. "Care to place your bet?"

Nathaniel narrowed his eyes, clearly undecided as to whether he should believe such a convoluted game of risk. "You said that was *almost* your last gamble."

"True enough," Asher replied, his experienced eyes scanning the tree line beyond Nathaniel. "My *last* gamble is on myself." The ranger caught the red of a man's cloak, between the trees. "A sure thing..." He grinned, spotting the drawn bow in the stranger's hands.

Nathaniel opened his mouth, struggling to ask what was likely the first of multiple questions. He never had time, however, to voice his concerns over the ranger's recklessness.

Asher pushed on the knight's chest, arching his back so far that he fell off his horse. The arrow that had been whistling towards him instead skimmed Asher's leathers and continued into the vale.

"Wands!" Kassian yelled from the rear.

Before the Keeper had retrieved his weapon of choice, Asher had already swung his leg over the saddle, removed his bow, and hit the ground with a nocked arrow. He rounded the back of his horse and released the missile with practised ease, catching the red-cloaked hunter in the neck.

Nathaniel rolled across the ground, evading two more incoming arrows, before jumping up with his own bow in hand. Asher was quickly reminded of the knight's archery skills when he let loose three arrows in quick succession, bringing down three hunters as they charged out of the tree line.

"You've gambled our lives because you saw something in Vighon's eyes!" Nathaniel growled.

By now, the Keepers in Kassian's band of vigilantes had unleashed their destructive spells upon the wood. More arrows were hurled from the hunters in response, forcing the mages to change tack and use defensive spells. Two groups wielding swords emerged at each end of their caravan, roaring in a bid to disorientate them.

It wasn't a tactic known to work on Asher.

The ranger discarded his bow and pulled his two-handed broadsword free. "I'll admit," he replied, parrying two of the hunters, "there's more of them than I thought." He swung across one of the hunters, slicing through most of the vital parts that connected his upper body to his lower body.

"Look on the bright side," Nathaniel grumbled, drawing his sword now. "At least they're not orcs."

Asher beat back the next hunter with his spiked pommel. "They're not even Darkakin!" he grinned.

With his head low, Vighon spurred his horse to continue its rapid gallop along the tree line. Thunder filled his ears but it wasn't from the sky nor his mount's beating hooves. Beside him, matching the horse's speed, Sir Borin's gargantuan frame was defying its size and running flat out.

It only made the Golem more terrifying in the northman's eyes.

It wasn't fear of Sir Borin, however, that kept Vighon riding, but the fear of his friends being set upon by the Bailey brothers. Judging by the tracks he had found, there were many of them and they had disappeared into the trees not far from the inn.

Then he heard it, a familiar sound that quickened his heart every time: steel clashing with steel. The northman navigated the base of a steep rise that cut into the forest, and rounded a cluster of rocks to find the fight he had heard.

At the back of the group, Kassian's mages were making short work of the hunters who had clearly rushed them from the woods. Their wands cast destructive spells of every colour, launching the foolish hunters in all directions. Those that slipped past the magic defences were met by swords and staffs.

Vighon directed his horse to maintain its speed, galloping further up the line, until he found Nathaniel and Asher. They were at the head of the group and battling a cluster of bounty hunters on their own, three of whom were the Bailey brothers themselves.

The northman prepared himself to leap from the saddle and join the melee, adding the sword he had taken from the dead Yarls to those who didn't possess magic. His mental preparation was for nothing, unfortunately, when an arrow sailed between the fighters and caught his horse in the side of the head.

As the horse dived head first into the muddy snow, Vighon's momentum propelled him from the saddle, promising at least one broken bone. Before he could crash into the ground in a battering of limbs, a pair of enormous arms wrapped around him and pulled him into a chest that might as well have been a solid wall.

Sir Borin hit the ground hard and rolled with all the care of a mother holding her baby. It was chaotic for a moment and not without pain, but when the Golem finally came to a stop, the northman was released from his grip without serious harm - a miraculous feat.

A thank you was on the edge of his lips until he locked eyes with Sir Borin. Seeing those dead orbs looking back at him quickly reminded Vighon that his guardian was a Golem, a creature that neither required nor warranted such thanks.

"Maybe I *will* keep you around," he remarked instead.

The sound of a man dying turned the northman back to his reason for being there. Indeed there was a man dying, quickly followed by another thanks to Asher's sweeping broadsword. The ranger never failed to impress Vighon while wielding a blade.

Not far from Asher was another considerable fighter. Nathaniel Galfrey was a model of swordsmanship and form, his discipline visible with every parry and strike of his blade. He was also outnumbered...

Vighon drew his sword and charged with both hands gripped to the hilt. He could see the impending danger behind the old Graycoat, his head seconds away from meeting the edge of a blade. The northman thrust his weapon out and blocked the hammering blow only inches from the back of Nathaniel's head.

"You took your time!" Nathaniel jested, parrying two of the brothers in quick succession.

Vighon pushed back the third and countered with a low swing. "I couldn't decide what sword I wanted!" He fell into the rhythm of combat after that, barely registering that his opponent was one of the three Bailey brothers.

Sir Borin waded in, using his hulking body to keep more than one stray arrow from bringing Vighon down. He picked up one of the hunters trying to find an angle of attack against the northman's back. Even through all the sounds that accompanied such a battle, Vighon still heard the man's skull cave in...

"Come on then!" the Bailey brother snarled, coming at the northman with a dagger now as well as his sword.

Vighon had to work twice as fast to evade and parry while searching for his own angle of attack. The dagger sliced across his forearm, almost causing him to drop his blade.

"You're out of practice," Asher commented, walking towards them as if there was no danger.

Vighon parried low then high before twisting his body to try and strike at the brother's back. The hunter's sword was already there, waiting to block the attack. The northman grunted with frustration and stole a glance at the ranger's approach.

Asher's broadsword was held casually by his side while his eyes assessed the northman's form. Vighon met his opponent in a flurry of sweeping attacks before he caught sight of a hunter emerging from behind one of the distressed horses. He opened his mouth to warn the ranger who was already ducking under a swing he couldn't possibly have seen. His broadsword came round with him and passed violently through the hunter's ribcage.

Asher came out of the melee and resumed the watchful eye of a mentor. "You're overthinking it," he stated, as if he hadn't just killed a man.

Vighon parried two more attacks and kicked a second hunter who came at him from the left. "Stop... talking." Sir Borin stormed through the gap between the northman and Nathaniel and back-handed that second hunter, cracking his neck in the process.

"Your aggression is getting in the way," Asher continued. "So too are your doubts. Stop thinking about *you* and start thinking about *him*."

Vighon roared, eager to be rid of his foe as well as the ranger's condescension. Again, Asher was set upon by the wild swing of a hunter who had no idea who he was attacking. The ranger tilted his head, avoiding the edge of the blade with minimal effort. His own sword came up, partially flicked into the air by his boot, and cut a red line from chin to brow, dropping the hunter at his feet.

Only feet away, Nathaniel knocked one of the Bailey brothers to the ground and pushed the other one back with an elven style of swordplay. By comparison, Vighon felt as if he were moving through sludge. His attacks were clumsy, relying on strength more than form. Asher's scrutinising eyes didn't help matters.

"Stay back!" he commanded the Golem, who appeared eager to intervene.

As he fell into a circling pattern with the brother, Vighon started to actually think about his actions. He envisioned his attack, followed by his enemy's counter, and then his own devastating reprisal that would end the fight.

A flash of red light tried to blind the northman, but he managed to maintain enough of his vision to capture the gory details of his opponent's death. The spell impacted the side of the brother's head and obliterated half of his skull and everything inside of it, knocking his remaining eye out of alignment.

Kassian Kantaris lowered his wand with a disapproving scowl on his face. "What is wrong with you?" His venomous question was directed at Asher. "We haven't gone through all this so the king of bloody Illian can die in his first fight!"

His chest heaving, Vighon looked over his shoulder to see the surviving brothers gawp at their sibling's death. They backed off from Nathaniel despite the burning hatred that lived in their eyes. Between the skittish horses and chaos of battle, they slipped away and vanished back into the forest, leaving their gang to the superior fighting skills of the Keepers and their magic.

Soon after, the sound of discharging spells dispersed and the clash of swords stopped altogether. The Keepers worked to get the horses under control while Vighon did the same with his breath. He looked down at the dead Bailey brother, disappointed with himself.

"Who in all the hells were they?" Kassian asked to anyone who could answer.

"The Bailey brothers," Vighon answered. "Bounty hunters."

"How did they track us out here?" Kassian used his boot to roll one of the bodies over. "We're in the middle of nowhere."

"They mentioned something about Skystead. I think they've been tracking you for some time."

"It doesn't pay to have so many wanted faces in the same place," Asher observed. "Though it doesn't help that you move with such numbers," he added, gesturing to the numerous Keepers.

Kassian, easily offended, replied, "It's our numbers that just stopped us from being overwhelmed. You're welcome."

"Did you lose anyone?" Nathaniel interjected before Kassian became irate.

"Of course not. We're mage knights, not herbalists. A ragtag group of bounty hunters is no match for our magic." Turning on the northman with some of his temper, the Keeper asked, "What are you doing here anyway? I thought you were seeking the bottom of every tankard from here to The Arid Lands."

Vighon stood up straight and sheathed his sword. "I came because..." The northman looked briefly from the Keeper to Asher and Nathaniel. "Because I thought I could help."

"And you did," Nathaniel replied with a sideways glance at the ranger. "You saved my life."

"At nearly the cost of his own," Asher pointed out. "The Rebellion doesn't need a figure head to lead it, it needs a warrior. You need to remember your way around a sword and quickly."

Nathaniel subtly flexed his fingers in Asher's direction. "There will be time to reacquaint yourself with the ways of battle." He looked the northman in the eyes. "Are you with us, Vighon?"

Seeing the body at his feet, Vighon wasn't sure what he could offer, but saving Nathaniel's life was an intoxicating feeling. It filled him with the need to do more.

"I will return with you," he said. "I can promise you no more than that."

Again, the old Graycoat used his eyes to hold a private conversation with Asher, before looking back at Vighon. "I will take that promise," he replied with an affectionate smile. "Come then. Pick a horse."

Vighon climbed onto the saddle of a stray horse, its rider likely killed by one of the mages. He didn't know what fate awaited him taking this path, but he was content to know that it was his choice.

Perhaps that was all he had left...

## CHAPTER 27
# HOLLOWED OUT

For two days, the dusty red cliffs of The Narrows had robbed Queen Adilandra of any horizon. The towering ravine weaved like a snaking river along Illian's western coast, challenging any foolish travellers to find The Hox.

Only the dwarves had been able to lead the way, their uncanny ability to read the rock invaluable in such terrain. Upon enquiring about such skill, they had merely replied, "The rock talks to us, me Lady..."

Adilandra was quite sure this wasn't the case, but the queen had no intention of insulting the children of the mountain while they were leading her people through a maze.

Doran had informed her that they had already turned back on themselves, heading north for the cut in The Narrows that led to the coast. Over the course of the last day, the heat had abated, reminding them that winter was quickly approaching all but The Arid Lands.

It was certainly a reprieve for the elves, who preferred a cooler climate, though Adilandra was most grateful for the state of dress the dwarves resumed, returning their shirts to their broad backs. Faylen had threatened to abandon her duties and find her own way to Qamnaran if she had to look upon Doran's hairy chest, glistening with sweat, one more time.

As night settled over The Narrows, the gorge was filled with a camp the likes of which hadn't been seen for five thousand years - elf and dwarf united under one cause. Fires were dotted from cliff to cliff between their makeshift tents where both cultures came together.

It brought a brief yet genuine smile to Adilandra's face, seen only in the flickering flames that danced across her fair face. Continuing her stroll, the queen noted Doran outside his tent as she weaved between the tents. She made for the War Mason, soaking up the unique atmosphere found only when these two peoples came together. There was no end to their differences, but they shared food, water, and more than a few laughs.

"It doesn' seem like a lot, does it?" Doran Heavybelly asked, soaking his hands in a bowl of water. "But this is what we're fightin' for," he continued, nodding at the nearest group of elves and dwarves seated around a fire. "I don' know what this world's goin' to look like when this war is over, but I pray to the Mother an' Father that it looks somethin' like this..."

Adilandra cast her eyes over her people, noting their gentle laughter in light of a dwarf's story. "A realm for us all," she replied wistfully, believing it to be no more than a dream of the foolish.

"I never thanked ye," Doran said, changing the subject.

Somewhat startled, Adilandra looked down at the dwarf. "Thanked me?"

"Ye've come a long way an' lost a lot to help me save me kin. I know that can' be easy when yer own are out there, sufferin'." The War Mason dried his hands on a cloth and stepped out from under the awning of his tent. "Ye an' I haven' really known each other for a long time, but I've known yer family for decades. I jus' wanted ye to know, me Lady, they're like family to me. If there was a path to victory that spared Alijah, I would surely take it."

Adilandra took a moment to absorb all that there was about

Doran Heavybelly, appreciating the dwarf for more than the sum of his parts. He was, indeed, unlike any dwarf the queen had ever met.

"I can see why my family speak so highly of you, Master Dwarf. I dare say I can see why they love you. I believe it is I who should be thanking you."

Doran raised the bushy eyebrow above his only eye. "How so, me Lady?"

"You have been there for them, so many times, when I could not. The house of Sevari will forever be indebted to you, Doran, son of Dorain."

The War Mason shied away and tried to shrug off her compliment. "I've done what any other would, me Lady - there's few who would deny yer daughter."

Adilandra placed a gentle hand on Doran's shoulder, mesmerising the dwarf by the look of him. "Never compare yourself to another, son of Dorain - there are *none* who could match your stature." The dwarf averted his gaze for a moment. "I would retire for the night," the queen added. Without waiting for a reply, she walked away, leaving the War Mason with a glassy eye.

As per Faylen's commands, two elves stood guard outside Adilandra's modest dwelling. Seeking privacy, the queen dismissed them both, instructing them to seek either companionship amongst the dwarves or rest for the day to come.

Alone at last, Adilandra positioned herself in the centre of her tent, legs crossed. Her hand hesitated over the pouch on the right of her belt. Inside was the crystal, only partially filled with magic. Looking to the pouch on her left, the queen pondered on the diviner housed within. She had possessed that particular diviner since one of the Mer-folk had delivered it into her hands, sent by Alijah.

The crystal demanded her attention, but Doran's words lingered in her mind, swirling into a storm that surrounded one question: could she kill her grandson? She needed to speak to him...

Removing the diviner, Adilandra cupped it in one palm resting on top of the other. Her eyes closed, the queen waited for the familiar pull in her mind as the diviner invited her consciousness to be absorbed within. Giving in to the feeling, Adilandra opened her eyes to the shadow realm, a place that existed between worlds.

Then she waited.

There was no way of knowing what Alijah was doing, but if he had the matching diviner on his person, it would be emitting a hum, set to a pitch that made it very hard to ignore, especially for one with the ears of an elf.

The shadows before her eventually gave way to white fog that began to rise and take shape. Within seconds, that fog bore the ethereal image of her grandson.

"Hello, Grandmother," he greeted with all civility.

Mirroring him in tone and formality, she replied, "Hello, Grandson."

Alijah gave a jagged grin, distorting some of the fog that formed his face. "I'm impressed," he confessed. "There were so few who survived among your fleet."

"I have been surviving for a long time," Adilandra said coolly.

"That you have. And I am glad of it. It saddened me to think you had perished so needlessly. As the queen of your people we will need to work together very closely if we are to build a better future."

"You are referring to a future in which I, and all my kind, bow to you as the king of Verda?"

Alijah tilted his head, eyeing her with curiosity. "Do I detect a hint of hostility there? Would it be so bad to have every country and race under one banner?" The half-elf waved his own question away. "You know what motivates me. Why are we speaking?"

Adilandra required a moment to compose herself, ensuring her ability to speak without her emotions causing her to quaver. "To see if there is anything left of my grandson to be saved."

Alijah narrowed his eyes. "Do you mean to kill me, Grandmother?"

"I have not decided," she answered honestly. "Though I would not hesitate to kill that beast of yours."

Alijah took a deep breath, puffing out his chest of dragon scales. "Malliath wants nothing but peace, a world where he can finally rest. He has witnessed eons of bloodshed and war and has paid for his assistance dearly. It is his steadfast resolve that keeps me on the path I was fated to take."

Adilandra recalled what Inara had told her of the last conversation held between the twins. "This fate you speak of - you told your sister you were going to *break the scales*. What did you mean by that?"

"Does that concern you?"

"You hold immense power at your fingertips, Alijah; the thought of you breaking anything concerns me."

"You couldn't fathom my plans, nor could Inara. You cannot see the past, present, and future as I can. Only through Malliath's eyes can one truly understand the nature of the world."

"You are a child to my eyes," Adilandra retorted. "Do not insult me."

Alijah leaned forward. "I have lived every day of Malliath's life. I have felt the passage of time as a fallen leaf sails on the wind."

"Feeling it and living it are two different things," Adilandra instructed.

A crack began to appear across Alijah's perfect composure. "The scales that have forever governed our realm - they are tipped one way. As things stand, however, there can never be balance no matter what we do. So the scales must be *broken* and a new order pressed upon the land, one that will ensure everlasting peace."

"That is hardly an explanation."

"Your failure to grasp the truth of things is *your* problem. I am not so foolish as to reveal my plans before they can be enacted - the realm is relying on me."

"The realm wants you dead," the queen corrected.

"That is a skewed point of view, typical of someone who sympathises with The Rebellion. Under my reign, the laws of Illian are actually being adhered to. Peace is finally starting to become more than just an idea."

"Open your eyes, Alijah - the only skewed point of view is your own. You're seeing the world through Malliath's eyes! Every thought you have is stained by his own!"

"You are the one who speaks without thought! You know nothing of me and you know nothing of Malliath!"

Adilandra held back her barbed retort and, instead, took a calming breath. "Please, Alijah, I beg of you: show me something of the boy I love. I want to save you."

The king of Illian shook his head. "I was saved the moment I locked eyes with Malliath. I beg of *you*, Grandmother: walk away from The Rebellion, leave me to my work, and let *me* save *you*."

Any hope Adilandra might have been harbouring was steadily fading - Alijah belonged to Malliath now. "I cannot walk away while my grandson uses dark magic to shape the world my ancestors bled to uphold. Whatever you're doing on Qamnaran, whatever you're doing in The Moonlit Plains, they come from a place of darkness you have let take a hold of you. Even if you are my kin, I cannot let your *work* continue."

Alijah's confident demeanour returned as he found control over his emotions. "While my heart beats, I will never stop. I hope this informs you on the decision you need to make. But know this: should you come for me, Queen Adilandra, I will not hesitate to kill you; I am the king before all else, including your family."

Adilandra could feel tears welling behind her eyes in the real world. "Then you know nothing of being a king," she said. "To rule, one must have love in your heart before all else. It seems Malliath has hollowed you out of such a thing."

Alijah's mouth moved to speak but the half-elf paused, his ethereal eyes shifting towards the shadows that surrounded them. Then the queen felt it, a third presence in the dark. From behind her grandson, a new shape began to form out of the mist, only it was much larger than him and also more... *real*.

Malliath's head hung over the king and looked down on Adilandra with blazing purple eyes. She had never known a dragon able to pierce the shadow realm while their companion used a diviner. A low rumble resonated from the dragon's throat and his fangs clenched together between curled lips.

A quiet rage emanated from Malliath, reminding her that emotional control was a dragon's primary form of communication with those who weren't bonded to them. His feelings were crossing the shadow realm and directly affecting Adilandra, filling her with the hatred and wrath that lived within him. In that moment, she wanted to lash out at everything and scorch the earth with her magic.

"I love the realm." Alijah's words felt distant, too weak to penetrate the fog of rage that clouded Adilandra's mind. "I love the realm more than anything." The queen's attention was fixed on those purple eyes. "To attack me is to attack the realm. Bear that in mind the next time you believe yourself to be the hero." Alijah smiled knowingly. "I'll see you soon, I'm sure..."

The king severed the connection, propelling both of them back into the real world. The queen felt her every muscle tense beneath her sweating skin. Malliath's anger rested on her heart, which now hammered against her chest.

"Adilandra?" The voice was just over her shoulder, too close given the heightened instincts Malliath had instilled in her.

The queen snapped and twisted her body like a snake, coiling around its prey. The yelp of her prey was barely audible beneath Adilandra's heavy breath and heaving chest. Her forearm pinned the insignificant creature down by the throat, allowing the queen satisfaction in watching the life fade from its eyes.

Then the fog began to clear.

The small voice pleading for help became familiar. Adilandra's heart rate started to slow down as the pressure she applied began to let up. The queen sagged, letting her muscles go limp as she realised Faylen was beneath her, desperate for breath.

"Faylen!" she panted.

The High Guardian gripped her own throat and held up a hand to keep Adilandra at bay.

"Forgive me," the queen begged. "I don't... I don't know what happened."

Faylen coughed several times and rubbed her throat. Her eyes darted from Adilandra to the diviner on the ground and back.

"You spoke... to him?" It clearly pained Faylen to speak.

Adilandra tentatively moved closer to her oldest friend and placed a hand on her leg. "I am so sorry, Faylen. I didn't have control. I wanted to... I needed to speak to him. I needed to see if there was anything left of him worth saving. Somehow, Malliath was there, in the shadow realm. I could feel his *monstrous* rage. I couldn't resist it. His mind is a well of hatred that knows no end."

Faylen visibly swallowed and stretched her neck. "What of... Alijah?" she managed.

Adilandra considered her grandson's words as well as his tone and demeanour. "I have lost all hope. He is bonded to rage itself." A thought occurred to the queen then and she recalled Alijah's last words. "I have doomed us all," she whispered. "I think he knows we are coming."

Faylen abandoned her throat and embraced Adilandra. They remained this way for some time, contemplating the inevitable conflict. It was going to end with death...

# CHAPTER 28

# WHY WE FIGHT

It didn't matter how many days had gone by since they left Dragons' Reach, Inara's mind was cast to the west, where she could only imagine the worst of things happening to Gideon Thorn. Athis had tried many times on their return journey to remind her of the wisdom Gideon and Ilargo possessed, but her concerns did nothing but grow. After all, Gideon's ability to wield magic had been diminished since he destroyed The Veil.

Eight years...

How could he have been in Erador for eight years and Alijah not know of it? How could Gideon not know of Alijah's plans? Unless something terrible had happened to him, he would be in Illian right now.

Again, Athis tried to share his soothing emotions with her, offering a degree of comfort she had persistently declined. She wanted to worry. It motivated her, gave her purpose. She would need such things if she was truly going to leave Illian and The Rebellion to fly to Erador.

*Take heart, wingless one - we are home...*

Inara looked up for the first time in hours. There before them were the welcoming white cliffs of The Shining Coast. Athis caught the currents and glided high over the tops of those cliffs, revealing a land of rolling green fields, dotted with patches of yellow.

A mix of emotions plagued the half-elf upon their return. They were supposed to be in the company of the entire Dragorn order, a congregation of dragons powerful enough to turn the tide. Instead, they returned alone with nothing but bad news.

Looking around them, Inara was disorientated by the landscape, unsure of where they were entering Illian. Her silent question was answered in less than a second by her bond to Athis. The dragon imparted his knowledge as if it were her own and she knew they were just north of Darkwell. Looking left of Athis's horns, she could make out the snowy peaks of The Vrost Mountains. There was half a day at most before they reached The Black Wood.

*What do we do if my father hasn't found Vighon?* she asked with a touch of despair.

*If Rainael believes Ilargo to be alive, we are obligated by more than just duty to discover the truth. Gideon and Ilargo would make a great difference to The Rebellion's cause. We must go to Erador, and soon...*

*Rainael gave you her knowledge of Erador's terrain,* Inara replied. *Besides the fact that such knowledge is ancient and everything could be different, how do we find them in a land equal in size to Illian?*

*Hopefully, I will be close enough to Ilargo that our minds can connect.*

Inara's face dropped. *So we just have to fly around and hope they're close by? That could take weeks, months, perhaps even years. There has to be a better way. If they have been in Erador for eight years, there must be some trace of them, something we can use to track them down.*

*I am an excellent hunter,* Athis spoke as a matter of fact, *but the traces of what you refer to are likely to be in places I cannot go.*

Inara thought of Valgala, Erador's capital from which Alijah had reigned. *You mean the cities.*

*Yes. If Gideon was truly investigating Alijah, he would have ventured into civilisation in search of answers.*

Inara began to question her own tracking skills. ***I agree that finding Gideon and Ilargo would not only soothe our concerns but also aid The Rebellion - but how long can we leave them to fight alone? We are needed here. Even now, our friends and family prepare to attack the tower at Qamnaran.***

*I have no answer to that. For all the innate wisdom my kind are renowned for, some things cannot be known. Only we will know when to return, wingless one. Trust in us, as others do.*

***Hope. Trust. Blind faith. These are ideals that Dragorn are supposed to instil in others. Given that I no longer hold such a title, I'm not sure how I possess them myself let alone continue to inspire others.***

*We have made a new role for ourselves, a role that is new even to Illian. We are the Guardians of the Realm - that means something now. We cannot tell the people what to take from our presence, be that hope or trust. Their lives will be affected by our actions alone, as they always have been.*

Inara closed her eyes, enjoying the harmony that existed between their two minds. *Guardians of the Realm,* she repeated. *To want for nothing. To give everything...*

They flew north, casting their mighty shadow over the land. Whatever was to come, Inara swelled with confidence that they would face it together, for what could stand against them when they stood together?

The remainder of their flight took a little longer than expected - the northern winds blowing south off The Vengoran Mountains were a force to be reckoned with.

They eventually soared over the town of Dunwich and on to The

Black Wood beyond. Athis flew low, revealing his incredible speed as the tops of the trees whipped past below in a blur of green.

Coming across The Rebellion's camp in the heart of the forest, the dragon climbed again and circled round, bringing his speed down until he was able to hover over the space that had always been allocated to his bulk. Those below were battered by his beating wings, but none moved from the awesome sight of watching Athis descend among them.

Jumping down, Inara could sense the exhaustion that weighed on Athis. The muscles around the joints of his wings ached and his claws felt heavy. She patted him on the side and walked up to stroke under his jaw.

***Rest a while before you hunt.***

*You will hear no argument from me...*

Inara left her companion and made her way further into the camp, where King Dakmund's tent stood above all others. With every step she could feel the discomfort of her trepidation. She had faith in her father to find Asher, and the ranger had proven time and again that he could find anything, man or beast. Still, the Guardian couldn't help but fear the worst. If they were yet to return, she would give them the night. After that, Athis would fly them to Erador, alone.

Along the way, she tried to take her mind off what she might or might not find at the end of her walk. There were still dwarves, mostly families, in the camp. Inara greeted as many as she could, offering reassuring smiles and nods of the head.

The sound of children laughing was heartwarming and it brought a smile to Inara's face when they came running out in front of her, halting her stride. Watching them run off between the tents, she was reminded of her own youth and days spent running around with Alijah.

Then, for the very first time in her life, Inara Galfrey thought about children. As a young girl, she had likely dreamt of having a family one day, much like her own, and raising children in the same manner as her parents. Such thoughts had faded since bonding with Athis, making her indifferent to the idea.

The Guardian sighed. She still had so many new emotions and thoughts to deal with as her human side emerged all the more. Life had certainly been simpler under Athis's guiding influence...

Leaving the dwarven children to play, Inara returned her attention to the path. She was stopped again by the figure standing in her way.

Vighon...

Inara was instantly elated and disappointed at the same time. The northman stood before her, a shadow of his former self. His clothes were filthy and the fur-lined cloak that hung over his shoulders was tattered and caked with mud. A neglected beard concealed the lower half of his face and a fine layer of dirt did its best to conceal the top half. A mane of dark hair reached out in every direction with matted clumps throughout.

"They found you," she said, in place of saying all the things she really wanted to tell him.

Vighon gave a subtle nod of the head. "We weren't expecting you so soon. You look good," he croaked before clearing his throat.

"I cannot say the same," Inara replied honestly.

Vighon looked immediately self-conscious of his appearance and shrugged his cloak back off his shoulders. "We haven't long arrived ourselves. I haven't had a chance to..." He ran a hand through his beard and looked somewhere between surprised and disgusted with what he discovered.

"A timely reunion then," Inara concluded. This had not been the conversation she had been rehearsing in her head for the last year.

"I've had a few of those recently," the northman quipped, gesturing to a hulking form standing outside King Dakmund's tent.

"That can't be who I think it is."

"Unfortunately it is," Vighon said, gaining some confidence by his tone. "And I can't get rid of him..."

Inara was sharp enough to put the picture together, and privately applauded Asher's tracking tactics. "Can he be trusted?"

"As long as no one threatens me," Vighon shrugged, "he'll just stand there."

Without blinking, Inara looked from Sir Borin to the northman. "I may test that."

Vighon was left clearly uncomfortable at the remark. "I would deserve—"

"Where are the others?" she interrupted.

Vighon thumbed over his shoulder, directing her to the king's tent. "I just came out for some fresh water," he lied, having most likely heard Athis's descent. He also lacked any water, be it in a cup or a jug.

"I have news that cannot wait." Inara strode past the north-man, eager to get out of the conversation - if it could be called that.

He quickly fell in behind her where, thankfully, his odour could not be caught. Sir Borin's particular stench, however, could not be avoided. He looked down at the Guardian from within his leather hood, laying cold eyes on her. Ignoring the brute, Inara nodded at the new shield guards appointed to protect the king of Grimwhal and entered the tent.

To her left, as always, lay King Dakmund. He lay deathly still within the glimmering cocoon of elven magic. Kneeling dutifully by his side was the queen-mother, Drelda. The king's sickly condition diminished her every day.

A new, and unexpected, sight was the Drake next to her. Adan'Karth's hands had pierced the glittering bubble to touch Dakmund's injured leg. Healing magic was among the hardest - comparable, almost, to portal magic - but if anyone could perform the miracle of saving the king's life, it would be a Drake.

"Inara!" Nathaniel approached from the other side of the tent, where a group surrounded a table of maps and reports.

"Father," she replied with a tight smile. They embraced briefly before each pushed away, giving the Guardian a better view of those behind him.

Asher was seated casually on a stack of crates in the corner, his green cloak draped over his shoulders. Between his legs, he twisted his silvyr short-sword on its pointed end. His blue eyes found her own, though he was an impossible person to read.

Leaning on the table, Kassian Kantaris turned his head of shaggy blond hair towards her. Comparing him to a dishevelled Vighon, he was a handsome rogue now. Inara recognised a few of his mages clustered around him, though their names escaped her.

As one, they looked expectantly to the tent's opening, past Vighon.

Nathaniel hesitated. "You are alone?"

Inara swallowed and nodded gravely. "I am alone." The Guardian approached the table, bringing her father and Vighon with her. "I have been to Dragons' Reach." She took a breath, looking from one to the other before settling on the map instead. "We have already seen the last days of the Dragorn - they are no more."

There was more than one frown amongst the gathered. "No more?" Nathaniel echoed. "I don't understand."

"Their time among the older dragons has shown them a different life," Inara tried to explain. "They have walked away from the affairs of the realm. Athis and I have been forbidden from returning."

Kassian's head dropped. "There goes any real chance of victory," he groaned with an air of exhaustion.

Nathaniel waved the remark away. "What about Gideon?" he asked with some aggression. "I refuse to believe that he has abandoned his duty."

Inara took another breath. "Gideon left Dragons' Reach eight years ago. He feared what was truly becoming of Alijah in the west."

Nathaniel's brow pinched in confusion. "He... Where is he then?"

Asher stopped twisting his short-sword. "He went to Erador," the ranger concluded.

Inara nodded. "I don't know what has become of him," she said, fighting to maintain her tone of control. "Ilargo's mother, Rainael, believes he is still alive and Gideon with him."

"She believes or she knows?" Kassian pressed.

"Dragon's intuition," Inara replied. "It's as good as we're going to get... *unless* we discover the truth for ourselves."

Nathaniel tilted his head. "You're talking about going to Erador. Now?"

"I cannot fight Malliath *and* the Dragon Riders," Inara asserted. "Without the Dragorn I will fall to them and what follows will be the end of The Rebellion."

"I thought you hero-types were above arrogance?" Kassian jibed.

"She's *right*," Vighon snapped, coming to her defence. "How many times have we claimed victory or survived a defeat because of Inara and Athis?"

"*Is* there a *we*, northman?" Kassian retorted, his words barbed.

"I'm here aren't I?" Vighon growled.

Nathaniel waved their argument away, focusing his attention on his daughter. "You want to find Gideon and Ilargo?"

"I don't see how we can win this without them. I'm not even sure we can win this with them," she added with despair. "Having two dragons on our side is better than one though. Especially when our enemy has *five*..."

"Alright," Kassian said, holding his arms up as a sign of truce. "I only know what I've read about Gideon Thorn, but I agree that he would be just as valuable as you are in this fight. If you go to, Erador, however, The Rebellion will be without any dragon for even *longer*. A large bulk of our force is about to attack Qamnaran. Now is the time for some dragon fire, not a hopeless quest in some far away land."

"The last I recall," Vighon began, "you didn't much care what The Rebellion did. At least that's what you told me before taking your Keepers and leaving."

Kassian gave the northman a pointed look. "I'm here aren't I?"

Inara spoke again before Vighon could continue their petty argument. "I have to assume that Gideon and Ilargo are in trouble - why else would they not be here? Neither Athis nor I will allow such a condition to continue. We *are* going to Erador," she said, looking at Asher, "and I do not wish to go alone." Inara's last words came to her in the moment, a product, she decided, of her shared wisdom with Athis.

Nathaniel looked from one to the other. "You want Asher to accompany you?"

"I'd say he's proven himself an excellent tracker," Inara observed.

"As it turns out," Kassian chipped in unhelpfully, "*Sir Borin* is an excellent tracker. Maybe you should take him instead."

"Kassian..." Nathaniel turned an exasperated look on the Keeper.

Inara directed her words to Asher himself. "I do not wish to rob The Rebellion of another fighter, but Erador is a big place and I could use another hunter beside me. The quicker we find them, the quicker we return. The choice is—"

"I'm in," Asher announced in his casual manner. The ranger shared a knowing glance with Nathaniel, who mysteriously nodded in return.

"Well I'm out," Kassian declared. "This is exactly the sort of ridiculous nonsense that gave me cause to leave the first time. You don't know where the fight is. You think you're making the brave decision, the bold choice that will win the larger war. You're *not*. You don't get to win the war if you can't fight the battles - it's that simple."

"You don't even know what this war really is," Vighon fumed. "It's just vengeance for you."

"At least the realm will benefit from my vengeance," Kassian spat. "How much will they really gain from your return to the throne? I'm starting to wonder why bringing you back was such—"

"Enough!" Nathaniel scolded. "Kassian, you claim to have found a new reason to fight, one that not only brings you in line with The Rebellion but also Vighon as our king. If that is truly so, then for Clara's sake start acting like it. Vighon, Kassian and his Keepers have walked away and saved more lives than The Rebellion has - they are powerful allies that, despite the patience required, are to be respected."

Inara contained her smile, though it felt good to see something of her father's *iron* return. He was as much an ambassador as he was a warrior after decades of walking side by side with Reyna. His voice carried as much authority now as his words, evident by the silence that followed, rather than the bickering.

"War is never simple," the old knight continued. "Battles must be fought on many fronts: such has been our downfall in months of late. Inara is right; without the Dragorn, we must look to Gideon alone for aid. But there are other battles to be fought, battles right here." Nathaniel looked across the table at Vighon. "First we need a king to lead us..."

All eyes fell on the northman.

"I..." Vighon held his gaze on the map. "I fail to see how I can do that."

Nathaniel leaned in to the table. "You and you alone can rally your soldiers, the realm itself."

"Do you know how many of my soldiers have even seen my face up close? To most I am just a man."

"And a scruffy one at that," Kassian added quietly.

"You have but to speak and they will *know* it is you," Nathaniel continued in earnest.

"No, Vighon's right," Inara said. "There isn't time for words. They need to see him and know the real Vighon Draqaro stands before them - and *with* them."

The northman took a tentative step back from the table. "Perhaps, for now, it would be better if I helped coordinate from here. Or I could go to towns and cities and rally in secret?"

"We didn't dig you up to do anything in *secret*." Kassian was already holding up his hands to let everyone know he wasn't attacking Vighon. "You're the *king*," he continued in a serious tone. "Kings are supposed to be seen."

"His sword," Asher voiced from the corner, turning every head. "The one with the flames - it has a name I think…"

"The sword of the north," Inara stated, watching Vighon's demeanour fall all the more.

"I lost it fighting Alijah," he recalled. "The last I saw of it, the blade fell into the courtyard of The Dragon Keep."

"Then it's likely still there," Nathaniel reasoned, a glint in his eyes that Inara recognised all too easily.

"What you're thinking," she quickly replied, "carries more peril than going to Erador, Father."

Catching on, Kassian gave a short, manic laugh. "You want to break into The Dragon Keep? Maybe you *do* belong among my Keepers."

"You said it yourself," Nathaniel argued. "A king needs to be seen. The people need to know that Vighon Draqaro stands before them. That sword is your banner," he added, talking directly to Vighon, who was shaking his head.

"I've been here less than a day and the first thing you suggest will see us all to our deaths. You want me to go to Namdhor and reclaim my sword. Any who follow me there will *die* and any who rally to me there will *die*. I can't… I can't do that again."

"Then why are you here?" Kassian challenged.

Nathaniel raised his hand to silence the Keeper. "Vighon. This is how we win. And this might be our only opportunity. We were in Namdhor a few days ago and we all witnessed Alijah and Malliath flying south, likely to Qamnaran. We must act now."

Vighon clenched his jaw and stole a glance at Inara before turning his resolve on Nathaniel. "No." With that, he turned and left the tent.

Inara shared in the collective despair that filled the royal tent. They had all pinned their hopes on the northman, but he appeared a shadow of his former self.

"Now what?" Kassian asked. "What's the next great plan Inara Galfrey has for us?"

Inara would have shot daggers at the Keeper, but her mind was too busy trying to think of a way to fix this - Vighon *was* the realm's only hope. "Start thinking of a way to infiltrate The Dragon Keep," she told them. "This isn't over."

"Where are you going?" her father called as she turned to leave.

"To find the king of Illian," she replied simply. "We leave in the morning," she added for Asher's benefit.

Emerging into twilight, Inara searched what she could see of the camp for any sign of Vighon. After receiving directions from a dwarf washing clothes in a bucket, the Guardian made her way to the western edge of the camp, where Vighon's tent had always been. She just caught sight of the northman as he disappeared beyond the flaps of the entrance.

Her confident stride faltered under hesitation outside his tent. Before entering, Inara closed her eyes and distanced herself from Athis, who was currently sleeping. She continued in this vein until the dragon was no more than a speck in her mind, his thoughts and voice as indiscernible as hers were to him now. For the first time in a while, she was alone inside her mind.

Inara took a breath and, without permission, entered Vighon's dwelling. The northman turned immediately to see her, his contracted brow easing at the sight of her.

"I thought you would be in the woods, *sulking*." Inara knew she should have taken a gentler approach, but her feelings demanded their day.

Vighon feigned a smile. "Everything is just as I left it," he observed, taking in his tent.

"There were many who held hope that you would return," she replied, her tone blunt.

"Were you among them?" he asked.

Inara allowed some of her irritation to settle. "I still am," she answered honestly.

Vighon removed his cloak and left it in a pile on the ground, exhausted by the look of him. "Do you know *why* I walked away?"

"Of course, I read your note," she replied sarcastically. "Or did you tell me why? Oh, that's right, you did neither. You just left."

"You're angry," Vighon reasoned. "I understand—"

"You understand *nothing*," Inara interrupted. "You took the easy path and convinced yourself it was the right thing, that it would save lives. You were wrong, Vighon Draqaro. We needed you. *I* needed you."

The northman wouldn't hear it. "You know what I did was—"

"Infuriating?" Inara finished. "Selfish? You didn't just walk away from me. You walked away from your *duty*. Your *people*. Kings don't get to do that."

With tears in his eyes, Vighon argued, "I was throwing lives away, Inara! I was calling on every man and woman who could lift a sword to fight beside me and die for me. And they did, by the score! I watched them fall to steel and fire on every battlefield."

Inara's shoulders sagged, her anger struggling to hold up against Vighon's despondency. "You fool," she uttered. "That crown has closed your eyes. Do you really not know? Those men and women you called upon, the ones who fought and died beside you - they weren't there for *you*. They weren't even there for the realm. They were fighting for their *families*. They still are. They died fighting for their loved ones, so that they might live in a world under your reign. Their lives have always been their own, and each and every one of them wanted to fight for what they held in their heart. You were their king, not their god. They were *never* your lives to throw away..."

Tears ran silently down Vighon's face now, but he maintained his solid composure as he slumped down to the ground beside his cot.

Inara could feel twelve months of disappointment and infuriation melting away. She joined him on the ground, shoulder to shoulder. "I know why you did it," she said softly. "In truth, were I in your place... I might have done the same."

"No you wouldn't," Vighon was quick to reply. "You've always been the strongest person I know. It's *one* of the reasons why I would have had you beside me, on the throne..."

A lump formed from nowhere in Inara's throat and her stomach tried to rise to meet it. How long had it been since they had had this conversation, standing in the freezing cold at the very apex of Namdhor's rise? Vighon hadn't been a king at the time and Inara had known nothing of the cave inside her sanctuary. For years they had both ploughed through their lives, side by side yet still apart.

"I know," Vighon continued before she could say anything. "I remember your every word. We can never be. I just wanted you to know... I still—"

"Love you," Inara beat him to it, her gaze turning his eyes to hers. She wasn't sure if she had finished his sentence for him or declared it herself. But seeing his dark eyes now, the Guardian could see something of the man she had always loved, the man who had stood up for what was right and just. There was a king behind those eyes.

"Neither of us are what we once were," she said, referring to the many changes they had both undergone since that distant night, overlooking The King's Lake. "But you cannot fight your fate. You *are* the king."

Vighon stared at her, perhaps wondering, as she was, whether a declaration had been made. "I don't believe in fate," he said.

Inara stood up then. "That's a shame, because Fate believes in you, Vighon Draqaro..."

The feelings that rushed to the surface were new yet old, familiar from a time she had almost forgotten, a time when Vighon had been her whole world.

"Think on what I have said," she advised. "Stop fighting for the realm and the people - no one can fight for all that. Fight for what's in your heart, as every man and woman in The Rebellion does. Only then will you find your strength, *northman.*"

Inara turned from him and made to leave. She paused with one hand opening the flap. "And Vighon, if your face wasn't a knot of hair and your odour not so foul, I *might* have kissed you..."

# CHAPTER 29

# TAKING FLIGHT

Asher's eyes flickered open for the briefest moment before a sixth sense told him he wasn't alone in his tent. All instinct, the ranger's arm shot up with his curved dagger, already in hand. It came to rest under Adan'Karth's throat.

The Drake, crouched far too close, stared back at him as if there wasn't a blade touching his skin. "I'm going with you," he declared.

Asher sighed and lowered his dagger. "What have I told you about sneaking up on me?" he groaned, swinging his legs off the side of the cot. Adan was the only person known to the ranger who could sneak up on him whether he was awake or asleep.

"I'm going with you - to Erador," the Drake clarified.

Asher cracked his neck and sheathed his dagger on the back of his belt. "The hell you are," he replied gruffly. The ranger winced at the glare of light that found a gap in the tent's entrance. "At least you waited until dawn this time..."

"You were most displeased when I last woke you in the middle of the night," Adan'Karth commented quietly with a subtle shrug of his toned shoulders.

"Some of us need to sleep," Asher pointed out, and not for the first time.

The ranger rose from his cot and began dressing himself in his leathers and weapons. Donning his weapons had become something of a soothing ritual that made him feel prepared for the day.

"You cannot ignore me, Asher. I *am* coming with you to Erador."

Asher stroked his face of stubble as he searched the tent for his green cloak. "I have no idea what awaits us in Erador, but I'd bet my life there's going to be some violence."

"There usually is," the Drake quipped, holding out the ranger's cloak.

"Then why would you come?" he enquired with irritation. "You'll either get yourself killed or get me killed protecting you."

"I *know* why you are going," Adan said, surprising Asher. "I overheard your conversation with Nathaniel Galfrey."

Asher cocked an eyebrow. "That's called eavesdropping, and it's *rude.*"

Adan repeated the word silently to himself as if he were tasting it in his mouth. "An unusual word," he remarked offhandedly. "And I cannot help it. I have sensitive ears, both of which have become highly attuned to your voice."

Asher continued to busy himself, checking the contents of his belt. He had a small pouch with coins that he considered leaving behind, given that Erador more than likely had its own currency.

"You're running away from the hunt," Adan'Karth continued, oblivious to the ranger's mounting irritation. "I am glad you have chosen this path, for I too believe you would have found your end at the hands of an Arakesh. Furthermore, I believe you would have died with hatred in your heart, your last days spent as an assassin yourself."

Asher didn't particularly wish to speak on the topic. "I'm glad you approve," he said, his tone out of step with his response. "Why are you insisting on accompanying me then?"

"Because we both know you cannot outrun Nightfall forever.

Your fate has been entwined with theirs since you were a child. You will always seek their destruction and you know of only one way to achieve that goal - the way of the assassin. So you run. But it is what you are running towards that concerns me."

Asher wasn't one for rolling his eyes, but roll they did. "When did you start using ten words instead of one?"

Ignoring the comment, Adan continued, "You are running towards death, Asher. You seek a warrior's death, perhaps even a hero's death. You don't want to die an assassin, but you know if you don't meet your end soon, that's exactly what's going to happen. I fear you are throwing yourself into anything that brings great risk."

The ranger held his tongue for a moment. He couldn't deny the truth behind Adan's words for every one had sunk beneath his skin and settled with familiarity. He knew it to be true, just as the Drake did.

"So why are you coming?" he finally asked.

"You are my maker. I do not want you to die."

Asher considered arguing the first point, as he had many times before, but he remained quiet and allowed Adan to finish.

"You will not live forever though," the Drake stated. "Death is inevitable and I do not want you to die as an Arakesh - you deserve more than that. So I will remain by your side until your death is a worthy one, or you have found a new path, one that sees you rise above your past..."

Asher was done with the conversation. "Well now I can sleep a little easier." Without another word, he turned on his heel and walked out of the tent to greet a pale sky of thick clouds.

"I am still coming with you!" Adan called, trailing behind.

Asher marched off into the camp having already glimpsed the red of Inara's cloak in the distance "No you're not," he said over his shoulder.

Crossing the camp, the ranger navigated the children, all of whom displayed remarkable energy, until he met the Guardian of the Realm. She was just walking away from a human family having spared a moment to talk to them. Inara reminded Asher, in many ways, of Reyna, her mother. They were both as caring as they were fierce.

"Good morning, Ranger," she greeted, her mood elevated since yesterday.

"Do you know something I don't," he remarked.

"Many things," Inara jested, looking past him to give a friendly nod to Adan'Karth.

"He wants to come with us to Erador," Asher stated, giving an almost imperceptible shake of his head.

"And I thank you again for accepting me," the Drake said, looking at Inara. "I will wait with Athis."

For all his training, Asher couldn't conceal his surprise as he looked from Adan to Inara.

The Guardian shrugged apologetically. "He came to me in the middle of the night - my judgment was impaired."

The ranger pinched the bridge of his nose. "He does that..."

"He's aided us before if you recall. It might not hurt to have someone who can *see* magic."

Helpless to change events, Asher did his best to forget the whole thing and focus on a more immediate situation. "You spoke with Vighon?"

Inara began walking towards the royal tent, where Nathaniel was likely discussing any potential next move with Kassian. "I did," she confirmed. "Though I have seen nothing of him this morning. I fear all the words in the world won't push him to make that choice."

Having fallen in beside her, Asher asked, "Choice?"

"It occurred to me before I spoke to him," Inara explained. "Vighon never *chose* to be king. He challenged his father because Arlon killed his mother, among other nefarious deeds that warranted action against him," she added with disdain, despite the passage of time. "But he didn't do it to become king. We entered the battle of our lives only minutes after he defeated Sir Borin and won the crown. After that, he *was* king. It was thrust upon him and he couldn't say no. I think it's time he actually *chose* to be the king of Illian..."

Asher had never thought of it that way, but it made sense to him. In many ways, he was similar to the northman having never really chosen any of his careers. The most pivotal decision he had ever made was to leave the order of Arakesh. Vighon had a slightly bigger decision to make.

The dwarven guard stood aside and allowed them entry to the royal tent. The ranger bowed, along with Inara, in sight of Drelda, the queen-mother, and her son, King Dakmund. For a moment, Asher let his thoughts wander to Doran, his oldest friend, and sympathised with the dwarf. The stout ranger had taken on a lot since receiving that simple two-worded note from his brother.

Alijah had forced so many of them into positions they had avoided for years...

"Morning," Nathaniel greeted, his mood failing to match his daughter's. "We were just trying to decide on the quickest route to Qamnaran."

Kassian was already shaking his head. "We could have left with Doran and the others."

Nathaniel glanced at the Keeper, frustration visible in his eyes. "With any luck, we'll reach the island before they attack the tower."

"We're not going to Qamnaran." The declaration came from the tent's entrance, turning every head to Vighon Draqaro.

Asher didn't miss the hint of a smile that pushed at Inara's cheeks. Indeed, the northman was not as they had last seen him. Gone was his forest of a beard and the fine layer of dirt that coated his face. His long raven hair had been washed, cut to his shoulders, and tied back in a similar manner to the ranger's. Even his leathers had been scrubbed and his tattered cloak replaced with a new one.

"Vighon." Everything about Nathaniel's demeanour brightened immediately. "You're with us then?"

The northman approached the table, his eyes on Inara before he came to a stop. "I know what I'm fighting for now. And I want my sword back," he added boldly.

Leaning against the table, Nathaniel wrapped his knuckles twice against the surface. "Then let's go get it."

"Finally." Kassian clapped his hands together. "I've got a couple of ideas that might get us into the keep."

Vighon raised a hand to stop the Keeper from going any further. "*I* know exactly how to get into my keep."

"I'm afraid we cannot stay to aid you in your plans," Inara said, glancing at Asher. "Erador awaits..."

Nathaniel rose from the table and walked over to his daughter. "I hope you find Gideon," he said, his tone serious. "I would tell you not to do anything dangerous, but we both know such a warning would fall on deaf ears. Instead I would implore you to be swift - all of you are needed here." The knight embraced Inara and planted a fatherly kiss on her cheek. "And try to keep the old man alive while you're at it."

Arms folded, Asher mirrored his friend's grin poking over Inara's shoulder. There weren't many the ranger considered his better - or even his equal - when it came to combat, but he had no problem believing that Inara Galfrey surpassed him in every area, from speed and strength to form and discipline. He only hoped *he* could be of help to *her*.

"It's been too long since I've witnessed Reavers falling under a rain of dragon's fire," Kassian voiced, his own way of telling them to be safe.

Vighon placed a rough hand on Asher's shoulder. "Thank you for finding me," he said, under the hubbub of farewells.

"Don't thank me yet... *boy*," he said with humour, bringing out a smile from the northman.

Taking back his hand, Vighon puffed out his chest. "The next time we meet, you might even refer to me as *your Grace*."

Adding an edge to his tone, Asher replied, "Earn it... and I might even bend the knee."

The northman laughed quietly to himself. "I wouldn't want you to break anything."

Asher enjoyed the banter, something Doran had originally fostered in him decades previously. It certainly wasn't something that had developed between Adan'Karth and himself. For all the Drake's ability to absorb the culture around him, he simply didn't understand sarcasm.

Nathaniel broke away to step in front of the ranger as Inara took a private moment to converse with the queen-mother, away from the table and Keepers.

"Don't worry," Asher said to the knight, "I'll be sure to always let Inara put herself between danger and me so that I might return to you."

Nathaniel laughed, a sound long missed by the ranger. "I would expect nothing less from the cowardly kind of a lowly ranger." They clasped forearms, meeting eye to eye. "Listen." The knight's tone was just above a whisper. "Gideon would make a fine ally and, as a friend, I wouldn't want him to suffer. But I don't want to lose either of you rescuing him. Gideon's a damn good warrior; whatever he's got himself into I'm sure he'll find a way out. Don't be reckless."

Asher held his hands up. "Have I ever been one to be reckless?"

Nathaniel stifled his smile. "I mean it. You both mean too much to be lost in some far off land. Get back to us and add that sword of yours to the fight."

Asher could see it on his friend's face - the cracks in his armour. Nathaniel had more than just their journey to Erador on his mind. Friends and family of his were days away from attacking a heavily guarded island. His daughter and oldest friend were entering the unknown. He himself was about to break into the enemy's home, a place where his wife was being kept.

It was too much and it was all over his face, evident to an experienced eye such as one trained to assess a man and instantly know everything about him. Nathaniel was cracking, his entire being held together by sheer will built upon by decades of discipline.

But Asher could see it...

"Keep your mind where it needs to be," the ranger warned, steering the knight towards the tent's entrance. "Don't be concerned with *Inara* or *me* or *Gideon*. There's not much we can't handle between us, not to mention Athis. You're going to *Namdhor*. There's no worse place to be for a rebel right now. Stay focused."

Nathaniel nodded reluctantly. "I know..."

"You're going to be tempted to rescue Reyna," Asher continued. "We both know the only thing keeping her there is herself. Don't stray from your task."

"I know," the knight repeated. "We're going for the sword and The Rebellion," he affirmed, applying what remained of that iron will of his.

Asher frowned. "If you get yourself killed doing something stupid, I will bring you back and kill you myself."

"I would echo that," Nathaniel replied with amusement. "What do you suppose is going on there then?" he asked, changing the subject to Inara and Vighon.

Asher looked at the northman's back as he leaned over the table. "You're asking the wrong man."

Inara returned after paying her respects to the king and the queen-mother. Vighon turned from the table to see the black orb in the Guardian's hand.

"A diviner?"

"It was Gideon's," Inara explained. "They gave it to me in Drag-ons' Reach." The half-elf touched a small pouch on the right side of her belt. "I have its twin. Contact me when you have the sword and you're out of Namdhor."

Vighon reached out to take the orb. "I will," he assured.

Asher was often oblivious when it came to matters of love, but even he couldn't miss the look both northman and Guardian held for each other. Their eyes were locked, speaking a silent promise to finish something that eluded the ranger. Whatever was going on between them, they didn't have time for it right now.

Vighon's hand was slow to retrieve the diviner from Inara, his fingers running over her palm to prolong the moment.

"We should go," Asher suggested, breaking the moment between them.

Their last farewells continued as they collectively made their way through the camp to Athis. As always, many gathered to see the red dragon take flight. Inara embraced her father one more time while Asher climbed his way up to find purchase between Athis's spikes, in front of Adan'Karth.

"I have never seen the world from the sky before," the Drake bubbled with excitement.

Asher's memories of riding on the back of Malliath were all too crisp. He rarely dwelled on such a time, for when he did he saw dragons dropping out of the sky, their throats torn.

He blinked hard and anchored himself in the present, wary of falling into Malliath's memories...

Inara was soon to join them, her climb appearing effortless as her feet and hands found their familiar grooves in the dragon's musculature. She draped her red cloak out behind her and looked back, over her shoulder, at the ranger and Drake.

"Are you ready?"

Asher's nod was far more casual than Adan's.

"It's going to be very cold up there," the Guardian warned. "Adan, I'm sure Asher would appreciate your magic to keep him warm."

The ranger blinked very slowly, though he didn't miss the smile pushing at Inara's cheek.

"Don't worry," Adan reassured, wrapping his arms around Asher's waist, "I won't let you freeze."

"Let's go," the ranger insisted with a groan.

Athis pushed up to stand on all four of his legs. Two magnificent wings unfurled, revealing tears here and there from battle. Preparing for flight, his legs crouched again and his wings flexed high. Asher braced himself before the dragon jumped and beat his wings at the same time, launching them over the tops of the trees in a single movement.

The ranger felt everything plummet into his boots and his knuckles became bone-white against Athis's spikes. He didn't need to look to know that Adan was beaming behind him.

Having quickly cleared the tip of The Black Wood, Athis banked to the west and found a comfortable altitude, allowing his occupants to acclimatise to the extraordinary form of travel. Every beat of his mighty wings carried them further from the wood and closer to The Vrost Mountains, a snow-tipped range that dominated the horizon.

Asher finally relaxed enough to take it all in, something he hadn't been able to do under The Crow's enthral. The world was incredibly beautiful from the sky - it filled the ranger with a sense of freedom he had never quite known.

"We're going to begin climbing now!" Inara called back. "The fastest way is over The Vrost Mountains!"

Asher nodded his understanding and hunkered down a bit more. He could already feel waves of heat washing over his back from Adan'Karth.

Below, the town of Dunwich was so small it could fit inside Asher's palm. The White Vale stretched out to his right, reaching for Vengora, a mountain range they would inevitably have to cross as it curled down along Illian's western coast. Then again, it occurred to the ranger that he had no idea where they were going. He knew they had to fly over The Hox but, beyond that, he couldn't fathom the best route to a land he had never even seen before - especially from the sky.

He decided, for the first time in a very long time, to let go and simply enjoy the adventure of his travels, just as he had done in his earliest days as a ranger. After all, the further from Illian they journeyed, the further from his past he journeyed.

It felt good to leave it all behind...

CHAPTER 30

# ESSENCE

Doran brought his trusty Warhog to a halt, his eye cast to the west and the end of The Narrows. Between the two cliffs, the canyon opened up to a beach and beyond that the lapping waves of The Hox. Further still, the dwarf could make out the rocky terrain of Qamnaran, overcast with thick grey clouds.

It wasn't a welcoming sight, but it was better than rounding the corner to find yet more of The Narrows' sheer walls.

The War Mason turned in his saddle to face Thaligg. "Send scouts to the beach. I don't want to leave the cover of the cliffs to find some undead dragon waiting for us."

"Aye, me Lord."

The loyal Heavybelly guided his own Warhog to a cluster of warriors on his left and instructed two of them to ride ahead. With any luck, they would find the boats Galanör had spoken of if not some of the elves of Ilythyra themselves.

Having taken himself off to the side, Doran could see the dwarves that marched westward, their line disappearing around the last curve in the cliff. They were weary after such a trek, some of them having accompanied him from The Black Wood. There were still those, despite his stirring speech in the eye of Grarfath, who believed they would have been better attacking the dig site in The Moonlit Plains.

How long, he wondered, before he had earned back the loyalty and respect of his own clan? Only in death, he feared.

Grouped together, in the middle of the dwarven line, were the elves. Whether they be exposed to the heat or cold, their beauty and composure never faltered. Compared to his kin, they glided through the world, even from atop their mounts. Adilandra led their procession, a warrior queen if ever there was one. Her elven features were just as sharp as her exquisite scimitar, a weapon the dwarf was very much looking forward to seeing in action.

"Got a thing for elves now, have you?"

Doran's bushy brow contracted with embarrassment as he looked upon Russell Maybury. The old wolf wielded his coy grin like a weapon, reminding the son of Dorain that his friend was a different man while the moon slept.

"Ye know where ye can stick yer question," he muttered, still struggling to look anywhere but at the queen of elves.

"No judgment here," Russell continued, his hands in the air. "I still remember the first time I saw Reyna and Faylen, back at The Pick-Axe. I thought the gods had sent angels from the heavens..."

"I don' know what ye're talkin' abou'," Doran lied. "They're too tall, too bony, and their skin is too smooth, like *silk*..." The dwarf lost himself for a moment after that. "Bah! What 'ave ye got me talkin' abou', lad?"

Russell refused to relinquish that grin. "You're the one talking himself into knots, Heavybelly. Why don't you tell her how you feel? You're a War Mason now!"

"Don' be stupid, ye can' afford to sound the same as ye look. Besides, even if I did like her, which I don', it could never work between us."

Russell cocked an eyebrow. "You mean because of..." His hands started to come together.

"No!" Doran spat. "Not because o' *that.* Ye dolt! It wouldn' work because she is the queen o' elves, the Lady o' Elandril, an' the ruler o' a nation that historically does *not* get on with me kin. It doesn' help that I'm a one-eyed dwarf half her height either," he muttered to himself.

Adilandra rode past him, sparing a glance and a brief smile. It was barely anything, but the son of Dorain still found a lump appear from nowhere in his throat.

"I dare any man, dwarf, elf, or even a damned orc, not to be taken in by her beauty," Doran commented to his friend.

With no reply from the old wolf, the War Mason twisted in his saddle to find him. Russell had stepped away and pushed back his hood, his nose pointed to the cliffs - not a good sign.

"Talk to me, Rus."

The weathered ranger continued to inhale the scents around him until his head snapped to a plateau high on their right. "Sandstalkers!" he bellowed.

The son of Dorain craned his neck and winced as the midday sun looked back at him. Sheltering his face with a hand, he soon found the monsters, leaping from the plateau to scurry along the cliff wall. Their six-pincered legs dug into the rock with rapid speed as they ran down towards the rebels.

"SANDSTALKERS!" Doran's voice boomed. "Make for the beach!" he commanded, reaching for Andaljor on the back of his saddle.

Russell rolled his shoulders, freeing himself of his cloak while taking his pick-axe in both hands. He crouched like a predator stalking in the long grass, his notched weapon twisting in his grip.

Dust and loose stones rained down from the cliff face, ahead of the Sandstalkers. There were so many that they began to scramble over each other in a bid to reach the walking buffet on the canyon floor. One of the monsters, not content to run down the cliff, leapt away from the wall, its spider-like body casting a shadow over the back of the elves.

Mid-air, its grotesque form was clear for all to see. Though the bulk of the body was horizontal in the manner of a bug, its torso rose up, not dissimilar to a Centaur's. That was where any comparison ended. Two thin, but toned, arms extended from its shoulders with razor sharp claws for fingers, designed to slice through flesh as if it were butter. Its head, an amalgamation of man and spider, was predominantly taken up by two curved fangs that concealed a smaller mouth of serrated teeth.

They were killing machines...

In his heyday, however, the same had been said of Russell Maybury. Proving that he still had what it takes to be a ranger, the old wolf used his supernatural strength to launch himself over the elves, where he met the falling Sandstalker with his swinging pick-axe. The beast was dead before either hit the ground.

"Make for the beach!" Doran repeated for the last dwarves rounding the curve in the gorge.

The elves were quicker to react, their bows nocked and aimed high. Arrows targeted the spread of Sandstalkers, causing dozens to fall rather than run. It created chaos amongst the monsters but it also made it hard to see which were hitting the ground dead and which were about to explode from the mass to charge their line.

The dwarves at the back were forced to join shoulder to shoulder and repel the Sandstalkers with axe and spear. The elves backed up with them, keeping pace, while never failing to miss with their deadly bows.

Doran, never one to hold back from a fight, sent Pig to the beach and waded in beside his kin. Andaljor had been separated into its two halves, allowing the War Mason to hack and hammer his relentless foe.

"To the beach!" he hollered between blows.

The Sandstalkers reared up, raising their already impressive height, to come down on the dwarves with their sharpened legs of bone.

"Shields!" Doran yelled. Absent a shield himself, the War Mason was forced to step back as his kin did their best to protect themselves against the spear-tipped pincers.

Looking over his shoulder, the majority of their force had made it to the beach, but they would never get everyone across the water while Sandstalkers picked them off.

Doran growled, deeply angered by their bad luck - this was the last thing they needed before a battle. Pushing his way back into the front line, he renewed his attacks and swung with left and right, leaving a mangled trail of monsters in their wake.

Russell appeared by his side, not easily missed, with his pick-axe thundering into the Sandstalkers again and again. There was something feral about him, an abandon in his yellow eyes that spoke of animal rage. Doran only hoped his friend would benefit from such an outlet. He hated to think of the wolf gaining more ground...

Three dwarves to his left cried out and a spray of blood hit the side of Doran's face - a Sandstalker had breached the line. The son of Dorain called on Grarfath's strength and prepared himself to send the monster back to the hellish depths it had crawled out of.

A flash of steel, cutting from low to high, split the Sandstalker open from gut to head. Doran marvelled at the elves bolstering their ranks. It had been Faylen's scimitar that had ended the beast's life, but her kin moved up to join her with swift precision, their blades whipping through the monsters.

"Back to the beach!" Doran shouted repeatedly, encouraging both dwarf and elf to steadily retreat.

As the Sandstalker bodies began to sprawl the width of the canyon, the monsters still rushing the line were gaining height as they trampled over their kin. Elven archers, standing on the threshold of The Narrows, let loose their arrows, aiming them just over the tallest elves. The monsters coming down on the defensive line were easy targets and soon added their corpses to the growing pile.

As they reached that threshold themselves, Doran did a double take seeing Queen Adilandra, a sentinel in the middle of the melee.

She had no weapon to hand, standing as a rock that withstood the tide passing around her.

"Leave her!" Faylen warned, tugging on Doran's pauldron.

The son of Dorain continued his retreat with the others, but he couldn't tear his eye from the queen. "What are ye abou'? They'll rip her to shreds!"

"Trust me!" Faylen pulled him back further until Adilandra was in line with the shield wall of Heavybellys.

"Fall back!" Doran ordered.

The dwarves turned and rushed towards the sea, leaving the Sandstalkers to face nothing but an unarmed elf. The monsters reared up - they would kill her in seconds and continue to assault the dwarves for sure.

Adilandra raised her arms to the side and her face to the sky. That was the last Doran saw of the queen.

A blinding light filled The Narrows as if the sun itself had risen from within Adilandra. Doran raised his hammer to shield his eye from the white glare. He tried several times to steal a glance, hoping to spot the queen, but his eye couldn't take the light.

"What's happenin'?" he cried.

Then, as suddenly as it appeared, the terrible light vanished and all the colours of the world rushed back in to fill the void. Adilandra was standing exactly where she had been, unmoved by the nest of Sandstalkers. The monsters themselves were gone, leaving only their dead behind.

Adilandra stumbled backwards.

"My queen!" Faylen darted forward and caught Adilandra before she fell. "Easy," the High Guardian bade.

"Is she a'right?" the War Mason enquired with unease.

"I will be... fine," Adilandra answered for herself. "I just... need to rest a while."

"There's boats!" came a shout from the shore.

Turning back, Doran spotted elves approaching from a hollow dug into the base of the northern cliffs. Between them and the dwarves filling the beach, there were indeed boats resting on the sand. At least Galanör was ready for them. Faylen handed Adilandra's care over to a pair of trusted elves, who escorted her to the nearest boat.

Doran turned back to The Narrows and took in the breadth of the canyon's entrance, scanning the cliff for any sign of the Sandstalkers. "What was that?" he asked the High Guardian.

"Magic, Master Dwarf," Faylen answered. "Very *powerful* magic. I have never seen it done before, but I could feel it - her essence."

"Her *what?*"

"The realm of magic flows through every elf like water flows through a valley," she explained. "The older we get, the more intense that connection becomes. I have heard of our oldest being able to release a portion of that magic, to have it manifest in our world. My Lady has walked the earth of Verda for over a thousand years..."

Doran looked at the site where she had stood and unleashed the power of the sun. The ground had been blackened, matching the charred Sandstalkers. "That was inside her?" His tone spoke of utter disbelief.

"Not anymore," Faylen replied. "She will need time now to absorb more from the realm of magic."

It was all above Doran's ability to understand, though it did remind him of Reyna, whose magic had been poured into the Moonblade years earlier. "If ye say so. Let's cross the water an' be done with this place."

What followed was a very slow process that involved a lot of waiting while the numerous boats ferried the dwarves and elves to Qamnaran. Thankfully, there were only five to bury on the beach, lost to the Sandstalkers. Doran spoke over their graves and took heart knowing they had fallen as heroes and would now reside in the Hall of Grarfath.

The War Mason insisted that he go last, in case the monsters of The Narrows returned. He encouraged his forces to rest and play simple games while they waited their turn. The last thing he needed was dwarves filled with Grarfath's battle-lust when there was nothing to fight - they needed occupying, like children.

The dark clouds had spread across The Hox by the time Doran found himself pushing off from Illian's shore, Russell beside him. A light rain welcomed him to Qamnaran and a much heavier rain accompanied his first step onto the island's beach. The elves that had once resided in Ilythyra were there to greet them, but one familiar face was visible, even through the battering rain.

"Galanör!" Doran cheered his name.

The elven ranger beamed and crouched on one knee to embrace the son of Dorain. "It has been too long, my friend."

"As was our journey to this wretched island."

Galanör looked over Doran's shoulder, to the shores of Illian. "I heard of the Sandstalkers. Have you suffered losses?"

"Five," Doran declared sourly. "If it weren' for the queen that number would surely 'ave swelled."

Galanör turned to the tree line, where the dwarves were being shown the way. "Adilandra has been seen to. She will have a place to rest in our camp, as will you and your kin."

Russell navigated the rocky beach. "Is there room for an old man?" he asked, soaking wet.

Galanör had a smile waiting for him. "Russell. It is good to see you." Rising back to his full height, the elf grasped Russell's forearm and pulled him in for a tight embrace. "There will always be a place for you among my people. I have already heard whispers of your efforts in The Narrows."

"Aye, he's very brave, blah blah blah. Let's get out o' this damned rain before me armour rusts..." In truth, Doran was eager to see Adilandra and make certain the queen was alright.

Not that he would tell any of his concerns...

CHAPTER 31

# THE BEAST OF QALANQATH

The White Vale. Home. Vighon breathed it in. For all the land in the realm, *his* realm, nowhere captured his heart so much as the north. He had been born here, as was his mother and every ancestor before her. The icy cold of these white plains was in his blood and he embraced it.

As bound to the land as he was, the northman knew that he wasn't fighting for it anymore. Such a belief had held him down, weighted beneath a responsibility as heavy as Illian itself.

Now he fought, as every other man did, for what was in his *heart*.

Vighon looked to the sky, a floating ocean of clouds far darker than the white of the vale. He didn't know why he looked up - he wasn't going to see Inara up there. Athis had set off for Erador almost two days ago while they had set out from The Black Wood, heading west for Namdhor.

Fate had separated them again...

The northman shook the thought from his mind. He didn't believe in fate, a notion tied to the gods; deities he, and a few others, knew not to exist. They had been separated because circumstances demanded it, nothing more.

Doing his best to think of something else, Vighon turned in his saddle to observe the men and women he rode with. Keepers all, regardless of their ability to wield magic. He liked that. It wasn't magic, after all, that bound this particular group together. Like the one who led them, they had all suffered a loss of some kind. They weren't just fighting for those who needed them, but for those who had already fallen.

From what he had heard, they were a hardy bunch. Kassian had kept them on the move, travelling from city to city in search of others to save and enemies to slay. In many ways, they had each lost more than he had, but they had still found the courage to keep up the fight. He envied that strength.

Riding to the capital now, the northman only hoped that his new found courage would hold up. There was going to be blood after all - there always was. He just needed to hold on to Inara's words, to remember why the men and women around him picked up their swords. If they could do it, then so could he.

Vighon tightened his grip on the reins and took a deep breath as he embraced that belief. It was time to get back in the fight...

"The Watchers!" Nathaniel shouted over the growing winds, his finger pointing to the black outposts that guarded the mouth of The Iron Valley. "We should take shelter and wait out the storm!"

"What storm?" Kassian questioned.

"He's right!" Vighon voiced. "There's a storm coming!" He turned in his saddle, getting a feel for the weather. "From the east! It'll be on us soon!"

Kassian shrugged, clearly irritated by the idea of camping for the night - he wasn't one for staying still. "As you say," he conceded.

"Sir Borin," Vighon addressed. "Go on ahead and scout the ruins."

The walking block of dead meat broke into a sprint that no man or elf could compete with. The Golem quickly overtook Nathaniel in the lead and kicked up plumes of snow in his wake.

"Can't you order that thing to check the depth of The Adean instead?" Kassian suggested.

Ignoring the Keeper, Vighon crossed the snow beside Nathaniel until they all reached the eastern Watcher, its black stone gripping the mountain side. The northman couldn't help but remember the last time he had been here, inside this very outpost. With Asher and Ruban by his side, they had taken shelter for the night on their way to meet the elves on the banks of the River Adanae.

It seemed a lifetime ago...

They passed under the broken archway and steadily filled the courtyard with their horses and supplies. Vighon scanned every corner, searching for the bodies they had left here, Ironsworn all. The northman jumped down from his horse and walked over to the exact spot where he had been told his father was responsible for his mother's death.

Of course, after seventeen years, on the border of barbarian territory, there were no bodies to be found. The valley's inhabitants had likely taken the bodies, known, as they were, for leaving nothing for waste. They would have found a use for every Ironsworn bone no doubt. Either that, or something had eaten their remains. Vighon was satisfied whatever the cause - vengeance had had its day.

Sir Borin was standing in the middle of the courtyard, draped and hooded in his muddy leathers. If he was satisfied with their safety he didn't voice it.

"Put the horses in there," Vighon instructed the others, gesturing to a chamber off the courtyard. It had long been emptied of its contents and its doorway was shattered, making it easy to fit the mounts through. "They'll stay warm in there."

"And what about us?" one of the Keepers voiced, their eyes running over the jagged walls of The Watcher with trepidation.

"We will have to go up," Vighon answered, nodding at the lowest steps of a spiral staircase built into the wall. "There's a church near the top - it should be large enough for all of us to camp."

"A church?" Kassian questioned, craning his neck.

"For Atilan," Vighon explained. "So the soldiers posted here could pray to him."

"Alright, come on," Kassian cajoled, responding to the caution on every Keeper's face. "We've stayed in worse places. Get inside."

The northman heard more than one of the mages disagree with Kassian's observation. Still, they did as he commanded and took their supplies into the outpost, their wands providing the light. With most of the walls missing from the face of the keep, they could be seen from the courtyard, exploring what remained of The Watcher's skeleton.

Nathaniel came to Vighon's side. "Is there a problem, your Grace?"

Vighon almost winced hearing the title. "I'm not king yet," he corrected.

"You will always be king to me."

Vighon nodded, appreciating the affection. "I know. But let's save the formalities until I actually have a crown on my head. It would be nice just to hear my name for a spell." He exhaled a long breath of vapour into the chill, his gaze cast to the stone where Godfrey Cross's head had hit the ground, absent his body.

"What's wrong?" the knight asked.

"I would not stay here any longer than is needed. Were it not for the storm I would have us camping on the vale."

"One night," Nathaniel reassured. "We'll leave first thing and be in Namdhor in less than two days."

Vighon couldn't shake that bad feeling. "It's the one night that troubles me..."

Within a couple of hours, Illian's night sky had brought forth a thunderous storm from the east, its black clouds rolling over the land with unbridled rage. Lightning lashed out across the horizon, striking The White Vale and even some of the taller spires that remained on The Watchers. An incessant rain hammered everything, moving in waves with the billowing wind.

Leaning against a side wall, Vighon watched it all unfold from five floors up, his cloak wrapped around his shoulders. There was no front to the outpost, offering him a view of it all. Flashes of lightning revealed the snowy plains in the distance, but the rain drowned out every sound.

Vighon decided that was the only reason he didn't hear Kassian Kantaris before the mage was by his side. Without a word, the Keeper offered him a pipe. It had been a long time since the northman had enjoyed the habit and his hand instinctively reached for it.

"Thank you." He brought it to his nose and inhaled the contents. "Calmardran Spice," he said, somewhat impressed by its exotic nature.

Kassian shrugged. "We get around." Using the end of his wand, the Keeper ignited his own pipe before doing the same for Vighon.

Standing there, dry under the canopy of a broken ceiling, watching the world before him with a pipe in his mouth, Vighon could almost imagine he was a younger man travelling the realm with Alijah again.

Almost...

"You know," Kassian began, his pipe clenched between his teeth, "shaving your beard and having a wash doesn't make you king."

Vighon blew out the flavoured smoke. "Damn..." he drawled.

Kassian continued to smoke his pipe and the pair stood in silence for a short while. "Can you really do it?" he finally asked.

Vighon gave the man a sideways glance. "Can I do what?"

"Can you take the throne? Can you be the king everyone keeps telling me you are? We're about to risk our lives just to get you a *sword*. I need to know that you can do more than *swing* it."

It would have been easy to give a quick reply, reassuring the Keeper that he was ready to resume his duties as king and that the sword of the north would rally the entire realm to their cause. But that would be an injustice in light of the aforementioned risk that Kassian and all of his Keepers were taking.

"No man has ever been able to stand up and *tell* the people that he is their king - even if his sword is on fire. That man must have supporters, champions, loyal men and women around him to lift him up. The throne is more than the person who sits beneath the crown. It is the people around it who *believe*." Vighon turned to lay both eyes on Kassian. "The question is: can I rely on you to be by my side when I stand up? Are you with me?"

Like Vighon, Kassian didn't answer right away, but continued to smoke his pipe and watch the storm hit the world. "You'll have my support when you've earned it," he replied gruffly. "I've heard all about your past deeds - most books refer to you as a *warrior-king*. For that you have my respect. But I see nothing of that man before me. It's easy to find your courage when you're surrounded by allies, and *powerful* ones at that. Wait until you're alone, the odds are against you, and you have *everything* to lose. Stand up *then* and I will rise with you..."

Without another word, the Keeper turned to leave the shell of a room and the northman to his thoughts. "Oh," Kassian added, pausing before the doorway. "You commanded Sir Borin to stand guard inside the church."

"What of it?"

"I would very much like for everyone to get some sleep while they can. That isn't going to happen so long as there's a Golem in the room. Have him stand outside, preferably outside The Watcher's *walls*."

Vighon nodded his understanding and promised he would follow the Keeper shortly to do just that. Until then, he wanted to enjoy a few more minutes to himself. It wasn't easy talking to people after a year of keeping to himself.

Inhaling another cloud of Calmardran Spice, he let his eyes wander over the ruins below.

Movement.

He just caught it through the rain - something white moving against the black of The Watcher's grounds. He started forward, careful to stop before the edge, where the stone was severely cracked.

"Wait," he called back, halting Kassian's departure.

"I need to rest, northman," the Keeper replied from the doorway.

"Wait," Vighon repeated, his tone conveying a sense of urgency and danger. "Look…" He narrowed his eyes, searching the darkness below in the hope that his eyes had been playing tricks on him.

Kassian joined him by the edge again and followed his gaze to the grounds. Lightning struck the tallest spire on The Watcher, illuminating the shadowed corners and sheets of falling rain. It also illuminated the white furs draped over the backs of several barbarians sneaking into the courtyard.

"They're going for the horses!" Kassian growled.

Vighon's spirits sank - the outpost was cursed…

"Quickly!" Kassian urged, running from the chamber.

Vighon dropped his pipe and drew his sword, hoping his muscles would remember how the barbarians of The Iron Valley fought - it had been years since he had faced them and their brutal combat style.

With the Keeper by his side, they dashed through the dark halls, warning a few others as they came across them. Kassian ordered them to rouse the others in the church and prepare to repel the barbarians, lest they steal the horses and add days on to the group's journey to Namdhor.

"This way!" Vighon called, correcting Kassian's wrong turn. The northman led them down a spiral staircase that required a small jump in the middle to avoid the missing steps.

Down two more floors, they ran along the next hall, illuminated by the flashes of lightning that poured through the archways and shattered doors. Vighon stole a glance at random, looking through one of the devastated rooms. He could see the black of night beyond, brought to life by one almighty crack of lightning.

He skidded to a stop.

There, existing in that single moment of light, a silent nightmare was revealed. The northman had seen such a vision before, on the icy fields of Grey Stone.

"What are you doing?" Kassian questioned, his wand held high. "The horses!" he reminded.

With cautious steps, Vighon slowly approached the jagged edge of the chamber, his hand sliding along the wall, slick with rain. The entire floor protruded further than the levels above and the chamber had lost its ceiling, as well as its outer wall, in the ancient assault that ravaged the outpost. As a result, the northman was soaking wet by the time he reached the lip, his dark eyes blinking rapidly through the downpour, determined to see what approached from the dark.

He waited with bated breath.

"Vighon!" Kassian stood by the threshold.

A flash of lightning, this time in the north, brought Vighon's fears to life. On war-torn wings, a monster, older than Illian itself, emerged from the storming skies.

"Dragon!" Kassian hissed.

The undead dragon came to land on the southern ramparts, its bulk reducing most of the wall to a crumbling waterfall of stone. Its front legs rested in the courtyard, curving its body down low so its eyes could survey its prey amongst the ruins.

The barbarians froze, seeing death given form.

The dragon unleashed its unnatural shriek, filling every nook and cranny of The Watcher's remains. It put dread in the bones and seized the heart, reminding Vighon of numerous battles where the Dragon Riders had wiped out countless men.

Both northman and Keeper retreated from the room and rested with their backs to the flat of the wall on the other side.

"Barbarians *and* a dragon!" Kassian complained.

Vighon was shaking his head. "I'm never coming back here."

Kassian turned a serious look on the northman. "You might never *leave* here." A pair of Keepers came rushing out of the spiral staircase up the hall. "Stop!" Kassian urged, raising his voice as high as he dared.

His warning was punctuated by a torrent of fire, expelled from the dragon's maw. The flames curled up, finding the cracks and holes in the stone until Vighon felt the heat on his skin.

If the barbarians screamed, they couldn't be heard over the roaring fire.

Vighon sheathed his sword and pivoted back into the doorway, crouching low as he used his hands to help him crawl back to the edge of the chamber. It was chaos below, with barbarians running in every direction. Some abandoned the outpost, jumping over the charred remains of their comrades, while others sought refuge inside the ancient fort itself.

A brave few, quite foolishly, challenged the dragon head on. The first disappeared behind a jaw of fangs, the body reduced to pieces in a moment. Those behind found their way blocked by the Dragon Rider, a forbidding figure in the rain.

Vighon narrowed his eyes as the rain did its best to mask the ancient warrior, but a horned helm and a two-handed battle-axe informed the northman of the Reaver's identity: Rengyr, the beast of Qalanqath, as Alijah had named him.

It was known amongst The Rebellion that this particular Dragon Rider patrolled the north, but Vighon hadn't seen him since... The Carpel Slopes. Rengyr's dragon, Karsak, had added his fire to Malliath's and torched hundreds of his men that night.

Vighon's hand wandered back to the hilt on his hip. He wanted to slay them both with every fibre of his being.

That battle-axe came up in a sweeping arc, propelled by the hands of a dead man. Two barbarians were cut down by a single strike, their white furs instantly bloodied. What followed was an impressive display by Rengyr, who evaded, parried, and countered every one of his surrounding foes. Within seconds, he had chopped them all down, sending them to the next life without all their limbs.

Following the slaughter, the beast of Qalanqath stood motionless in the rain. Vighon had the good sense to back away only a moment before the Dragon Rider looked up in his direction. Scrambling backwards on all fours, the northman returned to the hall and the Keepers therein. Kassian was silently directing them into different parts of the outpost, spreading their numbers out.

Nathaniel appeared at the end of the hall. He crept from wall to wall, pausing every time to peer through the doorways. Before the knight could reach them, Vighon watched a pair of barbarians rushing up the steps, behind the knight, oblivious to their presence.

"No magic," the northman warned, gripping Kassian's arm. "Too loud," he whispered.

Nathaniel finally joined them and pressed his back to the wall on the other side of the door. "We need to disappear inside these halls," he advised, just loud enough to be heard over the rain. "They've seen barbarians, not us."

Vighon nodded in agreement and gestured to a room in front of them, its walls crumbled into a pile that could be climbed, taking them to the next floor up—

The stone beneath their feet shook. Debris rained down from the ceiling and slabs of rock could be heard toppling into the courtyard below.

The northman tensed every muscle in his body, his breath caught in his throat.

Nathaniel closed his eyes and slowly shook his head, signalling them all to remain still for the moment. Vighon slowly turned to the doorway on his left - something wasn't right inside the chamber. It took a moment to realise he could no longer hear the heavy rain against the stone floor, but it was certainly still raining...

His eyes went wide when the revelation took hold. He subtly tilted his head towards the chamber, his expression full of alarm. Nathaniel nodded his understanding and flexed his fingers at the Keepers, warning them to stay calm.

The northman did his best to match Nathaniel's courageous display, despite the fact that there was only a single wall of cracked stone between them and what could only be Karsak's head. It wasn't the first time Vighon had endured a close encounter with one of the Reaver dragons. Like then, he was thankful that the beast was, in fact, dead, and had no sense of smell since it didn't breathe. Had it been Malliath hunting for them, their fate would have been sealed.

Somewhere inside the dark outpost, a barbarian cried out before death made them quiet forever. Vighon had to wonder if they had escaped Karsak and run straight into Sir Borin. The rain continued its relentless hammering on the chamber floor after the dragon removed its head. The Watcher shook again as the giant Reaver ascended another floor to pursue more prey.

Vighon gulped on precious air.

"Come on," he bade, leading Nathaniel and the Keepers on light feet.

They crept down the passage until they ran out of ceiling. The passage, however, continued into the eastern block, an area of the outpost that was exposed to the harsh weather, with brittle columns and pocked walls between chambers.

Kassian edged himself along the wall so that he could look up at the floors above. The rain, predictably, prevented him from looking up for any length of time.

"I can't see a thing." The Keeper stepped back under the shelter of where the ceiling ended in a jagged line. "We need to warn the others."

Something akin to the sound of an explosion erupted above them and a barbarian came crashing down onto the stone where Kassian had recently been standing. The body snapped in many places on impact, but the barbarian was already dead judging by the burns that covered him from head to toe.

"We need to avoid that dragon," Kassian remarked.

Vighon was just as concerned with Karsak's axe-wielding Rider. The northman stepped out into the rain and explored two of the ruined chambers, moving easily from one to the other. From his position, he could see most of The Watcher laid out before him, including Karsak, whose sickly body concealed the upper levels.

Crouching behind the remains of a low wall, Vighon narrowed his eyes through the rain and scanned the outpost for any sign of

Rengyr. Lightning struck the western spire, its flash offering a brief glimpse of The Watcher's etched stone.

The beast of Qalanqath was standing on top of a broken pillar, surveying the outpost as Vighon was. His ferocious-looking battle-axe caught the flash, making him easy to spot.

The Reaver's head turned.

Vighon ducked below the wall, almost placing his face to the wet stone. Deciding it would be unwise to take a second look from the same place, he crawled along the wall until he found a hole the size of his hand.

Rengyr wasn't standing on the pillar anymore...

The northman made a dash on his elbows and knees and didn't stop until he had entered the room closest to the hall. He found Nathaniel and Kassian by the edge, sheltered from the rain. With one frantic hand, he gestured for them to get away as fast as possible.

Kassian responded with a confused expression, his feet, stubbornly, rooted to the spot. Nathaniel saved his life, tugging the Keeper back into the dark hall only a second before Rengyr scaled the wall and dropped down into the eastern block. Vighon heard the sound of the Reaver's axe knocking against the stone.

Checking on his companions, the northman was glad to see they had vanished from the end of the passage. He backed up to a wall and slowly pushed himself up onto his feet. A quick glance informed him that Karsak was still clinging to the main face of the outpost, his head inspecting various chambers higher up.

He also saw glimpses of surviving barbarians, rushing along the ruins to escape the dragon's wrath. He feared what would happen if they bumped into the rest of the Keepers hiding in the depths. It would most likely come to a fight, alerting the Dragon Rider and his mount to a second faction within the outpost.

Something moved in his peripheral vision, turning Vighon's head to the right - Rengyr was passing between rooms. Taking advantage of Rengyr's cumbersome helm, the northman slipped round the corner of the wall before he could be seen.

He dared to peek around the edge, hoping that the Dragon Rider would make for the shelter of the passages. Indeed, Rengyr was no longer where he had been standing, but he wasn't under the ceiling of the nearest hall either. That meant he was still out there...

Vighon crept along the ruins, pausing to peer through every hole he could find. Rengyr was nowhere to be seen. He cursed the rain and its constant barrage against his eyes and ears.

Fearing that his foe was behind him, Vighon turned quickly on his heel, half expecting to see the edge of Rengyr's axe flying towards his head. There was nothing but shadows and rain. However, in turning without care, the metallic tip of his scabbard scraped across the wall, tearing through the sound of constant rain.

He dashed forward, hoping the rain drowned him out as much as it did Rengyr. Slipping behind a pillar just taller than himself, Vighon pressed his back to it and cautiously moved around. Looking back at where he had knocked the wall, the Dragon Rider was now standing there, his undead eyes scanning the area.

Vighon concealed himself fully behind the pillar once more.

He counted to five.

Looking back, Rengyr had vanished again. The northman swore under his breath. Crouching low, he moved away from the pillar, using the broken walls as cover to enter another chamber near the very edge of The Watcher. He still couldn't see the Dragon Rider, but he did have a clear view of the passage where he had left Nathaniel and the others. He could make it.

Steadying his breath, Vighon readied himself, hands braced either side of an ancient archway that failed to meet in the middle. He made it three steps before a dark mass barged into him, launching him over the side of a low wall and into another exposed chamber. The hard stone awaited him, as he tumbled across the wet floor.

Pushing himself up, blood dripped from his right brow and swirled in the puddle beneath him. Now was not the time to take stock of his injuries as there were likely more to come...

Rengyr levered himself over the wall and dropped down into the rain water. Dead white orbs looked through the slits in his helm, watching Vighon rise to his feet and draw his sword.

Was this it? the northman thought. Had he overcome his crushing doubts and finally found the one thing he would always fight for, only to die now, in the hollow halls of a Watcher? And to a Dragon Rider no less. He had expected to die at Alijah's hands if he was going to perish at all in this rebellion.

Rengyr hefted his battle-axe in both hands, preparing to answer all of Vighon's questions with a single swing. The northman raised his sword - he wasn't going to leave this world without a fight. He braced his knees, ready to parry the heavy blow that never landed. In fact, the axe went higher still and with its wielder firmly attached.

With all the grace of a charging bison, Sir Borin had slammed into the beast of Qalanqath. Rengyr was lifted clear off his feet and hurled through the remains of a wall with the Golem's arms wrapped around his waist. Undead, both creatures recovered quickly from the trauma and picked themselves up. Before the Dragon Rider could find firm footing, Sir Borin picked him up by his leg like a rag doll.

Using Rengyr as a bat, Sir Borin swung him into the adjacent pillar, shattering it to rubble. Letting the Dragon Rider go, Rengyr landed in a heap and slid across the wet floor until he hit the corner. Remarkably, the beast of Qalanqath maintained his grip on the battle-axe and came up twisting it between his fingers.

Fearless, Sir Borin strode towards the threat to his master. With space between them, the Dragon Rider was now able to display his superior fighting style and dexterity. Rengyr easily ducked under the Golem's thundering punches and swiped at his legs and hips, every strike taking chunks out of Vighon's bodyguard. One blow knocked Sir Borin down to one knee, lowering him to the perfect height for a clean decapitation.

That deadly battle-axe cut through the rain, aimed for the Golem's pale neck. But Sir Borin wasn't without his speed. Dipping one mountainous shoulder, he rolled aside and evaded the axe. With a vengeance, he rose. Mid-swing, Sir Borin snatched the battle-axe. The Dragon Rider pulled hard, heaving with all his strength to come away with his weapon. The Golem's free hand shot out and wrapped a vice-like grip around his opponent's neck, pushing Rengyr away with a superior arm span.

The beast of Qalanqath relinquished his battle-axe and, instead, turned his attention to freeing himself of Sir Borin's grip. The Golem discarded the weapon and hefted Rengyr in the air. With supernatural strength, he threw the Dragon Rider into the archway where Vighon had briefly hidden. The stones came down on Rengyr, slowing his rise.

Taking advantage, Sir Borin reached down and took the Dragon Rider by the ankle. A rough yank freed him of the fallen stone but the Golem continued to drag the beast back into the other chamber, away from Vighon. Whether he didn't care or he lacked the intelligence to realise it, Sir Borin did nothing to prevent Rengyr from retrieving his axe, discovered by the Reaver as he was scraped across the floor.

A solid boot connected with the Golem's arm and Rengyr was free to leap to his feet once more. The two fell into a cumbersome melee, each delivering strikes and blows that would kill any man. Their combat came to a grinding halt after Rengyr lodged his battle-axe in Sir Borin's slab of a back. Try as he might, the weapon refused to come free.

Without that menacing axe, Vighon was sure the fight was nearing its end, Sir Borin more than capable of destroying the Reaver with his hands alone. Rengyr, however, had been resurrected with all the prowess he had possessed as a living breathing Dragon Rider. His fighting form was magnitudes beyond anything Sir Borin boasted. Such a demonstration was given in the form of an exotic manoeuvre that saw the beast of Qalanqath twist around the Golem's hulking body. With one hand on the haft of his axe, Rengyr threw all of his weight into the acrobatic strategy.

The battle-axe came free...

Furthermore, Rengyr broke into a sprint, ignoring Sir Borin completely. Now he was coming for Vighon.

The northman braced himself again, his sword held steady in both hands. He only had to survive long enough for Sir Borin to get back in the fight. Using the ruins, Rengyr stepped up and leaped into the air, his axe raised over his head in both hands.

Saving his life for a second time that day, Sir Borin brought the Dragon Rider down by both ankles, flattening the beast of Qalanqath to the stone.

"Vighon!" The northman turned back to the passage where Nathaniel was waving for him to join them. "We need to go!" the knight called.

The stonework exploded behind him, returning his attention to the undead behemoths. Sir Borin and Rengyr were locked in a grappling match that had them pushing each other through every broken wall, archway, and pillar.

Using the time his bodyguard was granting him, Vighon ran for the cover of the passage and fell in beside Nathaniel and Kassian, both perched by the edge of the spiral staircase. Above them, the ceiling cracked under Karsak's weight and constant movement.

"This whole place is coming down," Nathaniel remarked, skipping down the stairs.

In the courtyard, Vighon discovered the rest of Kassian's mages, all wise enough to use the barbarians' distraction to their advantage. Even now, Karsak exhaled his fiery breath into The Watcher's highest levels.

"We ride west," Kassian instructed, mounting his horse.

They wouldn't reach Namdhor that night, or even the following one, but at least they would be far away from the cursed Watchers.

Vighon clambered onto his horse as he guided it towards the entrance. Looking up, over his shoulder, Karsak's attention had turned to his Rider's dilemma. The cumbersome dragon adjusted his position on the face of The Watcher and began climbing down, towards Sir Borin. The ruins could take no more. One of Karsak's front legs pushed straight through the stone into the floor below. His falling weight then brought down the entire floor beneath his skeletal ribs.

Unable to take any more, The Watcher was reduced to nothing more than a roaring landslide...

"Ride!" Vighon bellowed. With a few barbarians amongst them, the companions moved away at a gallop and turned their horses west, to the capital.

The northman was mesmerised by the scene of destruction, his head fixed over his right shoulder. Karsak shrieked as the top half of The Watcher came down on top of it, burying its bulk and wings beneath tons of stone. The outpost's ancient grip to the mountain was undone, tearing chunks of Vengora away with it. Within seconds, the structure had lost its shape, distorting any impression that it was man-made.

Karsak's head reared up, only to be engulfed by a sea of mud that had slipped away from the mountain above. From such a distance, there was no way to tell if Sir Borin and Rengyr were still bound together in battle, but the eastern block, already the weakest structure within the ruins, soon fell away, consumed by the debris.

As the companions rode across the mouth of the valley, the landslide crashed into the ground, wiping out the outer walls. Through the rain and battering wind, a plume of black dust and dirt reached for the heavens, masking the Vengoran mountainside. It was a sight to behold, the details brought to life in every flash of lightning.

Sir Borin's fate was his own now, lost to Vighon. The northman could only hope that he was free of Rengyr and Karsak with him...

CHAPTER 32

# ERADOR

After two days of watching the world slip past beneath Athis, Inara greeted the shores of Erador with the new dawn. Her eternal companion glided down, leaving the clouds behind, as he approached the eastern coast of new land.

Unlike the sheer white walls of Illian's Shining Coast, Erador possessed a jagged line of beaches and black cliffs. Beyond lay fields of green, a familiar sight, and beyond them a hazy line of mountains. Though familiar terrain, it was still alien to the Guardian. Inara didn't know the name of those mountains or the region that sprawled before them.

This was the adventure she had always craved!

The circumstances were not as she had dreamt. There would be no exploration just for the sake of it. Gideon was somewhere in this vast land and he needed help. Then, if they found him, The Rebellion needed them urgently in the fight against Alijah, so they would have to return home immediately.

Adventures were a romanticised idea conjured by writers who knew nothing of them. Inara knew the truth - they were hard and fraught with peril...

Athis finally crossed from sea to land, bringing the lush realm beneath them. Inara could feel the deep ache in Athis's joints where his wings met his body. She no longer shared that pain, as she once did, but she easily recalled the ache and knew her companion needed rest, and soon. Rubbing his scales, Inara poured her sense of pride into the dragon, letting him know how impressed she was with his efforts.

*I would keep you in the heavens with me forever, wingless one...*

Inara beamed and patted his side. ***Is there any better place to be?***

They continued to fly inland for several minutes before Athis dipped and banked to the south. Inara noted the new direction and looked around at their environment, wondering what had initiated the change.

*Do you see that lake?* the dragon asked.

Inara looked to her right, where a body of water - larger than The King's Lake - stretched out along the base of the mountain range. It glistened in the rising sun, revealing an island in the middle with its own mountain.

*That's Lake Kundrun,* Athis told her, referring to the knowledge Rainael had imparted to him. *The mountains behind it are known as The Spine of Erador. They touch both the north and south of this realm, but they also divide the east from the west.*

Inara was truly fascinated. She wanted to know everything about the ancient land, the true birthplace of humanity and civilisation. ***Why are you heading south?***

*We would be better starting our search in Valgala, the capital. Beneath us is The High Plains,* he continued, directing Inara to the rolling hills of green that engulfed the land from The Spine of Erador to the eastern coast. *Even your eyes cannot see it from here, but The North Road cuts through this region. It will take us to Valgala...*

Inara looked ahead, between Athis's cranial horns, with great anticipation. "We're heading to the capital!" she called over her shoulder, informing Asher and Adan'Karth.

The ranger was in the middle of tearing some bread into three pieces, one for each of them. Inara had been impressed by Asher on their travels. While Adan and herself required no sleep on the journey, the ranger had tied himself to Athis's spinal horns. With Adan's added arms, for stability, he had managed to sleep in small chunks.

There couldn't be many who could fall asleep astride a dragon.

"Make sure we're not seen," Asher replied.

Athis acknowledged the ranger's instruction and glided on a south-westerly heading, taking them closer to the mountains. Inara tried to absorb everything around them - it was all so new! Her curiosity rose and she desired to know everything about the world beneath them.

Her curiosity was soon overshadowed by awe. Interrupting The Spine of Erador was a mountain so gargantuan that all the kingdoms of Illian could reside inside it and never touch borders. Its peak was swallowed by the clouds and its base was carpeted in forestry for miles around.

Mesmerised, she asked, **What is that?**

Athis turned his head to regard the god-like formation. *Mount Kaliban,* the dragon declared ominously.

Inara repeated the name in her mind. That name had haunted Illian's history for millennia, yet so few knew the truth. **I can see why the Eradorians named it after their god...**

Athis grunted his agreement. *By Rainael's reckoning, it is the largest mountain in the world, dwarfing even Mount Garganafan in Ayda.*

An hour after sighting Mount Kaliban, Athis began his descent. Eradoran soil rose up to meet them with some speed, a sign of the dragon's exhaustion. All four of his claws thundered into the ground, sending a jarring shockwave through to his riders.

The land was higher here, offering them a view of a vast and shallow basin that dominated the heart of Erador. In the middle, surrounded by farm land, rested a city that could sit in Inara's palm. She didn't need to ask Athis to know it was Valgala.

*I must rest.* Everything about Athis was weary, from his bowing head to his tone.

***There is truly no dragon that can match you,*** Inara complimented, watching her companion lay flat against the ground.

Along with Asher and Adan, the guardian climbed down, eager to use her legs and stretch her muscles. The moment didn't escape her. The second her feet touched down on Erador, she was officially in a foreign land. Again, her excitement was dampened by their errand.

Asher contorted his body into various shapes, cracking his back, neck, and arms. Adan'Karth looked to have suffered no discomfort and simply removed his hood to better take in the new world. His reptilian eyes displayed the same sense of wonder that swelled within Inara.

"Isn't it amazing?" she remarked, gesturing to The Spine of Erador behind them.

Unimpressed, Asher ceased his stretching and cast his old eyes over Erador. "The sun rises in the east, the wind blows cold, and the ground is hard," he observed with all the wonder of a rock. "Not that different…"

Inara chose to ignore his description and walked towards the edge of the rise, where the shallow basin could be seen in its entirety. "That's Valgala, the capital. It's as good a place as any to begin our search."

Asher joined her, the Drake beside him. "We should take the day to recover and enter the city at night. We have no idea what's going on inside those walls - we'll blend in better with the shadows on our side."

Feeling Athis's fatigue, Inara was inclined to agree. "We should scout the area."

Asher removed the folded bow from his back and snapped it to life. "I'll find us something we can cook." The ranger was already raising his hand to Adan as the Drake prepared to protest. "I know," Asher said, "you don't eat meat. I'll see if there's some *leaves* for you…"

Inara instinctively wished to accompany the ranger, if for nothing other than the safety of their numbers. But she had asked

Asher to join her for a reason - he was a man of particular skills and he didn't need protecting in the wilds of any realm.

Athis heaved himself up onto all fours and lazily wandered away from the edge of the rise. He moved closer to the trees that dotted the area between them and the mountains, where he could conceal himself better. Inara took a step to trail him, but her eyes refused to let go of Valgala. Even from this distance, she could make out the circular white wall that protected the city. It shone in the sun, like a jewel in the muted colours of the land around it.

It was much later before she pulled herself away from the view and joined Athis and Adan, down the other side of the rise. The dragon was on the verge of sleep when Inara requested one last thing from him. Slowly, and very carefully, Athis allowed a portion of Rainael's knowledge to pass between their bond. The weight of it forced Inara's eyes closed and she dropped to her knees.

New sights, sounds, and even words took hold in her memory, as if she had always known of Valgala and the land around it. When next she opened her eyes, the sun had moved across the sky, though Asher was yet to return. Athis laid one startling blue eye on her before succumbing to a much-deserved sleep. Inara rose to her feet and ran an affectionate hand over the dragon's snout and over the ridge of his eye.

Not far beyond Athis's curled tail, Adan'Karth stood between the trees, his hands held out as if in prayer. Inara felt the call for more sleep, especially since they were to enter the city that night, but her curiosity was already piqued upon noticing the Drake.

"What are you doing?" she asked on approach.

Adan slowly lowered his arms and waited for the Guardian to join him. "The trees here... They only dare to whisper."

Inara inspected the closest trunk. She saw nothing to suggest it possessed intelligence and she heard nothing but the rustle of its branches and leaves in the wind. "You can talk to trees?" She couldn't help her incredulous tone.

"I would like to," Adan replied, "but I can barely hear them."

The Drake turned away from the trees and let his gaze sweep across the land. "Magic here has been stamped out." He crouched down and placed an open hand to the ground. "But there is magic in Erador's roots. It goes deep and spreads far." Adan rose again, his expression telling of his depression. "Fear has gripped this realm…"

Inara thought of home. "I can believe it - they've lived in the shadow of Malliath for fifteen years."

"You should get some rest," Adan advised, changing the subject. "You will need your strength for what comes next."

Inara cocked an eyebrow, aware, suddenly, that she was talking to a being of great magic and wisdom who could commune with nature. "And do you know what comes next?"

The Drake raised his hood again. "With Asher, there is always blood…"

Inara's eyes snapped open to see the last rays of light, dying in the west. Stars encroached on the sky, covering Erador in a blanket of heavenly lights and a beaming moon. Seated with her back to Athis, she moved backwards and forwards with his slow breaths.

"You're a heavy sleeper," Asher commented. His tone was flat, but Inara was certain the ranger was criticising her.

Finding her feet, the Guardian scanned the area and found a small fire between herself and Asher. Adan'Karth was seated with his back to her, his arms folded around his knees. The crack of the flames drew her to the rabbit being slowly roasted on a makeshift spit. Her eyes weren't required to know that Athis was still sleeping - he would need more hours to come.

Joining them by the fire, Inara gladly accepted the meat offered by the ranger. "You scouted the area?"

"I did." Asher took a swig of water before handing it to Inara. "There's a small homestead just south of here - simple farmers. If I hadn't known we were in Erador, their appearance and manner would suggest we were still in Illian."

Inara glanced at Athis, an unmissable sight. "Is there any chance they would wander this far?"

"Possibly, but not tonight. I stayed long enough to see them call it a day. They won't be leaving their home after dark."

Inara decided to trust the ranger's instincts. "Athis has shared some of Rainael's memories with me." The Guardian removed the Moonblade from the back of her belt. "Valgala sits in the middle of a crossroads, six roads to be exact." It wasn't befitting of a weapon so powerful, but Inara used the opal blade to carve into the dirt between them. "This is the city," she said, gesturing to a stone. "The roads intersect here." Using the Moonblade, she drew six lines out from the stone at specific angles. "We're here, in the north-west, between The North Road and The Spoken Road."

Asher edged around the fire and looked closely at the crude map. "This is The Spoken Road?" He pointed at the line that ran into Valgala from the west.

"Yes. We can see that from the ridge."

"I watched this road today," Asher informed her. "I only saw one cart journeying west. I don't know where it leads," he added, glancing at the mountainside in the west, "but I'd say it isn't used much."

Adan nodded in agreement. "We could look suspicious arriving via this road."

"It could also be the least guarded," Inara pointed out.

"What about scaling the walls?" the Drake suggested.

"Too high," Asher replied.

"Portal?" Adan came back with, looking to the crystal on the end of Firefly.

"Too much magic," the ranger rejected. "I'd bet my life there's Seekers down there."

Inara closed her eyes in a bid to see what lay at the end of the western road, but Athis had only given her so much, blurring the edges in her mind. "There's another way in, just south of The Spoken Road. I can't make out the name but it is a road. It cuts through the mountains." Again, she couldn't recall where it led. "I know there's a city on the other end. That would suggest merchant travel at least."

"Do we look like merchants?" Asher asked rhetorically.

Becoming frustrated with the ranger's stream of problems and lack of solutions, Inara sighed and gave the man an expectant look. "What would you suggest?"

Asher looked her in the eyes. "I would scout the perimeter for at least three days, noting the patrols on the walls and around the gates. I would get a lay of the land and see where each of the six roads lead and from there find a suitable cover that allowed me to enter the city undetected or at least unsuspected. Once inside, I would take a few more days to become acquainted with the city itself, its layout, its routines, and the people who inhabit it. Then I would scout the palace, which I presume is the building with the central spire. Infiltrating it would be next on my list..."

Inara's exasperated expression was enough to declare her thoughts on the ranger's very long plan. "We don't have time for even one of those things."

Asher shrugged. "Then let's walk through the gate..."

At least another hour passed before the three companions found themselves on The Spoken Road, Valgala dominating their view. Leaving Athis to rest, out of sight, they had walked down the gentle slope until the grass gave way to the road. Inara had woken the dragon, briefly, to inform him of their plan, or lack thereof.

*Wait until I am rested,* Athis had requested.

Inara reminded him that in a very short space of time, he had flown to Dragons' Reach and back before flying all the way to Erador. Athis had protested but his weariness won out, unable to challenge Inara's stubbornness for once.

Keeping to the road, three to four hours passed before they were craning their necks to see the top of Valgala's walls, lined with torches. The impressive archway, set into the western wall, was similarly illuminated and visibly guarded by four soldiers in black.

"Reavers?" the Guardian questioned on their approach.

"Too far to tell," Asher said. "Adan?"

The Drake employed his superior eyes and reported, "They wear the same armour certainly."

"Are they moving?" the ranger asked.

Adan waited a moment while he observed. "Not at all."

"Reavers then," Asher reasoned. "What about Seekers?"

The Drake's reptilian eyes twitched as he focused them on the shadows around the edges of the light. "One," he relayed. "Resting on the right."

Inara gripped Firefly on her belt but refrained from withdrawing it. "Four Reavers and a Seeker," she concluded. "There's no way we're getting through there without making a lot of noise. All three of us have magic in our bones and Seekers are loud. We'll have to dispatch them and move with haste - hopefully there's somewhere we can hide inside before reinforcements arrive."

The Guardian turned to Asher, expecting some revisions to her plan. The ranger was gone. Immediately concerned, Inara stopped and looked around only to discover the darkness that settled over the land was impenetrable.

Maintaining his steady pace, hood concealing his flat horns, Adan remarked, "You will get used to that..."

Inara groaned and quick-stepped to fall back in beside the Drake. "We could accomplish more if we coordinated."

"He is more accustomed to the shadows," Adan explained. "You, I feel, are better in the light - best you stay that way."

Inara was shaking her head. "I thought he had chosen to accompany me to get away from the call of the *shadows*."

Adan turned to give her a sideways glance.

"My father told me," Inara confessed. "I know he has concerns regarding the manner of his death."

The Drake folded his hands into the sleeves of his robe. "From what I know of Asher, it is not death that concerns him, nor has it ever. What really troubles him is the manner in which he *lives*. He is here to do the one thing he believes he can never do..."

Inara looked from the Reavers to Adan and back. "And what's that?" she asked, her eyes shifting across the darkness in search of the ranger.

"Atone," Adan said simply.

That truly surprised the Guardian. "He's already died for the realm once. Besides that, he helped turn the tide in The Ash War."

"Nevertheless," the Drake continued, "he feels his soul is still tainted. The scales are still tipped against him. He may never truly forgive himself for the lives he has taken."

Inara had never felt sorry for the ranger - after all, he was a man of great skill who had overcome more than most in the years he had been given. But knowing he lived a haunted life saddened her, for, in her heart, she knew he deserved much more for his service to the realm, whether that had been given willingly or not.

"You seem to know him very well," Inara commented.

"I have healed him many times," Adan explained. "It has given me ample opportunity to see what lies beneath his rough exterior."

"He's very lucky to have you by his side," Inara opined. "I say that because I'm sure he would never admit to it."

"It is not me he needs."

Inara dared to take her eyes off the Reavers for a moment and glance at the Drake. "If not you, then what?"

Adan'Karth turned his yellow green eyes on her, a sombre expression darkening his face. "I do not have an answer to that. The only companion he has ever known is Death - it has followed him everywhere. I fear he will not be ready the day it comes for him. I do not want him to die as a killer..."

Inara wasn't sure Death was ready for Asher; it had already lost its grip on him once. Either way, the Guardian was forced to push such thoughts from her mind - the Reavers were close now. Of the four, the two closest to the centre of the archway broke away to meet them, hands on their sheathed swords. Inara had no idea what Asher was doing in the dark, but the Seeker was already pushing up onto all four legs, clearly interested in the two magical beings on the road.

Inara pulled Firefly an inch from its scabbard.

"Stay behind me," she warned Adan.

The two patches, either side of the Seeker's head, began to vibrate, emitting a low-level drone. Any second now, it was going to detect the wells of magic that existed in both Inara and Adan'Karth and then that drone would elevate to a crescendo, calling every Reaver to their position.

Inara's keen ears heard the familiar sound of a whistling arrow before her eyes tracked its last moment of flight. The missile ended in the Seeker's skull, fired from somewhere in the surrounding dark-ness. The beast collapsed under its weight, dead, turning all four Reavers to the north. A second arrow caught the torchlight before sinking into the head of a Reaver. Before it fell to the floor, a third arrow was already on its way to the Reaver who had been holding the Seeker's leash.

Whether Asher had expected her to or not, Inara saw her moment and exploded into action. Firefly slid from its scabbard with a satisfying sound - it was also the last sound the two Reavers in front of her ever heard. Their attention split, they only glimpsed Fire-fly's edge before it sliced through the head of one and then the neck of the other.

As Inara sheathed her Vi'tari blade, Asher emerged from the darkness by the side of the archway. He flicked his bow and the limbs collapsed in on themselves making it easier to latch onto his quiver. With one hand, he gestured for them to join him by the threshold.

Inara stepped over the bodies whereas Adan'Karth gave them a wide berth. "Maybe next time we can *talk* about the plan," she chided.

Asher ignored her remark altogether. Instead, he entered the city and scanned the streets before turning his gaze to the tall buildings and towers that filled it. "We should go up - they won't expect that. Find a secluded spot, preferably sheltered. From there, we can scout the city and plan our next move."

Inara trailed behind the ranger, trying not to become distracted by the grand architecture of her ancestors. "Scout? I thought we were breaking into the palace tonight?"

"There won't be time to get in and out before the alarm is raised," Asher replied, thumbing at the bodies in their wake. "I know time is against us, but if we don't do this carefully, we might never return to Illian, never mind find Gideon and Ilargo. We find shelter, let the Reavers fall back into their normal pattern, *then* break into the palace. Trust me," he implored. "This isn't the first time I've been somewhere I'm not supposed to."

Inara was desperate to move things along. She needed to find Gideon and Ilargo. She needed to get back to Illian. She needed to stop her brother...

Voicing her needs was useless since Asher shared them all. "I trust you," she said reluctantly.

Asher nodded his appreciation and led them to the nearest alley-way. The building on their right was cathedral in size, a possible place of worship Inara reasoned.

"We're going up there?"

The ranger cracked his knuckles. "Yes," he replied gruffly. "It's tall so it should give us a better view of the city come sunrise. Also, it has lots of arches - potential shelter."

Inara sighed. "As you say..." She looked down the alley, wondering if she had made a mistake in bringing the ranger. With her power, if she moved now, she could be in and out of the palace in one night and possess all the answers that might come with it.

Adan tackled the sheer wall first, displaying exceptional climbing ability. Asher didn't follow after the Drake but, instead, turned to the Guardian.

"I know," he said, as if he could read her mind and the frustration that dwelled within. "I know what you mean to do," he continued, looking to the end of the alley. "But there comes a time when we have to make a choice. That choice has the power to define us—"

Inara raised a hand to stop him. "Are you seriously using *that* speech?"

Asher moved his head back. "What speech?"

"That speech!" Inara hissed. "Those are *my* words. I said that to you two years ago, in Namdhor, before you put that ridiculous blindfold on and tried to kill Alijah. You cut me off and gave *me* a speech about knowing the consequences..."

"And what did you think of me?"

"I thought you were being an *ass.*" Inara took a breath and glanced down the alley again. "I thought you were wrong."

"And I was," Asher admitted, taking the Guardian by surprise. "I should have listened to you. We do get to choose what road we take. I should never have put that blindfold back on and I shouldn't have tried to take Alijah on my own. It sent me down a dark path. I've had to leave the country to get away from it." The ranger nodded his chin at the street. "You could go and do this your way. You could take the palace by storm and demand answers. But if you fall, so too will The Rebellion."

Inara met his eyes, dark orbs in the shadow of the alley. "We do this your way," she agreed. "I trust you."

Asher responded with a mischievous grin. "Now that would be foolish..."

# CHAPTER 33
# A WARNING

Seated exactly in the centre of the tower, within a column of midday sun, Alijah Galfrey maintained a disciplined posture, a rigidity that reflected the life he led. His eyes were closed but his mind was open.

He sighed...

Opening his eyes, the half-elf cursed under his breath. He had been on Qamnaran for days now, overseeing the last preparations as well as meditating to ensure his own readiness. They were so close now. Yet here he was, unable to settle his mind and simply think.

*What is wrong?* Malliath asked from the skies.

Alijah took a steady breath, examining the circular wall of ancient glyphs that surrounded him. As instructed, the dwarf, Malankor, had painted the necessary runes with the Fenrig's blood, one of the spell's many demands. ***Every time I close my eyes I see him...***

*Vighon,* Malliath replied, his tone edged with impatience.

Alijah didn't need to answer for the dragon to know the truth. Through the eyes of Rengyr, he had seen his oldest friend and greatest enemy amongst the ruins of The Watcher.

*He's back,* the king lamented.

*It makes no difference,* Malliath told him. *The northman can do nothing to stop us now, none of them can - our hold on the realm is secure.*

Alijah turned his head to the left, aware that the east lay beyond. **Adilandra is already here - I can feel it. She has likely reinforced the elves with dwarven warriors. An attack is imminent.**

*Let them come,* Malliath growled. *Clan Heavybelly needs eradicating - a lesson for the others.*

Alijah agreed that the dwarves needed breaking before they could be trusted to integrate with the rest of Illian. **I am more concerned with Vighon's presence in the north,** he confessed.

*You should have killed him when you had the chance,* the dragon chastised. *You have allowed your feelings to get in the way. There are some who will never accept the world we are building. What do we do to those who stand in our way?*

Alijah heard Malliath ask the question, but he heard The Crow's voice answer it in his mind. **Sacrifice without hesitation,** he recited.

*Do you fear your enemy?* the dragon continued.

**No.**

*Do you fear slaying those you love if they threaten the peace?*

Again, Alijah replied, **No.**

*Why not?* Malliath asked.

The Crow's teachings, never far away, rose to the surface with ease. **Because fear is not real,** Alijah stated. **Fear is simply a product of the mind. Danger is real.**

He could feel Malliath's approval through their bond and he relished it. There was something else in his mind, another presence on the periphery. Alijah closed his eyes and quickly discovered that Lord Kraiden and his mount, Morgorth, were on approach.

*Perhaps,* Malliath posed, *we should put our enemies off balance...*

Alijah instantly knew what his companion had in mind. Turning his attention to the book laid out on the silvyr floor, the half-elf waved his hand over its leathery cover and flipped it open with magic. His fingers wiggled in the air as he flicked through the pages in search of the right spell. He had seen it before and only used it once to test the validity of the spell but, as always, the Jainus had unlocked every crevice of the magical realm.

Alijah finally arrived at the right page and read through the text a couple of times to familiarise himself with it. He already knew, from the Fenrigs' reports, that the elven rebels always disappeared on the eastern side of Qamnaran - that would give him somewhere to start.

Galanör couldn't help but wince at the noise that accompanied the dwarves of clan Heavybelly. For a year now, their camp had been a place of serenity; no easy thing considering their task on the island and those they had shared it with.

Now it was a clamour of hard sounds, raucous singing, and a language all too abrasive to the sensitive ears of a woodland elf. Then there was the smell. The odour that clung to sweating dwarves had become a daily assault on Galanör's olfactory senses, and he was the most accustomed of all the elves, having spent time with Doran.

Despite their many differences and the way both races were destined to grate on the other, Galanör could see a bond forming between them. He had expected to see clumps of elves and clumps of dwarves, all busy seeing to their separate activities, but that wasn't the case. Even now, moving through the camp, he watched as a pair of elves were advised by a dwarf to swap their arrows for ones crafted of Heavybelly design. They thanked him for them and fell into further discussion with the Heavybelly.

Galanör smiled to himself.

Following the sound of the waterfall, the elven ranger entered the heart of their camp. Standing in front of the pool was a vision of beauty. Aenwyn, he was sure, had beauty enough to mesmerise the entire realm of man. He paused to simply watch her as she directed a dwarf to their makeshift armoury, just west of the small cliff they inhabited.

Having waited for the Heavybelly to move on, Galanör approached his love. "Strange times," he observed.

"Indeed," Aenwyn agreed. "Though I think we will make for great allies. Our skills complement each other."

Galanör couldn't help but smile, always amazed by Aenwyn's insight and perspective - there weren't many who would view the dwarves as she did. Even he found Doran to be trying at times.

"You have seen the queen?" she asked.

"I'm on my way now," he replied, gesturing to one of the caves that pocketed the cliff face, beside the waterfall. "I have been speaking with Doran and Russell. They are concerned for Adilandra."

Aenwyn began walking towards the cliff, bringing Galanör with her. "I spoke briefly with the High Guardian. The queen used her *essence* to repel the Sandstalkers."

Had Galanör reported such a thing, he too would have used a grave tone. He had heard of ancient elves releasing this incredible power until it left them a shell, too broken to even reabsorb their magic.

"Adilandra is strong," he understated, his own concerns weighing on him. "She has overcome more than this."

Aenwyn nodded in understanding. "Of course. How could I forget of your adventure with the queen and the master of the Dragorn? You have lived an unbelievable life, Galanör Reveeri."

Galanör began to ascend the winding slope that zig-zagged up the cliff face. "I wouldn't call it an adventure. Especially in front of Adilandra," he warned, aware that her time among the Darkakin was far worse than his own. "Also, Gideon Thorn wasn't the master of anything back then," he added, wishing to introduce some levity rather than dwell on the queen's mistreatment. "He was barely a man, in fact. Though, he was still of better quality than myself..."

"I can believe it," Aenwyn quipped with a melodic laugh.

Halfway up the waterfall, the queen's dwelling was made obvious thanks to the armoured sentinels that stood outside. Neither prevented Galanör or Aenwyn from entering, where they were quickly greeted by Faylen Haldör. Her raven hair fell over golden pauldrons, adorned in armour as she was.

"How fairs the queen?" Galanör enquired.

"The queen fairs well," Adilandra answered for herself. With visible effort, she pushed herself up to sit on the edge of the cot. Galanör and Aenwyn bowed their heads until Adilandra waved the gesture away.

Faylen rushed to her side, clearly fretting. "You should still be resting," she insisted.

"I have rested enough," the queen croaked. "My magic returns with every passing moment." Holding her hand out, palm up, Adilandra narrowed her eyes and summoned a living flame of orange and yellow. It flickered and died as fast as it appeared, leaving the queen to ball her fist and wince.

"A simple spell still drains you," Faylen remarked, the only one brave enough to say it.

"Evidently," Adilandra uttered, letting her head hang for a second. When next she looked up, her expression had an element of forced exertion. "It is good to see you again Galanör." Despite the obvious effort, her tone was genuine and matched her smile.

"It has been too long," Galanör replied, matching her warmth. "How did you find your first night on Qamnaran?"

Adilandra's eyes made a cursory scan of the cave's entrance, as if she could see the dwarves of clan Heavybelly. "Loud."

"And wet," Faylen added.

Amusement flashed across his face. "There is little luxury here, I'm afraid. Only good company," he added, briefly meeting Aenwyn's eyes as a smile brightening her sharp features.

"You and I have endured worse together," Adilandra recalled. "I can still remember baking under a desert sun on a Darkakin rooftop..."

Galanör fidgeted on his feet - those particular memories would stay with the ranger all his long life. "I can assure you, your Grace, the last thing you will experience on Qamnaran is a hot sun."

"I have always welcomed the rain," the queen said offhandedly. Faylen reached down and attempted to help her up, but Adilandra managed it on her own. "It is fatigue, nothing more. I will be ready for the assault on the tower."

Galanör folded his arms around his ribs. "Doran would like to talk to both of us regarding the assault - when you're ready."

Adilandra inhaled a deep breath, steadying herself. "Ah yes, our dwarven cousins. They will be eager to meet the enemy in battle, I'm sure."

Faylen hovered around the queen. "I believe Doran has already been forced to hold some of them back."

Adilandra held a pensive gaze at nothing in particular. "For all his efforts, the son of Dorain is still being tested by his brothers."

"Your Grace." Aenwyn stepped forward. "Now that you are here, those of us who resided in Ilythyra would like to commemorate Lady Ellöria. We thought, perhaps, that we could have a pyre in her honour."

A sad smile preceded Adilandra's response. "I would like that."

Their conversation went no further, halted by the rushing feet of another elf. Turning to the entrance, Tyren, one of Galanör's best scouts, skidded into the cave and quickly bowed his head. "Your Grace," he greeted with a heaving chest. Looking to Galanör, he reported, "Dragon Rider."

Alarm spread among them. "Where?" Faylen demanded.

"Three miles north of here," Tyren answered. "We can't be sure which Rider it is, but we know the dragon isn't Malliath."

Galanör gripped the hilts on his hip. "Pull everyone back to the trees!"

Tyren hesitated, unsure who he was supposed to be speaking to. "They're not looking for us - at least they're not moving. It's the Rider. He's calling your name..."

Galanör had never heard of Reavers speaking before, let alone calling his name. "Take me to them," he commanded.

"It could be a trap," Aenwyn blurted.

"My thoughts exactly," Faylen agreed.

"I will approach from the west so as not to give our position away," Galanör reassured.

"That is very noble of you," the queen reasoned, "but what about yourself?"

"The Rider's calling *my* name - there's no reason to endanger anyone else; I will go alone."

"The hell ye will, laddy!" Doran's armoured silhouette did its best to fill the cave's entrance. "Thaligg an' Thraal can handle the clan 'ere. How abou' a couple o' *rangers* see to this..."

Galanör masked his reserve and thanked the War Mason.

"You will not go without my bow," Aenwyn told him. Galanör knew better than to argue with her where his life was concerned.

"Then let's go," he said.

Faylen cleared her throat, stopping the three of them in their tracks. Galanör looked back to see the High Guardian giving the queen a sideways glance. The elven ranger was suddenly filled with embarrassment as well as some irritation.

"Apologies, your Grace," he offered.

Adilandra held the moment, drawing all eyes on to herself. "Do not be blind to this, Galanör. That Dragon Rider has been dead longer than I have been alive. It does not wish to speak to you - this is one of Alijah's games. Be steadfast."

Galanör bowed his head, taking the queen's words as permission to leave with Aenwyn and Doran. On horseback and Warhog, they set out from the camp, led by Tyren. They travelled a longer route, taking them out wide, to the west, where they then curved back around to the north and into the embrace of rain clouds. Tyren brought them to a ridge, covered in dense foliage, giving them a view of the rocky terrain below.

"GALANÖR!" The voice that boomed his name was unnatural and stale.

Crawling, the four made their way to the edge and looked down on the owner of that terrible voice. It boomed again as they took in the sight of the Rider, clad in black armour, draped in a tattered cloak, and crowned with a helmet that covered his face and rose up into five sharp spikes.

Doran almost exploded with rage.

It took all three elves to physically hold him down as well as cover his mouth. Galanör looked him in the eye, his expression stern. "Our magic will not stand up to the wrath of Morgorth," he hissed.

"That's Lord Kraiden down there!" Doran spat through gritted teeth. "I owe him an axe to the head for what he's done to me brother!"

"This isn't how we beat him," Galanör dictated.

Doran huffed, struggling to dampen his anger. "I need that blade o' his. We need to know what the poison is before we can cure Dak. I *need* it."

"Lord Kraiden will fall with the tower," the elven ranger assured. "And Morgorth with him. Then we will retrieve the blade and save Dakmund. *Only* then."

The son of Dorain clenched his fist and pounded the dirt. "The lady was right - this is jus' one o' Alijah's games. If it ain' a trap he's jus' messin' with us. I say we go back, rouse the boys, get some o' yer archers on this ridge, an' we slay that beast right now."

"GALANÖR!" Kraiden bellowed.

The elf ignored his name for the moment and looked at Doran. "Alijah isn't the only one who can play games." With that, he moved away with barely a sound and made his way down to the slab of earth.

Suddenly, Morgorth seemed much larger. His dead white eyes quickly found Galanör and his great maw opened just enough for the ranger to see the two glands that would produce an inferno. He had to wonder if he really had made a mistake...

Lord Kraiden was standing in front of Morgorth's ruined form, a creation of evil himself. There was something about the way the Reaver held himself, however, something all too human.

"I didn't think the dead had need of words," Galanör began.

Lord Kraiden tilted his head, taking the ranger in. "I knew you would be here." The Reaver's voice was strange to his ears, as if there were two people speaking as one.

He recognised the more dominant voice.

"Is that you in there, Alijah?" he asked, without concealing his disgust. "Inhabiting the dead is a new low, even for you."

"Is *she* here too?" Alijah asked, moving Kraiden's head around.

Galanör said nothing, which was, perhaps, an answer in itself.

Kraiden let loose a menacing, if unnerving, laugh. "How many did she bring - my grandmother? Hundreds? Thousands? Has The Alliance been renewed to bring me down?" he asked with amusement. "It won't be enough," the king continued, lowering Kraiden's voice. "You're going to throw away all of their lives. And for what? You don't even know what I'm doing here."

"You have shown your true colours time and time again," Galanör protested. "You talk of peace yet do nothing but spill blood. You hold the realm in the grip of Reavers! Reavers, Alijah! Do you remember when we used to hunt them? Do you remember when we called The Black Hand our enemy? Now *you* are a necromancer. You use the worst of magic..."

"Do not lecture me on matters you know nothing about. Five centuries of life behind you and what do you have to show for it? You should have taken the time to study magic not the sword. There is no *good* magic just as there is no *evil* magic. The wielder's actions determine everything. I have used magic that displeases you, but I use it to maintain peace. Because of my Reavers, no man or woman will ever again have to pick up a sword and defend what is theirs."

Galanör shook his head in pity. "It has already corrupted your mind. We once stood together, agreed that what you're now doing is evil. How could you have fallen so far?"

Lord Kraiden remained very still and the ranger began to wonder if Alijah was still in there.

"You're just like all the others then," the king finally replied. "Are there none who can see as I do? Are there none left to have faith in me? My future has already been determined. I am *fated*, Galanör, to bring the entire realm together."

"The Crow's words," Galanör said. "The ramblings of a mad man, nothing more."

Kraiden took a step forward and Galanör's hands instinctively embraced his scimitars. "I came here to warn you, as an old friend. I have great respect for what you've done for the realm. You are a warrior I would gladly have welcomed to my side." Kraiden's voice distorted into a growl. "But I see you are too narrow-minded to share my vision. Instead, you will throw your life away for nothing."

"Dying to stop you isn't nothing," Galanör retorted, relaxing his posture. "There was a time when you would have said the same."

The Reaver squared his armoured shoulders. "I promise you one thing, Galanör of house Reveeri: before your end, you will watch her die on the battlefield. I hope in that moment, you realise your mistake making me your enemy."

The elven ranger furrowed his brow. "I have seen Queen Adilandra on the battlefield. I hope that when that moment comes, *you* realise you are nothing but a boy playing a game he doesn't understand."

Kraiden tilted his spiked head. "I wasn't talking about my grand-mother." Alijah turned his puppet's head to survey the jagged envi-ronment. "Did you bring her with you? Her name has eluded me since your little rebellion began, but I do not forget a face. She was so heroic on the walls of my keep - her skill with a bow is commendable."

Galanör could feel knots forming at the end of his arms. His knuckles cracked and his jaw clenched as his warrior's mind deter-mined the quickest way to part Kraiden from his head. The hunter Aenwyn had helped him to bury was eager to come out and tear through anyone who threatened the one who held his heart.

"I will face you soon with magic and steel," he said with fury behind his words. "Then you will see what I have to show for five hundred years of killing monsters. At my back will be a force not seen since The Great War. We will wash your stain away just as we did the orcs. Then, as I wipe my blades clean of your blood, I will grieve for you…"

"So there is a little bite behind that angelic face," Alijah jibed, determined to provoke the elf. "Good. You're going to need it. Whatever your force, you do not have what it takes to claim victory against two dragons and my Reavers. Leave me to my work and you will see that what I'm doing is—"

"I don't care what you're doing," Galanör cut in, his anger spilling out now. "Vighon Draqaro is the king of these lands. Not you. I will not rest until he is back on the throne and you are buried with that beast you call a companion."

"Heroes die," Alijah stated, his words as blunt as his tone. "I learnt that lesson a long time ago. You would do well to heed those words." Without waiting for a response, Kraiden turned back to Morgorth and ascended his thick neck.

Galanör held his ground and watched the dragon push off into the sky, its wings displacing the rain. Unable to maintain his gaze in the face of the rain, the elven ranger lowered his head and opened the palm of his right hand. His nails had dug into the skin, leaving four red lines that would begin to sting soon enough.

His ears detected the fall of loose pebbles, informing him of Doran's approach. It required some effort, but he managed to slow his breathing down and temper the thundering of his heart. Deliberately, the elf refrained from looking at Aenwyn as she jumped down off the nearest ledge. Seeing her, right now, would bring Alijah's threat to the forefront and he would lose what semblance of control he had found.

"What were all that abou'?" Doran asked, looking up at the ranger.

Galanör unclenched his jaw. "I think he believes he is threatening us - perhaps to unnerve us; that's what I would do. But, in truth, I think he is concerned we will ruin his plans here. He wants us to back off."

Aenwyn placed a hand on his shoulder and gave him the subtlest of squeezes. Of course she knew something wasn't right with him. They had unravelled themselves and revealed to the other what lay beneath.

"Are you alright?" she asked gently.

Galanör finally met her eyes. His heart ached, plagued by the fear of losing her. He often wondered how he had lived for so long without her in his life.

"We should return to the others," he said, aware that Doran and Tyren were present. "We have a battle to plan..."

# CHAPTER 34
# HOME SWEET HOME

Kassian Kantaris tugged on his coat, its length almost grazing the frosted ground. He looked upon the gentle rise of Namdhor's slope with apprehension. It was easily a mile or more from its base to the looming Dragon Keep, a hazy image at its apex.

The Keeper took it all in from the lower town which was sprawled across the flat vale around the city's base. From his position, leaning against the corner of an alleyway, he could also see other members of his band. They had split up, shortly before arriving at the city, and taken different routes to the main street - together, they were just asking for the Seekers to find them.

He looked at a few of them, encouraging them with a nod to slowly infiltrate the city in pairs. It would take time, but, eventually, they would all be further up the rise where they could more easily come to each other's aid.

It was dangerous.

Kassian had to remind himself that every one of his Keepers was willing to die to crush their enemy. There were, in fact, many who welcomed the idea of dying in the fight, eager to be rid of the grief that plagued them. Kassian himself was plagued this way, his every action motivated by the death of Clara. He no longer feared death, too angry to be concerned by such a trivial matter.

He couldn't, however, ignore the calling in his heart. It was as if Clara had reached out from the afterlife and pressed upon him a cause so strong it tempered his wrath and cooled the fiery vengeance that ran through his veins. He didn't want a body count to be her memorial - she had abhorred violence, often voicing concern about certain aspects of his training as a Keeper.

Clara deserved to have lives saved in her name. Kassian wanted something extraordinary to be established in her name. What that was, unfortunately, still escaped the Keeper. For now, he was confined to the plans of others which, at this moment, placed him on the cusp of yet more violence...

"Between us and that sword of yours," he began, "there have got to be more Seekers than I can count. Not to mention the Reavers and Fenrigs who have been let off the leash..."

There came no reply from Vighon, stood beside him. Like the Keeper, the northman had a thick scarf concealing his nose and mouth. Unlike the Keeper, he also had his hood up, an added measure of concealment where the true king was concerned. Kassian tilted his head to see inside Vighon's hood, wondering why he had failed to reply.

The look in his eyes told Kassian everything he needed to know. The city was more than stone and mortar to the northman - it held memories, though the Keeper suspected the sight bolstered the responsibility Vighon shouldered.

"Are you with me?" he asked, his tone enough to break Vighon's reverie.

"A part of me thought I would never see it again," the northman croaked. He hadn't said much since they fled The Watcher.

"I need you focused," Kassian emphasised. "Once we're up there, getting back down here is going to be damn hard. And that's *if* we succeed in breaking into the keep and retrieving your sword."

Vighon raised a hand to halt the lecture. "I told you: we don't need to break in. We just need to reach the church of Atilan…"

"Right," Kassian said sceptically. "Your *secret* door."

Vighon finally tore his eyes from the main street. "You doubt me?"

"You said you've never used the door," Kassian pointed out, his words slightly muffled by the scarf.

"I've read about it." Vighon shrugged. "Gal Tion himself had it built as a means of escape, should the city come under prolonged siege."

Kassian caught sight of two Reavers cutting across the main street and quickly pulled Vighon further down the alley. "And where exactly is this church?"

Vighon tried to hide his wince. "Not too far from the keep's outer wall…"

Kassian opened his mouth then closed it again. He moved back to the corner of the alley and peered up at the massive city. "It's at the top! Why would Gal Tion build an escape tunnel that only brought him beyond the keep's walls?"

"I found some entries regarding the stubbornness of Namdhor's stone," Vighon explained. "They could only dig so far with the tools they had. His court mages considered magic but there was concern for the stone's integrity if they dug too far down the slope. He opted for escaping the keep and taking his chances in the streets. Not that he ever needed to," Vighon added with a sour note. "Before my reign, The Dragon Keep was never taken by an enemy…"

Kassian groaned and rested the back of his head against the wall. Nathaniel appeared at the other end of the alley having paid the local stables to tend to their horses. He noted the Keeper's mood and enquired as to the problem.

"The church we're looking for: it might as well be *inside* The Dragon Keep."

Nathaniel looked from Kassian to Vighon. "There's no other tunnels?"

The northman shook his head. "Just the one."

Not unaccustomed to difficult situations, the old knight took it in his stride. "It's still our best way inside. We would never survive a frontal assault and we could never scale the walls before being spotted."

"We'll have to advance slowly," Kassian advised. "I wouldn't be surprised if some Seeker out there already has our scent."

Nathaniel adjusted the collar on his coat. "Let's go."

Abandoning the main road that rose up through Namdhor's tiers, the three companions climbed up a small rock face and entered the city proper, from the eastern edge. The side streets offered a multitude of routes up to The Dragon Keep, but they deliberately chose the winding paths, sometimes doubling back on themselves when they came across patrols of Reavers.

"Is it just me," Kassian began, "or are we not the only ones keeping our heads down?" His simple observation had been compounded at every turn, as the Namdhorian people averted their gaze, always appearing too busy to share so much as a glance.

"I don't think I've seen another's eyes yet," Nathaniel added.

Proving the Keeper's point, a woman and her young son rounded a corner and, upon sighting the three men, quickly disappeared inside the butcher's shop. Kassian was tempted to go inside himself and find out what the source of her obvious anxiety was.

Vighon put a hand out, across the Keeper's chest, halting their progression. "It's that," he said, gesturing to the wand holstered on Kassian's thigh. "You need to keep that thing hidden."

"You see," Kassian seethed. "This is what he's done. People are afraid of magic because Alijah murders anyone who can use it. They're even afraid of just being around it."

Nathaniel clapped a hand on his shoulder. "Stay focused. And keep it hidden."

Kassian was in the mood for an argument but, instead, tugged on his coat to better conceal his right leg. They continued up the rise, weaving through the busy streets, no longer able to see The Dragon Keep. Here and there, Kassian glimpsed other Keepers who tried to blend in by trading with the merchants and buying simple goods from the markets.

He wanted to tell them to keep moving for the Reavers were ever on patrol. But clumping together would be suicide. Kassian himself brushed off the enquiries of a sword-smith who took an interest in the blade hanging off his waist. Vighon, the king of these people, was never stopped by anyone. The hood and scarf disguised him perfectly - if anything, people avoided his menacing appearance. The northman, however, *was* stopped by what he saw.

Kassian tapped Nathaniel on the shoulder to hold him back. "Vig —" The Keeper's call was cut short by a hand squeezing his arm.

The old knight was shaking his head. "Don't say his name."

Kassian shrugged. "He was the king - there's got to be hundreds of Vighons around."

Nathaniel had no reply but to watch the northman, ten feet away. Vighon had been distracted by a scene not far, on the other side of the market square. Two young men, in a hurry by the look of them, were painting the flat wall of a church dedicated to Lethia, the goddess of luck.

"We need to go," Kassian urged Nathaniel, who was content to let Vighon watch the young men.

"Wait," Nathaniel replied. "He needs to see this."

The Keeper stepped to the side of a stall, draped in onions and herbs, to get a better look at what the young men were actually painting. It all clicked into place for him when he saw the image between them taking shape: the flaming sword. Turning to Vighon, he could just see the northman's eyes, transfixed by the sigil, *his* sigil.

The moment was broken with the sound of marching feet and scraping armour. From the far corner, six Reavers emerged with swords drawn and two Seekers between them. The crowd began to scatter and the stall owners took shelter amongst their goods.

Kassian dashed forward and snatched at Vighon's arm, pulling him away from the scene.

Through the chaos, the Keeper saw the two young men fleeing the scene of their own making. Three of the Reavers broke away and pursued them with one of the Seekers, its bony legs stretching its skeletal body. The remaining Reavers and Seeker immediately spread out, cutting three paths through the market.

"Come on!" Kassian hissed.

Together with Nathaniel, they half-ran from the area and entered into the maze of alleys and small streets. They ascended a set of stone steps and explored the next level up, always checking over their shoulders for Reavers.

"That was close," the Keeper remarked, catching his breath.

His last word caught in his mouth as he collided, shoulder to shoulder, with a Reaver walking round the corner. The undead soldier wasted no time asserting its authority and pushing Kassian back with a strong hand. In doing so, his long coat moved aside, revealing his wand...

There was a pause, as if the world was taking a breath.

Nathaniel reacted first, his instincts and experience shining through. Using the full weight of his body, he rammed into the Reaver and carried on through the door of a tailor's shop. The second Reaver gripped the hilt of its sword but failed to pull it free before Kassian shoved it hard into the wall, his forearm pressed into its armoured chest. His wand was out in the blink of an eye. He thrust the tip under the gap where the Reaver's helmet met its neck. The destructive spell ripped asunder the top of the soldier's helm and sprayed the wall with putrid innards.

He let its rotten body fall to the ground and turned to see Vighon, who had already drawn his sword and was pivoting on the spot, wary of reinforcements. Their attention was captured by the brawl taking place inside the tailor's shop. Therein, Nathaniel was crashing from one wall to the next, locked into a vice-like grapple with the

Reaver. The shop owner dived over his counter and only dared bob up to reveal a pair of terrified eyes.

"We don't have time for this!" Kassian insisted, hurling his words from the threshold. "More will come soon!"

The old knight found a moment to look at the Keeper with daggers in his eyes. Tapping into an element of his rage, Nathaniel flipped the Reaver on to its back and dropped down to plunge a dagger into its head, through one of the slits in its helmet.

"I can hear more coming!" Vighon warned from the street.

Nathaniel dusted himself off and followed Kassian outside. They could all hear the approaching Reavers. They would soon arrive to an empty street as every Namdhorian had fled the area after Kassian blew the top of the Reaver's head off.

"Which way?" the Keeper asked, seeing two paths ahead of them.

Vighon looked back at the sound of marching feet. "Either will take us up, but they'll just keep hunting us."

"Kassian!" Quaid's familiar voice turned the Keeper to a side alley that led to the main street. Beside the older mage was Fin, the youngest and most reckless of their merry band.

"We heard the discharge," Fin told them, referring to Kassian's spell.

Nathaniel pointed to the street on his right. "We need to get out of here, *now*."

Fin and Quaid both turned to the sound of Reavers. "*You* go!" Fin insisted, pushing Vighon towards Kassian.

Quaid nodded at the street to the left. "We'll get their attention and lead them west!"

Kassian hesitated - if anyone was going to throw themselves at the enemy and die doing it then it would be him. But he couldn't deny them the opportunity to do exactly what they had set out to do: make a difference.

"Be swift on your feet, brothers!" Kassian offered before trailing Nathaniel and Vighon.

The Keeper paused by the next corner, hearing the Reavers

breach the small courtyard. A staccato of spells wreaked havoc on the stone, Fin yelled some profanity, and their escape began in earnest. Vighon lowered the scarf from his mouth and encouraged Kassian to keep up with them as they reached the next set of steps.

He caught up with his companions and muttered, "This city's going to be the end of us..."

# CHAPTER 35

# WHAT LIES BENEATH

A biting breeze swept over Asher's sleeping form and freed him of his torturous slumber. Most would complain of waking up on a high rooftop on the cusp of winter, in a foreign land no less, but the ranger welcomed the challenges of life over those he faced in his dreams.

A clouded sky greeted him from between the arches of Kaliban's church. It looked like rain. Asher rose to his full height and cracked the various parts of his body that had seized up on him while he slept.

He cupped the rough stubble on his face; an extra moment required before he spotted Adan'Karth, perched on the lip of the church like one of the gargoyles situated on either side of the Drake. His hood had flown back in the wind, revealing his mane of black hair and flattened horns. What he was looking at was just as much a mystery to the ranger as what he was thinking about.

Moving from his sheltered position, the ranger walked out onto the flat roof, one of many that surrounded the church's main spire. Valgala sprawled across the horizon in every direction, its reaching towers and grand architecture eclipsing the green fields that lay beyond.

In appearance, Valgala was the perfect opposite of Namdhor. Illian's most northern city was a tidal wave of black stone, a rising monument on a sea of contrasting white terrain. Erador's capital, however, was a ring of white stone and dotted spires. Its royal palace was situated on the edge of a lake that dominated Valgala's heart.

It was beautiful, if a humble ranger could make such an observation. Taking it all in, he had to wonder how many times it had been built and rebuilt over the untold millennia. There was every chance the stone beneath his feet had been carved eons before humans even settled in Illian.

Of course, it was impossible to miss the numerous banners that hung from various buildings, visible from every street. Blood red and stamped with a black dragon; the house of Galfrey ruled this city and all the land around it. The same banners now decorated every city and town in Illian, extending Alijah's grip on Verda.

It was the reminder of Alijah's reign that made the ranger notice it - her absence.

Asher turned left and right, searching the gothic structure. "Adan. Where is Inara?"

"I'm here," came her voice, a hint of amusement behind her words. The Guardian of the Realm appeared, her red cloak billowing out behind her as she crossed the gap between the arches. "Did you think I had left while you slept?" Her smile was clearly visible now.

Asher cocked an eyebrow. "For all your fancy titles, you're still a Galfrey and, like your parents, that makes you *unpredictable.*"

"Good." Inara's response was clipped yet satisfied. "I've been on the western side of the church, monitoring three of the roads that enter the city."

"And?"

"For a city whose ruler considers himself a Dragon Rider, Valgala has defences that would bring even Malliath down." Inara wandered over to the edge and pointed at a building top half the size of the church they were on. "Can you see it?"

Asher narrowed his eyes until the object he was looking at took on a familiar shape. "Ballistas."

"They're positioned all over the city," Inara reported. "And they're all on building tops, pointed to the sky."

The ranger assessed every micro-movement on Inara's face, discerning her thoughts. "You think this is further proof that Gideon and Ilargo are here."

"I think it's proof that they were here, at some point. The ballistas are all manned, so Gideon and Ilargo are either out there, posing a threat, or they're prisoners and Alijah doesn't want them to escape."

"Or," Asher suggested, "it just means that Alijah and Malliath were wary of other dragons arriving on their doorstep."

Inara seemed to shrug off his pessimism. "I also discovered a concentration of Reavers at the gate where we entered, but we're too high to see much more than that. The other roads are busy. I've been speaking to Athis; he says they both lead to large cities."

Asher groaned quietly. "We've got a lot of territory to search."

"There's still a chance Gideon is here, in Valgala."

The ranger didn't share her optimism. "Then why can't Athis reach out to Ilargo?"

Inara's hope slipped off her face. "There could be any number of reasons..."

Asher caught sight of Adan's dragon-like eyes boring holes into him. The ranger sighed and his cheek twitched. "You're right," he said gruffly, addressing Inara again. "He could be here. If he is, and he has fallen prey to Alijah, it makes sense that he would be inside or around the palace." He finished by pointing at the collection of domes and spires that shone in the distance. "That's why we're going to break inside tonight."

"We are?" Hope had returned to Inara's voice.

Asher had to remind himself that he was with Inara Galfrey, a Dragorn, the Guardian of the Realm, and a daughter to heroes: she wasn't accustomed to breaking in to anywhere. "We know Alijah is in Illian. In my experience, that means less guards."

"Less guards doesn't mean no guards," Inara countered, looking now to Adan. "Perhaps you should remain up here."

Adan tilted his head to see her. "I have not come all this way to observe. Where Asher goes, I go…"

Inara looked at Asher, who could only shrug in the face of her plea. "He has the stubbornness of both an elf *and* a dragon - he's coming with us."

The Drake split his stony expression with a coy grin. "I will take that as a compliment."

"Take it however you like. Just keep that hood up and your head down." Asher turned away and began to check through his gear, inspecting his daggers and throwing knives. The blades were sharp and his silvyr short-sword was as exquisite as ever, its hourglass edging perfectly intact, even after decades of use.

The wind caught the red blindfold on his belt and blew it out in front of him. He pulled it free and wrapped one end around his hand so he could examine the length of it. It was tired: stained with sweat, dirt, and flecks of blood here and there. The edges were frayed, but the fabric was still strong and it would cover his eyes sufficiently.

"What were you saying about choices?" Inara asked from the corner of his vision.

Asher sighed before setting his blue eyes on the Guardian. "I liked it better the way I said it." He flashed a smile that came and went in the blink of an eye.

Without further discussion on the matter, the ranger wrapped the red cloth around the hilt of his broadsword and tied a strong knot.

He *had* made his choice.

"Let's make our way down," he suggested. "We can spend the day scouting the palace."

The streets of Valgala reminded Asher of Velia. In fact, Valgala could easily have been a city within Illian's borders. The people moved the same, their mannerisms were the same, and they even dressed the same, their materials crafted using similar, if not identical, techniques. Their language was entirely lost on the ranger, though he did enjoy the sound of it in his ear.

They possessed shops that sold food, general supplies, and clothes of every colour. Dogs and cats roamed the alleys, searching for scraps, and beggars huddled under blankets with naught but their prayers for comfort.

The companions were stopped more than once by children darting out into the street, lost in their games. Horses and carts trailed up and down the main roads that all converged on the palace, close to the centre.

Of all the shops and activity that surrounded them, Asher's attention was only captured by the bladesmith's dwelling. Swords of every kind were chained to wooden stands outside the entrance. The ranger was tempted to go over and browse, curious to see if their forging was any better.

There was the issue of payment, however, if not the language barrier. Hanging off his belt was a purse of coins, all stamped with the seal of Stowhold, Illian's bank. He had no idea what passed for coin in Erador, but he suspected it wouldn't be anything he possessed.

Keeping up with Inara and Adan, they continued their journey in relative peace. From inside, the city felt boundless, its limits immeasurable. Through the crowds and hubbub, Asher spotted the black garb of Erador's infamous knights. They patrolled in groups of six or, at least, that was the only configuration he had witnessed thus far.

"Seeker." Inara's only word cut through the pleasantness of their environment.

"Keep moving," Asher warned, as he slowed down. Experience

told him that coming to a complete halt amidst a moving crowd made one stand out almost as much as running. "Down there."

With a gentle hand against Inara's arm, he directed them down a side street, shaded by the towers on either side. Inara made to look back over her shoulder until Asher suggested, quite firmly, that she refrained.

With practised effort, the ranger kept his movements fluid yet smooth and controlled so as not to tell of any alarm. "This way."

They cut down an alley and emerged onto another side street. Following it, they soon found themselves returned to a main road at least four carriages wide. A sign, bolted high on a corner wall, informed them they were now walking along a different road, but the written words were unintelligible to the ranger.

Asher didn't dwell on it. His mind had relaxed, allowing elements of his former training to rise to the surface. Evasion had been one of Nightfall's most important lessons, often taught in the scorching cities of The Arid Lands.

"There's more," Inara announced gravely.

Asher found a gap between the throng and located the Seeker for himself. Its collar and leash led him to another group of six Reavers. The people parted like long grass, allowing the knights ease of passage. The pale beast sniffed the air left and right, searching for its magical prey.

There was another figure, leading the Reavers, that caught Asher's attention and held his gaze longer than he liked. By their movements he immediately knew it was a living person, not a resurrected corpse. Only the eyes were visible between the hood and mask, though it revealed the figure to be a man. Robes of red and black were fastened by several leather belts that held a pair of crescent blades.

Dead or alive, the ranger categorised the leader as an enemy.

"Do you both know where the palace is?" Asher asked, his attention now turned to finding the gaps he could utilise in the crowd.

"Yes," they both replied quietly.

"Split up," he instructed. "We'll meet on the western side."

Without pause, all three of them drifted apart as if they had never been with each other in the first place. Asher didn't glance over his shoulder, trusting both of them to accomplish their task without aid.

Taking a rather long route, one that weaved throughout multiple districts, Asher eventually exited an alleyway that opened up to the lake. The palace was to his left, an image lifted right out of some fairy tale that ordinary people were told as children.

Assessing the structure with a nefarious eye, the ranger was immediately interested by the scaffolding that crawled up the western walls. An extension or refurbishment, it mattered little to Asher. What it represented was a weakness: one he intended to exploit.

The surface of the lake reflected the orange hues of a tired sun. Small sailing boats were beginning to return to their moorings and the labourers working on the palace were packing up their tools, ready to call it a day.

He saw Inara and Adan before either of them saw him. They slowly came back together, huddling close outside a tavern called The Black Dragon if the picture displayed prominently on its sign was any indication. Others were doing the same, enjoying an early drink in the sunset before the night took on a life of its own. It was all so familiar...

"It took me a while," Inara began, picking up a discarded tankard to blend in, "but I finally realised: there's no crime in this city."

Now that Asher thought about it, he hadn't seen a single person who made him feel on edge - the Reavers took care of that all by themselves. He wasn't, however, about to give them or Alijah credit.

"There are plenty of Seekers," Adan commented. "Even now, I fear they have my scent."

Asher nodded his acknowledgement of both statements, but his focus was unwavering. "That's our way in," he told them, nodding at the scaffolding.

Inara casually turned her head to glance at it. "More climbing then. Are you sure your old bones are up to it?" she asked with half a mischievous grin.

Asher took the ribbing in his stride, accustomed to the Guardian's humour - much in the vein of her father's. "There's enough life left in these bones to put you on your back." Judging by Inara's expression, she didn't believe that any more than Asher did.

Cutting through their banter, Adan'Karth held out a small sack of what sounded like coins. "Perhaps a drink while we wait for true dark..."

Asher eyed the sack suspiciously. "Where did you get that?"

"I believe you call them highborns," Adan replied with an innocent tone. "It was just hanging off his belt."

Now the ranger's brow knotted in confusion. "You stole it," he concluded.

"I'm thirsty," the Drake stated simply.

"Doesn't this count as an act of violence?" Inara pointed out.

Adan gave the slightest shrug of his toned shoulders. "Not at all. I inflicted no physical or mental harm upon him. And, by way of his dress compared to those around him, I doubt such a small sack of coins will be sorely missed."

Asher was impressed, if a little disappointed. "We're corrupting him, *again*."

Inara waved the notion away and took the coins from Adan. "I'll get the drinks."

Over the next few hours, they soaked up the atmosphere inside The Black Dragon and sipped on their drinks. Inara had discreetly twisted the spinning top in order to communicate with the man behind the bar, lest their foreign words gave them away.

Still, the ranger didn't miss a single one of the curious looks they received. Of all the patrons filling the tavern, they were the only ones with weapons on show and Adan was the only one with his hood up, concealing most of his head and face.

Being so close to the palace, the district was clearly for the wealthier classes of Valgala. Asher couldn't say what any of their titles were, but there were more than a few inside The Black Dragon right now. The attire of any one of them was more expensive than all the clothes the three companions possessed between them.

"Maybe it's time we saw to our task," the ranger suggested, noting another patron enquiring about them at the bar.

With smooth ease, they slipped out of the tavern and welcomed the brisk night air as it captured their warm breath. It was with frustration that Asher observed the Reavers now stationed at the entrance to the scaffolding. They stood like statues, still as the dead.

As always, his mind worked more efficiently when faced with an obstacle. He quickly discovered the three rowing boats on the shore of the lake. From there, they could cross the water and scale the rocky foundation that formed the base of the palace. Past that, they would have access to the scaffolding and from there the palace's interior.

"We're too exposed to dispatch them," Inara said, her assessment only seconds behind the ranger.

"Follow me." Asher led them to the simple rowing boats and quickly explained his plan.

Adan obliged with the use of his magic to propel the boat, lest the oars create too much noise breaking the surface of the water. Asher kept his eyes on the Reavers at all times while his left hand rested on the folded bow clipped to his quiver. As they approached the palace foundations, Inara held out a hand, signalling Adan to slow down, before using her other hand to reach out and intercept the rock. Without a sound, they climbed out and began their ascent.

Asher winced with every creaking panel of wood that made up the scaffolding. More than once, they were forced to stop and check that the Reavers hadn't been alerted to their infiltration. Near the top of the scaffolding, they came across a large sheet of tarpaulin that had been fastened to the palace stone. Earlier that day, Asher had seen no such tarpaulin...

With tentative fingers, he pulled back the edges and peered beyond. An empty room greeted him and he greeted it with a broad smile. Removing one of the clips, they moved through the gap and entered Alijah's home.

The door inside the room was locked. Instinctively, Asher reached for the pouch on his belt that contained all of his lock picks.

"Allow me." Inara stepped forward and waved her hand over the lock, flicking the bolt out of place with a touch of magic.

It wasn't often that Asher found himself missing Paldora's Gem...

Cautiously, they entered the hall beyond the door. The walls were lined with torches but none had been lit, suggesting that this area wasn't in use. On light feet, they moved to the end of the passage and continued to explore the area until they found halls illuminated by flaming torches. Inara had them pause on occasion, her exquisite hearing detecting servants nearby.

When faced with the option to go up or down a set of spiral steps, the companions stopped and took a moment to assess the situation.

"This place is twice the size of The Dragon Keep," Inara remarked.

"If not more," Asher muttered, peering out of a window at the winding ramparts below. "We need to find Alijah's private quarters."

"Agreed." Inara glanced round a corner to make certain they were alone. "He's always been one for notes. As children I would always find him scrawling something down on a piece of parchment. But where do we start? We could be searching these halls until dawn."

"That way," Adan announced, directing them to the ascending steps.

Asher looked from the steps to the Drake. "What makes you so sure?"

"Like Inara, Alijah is bonded to a dragon - his connection to the magical realm is strong." Adan nodded at the steps. "I can see his aura, where he's been." The Drake waved his hands in the air as if he was touching something that simply wasn't there to Asher's eyes.

"You can see where he's been?" Inara enquired with the same tone of curiosity Asher had heard in Reyna a hundred times before.

"Yes. The stronger the magic, the stronger the echo. It dances in the air..."

The ranger waved the conversation away. "Alijah hasn't been here for a long time. Are you sure you're seeing it right?"

"Much like this land, the palace is absent magic. His presence lingers with ease, undisturbed by others."

"Can you follow it?" Inara asked.

"I believe so, though I must ask that you remain behind me. Your aura is powerful and very similar to your brother's - I am concerned it will interfere with what remains of him."

Asher naturally doubted what he couldn't see, but he had spent enough time around Adan'Karth to know that Drakes were nothing if not surprising. Taking up his position between them, he trailed Adan up the winding staircase and through the palace interior. They crept from passage to passage and hid where they needed to, avoiding the occasional patrol of Reavers.

Somewhere in the west wing, the Drake finally brought them before a pair of ornate arching doors. The wood was of fine craftsmanship with an intricate pattern carved across both doors to form one whole image that resembled a dragon.

Adan'Karth looked around. "This is the strongest..." His lips pursed as he searched for the right word. "*Concentration*," he eventually said in elvish.

Asher tried the doors but they were locked, as he had suspected. He stepped back and welcomed Inara to open them, leaving his lock picks right where they were. Again, Inara applied her silent spell and the lock relented its grip on the doors.

Inside, the chamber opened up to a spacious living area with multiple adjoining rooms leading off from the circular foyer. Both Adan and Inara breathed life into a pair of torches, sitting idle on the wall. The Drake handed his to Asher having no need of the fire to see in the dark. Together, they entered the first room, Alijah's bedchamber, and followed it round to another door that brought them to a long dining table topped with spires of books.

There was only one chair.

Leaving the dining room behind, they next entered a luxurious seating area that looked to have never been used for anything other than stacking yet more books on every flat surface. The last room was part study, part library. An ornate desk, larger than the boat they had recently used, dominated the middle of the chamber. Half-written scrolls and scrunched up parchments littered the ground around it and the surrounding shelves were stuffed with more books than they were designed to display.

"If there are any clues," Inara said, "this is where we're going to find them."

They split up, each taking a different part of the room to begin searching. Asher walked slowly along the nearest bookshelf, noting the new labels that had clearly been stuck to the old spines. The ranger could read the labels, marked with Illian's writing, unlike the spine beneath which possessed unknown symbols.

"He's done a *lot* of reading."

Inara was crouched beside the desk, sifting through the discarded parchments. "I've seen him devour books as thick as my arm in a day..."

Asher noted that many of the books concerned either the art of warfare or the history of Erador. A lot of them covered both topics in a single volume.

Turning away from the books, Asher took in the room from the back corner. His training demanded that he routinely check the entrances in and out of a room so as to prevent a blade in the back.

He failed to acknowledge the empty doorways, however, his eyes drawn to the object displayed above the archway to the foyer.

"Inara…"

The Guardian looked at the ranger before following his gaze to the object. Inara immediately stood up, her emotions visibly rising to the surface across her face. Three quick strides placed her under the archway where she used a low cupboard to climb up and take the object for herself. Asher and Adan'Karth gathered around her, entranced as she was.

"Mournblade…" Inara uttered the weapon's name as she pulled the elven scimitar a couple of inches from its scabbard.

"The significance?" Adan enquired.

Asher admired the red hilt, pommelled with a golden dragon's claw. "This is Gideon Thorn's blade."

Inara's jaw was set. "He's a prisoner then," she concluded.

Asher knew there was another, very obvious, reason Gideon's sword would be mounted on Alijah's wall, but he kept it to himself. "That's a Vi'tari blade," he said instead. "You should be the one to care for it until it returns to Gideon."

Inara blinked hard, falling back on her resolve. She had no response but to fashion a strap for the scabbard and sling it over her back.

"At least we know he was here," Adan commented, returning to the bookshelves.

Asher waited beside Inara a moment longer, seeing that she intended to speak. "Don't even think it," she said quietly to the ranger.

There were multiple avenues of dialogue that Asher could have chosen to use, all of which spoke of the logical conclusions concerning Gideon's fate and Inara's need to accept the worst.

"We *will* find him," he reassured, hiding his true beliefs inside a vague response.

Inara nodded her thanks and returned to searching the desk.

Asher continued his route around the bookshelves, intending to meet Adan in the middle. All the while, he suffered a horrible feeling in his gut, one which told him they would find nothing but death in Erador.

"There is no mention of magic here," Adan said from across the room, his sharp finger stroking along the leather-bound spines. "Given everything we know of Alijah, I would have expected there to be a considerable number of books concerning magic."

The ranger moved his torch up and down, examining other books above and below. Indeed, there was nothing about magic at all. "If his actions in Illian are anything to go by, he considers those who wield magic to be a threat. Perhaps he did the same thing here and removed any books so no one else could learn of it."

Doubt creased Inara's face. "He had to learn necromancy from somewhere. The Crow broke him down and filled his head with prophetic nonsense - he didn't teach him magic."

Asher pulled out a book with the title *A Time of Dragons* scribed on the side. "Well, he didn't learn it here..."

Adan continued around the edges of the room, muttering various book titles to himself. "Erador has a *long* history," he remarked offhandedly.

"A long history of *war*," Asher added, coming across more volumes that recorded something called *The Andaren War*. He had no idea what an Andaren was. Inara looked to be engrossed as she poured over Alijah's notes on the desk top. "Have you found something?" the ranger asked.

The Guardian's hands danced over the surface, moving notes around as they did. "He's referenced a lot of older maps. They all seem to be connected to dates and..." Inara narrowed her eyes to read Alijah's writing. "Wars. I think he spent a long time tracking down landmarks where great battles were fought." She lifted a strip of parchment to the light of her torch. "This is a list of historical events and people. Lord Kraiden's name is here," she relayed with disdain. "The Red Fields of Dunmar, The Glimmer Lands of Qalanqath, Arrow

Helm, Freygard - these are regions on the map that have all seen war at some point."

Asher joined her by the desk and browsed through the maps and parchment. "That's how he built his army. He exhumed the dead from Erador's past, suited them in armour, and marched them to Illian."

"This might be where he found them," Inara agreed, "but there's nothing that explains *how* he resurrected them."

Without really thinking about it, Asher had been walking around the desk with his free hand gliding just beneath the lip of the wood - old habits. Beside the chair, where Alijah would sit, his finger found a single piece of resistance. He explored its edges, building a picture of it in his mind. A latch. It took a simple flick, barely audible over the sound of fine bolts sliding out of place somewhere inside the desk.

Inara looked at him questioningly and the ranger answered her with an action - raising the surface of the desk with his free hand. Books, notes, and maps slid off the other side of the desk as he lifted what was now obviously a lid. Two mechanisms fitted into place at each end, holding the surface of the desk upright and allowing Asher to step back and examine the secreted contents.

Inara and Adan moved quickly to stand beside him. Inside the desk were more parchments and bound scrolls with an array of quills and crusted bottles of ink. The three companions merely glanced at them, their attention seized by the single piece of jagged parchment that had been pinned to the underside of the lid.

"What is that?" Adan asked.

To Asher's eyes, it was the scribing of a madman. Names and dates marked every inch of the parchment. Some were circled and tied to another by pieces of string. Others were crossed out with enough force to tear the parchment. So much of it had been written over itself as to be illegible. There was only one thing that stood out, in the very centre of the chaos. It was ringed with red ink and almost everything was pinned to it by a piece of string.

"The Tower of Jain..." Inara's words cut through the sound of flickering flames.

"Is that supposed to mean something?" Asher asked.

Adan moved closer to the desk, his hood lowered to reveal his unusual features. The Drake delicately moved the top pieces of blank parchment away, removing them from the piles that had been stacked on top of each other inside the desk.

Asher's face dropped. "Inara..."

The Guardian tore her eyes from the lid and looked into the desk, her brow wrinkled in horror. Every sheet of parchment had a single drawing on it, made with black charcoal. Adan pulled back every one in desperate search of anything other than the reptilian eyes that looked back at them.

Asher knew those eyes, even without their purple tint. "Malliath," he confirmed.

Inara took a breath, employing another layer of the famous Galfrey armour that had kept her parents on their feet through the hardest times. Asher recognised the look and silently commended her for holding back the grief that so clearly wished to rule her.

"He is haunted," Adan observed with a whisper, his fingers having scattered numerous drawings of the dragon's predatory eyes.

"Athis knows where this is," Inara announced without a comment for the drawings.

Asher's mind let the drawings go too. "Does he know what this tower is?"

Inara looked away for a moment. "No. He says it's at the end of The Spoken Road."

"The road no one uses," Asher mused.

"Are we to go there?" Adan'Karth enquired.

Again, Inara looked away for a second. "We're likely following in Gideon's footsteps," she reasoned. "If he was suspicious of Alijah, it makes sense that he would have discovered my brother's interest in it."

Asher agreed with the logic. "Then let's not linger." Using his free hand again, the ranger closed the desk back up, sealing the hundreds of drawings therein.

All three companions froze.

On the other side of the desk, standing in the doorway to the foyer, was a man dressed in red and black robes, all tightly bound by several belts. In his hands were a pair of crescent blades, each catching the light from their torches.

Asher reached for his broadsword.

# CHAPTER 36
# THE PATH TO WAR

Doran did his best not to fidget in the light of the roaring fire. It dominated the beach beneath a dark ocean of stars where, perhaps, Lady Ellöria looked down on them from the heavens. Surrounding the bonfire, every elf who had called Ilythyra their home was stood with heads pointed to the night sky in reverence.

Beyond them were the armoured elves who had accompanied Queen Adilandra, who was currently standing beside the son of Dorain in the inner circle. On the other side of her was Faylen and Galanör, both of whom held sombre expressions.

Doran couldn't say he had known the queen's sister, having only met her for a short time at the end of The Ash War. He had certainly heard much of her though, informing the dwarf that she had been wiser than most and that she had faced Alijah and Malliath with great fortitude. How close the queen had been to the lady was unknown to Doran, but there was pain on her face.

For all the respect he could muster for a person he had never really known, Doran found himself more concerned with the beacon they had lit on the southern beach. They knew the enemy had two dragons on the island and yet they had insisted on using fire in an open area.

The War Mason chalked it up to the nonsense of elves...

Had this been for a dwarf, they would have buried them in the ground of Grarfath's making and laid stones. Without a body, they would have crafted a headstone or created a cairn in memorial.

Doran rolled his shoulders and cracked his neck in an effort to keep himself rooted to the spot. He was eager to return to the camp and ensure that Alijah's conversation with Galanör hadn't rattled his warriors too much. Before setting off for the beach, he had heard rumblings from his fellow Heavybellys, concerns that their enemy was well prepared for their attack.

Adilandra stepped forward, into the gap between them and the bonfire. Doran stood a little straighter and squared his jaw, dispelling his thoughts like a hammer striking an anvil. Even with her back to the flames, her features in shadow, the queen was majestic.

"Lady Ellöria, my sister... She did not die just so we may live. She died for us because of what we live *for*. We have ever stood up to the darkness that would claim our lands and our hearts. Ellöria did just that when she drew a line and denied the evil that would have taken us all. Those of you who resided in Ilythyra, those of you who lived by Ellöria's wisdom and guidance, you now walk the earth with expectation on your shoulders."

The queen glanced at Galanör. "My sister died with a single word on her lips: resist. No longer do we hunger for the clash of steel and blood on our swords. We do not take war to the dark. The dark brings war to us, and we *resist* it. We rise up like these very flames. Here, on this island, we will make our stand against evil. We will declare *no further!*" As one, the armoured elves beat their fists into plated chests.

Even Doran was getting swept up in the rousing speech. "She's good," he muttered to Faylen, who was too engrossed in Adilandra's words to take note of the dwarf.

It wasn't long after the queen's speech that the ceremony came to an end and the elves steadily disappeared from the beach. They left the fire roaring, a beacon to Ellöria in the heavens that they would stand up to Alijah's might, just as she had done.

Doran was about to straddle Pig and take the path back to the camp when he saw Adilandra, Faylen, and Galanör lingering behind.

"Join us," Faylen invited.

The three elves slowly made their way a little further up the beach so as to utilise some of the light from the bonfire. Curiosity gnawed at the son of Dorain and he accepted the invitation.

"What's this abou'?" he asked, turning their angelic features on him. "Is this to be a time o' mournin'? Because I can leave ye to—"

"No, Master Dwarf," Adilandra interrupted. "I have and will continue to mourn for my sister. Should I survive the battle to come, I have no doubt my grief will live with me for many years to come."

Doran nodded his understanding. "So what's all this then?"

"We mean to spar," Faylen explained.

The son of Dorain scowled at the words. "Do we not 'ave a battle to plan?"

Adilandra drew her scimitar and plunged it tip first into the dense sand. "And so we shall, War Mason. We will proceed with planning at once."

The dwarf hesitated. "Ye can call me Doran, me Lady," he uttered.

Adilandra flashed a brief smile in his direction. "Doran," she announced, without offering the same courtesy.

Brow furrowed in confusion, Doran looked from the queen's upright blade to Adilandra herself. "Ye're goin' to spar?"

"I prefer to be moving while I strategise," the queen answered. "I also need to test myself after repelling the Sandstalkers. If I am unfit to lead, I will step back rather than compromise our plans and risk lives." Faylen moved to stand opposite the queen, her fingers working to remove her cloak. "No," Adilandra instructed, halting the High Guardian.

"My Lady?" Faylen questioned.

"You are my equal, Faylen," the queen stated factually. "I wish to truly test myself." She said the latter while turning to Galanör.

"Is that wise, my Lady? You haven't long recovered enough to walk. Perhaps *we* should begin before—"

"I will spar with the greatest sword master in Verda," Adilandra finished, her own cloak now removed. "Our enemy will show no quarter, especially Alijah. His Vi'tari blade already gives him the advantage. Galanör..." The queen gestured for the ranger to take Faylen's place. "If you hold back I will know it - I have seen you fight."

Galanör took a breath and shared a look with Faylen. Any hesitation, however, was brief, and he soon replaced the High Guardian opposite the queen. He opted to keep his cloak on and removed one of his fine scimitars, a gift from the woman he was about to fight.

"I told you not to hold back." Adilandra was looking at his scimitar's twin, sitting idly on his hip.

"Alijah fights with only one blade," he pointed out, "as do the Reavers."

"I am not fighting Alijah." The queen's tone was calm and even, but not to be argued with.

Somewhat reluctantly, Galanör pulled his other scimitar free of its scabbard and mimicked Adilandra's battle form. Doran left Pig to lie in the sand while he joined Faylen, who was perched on an outcropping of rocks. He couldn't deny his interest was piqued by such a sparring match.

Without a word, both combatants closed the gap between them and collided with such grace and elegance it could have been called a dance. Steel struck steel, ringing out across the beach. Adilandra set upon Galanör with an aggressive advance, pushing him back several steps. His hands came up one after the other, his wrists twisting in every possible direction to ensure his blades parried the incoming attacks.

They were considerable fighters, their style enhanced by their natural strength and speed that surpassed humans and dwarves. It certainly wasn't a battle Doran felt he belonged in, though his personal fighting style would most definitely get in the way of their fluidity.

Coming up on a minute, it became clear, to Doran at least, that Galanör simply wasn't trying as hard. The ranger moved as if he already knew Adilandra's every angle of attack before she made it. His expression was one of stone with no sign of real exertion, while Adilandra fought with a hint of untamed rage, presented in the baring of her teeth. It suited her more aggressive form but, mostly, it reminded the son of Dorain that the queen had spent a lot of time in the Darkakins' barbaric arena.

Galanör intercepted her scimitar, locking it between his own, before executing an unorthodox twist of his body that brought him round to her back. In a flash of steel, he freed one of his blades and rammed the hilt into Adilandra's back, pushing her several feet across the beach. She cried out and Faylen shot the elven ranger a look that prevented him from pursuing the queen.

Stretching her injured back, Adilandra turned around to face her opponent again, her scimitar gripped in both hands. "You were clan Heavybelly's War Mason for many decades yes?"

It took Doran a moment to realise she was talking to him and that they were actually going to have a discussion while they sparred. "Longer than I would 'ave liked," he admitted.

Adilandra fell back into the match, her limbs retracting and extending in a bid to evade and attack. "I imagine you have planned and taken part in many battles then. You know your people and what they are capable of."

Doran adjusted his position on the rock and glanced at Faylen, the whole scene somewhat bizarre to the dwarf. "I 'ave an' I do," he claimed.

The queen used one of Galanör's thighs to raise herself up and plant a solid boot in his chest, throwing him into a backwards roll.

"Would it be fair to say that they adhere to a rigid battle strategy, given their previous campaigns in Dhenaheim?"

The War Mason wanted to protest against such a suggestion, but he gave the question an extra moment's thought. Indeed, the clans of Dhenaheim had been fighting for centuries, their techniques and strategies handed down through the generations. Theirs had always been a battle of invasion or defence depending on which clan they were at war with. The terrain had always been the same: cold and mountainous. Qamnaran was wet, its terrain varied with its jagged rises and muddy pits, and the only mountains it boasted was a ridge of pointed cliffs at its heart.

"I only ask," Adilandra continued, her arms working furiously to meet Galanör's slicing blades, "because you have the superior force. We will bow to your strategy and adapt where necessary."

Galanör found a gap in her defences and spun on the ball of his foot, his dark hair and blue cloak whipping out around him. In a heartbeat, one of his fine scimitars was resting against the soft skin of Adilandra's neck.

Their chests heaving, the elves paused. The queen pushed his blade away with one finger and moved to separate, defeat spoiling her demeanour.

"You're thinking too much," Galanör commented.

Faylen stiffened. "Galanör," she chastised.

Adilandra waved the High Guardian's concern away. "There is none better to give me instruction." She looked at Galanör to continue with his lesson.

"Observe my every movement. My feet will tell you where I'm going next. My stance, my shoulders, even the way I hold my swords; they all betray my actions. Watch me and learn to anticipate."

Adilandra nodded once. "As you say."

They assumed their rigid forms and prepared to fight once again. This time, Galanör came at the queen with a spinning jump. His blades, slightly curved towards the tips, came down one after the other onto Adilandra's defences. After recovering from his initial attack, she found her rhythm and fell into the flow of their fight.

"As I was saying," Adilandra continued. "I would know of your strategy, Doran."

The son of Dorain cleared his throat. "I've been lookin' at the maps o' the island," he began, gesturing pointlessly at Galanör who had supplied him with the drawings. "A direct attack from east to west is out o' the question - me kin can dig but they can' climb, especially with armour. That leaves us with either a north or south approach," he concluded.

Galanör ducked under his queen's cutting attack and came up with a flurry of spinning blades. A brief gap in their spar offered the ranger a chance to speak. "The southern path, around the cliffs, would be treacherous for flat feet and heavy armour."

Doran arched an unkempt eyebrow. "Flat feet?" he grizzled.

Galanör flashed a mischievous grin. "If the flat boot fits..." His last word was punctuated by the clamour of steel, their fight renewed.

Doran couldn't keep the amusement off his face, his love for playful banter always at the forefront. "Perhaps lighter feet would make better work o' the southern pass then. I propose a two-pronged attack, staggered so as to surprise the enemy."

Adilandra weaved between Galanör's scimitars but failed to land a successful counterattack. Instead, she raised her free hand, palm open to his chest, and unleashed a wave of distorted air. The ranger skidded back on his feet, managing, somehow, to stay upright. The queen retracted her hand and clenched it with a wince marring her features.

"My Lady?" Faylen started from the rock only to be halted by a gesture from the queen.

"I am fine," Adilandra stated, flexing her fingers. "It was just a pinch. I need more time it seems..."

"Draw power from your crystal if you must," Faylen advised.

Adilandra gripped the pouch on her belt. "No. I would not use it so frivolously." She straightened her posture and faced Galanör with resolve. "I will rely on my skill with a blade for now." After the contest began again, the queen said, "I am intrigued by your tactic, Doran."

Unaccustomed to such a winding conversation, especially where battle plans were concerned, Doran required a few seconds to compose his thoughts on the matter. "Aye, a two-pronged attack. I suggest we split our forces. I will lead me kin an' navigate around the northern tip o' the cliffs. We'll then march south, to the tower, an' make as much noise as we can, turnin' the enemy towards us. With their attention on us, ye can bring yer forces up from the south. Between us, we'll chew 'em up an' topple that blasted tower into The Hox!"

Galanör dashed forwards and skidded low in a bid to swipe Adilandra's legs out from under her. The queen somersaulted over the attack and landed gracefully on her feet. She tried to back hand the ranger but one of Galanör's scimitars was already waiting for it.

"A sound plan," Faylen praised.

"I agree," Adilandra added, her breath laboured. "And what of the timing?"

Doran gave that some thought. "Galanör, ye said ye've found King Gaerhard. 'Ave ye been watchin' the other dwarves? Their routines?"

"Of course," he replied, evading three successive blows from the queen.

"Does me kin toil under every hour that Grarfath gives?" Doran probed.

"There are always dwarves working on the tower," the elf reported. "Less so at night."

That informed the son of Dorain. "We attack at dawn then. I 'ave no doubt that King Gaerhard an' every dwarf in that camp will rise up when we attack. It will serve us better to 'ave as many o' them rested when we do."

Faylen was nodding in agreement. "That would also help in

spotting Malliath and Morgorth. At night, they blend in to the heavens."

Hearing of Lord Kraiden's dragon ignited fire in Doran's veins. "Ye all know o' me grievance with the Dragon Rider. Whatever comes o' this battle, I *must* possess his sword. We can' cure Dak if we don' know what the poison is."

"It is certainly among our priorities," Faylen assured.

Doran wished to argue where it stood amongst their priorities, but they hadn't come all this way to save Dakmund Heavybelly. Alijah's plans had to be stopped and the half-elf himself had to be brought down. The son of Dorain let his shoulders sag and he nodded his understanding.

Again, the elves came to a natural pause in their sparring match when Galanör exposed a weakness in one of Adilandra's openings and brought his blade to her throat. The irritation that crossed the queen's face was momentary before she stepped away and composed her next fighting stance.

"How will we know when to attack from the south?" she queried.

Doran waited for the first two blows to ring out into the night. "Hold yer attack until we've met them in battle - the sound will help to mask yer charge."

"What of the dragons?" Faylen pointed out.

The War Mason shrugged his shoulders, both hidden beneath his pauldrons. "We've been fightin' this war for nearly two years an' I still don' know how to bring one o' 'em down. That's why we needed Inara an' Athis..."

"In the past," Adilandra said between attacks, "it would have been prudent to locate and kill a dragon's rider. However, given Inara's revelation regarding the change in her bond to Athis, harming Alijah will not harm Malliath."

"The same can be said of Lord Kraiden and Morgorth," Faylen noted.

Doran ran a gloved hand through his beard. "I'm afraid we dwarves 'ave little experience when it comes to battlin' dragons.

They're creatures o' the sky an' magic to boot - neither agrees with us."

Adilandra used a spell to fling a small rock at Galanör. The ranger dodged the missile at the expense of opening up his defences. His carelessness cost him a swift kick to the midriff, knocking him down to one knee.

"Leave the dragons to us," the queen asserted mid-victory. "Without Athis to occupy them in the sky, we will rely on our magic to keep them at bay if not slay them." Adilandra put some distance between her and Galanör, though her action failed to hide the tremor in her hand.

A groan escaped Galanör's lips as he rose to his full height. "Can *I* use magic now?"

Adilandra answered *yes* as Faylen replied with an authoritative *no*.

"You are not my shield, Faylen; I cannot stand behind you in battle. I *must* be tested."

Reluctantly, the High Guardian backed off. Doran was instantly reminded of a time, decades earlier, when Faylen had been Reyna's protector. Indeed, the authority of a queen was required to oppose the fierce elf.

"What of Alijah himself?" Galanör posed, an edge to his voice.

Adilandra flicked her sword so it ran up the back of her arm. "We have to assume he's on the eve of enacting whatever plan requires the tower. It has to be magic in nature or he wouldn't need Qamnaran's natural Demetrium deposits or the ancient runes you discovered."

"It has to be powerful magic," Faylen added. "I would say he's still preparing for whatever the spell demands of him, otherwise he would have done it by now."

"All the more reason to press the attack *now*," Doran chipped in. "Every second we give 'im the closer he gets to bein' ready."

"Agreed," Galanör said, falling into a circling pattern with the queen.

"We take him *together*," Adilandra emphasised. "He's too dangerous for any one of us. We few will challenge him."

"Preferably inside the tower," Faylen said. "He will be easier to best without Malliath by his side."

"I can attest to that," Galanör stated boldly. "I would have beaten him in Ilythyra had Malliath not intervened."

Adilandra was quick to quash his line of thinking. "It would be folly to consider yourself Alijah's better. Cursed or not, that blade he wields holds a Vi'tari enchantment. Besides that, The Crow had him train against Arakesh during his time in The Bastion. Couple those with his natural talents and combine them with his bond to Malliath and he's—"

"One of the best killers in all of Verda," Galanör finished in his own words. "I *know* I can beat him."

"He's got under yer skin, lad - listen to the Lady."

Galanör shook his head. "He's inexperienced," the elf insisted. "Just get me into that tower and I can—"

"Die for nothing," Faylen interjected. "Your skill counts for more than one on the battlefield, Galanör; but Alijah will require all of us."

Doran didn't need two eyes to see that Galanör disagreed. Rather than further his argument, however, the elven ranger refocused on his royal opponent. The tension was palpable enough that even the dwarf could detect it.

"It seems we've got the bones o' the plan," Doran surmised before their duel began anew. "I'll need to hammer out some o' the details with the clan - marchin' 'em around the cliffs will take a couple o' days an' I don' want 'em meetin' the Reavers after the trek."

"Can your warriors be ready to leave the camp at first light?" Faylen asked hopefully.

"Aye, they've had the night to themselves so there'll be no complainin'. Besides, promise o' a good fight will keep 'em movin'." Doran rose from the rock and glanced at the tree line. "They're still goin' to need some o' the details before then so..." He thumbed at the natural break in the trees that would lead back to camp. "I'll let you finish yer tests an' what not." He paused to bow at the elven queen. "My Lady."

"Doran," the queen called after him. "You may call me *Adilandra*..."

"In the right company," Faylen added softly, if firmly.

Doran bowed his head again, a boyish grin pushing his beard out. "An honour, *Adilandra*." The son of Dorain mounted his Warhog and nodded at Galanör. "Two blades or not, he favours his left. Attack him from the right," he suggested with a wink.

# PART FOUR

# CHAPTER 37
# THE TOWER OF JAIN

In the time it took Inara to discard her torch, push Adan'Karth back, draw Firefly from its scabbard, and leap over Alijah's desk, Asher had already rolled across the surface and leaped at the foe standing in the doorway. Their fight had become a frenzy of clashing steel, the ranger's broadsword pitted against the stranger's crescent blades.

As Inara moved into the foyer, intending to aid Asher, the open doors to Alijah's chamber were filling with Reavers and more men robed in red and black. The Guardian broke away from their duel and placed herself firmly in the middle of the foyer.

As Gideon had taught her, so many years ago, Inara called on her magic - a Dragorn's greatest advantage - to level the playing field. Before Firefly got a taste of the enemy, her free hand shot out and expelled a wave of concussive energy so powerful it stripped the walls and blew the doors from their hinges. Every being in between, dead or alive, was launched out of the foyer and into the adjacent wall.

Only the dead rose again...

A gargled cry, followed by a heavy thud, preceded Asher's

company at her side. The ranger lifted his bloody broadsword in both hands and presented the Reavers with a grimace that would turn the living away. Together, they collided with the resurrected knights in a flurry of unorthodox forms, their blades twisting and slashing in sweeping arcs.

The Reavers made not a sound as they were relieved of their limbs and heads.

Inara slew the last of them with a two-handed swing of her Vi'tari blade, its enchantment guiding her through the Reaver's neck.

"More will be coming," Asher panted, removing his sword from a corpse.

"Who in all the hells are *they*?" Inara pointed Firefly's tip at one of the robed men.

"I don't know, but they're trained," Asher replied, giving his basic assessment. "We need to go."

Adan half skipped out of the study, his attention still drawn to its contents. "There appears to be a fire," he observed. "Should I put it out?"

Inara watched as the torch she had dropped spread its flames up the nearest bookcase. From there, it would easily spread around the entire chamber and most likely burn every room on the floor.

"Leave it," Asher growled. "It will give them something to do." The ranger exchanged his broadsword for the silvyr short-sword on his back and made for the main doors - or what was left of them.

Stepping over the bodies, both inside and outside the foyer, the companions rushed down the hall. Asher led the way, keeping them at a quick walk rather than the flat-out run Inara would have preferred.

Passing a window, movement outside caught Inara's attention, holding her back. She drew closer and peered out, turning her gaze to the large courtyard at the front of Alijah's palace. There she discovered dozens, if not hundreds, of Reavers marching through the gates and into the palace itself.

"When was the last time you fought off an army, Asher?"

The ranger doubled back and joined her by the window. "It's been a while," he replied gruffly. "Come on."

Leading them through the passages, Asher instructed them to hide at every other corner, allowing their enemy to pass them by on their way to the king's chambers. When at last they arrived at the turn that would take them back to the scaffolding, the ranger continued through the palace halls.

"What are you doing?" Inara demanded. "The way out is back there."

Asher took one long step back and pressed himself against the wall as his hand gestured for them to do the same. Inara contained her exasperated sigh and followed his instruction, along with Adan. A moment later, three servants hurried down the passage that crossed the companions. All three of the women were speaking at once in hushed tones, obviously aware of the intrusion. The ranger let a few more seconds go by after they vanished before continuing their escape.

"Where are we going?" Inara hissed.

"Even if we make it back to the lake, or the shore if we're lucky, there's no way we're getting out of this city on foot - we just set the palace on fire. Very soon, every road out of Valgala will be blocked and every street will be swept in search of us. We need speed if we're going to get ahead of that."

"Athis can't come anywhere near the city," Inara was quick to reply. "Not while Valgala is ringed with ballistas."

*I would burn them all to reach you,* Athis stated boldly.

Inara believed him. In fact, she could imagine with horrifying clarity what her companion would do to reach her, as she would do exactly the same.

"I wasn't thinking about him," Asher admitted, before throwing himself into a Reaver that suddenly crossed their path.

The two rolled across the ground in a tangle of limbs that ended with the ranger driving a dagger into the creature's head. Inara turned the corner and discovered a second guard, concealed within its black armour. Her Vi'tari blade flicked up, ready to drop the Reaver into a pile of pieces, but her free hand shot out first and expelled a fireball that engulfed its head. The undead fiend hit the wall and slid down in a writhing inferno until it became very still, succumbing to true death.

"That was loud," Adan commented unhelpfully.

Asher flashed him a look as he got to his feet again. "Follow..." His next words died on his lips and all three of them turned to the long passage on their left.

"It sounds like an entire garrison," Inara opined, detecting more marching feet than she could count.

Asher smiled. "Good."

"Good?" Inara questioned, wondering if the ranger had lost his mind. "There's likely a hundred or more marching towards us and hundreds more outside. How is this good?"

Asher sheathed his dagger on the back of his belt. "Because they're all coming *here*. All we have to do is slip past them and the road out of here will be all the quieter."

Inara moved to the nearest window and saw, as she had suspected, dozens of Reavers entering the main gates, heading for the palace doors. "For those of us not trained in Nightfall; how do we just slip past a few hundred guards?"

Asher looked around, assessing their environment by the calculating expression on his face. At last, he settled on Adan. "Make us invisible," he commanded of a hesitant Drake.

Adan'Karth shifted on the spot. "I have told you before - I will not use my magic so that you can unleash violence upon the world."

"I know." Asher took a controlling breath, appearing rather exasperated. "This time, if you use your magic, we can *avoid* violence."

Inara was shaking her head. "That's powerful magic, Asher."

The sound of marching feet grew louder. "Make us invisible damn it!" Asher growled.

"Inara is right. I cannot hold such magic over all three of us for long..."

"You don't need to," Asher reassured. "Just get us to the courtyard."

"I will try."

"Do it or we won't all make it out of here alive," the ranger replied, adding pressure.

Adan'Karth closed his eyes and balled his fists.

Inara felt nothing as her hands and feet gradually faded into nothingness. Her arms were gone before her legs vanished, meeting in the middle and disappearing her leathers. At last, she lost sight of her nose, concluding Adan's spell.

"I can't see either of you," the Guardian complained.

"Good," Asher said in his gruff way.

Doors were flung open at the end of the passage and a steady stream of Reavers almost filled the hall from wall to wall. Inara felt a disconcerting hand press into her shoulder, pushing her back towards a statue that stood as a sentinel beside the window. Pressed to the stone, they waited for the Reavers to trek further into the palace, leaving them a clear path to the lower levels.

"Come on," Asher hissed, his voice coming from somewhere down the hall.

"The quicker you move," Adan announced from behind Inara, "the harder it is to maintain."

Regardless of their speed, the Drake finally relinquished his hold over the magic as they reached the main doors to the courtyard. "If I hold it any longer I will become a burden," he warned.

Inara squeezed his shoulder affectionately. "You did well," she praised.

Their sudden reappearance elicited a terrified cry from two male servants who had likely run from the palace when the Reavers stormed inside. Asher shoved them aside and continued to lead the way, taking them to the stables by the western wall.

"Someone will have heard them," Inara warned.

"Some *thing*," the ranger corrected, pulling open the wide door to the stables.

Seeing the horses, Inara fully realised Asher's plan and felt her stomach drop. "I'm not really a rider."

Asher was all movement as he saddled one of the mounts. "You know how ridiculous that sounds don't you?"

Inara sighed. "I'm aware..."

"You can ride with me," the ranger offered. "Adan, can you ride..." Asher never finished his question, seeing the Drake seated comfortably astride a horse without a saddle.

"We are friends!" he declared with a broad smile.

"Good for you," Asher muttered, climbing onto his own horse.

Inara wasted no time and accepted the ranger's hand to join him on the horse. It was immediately uncomfortable and she felt wildly out of control, but having the reins wouldn't have made her feel any more in control.

"This isn't going to be as easy as just riding out," Asher explained. "Keep that sword of yours to hand. Adan, stay close behind me."

As advised, Inara held Firefly out to one side. She could feel Athis's apprehension bubbling under the surface. It was killing the dragon to be so far away while she was in danger.

***We will see each other soon,*** Inara promised.

Athis had no response, his focus required to keep him grounded.

Asher had them launching out of the stables with a start. They had crossed most of the courtyard before the first Reavers, guarding the gate, noticed their fast approach. They were galloping past by the time the knights of Erador had drawn their swords, though Asher and Inara both swung their blades, knocking an enemy down on each side of the horse.

As they hit the street with thundering hooves beneath them, the first salvo of arrows was let loose from the ramparts. Inara raised her hand and clenched a tight fist, erecting a temporary shield over their heads before the second, more accurate, salvo rained down. The shield flared and rippled but succeeded in repelling the deadly missiles.

The ranger kept his head low and spurred the horse to keep going with all the speed it could muster. It wasn't long, however, before mounted Reavers were in pursuit. They emerged from the side streets on horseback with swords raised and bows nocked. One such rider came charging out of an alley and almost collided with them.

"Kill it!" Asher barked.

Inara deftly transferred Firefly into her other hand and met the incoming blade before it relieved her of everything above her shoulders. Their swords clashed high and low until the Guardian found the perfect angle to back-hand the Reaver with the edge of her scimitar. The top half of its head - the important part - was chopped away in one clean swipe.

"Hold on!" Asher yelled.

Inara gripped his waist as he brought their horse to a halt and steered it down a side street. Seeing the oncoming Reavers, all on horseback, the Guardian understood the ranger's reasoning. She looked over her shoulder to see that Adan was still in their wake, far more at ease on his mount than she was. The Drake ducked his head, narrowly evading an arrow that continued to bounce off the alley wall.

"I thought you said the roads would be *all the quieter!*" Inara snapped.

Rushing out of the other end, Asher ignored her remark and directed the horse back towards the west in search of the gateway to The Spoken Road. Candlelight began to illuminate various windows throughout the city as Valgala's sleeping inhabitants became aware of a disturbance. Inara ignored the curious looks that followed and kept her eyes on the streets around them.

"On our right!" the ranger bellowed.

Sure enough, three Reavers came running out of another street. With only swords in hand, they posed no threat while the companions were moving at such speed. Inara changed her assessment of the situation when a single rider burst through the middle of them and took up the chase. Adan guided his horse to the other side of the street, leaving the bloody business to the warriors.

A second look, behind them, informed the Guardian that this particular rider was one of the masked humans they had faced inside the palace. He was perched over his saddle, head and shoulders low, and most definitely gaining on them. His proximity, on their right, forced Asher to steer the horse closer to the houses and shops that lined the street.

"Get rid of him!" Asher's command preceded the leap their horse made over a barrel. Inara felt her stomach rise to meet her chest before slamming back into place with unease.

The human rider, now directly on their side, swiped with his crescent blade. Firefly whipped up and parried the blow, saving Asher's life. The rider attacked again and again, challenging Inara, who wasn't accustomed to fighting either astride a horse or an enemy wielding such an exotic weapon. More than once, the rider nearly succeeded in spinning Firefly out of her grasp.

Frustrated, the half-elf simply blasted the man with an ice spell, casting him from his mount and through a shop window.

"Perhaps," Asher called back, "you should start with that next time!"

Inara held back her barbed retort and checked on Adan, who was still keeping pace with them and thankfully absent any injury. Asher weaved through the streets, often forced to take the wrong turn to avoid larger groups. Winding as their journey was, their ultimate escape inevitably loomed ahead - the gateway to The Spoken Road.

Seeing their rapid approach, the Reavers guarding the way sprang into action, attempting to block the way using themselves as an undead wall.

"Shield!" the ranger commanded.

Grasping his intentions at the last possible second, Inara called on the magic stored in the crystal pommel of her scimitar. The added strength from the crystal allowed her to build a shield large enough to arc around the front of their horse, reaching from the ground to above their heads. Firefly's pommel glowed hot white and Inara felt the strain as the magic weighed on her muscles.

Asher kept the horse straight, ensuring its gallop never faltered. Four Reavers, occupying the middle of the line, were rammed by Inara's shield and thrown far across the ground in a mangled mess of broken limbs. Adan trailed closely behind, utilising the gap left in their wake.

Under a glorious ocean of stars, the three companions made their daring escape from Valgala, riding out on the lonely road steeped in darkness. Inara would have hollered at what felt like a miraculous evasion, but a glance over her shoulder revealed they weren't out of the woods yet.

"Riders!" she fumed, eager to leave the city behind.

"How many?" Asher enquired, keeping them to the road.

Inara turned back to further assess the situation. "Ten or more! Enough to slow us down and keep us busy until more arrive! We need to lose them!"

Asher looked around. "There's nowhere *to* lose them! It's open range for miles out here and I have no idea how far away this damned tower is!"

Inara was about to answer him when the solution to their problem spoke out into her mind. "Don't worry about it!" she replied, her smile informing her tone.

Asher threw her a curious look over his shoulder before turning back to the road. Inara wished she could have seen his face when Athis materialised out of the darkness ahead of them. The red dragon swooped low and set free unbridled fury across the land, torching the riders and their mounts. The inferno lit up the night, hiding the stars above and eclipsing the city beyond. Then, with a flick of his tail, Athis too was gone, returned to the sky.

His flames masked the sound of distant ballista fire, but her bond with Athis told the Guardian that two bolts had whistled past him.

*I will meet you up the road,* the dragon said. *I will watch for any who follow you.*

***Just stay high for now,*** Inara replied.

After putting a mile between them and Valgala, the horses could no longer sustain their dutiful gallop. They had ridden up and out of the shallow basin that housed the capital city and were trotting along The Spoken Road, guided mostly by Adan's perfect vision, when Athis landed in front of them.

"Easy!" Asher patted their horse's neck while Adan merely whispered into his mount's ear, calming the animal in seconds.

The dragon laid his exquisite blue eyes on Inara. *The tower is two days away on horseback.*

The Guardian understood and happily jumped down from their horse. "We fly from here on out," she relayed to the others.

Asher had no argument, but Adan appeared upset saying goodbye to both horses. After setting them off on a course back to Valgala, the three companions ascended to Athis's back and braced themselves for a forceful take-off. Inara was immediately more comfortable off the ground and welcomed the night air and the hanging stars.

A golden dawn graced Erador when at last they came within sight of The Tower of Jain. The land around it was barren and hard, leading into the mountains that dominated the horizon, including the unmistakable Mount Kaliban, far to the north. The tower stood tall in the foreground, backed by a cluster of smaller buildings and bridges that clung to the rising rock of the mountains themselves.

The light of dawn made it hard to discern the tower's colour, and that of the buildings behind it, but Inara knew from Athis's sharper eyes that it was a tired white with obvious scorch marks in places. It was only after they landed in front of the tower that they came to understand the sheer size of the structure.

The entry into the main tower was a set of double doors so big that Ilargo and Athis could have walked through side by side without having to dip their heads. The outer walls were twice the height of those that surrounded Valgala or even Velia. The buildings Inara had noted as being smaller were, in fact, as large as The Dragon Keep in Namdhor.

All of it, however, was ancient - easily observed by looking at any part of the complex. The stone had crumbled in places and lost its edge, while the top of the tower appeared to be completely missing, leaving a jagged circle in its place. One of the stone bridges, connecting the tower to a cluster of buildings, had been blasted by something powerful enough to remove most of the walkway.

"I know I am new to the world," Adan voiced, "but I have a bad feeling about this place..."

"The feeling's mutual," Asher uttered, while reaching for the folded bow attached to his quiver. It snapped to life in his hand and he thrust his chin at the ominous doors. "Shall we?"

Approaching the rest of the way on foot, with Athis behind them, the companions soon came to see that a series of long ropes and woven chains were hanging from both doors. "What are they?" Inara followed the curve in the tethers to where they attached to a rocky boulder on each side of the road.

Her question was answered in the most unusual way. Both boulders expanded in size as four legs unfurled from within, followed by a tail of spikes, previously unseen. A pair of bloodshot eyes blinked open from what had to be a head, though they looked more like misshapen rocks. From each, a dusty tongue slipped out of their mouths to taste the air.

Instinctively, Inara reached for Firefly and Asher nocked an arrow. The curious beasts looked at the strangers before them, easily spotting Athis and his hulking size. Without a fuss, the two creatures proceeded to stomp in nearly opposite directions. The ropes and chains soon became taut, revealing the harnesses that had been strapped to their rough hides. Their pace slowed, taking the weight of a door each, but they never halted, marching out into the barren land until the doors were fully open.

"Have you ever seen anything like them before?" Inara asked the ranger.

He shook his head. "They're as big as a house - if they were in Illian I would have noticed one by now."

Athis had never seen one before either but, in a typically dragon way, he was wondering whether his claws and teeth could penetrate their hard exterior.

"We're not alone here," Asher said gravely. "*Someone* has to be feeding these things."

That wasn't the assessment Inara wanted to hear, but she couldn't ignore it either. "Can you hear Ilargo?" She asked Athis the question out loud for the benefit of her companions.

The red dragon raised his head and closed his eyes for a moment. *No,* he finally answered.

That also wasn't something Inara wanted to hear. "Nothing," she relayed for the others. "There still have to be answers here, answers we *need.*" Without waiting, she led the way.

So close now, Inara noticed the size of each block of stone that made up the outer wall and even the tower. Each one had to be as big as a mountain troll and twice as thick, weighing several tons. Raising the entire complex would have taken centuries and, even then, she couldn't fathom the techniques required to move stone of such impressive weight.

*Magic,* Athis stated. *It's very old, but the magic used to create this place still lingers...*

Passing over the threshold, the light of dawn was confined to a single column that cut through the world of shadows and decrepit ruins. Cobwebs coated every surface, concealing the corners and clothing the sheer walls. Thick rounded pillars, riddled with chips and decay, supported the enormous atrium.

Athis walked between them with ease, his predatory gaze searching every inch of the interior for threats. In front of them, and to the sides, were deep cuts in the stone, offering something the size of a dragon multiple paths through the complex.

Adan glanced at all three fissures. "Which way?"

Asher gestured to the path dead ahead. "That way."

Inara scrutinised his choice and noted the differences. The cobwebs between the pillars were well above head height compared to the rest, and those that had been constructed lower down had been recently torn through. The ground was also worn, free of the thick layer of dust and debris seen on the other paths.

Inara was about to voice her agreement when her bond to Athis alerted her to an imminent threat. Before she could fully process the dragon's senses, however, he reared up on his back legs and unleashed an ear-splitting roar. Still in the column of light spilling in from the east, it was nearly impossible to see what lay beyond its borders. Trusting Athis's sharper senses though, Inara gripped Firefly firmly and positioned herself into the fifth form of the Mag'dereth.

Asher moved in such a way that Adan was placed between the two of them as the ranger aimed his bow into the shadows. Athis came back down on all fours with a thunderous crash, his wings fanned out beside him.

***What do you see?*** Inara asked of her companion.

*We are surrounded.* Athis's growl turned into another deafening roar that shook the stone.

***Surrounded by what?***

Athis relayed a description of their foe, informing Inara that the masked men, robed in red and black, were slinking out of the cracks in the outer walls.

Asher turned in every direction, blinded by the contrast in light. "Inara?"

"We're surrounded," she told them, readying multiple destructive spells in her mind.

Athis turned to their right and stormed between the pillars, out of the light. He expelled the darkness with a jet of fire, revealing the robed men stalking from the darkness. One of them failed to escape the torrent and was consumed by flames that continued past him to climb the walls. Athis quickly turned around, his tail sweeping debris across the chamber.

*They are fleeing,* he reported.

Inara let her muscles relax as she resumed her normal stance. "They would rather run than face Athis," she said to the others.

"They?" the ranger questioned.

"The same men we faced in Valgala. Their identity is becoming as much a mystery as their presence in this ancient place."

Asher grunted in agreement. "I would say their presence here is a good sign - they must be guarding something... or *someone.*"

"Careful, Ranger," Inara replied with some humour to her voice. "You're beginning to sound optimistic."

The human equivalent of a dragon's growl rumbled inside Asher's throat. "Let's push on."

As they had in the palace, Asher and Inara removed torches from the wall, both ignited by the Guardian's magic. There seemed little point in sneaking around when every resounding step taken by Athis would have informed any occupants of their arrival.

The generous passage opened up to another cavernous chamber lined with looming statues of hooded figures. Most were missing features, found in piles of rubble at their feet, or their details had simply worn away.

"I think this is as far as you go," Asher commented, looking up at Athis.

Inara turned in every direction, looking for another passage large enough to accommodate her companion. She discovered a set of arching double doors on their left, equal in size to the main doors, but they were sealed shut and absent the unusual beasts to open them.

"Why would they allow dragons to come this far but no further?" Inara voiced.

His face half in torchlight, Asher turned to the Guardian. "Who said anything about dragons?"

Inara then followed the ranger's gaze to a pair of vertical

handles, inlaid to the gargantuan doors. They might as well have been tree trunks to a human and they were higher than the top of Athis's head.

*Giants,* the dragon reasoned.

"Giants?" Inara repeated out loud.

"Perhaps," Asher said with little commitment. "This place wasn't built for them though," he added, gesturing to a human size set of double doors on the far side of the chamber. "If there are answers here, I suggest we start through there."

Inara turned back to meet Athis. ***Go back to the entrance - I don't like the idea of you waiting in a place like this.***

Athis bowed his head. *I will scout the buildings and search for any sign of Ilargo.*

It always pained Inara in some way to watch Athis walk away from her, but she had come this far; there was no turning back now. With Asher and Adan'Karth, she crossed the ancient chamber and entered the next via the double doors. The chosen path led nowhere but up, so up they went, traversing the winding staircases and maze-like corridors.

After rising through the tower for six floors, they saw the human guards for themselves. All three hugged the wall, hiding themselves successfully as a pair of men, attired in familiar robes, strode past without noticing them. The companions waited for them to be out of ear-shot before moving on. They slowed to make a better search of the nearby rooms but found nothing to suggest Gideon was there.

Every subsequent floor had an increased number of guards, all human. It made their progress slow, but it gave Inara hope. Without knowledge of the tower's layout, they wandered wherever they needed to in order to hide. Adan used magic for brief seconds at a time to conceal them when nowhere appropriate presented itself.

"They all seem to be in something of a hurry," Inara observed from a crack in a door.

"We're probably the first threat they've encountered here in a while," Asher replied. "Is the way clear?"

Inara moved her head to try and see both sides of the passage. "I think so."

"I hear nothing," Adan confirmed.

Continuing their exploration, Inara began to wonder if they were climbing into the clouds themselves. Having lost count of the rooms they had checked, Asher took to the first step on yet another staircase.

"Wait," Inara whispered with force. Something had caught her eye...

The ranger backed up and joined her, with Adan on his heels. Inara made for a passage they had almost discounted, drawn to the one colour the human eye could never ignore: red. The dark walls of the passage were covered in runes, all applied with red paint.

Inara ran two fingers over one of the glyphs and examined it. "This is fresh."

Asher cast his eyes down the hall and slowly raised his bow, the arrow ready to be released. The end of the passage was missing its outer wall, allowing the morning light to pour in. Inara rested her torch on the ground, careful not to make a sound. The ranger nodded ahead, suggesting she take the lead while also remaining on his left to keep his aim clear.

Naturally, Adan held back.

On light feet, they cautiously moved towards the light. Both warriors came to a quiet halt when the lever latch was raised on the door up ahead to their right. A robed man walked out reading from a piece of parchment. His head down, he didn't see the intruders until Asher's arrow was right in front of his face. That was the last thing he saw. The arrow fled through his head and continued out into the world via the jagged hole at the end of the passage.

Inara caught the body with one hand and lowered it to the floor. Asher gave her an approving look that the Guardian was ashamed to say she enjoyed.

"Too many doors," the ranger complained. "If we go any further, we risk being flanked. We'll have to check every room as we go, which will create a lot of noise if we cross any more of *them*."

"What do you suggest?"

Asher folded his bow. "We draw them out, *here*. Kill them. Find Gideon." He pulled free his silvyr short-sword, the perfect weapon for a close-quarter melee.

"What about those below?" Inara could imagine dozens of guards rushing up to meet them.

Asher looked back the way they had come. "Narrow passage. They'll be clumped together. Just make sure we take down those up here with speed. I'll hold off any reinforcements while you search the rooms."

Inara wanted to check that the ranger could handle that scenario but, sure of his answer, she held her tongue. Instead, she watched the ranger approach the first door on their left and kick it in with a solid boot.

"Gentlemen..."

The Guardian couldn't see who Asher was talking to but he soon disappeared after dashing inside. There was a brief clash of swords followed by something breaking and a man's pain-filled wail. A masked man then came flying out of the room where he met the adjacent wall with some force. He didn't get back up. While Asher concluded his business inside, Inara once more adopted the fifth form of the Mag'dereth, anticipating the inevitable conflict to come.

Sure enough, more masked men burst from two doors further down the broken passage. Seeing a human woman and a Drake must have been a confusing sight for them, explaining their brief hesitation, but still they charged with a crescent blade in each hand. Inara remained steadfast, holding Firefly in a vice-like grip. She didn't relish the taking of any life, but that didn't mean she wasn't highly efficient in doing so.

The man leading the charge was almost within striking distance when Asher exploded from the doorway and slammed into him. His weight crushed the man against the wall and the ranger used his rebound to crash into the rest of them, creating bloody chaos. His silvyr sword parried and slashed as he weaved between them, sending two stumbling towards Inara.

Firefly knocked their clumsy strikes aside while the Guardian spun through the gap, angling herself to kill both men in a single swipe. By the time they hit the floor, more had flooded the passage further up. Asher pulled his short-sword free of his last foe and presented the next wave with a grim reality should they challenge him.

Adan placed a gentle hand on Inara's shoulder. "More are coming," he warned, turning her back the way they had come.

Inara strode forward, past the ranger, and presented the oncoming men with her open palm. "We're running out of time."

Tapping into just a portion of the magic that swelled within her, the Guardian of the Realm released a shockwave that filled every inch of the passage. The men rushing towards her could do nothing but be carried away with the spell, launched from their feet and out through the hole at the end of the hall.

Asher motioned for Adan to take shelter inside the first room he had cleared. "Don't come out until I tell you to," he instructed. "You," he continued, looking at Inara, "find Gideon." In the silence after the melee, the half-elf could hear the guards running up the stairs to meet the intruders. "Go!" Asher insisted before turning to face the next threat.

Inara wasted no more time, realising that she could fill decades of her life with concern for Asher's wellbeing - the man attracted Death with his every action.

Turning her attention to what remained of the passage, she began to systematically search every room. There were no locked doors barring her entry, though every room failed to fulfil her hope. The guards who had been living here led a simple life given that all they possessed was a cot and food supplies; it seemed their only purpose was to exist in this place.

As she reached the last door on the right, reinforcements arrived from the floors below. Their pace came to a sudden halt when confronted with Asher, who stood defiantly amongst their dead.

Only when the handle failed to budge did Inara see the runes painted over the last door. None of the others had been covered, only the walls. Butterflies fluttered around inside her stomach. Her free hand hovered over the lock while her spell took a hold of the wood that surrounded it. One quick flick of her wrist broke that section of the door away, leaving it to swing easily on its hinges.

She opened the door as Asher collided with the bravest of the masked men. The room beyond was dusty, seen easily in the single beam of light that shone through a slit in the outer wall. Inara narrowed her eyes in the gloom, battling the contrast of light and dark. Passing beyond the beam, her sight adjusted, revealing the secrets that lay therein. Of course, there was only one thing to see. Such a sight was it that the Guardian could barely contain her gasp.

"Gideon..."

# CHAPTER 38
# THE PLANS OF MAGES AND MEN

His back pressed to the cold wall, Nathaniel Galfrey stopped and caught his breath. His heart - healthy beyond its years - thundered like a beating drum as his lungs pleaded for air. Tentative fingers reached for the hilt on his hip, pulling the blade out of its scabbard by a daring inch.

Under a still and starry night, the sound of marching armour echoed from the streets around him.

Vighon's hand snapped out and held the knight's sword in place. Without words, he guided Nathaniel's attention to the gothic spires that loomed over the buildings, on the other side of the main street. The church of Atilan. They had finally made it to the top tier of Namdhor's slope.

Kassian came skidding around the corner before flattening himself against the wall beside them. "We can't stay here," he warned with a spitting hiss.

"What did you do?" Nathaniel asked, concern etched across his face.

"It's not what I did," Kassian corrected with a shrug. "It's what I'm about to do..." The mage retrieved a small sphere, clay by its appearance, from his belt and kissed the ancient runes that ringed the surface.

Nathaniel reached out and gripped the Keeper's arm before any action could be taken. "What is that?"

"In a word: brilliant!" Kassian turned back to the corner and tossed the sphere underarm down the side street. "Get ready to run," he urged, gesturing at the church opposite.

There was no opportunity to ask anything else. An explosion rocked the ground beneath their feet, expelling dust and debris past the corner of the building. Glass shattered in the distance and the sound of tumbling bricks resounded throughout the alleys.

Kassian was already on the main street by the time Vighon and Nathaniel gathered their wits enough to join him. At a sprint, they crossed the road and dashed down the side street beside the church, avoiding the main doors.

Taking cover behind a stack of discarded barrels, Vighon gripped Kassian by the coat and pinned him to the wall. "What was that?" he demanded.

Kassian raised the tip of his wand to the northman's jaw. "Don't touch the coat," he instructed calmly.

Vighon clenched his jaw and stepped back. "What was that?" he growled.

"A diversion, obviously." Kassian sheathed his wand and adjusted his coat.

"A diversion that's cost lives?" the northman pressed. "This is my city, my *people*!"

"Why do you think I had to catch you up? I was checking the locksmith's shop was empty at the end of the street. Speaking of which." The Keeper thumbed at the door on the side of the church. "I would normally use magic..." he added with a shrug.

Nathaniel removed his lock picks - a skill Asher had taught him - and began working on the door. "What did you throw?" he asked, inserting the pick. "I've never seen anything like it before."

"A weapon of my own design," Kassian bragged, keeping watch

on the main street. "The runes are a type of trapping spell. I just have to cast a destructive spell inside the container and it remains there until the runes are broken. Elegant, if I do say so…"

"It's dangerous to use that in the city," Vighon chastised.

"It worked didn't it?" Kassian nodded his head at the Reavers rushing to the scene. "Can you get us inside?"

Nathaniel answered the question by unlocking the door and opening it a crack. He peered inside, checking the church was absent its priests. "Let's get off the streets," he urged.

Vighon was the last to enter, closing the door behind him. Nathaniel moved into the pews, beyond the row of pillars. Being a church to Atilan, its interior was nothing if not grand. The arching ceiling was decorated with murals and paintings while the walls were hung with tapestries between the tall windows. In the shadows of night, however, the church was lacking the lustrous colours that helped to accentuate its importance.

"Do you know where the entrance is?" Kassian's voice was almost lost to the vastness around them.

"Under the altar," Vighon replied, making his way down the central aisle.

Nathaniel checked the small room that led off from the dais, making certain they were truly alone. Finding naught but voluminous robes, he returned to his companions as they were lifting and moving the altar aside. Vighon kicked the long rug away, dropped to his hands and knees, and ran his fingers over the slab of stone.

He cursed, filling the church with his grievance.

"What is it?" the old knight asked.

"There's no handles or anything we can grip," he explained, struggling to fit his fingers in the groove around the stone. "I think it was only meant to be opened from the other side."

Kassian crouched and tapped the surface with his knuckles. "It's got to have some weight to it…"

Nathaniel rested his hands on his hips. The inescapable conclusion was logical if incredibly dangerous. "Use magic," he announced.

Kassian looked up at him with the face of a man both eager and cautious. "If I use magic they'll find us," he said as a matter of fact. "There's too many Seekers up here to miss it."

Nathaniel set his eyes on Vighon, a silent question behind them. The northman nodded gravely. "It *is* the only way in," he clarified.

"Do it," Nathaniel ordered.

Kassian drew his wand and stepped back from the slab of stone, ushering the others to do the same. The sound of scraping stone echoed throughout the church as the block was freed of its place in the floor. It wasn't as thick as Nathaniel had presumed it to be, but it was still heavy enough that without grips it required a magical touch. The Keeper guided his wand to the back of the church and the stone obeyed its given direction until placed on the floor.

"Well we've come this far," Kassian remarked, firing a white orb of light into the tunnel beneath their feet. It revealed steps carved into the bedrock and a narrow path leading from the bottom.

"I will move with haste," Vighon assured, moving for the hole.

Nathaniel reached out and stopped him. "You'll do nothing with haste. You're too valuable to go wandering off into The Dragon Keep alone."

"I didn't come this far *not* to retrieve my sword," Vighon argued.

"And you'll have it," Nathaniel promised. "It's what you do with it that truly matters. I know the keep's layout - *I* will go. If your position here is compromised just get out, leave the city. We'll meet up at The Black Wood. The same applies if I take too long."

"We'll find it faster if we both go," the northman countered.

"You'll live longer if you listen to me," Nathaniel told him with more authority than he would normally use with the king.

Kassian tilted his head, as if assessing the knight. "Perhaps I should go," he mused. "He's too valuable and you've got more than the sword of the north on your mind..."

Revelation crossed Vighon's face. "Reyna," he said with understanding.

Nathaniel held up a hand to silence them both. "I've been doing this kind of thing a lot longer than either of you. Trust me. I will find the sword and return - nothing more."

Kassian made to argue but Vighon halted him with a hand. "Let him go," he said softly.

Nathaniel nodded his appreciation and began to climb down into the tunnel. "That light won't last forever," Kassian called down.

Nathaniel looked up and nodded his understanding. "Just remember what I said - don't wait for me."

With that, he set off into the tunnel, moving with as much speed as his caution would allow. The tunnel was low, forcing him to bow his head at an awkward angle the entire way. Thankfully, there was only one way to go. Following the slight incline, Nathaniel moved through the shadows until he reached a solid wall. With his hand flat to the stone, he searched in vain for something to show him how to enter the keep. Like the stone in Atilan's church, however, it seemed he was going against the flow of the tunnel's design.

Kassian's light began to flicker.

With nothing left but brute force, the old knight rested his shoulder against one side of the wall and put all of his weight behind it. Inch by inch, the wall reluctantly gave way. By the time he was able to get his fingers around the outer wall and into the chamber beyond, the orb had extinguished, dropping him into darkness.

One last shove pushed the wall forward, opening a gap wide enough for him fit through. Unfortunately, he couldn't see a thing. His best guess, given the complete lack of light from either the moon or a torch on the wall, put him in the archives beneath the main keep - the distinct musty smell helping. Using his hands to explore the other side of the wall he had opened, his suspicions were realised. From inside, the secret door had looked like a book case, deduced by the numerous leather spines and scrolls he discovered.

Following the wall of the archives, he eventually came across the double doors that led up into the keep itself. It was comforting to find a passage lit by torches, showing him the way. Of course, he now had to contend with those who guarded the ancient halls.

Ascending into the main passages proved to be the easy part - the Reavers had no interest in protecting the archives, especially against infiltration. The hard part came with all the waiting. Nathaniel was painfully aware that Vighon and Kassian were likely going to be found and, in truth, he would have preferred to leave the city with them. But he had to wait in a number of spots while the patrolling Reavers walked by.

His progress was horribly slow. Time began to creep past while he himself crept through the halls, searching room after room. He had no idea where Alijah would think to store the sword, but he was confident his son wouldn't have got rid of something so exceptional as a silvyr sword that itself was a piece of history. He peered out of every window, dreading those first rays of sunlight - it would be very difficult to escape the capital in the light of day...

The old knight stopped by a single door. He knew from memory that it would lead up onto the ramparts and, from there, he could ascend to the levels that housed the throne room and the king's quarters. But the ramparts were too exposed. Cursing under his breath, he reconciled himself to the longer route, through the bowels of the keep.

More time slipped by and, with it, his hope was slowly replaced with doubt. The Dragon Keep was hulking in size and the sword could easily have been discarded anywhere; it was, after all, the weapon of Alijah's enemy.

Nathaniel turned a corner and realised he was in a very familiar part of the keep. This was where they would stay when visiting Vighon, their rooms lovingly maintained on the slight chance that they might be in the north. The old knight slowly approached the door he had passed through countless times without thought.

How had he arrived here? There were other ways to reach his destination. As hard as he tried to convince himself otherwise, the old knight knew he had come this way deliberately.

Every part of him wanted to open the door - she had to be inside. Nathaniel's hand came to rest lightly against the wood as he bowed his head. His emotions were turning him inside out. Every ounce of his self-discipline was required to take even a single step back from the door. That accomplished, he managed a second step. Turning his attention to the end of the passage, he set himself to the simple task of reaching it.

Ascending the other side of the keep, Nathaniel crossed a window that brought him to a halt. He backtracked a step and looked out at a pale blue sky. The earliest rays of dawn were just bringing the eastern horizon into view.

He would have sworn aloud were it not for the sound of marching feet around the corner. Nathaniel dashed to the nearest alcove and hugged the wall in the corner. Again, he was forced to wait, wasting precious time. The Reavers passed him by and were soon followed by another pair. It felt like a lifetime had come and gone by the time he was opening the doors to the throne room.

Inside, Nathaniel couldn't easily recall the last time he had stepped foot inside that room. He certainly didn't remember it being so cold, in both temperature and appearance. Vacant, the throne resided at the head of the chamber. He longed to see Vighon returned to his place upon it...

Walking a little further in, the dragon gate quickly captured the knight's attention. It was hard to miss, being so big that Malliath could fit his head and claws through. It was also open, the portcullis raised high into the arching ceiling. Letting his eyes roam around the chamber, it didn't take Nathaniel long to find the round shield on the eastern wall.

Before removing it, he observed a second bracket fixed to the stone. He had seen many like them, designed to mount swords. He looked around, searching for the sword of the north as he pulled the shield down and held it in both hands. A gentle finger ran over the runes that ringed the brown leather inside the iron frame. They had been put there by Hadavad to protect Vighon from magic so that he, in turn, might protect Alijah.

Nathaniel squeezed the shield until his knuckles whitened. How could his world have fallen into such ruin?

The old knight froze. That part of him he could never explain, a part that made him the warrior he was, informed him that he wasn't alone. His muscles stiff, Nathaniel slowly turned his head back to the chamber. There, he found a single figure standing in the gloom.

"Hello, my love..." came the sweet voice.

Kassian scrambled back inside the church and shut the side door with his body clamped to the wood. His eyes searched desperately for something, anything, that would be large enough and heavy enough to bar the way.

"I was beginning to think you were dead!" Vighon hissed from the altar.

"There was a moment I thought the same," the Keeper quipped. Without explanation, he began to drag a side unit, stacked with books, across the threshold.

"What happened?" the northman enquired.

Kassian groaned as he pushed the unit as close to the door as he could. "I tried to create some more diversions; lead them away from the church."

Vighon raised an eyebrow. "Why do I have a bad feeling?"

"There's a *lot* of Reavers out there," Kassian replied. "I evaded a few... killed a few."

The northman's shoulders sagged. "How many followed you?"

Kassian shrugged. "Two or three. Maybe all of them. I have no idea!" The Keeper strode towards the hole in the dais. "Why are we even still here? Nathaniel's been gone for hours!"

"We're not leaving without him," Vighon stated.

"He's either dead or so lost he might as well be dead. You heard him: you're too valuable. We should leave the city, regroup, and come up with a new plan."

"No!" Vighon growled. "I'm only leaving with Nathaniel and the sword."

Kassian's frustration was bubbling up. "I thought you ran away because you didn't want people dying for you. If we stay any longer, every Keeper in the city, including myself, is going to die. *For you.*"

Vighon leaned into one of the pews, shaking his head with grim determination. "You know what you're fighting for." The words came out as if forced. "So do your Keepers. If this *isn't* your fight, *leave.*"

Kassian looked away, his expression contorting. "It's *love* then," he reasoned, intoning some frustration.

"What?"

Kassian almost laughed. "It turns out we're fighting for the same thing you and I. A little twisted perhaps, but love all the same." He gave the northman a long hard look - he couldn't envision a future in which Vighon Draqaro and Inara Galfrey found happiness together like he and Clara had, for a time. "I hope this doesn't end for you how it ended for me. I really do." The Keeper sighed. "We both know you're going in that hole. *Go.* Find your sword."

Vighon made for the hole in the dais and hesitated. "What about you?" he asked, glancing at the main doors.

"Sun's coming up," Kassian replied casually. "The streets are about to get busy again. I'll wait for Nathaniel and we can slip away. Meet you at The Black Wood."

"I thought you said he was dead or lost."

The Keeper pursed his lips, wary of showing his hand and revealing any emotions. "I can wait a little longer. *Go.*"

The northman clapped a hand on Kassian's shoulder. A message of brotherhood passed between them, held in the eyes alone. The Keeper conjured an orb of light to guide the way. Then Vighon was gone...

～

Nathaniel couldn't prevent his eyes filling with tears at the sight of his wife. The last time he had seen her, felt the softness of her skin, enjoyed the pressure of her lips, they had been hiding in Dunwich with Kassian and Ruban Dardaris. The next time he had heard anything of her, she had taken a stray arrow to the chest and was left in the arms of their son. Since then, he had read nothing but reports of her on the ramparts, surrounded by enemies...

The old knight quickly rested Vighon's shield against the nearest pillar and engulfed Reyna in a crushing embrace. As always, her own embrace proved to be stronger. He inhaled the scent of her hair as he pulled her tight to his chest.

"I've missed you so much," he whispered.

Reyna moved to create a space between them, allowing her to cup his face and bring him down for a passionate kiss. "I've missed *that*," she replied with a coy smile.

"How did you know I was here?" he asked.

"Nothing gets by the nose of an elf," Reyna replied with love in her eyes.

Nathaniel couldn't help but smile, forgetting, for the moment, their circumstances. "Wait. Where are your guards? All the reports said you were escorted by Arakesh."

"I was," Reyna answered. "A few days ago, Veda Malmagol recalled *all* the assassins - I don't know why, though it might have something to do with Alijah's disappointment. Apparently, Asher has been dispatching them across the entire realm."

Nathaniel arched an eyebrow as an opportunity stared him in the face. "This is great!" he exclaimed in a hushed tone. "We can leave together."

The excitement of their reunion fell away from Reyna's face. "I cannot *leave*, Nathaniel. I cannot even stay long - the Reavers must not find me outside of my room."

As much as Nathaniel had expected this, he was still taken aback. "I don't understand," he confessed. "We need to go, Reyna. There's a war going on out there."

"I can't leave him," Reyna agonised. "I can get through to him. I know I can. Then there won't be a war—"

"There's no time for that," Nathaniel interjected. "There won't even be a realm left to fight for. Alijah is beyond reason now..."

"I refuse to believe that," Reyna argued. "How can you even say that? He is our son!"

"Our son died in The Bastion," Nathaniel snapped, tears rushing to the surface.

They were the hardest words he had ever said...

Reyna was shaking her head, blinking tears of her own. "No," she repeated again and again. "He's still in there. I can see it."

"You need to stop looking at *him* and start looking at what he's *doing* out there. He's killing anyone who shows even a hint of magic. He's enslaved the dwarves and put them to work doing who knows what. Bounties have been issued on every Drake in the country - he's rounding them up! And the elves... He had Malliath burn—"

"I know what he did," Reyna cut in, her eyes cast low. Her face quickly shot up again. "Is my mother..." The elf choked on her question and failed to finish it.

Nathaniel took a breath and gripped her affectionately by the arms. "She's alive. They both are. Your mother, Faylen: they've probably reached Qamnaran by now."

"Qamnaran? The tower?"

"Yes, they've gone to—"

"They can't be there!" Reyna warned. "Alijah and Malliath left for Qamnaran days ago!"

Nathaniel stepped back from his wife. "That's *why* they've gone. He needs to be stopped. Your mother might be the only one powerful enough to..." His words trailed away with his gaze, both dampened with guilt and shame.

Reyna tilted her head, forcing Nathaniel to look into her eyes. "To kill him," she finished. "We cannot allow that, for both their sakes."

"We cannot stop it," Nathaniel corrected. "There is more than just you and I in this conflict. Our son has wronged countless people, some of whom have the power to fight back - he's brought this on himself, Reyna. If anything, it *should* be us who stop him. Alijah is *our* responsibility."

"I won't give up on him," Reyna sobbed.

"You think I have given up on him?" Nathaniel retorted, losing his hold on the tears in his eyes. "I am fighting in this rebellion because I know there is only one way to save my boy, to give him some peace. This isn't the son I raised!" he spat, gesturing to the empty throne room. "Whatever evil rules him now will rule him forever, and I mean to *end* it. I don't know what will be left of me, but I can't let him live as a monster; it's killing me."

Reyna half turned away from him, tears running down her cheeks. "I cannot lose my son..."

Nathaniel glanced at the shield by his foot before confronting his wife. "We still have a son," he reminded, his voice almost pleading. "Vighon might not be ours by blood, but he's ours in every way that truly matters. We have more than just a duty to see him returned to the throne."

Reyna closed her eyes for a time, stemming the flow of tears. "Is that why you're here?" she uttered, regarding the shield.

"He's back in the fight," Nathaniel impassioned. "We have a real chance to undo everything. I came here for his sword..."

"You didn't come for me?" Reyna's question was delivered with an even tone, her emotions guarded.

Nathaniel recalled Asher's assessment of Reyna's captivity. "We both know you possess the skills to escape this place, Arakesh or not. You're here because you're clinging to hope. I beg you to leave with me, Reyna. If there is a way to stop Alijah without harming him then that's exactly what we'll do."

A pall of depression swept away the colour in Reyna's skin and the light in her eyes. She stepped further into the throne room, away from Nathaniel.

"I have to try," she whispered into the morning gloom.

"Then try, but try from our side," he pleaded. "In here, you're just a voice in his ear competing with Malliath - you can never win. Out there, challenging him, you will be heard. Please, come with me."

Reyna lifted her jaw, steeling herself. "You won't find the sword in here."

Nathaniel blinked as their conversation shifted. "Where is it?"

Reyna looked at the open dragon gate on the other side of the chamber. "Alijah cast it away, over the edge..."

Nathaniel marched across the stone and out onto the platform. The dawn was already being darkened by thick clouds sweeping in from the north, over the mountains. He ignored the chilling wind that whipped at his coat and peered over the lip of the platform. The rest of the keep was sprawled below, segmented by intersecting walls. He could see the main courtyard, the gardens, and the stables between the ramparts - the sword could have landed anywhere.

The old knight sighed and clenched his fist around the hilt on his belt. He didn't have time to keep searching and, even if he did, searching the grounds around the keep would be the end of him.

"I have to leave," Reyna announced from the throne room.

Nathaniel passed under the dragon gate once more. "You've already left," he said with disappointment. "The only way we were going to get through this was together. I fight for you, you fight for me - that's always been the way. Now, we're fighting for Vighon, for Inara, for the people, the very realm itself. This is it, Reyna. This is *the* war. Elves, dwarves, humans, and everything in between hangs in the balance this time. If you aren't fighting by my side now, it was all for nothing..."

He didn't wait for a response, for another rejection, another moment of madness from the one person who had kept him sane all these years. Leaving the shield and Reyna behind, the old Graycoat walked out of the throne room and began his journey back to the archives and the church beyond.

~

Lying on his back, beside the hole in the dais, Kassian stared up at the images that told the story of humanity's creation in the hands of Atilan. "I'm going to die in this city," he mused.

He couldn't count the hours he had spent alone inside Atilan's church, but his time there was coming to an end. Inevitably, he would be discovered by one of the priests - when they turned up - or the Reavers and their Seekers would sniff him out. What followed would be an epic battle, he knew, one in which he brought down as many of Alijah's knights as he could before Death showed its face.

The Keeper couldn't help but dwell on the peace that would finally bring him. Death would rid him of the grief that plagued his every waking moment. It would take the pain away and perhaps even reunite him with Clara, if there was such a place where they could be together.

That didn't sound so bad...

But what would he be leaving behind? There would be nothing good to have come from Clara's time gracing Verda's earth. There should be something, anything, that made a difference because she had been alive.

A noise from inside the hole disturbed his thoughts. Instinctively, his hand removed the wand from its holster and he sat up enough to aim it. He sighed a relaxing breath seeing Nathaniel's head appear over the lip.

"Finally!" the Keeper, exclaimed. He stood up and helped Nathaniel out of the hole, noting the discarded torch he had abandoned at the bottom of the hole.

"Where's Vighon?" they both asked at the same time.

Nathaniel's face dropped and he searched the church. "He was with you!"

"He *was* with me," Kassian agreed. "But then you didn't come back so... he went after you and the sword."

The old knight gripped Kassian by the shirt. "You let him go alone?"

Shoving Nathaniel's hand away, the Keeper growled, "I'm not his minder. It's his keep, his sword. I *told* him to leave you behind, just like you said."

Nathaniel groaned and turned back to the hole. "He'll never find the sword; Alijah tossed it away. We have to find him—"

The main doors to the church rattled as someone fiddled with the lock.

Kassian grabbed at Nathaniel and pushed him towards the side door. "If they find a hole leading into the keep they will flood it with every Reaver in Namdhor."

"We're not leaving him in there!" the knight argued.

Kassian rolled his eyes. "You sound just like him." Using his wand, he slid the stone slab back into place and quickly dragged the wooden altar in front of it. "This is the best chance we can give him now."

"I won't leave—"

"You will!" Kassian hissed, casting his wand to the left and removing the unit that barred the side door. "I'm using too much magic here - we don't have time for this!"

The main door opened, flooding the church with what light could pierce the dark clouds. A bald man in dark robes walked in with a large book under his arm. Nathaniel and Kassian froze. The priest hadn't noticed them yet, his eyes still adjusting to the gloom.

"Who are you?" he finally demanded, discovering them on his way up the central aisle. "What are you doing here?"

"Time to go," Kassian insisted, striding towards the side door.

"This is a house of Atilan - the king of the gods Himself! You are trespassing!"

Reluctantly, Nathaniel rushed to catch up with Kassian from where the two exited the church and shut the door behind them. "We need to put some distance between us and this place," Kassian warned.

"I won't leave the city," Nathaniel told him defiantly. "We come back tonight and open the tunnel up again. Hopefully, Vighon will be waiting for us."

Together, they walked down the side street and turned the corner as the priest opened the door and called after them. They kept moving, choosing a route that would take them further down Namdhor's slope.

Kassian glanced back over his shoulder, making certain the priest hadn't found his courage and decided to actually pursue them. His observation came to an abrupt end when his shoulder collided with that of another. The Keeper turned to apologise but the word never found life in the world. The man he had bumped into was one of two, and both men were unfortunately familiar.

The Bailey brothers...

Or, at least, the surviving two. They were absent any of their band, though most had been killed on The White Vale. Kassian bowed his head, grumbled an apology, and kept his feet moving alongside Nathaniel's. They turned down two more streets before the Keeper dared to look back again. They were following. More than that, the brothers each possessed a look of hunger about them.

"They know it's us," he whispered to the knight.

"We need to cross the main street," Nathaniel suggested. "Try and lose them in the east markets."

Kassian agreed and they made a left turn towards the largest street in all of Namdhor. Before they stepped out of the alley, the keeper looked back one last time - an act that saved Nathaniel's life. He barged the old knight aside, pushing him out of an arrow's path. The missile sailed across the main street and landed in the side of a passing cart.

Returning his attention to the Bailey brothers, Kassian could see that one of them had already nocked another arrow and was taking aim again. Wand in hand, he intercepted the next arrow with a spell and buried its tip into the ground at his feet.

"You're going to die for killing our brother!" one of them hurled.

The bowman lowered his weapon and retrieved a one-handed axe from his belt. Again, Kassian was forced to use magic to prevent it from flying into his chest.

Nathaniel drew his sword and prepared to meet the charging bounty hunters. "They're going to bring every Reaver in the city on top of us!"

Kassian had come to the same conclusion. The way he saw it, they had to dispatch the Bailey brothers with all haste and leave the area before all hell broke loose. Referring to his training, the Keeper knew several ways to maim or kill his enemy with speed. Unfortunately, they were all loud...

Holstering his wand, Kassian pulled free his sword. There was no time to ignite the spell laid into the steel and so he met one of the bounty hunters, blade to blade, with naught but his own strength behind it. Nathaniel quickly proved to be the superior swordsman in the alley and killed his opponent with a deft strike before the fight could even begin in earnest.

"NO!" the last Bailey brother cried, his rage driving every swing into Kassian.

The Keeper was inevitably pushed back into the main street in a melee of clashing swords. His foot slipped on a patch of ice and he fell down to one knee, bringing the Keeper under a heavy two-handed attack. Rather than meet it, he rolled to the side and came up with his tip pointed at the surviving Bailey brother.

Oblivious of those around them, their fight continued into the middle of the street, halting a trader on his horse. Nathaniel was shouting something, off to the side, but Kassian couldn't catch it between the blows and the gasps of those around them.

"You killed my brothers!" he yelled, coming at the Keeper again and again.

Kassian managed to spin away from an incoming thrust and back-hand his blade across the hunter's leg. It dropped the man down just enough to allow the Keeper a hammer blow using the pommel of his sword. More blood splattered across the ground before the hunter fell face first into the mud. Kassian raised his sword, tip down, and considered plunging it into his enemy's back, ending it there and then.

But his senses had come flooding back in the wake of his victory. Looking around, the street was steadily filling up with Reavers clad in their notorious black armour. Between some of them, Seekers were growling and snapping in his direction.

Nathaniel backed up towards him from the alley, his sword held defensively in both hands. "You couldn't have beaten him a little quicker?" he remarked.

Kassian scowled but ultimately ignored the knight's comment. Instead, there was only one thought, recurring as it was, that voiced itself.

"I'm going to die in this city..."

# CHAPTER 39

# SLIPPING AWAY

Emerging from his dwelling, set into the cliff, Galanör looked out on the dwarves of clan Heavybelly, their hubbub still audible despite the roaring waterfall. The children of the mountain had formed up into regimented lines of bulky armour astride their similarly armoured Warhogs. They were, indeed, a formidable sight to behold. It was a shame, the elf considered, that the Reavers were immune to fear...

"You can't get out of it," Aenwyn called from behind him. "You're not heading into battle with naught but ranger's leathers for protection."

Galanör tore himself from the dwarves, his eyes searching for Doran and Russell even as his feet turned him away. He wished to offer them some parting words before they rolled the dice and took their chance with Death yet again.

"I'm not wearing that," he articulated, looking at the ornate cuirass in Aenwyn's hands.

"You're already wearing the vambraces that match," she argued, pointing out the gauntlets that covered his forearms, now a dull gold.

"I had my time wearing that armour - those days are behind me."

"And that's all you will have if you get stabbed in the gut!" Aenwyn moved to hold it beside him, displaying the size. "It's perfect. I even had one of Doran's smiths add this."

Galanör took the golden cuirass in hand and scrutinised the emblem crafted onto the chest: a pair of crossed scimitars. "The detailing is exquisite," he admitted. "It's lighter than I remember too..."

"Why do I get the feeling your reluctance to wear armour has something to do with your dissatisfaction where the plan is concerned?"

Galanör stumbled over his response, still unaccustomed to being so understood by any other. "I have no problem with our strategy," he lied.

"Those were not your words when you returned from the beach," Aenwyn recalled.

"No plan is without its flaws," the ranger quipped, busying himself with filling his waterskin.

"The flaws, as you see them, appear to have got under your skin," Aenwyn observed, echoing Doran's words without realising it. "If you think us doomed then you should voice your concerns with—"

"The queen?" Galanör interjected. "My days of command ended the very moment Adilandra's feet touched Qamnaran. I told them what needed to be done, that Alijah should be our *only* goal. Defeat him and the Reavers will fall where they stand. Instead, we're attacking from the north and south, all our efforts aimed at his black knights. There is no plan to take down Alijah..."

"What would you have us do instead?" Aenwyn asked of him.

The ranger held his tongue then, cautious of showing his hand too soon. Instead, he envisioned his plan, one which would see him slip away and act alone. Then, while the battle raged, he would use the distraction to find Alijah Galfrey and end his reign of terror and ensure that his threats never came to pass.

"Adilandra and Doran have both led successful campaigns," he said. "Perhaps it would be arrogant of me to believe I know better."

Aenwyn stepped closer and cupped his cheek, her eyes penetrating his own. "I'm not sure you truly believe that, my love."

"Possibly," he replied with a coy smile. "But I know my place, and I would be happy to play my part in freeing the dwarves of Dhenaheim." Galanör made to step away but found his path blocked by a golden cuirass.

"Wear it," Aenwyn pleaded. "For me?"

The elven ranger saw an opportunity present itself. "I will wear it," he conceded. "But I have a condition..."

Aenwyn raised a curious eyebrow. "Then speak it."

"The queen is yet to recover from her stand against the Sandstalkers. Her magic returns," he continued, still feeling some of the bruises that attested to that fact. "And her skill with a blade is considerable, but she is too precious to lose. More than just our kin will need her leadership in the days to come."

"Speak plainly or not at all," Aenwyn commanded, her suspicion growing.

Galanör did his best not to smile. "Ride beside her and stand with her on the battlefield - your bow will keep the enemy at bay."

Aenwyn was already shaking her head before he had even finished. "No. I will go into battle with *you*."

"We will still share the same battlefield," he assured. "I only ask that you journey with the queen and Faylen; have them know that you are to be counted among her guard."

"I sense you trying to protect me: I have warned you about this before, Galanör of house Reveeri."

The ranger held up his hands in surrender. "Trust me, my love, sending you into battle beside Adilandra Sevari is not protecting you. As much as Faylen would like it, the queen will not fight from the rear."

Aenwyn looked deep into his eyes as if she could see the

thoughts that lay behind them. "And where will you be while I ride beside the queen?"

There was nowhere among his kin that his absence wouldn't be noticed and, if he stayed with them, he would likely be given some form of command. Confusion would be his only ally if he was to see his task through to the end.

But it broke his heart to lie...

"I will be beside Doran and Russell," he stated, thinking on his feet.

Aenwyn didn't even try to hide her surprise. "You will fight with the dwarves? Their part in the plan involves them smashing into the enemy's front line - something I would argue they were built for."

"If you're worried there won't be any Reavers left by the time you join the fight: don't worry; I will leave some for your bow."

"You know that is not my concern, Galanör! Doran suggested this plan because he knows his warriors can take the punishment. You should be with us."

The ranger took the cuirass in hand as if they were in agreement. "Please, Aenwyn. I have to do this."

Aenwyn took a moment to consider, clearly unhappy with the way Galanör had positioned her. "I had better find you on the battle-field. And you had better be wearing that armour too. Should I find you lost to me, know that I will be cursed to walk the earth in search of a way to bring you back... so that I might kill you myself."

Galanör beamed, his feelings mirroring her own. "I will be the one standing on the biggest pile of Reavers, so you can't miss me."

"Be sure that you are," Aenwyn added, her expression serious.

There came a booming horn from beyond the cave, signalling the Heavybellys' imminent departure. "I have to go," he whispered.

They enjoyed a tight embrace and a parting kiss, each trying to hold on to the memory of it. Galanör was confident that within Adilandra's guard, Aenwyn would be safer than anywhere else in the battle, but he couldn't say for certain what state he would return in, should he return at all. He wanted to remember the taste of her lips, the scent of her hair, and the feel of her soft skin.

Another horn blew, though its sound was distinctly different. Now the elves were readying to march south and navigate the cliffs.

The couple were forced to walk in opposite directions as their companions began their journey. Galanör held on to her fingers for as long as possible. Aenwyn eventually mounted her horse and rode away, looking back only once to see Galanör walking backwards so that he might see her until the world came between them.

Behind him, in the drizzle, the dwarves were already disappearing between the trees, just as unaware of Galanör's deception as the elves. With his blue cloak wrapped round his shoulders, a hood to keep the rain out, and his scimitars resting on his hips, the ranger began his journey that took him neither north nor south.

Leaving the cumbersome cuirass behind, he made for the jagged cliffs that separated the island's east from its west. Making the familiar climb, he would position himself before the silvyr tower and prepare for the fight of his life. He was only going to get one chance...

# CHAPTER 40
# TOGETHER AGAIN

Inara could scarcely believe the sight before her. Gideon Thorn, the strongest and most powerful person she had ever known, hung limp, chained to the wall - a shadow of his former self. His face was pale and gaunt, highlighting his cheekbones and eye sockets. What remained of his clothes were tattered and stained. His dark hair and beard weren't nearly as overgrown and messy as his appearance would have suggested, as if his body simply hadn't had the energy to even grow hair.

He was frozen in ruin...

The walls of his cell were covered in the same glyphs as those that adorned the walls outside, still a mystery to the Guardian. She quickly placed her sword on the floor and crouched down to Gideon's level. He was slumped against the wall, chained at the wrists and around the neck. Inara hesitated as her hand reached out to rouse him, afraid that her worst fears were about to be confirmed.

"Gideon?" she said again, running a soft thumb over his cheek.

Eyelids, paper thin, began to flicker and hazel eyes struggled to focus on anything. There was something missing from his eyes, the thing that spoke of an extraordinary life filled with adventure and wisdom. Gideon finally managed to settle on Inara's face but it only brought confusion to his own. His brow, speckled with dirt, furrowed as much as it could while he took in her every feature.

"Reyna?" he uttered her mother's name with a dry throat.

Inara tried her best to hold back any tears. "It's Inara," she blurted. "It's me, Gideon."

His cheek twitched in the battle to respond with a smile. "I'm dreaming again..." he croaked.

"*No,*" Inara replied with gentle force. "It's me. I'm really here. I've come to rescue you."

Now the Master Dragorn looked amused. "You say that every time."

Inara didn't know what else to say to convince him of the truth. Seeing no water in his cell, she took a small bottle from her belt and removed the cork with her mouth.

"Drink," she urged, pressing it to his lips and tilting it.

At least half of his mouthful trickled back out of his mouth to soak his beard. He tasted his lips and looked again at Inara as if reconsidering his previous conclusion. Deciding to hammer the truth home, she removed the scimitar from her back and placed the scabbard in Gideon's hands. He examined the weapon with great intrigue, though he barely moved an inch.

"I'm here to rescue you," Inara repeated, moving one of his hands to grip Mournblade's magnificent hilt.

Gideon showed his first sign of exertion pulling the scimitar an inch from its scabbard, revealing some of the runes that ran up the steel. There was a flicker of life behind his eyes at last.

"Inara?" His tone was filled with hope.

The Guardian nodded vigorously. "It's me."

Tears spilled down Gideon's face and he lurched forward to embrace her, only to be limited by his chains. Inara scrutinised the manacles, including the one that circled his neck - they too were engraved with ancient runes.

"What kind of prison is this?" she asked, surveying the cell.

"We need to get out of here," he rasped, lacking the energy to do anything but remain on his knees. "The runes," he continued, looking at the walls, "are there to keep me and Ilargo from reaching out, isolating us from other dragons." Gideon's head lolled back as he raised his wrists to display his manacles. "These runes drain me of life, but keep me from death…"

"Where is Ilargo?" she asked desperately.

"He suffers the same, somewhere else in this wretched place."

Inara couldn't shift the expression of horror that contorted her features. This was a prison designed specifically for a dragon and their rider. What made it worse was the one who had constructed such a hell: her brother.

Whatever love she still harboured for Alijah was beginning to be replaced by utter disgust. Her fond memories of their time together were quickly being replaced by fantasies of cutting him down.

"Can you still hear him?" the Guardian continued, gripping Gideon by the shoulder. "Can you speak to Ilargo?"

*I can still hear you wingless one,* Athis spoke into her mind. *The runes would explain why I could not reach out to Ilargo.*

"We can hear each other," Gideon confirmed. "They are but whispers…"

*Free him of the chains and get him far away from that passage. Beyond the runes, I may be able to use Gideon's bond with Ilargo to find his location.*

Inara moved swiftly, wielding Firefly with purpose - it wasn't the first time her blade had freed a powerful man from chains. Two surgical strikes sliced the manacles in half. The iron around his neck was another issue…

"I will have to use magic," she explained, wrapping her fingers inside the collar.

Inara heard the ice infecting the iron before seeing it spread out from her grip. Deciding that it was now brittle enough, the Guardian swapped her Vi'tari weapon for the shorter Moonblade. The magical dagger emitted a soft glow, its surface swirling with every colour of the spectrum. It cut through the frozen iron with ease and she removed it completely from his neck.

Her old master fell forward into her open arms and she pulled him away from the wall, giving him a moment to rest. "I need to get you out of here," she told him, barely aware of the battle taking place outside the cell.

"Wait..." he pleaded, watching the back of his hand intently.

Inara joined him and observed Gideon's hand. Her eyes widened at the miracle taking place. The scabs faded until new skin consumed them entirely. The bones, visible below his sharp knuckles, disappeared beneath a healthy hand that welcomed the returning muscles. His fingernails transformed and rounded themselves off into a flush pink. Regarding his other hand, she saw the same happening to his palm, revealing the ancient glyphs that had scarred his hand since destroying The Veil all those years ago.

"The spell is reversing," he stated, his voice a pitch stronger than previously. "We won't get out of here if I can't walk." A brief glimpse beneath his hair revealed a familiar face, absent the sharp angles of his skull.

Inara wanted to tell Gideon that she would carry him out of hell if she needed to but, the truth remained, they were in foreign lands controlled by the enemy - they needed to be strong.

Eventually, Gideon managed to pull himself up, away from Inara's hold. His legs were shaking under his weight and his breathing became ragged. Inara turned away while he doubled over and heaved on an empty stomach.

"Let me help," came a voice from the doorway.

Adan'Karth remained on the threshold until invited inside. He moved around Inara to better see Gideon, who was staring up at the Drake through a curtain of wild hair. He looked to Inara questioningly, having only seen Adan's kind at the very end of The Ash War.

"He is a friend, Gideon," Inara assured. "A powerful one at that." The Guardian collected herself then, recalling Asher's warning to the

Drake. She then realised the sound of fighting had ceased outside, plaguing her with concern for Asher's fate.

Leaving Adan to watch over Gideon for the moment, Inara hurried from the cell only to be halted by the sight that awaited her. The passage was littered from wall to wall with bodies, many piled one on top of the other. Blood was splattered up the walls, covering the runes, and pooling on the floor. Not one of the masked men had reached within twenty feet of Gideon's cell...

Seated on the cold stone, between Inara and the bodies, was the ranger, bloodied and bruised. His silvyr short-sword remained gripped in his fingers, the exquisite metal dull with the blood of his enemies. With his head rested back against the wall and eyes closed, Inara wondered if she was looking on what she thought was a dead friend for the second time in as many minutes.

Then his chest moved as he exhaled and so too did the Guardian of the Realm.

Rushing to his side, she crouched down and quickly assessed for any mortal wounds. Incredibly, he had only suffered minor injuries, at least on the surface.

"I'm getting too old for this," Asher complained without opening his eyes.

"I'm afraid you're cursed to live a little longer," Inara replied happily.

"Did you find him?" the ranger asked, at last setting his blue eyes on her.

A broad smile would have ruled her face but she was still perturbed by Gideon's condition and the mystery of Ilargo's where-abouts. "I did. Can you stand - he will want to see you I'm sure."

Asher rose to his full height with a pained groan and even a wince as he sheathed the short-sword over his shoulder. "You lead, I follow," he said simply.

Returning to the cell, Adan was casting his reptilian eyes around Gideon rather than looking directly at him. The Master Dragorn, if that was even a title he still claimed, tore his eyes from the Drake and greeted Asher with a warm smile.

"I should have guessed," Gideon said. "Fate refuses to let you go."

"Its claws go deep," Asher acknowledged passively.

Gideon's expression turned serious. "So it seems. You have my thanks for whatever blood you have given to free me."

"The blood isn't mine," Asher declared without an ounce of pride.

Gideon nodded his understanding and returned to Adan. The spectacle of the Drake brightened his face with wonder.

"You are bonded to a dragon," Adan remarked, "yet your magic is faded, fractured even."

"My magic was depleted decades ago," Gideon began. "A necessary sacrifice." He immediately looked up at Asher. "Though it pales in comparison to the sacrifice you made - accepting death," he added.

Asher shrugged. "It didn't stick..."

Gideon almost choked on the short laugh this elicited. He again returned his attention to Adan as he leaned against the skeleton of an old cot by the wall. "You are a *marvel*," he complimented, captured by the Drake's unusual existence. "I have always regretted leaving Illian so quickly and losing the opportunity to meet your kind."

Seeing a lengthy conversation ahead of them, Inara intervened. "Adan, you said you could help him."

"With his permission," the Drake said, "I would lay a hand and restore what I can of his health. At least enough for him to walk out of this dreadful place."

"I would be a fool to refuse," Gideon admitted. "Please, do what you can."

Adan reached out and placed the flat of his hand against Gideon's chest. Having never observed the Drake performing such a spell, Inara watched closely, curious to see veins pulsing on the back of his hand. Slowly but surely, Gideon's fists closed into tight knots, similar to his eyes.

Less than a minute later, Adan removed his hand and Gideon appeared to return to the room. "You are hard to heal," the Drake remarked. "Your fractured state of magic does not respond well to the magic of others. Luckily," he added with a sideways glance at Asher, "I have had much experience in the art of healing humans."

"He can walk?" Inara enquired, hopeful to see her old master moving again.

Answering her question, Gideon reached over his head, cracking his back as he did. "Healing magic is among the most taxing for any caster," he commented. "You truly are a being of great—"

"He's full of surprises," Asher interrupted. "We should leave this place before more arrive."

Inara nodded her agreement but her hand came up to slow their departure. "Ayana told me why you came here, to Erador. What did you discover? What happened here?" There were so many questions that she stumbled over the next. "You've been here for years..."

"I will tell you everything," Gideon promised. "But not before I free Ilargo of his torment."

Inara couldn't argue with that - she would upturn mountains to save Athis. "Can you lead the way?"

Gideon clapped Adan on the shoulder. "My strength returns with every beat of my heart." He strapped Mournblade across his shoulder and back. Leaving the dank cell behind, they were greeted by many obstacles, all Asher's doing. "You've met The Red Guard then," Gideon reasoned as he stepped over the bodies.

"Red Guard?" Inara repeated.

"That's what the people of Erador came to call them. They never claimed a name for themselves."

"Who are they?" Asher asked, retrieving his torch from the wall.

"Cultists," Gideon said with disdain. "They worship Alijah as Erador's saviour, blind to the atrocities he commits. They preceded the Reavers and helped him track down anyone connected to the magical realm."

As they neared the end of the passage, Gideon stopped abruptly, his eyes shifting as if a puzzle was being put together in front of his face. "If you're here, that means he actually did it - Alijah invaded Illian."

Considering the runes on the walls, Inara ushered them further down the hall until they were beyond their power. "Can you hear Athis?" Gideon looked away from her, listening for the dragon. *Can you hear me?* she asked him through the bond that the dragons shared.

"No, I cannot hear him," Gideon responded, ignorant of her second question. "You mean to share your memories with me," the Master Dragorn assumed. "This cannot be done while the same runes entrap Ilargo. It is the bond he shares with Athis that will allow us to communicate more intimately."

Inara cursed. "There isn't enough time to tell you everything that's happened."

"There's been something of a war going on," Asher chipped in.

A shadow overcame Gideon's face. "If only it were so simple as *war...*"

Inara didn't like the implications of his words nor his tone. "Ilargo first," she insisted.

"Indeed." Gideon flashed a hungry smile Inara hadn't seen in a very long time. "Follow me."

In the wake of his lead, Inara soon came to realise how long it had been since she *followed*. For nearly seventeen years, the span of her master's absence from Illian's shores, she had accepted a new title and led the people without any mentorship.

*He is not our master anymore, Inara.*

The Guardian welcomed her companion's comforting voice as they journeyed back down to the tower's ground floor. *He is still the master of the Dragorn order.*

*You speak of an order that no longer exists, wingless one. Like us, and even those of Dragons' Reach, Gideon and Ilargo are free of Elandril's Dragorn and its rules.*

**Gideon might not see it that way,** Inara pointed out. **He might wish to rebuild the order.**

*Impossible - there are no more dragons. Any eggs to be hatched will now be raised in Dragons' Reach, beyond Gideon's influence. Rainael will not allow him to bring potential riders to meet them. No, Inara, we have seen the last days of the Dragorn...*

Bounding down the stairs, it was becoming clear that Gideon was fast recovering from the magic of his chains. He led through new passages and into gothic halls left to ruin. "This way," he bade, having taken a few seconds to discern the right path.

Pushing through a partially shattered set of double doors, Gideon took the companions outside, to the back of the tower. Passing under a distressed portico, they moved from the tower to the next building, a derelict slab of stone so ancient its original purpose could only be guessed at. Exiting through a set of giant-sized doors, left open eons past, they traversed a large square courtyard that offered multiple paths.

Gideon paused.

"Which way?" Asher pressed, scanning the rooftops and visible doors.

"It's been years since Ilargo and I were together anywhere but our sanctuary. Even there I could hardly hear him..."

Inara turned her eyes to the sky, seeing Athis fly into view between the tower and the mountains. **Can you see a building large enough to contain Ilargo?**

*There is only one. Take the path to your right.*

"Athis says it's this way." Inara ran for the path between two buildings, following its winding route until she came across a structure built into the mountain. Thousands of years ago, it could have been described as a pyramid or a temple, but now its sides were ragged and its pointed apex had been broken, replaced with a mismatch of tarpaulins.

A shadowed entryway cut through one of the walls. "Yes," Gideon confirmed, "this is the place. Ilargo is inside."

Confirming the truth, four Red Guards strode out of the shadows and into the daylight, their crescent blades gleaming. Gideon flourished Mournblade and stepped forward to meet them.

"Are you sure?" Inara asked.

"There's only one way to find out," Gideon replied, a predator visible behind his eyes.

*I can be rid of them,* Athis offered.

**No. If it were me, I would want to free you myself.**

Inara kept Asher where he was with a look, allowing her old mentor the space to advance alone. Fearless as The Red Guards were, it wouldn't make up for the fact that they were about to face *Gideon Thorn* in battle.

Without a word, they set upon him like a pack of wolves, their curved blades coming at him from various angles. Mournblade swept in, lending its wielder the benefit of its ancient enchantment. He parried, blocked, and evaded the first two waves of attack as he slipped into the form of combat. Coming to understand the flow of his enemies, Gideon finally poured his desire to kill into the Vi'tari blade. It reacted dutifully, guiding his actions and, indeed, its edge to take down one opponent after another.

By the look of his strikes, he employed very little strength, relying on speed and precision instead. Steel sliced through all manner of body parts until Gideon stood among the dead, the last of their blood running clean off Mournblade's tip.

He was heaving...

For all the help Adan had given him, Gideon's recovery was incomplete. His shoulders sagged to the point that Mournblade rested against the stone floor. Inara moved to help him but Gideon's hand came up to stop her.

"I am well," he panted, his words barely audible. Taking a deep breath, Gideon straightened his back and resumed his advance.

"The Rebellion needs him," Asher mentioned quietly, as they

trailed at a distance. "Letting him die only minutes after freeing him would be a colossal waste of time."

Inara shot the ranger a look that implored him to both trust her and keep his thoughts to himself. Passing through the jagged entrance, the gloom therein demanded more of their eyes. It was the sound of ringing steel that drew their attention first. To the left, Gideon was dispatching two more Red Guards, spoiling the patterned floor with their blood.

Accustomed to the new level of light, Inara craned her neck to take in the despairing sight of Ilargo, chained down in the centre of the temple. Thick manacles bound his legs and a spiked collar encircled his neck, all engraved with identical glyphs to those that had imprisoned Gideon. Chains also pinned his mighty tail down and kept his wings tucked close to his body.

It was maddening.

Sudden movement in the corner of her eye turned the Guardian to another pair of Red Guards dashing around Ilargo's tail to meet them. One broke away to challenge Asher while the other fool charged at Inara, his weapon raised high. For serving her brother's wicked deeds, he would die, but for tormenting so magnificent a creature as Ilargo, he would suffer first...

Inara's hand flexed, unleashing a staccato of lightning to dance across the floor. The spell caught the bottom half of the Red Guard and threw him back, his robes singed and smoking. He writhed around, keening for the lifeless legs that weighed him down. Inara drew Firefly and carefully plunged it through his chest and into his heart. When the life left his eyes, she turned back to see Asher snapping his opponent's neck, having never even bothered to draw his sword.

"My friend..." Gideon was embracing Ilargo's jaw, his head pressed into the scales. "I have done naught but dream of this moment."

Inara gave them their time and examined the manacles around Ilargo's legs. "Adan," she called. "Can you remove the pins?"

The Drake studied the nearest manacle, observing the considerable bolt of iron that kept the two halves together. "Healing Master Thorn has reduced me somewhat. I cannot guarantee I can remove all of them."

"You take these two," she directed. "I'll go around and remove the others."

Approaching each leg, Inara pulled her hand away from the pin, steadily drawing it out with magic. Asher went about freeing the dragon's tail and wings, hacking through the chains with his silvyr short-sword.

Up close, Inara could see the effects of the ancient glyphs on Ilargo's body. His green scales were dull, absent their golden glitter. His claws appeared torn and brittle, much like his wings which spasmed to life, revealing his protruding ribs.

Inara ran an affectionate hand over Ilargo's scales, stricken with anger and guilt. **This should never have been allowed to happen,** she said to Athis alone.

*You must not take this on yourself,* the red dragon beseeched. *No one could have known such a fate would have befallen them. What matters, wingless one, is what we do next.*

Inara did her best to take her companion's words as facts, hoping it would ease her conscience and settle her emotions. It was times like this that she wished they still shared their previous bond, so that Athis could simply *make* her feel better.

Moving to Ilargo's head, Inara was pleased to see that, for all his suffering and torment, there was still a glint of ferocity in his blue eyes. Inside the temple, within the confines of the runes, she couldn't make contact with Ilargo via Athis, but the dragon still lowered his head to physically greet her. Parting from him, she discovered Gideon in the curve of his companion's neck.

"What are you doing?" she asked, afraid of the answer.

Gideon placed one of his hands to the flat of the iron collar. "*You* gave me the idea..." His hand began to glow white, then orange before waves of heat rose from his fingers. The iron slowly turned the same colour, melting under the pressure of Gideon's spell.

"You're pushing yourself too much," Inara warned.

"It's been *too long* since I pushed myself to do anything," Gideon replied through a clenched jaw. Inara made to help by adding her own magic to the collar, but he gave her pause with his free hand. "I can do it."

Drenched in sweat, Gideon finally melted his way through the collar - Ilargo's scales easily standing up to the temperature of his magic. The green dragon pushed up on all four legs and shrugged the broken collar off.

"A little light perhaps," Adan suggested, his hand held out to the temple's opening.

With an exhausted Gideon, Ilargo shifted his bulk and stumbled outside, blinking rapidly in the bright sunlight. Athis came down with a thundering impact and nearly barged into his kin with the excitement. The two touched heads, knocking their horns together. In the light, Inara could see Ilargo's body already filling out again, pushing back against the magic that had wasted him to almost nothing.

***Let them in,*** Inara eagerly instructed her companion. ***I want to hear him!***

*Thank you...* came Ilargo's regal, yet soft, voice, passed on through Athis.

*Yes,* Gideon added, speaking into their bond, *thank you. You have saved us both.*

***Where would the world be without either of you?*** Inara replied mentally.

Despite their bond, Ilargo gave no warning before he spread his wings, casting them all in shade. His neck flexed, pointing his head to the open sky where dragons ruled.

"Excuse us," Gideon begged.

The Master Dragorn climbed up onto his companion's back and settled into the familiar spot at the base of his neck. Inara couldn't help but smile in anticipation, watching Ilargo's legs crouch like springs.

"You might want to stand back," she said to Asher and Adan'Karth.

The moment they were clear, Ilargo beat his radiant wings to create a plume of dust and debris. His claws pushed off the ground at the same time and his whole body launched into the sky. With Gideon astride, he flew around the tower diving low before climbing high again. They danced a dance that only dragon and rider could know and, for a time, Inara swelled with the kind of happiness that could never be shattered.

Gideon and Ilargo were back...

# CHAPTER 41

# A LIGHT AT THE TOP OF THE WORLD

Since his crusade against Alijah had begun, Kassian Kantaris had found himself repeatedly in the middle of dangerous situations. Most involved hair-raising odds the likes of which would spell the end of any ordinary man. With his trusted Keepers by his side, however, the mage had time and time again repelled the enemy and delivered a sore blow to the regime.

Now was not one of those times...

Near the very top of Namdhor's rise, far from the open plains that offered a chance of freedom, Kassian stood shoulder to shoulder with a man he barely trusted, surrounded by Reavers and Seekers whose numbers could not be counted. They advanced from The Dragon Keep, behind them, and from the main road, trekking up towards them, swords drawn.

Kassian glanced down at the bounty hunter at his feet and cursed their bad luck. Were it not for the Bailey brothers, they would have made their escape by now.

"Any ideas?" Nathaniel asked, his sword held steady in both hands.

"You're asking me?" Kassian snapped. "You're supposed to be the war hero!"

"Fine. You take the few hundred from the south and I'll take the few hundred from the north."

Kassian was sure he had detected sarcasm in the knight's tone, but he was, indeed, facing those approaching from The Dragon Keep with a look of grim determination. "Have you survived so many battles that you've actually lost your mind?"

"Perhaps," Nathaniel considered. "Do you have a better idea?"

"I always have a better idea." Kassian aimed his wand into the air and expelled a brilliant flare that shone red against the grey clouds.

"What was that?" Nathaniel asked, unimpressed.

"You'll see!" Kassian grabbed the knight by the arm and dragged him towards the merchant's cart, abandoned in the middle of the road. "Get in!"

The Keeper was already firing destructive spells at the Reavers before he hunkered down below the sides of the cart. No sooner did he take shelter than the first arrow impacted the wood. It was quickly followed by another salvo, though the Reavers lacked the angle to hit their targets inside the cart. Kassian aimed blindly over the top and fired wildly into the street. The sound of exploding armour pleased him immensely.

"Like spearing fish in a barrel!" he hollered.

Nathaniel reached beneath his back and tugged at a sack of potatoes sticking into his ribs. "Look around! We're the fish in the barrel!"

"Wait for it!" Kassian urged, flinching from an arrow head that protruded from the wood.

The Keeper fumbled with his belt in an attempt to retrieve the rest of his spell traps. He took a clay orb in each hand and threw them backwards, towards the knights moving in from the keep. A single explosion rocked the city, scattering Reavers to the four winds. A piece of armour, indistinguishable from any other in its mangled state, pierced the end of the cart and cut Kassian's brow.

The knight marvelled at the smoking shrapnel. "I don't suppose you have any more of those..."

The Keeper wiped the blood away and held his answer - there had only been one explosion. If one of the spell traps had unleashed the other, he was sure the explosion would have been far more devastating. Using his wand, Kassian erected a temporary shield to allow him a daring look over the end of the cart. Two arrows immediately struck his shield before careening off at an angle. He desperately scanned the ground, his eyes searching furiously for any sign of the spell trap. Then he saw it.

Rolling...

The orb gathered some speed as it navigated the uneven road and small stones, making its way dutifully back to its master. "Jump!" the Keeper yelled.

Kassian dived out of the cart on one side as Nathaniel mimicked his actions on the other. The spell trap ricocheted off a slanted stone and smashed against the wheel of the cart, releasing the destructive spell. A deafening crack cut through the air, assaulting Kassian's ears, and the cart itself was upturned in a shower of splinters and debris. The Keeper barely registered the sound of its return to earth, replaced as it was with an irritating ring.

Through the smoke and flames, he could see Nathaniel rising on the other side of the mess. He staggered one way then the other, absent his sword. Kassian quickly reached for his wand only to find his holster empty. Both hands grasped at the dirt around him, feeling for the slender piece of Demetrium-laden wood that held the key to survival.

He found nothing but despair. Pushing up from the ground, he emerged from the smoke to discover a relentless force of Reavers. All his efforts thus far amounted to naught, save slowing the inevitable. This wasn't the end he had desired of late, but what man got to choose his manner and time of demise? With all that was left to him, he drew his Keeper's blade and ran it over the surface of his left vambrace. The steel came to life with the power of the sun inside it.

Glowing hot white, Kassian twisted the sword in his hand, composing himself into one of the fighting forms his order had drilled into him. "I'm coming, Clara..."

He uttered the words as he raised his sword, ready to slice through the first Reaver. His enemy, however, never made it within swinging distance. A flash of blue came between them and the Reaver was thrown backwards, into its foul comrades. Kassian wore a broad grin before even turning to see his saviour.

Reinforcements...

Whipping his head around, the Keeper quickly spotted Fin at the head of a side street, his wand glowing the same blue as the spell he had just cast. A moment later, Quaid emerged behind him, relieving Kassian of any fear that either one had perished.

From alleys and streets up and down the main road, men and women loyal to magic itself unleashed their power on the Reavers. Spells of every colour tore through the air, scattering the knights of Erador. Kassian saved the victory he felt like celebrating and turned his attention to Nathaniel, who he had last seen wandering blindly through smoke without a weapon.

The Keeper navigated the debris, expecting to find the old knight surrounded by foes and a blade to his throat. This was not how he found Nathaniel Galfrey. Displaying his roots as a Graycoat, Nathaniel weaved and bobbed between the hacking swords, narrowly, yet successfully, evading them all. Pivoting from defence, the knight rolled across the ground and came up with his fallen sword in hand and an aggressive air about him. By the time Kassian came to his side, all three of the attacking Reavers lay in a heap at his feet.

"Nicely done," Nathaniel remarked, admiring the dying flare above.

"The fight isn't over yet," Kassian replied grimly, his white-hot sword pointed at the Reavers fanning out around them.

"We just need to give Vighon more time," Nathaniel encouraged.

An inglorious cacophony of death and battle quickly came to

surround them. "We've already given this rebellion everything we have," Kassian declared determinedly, having decided which of the Reavers he was going to slay first. "Time is all we have left to give."

Nathaniel spared the Keeper a moment's glance. "We haven't given it *everything*..."

If Vighon wasn't sure that something was happening beyond the keep, the red sky and subsequent explosion confirmed it - his friends were in trouble. He swore and hit the stone beside the window. Where was his blasted sword? Where was Nathaniel?

Again, he was forced to hide as another group of Reavers dashed down the hall, making their way to the main road like the others. He wanted to get in their way and spare his friends the extra conflict, but he had to find the sword of the north.

With so many abandoning their posts to join the fight outside, the keep became increasingly easier to explore. The northman still kept light feet beneath him as he checked one grand chamber after another, wondering if Alijah would have put the sword on display as a trophy.

He began to curse the size of his old home...

Moving from one wing to another, Vighon chose to use the exterior bridges. He couldn't help but pause, however, hearing the sounds of battle so close. He leaned out from the railing, struggling to see anything over the outer walls. Flashes of brilliant light ran up and down the main road, dispersed between the ringing of steel and the blasts of devastating magic.

The northman was about to continue his journey across the bridge when the most peculiar sight kept him in place. There was an explosion of green light followed by the brief neigh of a distressed horse - the same horse that flew so high it topped the outer wall and crashed into the second floor of a tavern. It only made Vighon want to join what could only be a desperate fight all the more.

Snatching himself away, he turned back to the door at the end of the bridge. Again, he paused. There, standing on the threshold, was a man, marked by the tattoos of the Fenrig syndicate. He wore a smug grin as an axe slid further down his grip to give him the most leverage were he to swing it or throw it. Vighon looked back over his shoulder and, just as he had expected, discovered another Fenrig blocking any escape.

"And here we thought we was missing all the action," the axe-man sneered. "You're not supposed to be here, little birdie."

Vighon reached for his sword when he caught sight of two more Fenrigs behind the axe-man. Looking back again, the second thug was also backed up by more of their wretched gang. The northman couldn't decide who was the bigger fool: Alijah for employing murderers and thieves or the Fenrigs themselves for actually believing that Alijah would allow them all to live in his new kingdom.

It mattered little there and then - he was outnumbered on a narrow bridge. "I don't suppose any of you fine gentlemen have seen the sword of the north lying around have you? Made of pure silvyr, might be on fire..." Vighon was faced with blank expressions. "I'll take that as a no."

Without warning, he tucked up his legs and jumped over the side of the bridge. The Fenrigs ran to the rail and watched as he landed on one of the walkways that connected the outer walls to the inner walls. Vighon collapsed his body into a roll, taking some of the impact off his feet and legs. He came up only to be stopped by a flying axe, thrown from above. It remained buried in the stone, a testament to the Fenrig's strength, but did nothing to prevent Vighon from continuing his escape.

"After him!" came the call.

Vighon had no idea where he was running now, his route back to the royal chambers taken out of his hands. He heard more than one of the thugs follow his example and leap from the bridge to pursue him. That only meant he could expect the others to appear from somewhere inside the keep.

It wasn't very long before he literally ran into his next problem: Reavers. Not every undead fiend had left their post to challenge the Keepers, and the pair he barrelled into were heading towards the outer wall with a bow in their hands. The first he collided with was knocked from the walkway and into a small courtyard below, designed to do nothing but house a circular fountain. The second reached for its sword, but stumbled as Vighon had been forced to grip its cloak in a bid to oppose his momentum and join the fallen Reaver.

Then came the Fenrigs, their timing catastrophic as ever...

Vighon pulled himself onto a sure footing and shoved the Reaver into the oncoming thugs. The Reaver took the closest Fenrig down in a crash of limbs and cry of shock. The further of the pair proved more agile and evaded the collision to continue his hasty charge at the northman. Vighon noted the man's sica sword, distinguishable by its crooked shape, and decided he didn't have time to become tangled in a fight.

With bent knees, and crouched like a wrestler, the northman held out his hands as if he were prepared to grapple the thug. Of course, he had no intention of wasting time with the likes of a lowly Fenrig. At the last second, he shifted all of his weight to one side and simply watched as the man continued his charge off the walkway.

Rather than lose more time, fighting the recovering Reaver and Fenrig, Vighon shot off across the ramparts. Again, he had no idea where he was going - he was just running to escape those that wished him harm. Unfortunately, more enemies emerged from doors that led into the keep, driving the northman down a set of steps and off the ramparts.

There he met only more resistance. Reavers, making their way to the main gates, spotted him rushing between the inner walls. There was no other choice but to run in the opposite direction before the Fenrigs came down on him. Hurrying through the sparring yard, he came out into a courtyard that offered two paths: to his right, the gardens, and to his left, the outer walls and the option to ascend back onto the ramparts.

Neither would get him back inside the keep, leading him to turn back and hope there was somewhere to hide while the Fenrigs and Reavers passed him by. One step on his return journey placed him directly in the path of a Reaver, whose own momentum knocked Vighon to the ground. There was no time to consider the pain that followed for the Reaver was bringing its blade down that very moment.

The northman rolled to the side, leaving Death to observe him rather than claim him. On his feet once more, his sword drawn, there was no other option but to engage and dispatch them before the Fenrigs... Vighon felt any lingering hope fade away as the thugs rounded the corner, reinforcing the Reavers.

"Come on then!" Vighon roared.

As the superior fighters, the northman focused his first and most powerful attacks on the two Reavers. He cleaved half the head from one before kicking its body into the Fenrigs, slowing their advance. The remaining Reaver locked Vighon in battle, pushing him towards the gardens. The fight didn't last long. A two-handed axe swung high and came down in the middle of the fiend's head, dropping it lifeless on the ground.

"You're ours, little birdie!" the Fenrig exclaimed, yanking his axe out of the creature's head.

His chest heaving, Vighon made a quick assessment of the thugs spreading across the garden. He counted seven, killers all by the look in their eyes. The only way out was the arched entrance behind them. The northman considered climbing the large tree at his back, but he didn't know for sure whether the branches would take him back to the ramparts. He let the idea go, deciding that he would just end up with an axe in his back.

If he was going to die, he would be looking his enemy in the eye...

In the chaos that had erupted across Namdhor, Kassian's every sense had come under assault. For all his training and all his days fighting on the road, nothing could have prepared him for this. The spells of his companions blinded him, the sounds of the destruction deafened him, and even his skin crackled amidst the discharge of so much magic in the air.

Chopping down another Reaver - he had lost count - his arms began to jar from the constant impacts, regardless of his sword's ability to melt through everything. He kicked the next fiend away, booting it into the path of Aphira's wild spell casting. The Reaver took it in the ribs and flew from its feet and through a shop window.

Kassian thanked Aphira by blocking an incoming sword that would have seen the end of her. Due to the Reaver's pressure, the steel of its sword eventually melted and passed right through Kass-ian's. The Keeper adjusted his grip and swing and did the same thing to the Reaver's head.

Across the road, he saw Danika hunch over a spear thrust into her gut before being discarded through a tavern door, there to die alone in her own blood. It enraged Kassian every time he witnessed the death of another Keeper. They all possessed so much potential.

With a cry on his lips, Kassian charged into the middle of the fray without a care. He hacked, chopped, and swung at anything that got in his way - he didn't care if he put the Reaver down for good; he just wanted to lash out. His training and discipline were forsaken in the wake of his rage, and so he mistimed the stroke of his sword and received a Reaver's gauntlet to the face.

The pain was fleeting as the world lost all sound and colour for a moment. When next he opened his eyes, he was looking up at the tip of a Reaver's spear with the taste of blood in his mouth. His hand grasped at mud and debris, fingers clawing in an attempt to retrieve his sword. It was beyond his reach and with it any chance of saving himself. He almost smiled, sure that he was only seconds away from seeing Clara again...

As the Reaver raised the spear, ready to plunge it through Kassian's heart, a sword shot through its head, dropping the fiend to its knees. Now standing where the Reaver had been, Nathaniel Galfrey stooped to offer the Keeper his hand.

"Your fight's not over yet," he said, pulling Kassian back to his feet.

The Keeper found his blade and joined Nathaniel shoulder to shoulder. They were faced by an overwhelming force, perhaps overwhelming enough to seal their fate. Lacking any other options, however, they had but the swing of their swords and the grit in their bones.

That grit was tested by the quake beneath their feet.

The ground shook repeatedly, its origin turning both men to the slope behind them. There to greet them was a sight reserved for the damned. It came in the hulking form of a dragon, long dead and dragged from its grave.

The Beast of Qalanqath...

"DRAGON!" one Keeper bellowed.

Karsak's ragged and putrid body pounded its way up Namdhor's rise. The dragon was absent one of its wings and the other appeared so out of shape it would have been useless anyway. Though still distant, Kassian could make out the dark form of its villainous Rider, Rengyr, behind what remained of its mangled head.

Without its wings, the undead dragon had been forced to trek across the land, having pulled itself from the ruins of The Watcher like a demon clawing its way out of hell. Karsak's inability to fly was perhaps their only advantage, though Kassian was struggling to formulate a plan that would see them claim victory over the beast.

"We need to fight our way up," Nathaniel urged. "The keep is our only refuge now."

Kassian tore his eyes from what would surely be the death of them all. "Press the attack!" he commanded. "Make for the keep!"

Keeping his back to the approaching dragon, Kassian did the only thing he could. He swung his sword...

Vighon heard his sword clatter against the side of a rock before his knees followed that same devastating path to the ground. Blood trickled down his arm, over his vambrace, and along his fingers. He barely noticed it. The boot to the side of his head saw to that. The northman landed face down between two small skeletal trees, his senses fading fast.

From his skewed angle, he could see the two Fenrigs he had slain, their bodies flat to the ground. The big one with the axe had been the problem. One good slug from the back end of his axe had stunted Vighon's flow and doomed him. One of the others had swung wildly and caught his arm only to follow up their clumsy attack with a punch to his gut.

Rough hands gripped him and yanked him up, displaying him perfectly for the incoming fist. He wasn't sure what found him first after that: the ground or the boot. Either way, Vighon was forced further into the garden with agony racking his ribs.

"You see," the axe man began, "the problem with those knights is: they take all the fun. Anyone steps out of line and there they are to carry out the king's swift justice. They leave nothing for us."

Vighon groaned, drawing on the anger that bubbled in his veins. "I've got something for you." He pushed through the pain and leaped at the Fenrig with everything he had.

The big man jabbed the end of his axe into the northman's chest and knocked him back, absent the air in his lungs. Through his coughing and spluttering, he could just hear the Fenrig wittering on.

"I don't know who you are or what you're doing here, but I know you're going to regret it. Me and the boys are going to take our time getting to know you. Then we'll feed you to the Seekers."

His laugh enraged Vighon but he had no choice but to crawl

away and focus on his breathing - he wasn't going to get out of this if he couldn't even breathe. Making his way closer to the largest tree in the garden, he could hear the Fenrigs slowly trailing him, savouring their victory.

"Come on, little birdie! Get up and face us! We haven't had a proper fight in ages!"

The Fenrig's last words grew distant as the world drew in on Vighon, giving him a moment of quiet in the storm.

A snowflake landed on his bloodied hand, followed by another and then another.

The north wasn't without its snow, but a true northman knew the first snows of winter when he saw them. That light sprinkle was soon followed by a steady fall, released by the inky clouds above. Then he saw it, a vision to cut through his misery, standing upright in the dirt, between the thick roots of the tree.

The sword of the north.

Lost in the shadow of the tree, it was hardly noticeable, but he knew that sword like he knew himself. Without thought, he had crawled towards it, hounded by the taunts of his would-be killers. They were either too arrogant to see the weapon as a threat or too oblivious to have even noticed it. Vighon didn't care. There was only him and that sword now.

"That isn't going to save you!" the big man called, his axe resting over his shoulder.

Vighon's hand hesitated around the hilt, his eyes taking in the lion pommel that had adorned the sword for over a thousand years.

"*I don't believe in fate,*" he had said to Inara, days earlier.

"*That's a shame,*" she had replied, "*because Fate believes in you, Vighon Draqaro...*"

Seeing the sword of the north now, as if it had sought him out, Inara's words came back to him with an edge. His fingers wrapped around the black hilt and rose with the blade as he pulled it free from the earth. His touch ignited the sword, setting the silvyr alight with the flames of his house.

The axe-man stepped back. "Who are you?" he whispered, his expression contorted with confusion and trepidation.

Vighon embraced the power he felt, lent by the weight of his sword. He still didn't believe in fate. But he did believe in choice...

"I... am the *king*."

His declaration was followed by an almighty swing of his blade. The axe man was fast and managed to bring his weapon to bear, but Vighon had all of his weight behind the strongest metal in Verda. The silvyr intercepted the haft of the axe, chopping it in half with ease. A second swing in the other direction drew a cauterised line up the big man's torso, bringing a swift end to his time among the living.

The remaining Fenrigs dashed forwards, hoping to overwhelm the northman. Emboldened by the simple truth of his place in the world, Vighon moved with a confidence he had been lacking of late. Experienced from a lifetime of fighting, both honourably and dishonourably, he drew his enemies into a tangle of wild swings and missed blows, opening them up one by one to his attacks.

With fire and silvyr, he dropped them to the fresh snow. He trod over their bodies, oblivious to the pain they had previously inflicted on him.

He was the king of Illian, and he had a realm to reclaim.

Kassian heaved his sword from right to left, cutting through his opponent with a waning strength. The Reaver fell to the ground and behind it the dark walls of The Dragon Keep came into view, only feet away. He couldn't recall the exact path he had taken to reach this point or how long it had taken him - his focus had flitted constantly between the mass of Reavers and the approaching Karsak.

The dragon shrieked in its terrible way, promising an imminent death. The Keepers had retreated as commanded and were now gathering outside the walls of the keep, struggling to break away from the battle long enough to make it through the gates.

The fight beside him, between Fin and two Reavers, was growing beyond the young man's abilities. Kassian dragged one of the fiends away and lashed out at the second before turning to drag his heated sword across the armour of the first. It staggered back and into the path of Nathaniel's sword.

Kassian gave the knight a nod and returned his attention to Fin. "Get behind the gates!" he yelled, shoving him back.

Through the battle, there was no hearing the arrow before it impacted Fin's chest and threw him into the wall. A quick look revealed a trio of archers had taken up positions on a nearby roof. Without thought, Kassian retrieved the wand, dropped by Fin, and poured his never-ending rage into the spell. A burst of scarlet lightning erupted from the tip and tore the entire roof off the building, obliterating the archers in the process.

Such a powerful attack brought the closest Reavers down on him. Kassian flourished the wand, expelling destructive magic in every direction. All but one of the Reavers fell to the barrage. That last fiend came at the Keeper from an awkward angle, making it impossible to turn and defend himself with either wand or sword, but saved he was and by an unlikely source.

Karsak's ear-blasting roar rocked the city, halting every Reaver. Together, every knight of Erador began to back away from the walls, leaving the Keepers exposed to the dragon's glare. They all looked upon Karsak and Rengyr as the pair ascended onto the flat ground at the top of Namdhor's rise. They were all to be burned alive then...

Kassian's shoulders sagged and his body begged to do the same. Like those around him, he was exhausted and bloodied. He let the point of his sword rest against the ground where it sizzled under the peppering of snow. The Keeper looked twice at his hand, realising only now that he was missing his little finger. The bloody stump had stained the hilt and continued to trickle even now. He remembered a pain in his hand, not long ago, but he would never have guessed the entire finger was gone. That was going to sting, though he likely wouldn't live long enough to feel it.

Karsak opened its rotten maw, drawing out their inevitable doom. Kassian had no last words for either himself or his companions. Some twisted and grieving part of him found comfort knowing he would suffer the same end as Clara, consumed by dragon fire.

Stomping forward on its clawed feet, Karsak soon came to tower over them. There would be no escaping the Reaver's burning wrath. He shared one last look with Nathaniel. It wasn't that long ago he had distrusted the old knight, resented him even for bringing Alijah into the world in the first place. Now, however, he knew it was an honour to die beside him.

Karsak raised its head up, jaw pointed down at them. Kassian was about to close his eyes, knowing that he would open them again to the sight of Clara, when the most unbelievable sight kept him fixed on the view above. It was as if the world had slowed down, offering him a final moment of clarity.

There, above them, leaping from the ramparts, was Vighon Draqaro and his flaming sword.

The world caught up with itself when Vighon slammed into the top of Karsak's head. The sword of the north plunged straight down, through the dragon's skull, and into its brain. Karsak's shriek of surprise died in its mouth, along with the rest of its ravaged body, as it took three final steps backwards, away from the keep. Maw shut, it submitted to true death and its head hammered the ground, throwing Vighon and Rengyr aside.

Kassian was stunned. He looked to Nathaniel only to find the man smiling contently. That smile slid from his face, turning the Keeper back to the dragon's corpse. Rengyr and his wicked axe were rounding Karsak's splayed limbs and making for Vighon. The northman was still recovering from his jump and subsequent fall and had little to no chance of avoiding Rengyr's swing.

Along with Nathaniel, Kassian started forward as everything in him commanded the Keeper to protect Vighon. He raised Fin's wand, though they were too far to aid him...

Rengyr's axe came up over his head in both hands.

"YOU WILL NOT TOUCH HIM!" The voice boomed from the ramparts behind them.

Kassian didn't even have time to turn and look before an arrow whistled through the air and caught Rengyr in the face. The Keeper felt the ripple of magic that came with the arrow and saw its effects in the utter destruction of Rengyr's head and shoulders. What remained of his smoking body fell to the ground at Vighon's feet.

Nathaniel's smile returned when his wife leaped from the ramparts and landed between them and Vighon. Kassian winced at the fall, sure that such a drop would kill any human. Of course, Reyna's elven strength not only saw her survive the jump but also rise from her crouch with graceful ease.

As she approached Vighon, Kassian scrutinised the Reavers. Not one of the fiends dared to renew the attack while Reyna stood in the middle of them.

"I believe this is yours," she said, offering Vighon his rounded shield.

The northman accepted it, hefting its familiar weight. "You're with us then?"

Reyna's lips curved into a warm smile. "I'm with *you*."

Vighon embraced Reyna in a brief, yet squeezing, hug.

Kassian could sense that there was more both wished to express, but now was far from the time. They were still outnumbered by Reavers and there was no telling how long they would hold off their attack for.

Vighon flashed Nathaniel and Kassian a look of thanks before ascending Karsak's head and back. He looked out over Namdhor. His city. His kingdom.

With one hand he thrust the sword of the north high into the air, a flaming light at the top of the world.

Nothing happened.

The atmosphere remained tense, both sides on the verge of charging to continue their heated battle.

Then, one by one, the doors of Namdhor began to open. Up and down the city, soldiers forced into retirement, mothers and wives bereft of their loved ones, even the aged emerged from the warmth to see a sight they had long missed. Soon after, their numbers grew and they gathered in the streets, armed with everything from old swords to spades and torches.

The tide was turning...

Nathaniel greeted his wife as she returned to his side. His hand stretched out, revealing a small golden wedding band. Reyna pinched it between finger and thumb to better examine the trinket.

"I fight for you, you fight for me."

Her words seemed to deeply please the old knight. "Always," he replied.

Reyna fell in beside him, out of Kassian's sight, as Vighon jumped down from Karsak's back. He wielded his flaming sword, a lone figure between the Keepers and the Reavers. As one, the fiends took meaningful strides towards the northman and his allies.

"I'd say whatever was holding them back has faded," Reyna observed, likely aware that she had just been designated an enemy by her son.

Nathaniel puffed out his chest and turned to Kassian. "For Vighon," he stated.

The Keeper lifted his enchanted sword. "For the *king*."

# CHAPTER 42

# BACK TO THE BEGINNING

The Tower of Jain and its surrounding grounds had once held many secrets, but none so important nor more spectacular than its library. So grand was it, so extensive was its collection, that the top half of the tower had been dedicated to housing its ancient knowledge. This had all been reflected in Inara's eyes when Gideon led them through its doors.

To Asher, it was just a warm place to eat his food.

The ranger had utilised Adan's heightened sense of smell to locate the food stores used by The Red Guard. Now, seated at a long stone table, he filled his belly under the disturbed gaze of a Drake, who was clearly struggling to believe the amount of meat disappearing down Asher's throat.

"You should eat," the ranger suggested.

Adan cast a cursory glance over the variety of meats and chose a piece of bread from across the table. "I do not require as much sustenance as you."

Asher found that hard to believe given the Drake's toned form. "You look uncomfortable," he noted, sure that he would regret opening a line of dialogue while he was trying to eat.

"I have never enjoyed your appetite for meat."

"It's more than that," Asher observed, drawing a curious look from Adan. "You think you're the only one who can know someone?"

Adan shrugged. "I didn't know you were paying me so much attention all this time." The Drake tilted his head. "Are we *friends*?" he asked with some amusement mixed into his curiosity.

Asher picked his teeth as the regret sank in. "Don't push it," he replied, eliciting a smile from Adan. "What's wrong with you then?" he pressed.

The Drake became serious and pulled his shoulders in. His exquisite eyes scanned their lofty surroundings, always seeing something the ranger couldn't. "*It's this place,*" he said in elvish, as if man's tongue couldn't articulate it. "*The magic here is... wrong, twisted somehow. An enchantment has been placed over everything in here, keeping it all from rotting as it should. The malice lingers...*"

Asher's attention drifted to the many tiers that circled the tower. "*You don't need to be a Drake to know that nothing good ever came out of here,*" he remarked, matching Adan's elvish.

"How long will we have to remain here?" the Drake enquired, switching back to the common tongue.

The ranger finished a goblet of water before looking down the length of the table to Inara and Gideon. "It's hard to say," he answered.

"What are they doing?"

"Talking."

Adan didn't look convinced. "They are not saying anything."

"This is how they talk - *Dragorn*. Right now, Inara is likely passing her memories of The Rebellion and the invasion to Gideon." The ranger shrugged, indifferent to the whole thing. "It's a quicker way of explaining things than actually speaking."

Adan appeared impressed and all the more curious. "Can they do this with anyone?"

"Only if they have a dragon. It's something to do with the bond between... You know, I'm not sure *how* or *why* it works. There's probably a book around here that will tell you everything about everything."

Oblivious to the ranger's mounting frustration, Adan continued, "I do not think this place offers enlightenment. Dark magic lies within the pages of every book." Asher was saved from continuing their conversation when Inara and Gideon emerged from wherever they had been.

The Master Dragorn pushed his chair out and let his head roll back with a deep sigh. "I can't believe he did it..." he muttered.

"Ruthlessly," Inara described.

"I saw the dig sites," Gideon said. "I saw the dead - *thousands* of them - being removed from ancient battlefields. That was when I knew Alijah had discovered his lowest depths, that he was nothing more than a necromancer..."

Asher pushed his plate away. "Did you know he was going to invade?"

Gideon stood up and leant his hands against the head of the table. Behind him, flames were roaring in the ornate fireplace that had been built high into the wall. His features steeped in shadow, a grim visage overcame the Master Dragorn.

"I promised you answers and so you shall have them." Gideon's fingers tapped against the table. "It's hard to start a tale when you know it's littered with your own failings..."

"I know the beginning of your journey," Inara began. "I went to Dragons' Reach and I spoke with Ayana and the others."

Gideon nodded along. "I couldn't stay there any longer. Every day it pressed upon me that Alijah and Malliath had disappeared with naught but The Crow's words to fill their heads. I took my concerns to the others but they wouldn't hear it. The influence of the older dragons was changing them in ways I hadn't anticipated."

"So you left for Erador," Inara stated.

"Eventually," Gideon agreed. "I tried for years to continue their training, to make the order into something *strong*. One day I realised I was the last Dragorn in Ayda. I was too restless to stay among them. I couldn't accept the life they wanted, not when I knew Alijah and Malliath were still out there."

"What happened?" Asher asked. "How did you become his prisoner?"

"I wasn't for a time," Gideon shared. "Ilargo hid on the outskirts while I investigated Valgala and some of the other cities. I played my part as a citizen of Erador. They are *good* people. They've just been subjected to the worst kings and queens history could throw at them. They've endured more wars than I can count. But they're just as fascinating as the land they inhabit."

Gideon paused and made for the bookshelf that ran parallel to the table. He rifled through numerous scrolls that lay on top of the books until he found what he was looking for. Returning to the table, he laid out a map of Erador and weighted the corners down with candles.

"I was here, in Sunhold, when I first heard of the dig sites. Alijah commanded Valgala's army to put down their swords and pick up shovels. They marched to Freygard, The Ice Wilds, The Red Fields of Dunmar, anywhere that history denoted a great battle. While this was going on, The Red Guard emerged, a cult that considers Alijah to be Kaliban's vessel. Soon after that he introduced the creatures you've come to call Seekers."

"What are they?" Inara probed.

"They are creatures of the Andarens," Gideon revealed. "They hail from The Silver Trees of Akmar on the other side of the spine. I don't know what the Andarens called them but the Seekers were, *are*, gentle beings that possess a strong bond to the realm of magic. Alijah had his Red Guard hunt what they could of them and... Well, he used magic of his own to torment them into the beasts you know."

Inara kept her eyes on the map. Asher could see the continuing struggle she had with the acts of her brother. He wished to offer some comforting words, but he knew there was more of a chance that he would say the wrong thing and make everything worse.

"Who are the Andarens?" Adan'Karth's look of wonder had returned.

Gideon hesitated. "They're another story... and a *long* one at that. Thankfully, Alijah has avoided any direct confrontation with them. His attention was focused on building a new army, one that would never falter or question his orders."

"Well there he succeeded," Asher commented darkly. "All of Verda is crawling with Reavers."

Gideon had the look of a man haunted by his mistakes. "I finally revealed myself at The Red Fields of Dunmar. I had seen him resurrect a few soldiers on other battlefields, but when I saw him raise that dragon from the ground..."

"You tried to intervene," Inara reasoned.

"I couldn't let him resurrect a Dragon Rider," Gideon said tightly. "Besides the threat they posed it was just *wrong* - Dragon Riders were warriors. They should have been left where they fell." He controlled his fist as it came to rest on the table. "You've met Lord Kraiden and Morgorth - you already know I failed."

"What happened?" Inara pressed with a tone of sympathy.

"I made the mistake of trying to talk to Alijah," Gideon confessed. "I could still see that young man I had known for so long. But when I stood before him, all I could see was Malliath behind those eyes. We fought, *briefly*. We managed to escape, leaving Alijah to his insidious plans. Everything was harder after that. We were actively hunted by Malliath and The Red Guard. I took more chances and broke into the palace. That's how I came to learn of his interest in this place."

A subtle shiver ran up Adan's body and he pulled on his robes.

Gideon moved to take in all of their surroundings. "This is where my journey came to an end... and where Alijah's truly began."

Inara glanced at the library. "This is where he captured you?"

"I was separated from Ilargo," Gideon explained. "And The Red Guard was already embedded here. I might have bested them all but they weren't alone - Lord Kraiden and the other Riders were here. Their dragons were hiding high in the mountains - waiting for us."

"Why didn't he kill you?" Asher asked bluntly.

Gideon tapped his finger against the table, buying for time. "Alijah saw an opportunity having me for his prisoner," he answered. "You see, he knew a lot thanks to The Crow - he had books and notes taken from The Bastion. But this place... You could mine it for centuries and only scratch the surface of all the knowledge it houses. He kept me alive to do just that. I was to research specific areas while he committed himself to building the Reavers. Alijah would stay for days, weeks even, when he visited. We would research it all together, though he was often exhausted from endless resurrection spells."

"You *helped* him?" Asher contended, making no effort to withhold his judgment.

"Not in the beginning," Gideon corrected. "I refused to be a part of any of it. And back then I didn't know he was planning on invading Illian. I just knew he was using dark magic, *corrupting* magic."

"What changed?" Inara asked softly.

Gideon held her gaze for a long moment. "*Everything*," he replied emphatically. "It started with pain. Alijah kept me separated from Ilargo but he tortured us both, our pain shared. I don't know how long it went on for. Alijah left our torment in the hands of the Dragon Rider, Vilyra and The Red Guard's chief inquisitor. Neither of them ever spoke a word. They just carried out their master's will with dutiful diligence. Then, one day, when we were allowed to rest and heal before it all began anew, Ilargo and I decided there was only one way to survive." Gideon clenched his jaw at the memory. "We were wrong."

Inara narrowed her eyes at her old mentor. "You... You altered your bond," she concluded with revelation in her tone.

"Just as you have," Gideon replied. "Yes," he continued, answering Inara's questioning expression, "I could sense the change in your bond during the transfer. I know you and Athis are not as the Dragorn intended. That path is my own now too."

A flicker of suspicion crossed Inara's face. "Did you know?" she demanded. "Did you know *all* the dragons were influencing their riders?"

Gideon held a moment of silence before a firm, "Yes," was announced. "Ilargo told me decades ago, after Alastir bonded with Valkor."

Inara's face cracked. "You knew? You knew and you told no one?"

Asher relaxed back into his seat, sensing a diversion in their conversation that neither he nor Adan had any part in.

Gideon was shaking his head. "You weren't there, Inara - in the *beginning*. You have no idea of the responsibility I was taking on, the risk I was placing the realm under. Whether we like it or not, humans *and* elves are impulsive beings prone to acts of terrible and irrational violence. To say nothing of the greed and desire for power that lives in all of us.

"I was going to take a group of people and see them bonded to a dragon, giving them immortality and unlimited power. There needed to be a fail-safe, something that would prevent any of us from turning on the realm. For my sanity, Ilargo told me about the bond, a tradition amongst the dragons passed down from the time of Elandril. I slept better knowing that dragons couldn't be corrupted by their riders. Despite that, Ilargo still offered to change our bond and instruct the other dragons to do the same."

"But you didn't," Inara said flatly.

"I agreed with Elandril," Gideon replied boldly, holding to his wisdom. "We shared the same fears five millennia apart. So I continued his tradition; I didn't even change my own bond. I'm not blind to my weaknesses, Inara, to my potential to unleash destruction and death with the powers I have been granted. You must also know of our ability to influence our dragons. What if I turned Ilargo against the realm? What if Rolan's desires for power had brought fire down on Namdhor or Velia? Every single rider possesses the power to destroy on a scale from which there would be no return." He stopped and took a breath. "And I liked the man Ilargo made me," he added quietly. "It took the worst pain imaginable to finally change our bond."

"But it changed nothing," Asher chipped in, hoping to get things back on track.

Gideon maintained his eye contact with Inara for a few seconds more. "It turned out that *not* sharing our pain made the torment harder to endure. The mental toll it took on both of us was agonising. When Alijah was here it was worse. He could make Ilargo cry out in pain for days and I could do nothing but listen. So, after months and months of it, I agreed to help him..."

Asher wasn't one for pity - an emotion that required too much investment in the first place - but his heart cracked a little for the man. Of all the men he had ever met during his long life, no one had ever strived to do such good as Gideon Thorn. Every time he had been knocked down, every time he had failed to succeed, he got right back up and put himself in the middle of it for the sake of others.

He deserved better...

"That's how Alijah found out," Inara mused, her focus lost to the flames. "He changed his bond with Malliath after discovering that you didn't need to share the pain."

Gideon wore a pall of depression. "Yes," he said, as if confessing his guilt to a serious crime. "He became paranoid for a time after that - I didn't see him for weeks. Though he never voiced it, I knew he was concerned that there was a way Malliath could control him. When next he returned, he thought he needed to assure me that Malliath hadn't been influencing him as Ilargo had me. And that their bond was irrevocably changed: that he was, and had always been, his own man. Now they're much harder to kill," he lamented.

Asher wasn't blind to the tension that had built up between Inara and Gideon, but he decided to push through and get the answers they needed. "How did you learn the language?" he asked.

"I picked up quite a bit during my years among the people. I certainly didn't have Alijah's advantage. Erador's various languages have been locked away inside Malliath's mind since he was a young dragon. He imparted them all via their bond. I don't think Alijah even knew he was speaking a different language for a while."

Asher raised an eyebrow. "Then why did he label all of his books?"

Gideon glanced at Inara again, as if he was seeing that memory himself thanks to their recent bond. "He found speaking it to be very natural. The written word, however, proved a little more difficult. He conquered it all eventually though. It was Alijah who taught me the depths of their language."

"So he could use you," Asher concluded.

"Yes..." Gideon uttered.

"What did he have you researching?" the ranger pressed. "He already knew where to find thousands of dead soldiers as well as how to resurrect them."

Gideon stepped away from the table. "That brings us to the importance of this place," he declared with audible disdain. "The Tower of Jain: so named by those who inhabited it: *the Jainus*. They were the first mages: men and women who declared themselves wizards. There is no record of magic before them. They counselled the earliest kings and queens of Erador."

Inara physically stepped back into the conversation, her personal issues with Gideon seemingly put aside for now. "The Jainus - they were The Echoes, the priests of Kaliban?"

Gideon's tone lightened as he took on the role of storyteller. "That was what I suspected when I first began my research, but no; The Echoes were... well, an *echo* of the Jainus." Gideon opened and closed his mouth, struggling to find the words. "Erador's history is messy and violent. There are conflicting texts depending on who wrote the account. The best I can make out is that the Jainus were consumed by their study of magic. They became greedy - hungry for more. They delved deep into what we would call dark magic. To them, however, it was just a matter of degrees."

"So what happened?" Inara questioned, her interest piqued.

Gideon gave a light shrug. "Again, history was written by the victors who, in this case, were the earliest Dragon Riders. A few of the Jainus struck a bargain with them for their lives. I found a personal account written by a Rider called Joran Pendain. He stated that the remaining Jainus made a compelling case they couldn't ignore. They pointed out that magic would always exist and that people would always find a way to manipulate it, for good or bad. So, rather than slay the mages, they allowed them to live and start a school of sorts, not unlike Korkanath. You have to skip a few centuries and a few wars but, eventually, this particular institution emerges from some bloody war with a new agenda: unify the realm and prevent all future wars."

Inara folded her arms. "The Echoes..."

"Yes. It began with a noble cause, though their domination was secured when the king of Valgala adopted their beliefs. As we already know of The Echoes, they praised Kaliban. I think it was an easy god to invent given all the myths and legends that already surrounded the mountain."

"The wickedness of The Echoes is what turned Sarkas into The Crow," Asher remarked. The ranger could still remember hearing the necromancer's vile descriptions of what the priests did to him during his conversations with an imprisoned Alijah. "He learned everything he needed to know about dark magic during his time among them," he added.

Gideon was nodding in agreement. "As well as giving the masses a deity to worship and numerous hells to fear, The Echoes continued their hold over magic and even continued to keep the ancient works of the Jainus a secret. It was the Jainus's delving into necromancy that Sarkas found all those eons ago. How and when The Echoes descended into something twisted and evil isn't clear. Unfortunately, what came out of it was The Crow and his Black Hand. It's his world we're living in now..."

Asher pinched the bridge of his nose as he tried to follow Erador's history. "Wait," he said with some exasperation. "The Jainus came first, followed by The Echoes?"

"Yes. The Jainus were... *pioneers* of magic. They built this tower to study in private between counselling various rulers."

Asher was nodding along. "But the Dragon Riders destroyed them," he continued, ironing out the wrinkles in his mind.

Gideon maintained a patient demeanour, speaking volumes of his natural ability to mentor. "The Dragon Riders felt the Jainus were amassing too much power and influence," he elaborated. "This sparked a war between the two factions, though the Riders emerged the victors."

The ranger shut his eyes tight. "But they spared some of the mages, who went on to start a *school*..."

"The Echoes," Gideon confirmed. "But even they became corrupted by greed and power, the two ingredients that created Sarkas and, ultimately, The Crow."

Asher gently shook his head. "I think I'll just stick to swinging my sword at things."

"You still haven't answered his question," Inara pointed out, her blue eyes boring into Gideon. "What did Alijah have you researching here?"

"Apologies. To fully understand everything you have to know where it all began. Until Alijah named himself king of Erador, the Tower of Jain was forbidden to all - one of the only laws to have survived from the first days of The Echoes. He wanted me to help him uncover the past, to understand the Jainus. I thought he would want to know more about necromancy, but he had no interest in learning more than he already knew."

"Then what *did* he have an interest in?" Asher asked.

"Magic," Gideon articulated.

"Magic?" Inara questioned incredulously. "He wanted to research the very thing he already possesses."

Gideon pointed a finger at her. "That's just it - we already know that magic exists and that we can use it. No one ever questions it beyond that. Alijah wanted to know the *origins* of magic. Where does it really come from? Why are some people conduits and others not? I soon found out there was no end to his questions on the subject."

Asher leaned forward in his chair and caught Gideon's eyes. "Why would he want to know about the origins of magic?"

Gideon let his head drop as a long sigh escaped his lips. Asher knew shame when he saw it...

"Alijah's thinking was simple," he explained. "If he knew where magic came from, he could put an end to it..."

# CHAPTER 43

# THE BATTLE OF QAMNARAN

Having finally navigated the northern head of the cliffs and marched south along the coast, the dwarves of clan Heavybelly laid eyes on their destination, easily seen looming over the landscape. The silvyr called to every one of them, drawing them in astride their Warhogs. Nothing in the world was more coveted by the children of the mountain than precious silvyr.

Today, however, they weren't fighting for silvyr. Today, they fought for honour and blood. In preparation for the battle to come, they had rested on their journey around the cliffs and, now, faced their enemy with all the strength Grarfath could give them.

Doran only prayed it would be enough...

Bringing Pig to a halt at the top of a gentle rise, the son of Dorain observed the masses sprawled across the base of the tower. His kin, dwarves from the surviving clans, were being roused in the light of the new dawn. They would be put to work again, toiling over Alijah's designs until he was done with them or the labour killed them. Doran hoped that they too had awoken with all the strength Grarfath could lend.

"*Form up!*" he bellowed in his native tongue.

Either side of him, his clansmen lined up, mounted on their armoured Warhogs. They wielded spears, swords, axes, and hammers; bulky things one and all so as to inflict as much damage as possible. Many of the Warhogs carried extra weapons, strapped to their saddles, so that the captured dwarves below could be armed appropriately.

Russell Maybury appeared at his side, pick-axe twisting in his hands. The old wolf had walked beside them the whole way, displaying his superior strength and stamina. Doran had heard others talking about him, and not fondly, as well as noticing others who kept their distance. Russell was, indeed, an unsettling figure, but that was exactly what they needed today. The full moon was a little while off, granting the man more time in his own body and more time swinging that legendary weapon of his.

"Are ye good?" Doran asked him.

Russell glanced at his old friend. "You can count on me."

"Aye, lad. That I can..."

The son of Dorain set his good eye on those that would try and send him to the bosom of Yamnomora this day. Judging by the Reavers and Fenrigs running to form up at the base of the slope, the Heavybellys had made sufficient noise on their march to alert the enemy. With swords and spears, the Reavers created multiple lines to meet the dwarves while the human Fenrigs hung back.

Looking beyond them, to the south, there was no sign of the elves lying in wait. Doran took that as a good thing, having no doubt that Adilandra and her people were already in position. A cocky grin spread his blond beard - this was going to be a glorious battle.

From beside the tower, Morgorth took to the sky with Lord Kraiden astride. The undead dragon let loose its terrible shriek as it circled over the Reavers on bat-like wings.

Turning to face Thaligg, Doran commanded, "*Spears and cross-bows to the sky. We'll need to keep Morgorth off our backs until the elves get stuck in.*" Thaligg nodded his understanding and relayed the order to the various captains.

Curiously, Malliath remained on the ground by the edge of the coastal cliff. His purple eyes were trained on the dwarves but the dragon made no attempt to join Morgorth in the sky. Doran let his mind cast back to that black earth in The White Vale, where Malliath had scorched King Uthrad and so many others...

Doran retrieved the two halves of Andaljor and connected them into one devastating weapon. With axe and hammer, he would crush his enemies this day - he could feel the fight in him, aching in his bones to be unleashed. He stuck his heels into Pig and had the animal take him a little further beyond the front line.

"*This is the day, brothers!*" he yelled. "*This is the day we make our mark on history! It won't just be our own people who remember what we do here, but the entire realm! Our victory will be sung from here to Grarfath's Hall for all time! Today, brothers, we make the earth tremble!*" The clan cheered and hammered their fists against their armoured chests, creating a cacophonous beat. "*The stone will crack beneath our mettle! The sky will be torn asunder by our roar!*" Now, Doran's every statement was punctuated by their thunderous drumming. "*Today and forever more you will be known as the Father's vengeance! Today, you are the sword of Dhenaheim. You are the shield of our people! Let the enemy know they do not face the steel of just any warrior! Let them know they face wrath! They face ruin! Let them know they face -* HEAVYBELLYS!"

The response was deafening but, to Doran's ears, it was the sweetest sound in the world. He raised Andaljor into the air and a second wave of cheers punctured the realm.

Leading his people, Doran charged down the slope with a bristling Warhog beneath him. As Morgorth swooped down, spears and bolts were hurled from the dwarven wings, forcing the terrible beast back into the sky. The son of Dorain paid the dragon no heed as the gap rapidly closed between him and the Reavers.

He had nothing but rage for them.

From the base of the tower, Alijah watched the dwarves smash into his Reavers with a thunder-clap of violent sounds. The front row of Warhogs had leaped through the Reaver's defensive line and made an instant mess of things. With speed and sheer force on their side, the Heavybellys rammed their mounts tusk-first into the fray.

Alijah focused on his power over the knights and had every one of them rushing to the north. The dwarves needed to be held back for as long as possible.

*Let them fight as they will,* Malliath remarked. *Your energy is needed elsewhere now.*

Alijah agreed and turned to his faithful companion. **Bring the storm, old friend...**

His horned head lifted to the cloudy sky, Malliath flexed the joints where his wings met his body before they themselves stretched out. Alijah got a clear view of the ancient runes he had burned into the dragon's hide, each one a part of a combination that would split the sky.

**Remember to stay high. If you're too low the spell will fade.**

*You will have the lightning,* Malliath reassured. *Just be ready for it.* The black dragon paused to lay his beautiful eyes on Alijah. *Remember, this is our destiny. None but you and I can change the world - there is only us...*

His heart swelling, Alijah watched him ascend, climbing higher and higher until he became nothing more than a black dot against the grey clouds. After disappearing therein, the clouds darkened to near black, pulling on those scattered across the horizon. The storm grew with unnatural speed, swirling like the eye of a wrathful god. Soon, the light drizzle was replaced by torrential rain and the clouds roared as flashes of blue light pulsed from within.

Malliath's last words echoed throughout Alijah's mind. He had been preparing for this for days, but he knew that even a few more hours of meditation would have helped him. As it was, he couldn't be sure that he would still be standing when the spell was completed. Given The Rebellion's untimely assault, being incapacitated could spell his doom.

A single bolt of lightning struck the top of the adjacent cliffs, bringing Alijah's gaze down with it. Just as there was chaos above, so too was the world unravelling below. With so many Reavers and Fenrigs preoccupied with the Heavybellys' assault, there was no one to keep a hold over the dwarven camp nor those still working on bringing down the mountainous scaffolding. The prisoners added their war cries to the chaos, picked up the nearest tool, and added to The Rebellion's numbers.

Alijah seethed. This was exactly the kind of thing his reign would bring to an end. The half-elf reminded himself that this madness was only temporary. The kingdom would get his full attention as soon as his place on the throne was secured and the scales balanced.

"Your Grace!" The cry turned Alijah to Pelter, who was fast approaching with three other Fenrigs in tow. "Your Grace, my men aren't prepared to fight a whole army of dwarves!" he complained. "We need to flee - retreat that is!"

Alijah looked at the man like he was no more than filth beneath his boot. "Would you fight them if your reward was greater?"

Pelter licked his lips before hesitantly replying, "Yes, your Grace..."

Alijah glanced at the war-hungry dwarves. "Then today is an auspicious day for the Fenrigs. No longer do you fight for coin. Now, you fight for your *lives*."

Leaving Pelter and his bewildered expression behind, Alijah turned on his heel and entered the tower. He took the winding ramp that skirted the edge of the base and rose up to the only level inside. Rain hammered the centre of the circular floor, splashing out across the silvyr floor. The glyphs lining the walls remained dry, awaiting the power required to give them life.

Adjusting his cloak, Alijah shifted his Vi'tari blade, allowing him to sit cross-legged in the middle of the rainfall. He began chanting from memory the first line of the spell, as detailed in the Jainus's book. Even through the rain and the sound of his own voice, Alijah could hear lightning striking the tower all around him.

It wouldn't be long now...

~

Doran had ridden through ranks of Reavers with glee. Pig's tusks and considerable bulk had gouged and flattened the enemy while he had swung Andaljor with wild abandon.

Now, he was picking himself up from the ground with a face full of mud and no idea how he had got there. His Warhog was nowhere to be seen, though there were plenty running around the battlefield without a rider anymore.

Then there was the rain. It felt as if the heavens were dropping an ocean's worth of water on them, adding to the violent din and incessant clatter as it impacted their armour. Combined with the constant yell of his fellow warriors and the clash of steel, Doran's senses were on the verge of being overwhelmed.

The threat of death, however, had a way of honing his focus. Anticipating the swing of a Reaver's blade, angled to come down on his neck, the War Mason raised his hand to bring Andaljor to bear.

His hands were empty.

With no time to change his tactics, Doran clenched his fist and presented the Reaver's blade with his black and gold vambrace. The armour saved his life though his arm felt the sting of the cold steel where it had bitten through the edge.

A feral growl on his lips, the son of Dorain barrelled into his foe, taking it by the waist and lifting its feet from the ground. Coming down on top of the fiend, he was pummelling it with both fists when he noticed a fallen sword in the mud. Holding the blade in one hand and the hilt in the other, Doran pressed the weapon down across the Reaver's throat until its head was clearly separated.

Rising back to his feet was a battle in itself. The dwarf was jostled this way and that, barged by his kin and enemy alike. Doran scanned the ground where he could, desperately searching for Andaljor. The rain made everything harder to see and puddles were forming all around them, half-submerging the dead.

A Warhog sprinted past him, turning him back around where he watched Thraal save Thaligg from a Reaver's blade in the back. Both were good fighters, evident by the bodies mounting around them, but neither had seen the Fenrig stalking towards them, using the Reavers for cover. Shouting to them was useless, his voice lost among so many others.

Doran barged his way across the field, knocking one Reaver down before pausing to retrieve a discarded axe. He was running out of time, seeing the Fenrig closing in with a dagger in one hand and a mace in the other. Using a fallen body, indistinguishable in the mud and rain, the War Mason propelled himself forward and up, bringing the curve of his axe perfectly in line with the Fenrig's head.

Blood splattered across the dwarf's face as his axe buried the man's head into the ground. Since the battlefield was no place for thanks, Thaligg and Thraal continued their fight and Doran came up swinging.

Two more Reavers fell at his feet before Doran threw himself to the ground after them. Had he dropped down a second later, Morgorth's tail would likely have relieved him of his head. The fearsome dragon glided low over the battle, its body coated with spears and bolts, before gaining height again. Doran picked himself up and watched it turn around with an open maw.

"Grarfath save us," he muttered.

Morgorth drew closer and closer until Doran could easily see the back of its throat. The dwarf prepared himself to launch the axe in his hands. If he was about to die, he was going to leave that dragon with something to remember him by.

A flash of green light erupted across Morgorth's snout, forcing its head to roll backwards, knocking the monster off course. A flurry of spells followed the first, each colliding with the dragon's body and exposing its rotten insides. Now heading for the cliff face, Morgorth's limbs went wild before its body tumbled over itself and skidded across the ground in a wave of dirt. Doran ignored the spectacle, his attention captured by the figure who had fallen from Morgorth's saddle.

The moment Lord Kraiden met the ground, he was lost to the mayhem. Doran cursed, vowing to find the Dragon Rider. He cut down another Reaver before ascending the pile of bodies to survey the south where the elves were showing their quality. Adilandra led her people on foot, though their speed was comparable to a horse's.

With impeccable aim, the woodland folk released a salvo of arrows as a straight shot, felling Reavers and Fenrigs across the breadth of the battlefield. The elves that charged beside the queen remained unharmed by the well-placed arrows and leaped into the back of the Reaver force. Elegant, yet deadly, scimitars cut through air, rain, and foe, dropping more lifeless bodies to the ground.

Faylen skidded into action beside Doran and came up with a twisting kick to push back an approaching Reaver. Getting a sense for her flow, Doran arched his back forwards and allowed the High Guardian to roll over his armour and into a tangle of enemies. Her blade moved with an efficiency befitting of her station and reputation.

"Glad ye could make it!" Doran's last word was drowned out by a staccato of lightning strikes across the tower's silvyr surface.

"Watch your back!" Faylen warned.

Doran spun around and instinctively raised the two-handed axe to defend himself. There was very little defence, unfortunately, against a wild Warhog running rampant. The dwarf was rammed hard, freeing his hands of the axe, and thrown to the ground. The punishment didn't end there. His vambrace snagged on the Warhog's saddle, Doran was dragged beside the mount as it forced its way through the battle. He cried out and wrestled with his armour but there was no escaping while the animal was running.

At last, a Reaver's spear ended the Warhog's charge as well as its life. Doran spat mud from his mouth and did his best to ignore the new cuts and bruises added to his body. Tired of being pelted by the rain, he made to stand again only to discover his arm was trapped beneath the bulk of the Warhog.

"Come on ye damned brute!" he shouted at the animal. "Get off me arm!" There was no budging the Warhog, its considerable weight all the more while encumbered with armour.

Doran roared with all his might, pushing the beast with his shoulder while pulling his buried arm. Heaving as he was, slipping in the mud was inevitable. It did, however, save his life, when a Reaver brought its sword down into the Warhog's hide instead. The blade became lodged in the animal's armour, sparing Doran a few precious seconds. His hand scurried over the ground, grasping at anything that could be used as a weapon.

There was nothing but mud...

Amidst the chaos, the Reaver used both hands and yanked the sword free of the Warhog. It looked down at the son of Dorain through the black slits in its visor. Only the cold maleficent will of its master inhabited that helmet.

"Come 'ere then!" Doran growled, refusing to die.

His boot shot out and reversed the Reaver's knee, dropping it to within the grasp of his free hand. Doran's fingers hooked under the lip of its visor and dragged the Reaver down. A mad scramble took place between the two as the Reaver tried to stand and Doran tried to steal the slender dagger sheathed on the fiend's belt. Every time he found a firm purchase, the undead creature writhed just enough to displace him.

In the end, Doran settled for a swift elbow to his foe's head, shoving it aside. With a few more seconds added to his life, the dwarf extended himself as far as possible and tried to reach the Reaver's fallen sword. His gloved fingers clawed at the ground an inch from the hilt.

The Reaver's hand clamped down on his wrist.

Doran groaned, unable to do anything but watch as his executioner retrieved its weapon of choice. Sword in hand and balanced on one knee, the Reaver angled the blade to thrust down - a mortal blow. Tempted as he was, Doran kept his eyes open, determined to see his end to its last moment without fear. Then, as if Thorgen himself had stepped out of history's shadow, Russell exploded from the carnage with Andaljor in his hands. The hammer end slammed into the Reaver's head with such force its neck broke.

The son of Dorain looked from his would-be killer to his saviour. "Where in all the hells 'ave ye been?"

Russell ploughed the hammer into the ground and threw his body into the Warhog. A growl escaped his lips as he lifted the animal just enough to allow Doran a chance at freedom. "Move!" The War Mason rolled aside and the old wolf dropped the Warhog. After a much-needed breath, he gestured to Andaljor. "You're going to need this if you're going to beat me."

"Bah!" Doran battered the notion away and took Andaljor in hand. "No-one's cleavin' more heads than me today!"

Russell retrieved the pick-axe from over his shoulder. "We'll see about that!"

Together, they forged their way back into the heart of the battle. The elves darted between their foe, their spells creating beautiful colours as well as havoc. In the middle of it all, Doran couldn't help but notice how dwarves and elves complemented each other on the field. The swift and precise attacks of the elves combined with the heavy and brutish hammer strokes of the dwarves kept the Reavers fighting on all sides, high and low.

Russell brought his own style of fighting. Doran could see elements of his form instructed by Asher from the old wolf's earliest years as a ranger. Between these moments of finesse, he employed the fighting style of a brawler, a brawler made all the more terrifying by wielding a large pick-axe covered in notches.

Not to be shown up, Doran called upon his ancestral blood and brought Andaljor to bear. The hammer would knock legs out and the axe would follow across the neck, finishing the job. He saved as many lives as he could, intervening before that final strike. It wasn't long, unfortunately, before Doran began to notice the bodies scattered around him were captive dwarves - without armour, they were more vulnerable than the Heavybellys.

The War Mason gripped the nearest dwarf and yelled in his face, *"Find King Gaerhard! Find the king!"*

For the sake of their efforts going forwards, Doran knew it would be key to have as many leaders from Dhenaheim's hierarchy as possible. There were a lot of dwarves out there who identified as anything but Heavybellys and they would need someone like King Gaerhard to rally them.

Doran prayed they would find him fighting on the battlefield and not lying on it...

Morgorth's ear-piercing shriek blasted over the realm. Despite the chunks of flesh and even bone being ripped from its body, the dragon was pushing through the barrage of spells and arrows to enter the fray. A tail of spikes and bony protrusions curled round and swept through the edges of the battle, launching dwarves, elves, and Reavers into the air, never to rise again.

"Don't let it open its mouth!" Faylen cried.

"Aim for the glands!"

Doran turned to discovered Aenwyn, her bow nocked and held steady in one hand. The elf skipped over the dead and even used Reavers and dwarves, locked in battle, to ascend above the din. Midleap, her bow came up, the string pulled taut. Rather than watch her any longer, Doran whipped his head around to face Morgorth. The monster's maw, lined with razor-sharp fangs, opened beyond the normal limits of a healthy dragon, exposing its scarred tongue and the two glands that sat either side.

Aenwyn's arrow sailed over the top of the battle and sank deep into one of those glands. The dragon choked on it and shook its head, no longer capable of breathing fire. Of course, it still had four claws, a wicked tail, and the hunger of Death itself.

"Bring it down!" Doran roared.

Aenwyn landed in front of him, another arrow nocked, and renewed her attack on the dragon. Faylen took charge of a group of elves and challenged Morgorth from the left, while Thaligg and Thraal unleashed a savage mauling upon Morgorth's right, soon reinforced by more Heavybellys. That left Doran and Russell to the head.

Ploughing through, Morgorth flattened any too slow to get out of its way and flexed its wings to banish those attacking its flanks. Only when its head loomed above did Doran wonder if he was attempting to slay a monster that lay beyond his abilities.

Then, Morgorth stomped his front claw and crushed one of the dwarves Doran had come so far to save.

"Come on then ye ugly goat!" Doran bellowed.

Russell held out a hand to try and stop his charge. "No, Doran!"

Morgorth caught sight of Doran charging in towards its neck and raised a claw to scrape him from the face of Verda. There was no defending against those claws, talons that had travelled from eons past to take more lives. The son of Dorain raised Andaljor over his head, sure of only one thing: the dragon was stronger than him.

That threatening claw came down, intending to stomp him into the dirt, only to find something else in its way. Doran watched the shield flare beneath the points of Morgorth's claws, but his attention was quickly turned towards Adilandra, crouched beside him. The strain of her spell was written all over her face. Veins pulsed against the surface of her skin and a trickle of blood ran from her nose and over her top lip.

"I can't hold it..." she uttered, her magic still in shadow.

With no time to lose, Doran scooped a hand around the queen's waist and threw all of his weight behind him. Side by side, they leaped out from under Morgorth's claw, which shattered Adilandra's shield and thundered into the sodden earth.

Looking up from the ground, Doran met Morgorth's dead white eyes. Fire or no fire, the dragon was still going to kill them with the snap of its jaws. Coming to his rescue again, Russell jumped high into the air with his pick-axe raised above his head. The old wolf nailed Morgorth in the eye with a hammering blow that lodged his weapon. The dragon shrieked and violently shook its head until Russell was thrown clear.

"Move!" Faylen was pulling Adilandra back from Morgorth's shadow as Doran rose with Andaljor leveraged to swing the axe end.

He looked Morgorth in its only eye. "Welcome to the club!" he quipped. The dwarf clipped the monster's bottom jaw and, without meaning to, lined Morgorth's head up for Aenwyn's next shot. The arrow weaved through the beating rain and found its end inside the dragon's remaining eye.

The fiend went wild, blind to its enemies. "Take the head!" Doran bellowed at the elves.

Following Faylen's lead, every elf in the vicinity discarded their weapon and aimed their hands at Morgorth. Doran was nearly blinded by the stream of spells that competed with the lightning. Brilliant shades of green, red, and blue filled the air between the elves and the dragon, each spell exploding against its neck.

Doran lent Andaljor to the elves' defence and kept the Reavers at bay. He broke ancient bones and tore through putrid flesh, his every strike drowned out by the hurricane of spells and relentless rain. After caving one Reaver's skull in, he turned back and dared to take in the sight of Morgorth's final moments. Bombarded from all sides and blind to his attackers, the dragon finally lost its battle when its scales, flesh, and muscle gave way, exposing the spine. There was no way of knowing who cast that last spell, but it utterly destroyed the bones, severing the head.

Morgorth the doom was dead.

Doran felt the ground shudder as the horned head fell to its final resting place. Smoke tried to defy the rain and rise from both stumps. The son of Dorain lifted Andaljor into the air and cheered - they were one step closer to securing their victory on the wretched island.

Now to kill the Rider...

# CHAPTER 44
# ANCIENT HISTORY

Asher wasn't one to be shocked by much, his understanding of the world and its many facets comprehensive, but Gideon's words repeated again and again inside his mind, escaping his grasp.

By the look on Inara's face, she too was experiencing the same dilemma. "He wants to destroy... *magic?*"

Gideon closed his eyes and angled his head, as if pulling a distant memory. "When you confronted him, Inara - in Dhenaheim - he told you he was going to *break the scales*."

Inara nodded silently, her emotions regarding the memory kept far from the surface.

"He would talk to me often of the *scales*," Gideon continued. "He truly believes that the realm will always be in peril so long as magic exists for anyone to wield it. He would list various tyrants and villains from history, be it Erador's or Illian's, and explain how magic had allowed them to bring suffering to the people. *The scales are always tipped*, he would complain. The real truth is: Malliath hates magic. That dragon has been tormented by magic and those that use it countless times. It's *his* motivations that pull Alijah's strings, I'm sure of it."

Never had Inara looked more sceptical. "The entire concept sounds ridiculous. You can't *destroy* magic."

"I too thought it was absurd, a waste of time. I agreed to help him because I thought it would be better than helping him understand some other form of dark magic." Gideon craned his neck to look up at the highest tiers. "Then I found it, hidden behind the other books, the chronicles of some Jainus mage whose name I never discovered. They claimed to have found a way to... *physically* cross over to the other side - to the realm of magic."

"Cross over?" Inara echoed. "That makes no sense. Everything we know about that realm suggests it sits right on top of ours."

Gideon pointed to the higher tiers. "The Jainus spoke of the realms like *dimensions*. Even though it would seem they occupy the same space, they still have their own individual space, separate from each other."

Asher spared a moment to look at Adan, wondering if the Drake had a better grasp of the concept than himself. Adan, however, was still listening intently and without any sign of confusion. The ranger adjusted his cloak and did his best to keep any misunderstanding off his face.

"Do you believe any of it?" Inara asked her old mentor.

"It doesn't matter or, at least, it didn't matter when I found it - Alijah believed. He became obsessed with the idea of it after that."

"What else did this chronicle say?" Asher pressed, wondering if there was anything he might actually understand.

Gideon refrained from answering immediately. Instead, he walked over to the corner of the ground floor and retrieved a wooden box in both hands. He flipped the catches and lifted the lid. He stared at the mysterious contents.

"There was only one description from the other side," he finally said.

From inside the box, he removed a black leather book no thicker than his thumb. He opened it up on the table and pushed it away, displaying two pages of incoherent scrawls and a pressed leaf that had been kept between the pages. It was a vibrant red, redder than anything Asher had ever seen in nature. Upon closer inspection, the ranger couldn't tell if it was wet or not by the level of gloss it possessed.

"A tree," Gideon continued. "The Jainus described it as having bark as white as snow and leaves a blood red. They further claimed that this tree is the source of magic, the heart that beats it across both realms."

"Magic comes from a tree?" Inara repeated with disbelief.

"Trees give life to us all," Adan chipped in.

"What happened to this mage?" Asher enquired, his eyes drawn back to the scrawls of what could only be a very disturbed individual.

Gideon gestured to the diary. "The last entries tell of a desperation to survive long enough to complete their work. It seems this came at a time when the Dragon Riders had taken umbrage with the Jainus's practices. Since I have found nothing else in this vein, I have to assume this particular mage died in the purge."

"How did they do it?" the Guardian asked. "How did they reach the other side?" Inara's gaze was lost to time and space until she turned to her old mentor with a question in her eyes.

Touching his temple, Gideon replied, "Yes. The tower you showed me, on Qamnaran. The pit in The Moonlit Plains. They're connected to all this. The Jainus who made the initial discovery spoke of a doorway from this world to that one."

"Portals," Asher muttered to himself. "Where is this doorway?" he asked.

Gideon shook his head. "It isn't anywhere - it has to be made. How the Jainus did it is unknown. The details were never written down, even after the entire order became involved. But, from what I can tell, the only way to make one is to bring magic together in such a way that it distorts our reality to the point that it bridges the gap."

Inara's eyes lit up. "You mean—"

"Yes, like Dragons' Reach," Gideon confirmed.

Asher cleared his throat. "For those of us haven't been there..."

"Dragons are beings of magic," Gideon clarified. "When they congregate in large numbers, they affect the world physically."

"So there's a doorway in Ayda?" Asher surmised.

"No," Gideon replied as if the answer was obvious. "The dragons are too spread out and their numbers too low. They would have to be concentrated in a small space for a time."

"The pit," Inara announced.

A grave look returned to Gideon's face. "I suspect that's what Alijah is doing in The Moonlit Plains."

"His plan is flawed then," Asher asserted. "Alijah's not powerful enough to force all the dragons down that hole. I'm not even sure it's big enough..."

"Alijah came to that same conclusion," Gideon recounted. "But we have to entertain the idea that he has some kind of plausible plan, otherwise he wouldn't be going to the effort of having The Moonlit Plains dug up."

Inara turned away to slowly pace the length of the table. "He wants to destroy magic," she uttered, stuck in a well of disbelief.

Gideon made to interrupt her musings. "If it were, indeed, possible, it would come with grave consequences."

That stopped Inara. "Such as?"

"Without..." Gideon paused in a moment of distress. "I can hardly say it. Without magic... there can be no dragons."

Inara gave a slow blink, her reaction suggesting she had come to this dark conclusion.

"As magic ebbed away," Gideon continued, "so too would they." He turned to Adan'Karth. "I'm afraid I have no idea what would happen to your kind."

"If we didn't die with our cousins," Adan theorised, "we would certainly lose our minds..."

"Wait," Asher requested. "If he destroys this tree, magic dies and all the dragons with it. What about Malliath? Alijah isn't about to kill his own dragon."

Inara faced Gideon with a new sense of understanding about her. "The tower of silvyr," she said, as if this answered Asher's question.

Gideon nodded without a word.

"I don't follow," the ranger admitted.

Gideon attempted to elucidate the matter. "When I pointed out that every dragon, including Malliath, would die with the tree, I thought Alijah would let the whole idea go."

"But he didn't," Asher concluded.

"No. The Crow told him he had seen the future, one in which Alijah and Malliath ruled over all of Verda, unifying the realm. His belief in The Crow's words emboldened him. In Alijah's eyes, he would inevitably reign over everything with Malliath, just as he had been promised. As far as Alijah was concerned, that meant there *had* to be a solution that prevented Malliath's death... and there was." The Master Dragorn held his tale there, his fight with guilt and shame ongoing.

"Gideon." Inara looked long and hard at him. "Tell us *everything*."

Gideon almost laughed to himself. "This has all happened before. We're just an echo of the past, history repeating itself as it always does."

Asher was in desperate need of a simple answer. "What are you talking about?"

"Alijah's plan to destroy the realm of magic - that was the Jainus's plan." Gideon poked a finger into the open page of the diary. "When they discovered that one of their own had found a way to other side, they planned to burn the tree down, ending the threat posed by the Dragon Riders. But, like Alijah, they didn't want to lose their power in the process. So they found a way to shield their magic, trapping it inside themselves, never to fade. Can you imagine it? In a world without magic they would be gods."

"So the tower of silvyr has nothing to do with crossing over," Inara said. "It's going to help him...what? Shield his magic?"

"Exactly," Gideon replied. "The Jainus never accomplished their plan. And the Dragon Riders burned anything alluding to it. The only thing they missed was the diary and the spell book, which Alijah took with him. In it, the mage tells of a spell that, when combined with the right conditions, could bind one's magic to themselves forever, regardless of the tree's existence. The conditions, however, were so difficult to replicate that I thought Alijah would give up on the idea altogether."

"But he didn't," Asher repeated, becoming a little tired of Gideon's assumptions.

The Master Dragorn fingered some of the pages and turned to a crude drawing of a tower surrounded by ancient glyphs. "He needs a storm, a *big* one. Though, he found the answer to that in here as well. You recall Dolvosari the storm maker?" he asked of Inara. "Dolvosari had ancient glyphs burnt into his skin, beneath his scales. Once he rises above a certain height, those glyphs create the worst storms imaginable. Trust me, I saw one reduce a Darkakin city to rubble."

"So he has Malliath for that," Inara reasoned. "What about the rest of it?"

"The spell itself is complicated," Gideon explained. "A portion of it will amplify the lightning to a level that would destroy any structure, even stone. That's why he needs the silvyr - it has to attract *and* funnel the lightning to him and him alone without being obliterated. From what I could tell, it's no easy spell to survive either. He would need to meditate for days in preparation. That's also why he chose Qamnaran - because of its Demetrium mines. He believed the Demetrium would help his human side conduct as much magic as possible."

"So if he succeeds on Qamnaran," Asher enquired irritably, "he'll be immune to the tree's destruction?"

"In theory, yes. Malliath too thanks to their bond. Then, he would have the power to rule forever... *unchallenged*."

Asher spared Inara a moment's observation, sure that he could see the broken pieces of her heart shattering into dust. For them,

Alijah was the enemy, a complicated one, but still a foe who clearly needed vanquishing. To her, he was blood. Every blow carried a lasting sting for her. Should she survive this, the ranger knew they would stay with her forever.

"I tried to deter him at every step," Gideon added, his tone dripping with apology. "But there is only one voice he listens to now..."

All eyes fell on the Guardian, who had turned her back to them. "Inara," Asher said, cutting through the tension. "What are you thinking?"

The half-elf finally turned back to them, her hands resting on her hips. "I think we have nothing to worry about," she replied surprisingly.

Asher couldn't fathom her response having heard everything she had. "Oh good," he said sarcastically. "Can we go home now?"

"I mean it," Inara insisted, moving to the table. "This is the most ridiculous, outlandish thing I've ever heard. There's no real proof, just the ramblings of a mage we know nothing about. At least now we know there's nothing to fear from Alijah's plans. Now we can just focus on taking Illian back."

Asher maintained his steely gaze at the Guardian, his expression speaking for him.

"You think there's some truth to all this?" Inara challenged.

The ranger sat back in his chair. "I *think*... you're talking to a man who was born a thousand years ago, had a mountain dropped on his head, and is now sitting before you with a belly full of chicken..."

Inara closed her eyes and kept them shut for a moment - there was no arguing that anything was possible in light of Asher's story. "A tree?" she returned to. "A tree is responsible for all magic in Verda?"

Gideon straightened up and folded his arms. "There might be a way to prove it..."

As intrigued as Asher was, he had the feeling that said proof was at the end of a long road they didn't have time to explore. "We need to get back to Illian," he insisted. "The Rebellion is in sore need of a dragon and we have *two* of them outside."

Inara's mouth twisted, her urge to agree tempered by curiosity. "What kind of proof?"

Gideon approached the map again and placed his finger over a small mountain range in Erador's north. "Drakanan," he announced. "It's the ancient home of the Dragon Riders. Now, the Jainus never specified how they opened the first doorway, but they strongly believed the Riders were hiding one in the heart of Drakanan."

"Why would they believe that?" Inara queried, keen to poke holes in the whole affair.

"There's a complete chapter in the diary that describes the questioning of a captured Rider. I'll skip the gruesome details, but he apparently divulged this secret. That's why the Riders doubled their efforts to destroy the Jainus - they didn't want another doorway to protect."

"Under duress," Inara argued, "the Rider would have said anything they wanted to hear."

Gideon made an expression to suggest it wasn't beyond the realm of possibility. "The Jainus came to the conclusion that the Dragon Riders made Drakanan their home because the doorway *already* existed there."

Asher shook his head. "Dragorn or Dragon Rider... It's all just secrets built on secrets. Give me the life of a ranger any day."

"Did Alijah know this?" Inara continued, her tone argumentative.

"Yes," Gideon answered. "He even took me there a few times in an attempt to locate it, but we never did."

"This is sounding less like proof," Inara opposed, "and more like a wild chase that might keep us from returning to the fight."

"As you suggested," Gideon countered, "we need to know where our focus should be. Do we challenge Alijah and get between him and the tree? Or do we leave him to his own wild chase and concentrate on taking back the country while he's distracted? We could be in Drakanan in under two days by flight.

Then we would know for sure how serious a threat Alijah's actions really are."

To Asher's perception, there was still one problem. "None of that solves the issue of finding this doorway in the first place. Why would we succeed where you and Alijah failed?"

A sly smile crept across Gideon's face. "Because, as fate would have it, we have a Drake in our company..."

The ranger looked from Gideon to Adan and back. "What does he have to do with anything?"

Gideon pointed at the mountain range on the map again. "If this doorway really does exist inside Drakanan then its hidden, and hidden well. Those of us who can use magic can sense it when it's being used, but neither Alijah nor myself could detect it—"

"That's because it doesn't exist," Inara interjected, her opinion stated as fact.

Gideon held his breath, waiting to see if he would be interrupted at length. "*But,*" he emphasised, "if there is a doorway inside, it *must* be giving off magic. From what I saw in my cell, you can *read* magic, Adan, and on a level I never would have thought possible."

Silence settled over the companions as logic had its moment. Asher, however, was of a mind to keep the Drake safe, a natural instinct that had developed in the ranger during their time together. He could also see Inara's curiosity battling her personal issue with Gideon.

"We should go," Adan'Karth stated, his tone bolder than usual.

"No," Inara quickly replied. "We should return to Illian—"

"Stop," Asher commanded in his gruff voice. "Your judgement is clouded." Inara made to argue but the ranger held up his hand. "Whatever your problem is," he continued, gesturing to Gideon, "you need to put it aside."

Inara's brow contorted into a knotted frown. "*You* were the one who insisted we return to Illian and help The Rebellion!"

"And we should, but Gideon's right - knowing our enemy's motives and whether they're credible would shift the entire focus of

The Rebellion's efforts. Once we leave Erador there will be no coming back. We should return with *everything* we can, and that means more than an extra dragon."

The need to argue was written all over Inara - her mannerisms mirroring her mother's. It reminded Asher of his time journeying with Reyna and Nathaniel during The War for the Realm. As close as they had been, he had conflicted with Reyna more than once and seen her struggle with the urge to yell at him.

The ranger withheld his smile...

Slowly but surely, Inara's demeanour physically changed as she replaced her personal issues with duty, another trait her parents had instilled in her. She managed a glance at Gideon but, in order to maintain her appearance of control, she simply looked at the map on the table.

"To Drakanan then," she declared reluctantly.

# CHAPTER 45
# EYE OF THE STORM

Galanör braced himself in a crevice in the cliffs, his position held entirely by the tension in his muscles. He had beaten the dwarves and elves to the tower by a couple of days and watched his enemies with a keen eye. Having seen so many, he knew a battle-sized distraction was the only way he would reach his prey.

Now it was here.

It had taken every ounce of discipline to remain the observer when his kin joined the battle below. Aenwyn was down there somewhere, fighting for her life and The Rebellion without him.

Yet here he was, waiting for the battle lines to become clear so that he might find the best way to skirt around and reach the tower. All three sides, elves, dwarves, and Reavers, had knotted together to the north of the campsite, spreading out towards the edge of the cliff beside the tower.

At present, that left Galanör with a relatively clear path to the entrance. His sharp eyes could make out the cowardly Fenrigs holding back, by the base of the tower, reluctant to get involved in a real fight.

And inside - his prey. Alijah was at the epicentre of whatever spell was blasting the sides of the tower. Even now, countless bolts struck the silvyr from all sides, tearing through the scaffolding and setting the wood alight. Overhead, the storm looked to be the end of the world. Galanör had no idea what Malliath had to do with it, but the storm had only begun after the black dragon disappeared into the clouds.

The elven ranger cast the various distractions from his mind and narrowed his sight on the tower's entrance. Nothing mattered now but reaching it and killing Alijah.

A tormenting image flashed through Galanör's imagination, showing him Aenwyn's death amongst a sea of Reavers...

Action was the only thing for it. If he remained an observer any longer he would give in to his fears and fight his way to her side. He shifted his position and controlled his fall, using the cliff walls to prevent his descent from turning into a fatal plummet. With cat-like reflexes, he bounded from one rock face to another until he was returned to the hard earth.

Crouched behind a jagged boulder, the elf assessed his path again, making certain there was nothing standing in his way. His gaze, however, was drawn back to the fray. The concentrated burst of spells finally ceased and Morgorth's head fell away from its foul body. That gave the ranger some hope. If he completed his own task, every Reaver on the island would join the dragon.

Setting off at a sprint, Galanör darted through the campsite. He weaved between the soaking tents and jumped over the debris, his blue cloak billowing out behind him. As he ran, he visualised his duel with Alijah, recalling all that he could of the half elf's fighting style. He also visualised the details of running his scimitar through the young man. Galanör knew he had to be committed - to falter was to fail the entire rebellion.

The stretch of land between the campsite and the tower was devoid of all but four Fenrigs. By the look on their faces, they couldn't decide whether to stand and guard the entrance or turn tail and run for their lives.

Either way, Galanör wasn't slowing down.

In the few seconds it took him to close the gap, the ranger was briefly reminded of his time stalking the streets of Dragorn, a killer for the king of Elandril. He had moved with all the confidence of an apex predator, sure of his superiority. He was glad now to employ that same way of thinking for an honourable cause.

At the limit of his incredible speed, Galanör turned his momentum into a weapon. A single leap, a twist of his hips, and a solid foot broke the first man's jaw before breaking his neck. The elf came down, dropped into a roll, and came back up under the swing of a sword with Stormweaver in hand. The Fenrig, second from the back, hadn't even time to raise his weapon before Galanör's steel slit his back open.

In the blink of an eye, Guardian was in his other hand to create a scissor effect with Stormweaver. Together, the scimitars blocked the third Fenrig's high attack. A swift boot to the man's chest launched him towards the tower with at least three broken ribs. The last thug hesitated, his mace unsteady in his grip.

"Stay back!" he warned, his tone betraying his fear.

Galanör strode onwards, easily anticipating the man's first swing. Guardian deflected the mace while Stormweaver swept in to slice his torso. As the Fenrig hit the ground, Galanör twisted and dropped to one knee, bringing the tip of a scimitar down into the only surviving man, his broken ribs the least of his worries.

All four dead at his feet, the elf rose to his full height with red blades. The rain didn't have time to wash the steel clean before he had entered the tower. With one way to go, Galanör took the curving slope that led up to the only floor. Cautious steps brought the elven ranger to the top of the ramp. His head ascended above the floor first, giving him a view of the circular chamber. The silvyr walls resonated with every lightning strike as the storm pressed its vicious assault. A column of rain connected the top of the tower to the chamber floor - Alijah was sitting cross-legged in the middle of it.

Galanör steeled himself. It wasn't Alijah Galfrey but an enemy, a fiend wearing his old friend's face. The man he faced was the cause of suffering and death across the realm, his very existence a threat to Aenwyn.

He had to die...

As the elf stepped onto the chamber floor, he noticed the hundreds of glyphs carved into the walls were lighting up with every lightning strike. Sure to keep Alijah in his eye line at all times, Galanör scrutinised them. They weren't all being illuminated at once, though with every few strikes more came to life, suggesting the spell was working up to something.

In the heart of it, Alijah's eyes were shut and his lips were muttering incessantly, his voice lost to the rain and lightning. Galanör squeezed the hilts of his scimitars and took a step closer to the enemy. Could it be that easy? Could he simply creep up and drive his sword through Alijah and end the war? It wasn't how he had imagined killing him, or anyone for that matter; there was no honour in walking up to a foe and stabbing them while their eyes were closed.

Honour was forfeit when the entire realm hung in the balance. It would haunt Galanör for the rest of his immortal life, but seeing the world free of evil every day would keep him sane. One quiet step in front of the other, he closed the gap until he was inside the column of rain and his hair was being plastered back over his head.

His right arm came up and Stormweaver with it, the curved tip angled down at Alijah. He would never be able to look Reyna, Nathaniel or Inara in the face again. With true grit, Galanör clenched his jaw and accepted the path he was set on, regardless of whether history would note him as a hero or a murderer.

A blinding bolt of lightning found its way through the opening at the top of the tower. It struck the inner wall with an ear-piercing explosion and made Galanör flinch, averting his eyes from the light.

It was now or never, he told himself. He opened his eyes and thrust forward.

There was nothing but empty space.

Centuries of experience told him he was about to be attacked from behind. Guardian and Stormweaver came up together as he shifted his weight to the left with only a fraction of a second before Alijah's Vi'tari blade swung into them.

Through their locked blades, the half-elf offered a menacing smile. "One last dance then..."

As Morgorth's head hit the ground, Adilandra wiped away the blood from her nose. She blinked hard to banish the glare irritating her eyes, a result of so many spells in close proximity. Clarity returned, she first laid eyes on Doran Heavybelly and his ferocious Andaljor. The War Mason hammered and hacked at his enemies, cutting a path through the chaos.

Returning to the dwarf's side, Russell Maybury buried his pick-axe into one foe after another having reclaimed the weapon from Morgorth's eye. Together, the pair were a force to be reckoned with. Were their foe any other, Adilandra was sure they would run from Doran and Russell. As it was, they faced Reavers, the fearless dead.

The queen urged her royal guard to get stuck in as she herself advanced into the fray. Faylen's commands, however, had been drilled into the elven warriors - they would only leave her if Death demanded it.

In order to make a real difference in the battle, Adilandra had to push beyond the protective borders of her guard, and show them that a thousand years of wielding a scimitar made her more deadly than all of them.

Diving into the fray, her sword zig-zagged as she parried and attacked multiple enemies at once, saving two dwarves from being overwhelmed. The last Reaver came at her from an awkward angle and she instinctively relied on her magic to repel the creature. Only as the world began to close in on her, and a searing pain ignited in the centre of her head, did Adilandra opt to duck and evade instead.

Deflecting the continued attack, the queen positioned herself to turn on the Reaver with a powerful two-handed strike. Its head parted from its body, the knight from Erador fell at her feet.

"I saw that!" Faylen yelled, cutting her way through to Adilandra's side.

"You see everything," the queen complained.

"You were about to use magic again," Faylen continued, kicking another Reaver back. "You've already used too much saving Doran!"

"It's never too much if it saves a life!" she countered, before shoving the tip of her blade up and through a Reaver's head. Bracing herself against its armoured chest, the queen then used its body as a ram and knocked over two more behind it.

An arrow whistled past Adilandra's ear and caught an incoming Reaver in the visor, returning it to a lifeless corpse. The queen whipped her head around to see Aenwyn. Her quiver empty, the archer was dashing from body to body, removing arrows from the dead and firing them back into the chaos. To still be using a bow in the midst of such a heated battle was testament to her skill.

Seeing Aenwyn brought a searing question to mind: where was Galanör? The queen had shared a battlefield with the ranger before, on the plains of Alborn before the gates of Velia, and knew he was hard to miss. His skill dominated the melee and the enemy would always flock to him in a bid to bring him down.

Too far to call, Adilandra fought her way to Aenwyn's side. Faylen and those of the royal guard still on their feet were close on her heels, preventing any foe from attacking her back. By the time she reached the elf, Aenwyn was retrieving a slender dagger from a Reaver's faceplate.

"My Lady!" Aenwyn threw that same dagger and took down a Fenrig who had slipped between two guards locked in combat.

Adilandra offered her a nod of thanks. "Where is Galanör?" she yelled over the rain.

Aenwyn yanked an arrow from a body at her feet and nocked it. "He travelled with the Heavybellys, your Grace." Her answer came with a look of concern.

"So you said," Adilandra replied, recalling her report from their journey around the cliffs. "But *where* is he?"

Aenwyn shrugged her shoulders in defeat. "He must be in this somewhere..."

Adilandra held her tongue while pivoting to parry a Reaver's blade. Their swords locked against each other, but the queen twisted her grip into a sweeping arc, exposing her enemy's torso. A swift two-handed hammer-stroke cut the Reaver open from head to groin. The corpse fell away, revealing either Thaligg or Thraal on the other side.

Calling by neither name, Adilandra caught the dwarf's attention. "Have you seen Galanör?" she demanded.

Thaligg or Thraal swung his axe into the leg of a passing Reaver before delivering a second blow to its head. "No!" he shouted, pulling his weapon out of the skull. "Haven' seen 'im since we left ye lot at the camp!"

Adilandra's mouth hung open as she put the pieces together. Instead of responding to the dwarf, her eyes cast up at the tower. It was being assailed by lightning from every side, some of which was tearing through the scaffolding like butter. Chunks of burning wood were being scattered high into the air and thrown over those fighting closer to the coast.

The queen's jaw clamped shut. Galanör was in that tower...

Without warning her guard, she immediately began fighting her way towards the entrance, beyond the battle. "Where are you going?" she heard Faylen scream.

Adilandra sidestepped a falling dwarf that had taken a mortal blow to the head and slashed at his killer. "Galanör is in there!" she cried back. Aenwyn's face dropped and she too began fighting her way towards the tower.

The queen pushed through the raging battle, promising herself that if Galanör was still alive, she would kill him herself. Something told her she would have to get in line behind Aenwyn first...

The moment Alijah's foot connected with the side of Galanör's face, the ranger's only destiny was to leave the floor before crashing back down under the pelting rain. Every one of his limbs hurt with the impact, but it all paled in comparison to the pain in his jaw.

Groaning, Galanör pulled himself up with both scimitars still in hand. He lashed out with a wild back-hand to keep his enemy at bay long enough for him orientate himself. Alijah was stalking around the edges of the rainfall, his eyes honed in on Galanör like prey.

"You shouldn't have come, old friend," the half-elf warned.

Galanör bared his teeth. "I can beat you!" he snarled.

Alijah gestured at the silvyr walls. "I'm the least of your worries in here!"

The elven ranger dared to take his eyes off Alijah and examine the glyphs that surrounded them. Almost all of them were illuminated with the lightning strikes now.

"What is this?" Galanör challenged.

"This?" Alijah repeated with an amused smile. "This is beyond your comprehension, Galanör! You are wildly unprepared to be in here - I'm not even sure I'll survive!"

Galanör refused to believe the latter given that everything Alijah did was meticulously calculated. But he was beginning to wonder if this spell would kill *him*...

"Either way," the ranger called back, "you won't be walking out of this tower!"

Alijah flicked up his emerald blade and took a second to marvel at its edge. "Are you going to *kill* me, Galanör? We were friends once! Now, you're going to kill me over something you don't even understand? This is why I have to be the one! This is why the burden falls on me! Because the heroes like you are too short-sighted to see what needs to be done!"

"You had your chance to be something great!" Galanör snapped. "Your bloodline, your name, even the dragon you're bonded to... You could have been the best of us all!"

"Careful now, Galanör. Let too much emotion in and you might lose your nerve..."

The elven ranger leaped at his opponent, scimitars working in tandem. Guided by his cursed sword, however, Alijah deflected, parried, and countered every blow as if he knew where they going before Galanör took action. Of course, Galanör had more than steel in his arsenal. As Alijah batted Guardian from his hand, the elf thrust out his open palm and cast a fireball directly into his chest.

The flash was blinding and the heat intense, but it was all the worse for Alijah, who was launched from the column of rain with a smoking torso. He skidded across the floor and rolled backwards only to come up on his feet again. His look of anger faded into further amusement when he waved the smoke away, revealing a chest of undamaged dragon scales.

"You're going to have to do better than that!" Alijah taunted.

Without pausing to retrieve Guardian, Galanör darted from the rain and renewed his attack with one scimitar alone. The two weaved between the other's attacks and defences, their skills colliding like opposing storms. Their swords rang out, adding to the lightning and rain, and every few seconds, Alijah scored a new cut, slicing through the elf's leathers and flesh.

One particular wound, across Galanör's knuckles, caused him to drop Stormweaver and cry out in pain. Alijah shoved the elf back with a boot to the chest and gave no quarter as he pressed his attack with the pommel of his hilt. The steel clubbed Galanör above the eye and pushed him back further until he hit the wall. The heat from the glyphs instantly set his cloak alight and burned his leathers, forcing him to jump away from the silvyr.

Alijah was waiting for him.

A rounding kick to the ribs threw Galanör across the floor, where he immediately began to roll from side to side in an effort to extinguish the flames that licked his back. Smoking, burnt, and royally pissed, the elf rose from the floor with what composure he had left. He locked Alijah in his sights as he unclipped his ravaged cloak and let it crumple at his feet. With squared shoulders, he invited his foe to continue their fight with naught but a look.

An incredulous expression contorted Alijah's sharp features. "Is this supposed to be the part where I put down my sword, take off my cloak, and we fight hand to hand as *warriors*? You insult yourself for thinking me such a fool!"

Alijah crossed the floor in three meaningful strides, his last an obvious spring to give him height over Galanör. Watching his enemy, mid-flight, the elf's muscles tensed, succumbing to memory. Galanör couldn't count how many of his kin he had faced in the training pits in Elandril. His father hadn't allowed him to even wield a sword until he could disarm and defeat every opponent with his bare hands first.

Unlike most in his position, Galanör didn't step back or try in any way to escape beyond Alijah's reach. Instead, he moved forward, bringing him closer than the half-elf had anticipated when he left the floor. It was just enough to put him off balance on landing and drive his sword a few inches off Galanör's centre mass.

Like the claws of a predator, Galanör's hands snatched at Alijah's wrist and shoulder. Only a few pounds of pressure was required to place his wrist into a position of real agony. Alijah's fingers flexed as the pain shot up his arm and reached his expression. His Vi'tari blade fell from his grip and clattered on the floor before Galanör kicked it away and threw out his arm to deliver a blow across Alijah's chest.

The elf pursued his prey across the chamber, watching as he picked himself up and rotated his sore wrist. Killing Alijah with his bare hands hadn't been the plan, but he wasn't beyond improvising - it was just going to be a little more brutal.

The two locked together in a flurry of fists and kicks that quickly directed them back into the rainfall. Galanör felt his skin being shaved away every time he missed Alijah's face and punched his armour instead. As the fatigue began to set in, his speed came into question. One kick to Alijah's side was too slow and the half-elf gripped his leg and dropped a hammering blow to his knee. Galanör yelled in pain and collapsed to the floor with a splash. The rain blinded him but he could guess Alijah's next attack and rolled aside before a boot broke his jaw.

Getting up, he was forced to defend himself against three successive strikes, the third of which connected with his arm and threw him back down to the floor. Between the two of them, blood was dyeing the rainwater an alarming red.

"What a disappointment!" Alijah jibed, walking through the rain towards him.

Galanör raised his legs and twisted his hips, using his back as a pivoting point. One foot after another impacted Alijah's face, sending him sprawling away until he was face down in the bloody water.

"My thoughts exactly!" Galanör retorted, finding his feet again. "Don't get up!" he warned, seeing Alijah's hands pushing himself up. "You're only half-elf! You don't have what it takes to beat me!"

"Well..." Alijah said, his voice betraying his exhaustion, "You do have over four centuries on me, I'll give you that. But I have one thing you don't."

Galanör clenched his fists as he came to stand over him. "And what's that?" he asked, preparing to crack his opponent's neck.

"The power of a dragon flows through *my* veins!" Alijah twisted himself round and pushed his hands out, expelling a torrent of blinding magic directly into Galanör.

Only reflexes, honed over hundreds of years, kept the elf from being torn in two. Galanör's shield held up to the initial blast, but the power of it forced him back. His feet had no grip against the slippery floor and so he kept going until he was once again driven into the scorching glyphs. The impact and pain disrupted his concentration and he fell to his knees as the last of Alijah's spell spread up the side of the tower.

The silvyr came out of the ordeal without so much as a scratch - the same could not be said of Galanör. His palms burned and he felt an ache that went as deep as his bones. He had shielded himself against magical attacks before, but that was comparable to a dragon's breath. Looking through the gaps in his smoking hair, he spotted Alijah stalking towards him, his hands glowing from within.

"Damn you!" the half-elf cursed. "We're both going to need our magic if we're going to survive this!"

Galanör gritted his teeth and tilted his head to take in the top of the tower. He had no idea what was going to happen, but if draining Alijah of his magic decreased Alijah's chance of surviving, he was going to do whatever it took - even if it decreased his own chances of surviving.

The ranger stood up and hurled a spell under-arm without a hint of warning. The magic coalesced between them and took its true form in the shape of an icicle, its tip as sharp as any blade. Whether it would have pierced his armour or not, Alijah apparently wasn't taking the chance and erected a shield before him. The shield flared a multitude of colours as the icicle snapped on impact and bounced away in a myriad of shards.

Galanör wasn't going to give him an inch. Until his muscles gave way and his bones turned brittle from exertion, he would bombard Alijah with everything he had to give. Telekinetic blasts, balls of fire, spears of ice, and waves of lightning poured from Galanör's hands. Every attack was repelled, though the force of them pushed Alijah back a step, placing him well within the rainfall again.

By the seventh spell, Galanör's hands were numb, his fingers unresponsive. He roared with determination, pressing his attack, but the lightning from the storm was striking the inner walls and floor around them, drowning him out. One bolt tried to blind him, thundering into the silvyr beside him. Struggling to see his enemy, the elf swept his hand up and caught his discarded scimitars in a telekinetic wave. The swords whistled through the air and rain - which itself had been pushed back by the spell - only to be intercepted by Alijah's waiting shield. Still, it wore him down...

"Stop, Galanör," Alijah pleaded, raising his hand to block a jet of flames. "You're going to kill us both!"

The ranger could barely hear him and he couldn't say he cared much; this wasn't going to end until one or both of them were dead. The tenth spell, full of the elf's power and rage, dropped him to his knees inside the column of rain. How much more did he have to give? Galanör rid himself of the question and the biting doubt that accompanied it. Eventually, he couldn't tell if it was the relentless lightning strikes or the drain from his magic that diminished his sight.

He soon lost count of how many spells he had thrown at Alijah. His breathing had become laboured and he could hear blood pounding in his ears. A hard blink brought some of the world back into focus, but he was now looking directly up at Alijah. The half-elf snatched his hand, stopping him from aiming any further spells, and presented Galanör with an open palm brimming with flames.

With only seconds left to live, Galanör wondered if he had done enough to ensure Alijah died from whatever magic he had invoked inside the tower. He wouldn't live to find out, but he had to believe this was the case. He had to believe that he had done enough to save Aenwyn.

Then, all at once, the lightning ceased its blasting assault. There was no sound but for the rain on the floor.

Galanör looked up, beyond Alijah's face, and saw a spark of brilliant light in the middle of the rain. What followed was an instance of pain before the world slipped from his grasp...

CHAPTER 46
# VICTORY

D oran was getting sick of navigating the bodies that littered the battlefield. What disheartened him all the more, however, was the number of those bodies which belonged to his clan. A glance in any direction suggested there were more of his kin, and indeed elves, than Reavers lying in the sludge.

It boiled his blood.

Having now separated Andaljor into axe and hammer, the son of Dorain had entered a frenzy. His hammer broke legs, dropping enemies to their knees, and his axe parted limbs and heads with abandon.

Warhogs continued to ram their way through the fighting, though Doran never spared a second to see if Pig was among them. He trusted that wherever his loyal mount was, the animal would be spearing Reavers with his tusks and trampling over their corpses with glee. Either that or Pig had run away altogether - it was fifty-fifty in Doran's mind.

Since Morgorth's death, Russell Maybury had remained by the dwarf's side. Having hunted monsters together, and fought more than one battle shoulder-to-shoulder, their style of combat complemented each other. One would swing low, the other high, and Reavers would fall.

One such Reaver, its head still attached, crawled across the ground to grip Russell's leg. It had no legs of its own, but that wasn't enough to stop one of Alijah's fiends from seeing its task through to the end.

Russell's advance was stunted by the leach, causing him to miss his mark and open himself up to attack. He tried to shake the Reaver free from his leg while simultaneously defending himself against an incoming sword. The force of it knocked him off balance and the old wolf was sent down into the mud. One of the imprisoned dwarves, fighting for his life, accidentally kicked Russell in the face as he searched blindly for better footing.

Doran growled, launching spit across his beard. "Ye gonna get it now!"

He raised the hammer over his head and dropped it down with all his might, crushing the legless Reaver's head into the mud. Extending his axe across Russell's chest, he managed to block the sword before it cut his friend in half. Doran reversed the Reaver's attack and clipped its armour with the curve of his axe. Two more blows brought it down and relieved it of the burden Alijah had placed over it.

"Get yer arse out o' the mud!" Doran yelled, offering Russell a hand.

The old wolf accepted it and brought Doran's hammer with him. The dwarf gladly took it back, accustomed now to its weight. Russell flicked the haft of his pick-axe with his toes and grasped it in both hands.

"If this is how I die, Heavybelly, I'm glad it's fighting beside you!"

Doran wouldn't hear anything of dying today. "Ye jus' focus on yer swing, lad! Nothin' more!"

"Look!" Russell's yellow eyes were fixed on the top of the tower.

Doran shoved a fellow dwarf aside that had been knocked back into him and split the attacking Reaver's head in two. "What are ye talkin' abou'?" he demanded before turning his only eye to the storm.

The lightning had stopped pummelling the tower both inside and out. The black clouds continued to swirl overhead and spew rain by the ton. Then, starting from the edges of the storm, flickers of lightning danced inside the clouds until they met in the epicentre, directly over the tower. A single crack of lightning, far more powerful than anything the storm had previously produced, lashed out at the earth and disappeared inside the tower itself.

In the seconds that followed, everything changed. Dumbstruck, Doran looked across the battlefield and discovered that every Reaver on Qamnaran was standing still, frozen in their last pose. There was no way of knowing how long this would last for, but the son of Dorain wasn't going to waste the opportunity.

"*KILL THEM ALL!*" he boomed in dwarvish.

As one, the dwarves adopted Doran's frenzy and began hacking, slashing, and beating their enemy into the ground. Every dwarf still standing chopped down at least five Reavers each before Grarfath's generosity came to an end and the enemy regained their senses. Still, they had depleted their enemy's numbers to such a level that victory was on the horizon again.

"Doran!" Russell directed the War Mason to a narrow clearing in the battle. It led the dwarf straight to Lord Kraiden!

With a war cry on his lips, Doran ran towards the Dragon Rider, shoving his way past dwarves and hacking his way through Reavers.

He was going to enjoy this.

As he pushed his way past the last obstacle, he came face to face with the beast who had poisoned his brother and left him on the edge of death for nearly two years. Beyond Kraiden was the lip of the cliff and The Hox, its turbulent waves stretching across to the horizon. Doran barely took any of it in - how could he when the view was eclipsed by the death of King Gaerhard?

Some of the fight fled Doran's bones as he watched the Brightbeards' king and Bhan Doral's ruler slide off Lord Kraiden's jagged blade. The tip of that wretched sword came free of the king's throat and blood poured out, running down Gaerhard like a hellish waterfall. His eyes found the son of Dorain but there was no deciphering any last message as all life faded away. King Gaerhard, son of Hermon, found his end at Kraiden's feet...

Had Doran been able to think clearly in that moment, he would have seen what little chance there was of unifying the clans die with Gaerhard. As it was, he could only see red. Coherent thought evaporated in the burning light of his rage and he charged at Lord Kraiden.

The Dragon Rider took two steps back to take some of the sting out of Doran's initial attack. It also placed the combatants on the very edge of the cliff. Still, the son of Dorain gave it no heed - he had no fear of heights or even death right now: there was just him and the beastie that needed slaying.

Kraiden was nothing like his fellow Reavers. Retaining all his skills from life, he fought like a Dragon Rider, something Doran was quickly coming to dislike. His fighting style possessed a fluid motion to it that spoke of superior training and confidence born of many victories. There was also his blade to consider. As much as Doran wanted it, he had to work twice as hard to avoid even so much as a nick from its deadly edge, lest he follow in his brother's footsteps.

Tilting his head to the left, Doran just evaded the thrusting tip of that sword. It scraped across his pauldron before he batted it away with the flat of the hammer. A swing of his axe saw the Dragon Rider jump back along the cliff edge. His boot knocked loose a handful of pebbles and rocks, sending them down into the crashing waves.

"Now an' forever more, yer stinkin' head is goin' to adorn me saddle!"

Kraiden had no response but to sweep his jagged blade around and swipe at Doran's head. The dwarf parried the blow, only to realise the attack had been purposeful. The Dragon Rider planted a boot in his exposed chest and kicked him towards the edge of the cliff. What awaited him was a watery death. Of course, it always paid to have a werewolf for a friend.

Russell appeared from the periphery of the battle and gripped Doran's wrist just as his heels left the ground. With supernatural strength, Russell managed to heave the dwarf back, beating his momentum and substantial weight.

The son of Dorain hit the ground face first, his feet hanging over the edge of the cliff. Defying the rain, he looked up with a muddy beard and watched Russell stand between him and Kraiden. Doran tried to remind the old wolf that he needed the sword, but his words were lost in the ensuing fight.

Russell's pick-axe cut through the air and Kraiden shifted his shoulders one way then the next, avoiding the iron tip every time. When he pivoted from defence to attack, his jagged blade came at Russell like a dart, plunging at his vital areas with swift precision.

Doran groaned and fought against his aches - standing wasn't easy and his armour wasn't helping. Coming at Lord Kraiden from the side, the dwarf intended to hack through his leg and slow the fiend down. The Dragon Rider had anticipated such an action, however, and lifted his leg in time with Doran's swing. A quick back-hand beat the son of Dorain away, allowing Kraiden to focus on Russell alone.

Recovering with all haste, Doran turned back to renew the fight before his friend was overwhelmed. Kraiden brought his jagged blade down in both hands, a strike that would cut Russell open from head to groin. Stronger and faster than he looked, the old wolf raised his pick-axe horizontally and blocked the steel edge. The manoeuvre saved his life but his legendary weapon had slain its last monster: the haft snapped to the point that only a few splinters of wood kept it together.

The Dragon Rider drew his sword back, sawing through those remaining splinters, and prepared to gut Russell. Doran could see it all playing out as he charged at Kraiden from behind. He dropped Andaljor and leaped the last few feet to grapple the Reaver's arm before he could thrust. Now his weight played its part, proving too heavy for Lord Kraiden to stab or do anything but have his arm dragged down.

With two hands coiled around the Dragon Rider's wrist, Doran's back hit the ground and he kicked out, shoving one boot after another into Kraiden's face. Eventually, his helm and spiked crown was knocked free, revealing his nightmarish features. There was no nose to speak of and most of his left cheek was missing, though what skin remained was putrid and rotten. White eyes, devoid of life or beauty, stared down at Doran.

"Well aren' ye a pretty one!" the dwarf jested.

Russell grabbed Kraiden from behind and began pulling him in the opposite direction to Doran. The wrestle dragged them backwards and forwards through the mud and rain, none of them relenting their grip. Finally, the Dragon Rider threw his elbow over his shoulder and slammed Russell in the face, launching the old wolf towards the edges of the battle.

Rolling to one side, Doran broke Kraiden's wrist and the tendons that kept his fingers locked around the hilt. The War Mason simultaneously booted the Dragon Rider away and reached for the jagged blade. Rising to his feet with the prize in hand, Doran almost cried with glee. He had dreamed of possessing the blade since Dakmund had fallen ill and not a day had gone by that he wasn't plagued with doubt or despair.

Now it was his!

"I'm goin' to gut ye with yer own blade now!" Doran brandished the wicked sword, wondering how many times he was going to stab the fiend before chopping his ugly head off.

He lunged at the Dragon Rider, swiping first at his legs before backhanding at his midriff. Kraiden avoided both strikes, moving like a coiled snake. Doran's third and fourth strike were true, each one cutting through the undead creature. Unlike the sword's previous victims, this one was not only immune to pain, but also the poison. Doran didn't care. He just wanted to take chunks out of him.

Aiming for a gutting thrust, the son of Dorain prepared to ram his enemy right off the cliff. *Let the rocks smash his head in!* he thought.

With both hands behind the force, he plunged the jagged blade into Kraiden's chest and shoved him back, towards the edge. The Dragon Rider didn't bother fighting back until the balls of his feet were on the lip of the cliff. Doran quickly discovered that he didn't have the strength to finish the job. One step after another, Kraiden reversed their charge without an ounce of exertion on his gruesome face.

Finally, the Dragon Rider beat down on Doran's arms until he lost his grip on the hilt. A straight push-kick threw the dwarf onto his back, where he was forced to watch his enemy pull the blade free from his own chest.

The War Mason cursed and wearily found his way onto his feet again. "No bother!" he lied. "I'll jus' 'ave to take it from yer cold dead corpse!"

Lord Kraiden didn't attack as he should, a trait of all Reavers. Instead, he examined his blade and glanced back at Doran.

Then he tossed the weapon over the cliff.

"NO!" The son of Dorain watched his brother's only hope fly clear over the lip and disappear into the dark sea below.

Now it was gone...

Kraiden walked away and Doran dashed to the edge and searched frantically for any sign of it. Nothing. Just violent waves smashing into Qamnaran's western shore. Without the blade, there would be no identifying the poison and, without knowing the poison, there would be no cure for Dak.

The rain pelted Doran's face, masking the tears that streaked across his dirty cheek. The reach of his despair found new depths, plummeting him into emotional turmoil. He had but himself to blame - and one other. In that moment, the son of Dorain didn't know if his rage could ever be tempered again, but he knew where he would begin.

Turning back, he faced Lord Kraiden.

The Dragon Rider stared at him, expressionless. His wrist hung limply at his side, useless now. In his other hand he wielded a slender dagger. It wasn't intimidating, but Doran wasn't foolish enough to believe he couldn't be killed by such a pathetic piece of steel. He wanted to barrel into the fiend and bury him under his bulk. He would beat Kraiden with his bare fists until true death came to collect him.

But there was every chance that slender dagger would find its way between his armour and plunge into his ribs. Then, he wouldn't be able to take his grievances to Alijah, who was next on his list.

Unfortunately, the dwarf was too mad to formulate anything: his urge to kill and destroy too powerful. With no next move in mind, Doran broke into a short sprint and bellowed an incoherent threat at his foe. At the last second, before Kraiden could utilise the dagger in his hand, Doran spotted his hammer in the mud. He dived down, under the Dragon Rider's slashing strike, and rolled over the hammer, making sure to grasp it in both hands before jumping back up. Twisting on his heel, the dwarf brought Andaljor to bear with a mighty swing before releasing it into Lord Kraiden's face.

The Reaver's head whipped back with such force that the strands of his neck tore apart. Doran wrapped his hands around the back of Kraiden's knees and pulled hard, dropping the Dragon Rider into the mud.

"Doran!" Russell's cry preceded the axe he threw to the dwarf.

The son of Dorain caught the other half of Andaljor in one hand and dropped his knee into his enemy's chest. He wanted to savour the moment. Giving in to his urge, Doran drove the curve of the axe into Lord Kraiden's neck until the steel bit the ground.

It was over.

The foul magic that had given Kraiden a second life had lost its hold. But the Reaver wasn't the only one to have lost something this day. Doran tilted his head towards The Hox. How could he return to his mother now? How could he look her in the eye knowing his failure had doomed Dakmund?

His internal struggle came to a grinding halt when the very earth beneath him began to shudder. He heard bedrock cracking before the first fissure appeared, splitting the ground asunder. Returning to his full height, he turned to Russell questioningly.

"It's going to fall into the sea," the old wolf whispered. "It's going to fall into the sea!" he roared the second time. "Get back!" he warned, ushering the dwarves on the edge of the battle away from the coast.

Doran connected Andaljor into one weapon again and gripped Kraiden's head by the jaw - he was a dwarf of his word. "Get back!" he cried.

Looking out on the battle, there were barely any Reavers left now. Their unnatural pause during the final lightning strike had undone them. Now, elves and dwarves fled back from the towering cliff top, chopping down any stray Reavers who remained to challenge them.

It took the son of Dorain a few minutes before he realised something. "Where's Adilandra? Where's the queen?"

With Faylen and Aenwyn just behind her, Adilandra led the way up and round the winding ramp. Whether her bones were partially depleted or not, there was no ignoring it - she could feel it in the air - *magic*. It made her skin tingle, her hairs stand on end.

What had happened here?

As they reached the top of the ramp, their heads rose above the floor, allowing their eyes to catch up with their ears. Having only heard the rain, they could now see a thick column of it that ran from top to bottom. The chamber was surrounded with ancient glyphs, all of which held some kind of residual glow.

Before they could set one foot on the floor, the tower wobbled ever so slightly. Feeling the vibrations increasing beneath her feet, Adilandra looked questioningly at her oldest friend.

"Whatever magic has blasted this place," Faylen theorised, "I fear Qamnaran can no longer stand the tower's weight."

Adilandra couldn't even guess as to what spell had been enacted. Her concerns for Alijah's machinations faded fast when she spotted Galanör lying deathly still between the rain and the glyphs. Aenwyn cried his name and rushed to his side, beating the queen and Faylen.

"Is he alive?" Adilandra asked, her voice detached from her feelings for the moment.

"Yes!" Aenwyn exclaimed.

Adilandra took a breath, having not realised she had been holding it since sighting Galanör.

"Barely..." Faylen added, her voice just audible above the constant rain. "He needs the touch of healers, *now*."

Aenwyn stroked the side of his face as tears streaked down her own. "He will live," she stated boldly, as if challenging Death itself. "He's the strongest person I've ever met."

Adilandra was about to agree when she noted Faylen's gaze and the stiffness in her jaw. Following her eyes, the queen looked across the chamber, beyond the rain.

Alijah...

Her grandson was trying to get up, though his arms were shaking under his weight. "Get Galanör out of here," the queen commanded as the ground shook again.

"Adilandra." Faylen's tone questioned the queen's resolve.

"Get Galanör out," she repeated, not wishing to have an audience.

As Faylen and Aenwyn hooked Galanör's arms over their shoulders, Adilandra crossed the chamber and navigated around the rain. Alijah's right arm gave way beneath him and he fell flat to the floor. His dark cloak was soaking wet and twisted to one side.

"Dark magic takes its toll," she chided.

Alijah found the effort to roll onto his back and look up at her. His complexion was white as chalk and the veins under his skin created a black web. But Adilandra recognised those eyes. She had been present for his birth and that of his sister. She had seen him come into the world a babe and watched him grow into a beautiful boy, a boy who only ever wanted to help others, to be like his parents.

Her knuckles whitened as her grip tightened around the hilt of her scimitar. She had but to raise her arm and strike.

"Can you... do it?" he croaked, every word an effort.

"I should," Adilandra replied, her jaw tight.

"Then... do it."

"You think I won't?"

A crooked smile flashed across Alijah's face. "Love... gives you the strength to... transform *pain* into *power*. I understand this. But *your* love, Grandmother... it betrays you. It is misplaced. You are a queen... you should love the people... more than all others."

Adilandra could feel her heart breaking and the shards hardening. "You mock my love. But my love is the only reason you're still drawing breath."

"Then... do it. Misery and blood... have clung to our family for eons. Why should it stop now?"

The queen guided the curved tip of her blade to Alijah's neck. She could make it quick and painless. It was more than he deserved, but prolonging his death would haunt her for the rest of her days.

The ground shuddered again.

"You'll never get a better chance," Alijah told her, his hand edging across the floor to reach his Vi'tari blade.

"Don't," she warned, pressing steel to his neck.

"I won't stop," he continued, his last word almost lost when the tower physically moved and the ground cracked beneath the silvyr. "Do it!" he growled, as if some part of him truly wanted to die.

A single tear ran from each of Adilandra's eyes and she turned away, taking her scimitar with her. She cursed herself, her resolve, and her selfishness. Alijah had been twisted and left to rot inside - killing him would be a mercy. But she loved him... unconditionally - just like his mother.

Another quake threatened the tower's integrity and a monstrous, yet cowardly, thought entered Adilandra's mind. She didn't have it in her to kill her grandson, but maybe she did have it in her to leave him to his fate.

Absent the strength to do it herself, it was all that remained.

Looking back at him, she promised, "I will remember you as you were, before The Crow got his claws in you." More tears escaped her hard blink. "I love you, Alijah…"

The tower began to lean as Adilandra walked away. Putting one foot in front of the other was all she could do to reach the ramp. Try as she might, her memory refused to stop recalling every detail of Alijah's earliest years.

"Don't turn your back on me!" Alijah screeched.

Adilandra spun on her heel to see her grandson sprinting towards her, a face full of rage and his cursed blade held high over his head. He was even more powerful than she gave him credit for, a fact that greatly influenced her next action.

The queen's hand was a blur of movement, her fingers easily grasping the crystal from her belt. Now at a crossroads and with only seconds to choose a path, Adilandra played with Fate. To draw on the crystal would grant her a modicum of power, perhaps enough to see her survive until the tower buried them both. But that would mean Alijah's death. She required less than a second to realise that wasn't an option - he deserved a chance at redemption, a chance to see himself laid bare so that he might undo his dark plans.

That left her with one option.

She had poured into the crystal as much magic as she could before unleashing her essence on the Sandstalkers - it would have to do. A flick of the wrist launched the crystal at the floor between them. Adilandra felt a sharp pinch in her head as she used what remained of her magic to open a portal.

Alijah's speed worked against him, giving him no choice but to step into the nothingness. Adilandra saw the determination slip from his face, replaced immediately with panic. Unlike her, he had no idea what lay on the other side. Sadly, Adilandra knew it would be more darkness for the boy. But should he survive it, he might live to see the sun again.

Then he was gone, through the abyss.

Limited as her magic was, the portal closed the second Alijah was through it. The queen fell to her hands and knees in that same second. The world was closing in around her. Everything became dim and quiet. There was no fighting it any longer. Having pulled on the last thread of her magic, Adilandra closed her eyes and dreamed of playing with her grandchildren...

In the dwindling rain, Doran placed his boot on the Reaver's head and yanked Andaljor free. Russell was doing the same a few feet away, retrieving the two-handed hammer he had picked up from the battlefield.

They had done it. They had survived.

Looking around, there were hundreds of dwarves who had started the day as prisoners and were now free again. For all his personal loss, Doran took heart knowing they had liberated so many. And among them were his fellow Heavybellys, warriors all who had proven their mettle. Standing tall over them all were the surviving elves, an instrumental force in their victory. Morgorth would have crushed their attack were it not for the woodland folk.

Doran was patting one of the imprisoned dwarves on the back when a flash of blue light caught his eye. The lightning had ceased a while ago and so it drew his gaze, leading him to a patch of sky past the tower. It was much lower than the storm clouds but still high enough to be seen beyond the edge of Qamnaran's colossal edge.

Russell saw it too, his yellow eyes scrutinising the phenomenon. "It's Alijah," he observed, noting the black dot that fell from the flash.

"Alijah?" Doran questioned incredulously.

"He's just... falling."

Doran had never been stupid enough to challenge Russell's sharp eyes, but they both eventually lost sight of Alijah when he fell below the lip of the western cliff. Another object soon caught their attention, though this one was far larger and didn't require Russell's exquisite sight to identify. With mouth ajar, the son of Dorain watched Malliath the voiceless dive free of the clouds and plummet head first towards The Hox.

"What in all the hells has gone on in there?" the dwarf asked aloud.

Another earthquake rippled out from the base of the tower and sheets of rock fell into the sea. Doran's concern for the queen, Galanör, and Faylen was growing with every second. Looking around, he also couldn't see any sign of Aenwyn, leading the dwarf to wonder if she too was in peril.

"Look!" The owner of the voice was an elf, though Doran chose to follow everyone's gaze rather than search them out.

Emerging from the tower's entrance, two figures were trying to run with a third propped up between them. "Is it them?" Doran asked frantically.

"Aye!" Russell declared.

As much as the dwarf wanted to run towards them, he had no idea how much of the island was about to collapse into the sea. Deep cracks and chasms tore through the ground all around the tower, sending the flaming scaffolding into the waves.

Clearing what remained of the prisoners' camp, Faylen and Aenwyn came into focus with Galanör unconscious between them, his feet dragging through the mud. Exhausted as they were, the two elves were careful in the way they placed the ranger down.

"He's alive!" Aenwyn announced.

Doran looked desperately from one to the other. "Where's the queen? Where's Adilandra?"

With glassy eyes, her tears held back, Faylen turned to take in the tower.

"No…" Doran uttered.

At last, the island rid itself of the unnatural structure, toppling thousands of tons of silvyr into The Hox. The ground fell away one giant slab at a time until there was nothing left but a hole and a clear view of the ocean.

Now Faylen fell to her knees and let her tears flow freely. She wasn't alone. Every elf still on their feet began to grieve, their faces turned to the sky. Doran stumbled away and let Andaljor slip from his grasp. They had rescued countless dwarves from slavery, defeated the superior numbers of their enemy, and left Alijah and his dragon to the sea, their fate yet unknown.

But…

Kraiden's blade was gone, sealing his brother's fate. King Gaerhard had been slain and with him the hope of piecing Dhenaheim back together. And now Adilandra was gone, entombed in The Hox for all time.

If this was the price for winning the battle, he didn't want to know the cost of winning the war…

# CHAPTER 47

# ORIGINS

It was a cold dawn in Erador. Though rays of golden light pierced the rolling clouds, the land felt naught but the touch of winter, its cool light settling over the realm as snow drifted in the icy breeze. Seen from the sky, the green trees were steadily fading to white, creating a stark vista as blank as an unsullied canvas.

For nearly two days, Inara had watched Erador embrace winter from the comfort of a lofty vantage and warm scales beneath her. There was so much to see below and Athis did his best to call on Rainael's memories to inform her of the landmarks. Beautiful and fascinating as it all was, the Guardian of the Realm struggled to appreciate any of it.

After flying north from The Tower of Jain, they had topped the peaks of Erador's mountainous spine and passed into Akmar. Athis had informed Inara that the land belonged to the Andarens and their silver trees, but she had still felt the sting of betrayal, giving the region barely a glance.

Gliding over the northern cliffs that overlooked The Silver Trees of Akmar, they crossed The Red Fields of Dunmar. A colourful oasis left by the deaths of so many dragons, it had been partially concealed by the falling snow. Still, the parts that hadn't been turned into mass excavations by Alijah were undeniably winsome.

Yet Inara thought only of Gideon and his confession...

Now, with time and land behind them, Inara had let enough of the initial sting go to think clearly. Athis had counselled her most of the way and continued to offer her guidance before they reached their final destination.

*You forgave me,* the dragon pointed out.

**Gideon is not you,** Inara was quick to reply. She could feel Athis searching her depths and she didn't stop him, grateful to have someone who could understand her so completely.

*I believe you would have done the same,* he concluded.

Inara had considered that repeatedly on their flight. She wanted desperately to say that she would never have allowed such deceit, but the words hadn't fully formed in her mind yet.

**Perhaps,** she finally conceded.

*Focus on what really matters, wingless one. Though deceived, no Dragorn was ever harmed by their dragon's influence. The same could be said of the people, who knew nothing but their protection. Gideon had the weight of the world on his shoulders.*

Inara couldn't disagree with that. She had no idea of the hardships he went through to rebuild the entire order with both humans *and* elves - it hadn't been done before.

*I think you agree with Gideon's decision,* Athis continued. *What truly hurts you?* he asked, already aware of the answer.

Inara didn't want to say, but there was no shame or embarrassment where Athis was concerned. **He lied to me,** she admitted.

*As did I,* Athis said, bringing her back to the matter of forgiveness. *It takes greater magnitudes of strength to forgive than it does to hate. You have loved Gideon Thorn since before we met. Do not let that love turn to dust.*

In her earliest life, Inara had seen Gideon as a hero, an idol to look up to, and a father figure, despite the long shadow cast by her real father. After becoming a Dragorn, he quickly became a mentor to which there could be no equal, his wisdom and leadership beyond all others. After she passed the trials he had grown into something akin to a big brother. Her love for him had changed through the years, but it was love all the same.

*I will talk to him,* she promised.

Athis probed her mind further. *I feel a great unrest in you. Something beyond your quarrel with Gideon.*

Inara took a breath and glanced at Asher over her shoulder. She was just delaying her response in truth, but she also took the time to look west and see Ilargo. He appeared strong again, his muscles filled out and his claws as sharp as ever. He glistened with the faintest of golden specks that dusted his green scales. On his back, Gideon and Adan'Karth looked to be discussing some matter or another, each equally interested in the other.

*We're heading into a new world, Athis,* Inara finally began. *I'm not sure I like it. Our bond is different, our lives no longer bound together as they once were. Now Gideon and Ilargo share the same fate, yet so many others in Dragons' Reach know nothing of it. I know they're happy, but it bothers me.* She scrunched her eyes, frustrated with her own feelings.

*I don't remember emotions being so damned complex. A part of me craves the past, when you influenced my morality and I had no idea. And another part of me is so thankful, as if I knew all along that I had been missing a part of my life. I want both.*

Athis sighed, sharing her desires. *What is done cannot be undone, wingless one. We should both embrace our bold new future. Though we do not live by their code, we are as the Dragon Riders once were...*

Athis banked to the north-west, giving Inara a head-on view of Drakanan. She pushed herself up to see the ancient dwelling in all its glory. For the moment, her turbulent emotions were put aside.

This was where it all began.

The mountain range that housed Drakanan disappeared into the north-west, stretching further than either Inara or even Athis could see. Drakanan itself, the home of the Dragon Riders, resided inside the eastern face of the mountains. An enormous gorge pushed through, creating an expansive path that led to a variety of archways, platforms, and levels dug in and out of the rock face.

Having descended to come in line with the gorge, gargantuan statues took shape on either side of the path: heralds that spoke of the warriors who had once held order here. Giant chunks of them were missing, robbing Inara of their exquisite detail, but their heroic stances and broken weapons told her she was among the ruins of heroes.

Smaller statues lined the path beyond the gorge's entrance. Inara was immediately curious, her inherent wonder sparked past control. Were they famous Riders or simply statues to aspire to? How many had walked the road between them, heading into a future filled with adventure and dragons?

Through Athis, she could see his imagination filling the expanse with dragons of every colour, shape, and size. He fantasised of his kin, saddled and plated in armour, gliding between the gorge and diving off the platforms. There were also hundreds of Riders scattered throughout his reverie, going about their training and daily lives.

Perhaps those had been simpler times, she mused.

Picking up on her thoughts, Athis said, *I think every generation believes there were simpler times. All have known hardship, from the dawn of the world I'm sure. What defines them is their will to overcome such hardships and forge a better tomorrow.*

Inara smiled and patted him on the scales. She would forever adore his outlook.

Ilargo swooped in from above and assumed the lead, guiding Athis in and down towards the curved end of the gorge. There were many levels from top to bottom that disappeared into the gloom of the mountain. Inara wished to know where they all led and what secrets lay within, her thirst for adventure never far from the surface.

Both dragons touched down on the flat ground, their claws adding imprints to the land where thousands of others had once left theirs. Inara jumped down with Asher close behind. Her boots crunched in the snow as she walked further ahead and spun in a slow circle to see it all. Drakanan towered over them from all sides but the east, its walls far higher than even Namdhor's apex.

As cold and forgotten as it all was, Drakanan was beautiful.

Asher strode past her only to stop ten feet away and crouch down. The ranger shifted the satchel he had filled with food and water and placed his hand into the snow, a grim expression creasing his face.

"We're not alone," he warned.

Inara moved to join him and soon discovered the same tracks that had attracted Asher. "Boot prints," she concluded.

"Human boot prints," Asher added, rising to look back at Gideon.

"The Red Guard," Gideon began. "The reason there were so few at the tower was because Alijah had them come here."

"What for?" Inara asked.

"To continue his work. He believes there is a doorway inside these walls and he obviously had no plans for The Red Guard in Illian. He's probably forgotten about them..."

That wouldn't have surprised Inara - her brother had become accustomed to using everyone and everything to achieve his goals.

"This is fresh," Asher observed, his blue eyes scanning the numerous tiers. "Whoever left this was standing here only minutes ago."

"They're probably watching us," Inara reasoned.

Gideon joined them in searching the shadows. "They won't attack us while we're in the presence of Ilargo and Athis." The Master Dragorn adjusted Mournblade on his hip. "Come. What we seek is this way."

Inara fell in beside Adan and followed behind Gideon and Asher. Ilargo and Athis guarded them from the rear, trailing the companions at what was a leisurely pace for a dragon. Through her bond, Inara could sense Athis's apprehension as they walked under the ceiling of the first tier and entered the shadows. He wasn't afraid, an emotion rarely expressed by the dragon, but he had always distrusted what he didn't know, and Drakanan was nothing if not a mystery.

Except for Adan, the rest of the companions each retrieved a torch from the wall and used the flames to show them the way. Gideon moved with confidence, sure of the way. Inara tried to keep her eyes on the various passages that cut through the hewed stone, but her attention was captured again and again by the magnificent carvings, faded stone murals, and tired sculptures that came out of the walls. They were all telling their own story or perhaps historical facts, none of which made sense to the Guardian.

*You could spend years exploring this place,* Athis said with some amusement.

Inara smiled up at him, happy to hear his voice in this empty place. He was also right, of course: she would willingly spend decades exploring Drakanan's ancient halls. Though her roots were based in the ways of the Dragorn, the Dragon Riders were the origin of them all.

"Their origins seems steeped in violence," Adan remarked, as if he had been reading Inara's thoughts. "Every piece of imagery depicts a battle. I see death in them all."

Gideon glanced back over his shoulder before taking in some of the stone murals. "The Dragon Riders were nothing like the Dragorn - the same could be said of their dragons too. Elandril, and the elves who began the Dragorn order, considered themselves peacekeepers. They were slow to wield their Vi'tari blades, preferring their roles as deterrents." Gideon took a breath. "The Dragon Riders had a different code. They were warriors all. They lived by the sword and flame. Their dragons didn't look for empathy in their Riders as *we've* known. Instead, they looked for those who mirrored their own heart, a predator's heart.

"Throughout history their allegiance to Valgala's kings and queens kept them in perpetual war with multiple factions. In some ways, their lives were much simpler than any known by the Dragorn.

Personally, I think they could have shown some restraint and counselled Erador's rulers a little better. But the foundations were there. Over the past few years, I've come to the conclusion that something between the two orders would serve the realm as it deserves."

Inara stared at the back of Gideon's head. She could hear it in his words - there was more than just musings to his tone.

*Perhaps he does have grand plans for the order after all,* Athis chimed in, detecting all that she had.

*No,* Inara replied, thinking of the banishment that applied to all four of them. ***Those are just the dreams of someone who knows they're to be alone forever. Just like us...***

"Here it is," Gideon announced.

They came to a halt in front of a neck-craning archway blocked by two stone doors. The surface of the doors presented them with interlocking patterns, carved from the stone itself. Throughout the mural were several dragon heads decorated with ancient script.

Not one to be distracted by ancient marvels, Asher was drawn to the details that escaped Inara's first glance. "They're close." The ranger was inspecting the remains of a small camp off to the side. A small pot centred between four bed rolls was still steaming, its contents only now finding Inara's nose.

Ilargo and Athis each turned in a different direction and began sniffing the air, their heads low. Inara knew before the others that Athis had picked up the scent of at least five different humans, though they remained to be seen.

Recognising the look of a dragon who had caught the scent of their prey, Gideon turned to look down the shadowed tunnel to their right. "Alijah always made certain The Red Guard couldn't use magic. They only possess steel." He looked up at the red dragon. "Like I said; they won't bother us."

"You believe this doorway lies beyond?" Inara questioned, gesturing to the giant slabs blocking their way.

"We explored much of Drakanan - these were the only doors we couldn't open." Gideon traced a hand across the stone. "It would make sense. They have to be at least two-feet thick and the chamber on the other side would be at Drakanan's heart: the perfect place to keep a secret safe from the outside world."

Asher ran his torch over the doors, scrutinising every detail. "Were Dragon Riders known for their strength?"

Gideon gestured casually at Inara. "They were stronger than the average human, like us."

Asher rapped his knuckles against the stone. "Then they weren't opening these with their hands. There must be a mechanism, a weighted system perhaps, that moves them. We just need to find what triggers it."

"Not necessarily," Inara disagreed. "If there is a doorway in there, or at least something they didn't want anyone to find, there's every chance these doors weren't meant to be opened."

"Then why not build a wall instead?" Asher countered, stumping Inara.

In the absence of her reply, Gideon resumed the lead. "Alijah and I scoured every inch of the doors and the walls too. We didn't find anything to suggest there was a mechanism, though I agree there must be one." The Master Dragorn turned to the one he believed was their only hope. "Adan?"

Walking between them, Adan'Karth approached the doors in silence. His reptilian eyes worked their way up and down the stone, absorbing every detail. Inara didn't doubt that he was also seeing details they couldn't. They all watched him, giving the Drake his time, as he placed the palm of his hand against the door. His sharp nails rested gently in the curves of the intricate patterns.

"What do you see?" Asher asked, illuminating half of the Drake in torchlight.

"It's what I *don't* see that interests me," he replied ominously. "You said this doorway could only be made from a very concentrated place of magic..."

"Yes," Gideon answered. "It would have to be powerful enough to bridge both realms - at least that's what the Jainus claimed."

"There are currents of magic everywhere," Adan continued, his gaze drifting to the darkness. "But I neither see nor sense any around or behind these doors." His hand floated away from the stone and appeared to caress something that simply wasn't there. "There are powerful strands within the currents, but they disappear into several passages."

Inara looked from the nearest passage to the archway before them. "You're suggesting these doors are…what? A misdirection?"

"Of course," Asher said, the subtle hint of revelation behind his words. "This is what they wanted us to find. If you were hiding a secret your enemy already knew about, wouldn't you keep them busy elsewhere?"

Gideon looked at the doors with new eyes. "A misdirection," he echoed. "How could I miss that possibility? There's probably nothing but more stone behind here."

"We should follow the strands," Inara suggested, looking to Adan'Karth.

"There are too many," he replied. "Countless dragons called Drakanan home for millennia. We could be searching these halls for years."

"We don't even have days," Asher cut in. "We split up. Two go that way and two go that way." He pointed to both passages that led off from either side of the doors, neither of which were made with dragons in mind.

"That's exactly what our enemy wants," Gideon pointed out.

Asher drew his two-handed broadsword. "That's what I brought this for…"

Seeing only as far as the torchlight would allow, Inara kept her wits about her as well as Firefly in her hand. She hadn't been pleased to leave Athis behind, but she had been even less pleased when Asher paired off with Adan, leaving her with Gideon.

Together, they explored in silence, side by side. The tension between them was so palpable that even Athis complained of it. Deciding it would be best to focus on her issue with Gideon, Inara quietened that part of her mind where Athis existed, amplifying her human side. Without the dragon's natural calm, her emotions washed over like a tidal wave, increasing her grip around Firefly's hilt.

"You could have trusted me," she blurted a little louder than intended. "I understand why you kept the truth to yourself; I can't imagine the weight of it all. If you had told me... I think I would have agreed, for the sake of the realm."

Gideon dared to take his eyes from the passage and glance at her for just a second. "No you wouldn't," he replied with a hint of pride behind his words. "You have a better sense of morality than me - you always have. I could see the virtue in you as a child and I envied it then as I do now." He came to a stop and faced her. "I don't say those things because you are a Galfrey, I say those things because you are Inara, the Guardian of the Realm. You would have commanded every dragon to reveal the truth of their bond, their influence, and you would have been right to. We were following in the footsteps of an order made by elves *for* elves. It was never going to work..."

They naturally fell back into a steady exploration, their torches moving up and down the walls in search of new doorways.

"Thank you," Inara said quietly, appreciating his words and the sincerity behind them. "You know, if you had come to me, I would have journeyed to Erador with you. I... I would have followed you to the end of the world."

Half a smile pulled at Gideon's cheek. "I know you would. That's why I didn't come to you. I know it's hard to truly see oneself, so I will tell you what you cannot see." He came to another stop by the corner of a junction. "You are not meant to follow," he continued, pride now visible on his face as well as in his voice. "You are a warrior, a protector, and most certainly a leader. I don't know what your future holds, but I know people will be following you, not the other way around."

Inara averted her eyes from his, a touch of embarrassment flushing her cheeks. Her frustration towards Gideon was steadily melting away. Instead, she was reminded that her old mentor had spent years imprisoned and tortured, his mind and body broken repeatedly. And it was all because he feared for the people, even those of Erador whom he knew nothing about.

He was a good man.

"I'm sorry," she began. "I have been—"

"On your own path," Gideon interjected. "I'm sorry if you felt abandoned to that path. All these years, I have only hoped that you knew the reason I willingly left you in Illian was because I believed in you. Of all of us, you were the only one who *could* stay behind and watch over the people."

Inara reached out and embraced Gideon, careful not to burn either of them with her torch. "I missed you."

Gideon embraced her back. "Not as much as I missed you..."

They parted and continued their search with a new air between them, though the air they were breathing was incredibly stale. Every few hundred yards they were presented with new passages and murals. Signs in the ancient language marked the walls but Inara could only translate a single glyph in every other word. There was definitely nothing that read, *magic tree door this way.*

Inara couldn't help but think of Gideon and Alijah doing exactly as they were doing now - a very odd image. "What was the last thing you talked about - you and Alijah?"

Gideon made to speak but, instead, took a breath. "That was some time ago," he recalled. "It was an argument, perhaps our worst."

Her interest piqued, Inara asked, "What were you arguing about?"

"Between residing in my cell and studying in the library, I had a lot of time to *think*. There was one thought that scratched at the inside of my skull incessantly. After giving it quite some thought, I finally spoke it aloud to Alijah. He raged, reflecting the darkness that lives inside Malliath. We argued, then there was pain, and then he was gone. That was the last time I saw him."

"What was the thought?"

Gideon came to a halt at a crossroads between passages, his torch moving from one side to another. At last, he stopped looking for the next route and turned a serious gaze on Inara. With his scraggy hair tied back and beard trimmed, the small scars Alijah had inflicted were easier to see in the torchlight.

"What if we got it all wrong?" he said. "What if Alijah had it all wrong?"

"I don't understand," Inara confessed.

"I think The Crow lied to us." Gideon paused, allowing his words to sink in. "What if—" He cut himself short at the sound of a distant cry.

Inara's superior hearing picked up the distinct voice. "It's Asher," she told him. "I think they've found it…"

Gideon's face fell. "We should go to them!" he declared eagerly.

"Wait," Inara called, trailing after him. "What were you saying?"

Gideon slowed down just enough to keep them at a light jog. "I'll tell you everything, I promise! There will be time. But first I need to see it."

His answer displeased Inara, but she was disciplined enough to prioritise. They dashed from passage to passage, following the sound of Asher's call. At times, the echo threw them off and they were forced to backtrack. When the ranger's voice was crystal clear, they turned left and entered a tall chamber supported by two rows of pillars. There was a set of open double doors at one end and a stone mural at the other, its imagery filling every inch of the wall from floor to ceiling.

Standing in front the mural, Asher and Adan'Karth were inspecting the depiction of a dragon's claw. "He thinks this is it," the ranger said.

Adan waved his hand slowly over the stone. "There is magic radiating from within," he confirmed.

Gideon looked it up and down. "I have seen this before. Alijah and I studied it briefly, but we were hoping the imagery would reveal an element of the truth. We saw no way of opening it."

Inara looked it up and down. "That's because it's a wall..."

Asher crouched down by the mural and poked the tip of his finger down the gap that ran along the crease between floor and wall. Inara watched him follow that narrow gap and noted herself that it didn't run the entire length of the wall.

"I think there's a door here," he remarked. "You see this gap? It's possibly a hole in the floor where a segment of the mural descends."

Inara narrowed her eyes at the giant picture, searching for lines that might reveal the seams of any door. The imagery, however, was busy, telling the story of a battle between the dragons and a terrifying Leviathan.

"We examined everything in here," Gideon said. "Even the pillars. There's no obvious lever of mechanism."

As everyone cast their eyes around the chamber, Adan studied the wall. "Perhaps there is no lever, no mechanism." His words drew them back to him. "Perhaps it can only be opened by those who *can* open it..."

It seemed that both Inara and Gideon understood the Drake at the same time. "Could it be that simple?" Inara asked.

Some amusement flashed across Gideon's face. "I asked myself that same question before claiming Mournblade." He turned to look at Inara. "Together then?"

The Guardian joined him by his side, facing the mural. "Together."

As one, they reached out towards the centre of the wall and gripped the stone with their magic. It was stubborn, locked into place by eons of disuse. Inara drew on some of the power stored in the crystal on the end of her pommel. It was subtle to begin with - the slightest sound of grinding rock. Then, at last, it began to shift, running down into the floor in four columns. Judging by the size of the columns, it was going to offer them a doorway no wider than the one at the other end of the chamber.

Four resounding booms bounced off the walls as the columns fitted into place below their feet and became a part of the floor. Inara recovered almost instantly from the minor exertion, but Gideon required an extra second to wipe a bead of sweat from his brow. In time, Inara knew, he would recover some more of his strength where magic was concerned - he simply hadn't used it enough since his imprisonment.

Asher looked into the void that lay beyond the doorway, untouched by their torches. Beside him, Adan wavered on his feet and reached out for support against the wall. Inara stepped in and steadied the Drake who thanked her with a tight smile.

"The magic emanating from inside is... overwhelming."

Inara could feel it too, though clearly not to the same extreme as Adan. There was an unseen wave rippling over her skin, standing her hairs on end, and a tingle in the end of her fingers, as if a spell was itching to be set free. It was also unusually warm inside considering the rest of Drakanan had been so cold they could see their breath on the air.

"If we step through there," Asher posed, "are we going to end up... somewhere else?"

"There's only one way to find out," Gideon asserted, turning to Inara. "You lead, I follow."

With her torch held out in one hand and Firefly in the other, Inara passed over the threshold and into the shadows. Her heart was drumming with anticipation. Until a few moments ago, she had firmly believed Gideon's, and indeed Alijah's, theory to be based on naught but the fantasies of an ancient lunatic. But here it was, a secret door that could only be opened by those who could wield magic.

One foot over the threshold and her heartbeat reached new heights and her muscles tensed as an ancient spell was triggered.

Firefly came up and she dropped into a defensive stance. There was no attack, however. One by one, pyres and torches came to life revealing an enormous chamber that rose up like a one of the amphitheatres in Velia.

Inara's mouth fell open.

Firefly hung limply by her side and she moved her head to better see the curved chamber, its great height demanding Inara crane her neck. Behind her, Gideon, Asher, and Adan'Karth stood similarly frozen, their eyes lost to the chamber's contents. Even the ranger, who had the same reaction to almost everything, stared in wonder and amazement.

"It's not a doorway," she uttered.

Gideon beamed from ear to ear and said one word. "Eggs." His statement was followed by a light chuckle. "Dragon eggs!" He walked past Inara and turned left and right to see them all. "Hundreds of them! I can't believe it..."

Inara marvelled at the nearest row of dragon eggs resting on pedestals, each one a different colour and size. They were beautiful. Some could fit in her hand while others would clearly require two hands to heft. Some were shiny, as if they had been polished, and some were dull with bright speckles covering their scaled exteriors.

Steps had been carved and led up to the higher tiers, all with paths between that disappeared behind rocky outcroppings. There were potentially hundreds more they couldn't see from their vantage.

*I wish I could see them with my own eyes,* Athis whispered, his tone too soft to spoil the moment.

With glassy eyes, Inara blinked fresh tears down her cheeks, mirroring Gideon. This was the last thing she had expected them to find.

The eggs weren't the only things to surprise the companions. What could only be described as broken shards of mirror, each as large as any man, glided through the air. Others remained stationary, rooted to the spot by some unseen force. Their edges were always moving, changing the overall shape of the shards, but their interiors weren't transparent at a glance.

Inara turned to the broader chamber and discovered that some were even passing over the eggs. When seen on edge, they were practically invisible to the eye, thinner than a blade of grass.

Gideon crouched down and closely examined a silver coloured egg, his hands hovering around its shell. "This is a bonding chamber," he announced to an audience of confused faces. "Like me, you bonded with Athis upon meeting him - that's how every Dragorn bonded with their dragon. But unlike the Dragorn, the Dragon Riders of old were *called* to their dragons while they were still in their eggs. Their bond was fully formed right here in this room. They had to take the egg and care for their dragon from infancy." Gideon was shaking his head with a broad smile. "I can't believe this is still here..."

"Inara!" Adan's tone spoke of immediate danger and his eyes flashed over her shoulder.

Inara whipped her head around to see one of the jagged shards floating towards her. The Guardian quickly stepped back and tilted her head to avoid interacting with it. Besides the near collision, the phenomenon made no attempt to attack her.

As the shard rotated around, Inara narrowed her eyes at the image that rested between its jagged outline. It soon rotated again, taking the image with it, but she had been sure it held the image of a white tree...

"This *is* a doorway," she concluded.

"I think you're right," Gideon replied, getting a good look inside another shard. "It must be the number of eggs. Their proximity, their *potential*. They've..." Gideon struggled to find the right word. "It looks like they've *torn* through one realm and into another. Incredible."

"So it's real then," Inara reasoned. "The tree. Alijah can actually rid the world of magic."

Gideon shrugged. "We only have half an answer." He gestured to the nearest shard passing between two rows of eggs. "I think the proof lies just beyond."

Inara knew what she was going to do, what she *had* to do. Looking over her shoulder, the Guardian made certain that Asher, who had a good instinct for the impulses of those around him, wasn't going to stop her from doing something so rash. She quickly realised he wasn't going to get in her way, still wildly distracted by the spectacle before them. She had never seen the ranger in such a trance, but she wasn't going to waste her opportunity.

*Inara...* Athis's voice carried a warning.

In one fluid motion, she dropped her torch, sheathed Firefly on her hip, and ran up the closest set of steps. Gideon called out as Athis did, but her timing was perfect, her dive bringing her into alignment with a floating shard.

Then she was gone.

Gideon's voice sounded distant to Asher, as if the Master Dragorn was calling to him through a storm. It took Adan's strong hand on his arm to break his reverie and bring the ranger back into the present. The reality of his surroundings was dizzying, a most unsettling feeling for a man who prized himself on being in command of his environment.

Where had he been?

Adan's unusual eyes bored into the ranger's until he shook his head and the Drake away. The first thing he noticed had him reaching for his sword.

"Where's Inara?" he demanded.

Gideon's brow furrowed. "Didn't you see? She just jumped through one of these things!"

Asher wanted to chastise the man for allowing her to do such a thing, but who among them could really stop Inara Galfrey from doing anything? "Well where is she?" he growled.

Gideon's shoulders sagged. "I think she's on the other side."

"Can she come back?" Asher stormed across the chamber to join the Master Dragorn.

"I have no idea. I don't have all the answers, Asher."

"You had enough answers to get us here," the ranger retorted.

Gideon looked from one shard to another. "The Jainus who described the tree must have come back otherwise we wouldn't even know about it."

Asher drew his broadsword. "I'm not going back to Illian to tell Reyna and Nathaniel they've lost their daughter too."

"Asher," Adan'Karth called, his voice low and ominous.

The ranger didn't like the trepidation he heard. With Gideon, he turned around and laid eyes on a dozen Red Guards, their crescent blades already in hand. They remained as still as the eggs that filled the chamber, though their eyes were firmly fixed on their quarry. Naturally, Adan slowly drifted up the steps, away from the entrance and those that blocked the way.

Alijah's cult finally moved when another entered the chamber, emerging from the darkness with a flowing red cloak and black robes. Unlike the others, he wore the most unusual helmet Asher had ever seen. A single slit revealed the man's eyes, but the helm itself rose up from his head and stretched flat over his shoulders as if he wore a slender anvil.

This strange figure came to a halt between the Red Guards and the companions, his scythe hammering the ground beside him. He said something in his native tongue, but Asher knew a threat when he heard it, regardless of the language.

Judging by Gideon's clenched jaw, white knuckles, and dark gaze, the Master Dragorn had understood enough to come to the same conclusion. It also seemed there was some history between the two.

"Old friend?" the ranger enquired innocently.

Gideon dropped his torch and drew Mournblade. "This is *The*

*Inquisitor*, The Red Guard's auspicious leader. He oversaw much of Ilargo's time in the tower..."

The notion of killing one's torturer wasn't lost on Asher. "Fine. You take him and the five on the right. I'll take the seven on the left - don't get greedy."

The ranger pulled free his broadsword and leaped over the lowest row of dragon eggs while Gideon dived into The Inquisitor. Blood and screaming were soon to follow. Asher was more than accustomed to fighting opponents who favoured dual weapons and he was even more accustomed to fighting a better class of foe. Arakesh The Red Guards were not...

Still, they had the numbers and Asher knew better than to approach any fight believing he was invincible. He killed the first two with relative ease, neither having faced an enemy with quite so many fighting styles. The remaining five worked better together and forced the ranger to ascend the nearest steps. Out of the corner of his eye, he saw Adan retreat to an alcove on the far side of the chamber, his agility and climbing expertise more than enough to see him scale the rock.

Gideon was dominating the flat ground by the entrance. His Vi'tari blade had lain dormant for too long and its recent taste of action had it craving more. Gideon's seething rage was easily noted in his aggressive forms and the way his scimitar kept him on the attack. Three of Alijah's cult were already lying on the ground, their pools of blood merging.

The Inquisitor displayed a quality of skill that outshone the others, but his scythe was no match for a blade that had been killing monsters for five thousand years. Gideon came down with a two-handed hammer strike, splitting the scythe in half. A swift kick to the gut pushed The Inquisitor back through the entrance and into the antechamber. That would have left Gideon with only two to dispatch, but another four poured in from the shadows, replacing their leader.

Asher fell into the rhythm he knew so well and danced about his enemies, confusing them. Half of their blows missed him completely while the other half were easily deflected and countered. By the third tier of the chamber, he was facing three of the five, having left the other two strewn across the steps.

With every kill, however, the ranger noticed his hearing was diminishing. The world around him became dulled, its edge taken away and with it the sound of battle. The clash of his own blade, only a foot away from his face, sounded distant, as Gideon's voice had.

The ranger couldn't help but wonder if he had been poisoned...

After parrying one of them, he shifted his shoulders and narrowly avoided the swing of the second. It was only once the blade was beyond his ability to block that Asher realised he had left the eggs behind him vulnerable. The tip of the man's crescent weapon came down on a violet egg and the ranger flinched, sure that he was about to see a baby dragon sliced in half.

The sound of the blade hitting the egg was akin to steel clashing with steel. The egg fell to the ground and rolled away, unharmed, while the Red Guard examined his broken sword.

Asher shrugged, impressed with the little egg. Then he swung his blade, taking most of the man's chest with it. The last threw himself at the ranger, perhaps believing that sheer force would be enough to overpower him. His hearing now entirely gone, Asher brought his spiked pommel to bear and dropped the Red Guard with a broken skull for his efforts.

On the flat ground, Gideon was vastly outnumbered and The Inquisitor had returned with two crescent blades to replace his scythe. Without pausing to investigate his lack of hearing, Asher moved to help the Master Dragorn. He didn't make it down the first set of steps before a wave of dizziness almost took him off his feet.

The ranger cursed, though he couldn't hear the words. What was happening to him? When could he have been poisoned? He tried to correct his posture and put himself on course to join Gideon, who was being forced out of the chamber. Then the voices hit him - whispers from inside his own head. Asher dropped his sword and covered his ears but it did him no good. There were only the whispers, and the sound of his heart beating furiously in his chest.

Inara dared not move a muscle.

***Athis?*** she called out in her mind. Nothing.

Though the fundamentals of the world around her made sense, none of it was, indeed, of *her* world. She was standing in water up to her ankles and it was undoubtedly water: its look, smell, and temperature all very familiar. The air she breathed kept her alive and felt just as fresh as Verda's air.

The sky, though above her head, was unlike anything she had ever seen. Beautiful waves of greens and purples washed over a palette of stars, all of which appeared to be moving like flies. From certain angles, in fact, it actually looked like the sky was made from stalactites, speckled with dancing stars.

The ground crunched beneath her feet, drawing her attention back to the water. Crouching down, her red cloak became soaked as she scooped up the glittering rocks.

Crystals. There were thousands of crystals just like the ones she had spent hours creating in her own reality. A few seconds after removing them from the water, however, they lost their spectacular shine, their inner light fading away. Inara let them fall through her fingers and return to the water.

She looked over her shoulder and watched the shard she had come through drift away, carrying images of the bonding chamber within. Similar shards were dotted around, just as they had been in Drakanan. She recognised the images she saw in most of them, but some revealed new places where magic had formed a bridge, places she knew nothing about. Suddenly, Verda felt immensely bigger than Inara had previously believed it to be.

Looking past the shards, there was nothing but a shallow ocean as far as the eye could see. Of course, there were the roots. Inara was standing between them, but to follow any one was to get lost in the never-ending distance. Following them back to their source proved much easier, though no less unsettling.

Inara craned her neck to take in a tree that was more comparable with a mountain. Its bark was as white as snow and its leaves were a vibrant red. She had to wonder if its roots stretched out across the whole realm...

Finding her courage, Inara stepped over and between the twisting roots to approach the tree. Walking under a low-hanging branch, the Guardian paused to scrutinise one of the *leaves*. Hesitant to touch it, she reached out and caressed its surface between her fingers. It was like no leaf she had ever felt before. To her understanding, it was a crystal shaped like a red maple leaf. It was also very warm, uncomfortably warm in fact.

Releasing the leaf, Inara continued her approach and made for the trunk. So large was it that she could no longer make out its curves, giving the trunk a flat appearance. Cautiously, the Guardian placed the flat of her hand against the white bark. It was as cold as ice.

Inara covered her mouth in disbelief of it all. Her mind struggled to comprehend what her senses were telling her.

Magic had a source and this was it...

Stepping back from the tree, a weight of responsibility came crashing down on top of her. This tree wasn't just the beating heart that kept magic flowing throughout the realm, it was the very thing that gave Athis and every other dragon life. It needed protecting.

They needed to return to Illian and stop Alijah - nothing else mattered. Inara strode away from the tree, her mind working to formulate any kind of plan to defeat her brother. After getting out from under the red canopy, she searched for a shard with a familiar image inside it.

One shard glided past her with the image of a jungle inside, while another, rooted to the spot, revealed the snow-capped summit of a mountain. A little further out, three shards intersected and created a fourth, all of which held images of Drakanan. Seeing them drift apart, Inara broke into a run, though her speed was stunted by the need to navigate the numerous roots.

Placing herself in the path of a shard, she looked back at the tree, wondering if she would ever see it again. She hoped that no one would ever see it again. Entwined with her world, it was sacred, deserving of its own realm. There was so much of it to take in, but the Guardian did her best to commit every detail to memory; Athis would want to see it.

The shard passed over her, taking her glorious surroundings and replacing them with the fire lit gloom of Drakanan's bonding chamber. She watched that same shard drift away, reaching for the heights of the ceiling.

*Inara?* Athis's voice was sweet in her mind.

**I'm here,** she reassured.

"Inara?" Adan's voice came from lower down, returning her attention to those she had journeyed with.

The Guardian was immediately racked with concern, her sharp eyes spotting one dead body after another. Adan was spotless having clearly avoided the violence, but where were Asher and Gideon?

"What happened?" she demanded taking the steps three at a time.

Adan gestured to the bodies. "The Red Guard... They ambushed us."

Movement to her left stopped Inara in her tracks. Asher was crouching low to retrieve his broadsword. He appeared haggard if unharmed.

"You're back," he said somewhat surprised.

Inara wanted to tell him everything but she could only manage two words. "Where's Gideon?"

As if answering to his name, her old mentor walked out of the shadows, through the chamber's entrance. In his hand was a strange helmet she had never seen before, though he quickly tossed it aside before it became a topic. With a blood-splattered face, he looked up at Inara and found a smile to break through his obvious exhaustion. Mournblade was in his other hand, the steel pristine as always.

"You came back," he uttered, thankful to see her again. "For a moment there, we were—"

"It's real," Inara proclaimed, silencing the chamber. "The tree. It's real. I saw it, I *touched* it. I could feel it - I could feel the magic."

Gideon's smile wavered. "Incredible..." Mournblade fell from his grip and the Master Dragorn dropped to one knee.

"Gideon!" Inara rushed down the remaining steps and dashed to offer support.

"I'm fine," Gideon assured. "I took a hit across the ribs - nothing fatal."

Inara gave him a scrutinising examination from head to toe. "You've taken more than a hit to the ribs by the look of you." She could see various cuts where his leathers had been sliced through.

"I will help," Adan stated, coming to their aid. The Drake put one of Gideon's arms over his shoulder and guided him to the steps.

"I can help you," the Guardian proposed.

"I would have you save your strength," Adan said, placing his cloak under Gideon's head. "We don't know if there are more of them out there."

"Don't worry," Gideon managed. "I'm in good hands."

On the other side of the chamber, Asher made his way down to the entrance, his gaze set adrift like the shards that floated around them. "Are you hurt?" Inara asked him. "I'm sorry I wasn't here..."

The ranger blinked hard and his focus returned. "I'm fine," he replied in his gruff voice.

Inara meant to continue their conversation when she heard the faint buzz of the diviner on her belt. Opening the pouch, she could now feel its constant vibration.

"Vighon!"

Asher nodded at the entrance. "Talk to him. He needs to know The Rebellion is fighting for more than just the crown now."

Inara was about to hurry from the chamber, eager to speak with the northman. "Are you sure you're well?"

Asher pulled at the satchel over his shoulder. "I could do with food and water - some of us are more human than others."

Inara smiled at his quip and walked away. How she was going to explain all of this to Vighon she didn't know...

# EPILOGUE

Asher watched Inara disappear into the shadows of the antechamber. She had returned from another world with information that changed everything they were fighting for.

Yet the ranger couldn't find the heart to care...

His mind searched desperately for the eye of the storm, a place he could rest for a time and collect his thoughts before a torrent of uncertain emotions could bombard him again. But such peace eluded him.

Without real thought, he picked up Mournblade and took it to Gideon's side. The Master Dragorn said something to him, a question perhaps, but every word failed to register. Instead, he walked away and left the chamber altogether.

Passing from firelight to darkness and then entering the antechamber, littered with torches dropped by The Red Guard, the Nightseye elixir played hell with his senses for a moment. It was only for an instant, but he could taste Inara's sweat on the air and smell the blood of various people. He welcomed the light of a nearby torch and scooped it up, preferring to use his eyes for the time being.

Leaving the Guardian to her conversation in the antechamber, Asher walked aimlessly through half a dozen passages until he felt alone. He had no idea where he was or what the significance of this particular chamber was, and he didn't care.

Something had happened to him.

He couldn't say what it was, only that it was profound. All his long and unnatural life he had felt in control of himself, if not what Fate had in mind for him. But now... Now there was something inside him, inside his head.

Asher slid down the nearest wall and let his head rest back. He knew he should return to the others - none of them had any idea what dangers might still be lurking in Drakanan's ancient halls. Knowing what he should do and what he needed to do, however, were very different things. He *needed* to keep it safe.

That thought brought the ranger's head forward and his eyes opened with alarm. *Keep it safe*, he thought. Protect it. Where had that desire come from? What was he even talking about? Then, like a lightning bolt from the heavens, his memory caught up with his daze. He saw his hand reach out in the bonding chamber, though it hadn't felt like his hand.

It had seemed as if there was nothing else in all the world except for one thing.

A bronze egg.

A little larger than his hand, but still small enough to grasp, it had a rough exterior layered in scales. Of all the things he had done right in his life, including the lives he had saved, none of them had felt nearly as meaningful as the moment he picked up that egg.

Asher couldn't even bring himself to feel shame for leaving Gideon to fight so many. Had he not grasped that egg, the world would surely have come to a grinding halt. The sun would not rise, the oceans would dry up, and monsters would consume whatever remained.

It was fate...

Having relived the memory, Asher looked down at the satchel

beside him. He could feel it. Despite the cold air, his hands were clammy as he reached inside. His fingers felt around the curves of the egg. The scaled shell was warm. He didn't remember it being warm when he first touched it. Desperate to lay eyes on it again, he carefully removed it from the satchel.

It was the most exquisite thing he had ever seen. Though bronze in colour, it was a shade he had never seen before. Flecks of gold decorated the scales, reminding the ranger of Ilargo.

What was he supposed to do now? Whatever the answer was, he knew only that protecting it with his life was now the reason for his existence. He knew that Fate had dragged him through all manner of hell, testing him, to ensure that he was ready for this very moment. Nothing else really mattered.

A quiet sound fought against the licking flames of the nearby torch, competing for Asher's attention. It was coming from inside the egg. The ranger held it to his ear and waited. It sounded like bone breaking to Asher, and he had heard plenty of bones break. It came again and again until he actually felt a light thud against his thumb.

Holding it away from his ear, the ranger cupped it in both hands and watched intently. Nothing happened. The most precious thing in his life remained perfectly still, safe in his hands. Asher knew he could stare at it for hours. He wanted to shake his head, to push all these new feelings away before he was entirely undone. But then the sound came again.

The dragon egg cracked...

# PHILIP C. QUAINTRELL

---

Hear more from Philip C. Quaintrell including
book releases and exclusive content:

 PHILIPCQUAINTRELL.COM

 FACEBOOK.COM/PHILIPCQUAINTRELL

 @PHILIPCQUAINTRELL.AUTHOR

 @PCQUAINTRELL

# AUTHOR NOTES

*25th August 2020*

We're almost there! I've got all kinds of feelings going into 'A Clash of Fates', but the most dominant feeling is excitement. I can't wait to have my first epic fantasy series completed at last, as I'm sure plenty of you are eager to see how this all ends. Though, perhaps there are some of you who aren't ready for it to end.

That's mostly how I feel.

I've been writing in this world since 2014 and publishing it for all of you lovely people since 2017. It's fair to say that these books have changed my life and that of my family's. I've fallen in love with the characters and every part of Verda I've managed to get to. Indeed, I've made a point of trying to go everywhere I can within the confines of a good story.

These books have taken my imagination to all kinds of places and I hope they have done the same for all of you. It feels a bit surreal to be faced now by the final book after literally years of working towards it. I'm overcome with one simple recurring thought:

I don't want to leave it...

So I won't! Ha! I'm about to dive into 'A Clash of Fates' and I'm super excited to give this series the ending it deserves (EPIC), but obviously my imagination is projecting to the future and seeing what lies ahead. Guess what - it's more Verda! There's still plenty of places on the map that I haven't been to as well as certain points in the timeline I haven't explored.

I've mentioned before that I have ideas following this series (Asher prequel series, First Kingdom series, *maybe* an underwater series etc) and I fully intend on fleshing out this world in as many times and places as my imagination can conjure without it becoming stale (very important). I'll talk in more detail on this when we get to the end of book 9.

So, Last of the Dragorn! I think I enjoyed writing this book almost as much as Rise of the Ranger. And, like that book, it felt like a real adventure that took the characters all over Verda with no end of epic quests.

Though, I have to say, weaving them all together is definitely the hardest part of the job. I cast them all off across the world and throw them all into dangerous situations and then try to bring them all back together in such a way that they've complimented each other's story arcs. I'm aware that it put people off in 'Rise of the Ranger', considered to be too complicated or just hard to follow. So thank you to everyone reading this for staying with me and really investing in this world and these characters. I hope you feel rewarded for it as I do.

Getting back to this book, obviously there's been a time jump from 'The Knights of Erador'. I considered this gap carefully and went backwards and forwards over the exact passage of time. I didn't want to pick up directly where book 7 ended because the actual process of starting a rebellion is messy, complicated, and potentially slow where the pace is concerned.

In essence though, for me, this book was all about *choice*. It occurred to me - as it did Inara - that Vighon had never chosen to be the king. His story was swept away in the events of The Ash War and he simply responded to what was happening around him. 'Last of the Dragorn' gave me the opportunity to allow Vighon one last major story arc that would define him as king.

I enjoyed bringing him down and revealing some weakness and failures on his part. For some people those aspects can ruin a character but, without them, characters, like Vighon, can be something of a convenience. I wanted the weight of the crown to show, especially on a person who hadn't been raised or prepared to be a king. Plus, I love a good 'rising' story arc.

Asher too was presented with a choice. I'm sure a lot of you were thinking, "Asher's going to die!" throughout this one. At least that's the sense I got on my read through. I really hope the reveal at the end was a surprise to you all! I've been waiting anxiously to write this part of his story as far back as I can remember. Even my initial, and very rough, plans for 'Rise of the Ranger' intended for him to bond with a dragon, but it was never right. Only as book 7 began to take shape did I envision a way for it to unfold as I had always dreamed.

Obviously there's more to come from this particular story line and, yes, the dragon's sex and name will be revealed in 'A Clash of Fates'. I'm so friggin' excited!

Anyway, back to his choice. Asher was left on something of a dark path in 'The Knights of Erador' and I enjoyed writing that assassin aspect to his personality. It comes out in shades throughout the series, but I wanted to delve into that predatory mindset that Nightfall instilled in him as well as his extraordinary investigative skills. However, he has to make a choice, as all mortals do, about how he will be remembered in death.

Choosing to leave that path - hunting the Arakesh - showed a lot of growth in his character to me. He is always stating how he likes to be alone and that he works better alone, but he chooses to join Inara and take himself away from the dark. Once upon a time I believe he would have continued on that path until it consumed him or killed him.

Of course, we now know the one thing he was missing from his life - a fire-breathing companion! I also love that the revelation that he isn't meant to be alone is, in fact, a revelation to him as a character as well. I'll say no more on that for now...

Inara, bless her, has been plagued with making the right choices for some time now. There's still a way to go with her arc and the choices she needs to make, so I won't go in to them as they unfold better in the books themselves.

Gideon is back! It's been very strange not writing as him for so long. I hope the differences between the Dragon Riders and the Dragorn are becoming clear at this point. I realise that, essentially, they are very similar, but they were actually two completely different orders that existed at two very different times. Both the riders and, indeed, the dragons were different.

I know Gideon has already fleshed out some of these differences, but there will be a Dragon Rider series of some description that will tell the older stories in Verda and shine a light on their ancient order.

What I've enjoyed seeing is the way Gideon has been placed in the middle of both orders. A human Rider leading the Dragorn, an elven construct, is something of a mess really, and I think that shows in some of his past decisions and mistakes - it simply wasn't the way things were meant to be. This, in turn, reflects his ongoing evolution, which can be a hard thing for such an established character who is considered to be at the top of his game. His story, like everyone else's, will be concluded in the next book and I'm looking forward to tying up something that began for him so many years ago. I won't say any more in case I drop spoilers!

The Galfreys! I couldn't miss them out. They've been in this saga since the beginning and they too have had some serious choices to make as well some serious blows. Again, 'Last of the Dragorn' offered me an opportunity to present them with a choice that would go on to define their part in everything as well as their lives going forward. I think I'll always be sad that they didn't get to feature on one of the covers...

Adilandra. I remember my fingers leaving the keyboard when it happened. I couldn't really believe it was happening, but when I read through from start to finish I could see all the pieces falling into place as if my subconscious had been planning for it all along. I'm not a grandparent but I am a parent and I really sympathised with her 'choice' part in the story. The consequences of her passing will be revealed in the last book.

On a lighter note, while I'm talking about characters - Sir Borin the Dread! I loved bringing him back. I had this particular part planned since before he fell through the ice in 'Age of the King'. Again, I hope none of you saw that one coming. I have to say, it's really hard holding on to all these things until I finally arrive at the point at which I can write them. I think a lot of people reckon I took his archetype from Game of Thrones because of The Mountain character, but he's actually a homage to Frankenstein. I love all the Dracula, Mummy, Wolf man, Frankenstein stuff - it's a universe I wouldn't mind jumping in to at some point down the line. Anyway, we might not have seen the last of old Borin...

Doran, Doran, Doran... That poor guy has had hell of a time of it. Clearly his story still has some distance left in it and I won't go in to it too much, but his shoulders have got a lot sitting on them. He's gone full circle and ended up right where he didn't want to be - War Mason! If there was anyone I wanted fighting by my side though, it would be the son of Dorain.

I have loved writing every word of his tale. I had no idea, back in 'Empire of Dirt' that he was going to be such a major character. In many ways, he's become the beating heart of the saga. He has a lot of sides to him and I think I'm not alone in loving them all. I can tell you, quite confidently, that he will play a large part in book 2 of Asher's prequel series, detailing how they met etc.

Wow! Just looking back I've waffled on for some time. Thank you if you've got this far. I'm going to take a week or two off now and recharge before hitting 'A Clash of Fates'. If you've enjoyed this book and those before it, please leave a review on Amazon. I'm a self-publisher so your comments really help me to get the word out to others. At the end of the day, I'm just a guy with a simple dream really: to be *invited* to Comic-con San Diego.

Until the next time...

# Appendices



**Provinces of Illian:**

1. ***Alborn*** (eastern province) - Ruled by Lord Gydon of house Bairn, the steward of Velia, Alborn's capital. Other Towns and Cities: Palios, Galosha, and Barossh.

2. ***The Arid Lands*** (southern province) - Ruled by Lord Hasta Hash-Aseem, the steward of Tregaran, the southern capital. Other Towns and Cities: Ameeraska and Calmardra.

3. ***The Ice Vales*** (western province) - Ruled by Lord Barnish of house Yendyl, steward of Grey Stone, the capital of the western vales. Other Towns and Cities: Bleak, Kelp Town, and Snowfell.

4. ***Orith*** (northern province) - Ruled by King Alijah of house Galfrey from the city of Namdhor, the capital of Illian. Other towns and cities: Skystead, Dunwich, Darkwell, and Longdale.

5. *Felgarn* (central province) - Ruled by Lord Starg of house Hamish, steward of Lirian, the heart of The Evermoore. Other Towns and Cities: Vangarth, Wood Vale, and Whistle Town.

~

## Dwarven Hierarchy:

1. *Heavybellys* - Ruled by King Dakmund, son of Dorain. Domain: *Grimwhal.*

2. *Brightbeards* - Ruled by King Gaerhard, son of Hermon. Domain: *Bhan Doral.*

3. *Battleborns* - Leaderless. Domain: *Silvyr Hall.*

4. *Hammerkegs* - Leaderless. Domain: *Nimduhn.*

5. *Goldhorns* - Leaderless. Domain: *Khaldarim.*

~

## Dragon Riders and their mounts

**Lord Kraiden,** bonded with the dragon *Morgorth.* (Deceased)

**Vilyra,** bonded with the dragon *Godrad.*

**Gondrith,** bonded with the dragon *Yillir.*

**Rengyr,** bonded with the dragon *Karsak.* (Deceased)

~

## Orcish Tribes:

1. *The Sons of Gordomo* - Ruled by Chieftain Targ.

2. *The Berserkers* - Ruled by Chieftain Wuglaf.

3. *The Big Bastards* - Ruled by Chieftain Gargandor.

4. *The Mountain Fist* - Ruled by Chieftain Mezeg.

~

## Other significant locations:

*Valatos* (within the city of Velia) - School for magic - destroyed by Malliath.

*Ikirith* (inside The Evermoore) - forest home of the Drakes - destroyed by Malliath.

*Elandril* (northern Ayda) - Ruled by Queen Adilandra of house Sevari. The heart of the elven nation.

*The Lifeless Isles* - An archipelago in The Adean and home to the Dragorn.

*Korkanath* (on an island east of Velia) - The ruins of the once prestigious school for magic.

*Stowhold* (an island north of Korkanath) - The headquarters of Illian's largest bank.

*Syla's Pass* (south of The Arid Lands) - Entrance to The Undying Mountains.

***The Tower of Dragons' Reach*** (south of Velia) - The abandoned tower where once the rulers of the realm would meet with Gideon Thorn and the Dragorn.

***Ilythyra*** (in The Moonlit Plains) - Was governed by the late Lady Ellöria of house Sevari - destroyed by Malliath.

***Paldora's Fall*** (inside The Undying Mountains) - The impact site of Paldora's Star, a well of powerful magic.

***Qamnaran*** (An island off the west coast of Illian) - Under the control of King Alijah. Largest know source of Demetrium.

~

## Significant Wars: Chronologically

**The First War** - Fought during The Pre-Dawn (before elvish-recorded history). King Atilan started a war with the first Dragon Riders in the hopes of uncovering their source of immortality. The war brought an end to Atilan's reign and his entire kingdom.

**The Great War** - Fought during the First Age, around 5,000 years ago. The only recorded time in history that elves and dwarves have united. They fought against the orcs with the help of the Dragorn, the first elvish dragon riders. This war ended the First Age.

**The Dark War** - Fought during the Second Age, around 1,000 years ago. Considered the elvish civil war. Valanis, the dark elf, tried to take over Illian in the name of the gods. This war ended the Second Age.

**The Dragon War** - Fought in the beginning of the Third Age, only a few years after The Dark War. The surviving elves left Illian for

Ayda's shores, fleeing any more violence. Having emerged from The Wild Moores, the humans, under King Gal Tion's rule, went to war with the dragons over their treasure. This saw the exile of the surviving dragons and the beginning of human dominance over Illian.

**The War for the Realm** - Fought 47 years ago. The return of Valanis saw the world plunged back into war and the re-emergence of the Dragorn. Gideon Thorn became the first human to bond with a dragon in recorded history. Valanis was killed by the ranger, Asher, who died in their final battle.

**The Northern Civil War** - In the wake of The War for the Realm, the north, under the ruling city of Namdhor, was left without its king, Merkaris Tion. In the vacuum that followed, the lords and great families fell into civil war over the throne. The war lasted nearly twenty years and ended with Yelifer, of house Skalaf, seated on the throne.

**The Ash War** - Fought 17 years ago. The last war of the Third Age saw Illian transition into the Fourth Age. The orcs return to the surface brought with them war and blood on a scale Verda hadn't seen in ten thousand years. Resulted in the destruction of the Dragornian population and island, as well as the restructuring of Illian's kingdoms. The orcs were defeated and from the ashes rose a new species: Drakes - half-dragon, half-elf.

www.ingramcontent.com/pod-product-compliance
Lightning Source LLC
Chambersburg PA
CBHW030834190726
48285CB00004B/1222